MESS

Book One Of The Bar Kokhba Revolt.
132AD

Guy Aston

Copyright © 2022 Guy Aston

ISBN: 9798446057207

All rights reserved, including the right to reproduce this book, or portions thereof in any form. No part of this text may be reproduced, transmitted, downloaded, decompiled, reverse engineered, or stored, in any form or introduced into any information storage and retrieval system, in any form or by any means, whether electronic or mechanical without the express written permission of the author.

This is a work of fiction. Names and characters are the product of the author's imagination and any resemblance to actual persons, living or dead, is entirely coincidental.

The views expressed in this work are solely those of the author and do not necessarily reflect the views of the publisher, and the publisher hereby disclaims any responsibility for them.

www.publishnation.co.uk

Contents

Principio - Murder 3
Capitulum I - Arrival 7
Capitulum II - Apollinaris & Postumus 23
Capitulum III - Ambush! 45
Capitulum IV - Aelia Capitolina 62
Capitulum V - Silent Bells 79
Capitulum VI - First contact 99
Interludum I 118
Capitulum VII - A girl from the hills 124
Interludum II 139
Capitulum VIII - It begins 145
Interludum III 158
Capitulum IX - Revelations 162
Capitulum X - Assassination 169
Interludum IV 193
Capitulum XI - Training Camp 198
Capitulum XII - Tales from Home 212
Capitulum XIII - The Fourth arrives 218
Capitulum XIV – The end of a century 224
Capitulum XV – Death in the vicus 227
Capitulum XVI – Panic in Aelia 239
Capitulum XVII - Unrest in Galilee 251
Capitulum XVIII - Vengeance 263
Capitulum XIX - The storm breaks 280
Capitulum XX – A time to leave 299
Capitulum XXI - The column 322
Capitulum XXII – The junction 355
Capitulum XXIII - Decapitation 377
Capitulum XXIV - Aftermath 429
Interludum V 449
Capitulum XXV – Return to Caesarea 456
Capitulum XXVI – Herbs and lust 487
Interludum VI 505
Capitulum XXVII – Seeking the rabbi 510
Un breve interludio 539

Un breve interludio 546
Capitulum XXVIII - Parthians 547
Capitulum XXIX -Caesarea again 566
Interludum VII – *"They will rejoice in Heaven."* 581
Capitulum XXX – Postumus' sixth sense 587
Epilogue 592

Principio - Murder

23 Julius. Year 12 of Imperator Trajan.

At fifteen years old, the youth was not quite a man, so he was comfortable hugging his aunt and uncle farewell. His two girl cousins received lesser hugs as he became the subject of a developing sensitivity to young ladies. He must avoid the burning blushes he so often experienced at all costs – not that he did not enjoy their close presence. He gave an adult hand clasp to his cousin Ishmael, a boy of his age. His cousin was his closest friend. The boys had grown up together and shared many of the adolescent discoveries of life. His aunt was his mother's younger sister, and the two women had been close all their lives, though it had not been an easy relationship. Her choice of husband, a member of the *Telmedei Yeshua,* Judaic Christians, had not settled well with her Jewish kin.

The aunt's marriage to a follower of Yeshua saw her become a member of that sect. Yeshua, they claimed, was the long-awaited Messiah who would unite the tribes of Israel and restore the nation to its former position as the chosen land of the Lord God. Yeshua died nailed to a cross on a hill outside of Jerusalem, but his exhilarating creed spread by his followers permeated the Roman Empire.

The youth's Jewish parents were not enamoured with the marital choice and distanced themselves from his aunt. However, familial ties are strong, and discreet contact was maintained. One of their prime means of communication was the young man currently saying his farewell to his Christian relations.

The youth, a diligent boy, studied the Torah, the Talmud, and knew his scriptures. He had a brother, a strictly orthodox Jew several years older than he, who hated the Christians almost as much as he loathed the Romans. His sibling considered the Christians to be a perversion, a heretical betrayal of Judaism. The Christian Jews were of no concern to the youth but, if questioned, he might admit that his love for his aunt's family influenced his view of their beliefs.

"Thank you, aunt. The meal was lovely. Blessings be upon you all," he said after disengaging from the farewell rituals.

"You're always welcome in our home, *Gakhbar*." Gakhbar, the mouse. From when he first walked, he forever rushed about exploring everything in her home. From that time, he became her 'little mouse.' The 'little' may have disappeared as he grew in stature, but Gakhbar remained. "Go in peace."

Gakhbar turned and walked to the stone-built barn that sat detached from the house. Here he had left Shadoch, his pony, who would carry him home to Herodium in a matter of minutes. The pony neighed as he appeared. He had fodder and water aplenty, but now the shadows were growing longer, the animal wished to be back in its stable. Gakhbar checked the saddle and untied Shadoch's reins from the metal ring in the barn wall. Taking a grasp of Shadoch's mane, he pulled himself up and onto the saddle. Then, turning the pony's head to one side, with a gentle kick of heel to ribs, Gakhbar and Shadoch took the road home.

The horse and rider had travelled the route many times. Gakhbar's mind wandered as he rode, and his thoughts found their way to his cousin Mariah. A few months younger than himself, she had blossomed, and he couldn't help but notice she filled out in what, to a young man, were all the right places. He didn't know if his feelings for her constituted true love, but he found her presence intoxicating. As a well brought up Jewish boy, he ensured she remained unaware of his emotions. But should he tell her? What if she just laughed at him—he would feel such an idiot. But he so wanted her. Then an idea slipped into his mind. He wrote well. In fact, his teacher described his poetry as "passable". Yes, he would write to her, but *not* poems about God's creation. It would be a letter, accompanied by a poem about first love, the opening gambit in a game of courtship. In his head he began phrasing his lines.

"Damnation!" Gakhbar said, bringing Shadoch to a standstill. He could kick himself; his mother's letter to her sister was still in the knapsack that hung over his shoulder. To arrive back home with the missive undelivered would earn him the sharp edge of his mother's tongue. He turned his horse and rode back the way he had come at a fast trot. This would make him late home, but he decided it to be the lesser of the two evils.

Minutes later, Shadoch came to a stand in the barn. The youth leapt off him and secured him to the ring in the wall. Shadoch stamped his feet and snorted, not expecting this break from the routine. Gakhbar walked towards the house when he heard a commotion. It was not loud, but it was out of place and brought him to a standstill, listening.

A muffled scream penetrated the dusk; he hesitated and then sped forward. As he did, further screams filled the air — high-pitched female screams—Mariah's scream. The door, where he had exchanged fond farewells earlier, burst open, and Ishmael staggered out. Gakhbar froze; even in the failing light he could make out the distorted look of horror on his cousin's face. As he reached Gakhbar, Ishmael came to a standstill and flopped to his knees, looking up to Gakhbar.

"Gakhbar," he said, before collapsing to the ground at his feet. Mesmerised, the youth stared at the fallen Ishmael. A dagger protruded from his back. For what seemed a lifetime, Gakhbar remained paralysed, gazing at his fallen friend. Finally, reality returned, and he dropped to his knees, hoping to help. To make it all well again. He discovered to his horror that Ishmael lay stone dead. As he regained his feet, Gakhbar's body began to shake uncontrollably. He looked towards the door Ishmael had passed through and forced himself to walk towards it.

A few paces from the house a man appeared in the doorway. Dressed in dark clothing, he clutched a menacingly curved weapon. The light was too poor to make out much detail. The man's head, swathed in traditional garb, had a scarf pulled across his face. Both Gakhbar and the man froze, neither expecting the other. To a youth who was now expecting to join his dead cousin at any second, it felt like an age before the man spoke.

"Go back to the barn, boy. Get on your pony and ride away." He paused. "Do not return. Just go home."

The voice, deep, commanding, not threatening, expected obedience. Gakhbar knew he had little choice. Mariah was dead.

The family was dead; killed by unknown assassins in their own home. Yet his petrified body kept him rooted to the spot.

"I shall not tell you again, boy. Go! —Go now!" The tone had become more threatening, and it caused Gakhbar's brain to register the embedded threat. He took several paces backwards before turning and staggering back down the pathway, still shaking in shock whilst suppressing a rising desire to vomit. Making it into the barn and to Shadoch, Gakhbar tried to mount three times before getting into the saddle. As he left the barn, moving onto the track they called a road, he realised his vision was blurry. Tears streamed down his cheeks. He felt detached from himself. Then what control he had left him. Ravaged by deep sobs, his stomach convulsing, he leant over Shadoch's mane and vomited his aunt's fine cooking down Shadoch's shanks.

The pony knew the route home, which was as well because his rider had collapsed over his mane, his grip slack on the reins. But, for all the shock, the confusion and the sorrow, a tiny seed began to take root in Gakhbar's brain. He had no idea how it would come about, but Mariah and Ishmael would be avenged somewhere, at some time. The mouse would turn.

Capitulum I - Arrival

23 Martius. Year 16 of Imperator Hadrian.

The coastline appeared a coating of sandy brown, lying on a carpet of blue sea. Optio Lucius Decimus Petronius, late of Italia, was standing on the prow. The wind was stiff, stretching the sail of the *Fides*, a small military liburnian, pushing the galley through the water at a steady pace. The rowers sat at their oars talking among themselves and relishing the breeze. As the vessel closed towards the shore, the brown coating was marred by a lighter brown smudge, the first sign that the sea voyage of over sixteen days was ending. It had been a new experience, but Lucius was glad it was nearly over.

As Lucius strained his eyes, the smudge transformed into a distant sea wall with its great lighthouse. To the foot of the lighthouse was an opening in the wall, the entrance to the harbour. The trierarchus, the grizzled old ship's officer, had told Lucius what to expect; and there it was, the large, enclosed harbour and beyond it the colony of Caesarea Maritima, the administrative centre of Provincia Judaea, encompassing the regions of Galilee, Samaria, and Judaea itself.

A two-decker bireme passed through the harbour entrance and moved out towards the open sea, both decks of oars working in perfect unison, pushing the vessel forward against the breeze. The *Fides* altered her heading to give the bireme sea space, then sailed confidently landwards, close enough now for Lucius to see through the broad harbour opening and observe the military galleys and other cargo vessels moored within.

This was a busy port with small vessels criss-crossing the harbour and men toiling along the quays. Beyond the harbour, standing on a prominence, stood the great Temple of Augustus, brilliant white in the sunshine. The marble lighthouse towered above the small passing liburnian as it entered the harbour. The quays appeared to have lives of their own, seething with sailors, workers, and wagons. Here at last was Caesarea Maritima, a once royal harbour and one of Rome's largest ports to serve the *Mare Nostrum*. 'Our Sea', the name Romans called the great expanse of water that ran from Hispania all the way to the coast of Principia Judaea. Inside the protective harbour wall, the deep blue water of the ocean was replaced by water of a darker, green hue. On the surface floated the detritus of a busy port: sodden fruit, lengths of timber, old rope, and even a dead cat that must have run out of its legendary lives.

To the southern end of the harbour a jetty lay empty, and it was soon apparent that the captain of the *Fides,* while skilfully avoiding other moving vessels, had selected it as the ship's destination. A sailor equipped with several coloured flags joined Lucius on the prow and began to wave them in a specific sequence. On the jetty, still some distance away, flags were waved in response. The sailor ran back to his trierarchus with the instructions received and the *Fides* turned to close on the jetty. The ship continued to cut through the water at speed. Lucius was becoming more than a little concerned at the speed of the ship's approach when the captain cried out, "Lower sails – out oars." His fears were soon allayed as the oars dipped into the water, causing the *Fides* to quickly shed speed. As the jetty became close, oars were shipped as the boat slid slowly alongside. Lines were thrown and the shore men quickly reduced what forward motion was left, bringing the liburnian to a standstill, securing it to large bollards, lining the jetty. Lucius was impressed; throughout the journey he developed a respect for the navy, but now he would be back in *his* world; that of the Roman Army, or more precisely, Legio X Fretensis. After so many days of fresh sea air, the varied odours of the busy port overwhelmed Lucius. He smiled as he considered how he must smell, it having been several days since he had last enjoyed the Roman baths. The best he had managed since was several buckets of seawater.

Walking back towards where the gangplank was already being run out, Lucius adjusted his cloak and donned his helmet with its distinctive cresta running from the front to the rear. As he approached the gangplank, the trierarchus walked over to him. A squat, stout man with a tanned leathery skin, Trierarchus Amyntas was a man that had learnt his business over the last thirty years and had a look that conveyed he had been born at sea. During the preceding days, Lucius had many a chat with the man. He had concluded that when it came to the sea and boats, if Amyntas did not know it, then it was not worth remembering.

"So, it is a parting of the ways, Petronius," said the trierarchus. "I wish you well."

"You well know I'm no sailor, Amyntas," Lucius responded, "but your conversation and your wine have made the journey bearable. I shall, however, be grateful to walk on *terra firma* again. I'll also always appreciate the army's latrines from here on; I'm sick of hanging my arse off the side of a boat!"

Amyntas laughed. "A few days in Judaea, Petronius, and you may wish to be on board again. Always watch your back and your purse!" As he spoke, he glanced over his shoulder. "And here come your chests." Three sailors appeared, two carrying a large chest between them and one a smaller box. "Get those down onto the jetty boys, then bring the cargo of scutuae and piliae ashore," The shields and spears used the Roman army, "there'll be waggons arriving to collect them shortly." He turned back to Lucius. "Good luck, lad, and don't forget my words. Treacherous bunch of *mentula* in these parts."

"Good weather and safe seas," Lucius called over his shoulder as he descended the gangplank. The jetty was filling up with the workmen who would unload the *Fides*, and beyond them, he could see helmeted figures approaching, cutting a different bearing to the scruffy dock hands. It was good to be on land – though it was strange how the ground was behaving as though he was still on a rocking boat. Several of the dockhands glanced askance at the tall military figure. His *Lorica Hamata*, the mail coat he wore, the steel links of which appeared to sparkle in the sunlight, his military red cloak and his polished crested helmet all marked him out. What surprised them was that a man of a young age should be wearing the crested helmet of an Optio.

Barging their way through the dockhands came a small group of smartly dressed soldiers. The dockhands grumbled and once safely passed, hurled curses at them. The soldiers all wore Lorica Segmentata, the bodice of steel plates that was the trademark of the Roman legionary. The group was led by a wiry, balding, grey-bearded man wearing a battered leather cuirass and a cloak but no helmet. As he approached, he broke into a smile.

"Optio Petronius? Salve. We've been expecting you. A good journey I hope?" He paused a second, then, without waiting for a response, went on. "I am Tiberius Pullus, harbour master here at Caesarea. Welcome to Judaea." He extended his arm and Lucius clasped it.

"Salve, master Pullus. Neptune was merciful, and though the skill of Trierarchus Amyntas was exceptional, it's good to be on land, though strangely it seems to be moving!"

Pullus laughed. "That will wear off soon enough. I've seen experienced sailors walk along this quay as though they've had a day with Bacchus." He turned to the half dozen soldiers waiting in two files behind him. "Festus, get the Optio's chests down to the barracks and then report back to the office." He faced Lucius again. "There's accommodation arranged at the main barracks, Optio. You should find it comfortable after the Fides. Praefectus Faustinus shall be notified of your arrival, so I would suggest you report as soon as you can."

"It's top of my priorities, master Pullus." Lucius was aware that it wouldn't do to upset the camp prefect. Given his orders, the prefect is probably someone with whom he needed a lengthy conversation. "Is he as rigid as they say?"

"Well now, Optio," Pullus responded, "that depends on where you stand. Unlike yourself, I suspect, he's old school, and you don't step out of line with him. However, the men are fiercely loyal to him as he is to his men."

Lucius could not miss the reference to his age. At twenty-one years of age, he was young for an Optio, not having spent years grinding his way through the military ranks to his position. Army thinking had changed, and as the Empire consolidated, Rome needed brain as much as it required brawn. This did not always sit well with old hands who had fought for years to gain their positions. Lucius knew he would have to prove himself.

"So, tell me, Optio, you're the first of the new cohort. When do you expect the men to arrive?" Pullus was probing.

"That's very much a matter for army headquarters to decide," Lucius hedged, "and for centurion Crispus who has been knocking them into shape. That I'm here would point to the near future, I suspect." Crispus, a respected centurion of the Legio X Fretensis, with a handful of veterans, had been sent back to Rome to build the new IV Cohort, bringing the legion back up to full strength. The fact was that Crispus, with the new unit, would land within a matter of weeks.

"Right," said Pullus, "let's get back to the office, and I will arrange an escort to take you to the barracks. Anyone there will tell you how to find Praefectus Faustinus - though I am sure he'll find you." He guffawed. "Some soldiers will swear by Jupiter that he can be in several places at once!"

The pair walked down the jetty and onto the main quay which was a hive of industry. The two men had to avoid amphora of wine, sacks of grain, and many other goods moving along the quayside. Lucius, taken aback by the variety of languages he heard, could only recognise Latin and Greek amongst the different tongues. Pullus kept up a steady stream of talk about his role in the harbour, with a little exaggeration in Lucius' view but, clearly, he was an experienced harbour master. Most of the busy workers nodded as Pullus passed along the quay, some offering a smile or a relaxed wave of the hand. Popular *and* experienced, Lucius thought. The operation appeared efficient and organised so perhaps there was more to Pullus than just the affable front he portrayed.

Several workers nudged each other and stared at the sight of such a juvenile Optio. Lucius thought he would have to get used to this but was determined not to let it affect him. He had shared his concerns with Crispus some months back. "You were my choice," Crispus had told him, "So I know you have what is necessary. Just do it, Petronius."

By the gates at the back of the harbour was a white marble building of two stories: the domain of the harbour master. Two finely turned-out soldiers stood on duty by the columned entrance and inside the ground floor was expansive. Several clerks sat keeping records of ships and goods moving through the port; taxes would have to be paid. Behind them sat shelves of scrolls, records going back years, all well sorted and neatly stacked. Pullus' office was on the top floor and looked practical and efficient – Pullus was not one for ornamentation, there was nothing here that did not serve a purpose. A fine desk, a rack of scrolls, storage cupboards clearly labelled and hooks upon which hung his helmet, an oiled cloak and several leather satchels. On one wall sat the exception, a model of a Roman military galley, a three-decked trireme; no doubt a type of vessel with which he had a close connection. *If I mention it*, thought Lucius, *no doubt I will get another saga from the life of Pullus*. The Harbour Master sat at the large desk and gestured Lucius to sit opposite. As he removed his helmet, a soldier appeared in the doorway. Pullus spoke to him.

"Right, Sabinus, I need two men to escort Optio Petronius to the barracks. His chests have gone on ahead."

"I will see to it immediately." The soldier disappeared through the doorway.

"A drink while we wait, Optio?"

It was, in fact, three drinks before Lucius set out for the barracks accompanied by his escort. Lucius was sure that Sabinus had sought two of his most smartly attired men for the job, as these boys positively shone in the sunlight. Pullus had kept the escort waiting as he added to Lucius' little knowledge on what happens in a modern military port, sprinkled with some of his exploits as a younger man serving in the *Classis Romanus*, the Roman Navy. Concerning the Province of Judaea, Pullus had a low level of respect for the Jews, "irritating cac" as he described them, however he lived and worked in a military colonia that was very much Roman. He liked that.

As they made their way to Lucius' quarters, the ways parted for Lucius and his escort. Lucius felt naked without his hastile, his long silver topped stick for bringing his soldiers into lines – the clear badge of an Optio. It would arrive with the cohort as would his shield, but his rank was still clear to all.

"You've clearly been buffing metal today," he said to the escort.

The older of the two, who looked like he had been several years in the legion, replied. "If we're going anywhere close to Praefectus Faustinus, you get polished, sir. 'Pride of Rome' is what he calls us, and if we are that we should look it! That's what he says, sir."

"Well then, I think you have done him proud, men."

"Good of you to say, sir." The small group left the port and entered the town of Caesarea. "Oh, and welcome to Caesarea, sir."

Lucius' room at the barracks was practical and comfortable but far from luxurious. All the traditional furniture was present; cot, table, two chairs and plenty of shelves and hooks. In one corner sat his two chests, and the wall next to the doorway had a window with a view across the drill field - though it was not his plan to watch any military drilling when in occupancy; he had seen plenty of that over the last two years, and enough was enough. He poured a cup of water from the large pitcher on the table and poured some into the bowl that sat beside the pitcher. If he was to report to the Camp Prefect, a previous senior centurion of the legion, he wanted to be fresh and have his wits about him.

After a quick wash, he was ready to go. He straightened his helmet in the brass mirror that hung from the wall, adjusted his cloak, attached his sword, and strode through the door. He passed along a corridor and out through a large doorway that led to the drill field.

As Lucius moved into the morning sunshine, a legionary stepped towards the shade of the building. Lucius stopped in his tracks, the legionary swerved sideways, and they avoided colliding. The soldier spotted the plumes on Lucius' helmet and managed the feat of regaining his balance, standing to attention, and saluting in one motion.

"You Optio Petronius, sir?"

Lucius measured the man. He had the look of a seasoned soldier: leathery skin, ebony hair with heavy stubble, the classic 'thick neck', developed wearing the heavy Roman helmet.

"You're correct, legionary. What's your business?"

"Legionary Antonius Ligustinus. V Cohort. I am ordered to escort you to the Prefect's office, sir."

"Well then, we'd better not keep him waiting. Let's go."

They set off at a pace. The morning parade was over and on the large, dusty parade area, soldiers were going through their drills. Some were practising manoeuvres whilst others were working on combat skills. These were not recruits, practising sword strokes against wooden poles, these were trained professionals involved in one-on-one combat. The only small indulgence to safety was the use of wooden swords. Lucius smiled to himself. Wooden swords can hurt and leave a man black and blue for days.

"I suspect you're happier with this duty than that," said Lucius, nodding towards the battling soldiers.

"Not my unit, sir," Ligustinus replied. "Sorry for 'em though. Centurion Drax is a hard trainer. It's rumoured some of his victims survive training!"

"My trainer often said, 'train hard and live', Ligustinus."

The only response was a dry laugh from the soldier. As they walked around the perimeter of the drill field, they approached a small group undergoing sword practice. Each in turn, stepped forward to challenge a centurion, neither armed with shields. It was clear just who was getting the best of these interactions – it was not the legionaries. As they came closer, Lucius observed the centurion's technique. It was good but what appeared lacking was any instruction following the brief bouts.

As they passed close by the group, a legionary put up such a weak fight that it was little other than a submission. Lucius turned to Ligustinus.

"That could have been better!" he said. Unfortunately for Lucius, it was one of those moments when just before you open your mouth, the world turns quiet. Though not spoken loudly, Lucius' voice carried as far as Centurion Drax. As the beaten legionary pulled himself back to his feet and slunk off back to his rank, Drax turned in Lucius' direction. He stood legs apart and hands on hips, adopting a defiance stance.

"So, I could have done better, Optio? Am I right?"

"Apologies, centurion, I was, of course, referring to the soldier's efforts," Lucius called back. He did not like the tone of the centurion's voice.

Ligustinus muttered, "Fuck me, sir. Be careful. Lads call him 'the butcher'!"

"Optio, can I suggest you show the men here how it can be done better?" said Drax.

Lucius knew a challenge when he heard one – this was fast getting out of control.

"Centurion, I'd oblige but I'm due with the prefect shortly. Another time perhaps?"

"Come now, Optio. This should take just a few seconds!"

All eyes were upon Lucius; the soldiers standing in line were nudging each other and whispering, already taking bets on the outcome. Lucius suspected he was not the favourite. He was torn two ways; Drax was a senior officer, so in effect he was ordered to fight. If he refused, Drax would ensure the story of the cowardly "boy" officer would spread through the camp. If he beat Drax, there was no doubt he would make an enemy. Lucius decided. He would have to fight and cope with the outcome.

"I will not get around this Ligustinus. Take my cloak, will you," he said, handing his cloak to the soldier. Turning to Drax, he said, "Very good, centurion, let's do this." Lucius was not sure, but he thought he saw an expression of surprise cross the centurion's face. Lucius took stock of his antagonist. His medium height was countered by a barrel-like chest, bulging biceps and powerful thighs. He was the classic new recruit's nightmare. Lucius absorbed what he saw as he began a mental assessment; Drax had power, but how nimble would he be?

The centurion said something to one of his legionaries. The man jogged across to Lucius and handed him a wooden gladius. Lucius took it, nodding his thanks.

"When you are ready, Optio," said Drax. Lucius walked onto the drill field and stood facing the centurion. In the back of his mind, he could hear his first trainer, Atelius, talking to him. 'Watch his eyes. His legs and feet will tell you a lot about what is going to happen. Use your skill, not your muscles'. Lucius squatted down and picked up a handful of dust from the drill field, rubbing it into the handle of the wooden sword. Satisfied with the grip, he assumed a fighting posture facing the big centurion.

"I'm ready, centurion." Drax nodded and stood watching Lucius. A tensioning of the leg muscles signalled to Lucius that he was about to move and... he did. Drax came at him at speed, his gladius arcing through the air as he came on, targeting Lucius' neck. Lucius backed up and parried the blow. Drax pushed on and Lucius kept blocking and backing up, facing the onslaught. The attack was furious. Lucius wondered how long Drax could maintain such pressure. Smiling, Drax pressed on, confident he was on top of this fight.

Atelius' voice was telling Lucius to use Drax's strength to defeat him. Drax continued forcing Lucius backwards, sure he would shortly make his 'kill' against this impudent junior officer. He charged again, but to his surprise Lucius parried the blow across his front, leaving a path for him to step forward to Drax's side. Drax's momentum continued to carry him forward, allowing Lucius to spin inwards and kick him in the back of his knee. Drax, desperately trying to turn and face his opponent, collapsed to one side. Lucius dropped onto Drax's back and held the 'blade' of his wooden gladius against his neck.

Lucius looked across to the rank of soldiers who he expected to see smiling. They were not; they stood to attention. Out of the corner of his eye he noted that Ligustinus also stood still, expressionless. From underneath him, his victim swore.

"Fuck, fuck and damnation!"

Lucius stood up, turned to look around and understood the lack of emotion amongst the soldiers. Bearing down upon the small group was an officer, resplendent in a plumed helmet and a white, leather cuirass encompassing his chest. He was accompanied by an escort of four soldiers. Here was a very senior officer. At the same time Centurion Drax raised his head and repeated, "Oh, fuck -- the Prefect!"

Lucius offered Drax his hand to help him up. Drax responded with a silent snarl and rose to his feet. As the Prefect closed with the two men, both Lucius and Drax saluted. The Prefect looked both men up and down, shaking his head as he did so. The officer had the look of a well-seasoned soldier; he was stocky with weather beaten skin that carried scars on his arms and one on his cheek. He had a cheery disposition, but Lucius read this as a man who could afford to be genial but as hard as nails if needed.

"Salve, Optio, you are late." Turning to his orderly, he said, "Holy Zeus, Ligustinus, was it too difficult to get the optio to my office?"

The legionary shuffled uncomfortably.

"Apologies, sir. I was out ranked!"

"The legionary is correct, sir," Lucius said. "The centurion and I were responsible."

"Never mind, Ligustinus, I would have paid good money to see Centurion Drax on his back!" The Prefect guffawed. "Yes, good money indeed!"

Drax was not happy.

"More like a gladiator's trick, if you ask me," he said.

"It was an interesting move, Centurion," said the Prefect, "but as soldiers, we kill our enemies. Dead is dead - no matter how it comes about. Carry on with your training, Centurion. Optio Petronius, come with me."

Lucius took his cloak back from Ligustinus, threw it over his shoulders and joined the prefect. Ligustinus and the prefect's escort fell in behind. As they walked away, Centurion Drax's voice was heard admonishing the legionaries he was training. Lucius pitied them.

"It is good to meet you, Optio Petronius." The voice had all the timbre of a man who had spent years commanding cohorts.

"Yes, sir. Yours to be commanded!" snapped Lucius.

"Relax, man," said the officer. He stopped, turned to Lucius, and held out his right arm. "Caius Faustinus and I'm the prefect of this lot." He swung his left hand in an arc behind him, encompassing most of what was in view, including his small escort of immaculately turned-out legionaries. Lucius clasped Faustinus' right arm.

"I've heard a lot about you, sir. I understand you've been with the Tenth a long time."

"Correct. Done your homework, eh, Petronius?"

"I've spent quite some time with centurion Crispus, sir, and I must tell you he sends his regards and asks that you get the Falernian ready."

"Share a bottle of my finest with Crispus? Poor bloody waste that would be." Faustinas snorted. "He never could tell the difference between piss and nectar. I trust he keeps well?"

"He does," Lucius responded. "A touch of ague a few months back, but he's now fully recovered and should soon be in Caesarea."

"So, I understand. Let's go to the principia. We can have a slightly more formal chat in my office."

They exchanged niceties as they strode across the drill field towards the Principia: Lucius's voyage, the formation of the IV Cohort near Capua, and general gossip from Italy. There was no traditional Roman camp at Caesarea and the Principia, once the palace of King Herod Agrippa, now served as the headquarters of the Fretensis vexillation at Caesarea, many of whom were sneaking sideways glances at Lucius and the Prefect as they crossed the parade area. Conversation continued as they entered a courtyard. The porticoed entrance that then confronted them impressed Lucius with its splendour. As they entered the building the escort left them. The prefect led the way down a marble lined corridor, acknowledging several passing soldiers before entering an office. He stopped and turned, spreading his arms out, "This is my home, Petronius, from here I run my empire. Get yourself sat down," he said, pointing to a chair.

As he moved to the seat, Lucius quickly looked around. On one wall was painted a detailed map of Caesarea; buildings and thoroughfares identified. On an adjacent wall beside the doorway stood an armour hanger upon which hung the complete panoply of a centurion, all in immaculate condition. The third was covered in shelves housing a large collection of scrolls and several wax tablets. Finally, the last wall was positioned behind the prefect's desk and held a large window looking out over the town. This was the domain of a well-ordered man.

Another chair, another desk, thought Lucius as he sat. With a faint sigh, Faustinus collapsed into his seat and reached for a jug on the end of a meticulously tidy desk.

"Bloody country gets ever hotter it seems. Will you share some wine, Petronius – watered of course and not Falernian? We'll save that for when you make centurion, shall we?"

Faustinus did not wait for an answer, and the two goblets that sat beside the jug were promptly filled. As the prefect busied himself, Lucius looked around the room.

The two took a sip of wine when Faustinus leaned forward and rested his elbows on the desk.

"Petronius, Petronius, no relation to centurion Petronius of the VI Cohort by any chance?" Lucius knew this had to come and had been preparing for the situation for some time. It was not uncommon that some of the younger officers were the sons of centurions so there was nothing to be ashamed of, but the thought remained – it might be presumed he won promotion because of his uncle!

"Sir, Julius Petronius is my uncle." No matter how he tried to hide his emotions, they showed on his face.

"That is not a problem with me, lad. You are here to do a job; do it, and I will not give a *cac* who your uncle is. If you are half as professional as he is, then I will be a happy man and..." Faustinus paused, his eyebrows raised. "Holy Jupiter, that means you must be the son of *the* Lucius Felix Petronius? Marcus tells me if he was only half as rich as his brother, he could afford his own legion!"

Lucius shifted in his seat.

"Yes, sir, he is my father."

"So, what the fuck are you doing here in the legions? Working your way up the *Cursus Honorarium*, planning to be a consul? How come you are not a tribune?"

Thankfully, it was said with a smile. Lucius stalled. Faustinus was typical of his type; years in the legions, a Primus Pilus, the senior legionary centurion, before making his camp-prefect role. He could not be far from retirement. Though he was weather worn and tanned, he did not seem to have an ounce of fat on his wiry frame; in fact, he looked as fit as a much younger man. Lucius concluded the Praefectus had seen it all in his time and that his story would be in safe hands.

"As long as I remember, I had always wished to be a soldier," he began. "You know of my father. He built an extraordinarily successful business importing cloth and spices. Never satisfied, he added precious jewellery and stones to the business and over twenty years, he amassed great wealth, resulting in him being admitted to the ranks of the *Equites*."

Paradoxical, thought Lucius, that this social order's origins went back hundreds of years to when those rich enough provided their own horse when *soldiering* for Rome. "I always looked forward to the infrequent visits from my uncle Julius when he was on leave from the legions. He would regale me with tales of battles and glory, all in the name of Rome."

The Prefect laughed. "That's Julius, principally after wine! Damn fine officer, however."

"Well, I have to say, sir, such stories displeased my father. I was destined to be in commerce and trade, not the army. The one occasion they ever had a public row was about my uncle's martial tales of Roman valour. I remember it well."

"Families, Optio, families. You can choose your friends, but not your family."

"I know that to be true," said Lucius. "As I grew older, my father involved me in the business more and more; funnily enough, I didn't find any of it challenging. He was determined I should inherit the business empire. I tried, Prefect, I really did, but I became even more resolved to follow a military career. Matters came to a head when I was seventeen years old. My father made a critical comment about Uncle Julius. I snapped back with a comment about my uncle serving his country first and himself second. My father was furious and devised a plan that would, he thought, kill my military inspirations."

"Twenty-six-mile route marches!" the Prefect said with a chuckle.

"No, sir. Something a little more brutal. One of his clients was a lanista who ran a gladiatorial school near the Flavian amphitheatre. Father arranged for me to attend twice a week to learn sword skills. His logic was that if I had a hard time there, it would dissuade me from wanting a military career. The lanista arranged 'sessions' for me with his head trainer, Atelius, a freed gladiator who hailed from Egypt. He was to rough me up."

"Atelius?" Faustinus interjected. "You, my lad, are an interesting subject!"

"You know him?" Lucius asked.

"No, but I saw him fight some years back, not long before his award of the Rubus. It amused me to think that a steel gladius makes a champion, but freedom is given with a wooden version!"

"Let me go on, sir."

"Please, Optio, I'm fascinated."

"I met Atelius at the ludus twice weekly, not knowing at the time that Atelius was instructed to ensure I returned home black and blue each day. I was stubborn. A soldier had to be tough, so when Atelius regularly put me on my back, I arose again, sword in hand; moaning and grimacing perhaps, but I got to my feet. This routine went on for a month when, one day, Atelius' manner changed. He sat me down and asked me if I was serious about learning to use a sword and joining the legions. Naturally answered positively, and Atelius looked me in the eye saying, 'That being so, what I know, I will teach you.' From that point onwards, the nature of our meetings changed; the 'beatings' stopped, and we began serious training. When my father realised things were different, he threatened to stop funding the training, but Atelius offered me training in his own time for free. I don't know why, but I think he liked me and knew I was sincere. Giving in, my father continued to support the training."

"But surely, what Atelius taught you was not legionary procedures and drills, Optio?"

"Correct, sir, but he taught me to be confident in combat and I learnt a lot about sword-fighting." The Prefect nodded his head slowly.

"Go on."

"My uncle put in a word for me when I joined the legions; I was well educated, and my father had seen to it that I understood the principles of running an organisation. I went through two years of training and service, much in the field, before being appointed an Optio. It was planned for me to join the Auxiliaries, but just before leaving they directed me to meet with a centurion Crispus of the Tenth Legion. We had a good meeting; I had a high regard for him. He asked for me as his optio in the new IV Cohort he was putting together near Capua. The rest is history."

"He's a good man, Crispus, but never any good with the record keeping. I suspect he'll keep you as busy as a clerk. You will need a firm hand, or he will run you ragged!" Faustinus laughed.

"Very astute, sir - we have an understanding in that area," Lucius said.

Faustinus finished his goblet of wine with a flourish.

"Well, Optio Petronius, we must meet again tomorrow to discuss the arrival of Crispus and his crew. I have a plan which will see them initially quartered here in Caesarea; the Legionary Legate, Gaius Civilis, has approved it. But let's leave that until tomorrow. I intend to give you a small staff - two lads who will run and fetch for you - but more of that in the morning. I will arrange for them to join us after our meeting. Regrettably I cannot dine with you tonight, but there is a small taberna just beyond the barrack that is popular with the officers; you can't miss it, it's called the *Minerva*. The taberna's host is one Sistus, a veteran with some years of service behind the shield. Tell him I sent you and you can count on decent wine and fair food. It's very simple: if he upsets the Praefectus' guest, he gets closed!" Faustinus chuckled at his own joke. "I still have a few perks, Optio."

A beaming smile spread across Faustinus' face. Lucius smiled back, thinking Faustinus' waistline did not evidence regular visits to the Minerva.

Capitulum II - Apollinaris & Postumus

24 Martius. Year 16 of Imperator Hadrian

As arranged, the next morning Lucius arose and readied himself for the further meeting with Praefectus Faustinas. The previous evening had been uneventful. He ate at the Minerva where he mentioned Faustinus' name as instructed and consequently was served good wine and hearty food. While he passed a few compliments with other officers, no one seemed particularly keen to join him in his meal. Halfway through his dinner he noticed other officers were joined by none other than Centurion Drax, who had spotted Lucius before joining his comrades. A few minutes later, one of the officers said loudly,

"Well, Drax, young he may be, and his beard may make him look like a Greek, but he put you on your back!" Drax responded with a profanity and stormed out of the inn. Lucius finished his meal speedily and returned to his room in the barracks.

As a boy in one of his rare empathic moments, his father had gifted Lucius a copy of "Bella Judaea" by Josephus Flavius. The book was a history of the Great Judaean Revolt, which was crushed by Imperator Vespasian and his son Titus. The chief outcome of the war being the destruction of the great city of Jerusalem. Lucius had the book with him, removing it from his trunk. He spent some time reading through the account, thinking it might offer useful information on the region. There came an uncomfortable surprise with the retelling of the annihilation of the Legio XII by Judaean fighters.

Lucius never quite understood why his father had given him the book, bearing in mind his feelings about his son and the Roman army. Lucius remembered a heated discussion, one of several on the subject. Since Hadrian had become Imperator, his father argued that he had actively consolidated the Empire, even returning conquered lands won by Trajan. The Imperator was thinking like a Greek. Scornfully he talked of Hadrian building walls around the Roman Empire. His father was convinced there was still plenty of the world yet to conquer for Rome, enlarging the Empire and making its citizens much richer. He tried to persuade Lucius that in joining the army he would merely join a glorified urban cohort, pacing the walls of the Empire. They had lost the spirit of the glorious legions. In his father's view, there was no career for a son of the Petronius family in the legions of Rome.

His father had tried so hard to discourage him from following a military career, but at no time had Lucius wavered in his determination to carry the sword. It was just history now. Eventually, tired from his travelling, he fell into a dreamless sleep on his bunk.

Next morning, washed and dressed, Lucius was ready for his meeting. He was quickly back at the principia. Caesarea was an important Roman colony, and the principia reflected the town's standing. It was built of brick and fronted with gleaming white marble. The entrance was porticoed and left no one in doubt of the building's importance.

Even with his rank of optio, when entering a principium, Lucius always felt humbled, as though he was walking where he should not. As a boy, his uncle had told him many stories of the Roman army and its traditions, which had left him with a certain awe of the force. The principia, with the power and authority it held, was like a temple to him. It held the legion's money and even more importantly, it is where the standards were stored, along with the legion's precious eagle.

The awe soon dispersed as he entered Faustinas' office.

"Sit down, lad," he was commanded, "Did that old sod Sistus feed and water you well?"

"He did, sir. As promised, the wine was fine, possibly Falernian, and the food very good."

"Excellent, he didn't let me down," Faustinas said, "so he keeps his inn...for now! It's his wife, Octavia, that holds that place together. He was a proficient soldier though. Right, now to business."

He ran through his plan to move the V Cohort into tentage before they moved out to work on aqueduct repairs. The move would free up accommodation for the men of the IV Cohort so that they would arrive to some level of comfort – until Crispus got them out into the training field.

They talked through weapons issues, tent supplies, and the supply and stabling of horses where appropriate. Faustinus would introduce him to the Prefect Quartermaster, who had responsibility for supplying much of the sharp end for the cohort: armour, swords, shields, you name it. If anything required engineering, such as siege weapons, the Quartermaster was the man to go to. There was little that Faustinus did not touch upon, and in no time two hours passed.

"Right, Optio, we need a break. I think a stroll around the drill field might freshen us up, don't you?" No sooner had he spoken Faustinus was at the door, helmet in hand. It crossed Lucius' mind that Faustinus always moved with purpose; he was not one for ambling. Faustinus barrelled down the corridor placing his crested helmet on his head as he went, Lucius in his wake.

They stepped through the Portico into dazzling sunlight, though Lucius' eyes quickly adjusted. The air was pleasantly early morning warm, and the two officers set a pace. Fellow officers acknowledged the Prefect and soldiers developed straighter backs upon spotting the senior officer. They passed a century of legionaries being taken through drill postures; their centurion clearly aware they were under the gaze of the Prefect. Thinking to relieve the pressure on the soldiers, Lucius adopted a diversionary strategy and asked,

"Sir, I have heard a lot about Provincea Judaea from the cohort's seconded officers, but I would welcome your view?" asked Lucius, "Any insights would be welcome." The Praefectus' gaze left the nervous soldiers.

"Let's find somewhere in some shade." Suggested Faustinus.

They approached a bench situated under a cedar tree; grateful for the shade, they sat.

"Right lad – damn it, my apologies – Right Optio. We've been in these parts a long time. Provincea Judaea constitutes three regions: Galilee, Samaria, and Judaea itself. The Jews used to refer to it as Israel – many still do. The lads in Galilee and Samaria are generally as good as gold, but the Judaeans... The Judaeans don't like the Samaritans much."

"So, they are all Jews, but they don't get on?" asked Lucius.

"Yes. It seems the Samaritan view of the religion is different to that down south in Judaea proper and that pisses the Judaeans off. The Galileans? Well, they tend to keep to themselves and get on with life – and they live quite well off the back of us Romans here in Caesarea. Back in the Great Revolt, Vespasian hit Galilee very hard. They've learnt to live with us. If there's going to be a problem, it will come from Judaea. I sometimes think we get away so lightly here because the Judaeans spend more time fighting each other than us."

"But they have caused us some problems?"

"Yes, we've had occasional scraps with bandits, though of late, even that seems to have died down somewhat. Don't underestimate the Judaeans, they're a tough bunch; when they fight, they never know when they're beaten. Invariably, when it comes to a scrap, we kick the *cac* out of the *mentulas*, but sooner or later they come back for more."

"So, tough, but lacking in combat skills?" Lucius interjected.

"Don't misunderstand, Optio. They fight like demented lions and the way they go about it, ain't what we are strong at. They'll always avoid a major face-to-face fight. They usually hit us and run; appearing from nowhere and then disappearing as fast as they showed. We lost a good number of men in an incident last year. It was a cleverly planned ambush inside a small village. The lads got bombarded with roof tiles, so they formed a testudo. Next thing that hit them were huge rocks that even a testudo could not repel; then, once knocked about a bit, down at street level came the spears, crude I'll grant you, but they killed our boys all the same."

This took Lucius aback. The tactics sounded like behaviour beyond simple banditry.

"Were any caught?" he asked.

"Not one of the *cunni*. The villagers must have known what the bastards planned – you don't just stack rocks on a neighbour's roof and no one notices. The governor ordered the village razed, and occupants dealt with. A good part of the inhabitants was skewered, and the rest given to the slavers. Good riddance in my opinion."

"Reputationally, not good for us," said Lucius nodding his head in agreement. "If they believe they can beat us, then we'll have trouble."

"Precisely. Fortunately, it's not a regular occurrence. There's one crowd – sect, if you wish - that are as sweet as lambs: they're the Christian villagers. They try to keep a low profile as the Judaeans don't care for them much because they refuse to fight. Now and again, there's a fallout, and some throats get cut. They're good at that, are the bandits, an extreme and nasty lot. It seems they have an ally in a certain Rabbi Akiva. We'd particularly like to get our hands on him. It seems he's trying to stir up matters; he's been at it for several years, but it is damned hard to prove anything - just rumour. There's a man named 'Ben Koseba' who it's said is the bandit ringleader. He's a murky figure, and even our spies have been unable to give us much information about him."

Lucius had heard rumours but was surprised that such activity could occur in a Roman province.

"You're confirming some of what Crispus told me. I thought perhaps he was leaning toward exaggeration, but now it sounds not," he went on, "He's worked us all very hard on the practice fields. Even some of the centurions thought he might be bearing down a bit too hard on some drills."

"Oh, he would," said Faustinus laughing, "he was always one for the drill. *One day this gladius will save your life,* he used to say."

"That's Crispus! The very words. In the case of Judaea, perhaps he has some foresight!"

"Well, he may be right. However, things have generally calmed down, and it may well be that the Judaeans are finally getting the message; after sixty years! Of course, we get the odd incident, but even then, they are small fry, so hopefully, I might get to see my pension in a year or so."

"So, Crispus' efforts are wasted, sir?"

Faustinus sighed and shrugged.

"You can never say never, Optio, that much I have learned, but I think it may be the case, but we're an army and preparation is key; that time is never wasted. The Judaeans are sore over several issues. When he was first made Imperator, Hadrian passed through what remains of Jerusalem and announced that we'd build a new colony named Aelia Capitolina. It would have a Jewish temple built on the site of the temple that Titus pulled down years ago. Progress is slow, but it's coming together.

The Imperator's Greek mates brought pressure to bear about the temple, fearing it would feed Jewish nationalism and militant agitation. So, as a result, we're building a temple to Jupiter Capitolinus in Aelia instead, not the promised Judaean temple. It caused some upset with the Judaeans, but even that seems to have settled. I think as long as we keep reminding them of the power of Rome, they'll hold off – they can't win, you see."

"Well, maybe I should make an offering for that very outcome, sir," suggested Lucius.

"I'd kiss a goat's arse, if it got me what I wanted!!" said Faustinus. The conversation meandered around, but generally covered topics from the history of Judaea through to the legion's activities on a day-to-day basis. It seems the Fretensis had a fine reputation as aqueduct builders and produced some of the best roof tiles in the region. All in all, it left Lucius feeling he had walked into a complex situation, though one Rome seemed to be managing. "I'll arrange for you to meet the Quartermaster later today. Let's go back to my office. You'll remember I promised you some help and if all's gone to plan, they should be outside my office as we speak. Let me brief you before we meet them."

They arose from the bench and back into the now warming sun.

"They're both from a vexillation of the V Cohort detailed to my team for a month or two." Said Faustinas, "The first of them is Legionary Sextus Postumus who has twelve years' service in the Fretensis, so I thought he might be useful to you. He can also fight well, so he's a useful man to have at your side. The second is Marcus Apollinaris – his father was a Greek who gained citizenship way back. As soldiers go, he leaves a little to be desired, but, and it is a big but, if you need anything, Apollinaris will procure it. He's a good ear for what is going on – he does not miss a trick. He's also been here for some years. I imagine they will both be useful as the day draws nearer for Crispus' arrival. You'll need some organisational support."

"Thank you Praefectus; you've been a great help. But, you know, once I've met with the Camp Quartermaster, I suspect there'll not be too much to do here until we get closer to the cohort's arrival date. That'll give me a chance to get better acclimatised to the province and its politics."

"If that is the case, have you considered meeting with your uncle down in Aelia? You could use the excuse of visiting Quintus Vorenus, the legion's primus pilus, in Aelia. While Vorenus' I Cohort is here in Caesarea, he is with the Governor in Aelia. You represent Crispus, so you would be able to add detail to the formal reports the Primus receives from Crispus. Once the job's completed, you can look up your uncle."

"That sounds an attractive proposition and would be a path to getting better familiarised, sir."

"It would. I'll sort out authority for you."

They entered the porticoed headquarters building and made for the Prefect's office as he spoke. The air in the office was fresh as a steady breeze blew through an open window, shutters thrown back. Placing his helmet on his armour frame, Faustinus went back to the doorway.

"Sertorius, where in Hades' name are you?" he bellowed. Lucius heard a bench scraping on marble, followed by the sound of running feet. Faustinus strode to his chair as a young legionary came through the door quickly and skidded to a standstill, quivering at attention.

"Praefectus?"

"Where are the two legionaries I requested be here at this hour?" demanded Faustinus.

"I sent them to get some water, sir. They've been here a while. I'll fetch them, sir."

Sertorius turned smartly about and left the room as quickly as he had entered it.

"Legion's not the same Petronius; you just cannot get good staff anymore!"

"I can I take it that you are at least giving me *efficient* staff then, Praefectus?" Lucius feigned shock.

"So I am, hand-picked by me," Faustinus replied. In no time at all, two soldiers marched in and stood at attention in front of the Prefect's desk, followed by Sertorius, who hovered just inside the door.

Sitting to one side, Lucius looked the two legionaries over with a critical eye. They were smart, that was for sure.

"Well?" demanded Faustinus. Then, the taller of the two, who Lucius judged to be in his early thirties, dark, well built with muscled arms, Lucius took to be Sextus Postumus, spoke.

"Legionaries Postumus and Apollonaris reporting as ordered, sir." The two men stood rigidly at attention. It was not every day they met with the camp prefect, and they were both uncomfortable. These situations usually meant unwelcome news.

"Good. Enjoyed your water, did you Postumus?" asked Faustinus in a sarcastic tone.

"Yes, sir. There was no intention to keep you waiting, Praefectus, your clerk -"

"Forget it, Postumus. You and Apollinaris take a seat on that bench yonder," he said, waving a lazy arm at a long wooden bench pushed up against the wall of his office. The two legionaries sat as directed. "And in Jupiter's name, take your helmets off and relax, I am not about to crucify you!" The two men removed their helmets and visibly sagged.

"Right then, Postumus and Apollinaris, you're both seconded with immediate effect to serve as staff for Optio Petronius here," the arm waved in Lucius' direction. "You will know about the imminent arrival of the IV Cohort; the Optio here is making the arrangements for their settling in. I suspect he'll need some errand boys to do some running and sorting, and you two are it. Understood?" Both men nodded. "We have informed your officers – that is so, Sertorius?"

"Done, just as you requested, sir," the clerk responded.

"Good. It's not for me to brief you; I shall leave that to Optio Petronius. Optio Petronius is residing at an inn called the Minerva," a smile broke out on the Faustinas' face, "which I understand is to his liking?"

"Indeed, it is, Praefectus, especially Sistus' wine! But.... residing?"

"It's well you like it, Optio, as I have told Sistus that the army is taking two of his rooms. One for yourself, Optio, and," Faustinus turned to the two soldiers sitting uncomfortably against the wall, "you two will have to share. I thought it best if we billeted you as a unit; make life much easier for you on a day-to-day basis. Right, I have matters that need my attention. Sertorius?"

"Sir?"

"Have you alerted the Quartermaster? I expect the Optio is keen to get moving now he has a team."

"All arranged, sir," Sertorius replied, "I can brief the Optio as he leaves."

"Right then," Faustinus took in the documents on his desk, "I have things to do. Good day to you, men."

Secundus and Apollonaris jumped up and donned headgear. Lucius rose with a little more dignity, placed his helmet on his head, adjusted it and turned to the Praefectus.

"My gratitude, sir."

Following Sertorius, the trio left the office.

Once clear of the Headquarters building, Lucius and the two legionaries walked back to the barracks. Lucius quickly packed his two chests and tasked Marcus and Sextus to move both their belongings and his own to the Minerva. That done, he strolled back to the Minerva to find the inn almost empty. The smell of food reminded him that he had yet to eat, so he chose a table by a window and sat; Sistus saw him enter and once he was seated, walked across to him.

"Good day Optio. Are you settling into Caesarea?" he asked.

"I haven't seen that much, but I am sure that's about to change. You have rooms for me and my men, I understand?"

"Indeed, I have," Sistus responded, "You have my very best room, Optio. I am honoured that the Praefectus chose the Minerva for your stay."

"I am sure you are Sistus," He was conscious of a gnawing sensation from his gut. "Now, I have not eaten since your excellent dinner last night. What can you do for me?"

"My wife has a fine lamb stew just about ready. Stew, bread and a glass of wine, Optio?"

"That sounds good – the wine, though, not the usual piss! However, you can water the wine as I still have matters to deal with today." Sistus retreated towards a door beyond which Lucius presumed was the kitchen. The conversation with Sertorius before he had left the barracks with his "staff" had confirmed a meeting with the Quartermaster tomorrow morning first thing; Faustinus had been over-optimistic about a meeting later this day.

The IV Cohort would be bringing much of its weaponry with it, but many ancillary devices would have to be issued in Caesarea. At one end of the scale, these would include carts, tents, cooking utensils, through to the other extreme of scorpion catapults and small ballista. Equipping a four-hundred-and-eighty-man cohort so it would be ready for action was a significant task. Fortunately, Caesarea was a well-established Roman colonial town well supported for the job demanded. Lucius had a detailed list of equipment he meant to run through with the Quartermaster on the morrow.

Sistus arrived with a beaker of wine.

"Same as last night's Optio, though I've cut it as requested," he said, placing the beaker down. Lucius studied him swiftly. Sistus had the look of a legionary, but he had run to fat around the waist.

"Where'd you serve Sistus?" he asked. The innkeeper paused before answering and then sat down opposite Lucius.

"If I may Optio?" Lucius nodded, "My service was with the Tenth. Much of the time with Trajan in Parthia. I was at Hatras when Hadrian suffered from too much sun." He lowered his voice, "We then served under Quietus – a damn fine general in my opinion Optio – he certainly scared Hadrianus, who did for him once he became Imperator!"

"Probably best you keep that opinion to yourself, Sistus," Lucius responded.

"You're right, Optio. Hadrianus has done good for the empire, no doubt. After Parthia and Mesopotamia, we came back to the Judaean Province and Caesarea. About four years ago, I served my term and retired. I'd no family or ties, so I decided to stay on. I bought this place, married a nice local girl, and the rest should be obvious. The place pays well, and I appeal to the better class of customer – just like yourself, Optio."

"I will reserve that judgement for a few days, Sistus," Lucius responded.

"May I ask Optio; gossip says you're from the newly reformed IV Cohort; am I right?"

"Your intelligence is sound, Sistus."

"Are all the new officers… er, young sir?" Sistus was a little uncomfortable. "It's just that last night sir, when you was here eating your meal, some of the other officers were whinging – you know sir, "hasn't served his time, what do youngsters know about leading men" – you know sir, how they grumble."

"Sistus, you were- are, even - an experienced soldier. You must have seen a lot of change in twenty odd years?"

Sistus smartly responded,

"Be sure of it, Optio."

"Well, I am part of a changing army, selected to do a job in our new cohort. Now, do you think the command back in Rome is incompetent?"

"Absolutely not sir."

"So, rest assured, I will do that with which I am tasked."

"I thought so, sir. You see, I served under Aurelius Crispus. He was tough but dead straight, sir, and kept an eye out for the boys. So I said to 'em last night that if you are good enough for Aurelius, you're certainly good for the job!"

"Well thank you for that display of confidence, Sistus," laughed Lucius, "I'll call upon you if I get into difficulty. Seriously though, thank you for the tip-off." Then, almost out of nowhere, a good-looking woman appeared by the table, holding a large bowl of stew. She was shapely, hair tied back, big eyes and a remarkably smooth complexion; approaching middle age, Lucius thought she must have been a stunner when she was younger.

"Sistus Trianus, get out of that seat and get the officer some fresh bread!"

Sistus excused himself and disappeared off towards the kitchen.

"He's a good man, but he loves to talk – and they say women gossip! Enjoy your meal Optio; freshly cooked today." And she was gone. Lucius reckoned the prefect's comments about who ran this inn were accurate. Sistus arrived with the bread and immediately returned to the counter to serve soldiers recently arrived.

The lamb was good, the bread was warm and the watered wine refreshing. Lucius pushed the plate away from him and leant back, feeling content. He had some hours to fill before the sunset and wondered about a lazy tour of Caesarea. He had seen very little of the town since his arrival. His reverie was broken by a commotion at the door as five soldiers entered carrying Lucius' wooden chests along with an assortment of bags and other accoutrements.

Lucius noted that Marcus Apollinaris was free of any baggage and strode up to the counter where Sistus had just finished serving.

"Legionary Marcus Apollonaris, personal staff to Optio Petronius. We have both the Optio's baggage and the staff's baggage to place in the rooms arranged by the camp prefect."

Sistus looked down his nose upon the diminutive legionary.

"That's good. For a second there, I thought you were announcing the arrival of Hadrianus his self!" He turned toward the kitchen door. "Octavia!" Within a second, his wife appeared. "Can you show these men to the rooms for the Optio and his…servants." Marcus winced but did not respond.

"Follow me, please," requested Octavia.

"Right lads, you heard her, follow on," Marcus instructed his baggage party, "I'll be here when you comes down." The four soldiers, including Sextus Postumus, followed Octavia to the staircase and took the baggage up to the rooms. Marcus leant against the counter and surveyed the room. He jumped when a voice spoke up.

"Good work, Apollinaris!" Marcus stared toward the window table from which the voice appeared to emanate. Then, as he squinted against the bright sunlight pouring through the window, he realised who was sitting at the table. He straightened up quickly.

"Optio, sir, I didn't see you. The light – it's a bit dazzling. Your baggage is being taken to your room."

"So I gather Apollinaris. How'd you get the help?" asked Lucius.

"I -err – sprinkled the name of the Praefectus about a bit, sir." Responded Marcus sheepishly, "After all, he has organised our rooms, sir".

"Well, if it got the job done and the word does not get back to the Praefectus, then no harm done." As Lucius finished speaking, Octavia and the other four soldiers reappeared from upstairs.

"Thanks, lads." Called Marcus as three of the soldiers headed towards the door. They were not going to hang around for a quick beaker with an officer in the room. Sextus Postumus walked over.

"Chests in your room, sir. Nice rooms too if I may say so."

Lucius studied the two men. Sextus was a good head taller than Marcus; he was large by any standard. His hair was a dark yellow, his skin tanned but fairer than most and he had broad shoulders. Lucius was sure there was some Gaul in him. Lucius recalled the Praefectus' words about him being an excellent soldier and a fighter. Unfortunately, he didn't seem to be one for smiling much.

If you could imagine the opposite to Sextus, it must be Marcus thought Lucius. Short, dark, wiry with eyes that seem to be continually darting about, never quite looking you in the eye. Unlike Sextus, Marcus was always smiling though Lucius wondered how genuine the smile was.

"Right then," spoke Lucius. "Given we've only just met and given that we're going to be working closely as a small team, I'm going to break a rule. It'll be a one-off, and please do not misread my gesture. So, sit down."

Marcus looked at Sextus, who looked at Marcus, after which they obediently sat opposite Lucius, who turned towards the counter and Sistus.

"Sistus, a pitcher of wine; and ensure it's the usual wine too – oh, and please cut it generously!"

Lucius sat eyeing up the two men opposite who in response, stared back. No one spoke until Sistus placed the jug and two more beakers on the table then returned to his counter. The taberna had only two other customers, so he took to cleaning the worktops.

"So, men, who are you, and where do you hail from?"

"Family's roots are Gallic," said Sextus, "though my father served in the legions but got invalided out still a young man. My service has all been with the Fretensis, and I admit to liking the life. I'm thirty years old, so I've been with the shields for twelve years. I have Greek and a smattering of Aramaic, which I've picked up during service in Judaea. Judaeans? My advice is never to trust them. No matter how pleasant *some* of them can be, they all hate the Roman army. Having said that, a good number of the women are as beautiful as Venus." A smirk crossed Postumus' face.

"I hail from Antioch," chirped in Marcus, "where my Greek father ran an import business. He was a Roman citizen and proud of it. Unfortunately, the business went bankrupt when he made a stupid gamble on a shipment; it went to the bottom of the sea. The shame killed my mother, who died not long after, and I lived a wild life on the streets until I was sixteen. My father could not wait to see the back of me and persuaded me to sign up for the legions. He convinced me fortunes could be made with the shields. In Julius Caesar's day, maybe! Here I am twenty-eight years old, but I've found my true self in the army." Lucius felt that maybe he had made his fortune, but not via soldier's pay. Naturally, Marcus was fluent in Greek and spoke passable Aramaic.

Another jug ordered, and they talked about Judaea. Sextus believed that all the Judaeans should be enslaved and went on to recount some of the many skirmishes he had fought with bandits in the Judaean hills. "Nothing we couldn't handle, you understand." Lucius reminded him of the attack the Praefectus had mentioned. Marcus acknowledged that they were hit with a nasty one now and again. Had it quietened down? It appears over the last eight months it had done so – perhaps the bastards had seen the light!

Sextus sat listening then chirped in.

"Trouble is, Optio, we control the roads. We have toll houses and our Stationarii patrol the main routes looking for bandit activity. That way, trade and stuff continues, but what goes on in the hills in the hundreds of villages, well, we ain't got a clue. But, as Sextus says, it seems to have settled down, and many are happily trading with us. Used to be that the more extreme religious types would do for any of them what traded with us."

"What's all this about the temple in Aelia?" asked Lucius.

"Ah yes, the temple," said Marcus. "When he came to inspect his new colony a few months back, Hadrianus promised to build the Jews a temple. They worship one god and we screwed his temple, 'Holy of Holies' they calls it, when Titus and the boys flattened their city of Jerusalem after the Great Revolt. They yearn for a new temple on the site of the old one. You are following me Optio?"

Lucius nodded. Marcus continued.

"Well, a little while back, our Governor, Tinieus Rufus, announces that the temple will be built, but to Jupiter Capitolinus and not their god! It seems that Hadrianus under some political pressure had changed his mind. Well, that caused an uproar that is still grumbling. Then, to add insult to injury, the Tomb of Solomon collapsed. He was one of their prophets. They says it is an omen or something like. They blames the ground clearing works at Aelia for it."

"I was expecting an increase in banditry," added Sextus, "but it did not come. Of course, the legion was put on alert, we had the usual stone-throwing and wailing, but that was it. Pity really, a missed opportunity to rid the world of a few more."

The conversation meandered in and out of military matters and personal experiences, with Lucius making a small contribution and asking questions. The pitcher sat empty.

"I was thinking of taking some time to see Caesarea before the sun goes down. It's idle time since I shall not be meeting the Quartermaster today."

"Excellent idea, sir," Marcus jumped in. "Why don't Sextus and I show you around sir? We know Caesarea well."

"Nothing to worry about, sir," Sextus confided, "I shall keep Marcus here away from the dens of iniquity and ensure everything is respectable."

Lucius hesitated for a second and then smiled,

"Come on then, soldiers. We're wasting time." He tossed some coins on the table and arose. "Let's go and breathe the air of Caesarea."

The following day Lucius awoke early to a thumping headache. Leaving his bed, he staggered over to a table upon which sat a pitcher full of water. Lucius poured some of its contents into an accompanying beaker and downed it in one. Then he repeated the process twice before sitting on his stool and contemplating the cause of his headache.

As promised, Sextus and Marcus had shown him around Caesarea. Leaving the Minerva, they strolled past the baths, passed the Mithraeum to the Temple of Augustus. By the forum, Marcus suggested a swift drink, which indeed was swift. Up the Carbo Maximus they strolled and arrived at the amphitheatre. The little taberna on the amphitheatre approach was obliging enough to serve them more wine. The two soldiers regaled Lucius with tales from the legionary life along with some lurid details of life in Judaea and dealing with the bandits over the years.

They then strolled back again to view the Hippodrome, but they found themselves in another taberna along the way. At this point, they drew the attention of some scantily clad young ladies who made it quite clear that Heaven would be made available to them for the right price. Not being too far from where their exploration of Caesarea had begun, Lucius slipped away, leaving Marcus and Sextus considering the delights of Heaven. Lucius could not remember at what point he stopped watering his wine.

He regretted not drinking water before going to bed. The evening was not something he would do again, but he felt he had gotten to know his two 'staff' members and thought they could work well together. Of the two, Marcus might need the tighter rein.

After a light breakfast and with a much clearer head, Lucius raised his team by banging on the door and promising Hades' Fire if the two soldiers were not ready and presentable within ten minutes. Thirty minutes later, the trio entered the headquarters building. They marched down to the Quartermaster's office, several doors down from Faustinus; Lucius knocked and entered, leaving the two soldiers at ease in the corridor.

The meeting with the Quartermaster lasted about an hour. It appeared much of the equipment the IV Cohort would need was manufactured and waiting in the stores, including several carts to carry heavier baggage and the Cohort's Scorpios. These very useful catapults fire steel bolts, three-foot-long, capable of piercing two men at once. Lucius had lists given to him by Centurion Crispus before he left Italia and the two men worked through them quickly and efficiently.

Business completed, Lucius underwent gentle interrogation about his background and military career to date. He gave the Quartermaster a potted history before Lucius had the chance to ask some questions about the work done by the Quartermaster and his team at Caesarea. Lucius was a little surprised to learn that a good amount of the equipment manufactured was done so by Judaean artisans. The Quartermaster clarified that some contractors had supplied the Roman army for many years, and their workmanship was good. Except it seems where weaponry was concerned; their swords and spears always suffered a high rejection rate, but as the Quartermaster said, "You can't have it all ways." The meeting came to an end.

Lucius left the office and rejoined his men in the corridor. As he did so, a clerk walked towards them.

"Optio Petronius?"

"Indeed," responded Lucius. The clerk held out a small scroll.

"This is from camp prefect. He said you'd be expecting it." Lucius took the scroll and dismissed the clerk. He broke the seal and read Faustinus' message before handing it to Marcus.

"Documents are now your remit, Marcus. So you'd better get a bag to stow them in."

"Very good, sir," Marcus responded.

"Well, men, we are off to Aelia. I expect we shall be there for a couple of days. The objective is twofold. One, I meet with the primus pilus and brief him and secondly, I meet with centurion Petronius who, before you ask, is my uncle."

"Excuse me asking sir," interrupted Sextus, "but how're we travelling? It is a good two-day march."

"Don't worry, Postumus," Lucius smiled, "You won't be wearing down too many hobnails. The Praefectus has attached us to a supply convoy – if you don't mind sharing space with boxes of army provisions." He paused, then, "Right, Postumus, go to the market and get bread and cheese and anything else you think we may need. The convoy may feed us, then again, they may not. Apollinaris, we shall go back to the Minerva. Postumus, report back to the Minerva by mid-day, oh, and take this." Saying so, he handed Sextus several coins. "That should cover the food. Let's go."

"Excuse me, Optio, but I could really do with a piss," said Marcus.

"Get on with it Apollinaris," instructed Lucius. "Report to me at the Minerva."

At which point, all three went different ways.

Back at the Minerva, Lucius put some necessities into a leather bag and got ready for the journey to Aelia. He briefed Sistus, who promised to keep an eye on both rooms. A few minutes later, there came a knock upon Lucius' bedroom door, and he opened it.

"Just how many gallons did you piss, Apollinaris?"

"Sorry, sir, but…" his gaze moved to the rather splendorous leather despatch satchel that hung from his shoulder. Surprised, Lucius asked,

"In Jupiter's name Apollinaris, where did you get that?"

"Ah, well, sir, you see the route to the latrines passed by the commissariat. I just happened to look in, sir, they was all busy, but I did notice this bag lying near the door. Given the army –

that's you, sir – requires such a bag, I liberated it for your use, sir."

"I suppose it's army property in the use of the army, so arguably it's not theft, but I think the sooner we are on that supply train, the better, don't you, Apollinaris?"

"Wise words, sir!" Marcus responded.

An hour later all three were back at the Quartermasters' workshop complex where four covered waggons, each with two mules in harness, were at the later stages of loading. Stood a little distance away were eight legionaries propping up a wall; they were in full marching order though their spears and shields leant against the stonework, while their helmets sat in a row along the wall's top. Then, finally, Lucius spotted what looked like the waggon master.

"Wait here, men. I'll talk with the master and see what the plan is." At that, he crossed to the man busy issuing orders to the men loading the waggons. Although the day was still quite young, the work was hot. As Lucius walked across to the waggon-master, he noticed one legionary nudge his mates, who then looked in his direction. They were no longer lounging on the wall but standing a little more like military men.

The waggon master noticed the change in their posture and turned to see its cause. What he saw was a tall roman officer in a plumed helmet, Lorica Hamata, gladius, red cloak and leather boots fast closing on him.

"Ah, must be Optio Petronius," he said. "The Praefectus said to expect you and your men." He glanced over at Sextus and Marcus, who were approaching the group of legionaries. "You are joining us for our trip to Aelia? I am Lalius Galleo." He held out his hand. Galleo was dressed in a brown leather tunic and carried a sword in a baldric. He had dark hair and olive skin and looked about forty years old. Lucius took his hand.

"Lucius Decimus Petronius. Optio, IV Cohort of the Tenth. Do you have any plans for us?"

"Well, I have asked the lads to leave some space in the rear waggon for you," said Galleo. He shrugged, "A bit tight, I'll admit but I am sure you'll want to walk some of the way, and of course, Optio, you are most welcome to join me on the lead wagon."

"Where do you plan to stop tonight?" asked Lucius.

"We plan to get to *Antipatris* tonight – it'll be a late arrival. Tomorrow we'll strike out through the hills to *Aelia*." Galleo turned to look at his small convey. "We should be ready to move in a short while. Why don't you get your bags into the wagon? Meanwhile, I'll brief the decanus."

"Do you expect any trouble?" Lucius asked.

"You can never tell for sure, but it's been pretty quiet for a while, so I suspect not," responded Galleo as he turned to walk across to the soldiers. Marcus spotted the conversation was over, nudged Sextus and the two walked across to meet Lucius, who was heading in the direction of the last wagon.

"The boys are from the III Cohort, sir," Sextus said, nodding towards the train guard. "Came up with the last convey and going back down with this one. We will stop in *Antipatris* tonight."

"That I understand Postumus. Right, shall we get the bags stowed? We move off shortly. I'll go and have a word with the decanus." Lucius left the two soldiers sorting out the rear of the wagon while he walked over towards the soldiers donning helmets and handling their shields and spears. Lucius identified the decanus and made himself formerly known. The decanus snapped off a smart salute.

"Tesserarius Spurius Tetricus sir," the leader of the group introduced himself.

"I'm sure you've been briefed, Decanus, but my men and I are simply passengers on this trip. You carry on as you see fit."

"Of course, sir," he responded, "We heard you're from the new IV Cohort, sir?"

"That's correct," Lucius replied.

"Arriving shortly, are they, sir?" the decanus probed.

"I think that is for the army to tell, don't you, Decanus?"

"Sorry, sir, but my young cousin has joined 'em, sir. It would be good to see the lad. Ain't seen 'im in near six year, sir."

"Well then. Let's say you won't have to wait for much longer, Decanus."

"Gratitude sir," he turned to his men. "Right lads, form line. Quickly now!"

Lucius sat beside the wagon-master, and within a few minutes, the train moved south along the Cardo Maximus towards the South Gate and the road to Antipatris. The little convoy was flanked by its foot guard, four to a side while Sextus and Marcus walked behind the rear wagon.

Lucius learned that Lalius Galleo regularly travelled this route, moving military goods between Aelia and Caesarea. It seems they had little trouble of late, and he expected to arrive at the camp in Aelia by the evening of the next day. Lucius questioned Galleo about his experiences in the country and received the usual replies; don't trust them, and they've never forgiven us for destroying their temple. Galleo explained that many Judaeans had moved back into Aelia though it was not the great city it was before Titus devastated it after the Great Revolt. In addition, three years ago, Imperator Hadrian ordered the building of a new Roman colony on the site, hence the name Aelia Capitolina. Several new buildings were springing up, settling Roman officials, colonists, and their families.

Almost grudgingly, Gallo admitted that if you discounted the Bandits, many Judaeans just wanted to get on with their lives and find a working accommodation with the Romans. Still, they all lived in fear of the Bandits. Personally, Galleo was amazed the Bandits had allowed Judaean blacksmiths to produce weaponry for the Roman army. However, he never really understood them!

The countryside that passed by was not by any means a desert, but it was much drier than Lucius was familiar. Even so, there were trees and bushes alongside the road. Around the villages they passed, crops grew, along with orchards of fruit and olives, and always a quantity of livestock.

The day went quickly, helped by the conversations with Galleo and Tetricus and his small team at the rear of the train. They entered the northern gate, set in the low walls of Antipatris about two hours after sunset. Lucius and company did not have to depend on their cheese and bread supplies as Galleo took Lucius to a small taberna where he arranged a room for Lucius. It was clear that he and the taberna-keeper were on good terms, and Lucius suspected Galleo would get a kick-back for placing Lucius in the taberna overnight. Sextus and Marcus had straw beds in an adjacent stable along with Tetricus and the convoy guard. It was late, so activities were practical, and everyone ate and got to sleep quickly. Marcus may have had plans for sampling Antipatris' delights, but even he took to the straw.

Capitulum III - Ambush!

26 Martius. Year 16 of Imperator Hadrian

The following day was an early breakfast. The small convoy was moving in no time, and Antipatris was falling behind. The previous day had been a level ride through open plains. However, Lucius could see this leg of the journey would be different as the convoy began to enter the range of hills, heading onwards towards Aelia. As Galleo pointed out, they left Samaria behind and entered Judaea proper. The morning was uneventful, and the train halted for a rest at around midday at the small town of Gophna. The town had an auxiliary garrison. It took some time and shouting for the train to push through the populace going about their daily business. They eventually forced their way through to the market square and into a courtyard in front of an imposing building that was the garrison's headquarters. Two auxiliaries met with Galleo and exchanged familiar words before talking with Tetricus and the escort. Galleo ordered his drivers to dismount. He and his drivers saw to the mules while the escort fed on bread and cheese, as did Lucius and his two staff. Lucius took in his surroundings while Sextus and Marcus bantered with the soldiers.

Gophna was a hive of industry. People traversed the market while others were in and out of the shops lining the road. Loaded donkeys pushed their way through the crowd, and every so often, a couple of auxiliaries would march past going about their business. All this felt very different from Caesarea; Gophna was a Jewish settlement that suffered a Roman presence. Then, something caught Lucius' eye; a small group of men gathered in one corner of the market square. They stood out because they were static against a background of moving people. It seemed to Lucius that they were staring in the direction of the courtyard with some intent. Unfortunately, his view was disrupted by a passing donkey laden high with greenery and vegetables, and once it had passed, the men were nowhere in sight. Lucius simply shrugged and strolled back to the lead waggon, where Galleo checked the mule harnesses before moving off.

Within minutes, the train moved, and Gophna disappeared as they proceeded back into the hills. Lucius, riding with Galleo, jumped down and walked to the rear waggon. Then, falling in behind, he lifted the rear flap and climbed in to join Sextus and Marcus. It was a tight fit, but he managed to sit back to one side of the waggon facing the two men. The bulk of the vehicle was stacked with military tunics and other paraphernalia. Marcus noticed Lucius studying the cargo.

"Thought as how I might get me a new tunic, sir!" he joked. "We think there are even some *Segmentata* stowed at the front."

"Probably best you don't Apollinaris, I hear the camp quartermaster insists on flaying for theft," said Lucius, "or at least a hundred lashes." Of course, a little bit of exaggeration never hurts. "Right, I take it you're still in possession of the documents?"

Marcus rummaged around amongst the tunic bundles nearest to him and from under one produced his leather satchel, which he proudly held in front of him.

"Safe and sound with me, sir."

"Not sure you should let the Camp Quartermaster see that," chipped in Sextus, "or he may make bags from your skin – not that they would be up to much."

"I don't think…" Marcus was interrupted by a shout and the sound of a series of sharp thumps, and then mayhem outside.

"That's slingshot," Sextus said flatly. "We are under attack." There followed another series of thumps and more shouts and screams.

In the distance, a voice commanded, "On me, shields up!" It was Tetricus' voice. Lucius was suddenly conscious of being an officer, and he needed to decide for the three of them. It was simple; they had to help.

"Come on, you two; we can't leave them to it," rising as he spoke.

"Excuse me, sir," interrupted Sextus, "We don't have shields, sir, and they have slingshots. So if they are going to attack, they will have to come close, and the slingers will be disadvantaged for fear of hitting their own." It went through Lucius' mind that asking Sextus' advice should have occurred to him.

"Agreed, Postumus."

Another barrage of slingshots hit the train, coinciding with yet another yelp of pain. Lucius told himself to stay calm, especially in front of two legionaries, one at least who seemed to know just what he was doing.

"Also," said Lucius, "we may have the element of surprise, as I suspect they don't know we're here. If you lift the side canvas a little, can you see anything?" Sextus turned and did as suggested.

"Yes sir, the view's limited, but I can see two of our lads down. The bloody bandits must be hiding behind the bushes and the rocks as I am not seeing any of them. If we - oh *cac*! Here they come."

"How many?" snapped Lucius.

"Couldn't say a total, sir. Limited view," responded Sextus. "However, three of 'em are heading our way." In the confined space, the Romans frantically donned their helmets. The plumes on Lucius' helmet made it very difficult to stand upright. They constantly bumped into each other as they fumbled with their helmet straps.

"If this weren't so serious, I'd have to laugh," Lucius commented. As he spoke, a cry went up, shortly followed by the sound of steel on steel. Sextus arose, bent double under the canvas.

"I'll go first, as soon as some Jewish *cunni* lifts the flap. Marcus, get behind me. I suggest you follow sir." Lucius was not comfortable with Sextus taking control like this, but he was an experienced soldier and certainly acted as though he knew what he was doing. The big legionary stood up the best he could manage and waited by the flap with Marcus behind him. Lucius was unsettled. He had seen some action before, but not like this, only as part of an organised fighting unit.

"Let's do it", he said, and at that, they crouched down and waited, but for only a few seconds. The sound of combat raged then slackened; heavy footsteps were heard behind the waggon. Then, very suddenly, a hand pulled back the canvas flap at the rear. Lucius briefly caught sight of a heavily bearded bandit, a blue tunic, grey headscarf and what looked very much like a Roman gladius in his hand. However, the sighting was brief because Sextus, sword in hand, launched himself upon the bandit whose face took on the expression of extreme surprise; his expectation of booty had very suddenly been brutally altered.

Sextus' two feet landed on the bandit's chest, who fell backwards to the ground, with Sextus planted firmly on his chest. Behind the Jewish rebel was his comrade, also showing surprise at the easy pickings turning nasty. Sextus' momentum caused him to bounce forwards off the first Bandit and, in a flash, plunge his gladius into the chest of the second man. Meanwhile, Marcus leapt from the wagon onto the first bandit, desperately trying to regain his breath and slashed his gladius across the bandit's throat. Lucius, who was following close behind Marcus, caught a spray of blood from the man's throat.

The action lasted seconds, and all three Romans fell back behind the wagon. Sextus peeked around the side.

"Still some scrapping up front, sir. Not sure how many. About six *cunni* raiding the wagons from what I can see," he reported. Meanwhile, Marcus looked at the other side.

"Quiet this side, sir. Don't reckon there's that many of 'em!" he reported.

"Nothing for it, lads. We shall have to use brute force. I suggest we charge them, making a lot of noise as we go. We still have an element of surprise," suggested Lucius, trying hard to sound as though he was in control. The two legionaries nodded.

"On your command, sir," Sextus said. Then, kissing his gladius, Sextus said "Mithras, be with us." At which point Marcus fell to one knee. "Mithras," was all he said.

"Whichever god it may be lads," whispered Lucius. He took a deep breath. "On the count of three. One – two – three. Go!"

The three soldiers swung out from behind the wagon and quickly formed a line. Sextus spotted a Roman shield next to a fallen soldier and picked it up.

"Now I feel better," he said earnestly, "Let's do it."

With a roar, they charged forward. The bandits raiding the wagons leapt to the ground, grouped, and braced themselves for the onslaught. They were six in number, and after the initial surprise, upon seeing only three Romans, they regained an air of confidence – or so it appeared to Lucius. Within a heartbeat, they were in hand-to-hand combat. Lucius would remember little of the fight except that three bandits, keen to kill a Roman officer, faced him off.

Marcus and Sextus were facing three fighters. Sextus went at them full bore using his shield as a battering ram. But, caught in the act of sacking the supply train, the Jewish warriors were without shields. One of them leapt sideways, and his partner took the brunt of the Sextus' shield, staggering backwards. Sextus pulled his shield to his side, clearing the way for a forward thrust at the staggering fighter, piercing his stomach. One down.

Meanwhile, the diminutive Marcus came face-to-face with an opponent who was seriously larger than he, but unlike Sextus, he ground to a halt a few paces in front of the fighter. To the Judaean's surprise, Marcus smiled.

"Come on, cunni; I'm waiting!" Whether he understood or not, the Judaean smiled then rushed Marcus. The little man leapt sideways while at the same time his left hand whipped through the air, releasing a handful of grit into the fighter's face. His kneeling before the trio's charge had little to do with appealing to the gods but more about collecting a handful of dirt. You can take the lad from Antioch, but…. The half-blinded soldier threw up his arms to protect himself; it was almost as though he knew just what was coming. Then, Marcus drove his sword into the man's gut in a blur.

Sextus found himself up against a worthy opponent, and no number of feints or rapid thrusts would touch him. His opposition may not have had a shield, but he was very agile, and Sextus began to feel the sweat soaking into his tunic. Fortunately, Marcus appeared, and the tide turned. Just as the two Romans believed they had the man in a position to finish the fight, he made a rapid about-face and sprinted up the hill as fast as he could.

The two turned quickly to see Lucius thrust his gladius into the chest of one of two men attacking him. The third was already on the ground. As he withdrew his gladius from the man's chest, he pivoted around a full half circle, catching the throat of the third man who had been trying to flank him. The man dropped like a stone.

"Jupiter!" exclaimed Marcus, "did you see that?"

Panting, Sextus rested his shield bottom on the ground and leaned over it. The immediate danger was over.

"Right then, any more of 'em?"

Unbeknown to Lucius and his two legionaries, busily engaged with their fight at the rear, three Romans were fighting for their lives up at the front of the train, where Tetricus and two of his men were desperately holding off six bandits. No matter what training the bandits had received, no matter how committed and devoted they were to their cause, they were engaged with some of the most highly trained killers of their world, whose years of training had prepared them well for this. Tetricus' opponents, hearing the cries from the far end of the train, realised something was not quite going to plan, a fact reinforced as they saw one of their number fleeing back up the hillside. Tetricus noticed the slight waver in his enemy's resolution; this was the tipping point.

"Kill the bastards, lads!" he cried and pushed forward behind his shield, and his two allies did likewise. A gladius found its mark, and now it was five bandits they were facing. Another bandit, hit hard in the chest by a shield boss, fell backwards and was rapidly finished off by Tetricus, san his gladius in him as he stepped over the fallen warrior. It was now four. "Odds are improving, boys," he shouted, "*Fretensis* forward!"

At the rear of the train, it was over. Sextus' bandit had fled up the valley side where he, joined by half a dozen slingers, fled over the ridge and out of sight. Marcus stood atop a fallen bandit he had finally dispatched with the customary blade across the throat stroke.

"You're bleeding!" exclaimed Marcus as Sextus noticed a gash on his left arm. Sextus simply shrugged.

Meanwhile, fighting over, Lucius slowly started to take in his surroundings. Around him lay three bloody, dead bandits. What was so scary was that he could not remember it. Yes, he recalled the noisy charge and seeing the enemy coming for him, but just what happened.... he had the haziest recollection. Then, finally, he became aware of the sound of fighting from the front of the train.

Tetricus and men were still struggling; they had their backs towards the waggons pushing the bandit fighters back away towards the hillside. As he watched, much to Lucius' horror, a rebel appeared from the other side of the train. Lucius screamed out, "Behind you!" but as he did so, the rebel thrust a short sword into the back of one of the Roman soldiers, who immediately collapsed onto his knees. Tetricus turned in one smooth movement and pushed his shield at the bandit, deflecting a downward swing from the bandit's sword. The bandit raised his sword again to get over the top of Tetricus's shield. Tetricus swiftly pulled his shield to one side and drove his blade into the chest of the bandit, who joined the fallen Roman in the dust by the road. Tetricus turned neatly back to be beside his sole surviving comrade. A bandit was fleeing up the hillside bleeding badly, and the legionary beside Tetricus despatched another bandit, his gladius punching above his shield into the face of one of two bandits who tried to crowd him. The remaining two antagonists turned and sprinted back up the hill in a flash. The two Romans did no more than rest their shields on the ground and watched them flee.

"We'd better join them just in case the bastards come back," ordered Lucius as he bent down to pick up his helmet. The three soldiers walked up the length of the supply train, avoiding the dead and seriously injured as they went. Tetricus saw them coming.

"Well, that was not the finest hour of the Roman Army, Optio!" he exclaimed. He took in his surroundings. "We're it, I suspect. I believe all the drivers are dead, even poor Galleo, as are many of my men." He noticed Sextus' wounded arm. "Is that bad, soldier?" he asked.

"A scratch Decanus, a bit deep, but a scratch. Had worse in training," joked Sextus. Behind them, they heard a grunt. Turning, they saw a bandit lying on his back by a wagon. He had pushed himself up onto his elbows. His tunic was a black mat of wet blood. His face contorted in pain, he took a deep breath and spoke in a loud, clear voice before pausing, smiling, and falling back dead.

"That was not Greek," said Marcus, "Not Aramaic either...."

"It was Hebrew," stated a voice from behind them. The group swung round, and swords raised. Before them stood a Judaean, in a blue tunic adorned with two red vertical stripes on either side, he wore a headdress held in place by a crimson headband. He was dark-skinned with a close dark beard.

"Fucking bandit!" muttered Marcus. The stranger had excellent hearing.

"No, my friend; I have as good a reason to loathe them as you do." He spread his arms wide. "Apart from my small dagger, I carry no arms and do not wish you harm." As he said this, one hand moved to his dagger. The Roman group physically braced for a fight, but the stranger very slowly removed his blade using two fingers, held it out in front of him, and dropped it to the ground. "Please, you may search me if you wish."

"I'll do this," Marcus said. He stepped out of the group, sword in hand, and approached the stranger. "Don't you even flinch, my friend, or I will skewer you!" Then, with one hand, his left, he checked the stranger for a hidden weapon. "He's tellin' the truth, sir."

"Who are you?" asked Lucius.

"I am Matthias ben Shalev." The Judaean said in Greek, "My family lives in a village not far from here two miles beyond the hill. I was making for this road to return to Jerusalem – Aelia, when I heard the fighting. I sheltered until the bandits fled and then came to see what had happened."

"So then, Matthias ben Shalev." Lucius responded in the same language, "share with us just what our dead friend said before he expired?"

"Forgive me, but I will tell it literally. What our dead friend said was, *there is a storm coming that will wash all your Roman filth from our beloved Israel*."

Tetricus snorted, "More *cac* from one of their bloody books, I'm sure!"

"Well," Lucius replied, "wherever it comes from, we've more important issues right now. Tetricus, can you check our fallen and see to any survivors amongst them. Apollinaris, check the mules and the wagons; will we be able to carry on towards Aelia with the convoy? Postumus, come with me."

"If I may Optio," Matthias spoke.

"You recognise my rank?" Lucius asked.

"I have had some dealings with the Roman Army, and you have a distinctive helmet. Now, I studied with Rabbi Eliezer of Istra, a wise teacher, and a healer. I may be able to offer some little service?"

Lucius looked across to Tetricus, clearly signalling this was Tetricus' decision.

"Yea, why not? Come on, Matthias, isn't it?"

"I suggest you pick up your knife my friend," Lucius said to Matthias, who nodded, smiled, and said,

"Thank you, err...."

"Optio Lucius Decimus Petronius, IV Cohort, Tenth Fretensis," Lucius responded.

The survivors separated to attend to the allotted tasks. Lucius took Sextus back towards the rear of the train. Off to one side, lying face down in a pool of blood next to a bush, was an injured Roman soldier. Both officer and legionary squatted down beside the man and gently rolled him onto his back. The bloody soldier emitted a soft moaning sound; Sextus and Lucius caught each other's eyes, and Sextus slowly shook his head. Lucius could see the soldier had a severe stomach wound; it must have been a deep penetration by the amount of blood. Lucius knew what had to be done. He sat the man up and signalled Sextus by running a finger across his throat. He was beyond minding the blood that would stain his Hamata. Sextus nodded and bent over the wounded soldier.

Sextus untied the shoulder braces of the man's Segmentata and pulled the steel plates away from his shoulder, exposing the *subarmalis* tunic below, withdrawing his gladius from its scabbard.

"You're a lucky bastard lad, you are out of this bloody army, and it's time to get some rest. I'll pray to Mithras for you." He rested the blade gently upon the dying soldier's left shoulder as he spoke. Then, as he finished speaking, he thrust down hard, and the blade tore through the linen tunic into the wounded soldier's shoulder and penetrated the body by its left clavicle driving deeply into the heart muscle. The body twitched, and a little blood surged around the wound. "There wasn't much left in 'im, sir; poor sod!"

Lucius was quite affected by the killing. Ridding oneself of an enemy was one thing but slaughtering your own was not easy to handle, even if it was the kindest mercy. He took several deep breaths and lay the soldier down. He needed to take control.

"Once we sort out this situation, we'll see he is taken back to Aelia with the rest for cremation. Now, I'd like your opinion on something, Sextus. Come with me." The two men walked back to the corpses of the bandits they had slain at the rear of the train. Lucius stood by one of the corpses and stared down at it. "So Postumus, what do you see?"

"A dead Jewish *cunni,* sir," Sextus answered quickly.

"Apart from that. Look a little closer."

"Well, sir, he was a strong lad looking at his build. No shield, just a sword - hold up - you mean the sword sir?"

We got there, thought Lucius. "Exactly, Postumus, the sword. Look at it would you." So Sextus bent down and retrieved the sword which had fallen a little distance from the body.

"This is an army issue gladius, sir. Same pattern as mine. These boys must of done this before!" Sextus exclaimed.

"My thoughts exactly, Postumus. I want you to check every bandit corpse and tell me if they are equipped with army weapons. Do it now if you don't mind."

"Give me a few seconds, sir; this ain't going to take long." Sextus headed directly towards the other fallen bandit that the team in the rear wagon had dispatched. Lucius moved back up the train to find Tetricus. He found him squatting beside another injured soldier; Matthias was with him. Marcus appeared from between the wagons and apprehended Lucius as Lucius approached them.

"Sir. Wagons is alright, but a couple of the mules look like they was hit by slingshots. I don't think it is too serious, sir. Perhaps our Jewish friend can patch 'em up; they should get us to the camp sir."

"Good news Apollinaris. Let's see where we are with the wounded." Lucius strode over to where Tetricus and Matthias were treating the wounded soldier. Before he could ask, Tetricus looked up,

"Two men injured Optio. However, according to our healer here, they should be alright," he nodded towards Matthias.

"They are both victims of a slingshot, Optio," Matthias said, "Fortunately, Rome produces strong helmets. They are dizzy, and they are going to have painful headaches, but..." The wounded soldier turned his head to one side at this juncture, causing Matthias to jump back to avoid the fountain of vomited bread and polenta. "This is normal for such a head injury. He and his other injured comrade will not be able to walk for some while; they will need to go back in a wagon."

"Fucking good job they weren't using lead army slingshot," Tetricus said, "They'd be very dead by now!"

Lucius turned to Tetricus.

"Well, fortunately, Decanus, they are still very much alive. Put them in the rear waggon. Marcus give the decanus and this legionary a hand to move the injured. Matthias, would you help?" Matthias nodded and took hold of the casualty. Lucius felt that order and normality was beginning to return. Watching the legionaries and their newly found medicus shuffle the injured soldiers back down the train, he called out,

"Decanus, can you leave your legionary with the waggon to keep the men as comfortable as possible. He received an affirmative response from Tetricus, at which point Sextus arrived from his inspection of the dead bandits.

"Ten dead bastards, sir. There was eight when I started though." He smiled, looking very pleased with himself.

"You are every bit the warrior!" smiled Lucius, "But what of the weaponry?"

"Funny that. Five of our gladii, sir. I also spotted four pugio daggers, sir, all dead ringers for army issues. Two of 'em had issued auxiliary helmets, sir."

Lucius stroked his beard in thought.

"They've been at this for some time, Postumus."

"Looks as that might be the case, sir. Something else though. I noticed several the *cunni* seems to 'ave the top of the little finger on the left hand cut off."

"Can't say I noticed," Lucius said. "Can it be some sort of bandit initiation, right?"

"Well, these Judaeans seem keen on cutting certain parts of their bodies, sir" Marcus responded, grinning.

"I'll ask Matthias if he knows," Lucius responded. "Right, we need to get the wagons back to camp at Aelia. Can you get everyone together once they've dealt with the injured and we'll sort out a plan to get this lot moving? We need to collect our dead first and strip the bandits of their weapons. Postumus, would you collect all the army-issued weapons they were using."

It was not very long before the convoy moved off along the road. Matthias, a man of many talents, drove the first waggon with Lucius at his side, the remainder of the survivors split between the other three waggons. The two men said little initially, both lost in their thoughts until after several minutes had passed, Matthias asked,

"Were the dead all your men, Optio?" Lucius was not sure he wanted this conversation, but the Judaean had shown a willingness and helped the injured men so far.

"No, I was simply a passenger on a regular supply train. Postumus and Apollinaris are with me."

"You must hate us?" asked Matthias.

"I am not long in your country, and until today I had no reason to hate anyone."

"You know Roman, those people who attacked you; they don't represent us all." Lucius detected exasperation in his voice. "There are many of us with no great love for the Roman Empire, but we can accommodate you. To an extent, the Imperator has left us alone, and if we cough up his taxes, I imagine he will probably remain to do so."

Lucius laughed, cynically,

"So, what just happened was accommodation then, was it?" he asked quite sharply, "Those men wanted me and my comrades dead!"

Matthias sighed.

"There are some of us who are extreme. Filled with religious fervour; they speak of you Romans defiling God's land, and they must drive you from Judaea, Samaria - indeed all of Israel. What the dying bandit said was typical – even in his last breath, he condemned you."

"Who allows this to happen? I thought your Rabbis had control over your country." Then, it was Matthias' turn to laugh.

"Oh, we are a strange nation, we people of Israel. We argue, we debate – yes, and sometimes we fight. But, you know, in the Great Revolt, while you were besieging Jerusalem, within the walls Jewish sects fought each other! Yes, even while a common enemy was at the walls, determined to destroy us, we fought each other! Can you believe it?"

"I've read Flavius Josephus," said Lucius.

"Then you know we are not all like this. A few years back, you may also know that the Imperator Hadrian had planned to build a new temple for us in Jerusalem – err, Aelia. Regrettably, he changed his mind and the Judaeans, egged on by the Bandits and a new breed of Zealots, armed themselves and prepared to fight. It was the great Rabbi Yehoshua who managed to change their minds. He told them a story of a Lion who had a bone stuck deep in his throat, so much so that he could not swallow and would starve. The Lion saw a crane walk past and made an offer to the bird. 'If you remove the bone from my throat with your long bill, I will give you a great and rare thing that will be with you all your life. The bird immediately offered to remove the bone and indeed did so. Once the bone was free, he asked for his gift. The Lion said to the Crane; you can go about the world and tell all you see that you are the only living thing that has ever stuck its head deep in a Lion's mouth and lived to tell the tale! Your survival is your reward'". Matthias chuckled. "Yehoshua knew that carrying arms put the people in the lion's mouth. They saw sense, went home, and put their weapons away. Yehoshua was a peaceful man – always. He never saw sense in violence."

"Was?" asked Lucius.

"He died a while back, and though he had many followers and students, I fear that others of a more forceful nature are holding sway," said Matthias, "Even now, many of us are at loggerheads!"

Lucius shook his head slowly,

"You know, a good friend back in Italy warned me not to try and understand you people. He claimed no Roman ever has!"

"I was raised here, Optio," laughing, Matthias replied, "and at times I am not sure even I truly understand."

"So, what do you understand about bandits cutting the ends of their fingers off?" Lucius asked.

"You have seen this?" a surprised Matthias responded. Lucius nodded.

"Some of the dead back there were so mutilated."

"I had heard myths, rumours, of a force of great warriors who would do this. It has now just become a bandit token of bravery."

"Let's hope so," Lucius said, letting the subject drop.

They rode on in silence for a few minutes before Lucius said, "Tell me about Aelia, Matthias."

"Well, the conquerors, for that is the term we often use for you Romans, occupy a great camp that stands on some of the ruins of our holy city of Jerusalem, which is where you are heading. From there, you rule Judaea, but this you will already know.

Before the Great Revolt, Jerusalem was a beautiful city and the home of the temple built by King Herod, said by many to be one of the finest structures in the world; indeed, the city was often spoken of in the same breath as Rome. By the end of the revolt, buildings lay in ruins; some burnt, others ransacked, and yet even others destroyed; some out of pure vindictiveness during the internal disputes between the factions I mentioned earlier and others by upon Roman orders. Thousands of Jerusalem's inhabitants died or were taken into slavery. "Woe unto you, O Israel!" he quoted.

"Those who remained lived a hand-to-mouth existence, and many starved. However, as time passed, those with memories became fewer and fewer, and small numbers returned, being allowed to settle. Today, a small community in Jerusalem – Aelia, as you know it - lives side-by-side with the Roman occupation, yet the city is a mere shadow of its former self. Our priests no longer meet there; ever since the fall of Jerusalem, they gather in the town of Jamnia. When Hadrianus first became Imperator, he passed through Judaea and founded the new Roman colony of Aelia Capitolina on the site of Jerusalem. It was a slow start, but the colony is growing, and people are settling in.

The Jewish people long for a new temple in Jerusalem, and it was a bitter disappointment when Hadrian chose to dedicate his planned temple to a Roman god and not the one true God." He stopped speaking, wondering if he had gone too far with his words.

"It would sound as though we merely tolerate each other," Lucius said, keen to show no offence had been taken, "or at least we do so in Aelia?" He added, recalling the earlier incident back along the road.

"That might be one way of looking at it, Optio," responded Matthias.

"Aelia aside, Matthias, have there been violent incidents of late?" Lucius was aware he was moving onto sensitive territory with his question. Matthias took in a breath and replied,

"Of late, Optio, not much. Given you were so close to Aelia, I am surprised the bandits attacked you. Such things have been rare. There has been grumbling and protests, but violence of this nature has been few and far between."

"So, you are saying we were just unlucky then?" Lucius asked.

"I don't know," Matthias replied.

"Tell me then, Matthias, just who are these bandits?"

"They are those who cannot let go of the past, Optio." He paused, then continued, "They have a hatred of the conqueror and make a living from hurting you and stealing from you. They believe they are advancing the cause of Judaea, indeed the whole of Israel, but they are doing no such thing. On the contrary, since the last rebellion some years back, where they were crushed so totally, they have become a thorn in Rome's side – no more than that.

You know Optio, our scripture says that neither political manoeuvring nor armed resistance will bring redemption.

Furthermore, we are taught that until the ten tribes of Israel return to our land and until the temple is rebuilt, only until these things happen, then and then only a Mashiach – Messiah in Greek - will come to restore Israel in all its glory. Many of us merely want to worship the one true God and await the time that he determines for the coming of the Mashiach. Be assured; we know what armed resistance will lead to; Rome could stamp on Judaea as a boot stamps upon the scorpion." Matthias paused. "I am sorry, Optio; my mouth runs away with me again."

"Matthias, I'm a Roman soldier, and I love the army. However, my father taught me that when in negotiations, you must always understand the other side, for only through understanding can beneficial arrangements be determined. So, help me understand. The bandit who spoke to us just before he died. He sounded more than just a bandit who hates 'the conquerors?"

"Perhaps Optio," replied Matthias, "he was simply a man who only had words remaining to hurt you…" The conversation was interrupted by the sound of horse's hooves, and a cavalry Decurion drew up alongside Matthias' waggon in no time. Lucius observed that the supply train now had a cavalry escort on both flanks. A turma of thirty armed cavalrymen had overtaken them. Lucius experienced a feeling of relief, for each equestrian carried a large round shield emblazoned with the bull motif of the Tenth and a long cavalry spear. In addition, each was armed with Spatha, the long cavalry sword, giving the riders a better killing reach against infantry.

"Not often do I come across an Optio commanding a mule train!" called the cavalry commander. "Looking at some of the mules, I suspect you've seen trouble." He turned his stare to Matthias, "This one a Prisoner?"

"Stop the wagon, Matthias," instructed Lucius, and as the vehicle slowed, he jumped down onto the road. The Decurion dismounted and the two men drew to one side of the wagons. Lucius shared the details of the attack with the officer, along with its consequences. The soldier was all Roman military efficiency. He called a fellow horseman to join them, instructing him to send two riders to the fort at Aelia at speed. They were to alert the

Pilus Primus to the attack and the medicus there that two badly injured soldiers were on their way. The remainder of the turma would escort the supply wagons to the fort. In no time, two troopers thundered ahead of the convoy towards Aelia. The Decurion turned back to Lucius.

"If I may say, Optio, I am not sure that a Judaean driving a military supply waggon will be well received at the fort. Therefore, may I detail off one of my lads to take over the waggon? You can take his horse and the Judaean can walk."

Lucius called Matthias down from the waggon and explained. The Judaean accepted the situation; a cavalryman was quickly at the reins of the cart. Lucius mounted the driver's horse. The Decurion had remounted and rode up beside Lucius.

"Perhaps we should lead this procession, Optio?"

"Lead the way, Decurion...?"

"Caius Manlius, Optio. First Ala. Tenth Fretensis."

"Lucius Decimus Petronius. IV Cohort. Tenth Fretensis."

"Fourth? You boys have arrived then?" asked the decurion. He turned in his saddle, raised his arm, and called "Forward. At the walk." Once they started to move, Lucius responded to the decurion's query,

"Very soon, I am arranging the arrival."

Capitulum IV - Aelia Capitolina

26 Martius. Year 16 of Imperator Hadrian

Lucius turned his horse about a while later and headed to the rear, drawing up behind the last waggon.

"Legionary," he called to the soldier within, tending to the two casualties from the ambush. The cover on the waggon's rear drew back, and a soldier's head and shoulders leaned out.

"Yes, sir?"

"How are our two lads faring?" Lucius enquired.

"I'm not a medicus, sir, but I think Terentius isn't doing well. You know; very quiet and very pale, sir. He's lost a lot of blood. As for Quietus, sir, he's already whining about the ride, so I am sure he'll be fine. How long 'till we reach camp, sir?"

"The decurion tells me it isn't far off. Do your best. We've sent word so that a medicus will be ready to meet us when we arrive at the fort." Lucius returned to the head of the convoy, where he briefed the decurion. Both men decided that increasing speed would not be helpful but concluded that Matthias should intervene with the more poorly soldier. Lucius rode back to where Matthias was walking alongside Marcus' waggon. For someone who claims to hate Judaeans, Marcus was conversing freely in a language Lucius did not recognise. Lucius broke into the exchange.

"Matthias, I'd like to make use of your medical skills again. One of the soldiers in the rear waggon, Terentius, is in a bad way and getting worse. Would you look at him? Tell the soldier tending to him that you are there on my orders."

"I will, Optio," Matthias responded and, saying so, headed off to the rear of the small column. Lucius returned to the head of the column and fell in alongside the cavalry commander. The decurion turned to Lucius.

"Strange one that Judean," he said, "There aren't many of them who would actively help us. You say he just appeared after the scrap with the bandits?"

"Yes," Lucius responded, "He was on his way to Aelia when he heard the fighting and took cover until it was over."

"By now, nothing surprises me in this country," said the decurion with a resigned expression. Lucius steered the conversation to the decurion's past service, and the two men continued to share experiences until sometime later, cresting a hilltop, Lucius had his first view of Aelia.

Atop a large hill sat a township, and it looked very new. The entry was through a large gateway, though it surprised Lucius that the gateway stood in splendid isolation. On either side of it, there was nothing but large stone blocks, lying at all angles. It was strange to look upon this new colony without protecting walls. Lucius recalled how the Imperator Vespasian had instructed Titus, his son, commander of the legions which had successfully seized Jerusalem, to ensure the city's destruction was total. The Judaeans would never again use this town to fight Rome as a home or base. Now, it was becoming a new Roman Colony. As they closed upon the gateway, Lucius could see that the road ran through the wide gateway into a large square.

"This was one of the main gates to the old city, the North Gate. Titus' lads broke into the city through this gateway during the Great Revolt. Jerusalem, now Aelia, has been the Judean base for Tenth since Titus took the city," the decurion explained, "Apart from the new project and the fort, much of the rest of the place is ruins. A few manage to scrabble out a living amongst the stones. Outside the fort, there's a *vicus* where suppliers and their families live. Many soldiers have women living there too – along with the usual whores."

"What happens when their units return to Caesarea?" Asked Lucius. The decurion laughed,

"You should see the tail end of the march! Baggage, women, children – you name it. And there is a similar procession in the other direction coming from Caesarea. The whores stay put; they get a new supply of customers!"

"Once through the gate, just how far is the fort?" asked Lucius, thinking of the two casualties in the rear of the convoy.

"No distance at all," replied the horseman, "Once through, we pass down what is now the Cardo Maximus straight to the gates of the fort; we should be there very soon now."

As the convoy moved towards the camp, Matthias appeared alongside Lucius.

"Optio, I think it best that I take my leave of you all. Legionary Terentius will live, but I suspect it will be many days before he sees soldiering again. The other will be fine; he was well enough to complain about sharing 'his' waggon with a Judean 'scum'."

"I'm sorry, Matthias," said Lucius, "but understand who'd just killed his comrades and countrymen. But I thank you for your assistance. I hope you get to your destination safely."

"Farewell Optio. Should we meet again, I hope it will be under more pleasant circumstances." Matthias turned away and took a route that took him along the front to the ruined walls rather than through them.

"Do you trust him?" Asked the decurion.

"Well, he's gone now, but he gave me no reason at all not to trust him. It might well be that one of our casualties owes him his life. He tried to convince me that not all Judaeans are bandits and that many are happy to accommodate us."

"That may be Lucius," replied a sceptical decurion, "but don't be fooled. They'd offer you bread at the same time as they stick a knife in your back."

As they passed through the gateway, the view that greeted Lucius took his breath away. In front of him was a small, paved square of which ran a perfectly laid street, the Cardo Maximus, lined with bright new buildings, some of which were clearly in use and others in various stages of completion. Masons were erecting a large column in the middle of the square, and to the right lay more buildings and alleyways. An area yet to be developed, to his left, was devastation he had never witnessed. The contrast between this area and the newly erected colony could not be greater. Yes, he had seen enemy villages and small settlements destroyed, but never a city. He wondered how many men must have toiled to wreak destruction to this extent; the power who sanctioned such a project must have been entirely determined and driven by an intense hatred of the place and its people.

The damage was such that it was impossible to determine where one building started and the next one began. Amongst the ruins, weeds, bushes, and small trees grew between which small birds flitted; this, thought Lucius, was a definition of devastation. In the distance was the ruin of a great tower; between it and the convoy lay nothing but a desert of rubble. The perfectly constructed roadway upon which they moved accentuated the sense of destruction.

The decurion was watching Lucius with a smile on his face.

"Rome does not tolerate revolt, Lucius. Anyone who thinks they can best us should come here and see the consequences for themselves. These Judaeans may scratch and spit at us, but they know the price they would pay for revolt. We simply must remind them now and again."

"I confess, Caius, I have never seen anything like this. It must have been a great city once."

"It was. Do you see the ruined tower ahead? It's what remains of the fortress of Antonia; just look at the size of it. They tell me the Judeans great temple stood beside it and it dwarfed Antonia."

Lucius squinted in the sun but could only see the tower's remains.

"There's nothing there, Caius. Am I missing something?" The decurion shook his head.

"No, my friend, *you* are missing nothing, but the *Judaeans* are - their temple!" At which he burst out laughing at his joke.

"Hades," swore Lucius, "but there is simply nothing there."

"After the revolt failed, Vespasian ordered Titus to level it entirely, and being an obedient son, he did as his father requested.

"I knew Titus sacked the temple," Lucius said. "I remember as a boy being told by my father that Vespasian used the gold to fund the building of the Flavian amphitheatre in Rome. I hadn't realised just how far Titus had gone in destroying the city."

"Every single block that was the temple was thrown down," said the decurion, continuing his lesson in Jewish history, "and when levelled, Titus' men started upon the city. They were well motivated as many inhabitants had hidden gold and other valuable possessions during the siege. Using prisoners to search and scavenge, many soldiers became rich amongst the ruins. The only area still readily identifiable was the remains of Antonia."

As the topic of their conversation, Antonia's ruins drew closer, the mules developed a spring in their step and strained to up the pace. The decurion noticed the beast's determination.

"They've come this way many times, and they know that a feed and a stable is ready and waiting," he commented. The convoy crossed the square and headed along the *Cardo Maximus*, one of the main thoroughfares of the new colony. Both workers and residents glanced at them as they passed along the street. Those who gave them more than a glance sensed that something was not right; a cavalry *turma* of thirty riders does not usually escort such a small convoy, and why did legionaries drive the wagons? Where were the drivers?

They descended gradually downwards as they travelled along the Cardo, the road being a gentle slope. At the bottom, when they had crossed the expanse of the town, Lucius could see great wooden gates across their path; it was the entrance to the Roman fort that served as a base for the Tenth Legion in Judea. The gates opened, and two riders complete with shield and spears trotted clear of the gate and up to the head of the convoy; it was the two cavalrymen the decurion had sent on ahead to forewarn the camp of the convoy's situation. They stopped before the decurion and snapped off a salute with a nod to Lucius. Their message was straightforward. The convoy should stop inside the camp gates where the medicus and his orderlies would remove the casualties. At the same time, the bodies of the slain legionaries would be removed by a party detailed to arrange a funeral for the men. It crossed Lucius' mind that his opposite number in the dead men's cohort would soon be working on the men's funeral funds and arranging their savings to be sent home to their next of kin.

The decurion ordered the column forward.

A double file of soldiers appeared as the convoy passed through the gates. They were all dressed in military tunics, no armour or protection save the swords on belts around the waist.

At their rear, the soldiers carried some simple wooden stretchers. Behind them, bearing two leather stretchers, the medicus and his team came. As the convoy came to a halt and Lucius dismounted from his borrowed horse, a second party approached.

The leading figure was every bit a Roman officer. The red plumes spanned his highly polished helmet from left to right, broadcasting his rank. The eight golden disks, each depicting some martial image or scene, positioned on his chest on a leather harness, confirmed his considerable experience. His Lorica Hamata shone, as did his greaves about his legs; here was the Primus Pilus of the Tenth Fretensis Legion, Quintus Vorenus. Accompanying him was a small gaggle of officers and four armed legionaries.

Instinctively, Lucius snapped to attention and saluted. The centurion briefly raised the vine-stick he was carrying, acknowledging the Optio's salute, before letting it fall to his side again.

"It must be Optio Petronius... and you can relax Optio. I hear you've been in a bit of a scrap; looking at the state of your Hamata, I'd say the other side came off worse!" With everything that had occurred, Lucius had utterly forgotten that he had been liberally sprayed with other men's blood during the recent fight. What had been scarlet was now a dark, sticky stain sitting across the metal links of the hamata.

"Indeed, sir, but I regret to say that's not all Jewish blood, sir. Unfortunately, we lost legionaries today." At which point Tetricus marched over to join them, snapped to attention and saluted.

"Decanus Tetricus, sir. With the Primus' permission, sir."

"Speak," responded Vorenus.

"Sir, six legionaries dead an' two wounded. All the drivers killed. The wounded should recover, sir. The bandits got nothing. Seven dead, the rest fled. Swordsmen and slingers, sir. Much of the damage is due to slingers, sir. It might have been worse 'ad it not been for the Optio and 'is two legionaries being concealed in the rear waggon – took 'em by surprise you might say, sir." At that, Tetricus stopped. Vorenus turned to Lucius,

"Your two men unscathed?" Lucius looked over his shoulder at the short procession of stretchers leading away from the waggons; when he faced the Centurion again, he said,

"Compared to some, yes sir, unscathed." As Lucius spoke, the decurion rode across to them, brought his horse to a stand and saluted.

"Primus, with your permission, I would like to get the horses stabled; it has been a long day for us."

"Of course, Caius, go ahead," the Primus responded with a wave of his vine stick. The horseman turned and rode back to his column.

As the horses disappeared through the gate, a group of scruffy, unmilitary individuals appeared and walked towards the gaggle of officers and Lucius. Vorenus spotted them out of the corner of his eye, turned to them and in a peremptory manner said,

"Right, you men, get these waggons to the Praefectus' stores immediately." Sextus, Marcus and Tetricus' surviving legionary jumped down from their waggons, and the drivers took position; within moments, the creaking carts moved on through the gate. All that remained was Tetricus and his one surviving uninjured soldier, Lucius and, standing a little off, Marcus and Sextus. Facing them stood Vorenus, three officers and the four legionaries. Vorenus' vine-stick slapped his thigh – a sign to those that knew him well that he had come to a decision.

"Tetricus, get yourself and your man back to the barracks, get cleaned up and then report to the Praefectus' office," He broke out into a smile. "He'll want a complete account of what has happened to his beloved waggons. Tomorrow morning I'll want a detailed report from you." Turning to Lucius, "These two must be with you?" using his vine stick to point to Sextus and Marcus, "Step forward. I heard you played an important part in driving off the *cunni* today."

The two soldiers stepped smartly forward. The Primus Pilus developed a broad smile as he slowly shook his head,

"By Jupiter, Marcus Apollinaris. You are like a bad sestertius; you keep turning up."

Marcus filled his chest a little, stared directly ahead and recognised the Senior Centurion's comment with but one word.
"Primus."

The vine stick arose until it pointed to the leather bag that hung from Marcus' shoulder.

"And that, if I am not mistaken, is a despatch bag. Have you changed your role, Apollinaris? Are you now a messenger?" Marcus showed severe discomfort, but he held his ground. He assumed his best attention posture, puffed out his chest even further and replied.

"Primus, sir, I – err – I was asked to carry official papers concerning the IV Cohort for the Optio, sir. Official papers needs an official bag, sir, so I am using the bag as the army intended sir – to carry official papers like, sir."

Lucius, a guilty partner to Marcus' misdemeanour, quickly spoke up, keen to defuse a potentially tricky situation.

"Legionary Apollonaris was acting at my request, Primus!" The centurion looked at Lucius then turned to Marcus; after a few seconds of visual scrutiny, he relaxed, tension gone.

"Alright, no harm then but take my advice Petronius, keep an eye on that one."

"Of course, Primus, but may I say that both these legionaries fought with bravery earlier today, sir, they did the Fretensis proud."

Vorenus nodded,

"Remiss of me. You never cease to surprise me, Apollinaris and legionary....?"

"Postumus sir, Sextus Postumus. V Cohort sir."

"Well then, on behalf of the Fretensis, well done men," noticing the bandage on Sextus' arm, he asked, "Is that bad Postumus?"

"No, sir, just a scratch. I must be slowing upon my old age," Sextus quipped.

"Good to hear it's not serious. Now I am sure you'd all like to refresh and perhaps clean up?"

Within minutes, Lucius was ensconced in a room in what would be the Fourth Cohort's barracks in weeks to come. He had requested that his two men should stay in the same barrack block;

the request was readily granted, so the two men were nearby. Lucius requested Marcus to report once he was settled in, and he gave his hamata to the soldier with an instruction to return it cleaned first thing the next morning. As the evening was fast approaching, he gave both soldiers free time for the rest of the day.

Lucius washed and changed his tunic and felt ready to eat when there was a knock on his door. Just as he was beginning to relax, it looked like the army was intruding again. He walked to the door and swung it open.

"Well, well, well, if it isn't Optio Petronius!" Lucius' training kicked in and he snapped to attention in front of the centurion who stood outside the door. Though he recognised the visitor, his emotions were conflicted – once a Roman soldier, always a Roman soldier. "Hades, nephew, we are off duty. Relax." Lucius did as commanded,

"Uncle Julius, you look well. It is so good to see you."

"Army life Lucius, army life. You are an officer now, lad, so let's drop the uncle bit."

When a boy, his uncle had always been a larger-than-life figure. He was not a tall man but healthy and full of life. He wore his dark hair on the long side and always had dark stubble on his face. The one thing that impressed the young Lucius was his uncle's hands. They were large and his fingers thick, his party piece crushing nuts in his palm. A jovial character but one you did not cross, as when his temper flared, it was a thing to see! He had an excellent reputation as a soldier and had been the centurion for the VI Cohort for some years.

"So, I know a good taberna just outside the fort; have you eaten yet? Silly question: From what I have heard, you won't have had time. Grab your cloak and helmet, and let's go." Lucius was delighted to be with someone with whom he could truly relax and talk, as he had something he needed to share. Lucius quickly did as instructed. "Right, let's be off. I'm dying for a nice little Falernian." Only the finest for Centurion Petronius, thought Lucius.

In the vicus, built up over time by traders, there were several tabernas, and Julius headed to his favourite haunt. As they proceeded, Lucius shared some of his adventures experienced on his route to becoming an Optio. As he passed through the vicus, the smell of freshly cooked food assailed his nostrils. Lucius became aware that he was acutely hungry, and fortunately, the realisation coincided with the arrival at the doorway of Julius' chosen taberna.

The day was bright, so it was dark inside the taberna, but Julius seemed to know exactly where he was going.

"Your favourite spot, Centurion?" It was a soft, female voice. Its owner was about Julius' height, slender, long dark hair, and wearing a thin cotton dress did not leave much to the imagination.

"Indeed," replied Julius. "This is Optio Petronius," Her eyebrows rose, "and before you ask, Anaitis, he is indeed related."

"Welcome, Optio. Are you here to drink, or do you wish for food? Then, of course, afterwards, if you wish...." She pointed to a staircase becoming apparent in the gloom as Lucius's eyes adjusted.

"I think food is certainly in order, Anaitis," Julius said as he sat on a bench by a table in the corner of the taberna. Lucius sat opposite him, glad the table had a window view allowing a cool breeze to pass through. Anaitis went off and was soon back with a pitcher of wine – she knew what the centurion would drink.

"Don't mind her," Julius said, "She's a good lass at heart. They have rooms here, nice and clean, so if you need a night off, it's not a bad place. Anaitis' girls are also obliging. Now, food?" After some discussion, the two soldiers settled for a meal of lamb stew.

"Well then, Optio Petronius, I heard you were in a bit of a jam earlier today," Julius said. Lucius ran through the chain of events exactly as they happened.

"...and, what is more, Julius, it has just struck me that some of the Judaeans that attacked us may be the ones so interested in us in the market at Gophna." He explained how he spotted them observing the convoy and how suddenly they disappeared.

"They must have left and managed to get ahead of you," said his uncle, "No point in going back to Gophna to see if you can catch the cunni. They won't be from there; too smart for that!" He paused, staring at the tabletop where a small fly wandered looking for food. Then he said, "Why? We haven't seen an organised attack like that for quite some time, not the usual brigandry. The bastards went for an army convoy. Why?"

"Perhaps they had mistaken intelligence as to the contents of the waggons," suggested Lucius.

"Ha! That's for sure," laughed Julius, "You and your lads in the last waggon." He paused. Then in a quite different tone, "I am sorry Lucius, we lost good men to the *cunni*."

"We'll probably never know," Lucius stated with some finality. At that point, the lamb stew arrived. The fly from the table took to the air. As quick as a flash, the large hands of the centurion crashed together, ending the insect's life. For shovel-like hands, Julius's were amazingly nimble.

"I have not seen you do that since I was a boy," exclaimed Lucius, "Quick as ever 'eh?" Julius laughed as he rubbed his palms on his tunic.

"Got to be, to survive this life, Optio!" The two were silent for a fleeting time as they enjoyed the lamb stew. Anaitis always took diligent care of the centurion, which had paid dividends in the past. Any soldier who misbehaved in this taberna could count on retribution coming one way or another from the grizzled centurion. The consequence was that 'The Neptune' (Anaitis' father was an ex-sailor of the *Classis Syriaca*, based in Antioch) became known as a pleasant spot to relax and not to have to worry about rowdy off-duty legionaries spoiling your dinner.

Then Lucius put down his spoon, rested elbows on the table and his chin on his hands.

"Julius, can I share something with you – as my uncle rather than as the centurion of the VI Cohort?"

"Of course, this is between uncle and nephew. So, tell me."

"I'm a little cautious as I realise you and many others have been here for many years and have a much better understanding of this place. I also know that I'm young for an Optio and freely admit I don't have the experience of many serving soldiers here. But, sometimes, a fresh eye…"

"Lucius," interrupted Julius, "For Jupiter's sake, spit it out, lad."

"Apologies. When I related what transpired earlier in the day, I didn't recount what a dying Judean had said." Lucius went on to recount the event earlier that day. Julius listened, and when Lucius had finished, nodding his head deliberately.

"There's a storm coming..." he muttered to himself. He looked up and faced Lucius. "It sounds ominous enough lad, but these Judaeans, there are Jewish fanatics amongst them that will quote all sorts of religious *cac* at you. He has just lost a dice throw with a Roman, so he curses you. That's all."

"Julius, there is more..." and Lucius told Julius of the pristine gladii and daggers the bandits were using, not forgetting the two Roman helmets they possessed.

"They've killed our soldiers in the past; they're not going to walk away leaving good weaponry on the ground, are they?" said Julius.

"Uncle," said Lucius, his frustration overriding the agreed protocol on addressing each other, "Sextus assured me these swords were new – brand new! Do you know that the army rejects about half of the weapons the Jewish contractors offer because they are below standard? We Romans believed they would be reworked and resubmitted next time around. Suppose they are not? I wonder how well we check!" Julius sat back against the wall. Lucius barged on, "Why has the banditry and brigandry dropped off over the last year or so? Have we done anything differently to effect that?" Lucius suddenly stopped, realising that he was launching a verbal attack on his uncle, a senior officer. "Apologies, uncle, I didn't mean to offend."

"No offence taken, Lucius," Julius responded. "You've clearly given this some thought. So, briefly, you think the Jewish cunni are lulling us into a false sense of security while they prepare for another attempt to have a serious go at us?"

"Julius, I don't know what to believe precisely, but I feel that something may not be right here." Suddenly he began to feel a little foolish.

"Right then, Optio Petronius, I have a suggestion. Tomorrow, the five centurions have our informal weekly gathering in the

Principia. Come along to it; you'll have to wait outside for a while, then I will see if the others will hear you out. If you convince them, especially the Primus, we shall see what can be done. What you have is flimsy, but it is worth consideration."

Lucius suddenly felt his stomach turn. He had put himself in a position where he would be telling five experienced centurions and the Primus that they had missed something. Julius could see the discomfort that was beginning to show on Lucius' face.

"Don't worry, Lucius. I shall tell them that you shared your thoughts with me, and I insisted that you share them with the Centuriate, very much my decision."

"Thank you, Julius. At this stage, I would hate to appear critical."

'You won't and feeling as you do, it's your duty to report it. And you have, so let's get back to this excellent lamb and wine."

After a wide-ranging conversation covering many aspects of military life, the discussion moved towards the family. Julius suddenly sat back and stared Lucius in the face before asking,

"You know your uncle Aminus died a few months back?" Julius asked.

"I did. Regrettably, my service at the time did not let me get to his funeral. He had a fall?"

"A stupid thing. He slipped on some wet flooring, cracking his head on a table. But for that, he would be as right as rain. Killed him stone dead, I understand."

Lucius nodded sagely,

"The gods can be fickle, that is for sure."

"Well, it's not always just the gods. You must be aware that you upset your father by joining the legions. He always wanted you to take over the business and, in time, to be somebody in Rome. You'll not be aware that he blames me for encouraging you as a boy. I am now very much persona non-grata as far as he is concerned. It was after an argument with me some years back that he sent you to the ludus for sword training, where you were meant to be dissuaded from any idea of military life."

"I always knew he was not happy with you encouraging me," Lucius responded. "I had no idea he had declared you 'non-grata'."

"There is more," Julius continued. "Your father has formally adopted Antonius, your cousin and Aminus' son, and he declared him to be his rightful heir. You realise just what this means?"

Lucius let the information sink in before responding.

"I knew he had taken Antonius into the business. I know he had disinherited me, but I had not realised that he had declared him his heir. So that is you and me thoroughly in the *cac* then 'eh?" He paused for a few seconds. He knew this might come, and now it had, he was strangely numb; he felt little emotion. "Should I be shocked, Julius? I think in my heart I suspected this would happen. But I have chosen my path and must walk it." The gods were fickle indeed, but as one door closes, another often opens. He picked up his beaker of wine, "Damn it all! A toast, Julius. To the Fretensis!"

Later that evening, Lucius sat in his room unpacking his few personal belongings from his bag in the light of two small oil lamps. Then, there came a knock on his door. He rose, opened the door, and there stood Marcus.

"I hope you'd a good evening, sir. Heard you dined with Senior Centurion Petronius. I thought you might like your hamata back, sir."

It was then that Lucius realised that folded over his left arm was the hamata he had asked Marcus to clean. Marcus held up the hamata, gleaming, even in the weak light of the lamps.

"By the gods Apollonaris, you have worked a wonder. It's like new!" exclaimed Lucius.

"Well, sir, I knows the vicus well, and there's a few people that, like, owe me the odd favour. One of 'em is an armourer, after a fashion – not like ours – but he 'as a concoction he says is 'is secret for cleaning metals. So, I calls in the favour and here we are, sir."

"Well," Lucius said, "if we can break his magic concoction, we could become as rich as Crassus." Marcus passed the hamata to Lucius.

"There's a bit more, sir." He reached into the bag he wore over his shoulder and pulled out a small clay bottle stopped with a wax seal. "I got a bit of the stuff for your helmet, sir. If you let me have it, I will return it first thing tomorrow, sir."

"I have a meeting to attend early in the morning – it's the Senior Centurion's Meeting. Do you really mean the first thing?"

"Sun up, sir. My life is upon it!" Marcus retorted. Lucius went back into the room and took up his helmet, returned and handed it to Marcus. "Permission to ask the Optio a question?" Marcus said very formally. Lucius frowned,

"Of course, Apollinaris, go ahead."

"Well, sir, where did you learn to fight like that? Today I mean, that was not army training from what I saw. Those cunni didn't stand a chance as I saw it!"

The question caught Lucius off guard. He could have shrugged it off, but the news of his effective disinheritance had hit him a little harder than he let on to his uncle. He felt a need to talk to someone, so he said,

"Come in, Apollinaris, sit on that stool by the window." Marcus did as instructed. As Lucius sat on a second stool, his past flashed through his mind.

After military training and serving time as a legionary, Lucius took on the role of Optio and was destined to serve in a Roman Auxiliary unit in Dacia. Senior Centurion Aurelius Crispus then asked him to be his Optio in the rebuilt IV Cohort of the Legio X Fretensis. The unit was being constructed and trained outside of Capua.

Quite by chance, it was in a taberna in Capua that Lucius found his old sword trainer Atelius drinking wine with the very Lanista with whom his father had arranged his initial training. Business was excellent, and the Lanista had opened a new Ludus in Capua. By the time Lucius left the bar, he had arranged with Atelius for further training.

After a few weeks, Atelius decided to put Lucius up against a freed gladiator who he considered his top trainer. They would use wooden swords, but the fight was for real. His opponent was simply known as Furius. He was stocky, dressed in leather and wore a wide-brimmed steel helmet; just practice kit, you understand! Furius looked every bit the professional gladiator who intended to do his job - fortunately, in this case, only going as far as putting Lucius on his back. And so, the fight began. Lucius recalled everything until the first blow; next, he stood over his fallen opponent. He had no idea how long they had fought, only that the man was at his feet. After that, his recollection of the fight itself was just a blur. Finally, his opponent rose and looked Lucius over.

"If you ever need a job, lad...." he said and walked away, leaving the sentence hanging. Atelius led Lucius across the sand to a bench beside a bucket of water and a ladle.

"Take a drink," he instructed. Lucius did as commanded and then poured a ladle of water over his head.

"Lucius," said Atelius, "Can you tell me about your strategy for that fight? What were your moves going to be?"

"Atelius, believe me, I don't recall. I had a general approach just as you trained me, but then it began and...."

"I think you would make a fine gladiator," Atelius said. Lucius laughed. "I do not joke, lad. I know where you are right now. I was there some years ago. I trained extremely hard when I was a young gladiator; failure to do so would mean my life. Then I started to win bouts comfortably. My fellow gladiators would ask me about this-and-that, such-and-such to do with the fight. But do you know what? I couldn't remember. Like you, the training just kicked in and I did the job. There was rarely a choice of thumbs up or down because they were dead before they hit the ground. In the end, I was retired for one simple reason. No one made a profit betting on me anymore – the outcome was too predictable. My lanista thought there would be more money in it for him if I became a trainer. So now I get well paid and all the ladies I want!"

Lucius sat staring at the ground.

"It's rather unnerving Atelius," he said.

"You get used to it. It only kicks in when you feel threatened, but this is important, my friend. I have a rule that has served me well. Never draw your sword unless you intend to use it for the purpose for which it was made. The rule has worked for me. Meanwhile, I don't think you need any further formal training, but keep in practice." Atelius changed tack, "So how do you fancy some time in the baths? Get rid of all that grime."

Lucius sighed, "You know, that might not be such a bad idea. You mentioned lovely ladies?"

"Nothing wrong with you, lad!" retorted Atelius.

"Sir, are you well?" Marcus disrupted Lucius' reverie.

"Apologies Apollinaris. Let me tell you a story…" and he proceeded to outline his training with Atelius without going into personal family detail. "… and so, with the centuries I fight as we are trained, in solo hand-to-hand, I rely upon Atelius' training."

Marcus felt he was privileged to have peered through a window into the Optio's life.

"Well, sir, better you an' I don't fall out," Marcus laughed, "for my sake." He rose from the stool, "I'll be leaving you now, sir, helmet to clean. Sleep well, sir." He strode through the door and left Lucius to himself. Lucius remained on his stool, staring at the floor, his thoughts miles away. Eventually, he undressed and threw himself onto his bed after dowsing the oil lamps

Capitulum V - Silent Bells

27 Martius. Year 16 of Imperator Hadrian

Having not closed the shutters on the window the previous night, Lucius was awoken by the light of dawn filling the sky. He rose, washed, dressed, and looked across the room for his helmet. It was absent, but as the events of the previous evening flooded back, there came a sharp knock on his door. Upon opening it, he was presented with the sight of Marcus in a spotless segmentata and helmet, carrying an even grander glistening helmet. Lucius' face showed surprise.

"I got a bit for meself," the soldier declared. "Here's your 'elmet, sir," holding out the pristine piece.

"By Zeus, Apollinaris," he exclaimed, "how do we get our hands on that formula?"

"Not much hope of that, sir, locked away in his head it is, sir." He paused, "I have the despatch bag here, sir, as I thought you might want it this morning, like."

"Good work," responded Lucius, "you can bring it with us. Where's Postumus?"

"He's outside, sir. Ready when you are, sir."

Lucius donned his helmet and followed Marcus out to where Sextus was dutifully waiting.

"How's the arm, Sextus?" Lucius asked.

"Nothing that'll get in the way, sir," he said as he displayed his injured limb.

"Well, in that case, let's get going, shall we?"

As they approached the Principia, Julius Petronius was seen to be pacing up and down, swinging his vine stick back and forth by his side. He spotted the trio approaching and joined them. The two legionaries snapped to attention and Lucius saluted.

"Optio, you will accompany me to the meeting." He was formal, quite correctly for the situation. "I shall leave you in the ante-chamber and will call you when required. I suggest your men wait outside; there's shade and a fountain, so they should be fine. Let's go."

"Excuse me, sir," It was Marcus. He was holding forth the despatch satchel in Lucius' direction. "Just in case, sir." Lucius took the bag.

"I suggest you two take the Senior Centurion's advice. I will join you later." Marcus and Sextus left the two officers to their business.

As they approached the building, Julius said quietly,

"I see you are a customer of old ben Israel, the blacksmith," nodding at Lucius' pristine hamata. "God knows what his concoction is, but it works like a magic potion on tarnished metal!"

"It was legionary Apollinaris' idea, Julius. The blacksmith cleaned the hamata and Apollinaris the helmet, and yes, it does a respectable job."

The two officers reached the entrance to the Principia. The sentries that stood either side of the porticoed entrance nodded them through. Several clerks scurried by as they walked down the corridor, going about their business. Then, suddenly, the Primus Pilus appeared out of a side room, almost colliding with the two officers.

"Good day Julius, good day Optio," he greeted the two men in a deep baritone voice that echoed down the marble passageway. "I hear from Senior Centurion Petronius you may have something of importance to impart to us this morning. Won't keep you waiting too long. We have a few matters to dispense with first. Come in."

The three of them passed through a doorway opposite the Primus' office into a small anteroom. "Take a seat, Optio. Shan't be too long." Then, turning to Julius, "The others are here, Julius, let's go in and get on with it."

Lucius sat on a marble bench placed against the anteroom wall. Suddenly, he was overcome by feelings of doubt. Was he imagining things? Who was he, the new boy in the region, telling the five senior centurions and the Primus that they all might be missing something? He took a deep breath and let the air slowly leave his lungs. If it were nonsense, his uncle, a senior centurion, would surely never have suggested this meeting? The latter thought helped calm his nerves.

Lucius was mentally rehearsing what he would say to the Centurions. He was on the third iteration of his plan when the door opened, and Julius appeared.

"Come on in, Optio," he instructed. Lucius arose, walked to the door, took a deep breath, and followed his uncle into the room, looking as soldierly as possible. It was rectangular, large, and possessed a high ceiling and one wall lined with windows. At one end of the room, the wall was adorned with a bust of Imperator Hadrian. The legion's crest adorned the wall opposite; a yellow boar underwritten by '*Legio X Fretensis*', all on a red background. This is more than "just a room."

Five Centurions sat at a rectangular table that could hold twice that number. The Primus instructed the Optio to relax and indicated he should sit at the far end of the table, which Lucius duly did, removing his helmet as he did so. The Primus spoke.

"I have asked the Optio to attend at the request of Centurion Petronius. I have heard an outline of what the Optio says, and I considered it worth sharing. Can I suggest we hear him out before we comment?" He turned to Lucius. "We wait with interest, Optio."

Lucius visibly took a deep breath and began,

"You will all be aware of what happened to the supply convoy yesterday." Heads nodded. "What I saw and heard caused me a sense of unease...."

The door to the room opened and a soldier walked in, stood to one side, and adopting the sentinel stance, said, "Rise for Legatus Augusti Tineus Rufus." The population of the room promptly rose and stood smartly to attention. Like one used to power, a man who moved confidently walked through the door. His hair may have once been black but was now a mottled grey. He was of average height and slightly built. Upon meeting him for the first time, what struck one was the sense of a certain arrogance as he looked at you down his sizeable Roman nose. Everything signalled that this was a man comfortable with power. Tineus Rufus came from the old Etruscan town of Volterra and had been Governor of Thracia for several years.

Before arriving in Judaea, he had been a Consul in Rome. Rufus understood power.

"Please, please, do sit," he said as he moved to one of the several unoccupied chairs and sat down with a grace that was long practised. A second soldier entered the room and stood sentinel at the door with his partner. "Please carry-on Primus, as though I am not here."

"Very good, Legatus," snapped the Primus. Lucius was dumbfounded; it was bad enough sharing his thoughts with the Centuriate, but with the Governor of Judea? It was going to be exceedingly difficult pretending he was not there! The Primus nodded at Lucius, "Continue Optio." And so, Lucius did.

He repeated the words of the dying Judaean to them, the words that started his suspicions, then told them of the decline of hostilities over the last year. Finally, he shared his thoughts about the rejection of weaponry with no improvement in quality, mentioning the pristine roman army gladii, pugii and helmets the Judaeans were using, and he then concluded. As he finished summing up, Julius spoke.

"The Optio shared these thoughts with me last night, and I mentioned them in not so much detail to the Primus first thing this morning. We both thought you should hear them." There was a pause before one of the centurions spoke.

"Optio. I am Claudius Aginthus, III Cohort," he introduced himself. Aginthus was fair-haired, contrasting with his very dark olive skin, hinting at his Syrian roots. His eyes were a very noticeable green. "You will not have been here, of course, but a year or so back, we had a very vicious attack on a patrol in a village not far from Mizpah; we lost all the men. We responded by raising the village and leaving a few survivors for the slavers. I mention this because that may well account for the recent lack of serious attacks. Lesson learned, perhaps?" There were nods around the table.

"Good point Claudius," said one of Aginthus' comrades, "I am Flavius Gallianus. V Cohort. Good to meet you, Optio. I look forward to Crispus' return with his new IV Cohort," he paused ever so briefly. "You know over the last years we have lost, regrettably, some men to the bandits; indeed, Centurion Aginthus has just referred to one such incident. Invariably, when we find the bodies of our men, they are without arms or armour. On the other hand, we have found slain bandits with our weapons before yesterday, you know." Lucius had expected this.

"I understand, Centurion Gallianus," he said, "but the swords we recovered were of new issue." Then, to his surprise, the Primus reached into a bag and produced a gladius that looked new.

"I have to say," stated the Primus, "It was this that made me believe we should discuss the Optio's concerns; one of the swords recovered from the dead bandits involved in yesterday's incident. It had the modified pommel that was only introduced mere weeks ago."

Gallianus reached across and took up the gladius.

"I'll grant you that Optio. This looks pristine," he said, nodding his head, looking towards the Primus. Lucius was beginning to feel more relaxed, so he decided to clarify his thoughts further.

"With permission Primus?" Lucius said. The Senior Centurion nodded. "I readily accept that each point on its own does not constitute much of a case. However, when it is all considered together, I worry it points to something more serious."

A few seconds passed as the centurions considered Lucius' statement, but those few moments of consideration were disrupted by a man Lucius thought looked akin to an angry bull. Dark-haired, ruddy-faced, flat-nosed and facially scarred, Senior Centurion Octavius Secundus, forgetting the presence of the Legatus, banged his hand on the table.

"Jupiter. How many years of experience have we had between us brothers? How many of those have been spent soldiering in this god-forsaken land? Do you think we would miss the signs of a potential major revolt? We've had tales of Simeon ben Koseba, Rabbi Akiva and imminent revolts for years – have we seen one? No, we have not. These Judaeans are capable only of brigandry and robbery." He turned to Lucius, "With all due respect, Optio, you arrive in the country, newly appointed, and within a matter of days, you detect a revolt is developing; one that we've all missed? I have not seen anything to raise my sense of concern. Yet you come here, telling officers far more experienced -"

"Secundus!" it was the Primus. "You forget that it was I who requested the Optio to come before us. Therefore, it was not his bidding."

"Forgive me," Secundus said, "I believe my point is made."

"Indeed."

Lucius received Secundus' criticism as a deliberate highlighting of his lack of soldiering experience; it was what he was expecting. He felt uncomfortable again, exposed even when the Primus spoke up.

"I will be the first to admit the evidence is very circumstantial. I propose that we double the escorts on any convoys moving between here and Caesarea. If you have any contacts amongst the Judaeans, talk to them. Some of the workers in the *vicus* may know more. Simply put, be alert for anything out of the ordinary; I want to know of any matters immediately. If anything untoward happens again, we shall reconsider. None of this really should be difficult for any of us." He looked around the table and received nods of agreement from the centurions. Secundus smiled at the Primus,

"Common sense as always, Primus."

The Primus saw this as a veiled criticism of Lucius. Turning to Lucius, he said,

"Optio, you did the correct thing. Any officer having concerns should share them and my gratitude for raising them with Centurion Petronius." A thankful Lucius realised that the issue was being closed.

"My gratitude Primus, for the invitation to speak. My gratitude, officers, for your consideration." He was about to rise and leave when he caught a glimpse of a self-satisfying smile from Secundus. Lucius could not resist a Parthian shot as he stood up to leave. "I, too, pray to Jupiter that my concerns are nothing but observations of an inexperienced soldier."

Secundus sat up in his chair and was about to respond when the Primus, whose hand was flat on the table, raised his fingers an inch or so. Secundus spotted the gesture and sat back in his chair, body relaxed but mind seething. Julius released the tension saying,

"Would you wait for me in the ante-room Optio; we should be finished here in a while." Lucius stood, donned his helmet, and smartly saluted the group before turning and leaving the room. In the anteroom, he sat and reviewed what had taken place. He had not expected applause and support, but Secundus' response had quite shaken him, to the point of believing the centurion may well be right. However, the Primus' final words had restored his confidence. He was staring aimlessly at the door to the meeting room when suddenly it opened. The two soldiers of the Governor's guard marched through the doorway, followed by the Governor. He strolled over to Lucius, who jumped up to attention. Rufus gave him a cold smile.

"That numbskull Secundus shat on you lad, but pay it no heed, it how he is. My office, third hour after noon – do not be late. Until then." His guard escorted him out into the central passageway, and he was gone.

Lucius sat down with a thump. He had just received a summons to a meeting with the Governor, and his mind began to race. Why should the Governor wish to speak with him? Was the reason hidden in the Governor's words? Did the Governor give him more credence than the Centuriate? He was none the wiser when the door opened again, and the centurions walked out talking amongst themselves.

Lucius jumped to his feet. The Primus acknowledged him with a wave of his vine stick before disappearing into the passageway, followed by the other officers. Julius Petronius, wearing a beaming smile, joined Lucius.

"Jupiter Lucius! I asked you to outline your thoughts to the group, not to go to war with Octavius Secundus!"

Lucius frowned.

"It felt awkward!" he exclaimed. "Gratitude for your support."

"Ignore Secundus, he's all bluff and bore. Your concerns were registered, and I think we shall all be a bit more alert to anything going forward. You did well, Optio."

"If that was well, I would hate to fuck up!" Lucius retorted. "But I must tell you; the Governor wants to meet me in his office after noon. He did not say why." Julius showed surprise.

"Rufus, the Governor, wants to see you later today?" His brow creased, "That's interesting. I can only suspect something you said must have caught his attention. All I can advise is be careful with that one Lucius; he is devious to the extreme." He stepped back a pace. "I wish I had time to explore this further, but I have matters that need my attention. Keep me posted. I will find you this evening." He turned and walked out. Lucius followed a few seconds later, carrying the despatch bag full of yet to be utilised papers.

He joined Marcus and Sextus who engaged in a simple dice game outside. He briefed them about the appointment later that day and agreed to reconvene at Lucius' room after meeting with the governor. The two soldiers seemed delighted to have a good part of the day to themselves. As they walked off, it dawned on Lucius that he had little to do until his meeting, so he thought he would explore the environs around the fort.

The fort at Aelia may be long-established, but like every roman fort, it was laid out to a set of guidelines followed by forts over the last few centuries. It was divided into quarters by two straight roadways; the *Cardo Maximus* ran on a north/south axis, and the *Decumanus Maximus* ran east to west. Lucius knew the location of the various buildings; they would be in the same position in any Roman camp. Deciding the *vicus* might make a more exciting visit, Lucius headed for the northern gate of the Cardo Maximus, beyond which lay the small township.

The *vicus*, built around the camp walls, was a hive of activity. There had been little planning as the small township grew chaotically over the years, so while some streets were straight, others twisted and turned, but all were narrow. But, on the other hand, there had been no shortage of building material, it lay all around, and some of it was high-quality stone, so this *vicus* was like no other regarding appearance. Lucius smiled to see a small cobbler's shop with an open front – nothing strange in that – but each side of the opening holding up the roof frontage were two beautiful marble columns that stood just higher than a man.

In the *vicus,* a soldier could buy anything, from food, furniture, clothing through to sex. As Lucius strolled along the beaten, twisting pathways that fed off the main road, he drew salutes from the many soldiers busy about their business. Women ran quite a number of these establishments and Lucius knew several would be under the protection of soldiers from the garrison. He did not doubt that in time they would move into Hadrian's new city, Aelia Capitolina. The numerous odours assaulted Lucius' nose; urine from the fullers, sulphur from the blacksmiths, food from the several different establishments preparing meals for the day, and of course, every so often, the stench of latrines ready for emptying.

Lucius approached a small crossroads where a small smithy set in one corner. The blacksmith looked as old as Methuselah, but his body, stripped to the waist, was rippling muscle. He had three young boys working alongside him. He paused from beating a piece of metal, stood up and stretched, then he saw Lucius. He beamed a smile, not entirely toothless, as he recognised his work of the previous night. He waved and returned to his efforts.

"You too?" A voice asked. Lucius turned to face a fellow Optio dressed in similar attire to himself. "Once a month and the price is very reasonable," the stranger said, referring to his relationship with the blacksmith. "Salve. I haven't seen you around before. You recently arrived? I'm Porcius Fimbria, 1stCentury, III Cohort."

Lucius held out his arm.

"Salve, you must be Aginthus' optio then. I'm Lucius Decimus Petronius, 1st Century, IV Cohort." He watched the expression on his fellow Optio's face, one he was coming to expect.

"Fourth? I did not know you had arrived; I've seen no sign -"

"They haven't Porcius, I am, shall we say, the advance party."

"Oh, I see," responded Fimbria in a way that led Lucius to think that if he did see, it wasn't that well. Fimbria recovered and took back control, looking towards the smithy. "The old blacksmith has been with the Tenth man and boy. He says his grandfather, a Syrian, served Vespasian and Titus at the siege, regularly sharpening their swords – or so the story goes. That cleaning potion he uses saves a lot of work. He completely immerses a hamata into it, leaves it for a short time, and when it comes out, it is brilliant. He puts it on a cloth when he cleans helmets." He continued, "So, welcome Lucius Decimus Petronius. May I buy you a beaker of wine as a welcoming gift? There's a good taberna just around the corner." Lucius happily accepted. It would be good to talk with a soldier of his rank for a change. He had had a fill of Praefecti, Primus and Governors.

Lucius guessed that Optio Fimbria was a few years older than him. They were of similar build, and he had a temperament to which Lucius quickly warmed. They were soon sitting on a bench outside the taberna that boasted a large boar painted on its outside wall. Like much of the vicus, the establishment was built of recycled masonry from the ruins of Jerusalem. It was no time before beakers of wine sat in front of them.

"Good thing about this taberna," Fimbria said, "is that it is usually upwind of the cesspits!" It transpired in the conversation that followed, Porcius Fimbria had been in the Legion for nine years, joining as a young man and had held the rank of Optio for two years. His full service had been in Judaea, and he enjoyed his role.

"So, tell me, how does it all happen in Judaea?" Lucius requested. "To start with, just what forces do we have down here?"

"Well," began Fimbria, "as you must be aware, the Fretensis are split between Caesarea and Aelia, usually five cohorts at any one time in Aelia. We turn about on a three-month cycle. Judaea is where we are now – Caesarea is in Samaria – so we have just five cohorts in Judaea itself. Galilee is outside of our brief."

"All based in Aelia?" Lucius asked.

"No, not all. We tend to have centuries stationed in certain towns. Their role is to help the Tax Farmers and keep the bandits at bay. The locals do not like handing over money or amounts of their hard-earned produce, so to make sure it goes smoothly, they are usually accompanied by a patrol of twenty or so of our lads – the auxiliaries muck in too."

Lucius knew all about Tax Farmers. Back in Rome, they would bid to collect taxes in each area. They were expected to produce tax for Rome and keep whatever else they could raise. They would often double the official figure making their occupation very lucrative. Squeezing all he could from the natives, whilst avoiding a revolt as a consequence, was the tax farmer's most arduous task. The practice was a cause of much bitterness amongst the Jews!

"If there is any trouble," Porcius said, "we dispatch a couple of centuries to back up the patrol."

"Do you often get trouble?" Lucius asked.

"Every so often, there will be a protest, but knowing the consequences, the locals usually calm down and it is often settled before the support unit arrives."

"So effectively, the Fretensis is managing all of Judea?"

"Oh no, not at all. There are several auxiliary units in the area. Down at Beit Guvrin, that's about twenty miles or so south of here, near Hebron, we have two units: First Cohort *Milaria Thracum* consisting of Thracian infantry and a cavalry unit, the *Gallorum et Thracum Sagittaria*; Gallic and Thracian horsemen. Last I heard, a detachment of the *Milaria Thracum* was down at Ein Geddi on the Dead Sea looking after the Imperator's balsam plantations there. There are others, but I won't bore you. How's the wine?"

The question caught Lucius quite by surprise; he focused on absorbing the information coming from Optio Fimbria.

"Excellent Porcius, gratitude," Lucius replied and went on, "I understood that Legio VI Ferrata was also in the region?"

"Technically, yes, they are, but they are way up at Tel Shalem, which is not that far from Pella, in Galilee." responded Fimbria, "If you had marched due east from Caesarea, you would have bumped into them after about forty miles. So, we do not have much contact with them."

"So, we have two legions; the *Fretensis* and the *Ferrata*, assisted by a small number of auxiliary units?"

"Five or six at the last count, but yes, that's about it," Fimbria clarified. "Mind you, in the last year or so, there's not been too much trouble, just the usual hassle with the tax farmers."

"Quiet then?" queried Lucius. Fimbria was about to nod when he sat bolt upright.

"Hades, I am sorry. Of course, your convoy was hit, wasn't it? Lost some soldiers too, I heard."

"Yes, but don't feel badly," Lucius had not meant to come over as sarcastic, "My question was a genuine one, Porcius; is it quiet lately?"

"It is, but…" Fimbria hesitated, "this will sound silly, Lucius, but it is almost too quiet. Even my century was talking about it the other night. One of the men said how much he misses 'banging heads' of late."

Lucius felt the urge to share this morning's events with Fimbria but thought it best to leave it with the Senior Centurions.

"It's not like soldiers to complain about doing nothing!" quipped Lucius. Fimbria laughed.

"If that's the worst of it, I should be grateful, I suppose," he responded, "but here's a thing. It is probably nothing, but one of my tesserarius was out with the Tax Farmers a few days back. An aggrieved Judaean, an old man, said to him, "Take it, Roman, it will probably be the last time that you ever do; your time is coming to an end."

Lucius' eyebrows rose. Trying to stay calm and natural, he asked,

"And what did your tesserarius do?"

"Thumped him in the mouth, put him on the ground and moved on," Fimbria said as though it was just a natural occurrence. "But you know what, Lucius, that phrase keeps nagging me. It is probably nothing."

Lucius shrugged his shoulders,

"I guess I am in no position to comment, having arrived in the province a few days ago." The words belied what was going through Lucius' mind. He was convinced that he was not suffering from paranoia; something was afoot, he was sure of it. "To harm us, the Judeans would need a huge army, and you cannot magic such a force up from nowhere." Lucius was hoping that Fimbria might have more jewels to share, but he was disappointed.

"You are right, Lucius," he replied, "we would surely have noticed any form of military build-up. I mustn't get spooked for no reason."

The pair talked for another while before Fimbria declared he had to be back in camp for duty. They promised to look each other up, if not in the coming days, then once the IV Cohort was installed in Judea. Fimbria paid for the wines and left. Lucius also left the taberna and continued his exploration of the *vicus*, though his mind was distracted. He felt sure that something was going on but had no idea what it was. His earlier point was valid; you do not assemble an army overnight, so just what was the plot?

Later he found a place to eat. He sat on his own and reviewed events. He had come to the province as an administrator for his cohort. A visit to meet his uncle, the man most responsible for his military career, had turned into a small nightmare. Soldiers dead, a meeting with the Senior Centurions, and a meeting with the province's governor very shortly. For Jupiter's sake, he was only an optio of the IV Cohort, traditionally the cohort with the newest and weakest men! He ate his bread, cheese and chunk of lamb feeling like a man condemned.

Lucius decided to return to his quarters. As he left the *vicus*, he made for the north gate of the fort. Unfortunately, he was forced to wait to let a large waggon pass as he approached the entrance. Beside Lucius was a gate guard who watched his partner check the waggon. The guard noticed Lucius and came to attention.

"Contractors, sir. They bring in equipment every few days." The inspecting soldier appeared from the waggon's rear, walked to the front, and waved the driver forward. As the waggon disappeared through the gate, Lucius smiled, saying,

"I hope their workmanship is better than their artistic skill!" The soldier looked and laughed. On the back of the waggon was a small painting of what was supposed to be the outline of a gladius; it was recognisable, but in several places, the paint had run. The guard spoke up,

"If those drips were red Optio, it would look quite like blood running off that blade," at which Lucius followed the waggon through the gate and went in the direction of his quarters.

Just over an hour later, Lucius found himself standing outside the Principia. He had found time in his room to buff up his helmet and smarten up his kit. To say Lucius was nervous would be an understatement, but he took a deep breath and marched between the pillars. The sentinels saluted, and Lucius walked the length of the marble corridor, past the Primus' office to the end of the walkway where he knew the Governor's office resided. Two soldiers stood guard, and as he approached, they thrust their *pilum*, the military spears used by all legionaries, out across the entrance. Lucius stopped in front of them.

"Optio Petronius. IV Cohort to meet with his Excellency the Governor at his command." The soldiers had been briefed. The spears pulled back, and one soldier simply said, "Sir," as the two men resumed their sentinel positions. Lucius pushed the door open and passed into the antechamber of the Governor's office. A military clerk sat at a table and promptly looked up as Lucius entered.

"Must be Optio Petronius." Lucius thought he would not have been able to get through the door if he was not.

"Indeed, I am here at the Governor's command," he stated. The clerk stood up, telling Lucius to wait and disappeared through the heavily decorated doors that gave access to the Governor's office itself. He reappeared a few moments later, holding one of the doors wide open, instructing Lucius to enter.

The office may not have been palatial, it was only ever designed to be a functional part of a Roman fort, but it was comfortable. One wall held many scrolls, but the rest of the room was much more relaxed. One luxury was a glass window, supported by four ornate columns, which let the brilliance of the outside day into the room. Legatus Augusti Pro Praetore Tineus Rufus sat behind a large ebony desk, mostly clear except for several scrolls set to one side. Rufus looked relaxed and entirely at home. Lucius snapped to attention.

"Optio Petronius, welcome to my humble office." Rufus said, waving towards a chair that stood opposite him on the other side of the table, "Sit." Removing his helmet, Lucius did as instructed, sitting to attention in the chair. He was conscious of being told to sit, not relax.

"Relax, Optio. Now, I do not like these damned *lestai* doing us any damage," referring to brigands and bandits. "I am led to believe your action yesterday may have saved us from losing the contents of the convoy. Well done." I have been called here for a thank you, thought Lucius. He began to relax. "I am only sorry we lost some valuable men. However, the IV Cohort should be here soon, and their addition to the strength will be appreciated." Rufus paused; when he spoke next, the tone had become more serious. "I listened to what you had to say this morning, young man. In a matter of a few days of arrival in the province, you are detecting rebellion and revolt! No wonder old Secundus was steaming. Had the Primus not been present, you would have received much worse from that man!" Rufus stopped, staring at Lucius. The latter was unsure if this was a signal to say something, and as Rufus remained silent, Lucius spoke up.

"It was not my intention to ruffle feathers, sir. If I caused any offence, I apologise, but I felt it my duty to report my suspicions." Silence reigned for a few moments before Rufus spoke,

"Yes, well you did that alright!" Lucius was not sure if Rufus was referring to feathers or duty. "Frankly, I would probably side with that awkward old sod Secundus." This was not going too well, thought Lucius. "The saving grace is that Senior Centurion Petronius took the matter to the Primus, and they decided to have you share your suspicions, so we cannot blame you for that Optio, can we?"

"Gratitude, sir," Lucius responded with a feeling of relief. Rufus, who had been leaning forward, elbows on the table and chin in his hands, suddenly sat back.

"However, there are things you do not know, Optio." Lucius' stomach lurched; just as he thought the atmosphere was beginning to improve, "I do not rely on our good centurions for everything. Over the while I have been here, I have developed what I call my 'bells.' These are several, shall we say, informants who report back on what they hear out there in the countryside. Do you understand me? If anything is amiss, the bells ring."

"Yes, sir. Spies?"

"Not quite, Optio," responded Rufus, "as they are quite passive, they listen, and they send in reports every so often." He paused. "I must tell you that I have received no warnings of imminent revolt, not from any of them. Just the usual chatter about protests over tax and the occasional detail of bandits – the usual stuff. It enables the odd arrest here and there. We have sometimes learnt of secret stashes of goods they try to hide from us, but no revolts!"

Lucius' heart sank; he had been wrong. Rufus had stopped speaking again. Was this a signal that he should talk – it was beginning to look like it.

"Sir, I talked this morning with an Optio from the Cohort…" and Lucius told him of the comments from the aged Judaean to a III Cohort tesserarius. Rufus sat forward again when he had finished, looking pointedly at Lucius.

"That is interesting. You see, I have a minor problem, Optio." There was another pause, but Lucius was getting the hang of matters when conversing with the governor.

"Sir?"

"My 'bells'," the governor said very slowly, "have stopped ringing. We have had nothing from any of them for quite some time. Now, that is something else for you to add to your hypothesis, isn't it?" Lucius was aghast; to all intents and purposes, the governor supported his concerns. "Now, young man, what do you suppose I should do?"

"Logic, sir would say that either they have been silenced, or they have chosen of their own volition to cease communicating with you." Rufus smiled,

"My thoughts exactly, Optio, my thoughts exactly. And….?"

"It would be expedient to clarify which of the two possibilities reflect the reality of the situation," responded Lucius. But, as he said it, he suddenly had a feeling that he was drawn into something, and it was too late to avoid it.

"My thoughts exactly Optio, my thoughts exactly." Rufus' appearance was that of a cat about to enjoy a large fish. Lucius braced himself for whatever may be coming. "And I would like you to arrange that for me, young man." Lucius was stunned, but Rufus said nothing, so he spoke up,

"Sir, I have hardly arrived from Italia; only this morning I had the situation here in Judea explained to me-"

"I am only too aware of your circumstances, Optio, but you have a sharp mind, which is, after all, why the army recruited you. Unfortunately, however, much of the *Fretensis* is still 'old army,' warriors to the core but not always quite so sharp between the ears." He paused.

"But sir…" protested Lucius.

"Optio, I too have some sense between the ears! I do not intend to send you out alone, but I want you to be *my* man in this small venture, someone I can trust because you are Roman. Now, there is someone I would like you to meet before we talk further." Saying this, Rufus rose and went to the door, pushed it, and spoke through the small opening gap. "Mamercus, send in Mordecai." He came back to his desk and sat down, at which point one of the two doors opened wide and in strode a Jewish man wearing a cloak and hood, which he lowered as he came through the door. Upon seeing the man, Lucius stood up,

"Matthias!" he said as the man smiled.

"Good day to you, Governor." He turned to Lucius, "Optio, I apologise for deceiving you yesterday. I was your friend, but I am not Matthias ben Shalev. For reasons that will become clear to you, my friend, I could not reveal my true credentials. My true name is Mordecai ben Zakkai." The governor indicated they should both sit, and Mordecai fetched a chair from across the room.

"I believe you should explain yourself, ben Zakkai," said the governor, now sitting back in his chair, which Lucius read as a sign that things were going his way. The man known as Mordecai ben Zakkai shuffled awkwardly in his chair.

"Apologies again, Optio, but sometimes my role means I cannot always be open with people I meet. In this case, I appreciate that I shall have to be so. We talked on the waggon; you recall?" He waited for Lucius to acknowledge with a slight nod. "I mentioned that the Judaeans were often disparate in the way they accepted the presence of Rome in our land." Lucius simply nodded again. "Well, I represent one of those positions. I represent the viewpoint of a small number of the Rabbinate based at Jamnia, some of the most learned and wise men in Judea at this time." He paused, rubbing his beard while looking down at the floor. He then looked up directly at the governor. "We-err-I would prefer that my country was free and that we were not a province of Rome – but we are, and before the time of the Great Revolt, as long as tribute flowed, the Imperator left us in peace. It was the Zealots, the Sicarii and others who revolted against Rome, and we know the consequences; indeed, here we are, placed in the middle of those consequences in the ruins of Jerusalem and the Holy Temple." To Lucius' surprise, Mordecai, or at least thought Lucius, that's his name today, stood up. He continued his piece as he began to walk up and down the governor's office. "Indeed, my friend, your legion was one of those who crushed the rebellion all those years ago, and it remains here still."

Mordecai moved to the window, pausing to stare out at soldiers moving back and forth about their business. "Oh yes, you are still very much here," he emphasised, watching the legionaries. Mordecai turned to face the governor and Lucius, the latter sitting in anticipation. Something within Lucius told him he was getting involved in a business way beyond an Optio's usual role, and he suspected he might not like it. But he listened.

"Optio, my principals and I both know that should there be another uprising against Rome, and I am not talking about glorified banditry here, it would be extinguished with great violence; it is the way of the legions. The consequences for our people and our religion could be disastrous - no, not could, they *would* be disastrous. Therefore, it simply must not be allowed to happen."

Rufus sat upright in his chair and to Mordecai said,

"Sit down, Zakkai; you make me nervous wandering about like that." As Mordecai came back to his chair, the Governor turned to Lucius. "You see, Optio, I am the governor of this province, and I am personally responsible to Hadrianus, our Imperator. If I so much as smell a rat, I must check out the smell.

Am I facing a serious revolt? I cannot be sure, but I am smelling something going on, so it needs to be checked out. That is where you come in."

So here it comes thought, Lucius. He realised he was holding his breath, so forcibly exhaled and took in another breath.

"I want you and Zakkai to seek out a number of my 'bells.' I need to know why they have stopped chiming. If they are still alive, you are to interrogate them until you get the truth; I must know what is going on amongst the Judaeans." Rufus stopped, a signal that Lucius now understood.

"I will, of course, comply, sir, but I shall need a certain amount of information, who are these…"

"You shall have everything you need," interrupted Rufus, "Zakkai and I have talked this through, and he will brief you fully."

Lucius looked across the table at Mordecai. Here is a man who is much more than he seems and has the Governor's trust. He felt anger growing within; he had been manoeuvred into this position and left with no options. Rufus continued,

"Preparations are made, Optio, but if there is anything you need, go straight to the quartermaster who is briefed. Now, you two have a lot to discuss, so I suggest you get on with it. It goes without saying that time is of the essence, so the sooner you are moving, the better. Keep me informed." Saying this, Rufus stood, causing the other two men to jump to their feet. Lucius gave Rufus a salute, to which Rufus gave the two of them a wave of the hand and left the room. Lucius turned to Mordecai,

"Well, Matthias – or is it Mordecai? - I think I am owed some form of explanation. I don't know just what you and the Governor have cooked up between you, but I am feeling a little uncomfortable right now. So, just who the fuck are you? I am presuming Mordecai is the real person."

The Judaean faced Lucius holding out his hands, palms upwards.

"Optio, I am heartily sorry for misleading you that day we met. I will explain in due course. As for this task the Governor has asked of us, I too was manoeuvred into it, a little earlier than you, and I am uncomfortable. I am a Judaean and to be seen in any way working for an occupier against my people is not good."

Lucius thought he looked and sounded genuine, so he was prepared to give him the benefit of the doubt. He said,

"We need to talk, Mordecai. Being seen in public conversing with a Roman officer may not be helpful. Why don't we head back to my quarters in the barracks? We should not be overheard, and we can be there in no time." Mordecai nodded.

"I think that would work. Let's go."

Capitulum VI - First contact

27 & 28 Martius. Year 16 of Imperator Hadrian

As the Roman and the Judaean walked down the Decumus Maximus heading towards the officer's quarters, they drew a few glances from passing legionaries. A centurion gave Lucius a wave of his vine stick. It was only a brief time before Lucius closed the door behind them, and they were secure in his quarters. He offered a chair to Mordecai, removed his helmet and cloak and sat on a stool.

Only then he noticed an alien pitcher sitting on the table. He stood up to investigate to find the vessel full of wine.

"That is strange," he said to Mordecai, "This was not here when I left. Still, we can't let it go to waste – will you have a beaker?"

"With pleasure," the Judaean replied. "Then, if you sit again, I will share what I know about this task Governor Rufus has set for us."

Lucius poured the wine and sat with a beaker brimming with wine.

"Go ahead, Mordecai. You have my unswerving attention."

"I mentioned the other day that I was sent to Alexandria. I led a rakish existence, one I am not proud of, until the rabbis got me back to Judaea. After a while, I became a travelling emissary for a group of rabbis of a more peaceful persuasion. I spoke with communities across the land, in some places being welcomed while in others, being merely tolerated. A few days ago, while up in the country, I learned the Governor was in Aelia, so I returned discretely to the fort. He briefed the Governor on how many of the Rabbis in Jamnia saw the current situation across Israel. They did not want trouble and were doing what they could to avoid it. In summary, the two northern areas of the province, Samaria and Galilee, were settled, while Judea itself was decidedly mixed in its views of Rome. The latter was no great surprise for the Governor, as Judea had long been the main concern for both him and his predecessors.

Being Judaean, the Governor saw me as the best person to lead an investigation as to what had occurred with the informers, and we hatched the plot." Rufus passed the details of three of the informants to Mordecai.

"Our brief is to find and question these men; if Rufus was to avoid inflaming passions, he could not use the military for the task. So we devised a plan for you and me to pose as a Greek merchant and his Jewish agent looking to trade. The Greek merchant would have his servant with him and a bodyguard.

"You are involving Apollinaris and Postumus?" Lucius asked, taken aback.

"Look, the team would be entirely natural for such a trading expedition," said Mordecai, "Both you and Marcus speak the tongue well, so can pass off as Greeks. I can manage Hebrew and Aramaic; Marcus also has a command of Aramaic which will prove extremely helpful. Sextus could pass easily as a hired Gallic bodyguard." Lucius was listening intently. "The next morning, we will all report to the quartermaster, where suitable clothing would be available. A small two-wheel cart will be prepared and loaded with goods, cloth, quality leather belts, and other items." *If my father could see me now,* Lucius thought, *back in business, the very thing I ran away from!* "Our disguises will be as good as possible, even to the point of selling our wares. We will be given a sum of money to buy produce if it helps with our cover. The first port of call will be Beith Horon, about fifteen miles from the camp. I know the territory well and believe that we should reach their by sunset the next day given a clear run. The informer we are seeking should be easy to find; a shoemaker by the name of Mori ben Leizer."

Lucius, sipping his wine, had listened to the plan without comment. When Mordecai finished outlining the idea for the next day, he asked,

"You know Mordecai, the army has specialists at this type of activity. So why is the Governor entrusting the task to us? A newly arrived Optio and – with respect – a Judaean?"

Mordecai smiled.

"Politics, Optio, politics," he paused. "Look, we are going to be working very closely in the next few days. Under the circumstances, it would be madness to address you by your rank; may I address you as Lucius?"

"Given the nature of what we are doing, I think that might be a good idea," returning to the subject, "So, politics, you say?"

The smile reappeared,

"The governor's senior officers, the centurions, think there is no major risk of a revolt right now. I ignore the tribunes who are usually not the smartest and are only with us for a year. It would look odd if Rufus went against the centuriate's views and proceeded with a serious investigation that could come to nothing. His credibility would suffer. Don't forget; this is Tineus Rufus we are dealing with, a past consul of Rome. His reputation and status are everything to him." He paused to take a drink of his wine. "Hmm, nice wine. Also, as he has mentioned, he is responsible to the Imperator, so he must make the correct judgement. So, what Rufus does is get an unknown officer and a Judaean to do the job; that's you and me. If we find evidence, he positions himself as the man who rumbled the planned revolt – a hero. Should there be no evidence, then nothing lost," he frowned before continuing, "there is another factor, of course. Should it all go wrong, then we are dispensable."

The two men sat in silence for a few seconds before Lucius said solemnly,

"We had better not get this wrong, Mordecai."

"I would agree, Lucius," responded Mordecai. "It is arranged that we meet at the quartermaster's at sunrise. I am going to the *vicus,* where I have a few knowledgeable contacts. If I may be so bold, perhaps if you could brief your two legionaries?"

"I have arranged to meet them in a short while, a fortunate arrangement given the briefing I need to give them." Mordecai stood up, finishing his wine as he did so. Lucius also stood, and as the two men faced each other, Lucius held out his hand; they clasped in the Roman fashion, wrist to wrist, as Lucius said,

"I pray that my gods or your God is with us in the coming days, Mordecai." The Judaean simply said,

"So be it, Lucius, so be it," before donning his cloak and leaving the room.

As the door closed, Lucius poured another beaker of wine and sat back on his stool. His world was turned upside down. How had he gone from being the IV Cohort's administrative officer to acting as a spy, an *exploratore*? He expected to be working through lists and scrolls in preparation for the Cohort's arrival, yet he was about to go sneaking around Judea gathering intelligence for the Governor. What was worrying him more was Mordecai's comments about being dispensable; if anything happened, there would be no centuries of legionaries rushing to the rescue. The small team was on its own.

Lucius was still turning the situation over in his mind when there came a sharp rap at the door. He opened the door to be met with a beaming smile from Marcus, with Sextus standing at his shoulder.

"Reporting as ordered, sir," he said, as they both stood smartly to attention.

"Relax. Your timing is impeccable, men," Lucius replied, "I need to eat, and we need to have a conversation. Can I suggest we head to the *vicus*?" He collected his cloak and helmet, and the trio headed in the direction of the north gate.

As they made their way out of the camp and towards the *vicus*, Marcus asked,

"Did you find the wine, sir?"

"I guessed you were involved, Apollinaris," responded Lucius, adding, "a pleasant wine it was too. I must reimburse you. How much did you pay?"

"Ah, well…you see sir, Sextus and me sort of stumbled across it, you could say it was lost an' we rescued it. We thought you could use it, sir; we heard that you'd crossed swords with Centurion Secundus," Marcus sounded positively enthused, "the whole Legion knows what he can be like!" Taking a slightly more diplomatic approach, Sextus added,

"Few secrets in this camp, sir. Just gossip, you know how it is, sir."

"We didn't exactly cross swords," Lucius clarified, "just a mild disagreement-"

"And we heard you'd been in the Governor's office, sir," interrupted Marcus, "and I also hear-"

"Apollinaris, if I wish you to know anything, I shall tell you!" Lucius came back smartly, "Anything else you ignore. Clear?"

Marcus looked sheepish.

"Apologies, sir."

"As it happens, I have information that concerns you both; we are going to be rather busy. Firstly, let's find the Boar; it's a taberna I know, where the food is passable, and the wine is too. Then we can talk."

"Very good, sir," Marcus said smartly, "and I have the bag, sir."

As if we'll be needing that in the next few days, thought Lucius.

Marcus's thoughts were a bit different; officers buying legionaries drink and food again? They were in for something dodgy, no doubt about that.

As they entered the Boar and chose a discreet table, the taberna keeper nodded at Lucius and welcomed his return. Settling for bread, olives and cut wine, the three men settled down to talk. Lucius outlined the plan and their roles for the duration of their small expedition. Neither of the two legionaries spoke until Lucius had finished. Surprisingly the first to speak was Sextus.

"What's the chances of trouble, sir?"

"As long as people believe our cover, I would expect little trouble," Lucius said as confidently as he could, "Should our cover be disrupted, we will return straight back to camp as the mission would be impossible to fulfil. So I don't think we need be too worried."

Sextus pondered a few seconds,

"What arms shall we be carrying?" he asked.

"As our bodyguard, you will be well-armed. The rest of us will carry small daggers," Lucius realised he was inventing this as he went along as it was not a subject discussed with Mordecai, but it made sense. "I suspect we shall conceal our swords amongst the produce we are 'selling, just in case."

The answer seemed to satisfy Sextus. Marcus had a few questions about detail, but both legionaries accepted the roles they would be playing in the next few days.

"Jupiter, sir," Marcus said, "So much for acting as your clerk," as he spoke, he held up the despatch-case, "So far, I don't think we've opened this thing once!"

"Well, Apollinaris," Lucius quipped, "Never say life in the *Fretensis* is boring."

After sunrise the following day, he and the three men presented themselves at the Quartermastery. Apart from Sextus, they were simply clad in tunics and cloaks and armed with daggers. There was no role for armour or helmets in the forthcoming mission. A milites immunes met them; a soldier excused regular duties because he had a skill valuable to the Legion. He took the three into a small room where civilian clothing was awaiting them. The clothing suited each man's role: Lucius's tunic and cloak were superior, whilst Marcus, a mere driver and servant, wore much simpler fare. Sextus, however, looked the part wearing clothes acquired from a passing Gallic Auxiliary unit. *But, no doubt, thought* Lucius, *they would have cost the quartermaster dear!* Indeed, even the armoury had contributed to the venture, supplying a typically Gallic sword. Lucius was handed a pouch brimming with denarius coins, enabling the group to maintain their cover as merchants. However, he was pointedly reminded he would have to account for any monies spent.

Feeling as though he was ready, Lucius asked about the cart. He was told it would be by the forge in the *vicus* where Mordecai was waiting for them. Lucius now understood Mordecai's mission in the *vicus* last night. It made sense as it would not be good to see the Greek merchants leaving a Roman fort. So all three men knew the forge's location and set off to find Mordecai and the cart.

Mordecai smiled as the three approached, wearing unfamiliar clothing.

"Good job, you could have fooled me. I think it's best if we get moving."

The cart was a two-wheeled affair with high sides and a leather cover sitting on a frame, smaller than the military waggon that had brought the group to Aelia. It was pulled by a well-fed and watered mule, agitating to be on its way. Lucius was pleased to note they had the sense to choose a beast without a legionary brand emblazoned on its flanks. It was decided that Marcus would lead the mule, Mordecai and Lucius walking behind. Sextus would move between them. Before they started, they ran through the cart's contents. Then, once familiar with their 'wares,' the small group set out.

Lucius felt very conspicuous as they walked along the road out of the *vicus*. He was sure those they passed must be suspicious of them. He said as much to Mordecai, who advised him to relax; carts pass up and down this road daily. What is one more? It was not long before they were clear of the *vicus* and moving towards the hills of Judea. Mordecai hoped they would make Beith Horon by nightfall.

"We head north to Mizpeh and then head north-west across to Beith Horon. We may have to play being merchants in Mizpeh; it would help the illusion we are trying to create. We have some fine cloth on the cart and general leatherwork. Anyone else heading for Beith Horon that sees us trading will make it all the easier when we finally reach that destination."

Lucius nodded.

"My father's business was trading in, amongst other things, cloth. It will be a home from home." He jested. Mordecai smiled then frowned,

"Lucius, I have been thinking. Just suppose that Rufus' informers were not informers. Just suppose they were purposefully feeding him information." Lucius guffawed,

"Come on, Mordecai," he said, "You are way off the mark. Based on what they have fed us, we have been able to disrupt and apprehend bandits, brigands - you name it. Their information is good!"

"Think of the bigger picture, Lucius," Mordecai stuck to his hypothesis, "If you are planning something major, some minor sacrifices might be well worth offering if it shielded the main plan."

"So, let me understand," Lucius responded, "You are saying that someone may be fooling us into believing all is normal, just the usual scraps and raids, to hide a bigger plan; a smokescreen?" He paused. "Clever, if it's true because it gives us just what we would expect; minor trouble here and there, but Rome remains in control. So, to an extent, we can relax. Meanwhile…"

"It would be clever, wouldn't it?" asked Mordecai.

"It would, but I understand that Rufus, or at least his people, recruited these men, so they have not been 'planted' as such. Had they volunteered to inform, it would be different."

"Indeed," Mordecai came back quickly, "but suppose the other side discovered their activities and effectively took control of them, telling them what information to pass?"

"Mordecai, this is wheels within wheels," said an exasperated Lucius, "if, but – who knows?"

"I know it sounds outlandish, but if the informers had been deliberately turned against you, why has the information flow suddenly been 'turned off'?"

The dawning hit Lucius in the pit of his stomach,

"Because they no longer need them. Which mean something is about to -"

"Lucius, this is all supposition," Mordecai replied, "but the sooner we get to Beith Horon, the better."

With Aelia behind them, the group followed the road as it meandered through valleys between the Judean hills. They passed travellers heading south, acknowledging them but never stopping to talk. Mid-morning saw them take shelter from the sun for a few minutes as the day became warmer, but the break was short. They were keen to push on.

Though the aim may have been to reach Beith Horon as quickly as possible, around midday, the group spent an hour in the village of Mizpah. They left the town slightly lighter in cloth and heavier in the purse. Lucius was not surprised to find that Marcus would have sold his mother had he had the chance; he was a natural seller. His negotiation skills were also sharp as he negotiated a five per cent personal commission for what he sold with Lucius. Marcus' fluent Aramaic was also helpful. Surprised at Marcus' skillset, all Sextus could say to Lucius and Mordecai was, 'If you'd asked, I could have told you!' An hour later, the remainder of the team had to drag Marcus away, but he left everyone who had seen the small group in no doubt that they were merchants. Nevertheless, Lucius considered the five per cent was a worthwhile investment. As they left the village, Mordecai spoke up.

"Ironic, isn't it?" he said. "Many years ago, Judas Maccabeus mustered his army here at Mizpeh before crushing the Greeks at Emmaus and leading the way to Judean freedom. Yet, here we are now, pretending to be Greek merchants!" Lucius wondered if another Jewish army was mustering somewhere to crush the current occupiers. However, he thought it a question better left unsaid.

The small party moved on in a more westerly direction, moving at a steady pace. Mordecai was confident they would reach the village before nightfall. They had managed to obtain some food and drink in Mizpeh, so they were refreshed, and the pace was no problem. In addition, they had bought additional provisions for an evening meal. The plan was to camp just short of the village, enabling them to enter the settlement at sunrise. They would set up in the small square that Mordecai remembered, look for customers, and establish their cover. At some point, Mordecai and Sextus would slip away and find the cobbler's shop and, if all was well, the cobbler within it. This was a reconnaissance, and they would not engage with Mori ben Leizer at this time but report back to Lucius with his location and the fact he appeared well. They would then plan an approach.

The sun was lowering in the sky as the group laboured up a long incline at the top of which, Mordecai assured them, they would see the settlement of Beit Horon. The three Romans were well used to marches carrying a full complement of a soldier's kit; none of them found the journey arduous. Mordecai spent much of his life on foot, so he, too, was finding the going good. All were cheered by the fact that the journey's end was in sight.

The roadway ran through scrubland covered in rocks, stunted trees and bushes; it would be a hardy population that lived in Beit

Horon, thought Lucius. There may not be much demand for fine cloth here, but the leather may sell. He stopped his line of thought – there was more of his father in him than he thought.

As if from nowhere, two men appeared ahead, moving meaningfully in their direction. They had passed many travellers through the day, but the approaching men had none of the bearing of travellers. Mordecai caught Lucius' eye and quietly said, "Leave this to me." Sextus apart, they were all unarmed except for daggers, but their swords were hidden under the waggon's front seat. Marcus was leading the mule and committed, so Lucius fell back to walk alongside the vacant front seat in case he needed to react quickly. Mordecai moved forward across from Marcus, level with the mules' head. Sextus stayed just behind his legionary friend.

The two men stopped ahead of the group. Lucius looked them over. They were well built, bearded, dressed in tunics and cloaks and around their shoulders, they wore long scarves. Lucius recalled the bandits that attacked the convoy; those scarves could be wrapped around the head as both disguise and for protection. The group came to a stop, and one of the two men called out. Lucius recognised Aramaic but did not understand. Mordecai replied in the same language, and the taller of the two men replied in Greek,

"My apologies. Have you come far today?" It was said with a smile. It was a very crooked smile as Mordecai realised the man had a prominent, jagged scar running from the left corner of his mouth halfway up his cheek. Mordecai decided to avoid any mention of Aelia and responded,

"We've been trading in Mizpah today and are headed to Beit Horon next."

"I fear you will not get the people of Beit Horon to pass their shekels over as they do in Mizpah, friend," he looked across to the other members of the group. "So, you are Greek?"

"Indeed," said Lucius, "We are on a trading venture here in your country before moving on to Damascus and beyond. It has been a productive visit to date."

"You must be persuasive," laughed the tall man, "It's usually blood from a stone in these parts. So where are you off to next?" Mordecai jumped in quickly to answer the question.

"We often take advice from the town we are in as to where to go next. No one knows a country as well as those who live there."

The tall one laughed again. "It must have been someone you overcharged who sent you to Beit Horon!" He nodded in the direction of Sextus, "He don't look Greek to me."

"No," said Lucius. "Sextus acts as our security. By the end of a trip, we could be carrying a quantity of money and goods purchased for export, so we must be careful. He is from Gaul. Mordecai here is Judean and acts as my agent as well as a guide too." The man nodded.

"You have our life story, my friend," Mordecai said with a smile, "You live in Beit Horon?"

"My brother and I have lived here all our lives," was the reply. "We are just on our way to check some goats we have down the road. You probably passed the pens."

"Then let us not hold you up. It will be nightfall before long, and I am sure you would both wish to be home by then," Mordecai said. Both men readily agreed, and they went on their way down the hill. Marcus moved the waggon forward, and the group moved on.

"Goats, my arse!" spat Marcus, "My uncle kept goats, and those two did not smell like goatherds to me."

"They were not goatherds. On the contrary, they carried themselves like fighters," added Sextus, "As they passed, the breeze blew the shorter one's cloak against his body. He was carrying a sword. What is more important, the top of the little finger on his left hand was missing."

"I missed that," Lucius said. "So, a bandit or at least an ex-bandit then?"

Sextus nodded,

"Can't be a coincidence."

"This does not alter the situation," Lucius said. "They had no reason to disbelieve us, so we have to stick to the cover. Tonight, we camp outside the village, off the road, to minimise the chance of seeing those two coming back. Tomorrow we will enter the village and set up in the centre. First, we must ensure they believe we are who we claim to be. Then, that evening we shall see about Mori ben Leizer. We may glean some information from our customers about him." He turned to Mordecai, "What do you think, my friend?"

The Judaean nodded in agreement.

"If we lose our cover, then all is lost; if our suspicions are correct, it could turn dangerous. So, yes, your thoughts are good."

So that night, they spent encamped behind a wind-blown copse of short, wiry trees near the entrance to Beit Horon. They posted watches through the night, though the hours were uneventful. They saw no sign of the two men from Beit Horon. In the morning, after a breakfast of bread, cheese, and figs, all washed down with water, the group moved back onto the road and headed the last short distance to Beit Horon.

The village was well established and consisted of many low, square, brown stone houses surrounded by stone walls. The walls penned in the odd cow, chickens and some goats, all part of the resident's subsistence strategy. Though it was early morning, many people saw the cart with its four attendants move along the main thoroughfare towards the village centre where the marketplace was to be found.

Upon arriving at their objective, the group laid out their wares. Sextus was leaning casually against one of the cart's wheels, but he carefully observed any passing villagers. After the meeting on the road the previous evening, he was very wary of the situation in which they found themselves. It was agreed that Marcus would be the seller; he had a natural flair to help confirm their cover.

Soon, other merchants appeared, bringing fruit and vegetables amongst other products. Then, around the edge of the marketplace, shops began to open; a baker, a butcher, and what looked like a general hardware store. There were all types of buildings; the commercial buildings faced the market, while the residential area faced the rear. Soon, a few natives tentatively approached the cart and struck up a conversation with Marcus; Lucius began to relax a little. Finally, Mordecai joined him around the side of the cart. He nudged Lucius and nodded in the direction of the one store that was not yet open.

"If I am not wrong," he said quietly, "that is the cobbler's shop."

"Perhaps he has overslept," Lucius suggested. "Let's keep an eye on it for a while, I am sure it will open." And so, they did, but they saw no change. Finally, after an hour, Mordecai walked over to where Marcus was talking to a customer, a grey-haired elderly man.

"Excuse me, my friend," he butted in. Then, turning to the customer, he asked, "I have a pair of boots in the cart that need a small repair. Do you know what time the cobbler opens?"

"The cobbler? Well, now, I heard he is ill, so I am afraid you won't have much luck today. However, there is a good man in Mizpeh who could help you."

"Oh dear, poor man. Nothing too serious, I hope?" The old man noticeably stiffened a little before responding,

"Chest, yes, he has pains in his chest!" At which he turned and hobbled off on his stick. Mordecai strolled back to Lucius.

"Well, that did not sound too convincing," Lucius said. "The sooner we check this cobbler out, the better."

They had the rest of the day to hatch a simple plan. They would leave Beit Horon just before sunset and camp outside the town again. Then, early next morning before sunrise, Lucius and Mordecai would return to the village and attempt an entry into the cobbler's residence. Sick or not, they needed to talk with Mori ben Leizer.

The day wore on, and to everyone's surprise, they sold a good amount of cloth and leather from the cart; Marcus was in his element as a seller. One customer commented that most merchants were put off coming to Beit Horton, having been told that the potential is not good there, so it will be well supported when one does turn up. Marcus was wearing a constant grin and counting his commission. Meanwhile, Sextus was pacing around the cart like a mother cat protecting its kittens. Try as he might, he could not spot the two individuals they met the day before; rather than assure him, it seemed to leave him rattled.

Meanwhile, Lucius used the time to attempt to understand more about his new 'friend.' Mordecai was unhappy as a youth and was sent to Alexandria with an uncle from the age of sixteen. He appeared not to wish to go into much detail about his early years. While living in Alexandria, he was befriended by Rabbi Gamaliel and studied under the rabbi for two years. Then, he returned to Judea with a note of introduction to the famous Rabbi Tarfon. It appeared that from that time on, he became a trusted emissary for the Rabbis in Jamniah, travelling across Israel and further abroad to Jewish communities wherever they were settled. Lucius's ears pricked up at Mordecai's mention of following Rabbi Akiva to Mesopotamia a couple of years ago. Lucius recalled the army would like to question Akiva but could not find him. Lucius probed Mordecai on the topic, who told him that the Rabbi sounded out the Judaeans in Mesopotamia about supporting an uprising. To Akiva's disappointment, they wanted nothing to do with such a project. It seems messages that Mordecai carried to the Mesopotamian rabbis had influenced their thinking. The conversation ran on with no significant revelations, and Lucius shared his story in return. He was growing to like Mordecai. The Judaean suddenly developed a severe expression.

"My friend, I walk a dangerous path. I wish to prevent a senseless uprising; I have worked hard to achieve this."

"I understand, Mordecai," Lucius replied, "We all know what a rebellion would bring to this land."

"Indeed," said the Judaean, "but one day, I may have a difficult decision to make. If my people rise, do I disown them? Does a mother desert her errant children? Should Rome start to slaughter my people, do I stand aside and watch?" He fell silent. Lucius thought carefully about his reply.

"This makes it all the more important we prevent any uprising – or perhaps contain it locally," Lucius responded whilst considering the situation for himself; it would indeed be difficult if it came to violence. Nevertheless, he hoped that his fears would come to nothing.

The sun was lowering, and Marcus packed up the waggon, completing a last-minute sale as he did so until they were ready to move out of Beith Horon. Mordecai told Lucius that the next informer to check after Mori ben Leizer was found in the town of Emmaus, so they would leave in a westerly direction and camp a mile or so outside of Beith Horon. It did not take long to cover the distance, and soon they had pulled off the road and set up a basic camp. A small fire was burning in no time, and Sextus was preparing a simple broth for the group's dinner. They agreed on a watch schedule, and apart from the watchman, they all turned in.

    The first light was just observable when Sextus woke the others as agreed. All four would make their way back to Beith Horon. Whilst Marcos and Sextus stood guard, Mordecai and Lucius would enter the cobbler's premises. The previous day, while the others were busy being merchants, Mordecai had taken a stroll across to the cobbler's shop. It was closed, so he strolled around the back of the premises, surrounded by a wall of such a height that he could just see over the top. He did not observe much movement, but if the cobbler were ill, then there would not be cause for such. There was a gate in the wall, but the presence of passing locals prevented him from going any further. At least he knew exactly how to gain entry.

    The sky began to lighten as the group approached Beith Horon. It was still early, and apart from passing one man on a donkey heading out of town, they saw no one. Once they entered the town proper, Sextus insisted on leading the way as they tried to be as inconspicuous as possible. No one spoke, and Lucius wondered if their walking so close to walls was a natural reaction to a sense of threat. It was Mordecai who broke the tension by saying,

    "My friends, we are simply four people walking into a village; be as natural as possible, and it is fine to talk!" The others visibly relaxed, realising that Mordecai was right. It crossed Lucius' mind that Mordecai seemed quite at home in this environment, telling Marcus and Sextus to stand guard when they were close to the cobbler's shop.

    "But in Moses' name, lean against the wall, chat about women, the weather, the bloody Romans but *do not* look like you are standing sentinel. Do you understand?" They both nodded. "Marcus, if you suspect any trouble, fake a sneeze, and we will get out quickly." The two soldiers walked over to a dry-stone wall, leaned upon it, and started to chat. Lucius nodded towards the shop's rear, and he and Mordecai strolled around the corner. They followed the wall around to the back of the premises, where Mordecai stopped at the gate and lifted the latch handle. Although the early morning was cool, Lucius was nervous and could feel a damp sweat under his arms. *Let me face a horde of angry Dacians than this cloak and dagger stuff*, he thought. The gate opened with no fuss, and they both slipped quietly through the entrance, closing the gate behind them. So far, so good.

The two men walked carefully up the pathway that led from the gate to the shop's rear entrance. A small lean-to at the back of the shop gave shelter to several animal skins and small barrels. As they closed upon the rear entrance, they were overwhelmed by a strong odour of leather and wax. Lucius arrived at the door first and reached for the handle, a simple latch operation; he looked to Mordecai for reassurance that lifting the latch was the next move. Holding his breath and trying to suppress his nerves, he gently lifted the latch, and the door opened effortlessly. It may have been a redundant comment, but Lucius whispered,

"It's open."

"So it would appear," Mordecai responded. They passed through the doorway and quietly closed the door behind them. The room they entered was initially very dark, but they could see it was a living area as their eyes adjusted. Chairs, table, and a floor covered in carpeting; the smell of leather was overpowering. Ahead of them was a doorway that led to the shop itself. To the right was a further door. Mordecai mouthed "bedroom" slowly, and Lucius nodded. It was then that Lucius noticed that between entering the room and now, Mordecai had taken a dagger in hand. He followed suit.

Mordecai moved towards the bedroom door, placed his hand upon the latch, paused for a second before lifting the latch and bursting into the room. Lucius followed. It was very clearly a bedroom, but an empty one. There may not have been anyone asleep in the room, but the bed was unmade. Lucius felt the urge to laugh, not because anything was funny but in pure relief.

"Damnation!" Mordecai exclaimed, "He's not here. No wonder it was so quiet yesterday."

"He is ill. Perhaps friends are caring for him," Lucius suggested.

"Maybe," Mordecai said disconsolately, "but we have lost a day. Damn it!"

Lucius turned and walked back into the living area. The first beams of sunlight were falling on the village, and Lucius could get a much better view of the room. Several chests lay around the edge of the room, and various instruments of the cobbler's trade hung on the wall. Around the fireplace were some blackened pans and a kettle. The carpet was of exceptional quality for such a dwelling. Lucius wondered what the story was behind Mori ben Leizer, why did he turn informer?

Mordecai joined him in the living area.

"No point in searching. I doubt if we would find anything. We should get out of here." He looked around the room and, like Lucius, noticed the carpet. "Wouldn't expect to see this in here."

"A small luxury perhaps," responded Lucius. As he spoke, he noticed what he had initially thought was a shadow on the carpet but upon a second look seemed an odd shape for a shadow given the angle of the small window that allowed light to stream into the room. When he ran his sandal sole over the 'shadow,' the tufts felt stiff. Mordecai noticed, and as he looked down at the carpet, a suspicion hit him about the same time as the thought jumped into Lucius' mind. He promptly squatted down and ran a finger across the dark blemish in the carpet.

He looked at the finger and then turned his hand towards Lucius; in the sunbeam's light, Lucius could see his finger was a dark crimson.

"Blood?" he asked, knowing full well what the crimson substance was. His companion sniffed the substance on his finger, causing the back of his tongue to taste of iron; it was blood all right.

"Yes," Mordecai answered, "not dry, still a little moist. I'd guess it's been here a day or so. This time tomorrow, it will be dry." Lucius' mind was racing, trying to process the information.

"Where is the body?" he asked, then realised what a ridiculous question it was, "er… I mean, why remove the body?"

"Who knows? It all depends upon why he was killed. Was it intended to be more a disappearance than a murder – you know, a message sent? It may have become messier than planned." Mordecai stared at the patch of blood for a few seconds, his mind also racing before snapping into action. "Right, Lucius, we have to get out of here and on the road to Emmaus and be quick about it." As he spoke, he moved towards the external door. He peered out gingerly and determined that it was safe to signal Lucius to follow him. He peered over the wall at the gate, then gave Lucius a nod, and they passed through the gate.

A few seconds later, they were back on the main street and turned to leave the town. Sextus and Marcos spotted them and followed behind, leaving a gap between them. There were more people on the street by this hour, and whilst one or two gave the two groups of strangers a passing glance, most just walked on by engrossed in their thoughts this early morning. By the time they left the outskirts of the town, the sun was climbing into the sky, driving away the early morning cool. They walked on and, leaving the main road, quickly arrived back at the cart where they had left it earlier that morning.

Lucius briefed Sextus and Marcus about what they had found. The ever alert, ever suspicious, Sextus voiced what Lucius had thought as they returned to the cart.

"Excuse me, sir, but my nose is twitching. It's those two men we met as we approached the town. They didn't seem like goatherds to me, and I recall no goat pens as we approached - not forgetting the finger." Lucius looked across to Mordecai, who shrugged his shoulders,

"You may be right, my friend, but who knows. The timing may be about right, though." He then urged the team to get to Emmaus as quickly as possible.

"What," asked Sextus, "if our man is dead or disappeared when we get there?"

"A valid question, my friend," Mordecai responded, "I would suggest that we report back to camp as quickly as possible. But, first, we must get there, and quickly. If we move swiftly, we may have to overnight in Beitoannaba, arriving in Emmaus tomorrow sometime past noon."

Within minutes they were on their way. The carefree attitude of Beith Horon was gone as each member of the team understood they may well be involved in what had become a deadly game.

They covered several paces before Lucius suddenly stopped.

"Great Jupiter!" Mordecai and the others stopped suddenly, and Sextus grasped his sword handle. Lucius suddenly felt a little embarrassed. "Apologies, but I just realised that we have been in Beit Horon." Sextus wondered if the sun was influencing the young officer. "It was here that a rebel Jewish Army destroyed the twelfth legion under Sextus Gallius during the Great Revolt. Six thousand men died that day."

"All the more reason to move on then," Marcus said. "I don't like ghosts!" Mordecai said nothing.

Interludum I

The tax collectors

Forewarned, the village elder knew the tax collectors and their escort would soon be approaching. Yet again, they would expect to collect hard-earned coinage from the populace, and where that fell short, help themselves to much of the village's stores of grain, olive oil and other produce the community had worked to produce. It was galling for villagers to work in the hot sun, day in and day out, only to have these people come and help themselves to the fruits of their labours. To make matters worse, the collectors were often Judaeans who had learned that a good living was to be had working for the conquerors. This process had run for decades as the villagers were helpless to protect themselves. Any attempt to avoid paying the levy placed upon them by Rome would exact swift punishment. It was a tragedy that such attempts at avoidance were so often betrayed by one of their own.

The elder recalled when the tax collectors had uncovered a secret store of olive oil in a cave outside the village. They seized a family's daughter concerned as punishment, and the accompanying soldiers had taken her off. Despite appeals to determine her fate, the girl was never seen again, no doubt eventually sold into slavery. The old man had no love of tax collectors. Hearing the creak of a waggon and the banter of marching soldiers, he snapped out of his reverie.

Sitting in the village centre, the old man could look out across some stone two-storey dwellings, each surrounded by a low wall. Several of the populace, resting against their walls, waited for events to unfold. As he watched, a younger man who must be at least half his age came and sat beside him. The older man would have longed to be at such an age, but he consoled himself by knowing seventy-three years of age did not exclude him from playing a vital role in the plan for the very immediate future.

They sat upon the bench with their backs against the wall of a communal storehouse; opposite them was the opening into the village centre where the collector's journey would end. The younger man lightly grasped the elder man's arm and spoke gently,

"Have courage, brother. You know your part."

"I have been over it many times, believe me, I will not fail you."

A large waggon drawn by two white oxen pulled into the village centre as they conversed. Next, there came a second waggon, well loaded with produce, followed by two files of soldiers. Sitting upon the waggons were the drivers accompanied by the much-despised tax collectors. The two villagers stood up from the bench and took a pace forward.

As the waggons approached, two tax collectors jumped down and strode across to the two. Forty soldiers flowed around the waggons and formed up in two lines, fronted by a tesserarius. The formation was to overawe the locals, with the soldiers trying hard to look menacing. These were not legionaries but Roman Auxiliary soldiers, typical of such units whose members were drawn from across the Empire, often staffed with people from conquered nations. They were easily recognisable by their large oval shields and suits of ring-mail Hamata. Rome was cautious enough to ensure Roman officers led these units.

The tax collectors strode to where the two villagers stood. Like them, one collector was older than the other. The village elder wondered if it was a case of one teaching the other to turn upon their own people! The old man took a deep breath.

"Welcome to Bet Alin. I trust your journey has not been too arduous?" he said.

"It has been warm, so if you are offering us a glass of refreshment, it will be well received," the older collector responded.

"I am sure we can give you such comfort. It would be the only correct thing to do for a traveller; after all, we are God's children," he said, making a risky dig at what he saw as the betrayal by the two collectors. He continued, "In the storehouse, we have a full record of what our families have produced, and we have collected the due tax revenues for you. Where there is a shortfall, we will substitute with produce stored within. We will be happy to assist you in loading your waggons." After his irresistible dig at the two traitors, he became all smiles and subservient. "Meanwhile, we shall prepare refreshments for you. If you would like to step inside..." He pointed to the entrance to the storehouse.

The younger of the two collectors relaxed; this was looking straightforward. He loathed it when villagers protested; he cursed his father for pushing him into this job alongside his uncle even though it paid exceptionally well. He knew others would have given their back teeth for a chance at the role.

The older tax collector turned to the infantry tesserarius stood in front of the two rows of auxiliaries.

"Wait here, tesserarius," he called across to him, "We'll check what they have for us, and if all is well, we shall commence loading in a few minutes." *Not until you've poured a pitcher of wine down your throat,* thought the officer.

The elder opened the door and stood back to let the two collectors enter, while the younger villager then allowed the older man to enter before following him. Inside it was dark, blinding the two collectors for an instant, but that was all it needed. As the door closed behind them and the darkness enveloped, the older collector felt a hand placed on his forehead pulling his head backwards. There followed a tingling sensation across his throat and a sudden warm dampness on his chest. At that point, his world went black and stayed that way forever.

The younger of the two collectors, a pace or two behind the older man sensed, rather than saw, someone barge in front of him. His mind tried to understand what was happening when he too, experienced his head snap back and the cold tingle on the throat. He tried to struggle but found that his strength failed him. He blacked out as his body slid to the floor, never to awaken.

Outside in the sunlight, the tesserarius turned to his men,

"Stand easy and relax, men. Those two may be a little time attending to their wine!" A ripple of laughter ran through the ranks as the soldiers visibly relaxed. The officer spotted a well set off to one side of the village centre. "Not all at once, mind, but if you need a drink, fall out and get one from the well." The soldiers knew their drill; leaving their shields and spears with their mates, they strolled across to the well that sat sixty feet away from the body of men. The tesserarius took in the surrounding village, typical of many Judean communities with their two-storey buildings surrounded by low walls. Around the central open area stood small workshops and general traders selling their wares, but untypically today, it was tranquil. He noticed a handful of people leaning on homestead walls watching them, but none of the usual coming and going. As the thoughts ran through his head, an infantryman spoke up,

"A bit bloody quiet this one, eh tesserarius?" Alarm bells rang in the tesserarius's mind; it was much too quiet by far, so better safe than sorry.

"Form up!" he shouted. The men at the well turned and ran back towards their comrades. Four of the six fell to the ground. Two lay deathly still while the others writhed and cried out. The two left standing shouted in pain but kept running. Many of the soldiers in line also screamed and shouted, some falling and others gripping arms and heads. "Shields up – slingshot!" yelled the tesserarius. He knew only too well how these people learnt the sling from the age of six. The small shot they fired would travel through the air at phenomenal speed, tearing the flesh and shattering the bones of their target. The tesserarius spotted, with some dread, the slingers now visible, standing brazenly on the roofs of the houses. His command was in a mess; he had men on the ground, and while others were standing, some of them injured. He spotted blood red blotches on several men, and he realised this was turning nasty.

Some auxiliaries had raised shields but too few to block all the deadly slingshots - the orders had come too late. A further volley of shot arrived, and though the auxiliaries were better prepared, a late returner from the well without a shield fell to the ground and remained still. The tesserarius ran into the middle of the ruptured lines, gladius in one hand and shield in the other and called for the men to form up around him. The fight would be defensive, he thought, horrified that only half his men were in fighting condition.

The small band of auxiliaries formed up behind a circle of shields, raised to a height that would reduce the impact of the slingers. The auxiliaries wanted to get man-to-man with the enemy; they had trained for this and had a high sense of self-belief in fighting Judean bandits. True, they may have been taken by surprise, but now it was payback time. What happened next was even more horrific.

The main road that ran through the village centre was not the only ingress onto the dusty piece of ground. Alongside houses and walls, there lay several other pathways and alleys, and it is from these locations, Judean warriors appeared. It shocked the auxiliaries to see men equipped as soldiers, not bandits. Many of the new arrivals wore Hamata, and they carried shields and spears, with several equipped with the Roman gladius sword. The Auxiliary tesserarius tried to estimate the numbers and had only reached about sixty – nowhere near half the size of the enemy surrounding his small force – when a shrill horn sounded. His antagonists roared a war cry and rushed upon the tesserarius's small band.

Ferocious warriors flung themselves at the auxiliaries' shield wall, and the sheer weight of numbers told. The tesserarius fended off several of his antagonists, wounding a number who fell back bleeding. The fight was turning into a messy melee. It was then that a young adolescent boy came from behind him. The boy was armed with only a spear, positioned in a low hold. His target never saw it coming. The sheer mass of the boy's weight combined with his speed drove the point through the tesserarius's hamata, deep into his chest and into the heart. Silently, the tesserarius fell to the floor, where the remaining soldiers of his unit joined him in no time at all.

All was still – there was no rejoicing amongst the warriors. They had trained hard for this day, talked about it, planned it but to see forty dead and wounded Roman soldiers, killed by their hands, left them with a strange feeling – almost one of dread. What had they done? As they watched, one of their number went about the grisly task of finishing off the wounded. When it was done, a voice cried,

"Collect their weapons and armour!"

This game had now become very real.

The village elder and the younger Judaean stood in the storehouse door and surveyed the scene as the warriors turned to face the younger of the two. A bloodied soldier lifted his sword to the man.

"Commander, we have done as requested!" he cried. Then, the group came back to life and roared their success to the sky. "We have beaten the occupiers!"

The young man turned to the elder,

"Your part was as vital as theirs, my brother. We all thank you. Soon, Judaea, if not all of Israel, will be free of the vermin."

Capitulum VII - A girl from the hills

30 Martius. Year 16 of Imperator Hadrian

The group of four walked at a good pace, leaving the village of Bet Horon behind them. The events at that place were not to be dismissed. They suppressed even the usual buoyant behaviour of Marcus. No matter how many times Mordecai and Lucius talked through the experience, there were no clues whether the informers were genuine or working for the dissident Judaeans; if the latter, why kill them? No evidence related the suspect's death to anti-Roman activity. It could all depend upon what they found at Emmaus.

The sun was high in the sky when Lucius suggested they pull off the road and take a break. The mule needed water, and they had not eaten since very early morning. So they pulled over under a clump of trees that offered shade and sat around for a mid-day meal. Marcus and Lucius discussed how much money they had made. They had cleared several hundred denarii, a fact that made Marcus smile thinking about his commission and should also make the quartermaster happy when they return.

As they talked, a four-wheel waggon trundled past with two men on the seat. They acknowledged the group under the tree with a casual wave of the hand as they passed. Lucius responded with a wave and then set about a piece of dried meat. The sustenance had just passed his lips when his jaw dropped.

"*Cac!*" he exclaimed. The others turned in his direction, and Mordecai, amused at the surprised expression on Lucius' face, said,

"Are you about to explain, my friend?"

"That waggon, the one that just passed. Two days ago, I watched it enter Antonia. The gate guard assured me it was a contractor bringing in weapons for the garrison. There are no weapon forges out this way, so what is he doing out here?"

Lucius noticed puzzled looks from the others. "It's the painted gladius on the rear of the waggon; that's how I know it is the same waggon."

Sextus cocked an eyebrow,

"I know what you are thinking, sir." He went on, "The new gladii we found when we were ambushed?" Lucius was surprised that Sextus had made the connection so quickly.

"That's exactly what's in my mind, Sextus," he responded.

"Right," said Mordecai. "Break camp; the mule's had his fill. We follow – but at a distance."

The two soldiers looked to Lucius.

"I agree. Let's do it!"

Within a few minutes, the cart was moving, and the group set a pace to enable them to get the big waggon in view. The road twisted a lot, and it concerned Lucius that they might come around a bend and find themselves on top of the vehicle. He suggested that one of them walk a distance ahead of the cart to act as a scout and warn before they get too close. Mordecai volunteered for the role. They need not have worried, for about forty-five minutes later, Mordecai came around a tight corner and back to the waggon at speed, holding his hand in the air. The cart came to a halt.

"They have just taken a left turn, my friends," He shared with them, "it would appear to be a secondary valley. But, from my position, I could make out the valley head, so they won't be going far."

"Why would they do that?" pondered Sextus, "Unless they have an interest in that valley."

"Given our suspicions," Lucius said, nodding his head towards Sextus, "I believe we need to check this out." He received a series of nods from the others of the group. "So, the question is, how do we do it?"

"We could just stroll up the valley like we was lost." Piped up Marcus.

"I don't think we want them even to know we are here," Lucius replied, "It could jeopardise our mission." Then, he turned to Mordecai, "What're your thoughts, Mordecai?"

The Judaean stood with his arms crossed, head down in a position of thought. For a while, he did not respond, and the group waited in anticipation. Lucius was about to break the silence when Mordecai spoke.

"The road straightens around this corner. The valley entrance is about half a mile along the road to the left. There are several small clumps of trees up front, and I suggest we conceal the waggon behind one, then climb up the hillside that makes up the valley side nearest to us. From the top, we should be able to look down into the valley they've entered. We can see what the waggon is doing there."

Lucius turned to his fellow soldiers, eyebrows questioning.

"Makes sense," was Sextus' reply.

"If you agree, sir, I'm in!" said Marcus.

"That's sorted then. Let's get about the job," Lucius responded to the support.

Ten minutes later, with the cart concealed and the mule left with water and food, the four men moved off towards the hillside. Each had recovered their weapons from behind the seat on the waggon; they were taking no risks. It was not long before they were struggling up the barren hillside. In no time at all, they all ran with sweat. Mordecai wrapped the scarf he was wearing around his head, looking like a bandit. The ground was shale, whose slippery nature made the climb even harder, but after a few minutes, the ridge that dominated this side of the valley was in reach. Lucius came to a stop and signalled for the group to gather around him.

"Once we get within ten paces of the ridge, we crawl. We would stand out like virgins in a bacchanalian orgy if we were upright. I will go up alone and signal to you if it's safe to follow. Should I be seen, they may think there is only one of us, which could be helpful should they pursue."

Mordecai nodded sagely.

"Military thinking, my friend," he said, "lead on."

They climbed a few more paces, after which Lucius dropped to his stomach while behind him, the others followed suit but dropped only to one knee. The shale was sharp and made for an uncomfortable crawl, but Lucius headed for the top. Initially, he saw the ridge on the other side of the valley, but as he covered the last few paces, the valley side opposite became visible. He paused for a second, conscious of the sweat running down his back before he pushed forward to peer down into the valley below.

Mordecai had been correct. The valley was short, and its head rose steeply from the bottom. A brick building nestled in the bottom of the valley, backed up to the steep end wall, surrounded by six wooden shacks and some tentage. Smoke arose from the brick building, in front of which the waggon had stopped. Half a dozen men were transferring bundles from the waggon into the building. It was hard to be sure, but Lucius convinced the bundles were swords, had little doubt that the building was a forge. A little larger than the rest, one shack looked as though it might be a carpenter's shop. Outside the shop was what looked like a foot-powered wood-turning lathe. But it wasn't just the men unloading; wandering around between the shacks and the tents must have been another twenty men involved in various activities, including sharpening weapons.

He reversed down the slope before sitting up on one arm and signalling for Mordecai to join him. As the Judaean came alongside, Lucius said,

"You need to see this."

The two men edged forward, peering into the valley. The unloading had finished, and the waggon moved across to one of the wooden shacks. As they watched, they loaded the waggon with bundles of spears. It was difficult to estimate, but they watched the loading of a considerable number of spears onto the vehicle; Lucius thought well over a hundred. Mordecai turned to Lucius and whispered,

"This isn't banditry, my friend; this is trouble." Lucius nodded his agreement,

"I will wager this isn't the only such forge; there'll be others," Lucius said, "Wand we have to get this information back to the fort as soon as possible. We don't need informers – we've seen it for ourselves."

The two men slid back down the shale to where the two legionaries waited. Lucius briefed them on what they had seen, and they all resolved to get back to Aelia as quickly as possible. Mordecai said he knew a route more direct than retracing their steps.

The men that returned to the cart were dustier and dirtier than those who set out, but they cared not. There was now a sense of urgency prevailing, and in no time, the cart was doubling back until it would turn off the road and take the faster route south to Aelia. They kept the practice of having a scout out front that they had adopted earlier. The last thing they needed was a nasty surprise as they realised they were in enemy territory. Lucius insisted that they maintain the illusion of being merchants, so the cart driver's seat saw the swords returned. They left Marcus as the cart driver, so they shared the rota of scout duty between the remaining three group members. Sextus took first duty.

They walked along at speed. The three men with the cart discussed the implications of what they had learned. The conversation was serious until Marcus regained his usual personality,

"Well, sir," he said chirpily, "I can't wait to see Secundus' face when he learns you was right all along!" Lucius could not help but smile, as did Mordecai.

"Thank you, Apollinaris," Lucius retorted, "but I fear we are talking life and death here. Centurion Secundus is not important."

"Sorry, sir," replied a crestfallen Marcus, "Just saying."

It was approaching late afternoon when Mordecai, on scout duty, turned in the distance and raised his arm in the air, signalling a halt. Marcus pulled on the mule's rein, and the cart came to a stop. Mordecai beckoned to go forward. Lucius told Marcus to stay with the vehicle while he and Sextus ran ahead. Mordecai had positioned himself on a slow turning bend. The two men joined him.

"Come with me but stay in the cover of the bend. Something is going on ahead." At which he moved slowly along the bend, sticking closely to the inner radius so as not to be visible to anyone around the other side. Lucius and Mordecai followed.

"Why is it always him that gets us creeping around?" Sextus whispered to Lucius. The question was rhetorical, and he wasn't expecting an answer. Instead, Mordecai's arm went up, and they stopped. Upon being prompted, they crawled close to Mordecai to establish what had caused the Judaean such concern.

Several hundred paces away stood a farm; it was small and did not look prosperous. Around the front of the establishment was a large group of men; Lucius estimated thirty people. It was difficult to see the focus of the activity, but there was shouting and waving of arms. The one factor that caused most concern was that these men were heavily armed; some carried swords, many also had spears and a good number of shields. Lucius whispered to no one in particular,

"I will hazard a guess as to where they got their weapons from."

The shouting went on for a few minutes when they heard a long scream followed by almost constant wailing. There followed a cry, quickly cut short. Hiding just around the corner, the three men knew what had taken place: two, possibly three, deaths. They knew there was nothing they could do. Nobody was going to be saved today, it was too late, and the odds were suicidal. A thought hit Lucius like a punch, which he verbalised,

"Jupiter! Suppose they come our way?"

The question hung in the air, but as it did so, the group moved off further down the road; several sheep and goats went with them while other men carried flapping hens. The three men stood their ground until the last of the soldiers, for that was what they were, moved well out of sight. What remained in front of the farm was three heaps, one smaller than the others; the three observers knew they were looking at bodies. They waited a few minutes more before Lucius stood out in the road and signalled to Marcus to bring the cart forward and as a group, they approached the farm.

The farm comprised a small house in stone set back from the road a few paces; behind the house were two small wooden sheds. A simple stone wall surrounded the property, and the area at the rear appeared to house animal pens, all empty. As the group approached the building, the bodies became clearer and seemed to be two adults and a young girl. They stopped the cart opposite the building and walked to where the bodies lay.

No one spoke as they took in what lay before them. The girl was an adolescent and lightly built; Lucius estimated her age to be around seventeen years. Her throat cut, her blood had pooled in the dry dust. She looked serene in death which Lucius thought strange given her demise. Lucius felt anger rise within him. Why would thirty men wish to slaughter such a girl? A few feet away lay what Lucius presumed to be her parents. The mother, like the daughter, had her throat cut and like her daughter, she reposed in a pool of blood. Her dark hair was greying, showing her age - she would not be growing any older.

The father was different; he had lost blood from a stomach wound that soaked into his clothing, turning the grey tunic a dark shade of crimson. He had been finished off, like the rest of his family, by a knife to the throat.

"I don't understand," Marcus broke the silence, "Those men were Jewish, so why kill fellow Judaeans? I thought *we* were the enemy."

"There may be an explanation, my friend," responded Mordecai. "I shall need to look inside."

"Go ahead," said Lucius and turning to the two legionaries, "Find shovels. We can't just leave them in the sun."

Marcus and Sextus had just moved off toward the wooden shacks when an ear-piercing scream rendered the air. A young woman appeared from the other side of the building, her face a picture of horror as she staggered towards the corpses. Her full length, pale dress was crumpled, and the red and black striped shawl lay at an oblique angle across her shoulders. The crimson headscarf that covered long black hair slid back on her head.

The two legionaries disappearing around the side of the building swung around. Sextus had his sword in hand and Marcus his pugio dagger. Mordecai pivoted about, dagger in hand and immediately adopted a crouched fighter's stance, a point not missed by Sextus. Lucius had a full view of the woman, and though initially taken aback, he started towards her. She fell to her knees by the bodies, face in hands and wept, her body heaving with sobs. Seeing no threat, Marcus rushed and squatted beside her, attempting to get her to her feet, his intention to remove her from the gore. He was talking gently, trying to soothe

the woman in what Lucius took to be Aramaic. Marcus helped her to her feet as the others approached, turning her back towards the small farmhouse; numb with shock, she offered no resistance. Sextus placed his sword back in its scabbard.

"I'll carry on," he said, walking back towards the shacks. Mordecai joined Marcus and helped take the woman inside. As they disappeared through the doorway, Lucius called out to Marcus and asked him to assist Sextus once they had the woman settled; he was keen to get moving toward Aelia as soon as possible. Lucius did not understand what had happened here and hoped the woman might shed light on the three deaths. Meanwhile, he thought it might be wise to stay out in the front in case they had visitors. So, Lucius walked to the cart and led the mule up beside the farmhouse giving shade to the beast. It was then that Marcus reappeared and asked if Lucius would join Mordecai inside the building; meanwhile, he would help Sextus with the burial.

The interior of the farmhouse was divided into three; a room for eating and sitting, one for sleeping and the other a kitchen and general work area. The young woman sat with Mordecai at a simple square dining table, who whispered to her. She had calmed herself, and Lucius noticed the scarf was now properly positioned upon her head. Mordecai looked up,

"This is Miriam," he said slowly, speaking in Greek. "She's had a thoroughly unpleasant experience, and I've been trying to explain how important it is that we understand what has happened. She will tell us. I'm sure she would like a drink." He spoke in simple sentences as the young woman was clearly in shock. How much she understood was anyone's guess. He nodded towards a pitcher that sat on a side table, accompanied by two cups. Lucius responded, filled a cup and brought it to the table. He sat opposite the woman. Mordecai continued, "So Miriam, in your own time, can you describe what happened?" He received no response, so he repeated the question, this time in Aramaic.

Miriam took a deep breath and sat up in the chair – even with red eyes and a tearful face, Lucius, something about her, attracted Lucius. She had dark hair but a lighter complexion, a thing not so common in Jewish women. For a few seconds, she composed herself before speaking.

"This home of uncle, aunt and cousin, Sarah." Her tone was flat, "I here after parents die of plague for two years." Her lips quivered and eyes welled up, but she struggled on, in her broken Greek. "My uncle, send me back farm collect figs. I hear noise – shouting, many voice – it scare me, I hide. The shouting goes on and stops. Where I hide, I saw men take sheep and goats. I knew bad had happen. I should help...." Tears were flowing down her cheeks. Lucius looked across at Mordecai. To Lucius' surprise, Mordecai looked shaken. Lucius turned back to Miriam,

"Miriam, why do you think these men did this?" The woman replied in the same flat tone,

"We follow Yeshua, true Messiah." Lucius was baffled and looked at Mordecai.

"I had my suspicions," Mordecai said slowly, before repeating the words, "I had my suspicions." As he spoke, his eyes filled, leaving Lucius even more confused. However, Mordecai went on, "Christians, my friend, these people were Christians. You are familiar with them in Rome."

The girl's countenance quickly changed. She wiped her eyes and spoke forcibly.

"No! We follow Yeshua, not deceiver Paul who go to Rome. We true faith!"

"I apologise, Miriam," Mordecai said, "I meant no offence."

"I also apologise," Lucius said; he gave a deep shrug, "but I am completely lost."

Mordecai slipped back into his normal confident personality,

"My friend, the politics and beliefs in this part of the world are indeed complex. I will explain later, but Miriam said something that caused me grave concern. She used the term 'Messiah' in respect of her belief in Yeshua, a great prophet long dead," Mordecai recognised a confusion on Lucius' face. "It is complicated as always, my friend, but the Messiah is a Jewish king who, at the end of times, shall defeat the oppressors and establish a state of Israel, a Heaven on Earth. So, .groups of Judeans – Jews – see these 'Christians' as misguided heretics in believing Yeshua to be a Messiah. Christians have been assassinated over the years, and there are still many Jews who think they are fair game."

"They'll kill them, given a chance?"

"My friend, some will, not all, but some," confirmed Mordecai.

"*Cac*!" was Lucius' retort. Miriam did not respond to the expletive, either through shock or lack of understanding. Instead, she sat staring into space. "We need to move... and quickly." Then, looking at Miriam, he said, "We can't just leave her here; she'll have to come with us until we can find somewhere for her on the route."

"My friend," Mordecai began, "That may not be-"

"We got company: four men, all armed. Be here very shortly," said Marcus from the doorway. Lucius' mind raced as he took in the news.

"Right, we are traders, so we act like traders. Let's get outside. The girl can stay here. Let's move."

As they left the building, Marcus re-joined Sextus in digging the graves for the farmer's family. Lucius and Mordecai strolled towards the road and waited for the strangers to reach them, all four carried swords and wore leather jerkins over their tunics with bulky scarves over their shoulders. They were all heavily bearded and solidly built. These were not simple farmworkers. One of the group, shorter than the others but with a bearing that spoke of leadership, led them across to where Mordecai and Lucius stood.

"A good day to you," he said amicably, "What is going on here?" he asked in Greek, glancing at the bodies that were now attracting large black flies.

"A good question, my friend," answered Mordecai. "We came around the bend yonder to be met with this terrible sight. We felt the least we could do is bury the poor people before - well, you can see the flies already."

"And you saw no sign of who did this?"

"Nothing," lied Mordecai, "it is as I described."

"You are not from these parts?"

"We are not," Mordecai replied. "We are merchants, and we have been touring the area selling our wares."

"Those two?" the man asked, nodding towards Sextus and Marcus, who had stopped digging to watch. Mordecai went through the bodyguard and driver routine. The two men in question ambled casually across to the conversation as he did so. "Where have you come from?" was the next question.

"Bet Horon was our last market, and we had a busy day." Said Mordecai. One of the other men spoke up,

"You are selling fine cloths?"

"Indeed," Mordecai confirmed. The man turned to the shorter man, the leader, and said,

"My sister told me last night about these men. She bought cloth from them, showed it to me, a pale grey with red stripes it was." Before the leader could respond, Marcus burst into the conversation,

"I remember her, very nice lady she was. How would you like to surprise 'er?" Everyone looked askance at the question, "She liked a lovely deep green cotton, special it is, but it was a bit expensive, you see. However, I'm sure a man of your standin' would want to treat such a lovely lady!"

The target of the question flustered, showing signs of embarrassment when his leader spoke up.

"We are not here for trade!" he snapped. "I suggest you get the bodies buried and move on… fast."

Clever, thought Lucius, Marcus had stopped the interrogation and may have managed to get us out of here without a problem. Then the leader added,

"We'll stay and see you off." Lucius looked across to Mordecai, who had also realised the potential complication of Miriam's appearance. He asked Marcus and Sextus to finish the graves near completion while he and Mordecai talked to the four Jewish soldiers for a while. Though no one called them that as such, that is what they were. As the graves were readied, they talked meaninglessly about business, the spell hot weather and the usual whines about tax and tribute. Then Lucius deliberately asked a pointed question,

"It is strange, but we have noticed a lot of people carrying swords in these parts. Are you having banditry problems?"

"We are living in dangerous times," the leader replied, slapping his hand on his sword pommel. His other hand rested on his thigh, "we cannot be too careful these days." It was then Lucius spotted the mutilated little finger on the left hand spread out across the thigh. He was sure Mordecai had spotted it also. Beside him, his men looked decidedly uncomfortable. "It might be best you get away from the area, as you never know what might occur."

Lucius kept up the pretence.

"Thank you," he said with a smile, "We have valuable cloth and other materials with us, I would hate to see bandits get their hands on it." Mordecai looked across to the burial party; Sextus signalled they were ready to proceed with the burial; he and Marcus walked back to the bodies. Lucius turned to the leader.

"You know, with eight of us on the task, we can have them buried quickly. My men can then fill in the grave afterwards." Much to his surprise, the leader turned to his three men and signalled them to help. Within minutes, all that remained of the family was a mound above a common grave beside the farmhouse. Lucius noticed that none of the four soldiers had made mention of any religious rites to accompany the burial. Apparently, they were aware that the dead were not of the Jewish faith, implying the four soldiers knew more than they were saying. Having been to the waggon, Sextus passed a skin of water around; it had been hot work.

"You'll be on your way then?" asked the leader.

"We shall," Mordecai said, "but I must fetch my cousin. She was naturally very shocked at what we stumbled across." The four soldiers shared glances and watched Mordecai disappear into the farmhouse. Lucius was holding his breath, unsure of the response when Miriam appeared. However, he did not have to wait long.

Mordecai came through the farmhouse door with one arm around Miriam. She was composed, but her face was expressionless.

"We'll be on our way now, cousin. You must put this awful tragedy behind you," Mordecai spoke gently to her. They began to walk toward the waggon when the leader stepped in front of them, quickly followed by his compatriots.

"Your cousin?" he asked. "I don't think so. I've seen her about these parts."

Lucius thought hard and fast,

"You are both right. She has lived locally for a time, but she is my agent's cousin, and we planned to collect her and take her to her uncle who lives in Hebron." The leader spread his legs to get a firmer footing, and a hand moved across to his sword pommel.

"You take me for a fool, lad?" He stared at Lucius, who was acutely aware he was armed only with a dagger, as was Mordecai. Lucius was not sure of how much this man knew about the girl. A strategy took shape in his mind that might just extricate them all from a confrontation.

"No, I do not take you for a fool – in fact, far from it." He said. "None of us here are fools, so why don't we stop playing games with each other?" If nothing else, it took the leader of the group by surprise. The hand did not move from the pommel, but he was prepared to hear Lucius out.

"Go on," was all he said.

"She is just a girl and of no threat to anyone. If she comes with us, she disappears as do we, and the situation resolves itself." Lucius paused, but the man remained expressionless, so Lucius ploughed on. "There are four of us and four of you. So, we fight over her, and who knows who will win, but it will be a pretty hollow victory with a lot of blood spilt over what? A woman?" The man's face remained expressionless. "We are merchants, and we wish no one harm, least of all you, but we have given this poor girl our word we would remove her from all this." The man thought through what he had just heard. He looked over at Sextus and then nodded his head.

"I think there is wisdom in your words, Greek, if that is what you are. You will take your friends and," he sneered, "the 'woman', and you will leave here. Go fast before circumstances overtake you. Then, should we meet again, things will be very different."

Lucius nodded and signalled to Mordecai to take Miriam to the cart. Sextus and Marcus needed no bidding. Marcus went straight to the mule, removed the water bucket and prepared to move. Sextus took station by the side of the vehicle. Mordecai helped Miriam up onto the driver's seat. Once she was in position, they moved off. As they set off in a southerly direction, Lucius turned to see the four men move into the farmhouse. The leader was the last to go through the door, who looked back and stared a final time at Lucius. Lucius smiled and gave him a wave, but he was gone. A sense of relief flooded through Lucius; he had been readying himself for a fight, but they had managed to extricate themselves. Mordecai joined him.

"That could have been worse," Mordecai said, "but it confirms my worst fears. Our friend back there was not just confident but getting brazen. I take it you spotted the finger?"

"I did, and I'm sorry to say you're right. His last words, *should we meet again, things will be different,* confirms it for me. Something is starting, no doubt, but just how big it is, I don't know." Lucius turned to Marcus and Sextus at the head of the cart, "Lengthen the stride," he called, "we need to report back as quickly as we can."

"I'll scout ahead," volunteered Mordecai, "we don't want any more surprises today." Saying so, he took full strides and pulled ahead of the cart. As he drew further away, Sextus came alongside Lucius.

"When my nose twitches," he said, "I've learnt to respect it, sir."

"That's good to know Postumus, but can you be a little less obscure?"

"I will, sir. Do you remember when the girl – Miriam – screamed? When we first arrived like."

"I do indeed," Lucius said, "and I must admit it made me jump!"

"Yes, well, that's it, sir. It didn't make our Jewish friend jump." He paused for a reaction. Then, when all he received was a puzzled look from Lucius, he continued, "He dropped into a fighter's stance, sir. You'd not of seen it as you were looking at the girl."

"Well, what's strange about that?"

"No sir, not a fighting stance – a *fighter's* stance. It was real natural like and instant. That man has been well trained, sir, and I reckon he's well-honed. There's more to him than meets the eye."

"I didn't see it; you're correct. Perhaps we should be grateful he's on our side, don't you think?"

"I'm sure you are right, sir," was the terse response.

"Secundus?"

"Sir?"

"Feel free to keep me updated upon your nose!"

Interludum II

Hadani's end

The settlement was typical of the region; huddled along what passed for a road in a valley, it had eked out a meagre survival over the years, originally producing olive oil for the great city of Jerusalem and today for anyone who would buy it. The several square stone houses had been worn smooth by the elements and the low walls that surrounded each house, smoother still. Many dwellings emitted smoke trails into the air as their inhabitants prepared meals. What was atypical was the number of men and horses inhabiting the place. These were not the farmers or merchants so often seen here; they were heavily armed soldiers. They sat around in groups, cooking, cleaning and honing weapons whilst others groomed their animals. A small band of riders approached, and as they drew closer to the settlement, the riders could hear conversation, banter and laughter.

Heads turned at the sound of the approaching horses as five well-armed men casually rode towards the well that sat at the settlement's heart. The banter and conversation stopped as the men dismounted, their faces masked by the sudra headscarves they wore around their heads and neck, just leaving enough space for vision. One of the five, a stocky, tall man, unwrapped his sudra allowing the scarf to fall to his shoulders, causing a ripple of surprise through the watching men. Some stood up as one voice said, "The Big One," to a soldier by his side.

"Where is your leader?" the man asked. A soldier closest to the questioner stepped forward, pointing to a small cottage a few paces away.

"He is in there, General Koseba." Koseba turned to his four companions,

"With me, brother," and he strode towards the building in question. He did not knock but opened the door and marched in, followed by his coterie. Sat at a table were three men who had been drinking and eating. They looked agog at the five

interlopers who had disturbed their meal. About to protest, they recognised Koseba and rose to their feet.
"Which of you is ben Hadani?" asked Koseba.
Of the three men standing, one of them replied.
"I am he," he said, "and what brings the great General Koseba to our humble village?" Koseba nodded at Hadani's fellow diners.
"Out," was all he said. They picked up their knives and left the room. One of Koseba's lieutenants closed the door behind them. "Sit down Hadani." Hadani moved to protest but then sized up the four men now flanking Koseba and did as requested.
"Of course, you are welcome, Ben Koseba, but I ask again, what brings you to my village?"
"Johanon," Koseba said asked a companion, "has Hadani been briefed as to the plan and our aims? Have you not been precise about what we expect of our area commanders?" Johanon unwrapped his sudra. Hadani recognised him,
"Welcome Johanon, it is good to see you." Johanon ignored the greeting.
"As with all of our commanders, General, Hadani has been kept fully informed." Koseba bent forward, placing both hands upon the table until his face was a few inches from Hadani's.
"Who allowed an attack on a Roman supply train?"
"It was only a small one, General. You see, since you called a halt to the bandit raids, my boys have been restless. We saw the Romans at Gophna and followed the waggons until - "
"Answer my question Hadani," shouted Koseba, "Who allowed it?" The subject of Koseba's questioning showed physical signs of discomfort, shuffling on his seat.
"It was only a small – "
"Damn you, man! Who allowed it?"
"I - I - I did, General." Koseba gave a great sigh and shook his head. Then, he stood up and turned to his companions, raised his arms and shrugged.
"Brothers, here we are on a knife-edge, soon to launch a major attack on one of the greatest powers the world has seen, and this man pre-empts everything and attacks a Roman supply train," He gave a dry laugh, "and to top it all, the fool got chased

away! The Lord was with us that day. Had the attack succeeded, at this moment, many very pissed-off Romans may well be surrounding us."

"They surprised us, General. They had soldiers hidden in a waggon. They said one, an officer, fought like a devil, leading the defence. We tried but -"

Koseba spun around and landed a heavy punch on the side of Hadani's head in one swift movement. The bandit leader fell backwards off his chair onto the floor and lay still. Koseba shook his hand before turning to one of his companions, saying,

"Do it now." A man stepped forward and knelt beside Hadani. In doing so, he produced a knife, kneeled on the prone man's midriff, thrusting the knife sideways through Hadani's ribs and up into his heart. Then, the executioner withdrew his blade and wiped it upon the dead man's tunic before returning to his standing position.

"It is done, General."

"And done well, Isaac." Koseba leant across the table where three meals sat prepared and ready. He chose a leg of chicken and took a bite. "A small perk," he said, "Now the hard part." He moved towards the door. "You two stay with the body," he ordered, "When Johanon knocks on the door, bring the body out. Johanon, Matthais – with me." Koseba opened the door and stepped out followed by the two chosen men. Whilst they had been dealing with Hadani, Koseba saw that a crowd of about thirty men had gathered outside the house, waiting expectantly. He exchanged a knowing glance with Johanon and stepped just in front of his two men. Koseba said nothing whilst Hadani's bandits waited – the tension palpable. He looked across the group, back and forth, then took a breath,

"Brothers, I ask you, do you wish for freedom from the Roman yoke?" The group of brigands murmured and nodded. "I did not hear you, brothers!" This time the sound was clear and full of 'yes' and 'of course' and similar utterings.

"Do you wish to live free in the land of our ancestors, under the ancient laws of Israel?" The response was a clear affirmative.

"Do we rebuild the Holy of Holies in Jerusalem? Does Hebrew become our mother tongue again?" The response was clear, involving fists being raised into the air.

"Brothers, we can make this happen. We, you, me and all of us," he swung his arms out wide, "along with the help of the Lord of Hosts, can bring Israel back to its people. We have to believe and have faith. You have trained to do this." A slight pause before, "Whenever have you been so well armed?" The soldiers raised their swords, spears, and shields into the air in response.

"To free Judaea and all Israel, we must take on the force of the conqueror's army. We had to become an army, and yes, we are just that – an army. We have trained for years now, and we are ready." Koseba paused for a few seconds. When he spoke next, he dropped the tone of his voice. "Brothers, for an army to succeed, it has to be disciplined and obedient. This is something the Romans have taught me. The other day, against orders, some of you attacked a Roman supply train, potentially putting our plans at risk." The men turned to look at one another in the audience, not sure what was coming next. Koseba let matters hang for a few seconds. "The attack failed but not before some of our soldiers died; a stupid, wasteful loss." Another pause. The listening men showed signs of discomfort. "Brothers, you are soldiers, and you only did as commanded that day. In an army, it is the officer who is responsible." Koseba turned to Johanan, who nodded and moved to the door of the small house and gave it three hard taps.

The door opened, and the remaining two of Koseba's men appeared dragging the body of ben Hadani; the body was thrown down at Koseba's feet. Two of the brigands pulled their swords; as they did so, Koseba raised his hands and spread his palms. The effect left the men frozen, swords half out of their scabbards. Then, they saw the missing fingertip – he was one of them.

"Brothers, we are about to enter a fight for the life of Israel. This officer failed in his duty and deliberately disobeyed his orders, exacting punishment. We are no longer brigands or bandits; we are soldiers in the army of Israel, its liberators. I ask you, as soldiers whose trust must lie in your officers, would you have it any other way? Is there any one of you who would not stand with me?"

For a second, nothing, then a voice said,
"I am with you, General," followed by,
"Me too!" The dam broke. The two individuals with the half-drawn swords pushed them back into their scabbards and nodded. Some of their colleagues slapped them on the back. After a short while, the noise quietened down.

"Brothers, my heart bursts with joy, and I give thanks to the Lord of Hosts for this day. I will not let you down; we shall see Jerusalem liberated and the temple restored. I am so determined I will let nothing stop me. But had you rejected the cause..." He nodded to the man standing next to Johanon, who pulled a small brass horn from his tunic and blew a single, shrill blast.

A counterblast came from beyond the closest house, followed by the arrival of many heavily armed soldiers who marched into the village square and stopped in formation. Soon there were sixty men in the square with others waiting in the spaces between the houses.

"Today," Koseba called out, "The Lord has seen that these men are your brothers. I thank him it was not a different outcome. Come, let us arm ourselves and march out together and free this land."

The crowd broke up as soldiers went to pack up their kit and be ready to move. Koseba stood with his four compatriots and watched the hustle and bustle.

"My brothers, hear me. By the time this is all over, we shall wield an army of thousands of men. For complex plans to succeed – and believe me, if we are up against Rome, this will not be simple – we must have total obedience to orders. We must always maintain discipline. Our comrades will realise that we mean what we say when we issue orders. A dereliction of duty could be the death of us all."

"You are correct Shimeon," said Johanon, "but killing our own is difficult."

"Johanan," Koseba replied, "believe me when I say I did not find this easy."

"Apologies Shimeon, I did not intend to imply you did, brother."

"There is something else I have learned," Koseba continued, "If we give men a righteous belief, it is easier for them to carry out killings and abominations on behalf of the cause. Before this war is out, we shall ask all our soldiers to carry out some difficult tasks. When the Lord gave us the Promised Land, he instructed us to kill all that lived within it. Similarly, we are required to cleanse this land of all things Roman; we must purge man, woman, child. The heretical Christians must also burn in the fire."

Capitulum VIII - It begins

30 &31 Martius. Year 16 of Imperator Hadrian

As the small group and their cart headed south towards Aelia, there was no pretence of being merchants. On the contrary, Lucius felt an air of escape about them, unconsciously fleeing. They passed a few travellers on the road, but nothing resembled the armed men they left behind them. After a while, hunger overtook them, and Lucius realised they had not eaten since the day began, so they pulled off the road to eat and take a break. He saw to it that the mule was watered.

Marcus carried a basket from the waggon and dropped it on the ground where the others sat while Sextus brought a water skin across to the group and joined them. Seeing the food in the basket, Miriam took over and began to break bread and lay out cheese, nuts and olives upon the cloth that had covered the basket. Next, Sextus distributed small drinking beakers and filled each with water. Lucius noticed that Miriam had not said a single word through the whole process.

They all sat in a circle and the men ate, only now realising they were ravenous.

"Hungry work buryin' people!" Marcus joked and then choked on his olive as he realised just what he had said in front of Miriam.

"Don't mind him, lady," Sextus said, "His tongue always runs away with him before the brain has decided what to say." The young woman appeared not to notice, and Lucius wondered if she had missed what Marcus had said as it was spoken in Greek. She was making a half-hearted attempt to eat a piece of bread and was suffering; he thought it might help both her and the group if he could persuade her to talk.

"Miriam, I am so sorry about what has taken place. I appreciate it was a terrible experience, and it must have upset you. However, to help and keep you safe, we need to know more about you. Do you have any relatives in the area that may help?"

She put her piece of bread down and stared into space for a few seconds.

"My parents are dead. Now my aunt and uncle are dead. I live." Her words were a flat, monotone.

"Yes, Miriam, you are alive, and that is good. But to help you, we need to understand more about you-"

Mordecai leant forward slightly and raised his hand, signalling Lucius to stop. He turned to Miriam and spoke to her in Aramaic. A conversation followed, and Miriam seemed to become a little more responsive. As they talked, the others carried on eating but watching intently. Finally, the conversation ceased, and Mordecai summarised.

"My friend, Miriam's full name is Miriam bat Yahalom, and she is nineteen years old. As she has told us, her parents died of the plague. The bodies were those of her aunt, uncle and cousin. They are – were – Christians which is why they died. The only other relative she knows of is a distant uncle Jacob, who lives in Caesarea."

"Her Aunt was a healer, a doctor of sorts, and she describes herself as a soother, a name we would translate as 'nurse'. She learnt some basic skills from her aunt. After her parents died of the plague, she moved to live with her uncle, and she cared for local people when needed and acted as a midwife. That's about it, except she wished to thank you for your kindness." As Mordecai finished, Lucius detected just a hint of a smile from the young woman. Jove, he thought, she's a good-looking girl. Lucius was about to reply to Mordecai's statement when Miriam said, in Greek,

"Thank you all. I know not what to do if you no there. I am sad. I do not want to be burden. Forgive me. Yeshua will bless your kindness."

It was Marcus who spoke first,

"Look, lady, you needed to be away, and we was goin' to Aelia, so you're just another passenger on the trip, not a burden." The hint of a smile from Miriam seemed to grow just a little. "Don't you worry, my honey; me and Sextus will look out for you."

"Thank you, Apollinaris," Lucius said, not without a hint of sarcasm, "I am sure that Miriam will rest much easier for having such a champion as you. Let's get this food eaten and be on our way. Mordecai, do you think we will make Aelia by nightfall?"

"I doubt it, my friend," he said, "We shall have one more night under the stars. Then, when tomorrow comes, I shall have to leave you."

"I am sorry, Mordecai, I don't understand. Why?" Lucius asked as Marcus and Sextus exchanged puzzled looks.

"Like you, my friends, I have concerns. But, Lucius, you have seen all I have seen and can inform the Governor of the facts. My principal is Rabbi Eliezer, and he must know what I have seen, and quickly. There may yet be a chance to stop what is happening, or at least limit the impact."

"Well, not being in the service of Rome, so I can't order you to stay. However, we each serve a different master, so I do understand."

"Thank you," said Mordecai, "I will see you close to Aelia before I leave."

And so the small company moved on. The journey for the rest of the day was uneventful as they trudged through the Judean hills, pitching a small camp a small distance from the roadside just before darkness fell. Lucius had considered moving through the night, but Mordecai advised against the idea; the back route they had taken was precarious, and a misstep could cause injury. As Lucius lay on his blanket under the watchful eye of Sextus, who was on the first watch, he realised that he would miss Mordecai. He liked the man, feeling he was one to be trusted. However, Lucius also felt sadness for him too. Should matters turn belligerent and Judaea takes to arms, who side would he stand on? In addition, the matter of Sextus' nose was nagging away at the back of his mind. Mordecai seemed very comfortable in the current situation; was he more than Sextus suspected?

The following day at first light, they quickly moved on, wishing to reach Aelia as early in the day as possible. But, true to his word, Mordecai remained with the group until they turned onto a Roman road.

"My friend, close to here, just over that ridge," he pointed to the hillside that ran up and away from the road, "I have a contact who will give me a beast to ride. I will double back past Emmaus, Gezer to Jamnia." There I will find the Rabbis and make my report."

"Is that what you'd like me to tell the governor?" Lucius asked.

"Indeed, my friend, there is nothing to hide." Mordecai paused as though deep in thought before continuing, "My friend, tread carefully around that man. He cares not for Rome or Judaea; he only cares for himself. I wish you God's blessing, all of you, God's blessing, especially you, Miriam."

The two men clasped arms, after which Marcus and Sextus bade farewell. However, Sextus was in no hurry to release Mordecai's arm.

"We have your friendship Judean, and I thank you for it. But a part of me says we have not seen all of the man behind that friendship, but I wish you well, brother." Upon which he released the arm. Within seconds the Judean was walking up the hillside towards the top of the ridge. Lucius turned to Sextus,

"Your damned nose again, Sextus?"

"You could call it that, sir," Sextus replied. Marcus was standing with Miriam, both looking toward Aelia.

"Nose or no nose, all I'm looking forward to is a good meal and a visit to the baths. What about you, Miriam?" The young woman just gave a hint of a smile. Then, it occurred to Lucius that he had not thought through what he should do with the girl once they got to Aelia. In the back of his mind, he assumed Mordecai could see her settled somewhere, but that would not happen.

"Let's get moving," he said, and the waggon trundled down the road. Meanwhile, he pondered his problem with the girl and then rehearsed his report to the governor. As he ran through the words he would use, he found himself constantly distracted by the girl, frequently glancing across to where she sat, looking straight ahead down the roadway.

As they approached the ruined city, Miriam's eyes widened as she saw the massive ruins. No matter what you are told, only the sight of such devastation can bring home the enormity of it. She was visibly shocked. She spoke out to no one in a language that Lucius could not understand. Marcus listened and then turned to his officer.

"Aramaic, chief," he said. He screwed up his face in concentration. "And Yeshua said to them, "Do you not see all these things? Assuredly, I say to you, not one stone shall be left here upon another, that shall not be thrown down." That's if I get it right." He turned to Miriam and spoke to her in Aramaic. He turned to Lucius. "It seems 'er god predicted Jerusalem would be torn down," he said, "'s'funny, you'd think he would've 'elped them, wouldn't you?" The girl continued to take in the ruins.

Not much later, the waggon and its accompaniment approached the *vicus*. Lucius recalled his uncle's comments about the Neptune taverna where they had eaten. They had clean rooms, and Anaitis, the landlord's daughter, "had a heart of gold". All he needed to do was remember how to find the tavern in the narrow lanes of the *vicus*.

Miriam looked about her, quite amazed. Her environment had been the small villages of the Judaean hills. The vicus, close against the walls of the Roman fort, was a very different place. With its many artisans, taverns, small houses - its very 'busyness' – took her by surprise. The smells of cooking, tanning, foundries and fullers were overwhelming, not to mention the smell of human detritus. Lucius noticed her wide-eyed stare.

"You will get used to it," he said. Miriam nodded, but he was unsure if she fully understood.

Lucius slowly and carefully briefed Miriam about his plan for her, also telling Marcus that he would 'lose' a large chunk of his trading profits to fund the plan. Quite how long Miriam would have to stay at the Neptune was another question, but Lucius already had thoughts about getting her to Caesarea and her uncle.

It turned out they found the Neptune quickly. There then followed a discussion of terms with Agenor, the landlord, after which several denarii changed hands. They left Miriam with funds to purchase some additional clothing. Marcus handed over the money saying,

"What the Praefectus don't know about, the Praefectus don't miss!" He then gave Agenor another coin. "That's for Anaitis. My officer says she 'as a heart of gold, so ask 'er to teach this lass some Greek!"

Lucius promised to check on Miriam once matters had been settled at Antonia. The men then headed for the North Gate of the fort.

The gate sentries espied the cart and three dishevelled Judeans accompanying it. Uniformly, they left their posts at either side of the gate and met in the middle, barring entry to the fort. Marcus brought the cart to a halt, and Lucius approached the guards leaving Sextus with the cart. One guard spoke up in Greek,

"Sorry mate," he said, "but unless you got authority, you ain't coming through here!" Lucius stopped within a foot of the soldier, drew himself up to his full height and said in his best Latin,

"Lucius Decimus Petronius, Optio IV Cohort, accompanied by Legionaries Apollinaris and Postumus on special duties for the Governor, requesting immediate entry." The soldier's face was one of confusion.

"Right sir – Optio – err, do you have any authorisation?"

"Soldier," said Lucius, in an exasperated tone, "If I were to run into bandits with a Roman authorisation on my person, it would be my death warrant!" Nevertheless, the soldier had his regulations and was not one to break them; time had come to refer upwards. He took two steps back,

"Officer to the gate!"

Lucius could hear footsteps descending stairs, and within a few seconds, a fully attired Roman officer appeared in the gateway. He quickly took in the scene, and his face immediately adopted an expression of surprise; at the same time as Lucius broke into a smile,

"For the love of Artemis, Lucius Petronius!" said the officer. As he spoke, he held out his arm to the officer, who did likewise and they clasped wrists.

"Porcius Fimbria, what a stroke of luck," responded Lucius. Fimbria looked Lucius up and down,

"I can share a few tips about military fashion if you like! Where on earth have you been in that get-up?" asked Fimbria.

"An interesting story, but not for here." Fimbria understood the message and turned to the two guards,

"The Optio and his men are cleared to enter. Let them pass."

The waggon entered the fort coming to a stop behind the two standing officers.

"I am Officer of the Watch, Lucius, so I can't leave my post. But, before you go on, do you remember our conversation the other day?" Lucius nodded. "Well, I have heard a rumour that a taxation patrol has been reported missing."

"Do we know where?" asked Lucius.

"Over towards En Gedi, on the Dead Sea."

"But that's far from where we've been, or from where we were attacked coming here." Lucius let the possible implications of what he had heard sink in for a second or two. "Thanks, Porcius, but we have to move. Is there any chance you could send a runner to the principia to see how rapidly we could have an audience with the Governor? Then, when the runner has the answer, he shall find us at the Quartermaster's, letting him have his waggon back and getting back into some civilised clothing!"

"Not a problem Lucius. I'll see to it. How about sharing bread and wine tonight? It would be good to hear what you've been up to out there."

"That sounds interesting, but I'll get a message to you, Porcius as I'm not sure about my schedule right now." The two men parted.

The trio with their mule and cart made their way to the Quartermaster's building. Everything went smoothly. The quartermaster's accountant seemed amazed that there was a good profit made from the sale of the goods while those unsold were returned in good order. Marcus kept a straight face when explaining the finances of the journey. The three soldiers donned their uniforms and all three relaxed to be wearing them again. Marcus successfully moved a heavy purse from one tunic to another without being detected by the clerks. As they left the building, Marcus said,

"Well then, I've got a fat purse, young Miriam is nicely lodged in the Neptune, and we are all alive. I would call that a result, wouldn't you, Optio?" As Lucius was about to reply, a legionary marched across to the group.

"Optio Petronius, sir?" Lucius nodded. "The Governor will see you immediately, sir."

"Thank you, soldier. Dismiss." The legionary saluted again, turned on the spot and marched off. Lucius turned to his two compatriots. "You men get back to the barracks and get something to eat. Keep yourselves available." Lucius checked his uniform as the two soldiers departed and donned his helmet. As he strode off towards the Governor's office in the Principia, he decided he preferred the role of soldier to that of spy.

As Lucius moved through the porticoed entrance to the Principia, it occurred to him that not every Optio gets to hold a meeting with the Governor on such a regular basis, twice in a matter of days. He walked along the marble hallway towards the Governor's antechamber with more confidence than previously. This time Lucius had vital intelligence to share with the Governor, who also served as commanding officer of the *Fretensis*. He felt this would be unlike his previous interview, where he had only a simple hypothesis to share.

Lucius introduced himself to the secretary who was seated at the desk by the door leading to the governor's office in the antechamber. Informed the governor would see him shortly, Lucius removed his helmet and took a seat on a bench positioned against an adjacent wall, placing the helmet on his thighs; he was experiencing a strong feeling of life repeating itself. It was then that a fully attired Roman Tribune strode into the room. The officer acknowledged the secretary and strode over to Lucius, who saluted. He looked Lucius up and down.

It occurred to Lucius that the Tribune was not much older than himself. He wore a superb, embossed bronze helmet with a full red crest. Instead of the usual steel breastplate, he wore a brown, muscled leather cuirass. His tunic was a brilliant white, and an ornate gladius sat in a red leather scabbard. Not only does his dress show his rank, though Lucius, it also shows wealth and lots of it.

"So," the Tribune began, "You must be our Optio turned spy the Governor has told me about?" Almost as an afterthought, he added, "Oh, relax. Let's sit, shall we?" The latter was said in such a way it was not meant to be a question. The two men, Optio and Tribune, shared the bench. Lucius replied to the Tribune's initial question,

"Perhaps more a speculatore, sir, rather than a spy."

"Well, I shall look forward to what you have to tell us, Optio. I am Gaius Civilis, by the way. You are....?"

"Lucius Decimus Petronius sir, IV Cohort." Lucius replied.

"Ah, the 'Italian Cohort' as we like to call you. They're not here yet, surely?"

"No sir, I expect them soon. My role is – err, was – to prepare for their arrival, then I found myself on this mission for the governor."

"Twists of fate, Petronius." He paused and scrutinised Lucius, his face frowning. "Petronius, Petronius. As Venus is my mother! I don't suppose you are the son of *the* Lucius Felix Petronius'?" Lucius did not reply for a second as he was taken by surprise. He knew of no connection between the tribune and his family.

"I am he, sir. Do you know my father?" Tribune Civilis laughed,

"Nothing to worry about, Petronius, but that means you are an Equestrian. Your father is as rich as Croesus, I believe!"

"I am not sure about that, sir, but he is a wealthy man." The Tribune slapped his thigh,

"I've remembered now! You ran off to the army and he disowned you, I believe. Is that true, Petronius?"

"It is true, sir. He has not disowned me in the truest sense of the word, but my inheritance is questionable I suspect."

"Forgive me if I seem to intrude, Petronius. I was in Rome a while back with my father, and your story came up during a party at Senator Lexus' villa. My father is Equestrian and is also in trade, based in Antioch. It was merely a side conversation. You now know all I know about you. So, army before an inheritance, eh?"

"It must sound crazy, sir, but I was never a merchant. All I ever wanted to do was join the legions. I believe my uncle had a role to play in the decision, but – "

"Of course, Centurion Petronius, now it makes sense." Lucius dreaded that the Tribune would think he was where he was because of his uncle, so he rapidly followed up,

"Actually, sir, I was in the army for three years before Centurion Crispus asked for me as his Optio. So, naturally, I am pleased to serve in such a legion as the *Fretensis*."

"You must be an asset, Petronius, or I am sure the Governor would not have trusted you with such a mission as you have just completed." Or possibly, Lucius thought, maybe the reason for the 'trust' was that he was not a great asset but an expendable one. The Tribune continued, "Look, may I address you in private as Lucius, and you address me as Gaius? We are, after all, both equestrians, aren't we?"

Lucius processed the request. The Tribune was right. Their upbringing and education were very similar, as were the circles they moved in as children and young men. It was fate that chose different paths for them. Had his father been willing, Lucius could be a senior officer right now. He was sure that the Tribune's father was running his son through the *cursus honorum* on his way to a greater position in the Empire. Lucius swung in his seat to face the Tribune and held out his arm,

"I would be honoured to address you as such, Gaius." Then other man grasped the proffered arm,

"I am pleased to have met you, Lucius. However, we must talk further in a more relaxed environment." As he spoke, the door to the office opened.

"Enter." Lucius recognised Governor Rufus' stentorian tone, so he walked smartly into the Governor's office, helmet under arm, stopping before his desk and saluting. The Tribune adopted a more leisurely pace but came to a stop in front of the same desk standing to attention.

"Relax. Please, sit." The two soldiers pulled up chairs in front of the Governor's table. "Gaius, I have asked you here as my Tribune Laticlavius for a decision needs to be made, and your view might be helpful." First, he outlined the background to Lucius' mission in northern Judaea. This process took a few minutes as he explained the Senior Centurion's majority opinion that there was little to cause concern. When he finished, he turned to Lucius.

"You had better continue, Petronius. I await your findings with interest though I have to say you are back a little earlier than expected. No doubt you will also explain Ben Zakkai's absence."

Lucius related all that had happened when they left the fortress a few days earlier. The Governor and the Tribune listened, taking in what he was telling them and asking a few clarification questions. After about fifteen minutes, Lucius came to a stop. Rufus turned to the Tribune,

"Gaius, I need to determine whether we are facing a simple increase in banditry or is it something greater, so let me check my understanding of what we know." He paused for a few seconds before continuing, "We only *suspect* that *one* of my informants might be dead and nothing on the others. We have located a foundry where bandits make weapons or fix faulty weapons. A heavily armed unit of bandits operates not far from Bet Horon, responsible for killing a Christian family who lived in the area. I have to say, Petronius, this is not exactly an intelligence scoop, is it?" Lucius could see the direction this was going in. "And you rescued a Judean woman."

"Your excellency, once we met the brigands at the farm, we knew they suspected our disguise. So we had no choice but to return. However, the girl told us they slew her family because they wouldn't support the rebels - er - bandits. It would seem they're trying to build general support in the area; does that sound like banditry?" Lucius realised he had inadvertently pushed the Governor a little hard with the last question, the latter having stiffened in his seat. The Tribune spotted the tension.

"If I may, your excellency?" Civilis asked. Rufus nodded. "I, too, see little hard evidence beyond some determined bandits, but I do find it odd that mere 'bandits' are looking to build 'support' to the point of killing those that will not side with them. It is not exactly the bloodstained gladius we would like to have found, but I *do* share Petronius' discomfort with that element of the situation."

"Gaius," said Rufus, "if I believe there is a rebellion in the offing, I have to bring the whole legion to a war status and report to Rome. As a soldier, you would understand what is involved, and I need sound reasons to do that. I am simply not seeing those reasons. So let me ask you; if you were me, would you move on what we have?" Lucius watched as Tribune Civilis bit his lower lip and thought.

"Hard evidence, excellency? I have to say I see circumstantial evidence, but nothing firm."

"So," Rufus pushed him, "You are saying you would not activate the whole legion?"

"I would not, excellency...we need more."

Rufus turned to Lucius,

"I had hoped for more from your small expedition, Petronius," he said, "and you say Ben Zakkai has returned to Jamnia and the Rabbis?"

"He has, excellency," Lucius confirmed, "I know he was very concerned with what he had seen."

"Do you trust him, Petronius?"

"I was given no reason not to, and as he came from your good offices, excellency, it was not a thought that crossed my mind, sir. Only..." Lucius paused,

"Only what, Petronius?" Rufus shot back.

"Well, I was wondering if it came to a greater conflict, would he throw his support behind those he sees as his people?" Lucius added, "He is a Jew, after all." There was a silence for a few seconds, so Lucius fired off another question,

"Excellency, I understand a tax-collecting patrol near En Gedi is long overdue?" Rufus' eyebrows rose,

"You are well informed, Optio, to a point. It is overdue, as can happen when those greedy fellows see a new opportunity. They always turn up. I am sure a turmae of cavalry will be off to locate them." It occurred to Lucius that Rufus was thinking more about his reputation than about the safety of his province. He seemed determined not to see the significant threat facing him. If there was coordination between bandits north of Aelia and groups way across the Judean Desert at En Gedi by the Dead Sea, then it was far more than "enthusiastic banditry".

The conversation ran on for a while, during which Lucius sensed support from Civilis. Still, Rufus was adamant he would need further evidence to be convinced that anything serious was in the offing. Civilis was instructed to send a cavalry patrol to check out the hidden foundry that Lucius and Mordecai had observed. Rufus then suggested it may be time for Lucius to return to Caesarea and prepare for the arrival of the IV Cohort. Whilst concerned about the situation in Judaea, Lucius felt that it was not his place to push the case of a possible revolt any further. In fact, he would welcome getting back to simple soldiering. But, at least on the point of a return to Caesarea, Lucius was at one with the Governor.

Interludum III

Rallying cry

The one known to his comrades as the 'Big One' rose from the bench seat and stood up. His height of well over six feet would have been imposing, but he was also muscular and carried himself like a warrior, and that is what he was. He stared out across the assembled group. Some sat on benches, others on the ground under a huge cedar tree's shade. He estimated at least fifty people who had travelled from across Judaea. They were silent. They were waiting.

Looking out across the gathering, the Big One realised his life had been working towards this since he was young. He hated the Roman occupiers with a vengeance, but he realised that to throw them from the land of Judaea would require planning and forethought. By understanding them, getting into the Roman head, he would engineer their downfall.

The preparations began over a decade ago. The Big One recalled arguing, encouraging, and coercing village elders and others to accept the plan. Men would have to be well equipped to take on Rome and well trained. So he appointed regional leaders, men he could trust to mobilise their areas for the plan. There lay tunnels and caves under the many villages of Judaea, and these quickly became meeting places where local militias could plan and train.

Several foundries across Judaea produced weapons for the Roman Army. Many were manufactured with minor faults and suffered rejection. However, the flaws were quickly corrected, and weapons were sent out to the militias. The training was put into practice in time, usually involving small raids on provision trains and burning Roman facilities. The key was to keep the activity at a low level. Rome must never guess a revolt was being prepared right under their noses.

As the Judaean's self-belief grew, morale rose, and an element of fanaticism crept into the militias. To mark themselves out as loyal soldiers of the cause, it became a test to cut off the top of the little finger of the left hand. It became a badge of honour. Most of those sitting before him wore the badge – these were his key officers; reliable, dedicated and trustworthy. They all recognised there could be no going back on the commitment they had given the big man.

The officers knew this was to be no ordinary meeting; a tiny number had a clue, but no detail, the Big One played matters close to his chest. That he was attired for battle spoke volumes. They admired the beautifully muscled cuirass that adorned his chest, sitting over a fine linen tunic of snow white, the crafted sword he carried and the tall black leather boots he wore.

"Brothers," he began, "or should I refer to you as soldiers?" The crowd rumbled its approval. "For years, we have been planning a war of liberation. A war to take back Heirosolyma. A war to rebuild the temple. A war to give this country back to the Lord!" As he spoke, his voice rose, and the last few words were almost a shout. The audience reacted, waving fists and cheering. Then the voice returned to normal again. "I can tell you that yesterday, at Tel-al, near En Geddi, the local militia slaughtered a patrol of forty Roman auxiliaries and two accursed tax collectors. We suffered wounded, but no fatalities." Again, there was a roar of approval. "It has begun, soldiers; the liberation has begun."

He let the excitement that rippled across the audience calm down before holding up his hand for silence.

"Understand that we are not rushing off to war. History tells us we cannot take on Roman Legions on a battlefield, so we must move carefully. Many of you have been stung by a bee, and you laughed it off. Those stung by several bees will know you do not laugh it off. It causes you great pain and suffering. No one here has been stung by a nest of bees because if you were, you would be dead. We have stung the Roman once, and I am sure they will see it as a nasty piece of banditry and shrug it off. We shall sting them again and again, again and again until it runs them ragged. Then we unleash the bee's nest! We shall not allow them to fight as they would wish. This is our land, and we are all familiar with it; we shall sting and vanish, returning into our caves. They will not see us coming and will not find out where we have gone.

The village and area militias will have a crucial role in this opening stage. Meanwhile, as some of you are aware, I am creating mobile battalions that will move quickly to crush any attempt at Roman reinforcement from Caesarea.

I have asked you here, not just to tell you this news. I want to stress upon you all that no one moves without orders. Ours is not a simple insurrection; we must make our plan work if we are to defeat the Romans. Any leader, and I mean any, that deviates from orders will be punished. So far, you have all helped create the position we are at, with no Roman being aware of what we are doing, and I say well done for that. This adherence to the plan must continue. To deviate is to betray your comrades and your country."

A younger man sat at the Big One's right side, dressed as a soldier if not quite to the finery of the larger man, stood up.

"Since the Great Revolt, though sixty years have passed, our holy city of Jerusalem remains a shell. The Romans have allowed a mere handful of our people to resettle. Imperator Hadrian promised us he would rebuild our temple; yes, brothers, he did, but what do we see? Does he build a temple on the site of our Holy of Holies? Yes, he does; he builds a temple to a Roman god! If that was not sacrilege enough, he now promises to rename our holy city after himself and the self-same Roman god for which he builds his abomination, calling it Aelia Capitolina!" He paused for effect. A general grumbling went around the room. He looked to the big man by his side, "We, the soldiers of Shimeon bar Koseva, are about to rectify this." The audience rose as one, raised fists into the air and chanted the Big One's name several times.

"Koseva, Koseva, Koseva…!" The young man ploughed on,

"We shall no longer suffer the hobnailed soldier's boot on our neck. We shall no longer sit by as sacrilege occurs. Governor Rufus will no more freely use our wives and children. Joshua or Yeshua would not have endured such, watching their people wail and suffer." His right arm chopped the air with each statement.

"The Lord God gave us this land of Israel – we shall recover it, slaying the rabid wolf as we do so!" The chanting began again, "Koseva, Koseva, Koseva…!"

Shimeon bar Koseva, the 'Big One', smiled at his men; the time had come.

Capitulum IX - Revelations

31 Martius. Year 16 of Imperator Hadrian

As he left the principia, Lucius sought out the duty tesserarius and detailed him to deliver a message to Porcius Fimbra to say he would be in the 'Neptune' around sunset. Lucius planned to get there earlier and check up on Miriam before Fimbra's arrival. Before then, he planned to talk to Postumus and Apollinaris about exploring the options of returning to Caesarea. He was hopeful of a ride back on a waggon train. After that, the next item on the day's agenda was a bath to wash away the dust and dirt of the recent adventure in the Judean hills.

As he approached the barracks area, Lucius was fortunate that he spotted Postumus and Apollinaris, strolling out of the refectory having just completed the best meal since leaving the fort a few days ago. He briefed them to organise a return to Caesarea, reminding them that Miriam would accompany them. The two soldier's countenance lit up when they realised they were returning to the provincial capital, and they disappeared off to plan.

Lucius returned to his quarters to find it as he had left it. He changed into a clean white tunic and headed off to the baths. The bath house in Antonia was not a large one, but it was a fine building with marbled floors and decorated walls. Lucius' first port of call was the anteroom. He hung his clothes on a peg and allowed an attendant to apply oil to his arms, legs, and torso, wearing only his loincloth. That done, he moved through to the small gymnasium and spent half an hour lifting weights and then running up and down along the back wall. As he worked up a sweat, he felt the tension of the last few days flow out of his body. Having finished the session with a fast sprint involving kicking off the walls at either end, he stood panting, hands on knees, when a voice called,

"Bravo Lucius, Bravo!" Lucius looked up, having to shake his head as he did so to shake off the sweat pouring from his brow. Recognition took a second. The voice's owner had shed the leather cuirass, the red scabbard and the fine boots, wearing nothing but a loincloth but recognisable as Tribune Gaius Civilis.

"Tribu - err – Gaius," Lucius stammered, "I was not expecting to meet you here."

"It's quiet," Civilis responded, "and I like a freshen up. Shall we apply ourselves to the strigil and bathe? We can talk as we relax."

In a short time, slaves had scraped them both with sharp strigils, removing oil and dirt and hair from arms, legs, chest and backs, and they were lying in the lukewarm pool of the *Tepidarium*. The conversation turned around each soldier's background. As Lucius had suspected, Civilis was working his way into the upper management strata of Rome. He was a *Quaestor* – young for the role – and served as second in command to governor Tineus Rufus. Lucius smiled as Civilis talked about his duties; Civilis was not only the paymaster to the legion, but he was also taking much of the administrative load off the governor. This was like Lucius' role in supporting Centurion Crispus; they found the comparison amusing. If all went well, in a few years, the Tribune might be back to Rome to serve as an *Aedile*, one of the supervisors of public works across the city. He would be on his political way when that happened. But for now, he was doing as good a job as possible to maintain a spotless reputation.

Civils suggested they move to the *Caldarium*, the hot pool. Lucius felt the sweat run down his cheeks as soon as they sat. Then, the conversation took a different turn.

"What I am about to say is between us, Lucius," Civilis said in a conspiratorial tone. "I am worried the Governor is erring too much towards caution. You see, it is just possible you may have stumbled onto something. Perhaps I should explain." Civilis glanced around, but they were alone. "In the six months I have been in Judaea, I have concluded that the Fretensis has become somewhat lax. Many of its soldiers are recruited from the province and surrounding provinces, and whilst they have all gone through training, it has been a long time since they have experienced a real fight. The Imperator's comments when he visited the province were generally positive, but privately he had concerns about the quality of the legion and its leadership. It is the main reason a new IV Cohort was raised outside the region." What he was hearing amazed Lucius. Civilis was staring at him, gauging his reaction.

"Optio Petronius," Civilus said, "I could say more, but I would like to give you the opportunity for us to enjoy a bath and then to go our separate ways. We will have shared time together, nothing more. If I go further, I need your solemn word – your oath – that our conversation will remain private. I would add that the knowledge I am about to share could put you at risk." Lucius' level of amazement reached 'astounded'. "I have to say, should you betray my trust, your future in the Legion will be a short one, and it will disgrace you in Rome. What do you say?"

Lucius was eager to hear more, yet his heart told him to steer clear. His head, however, said that Civilus was to be trusted. So he took a centre course.

"Gaius, as an officer of Rome, I give you my complete commitment to privacy. However, in terms of actions, I cannot support what I do not know, so I would reserve a right to withdraw but in silence, and I would keep my commitment to silence."

Civilis gave a grim laugh,

"You truly are an Equestrian and possibly even a politician! But, for me, that is a positive." He held out a dripping arm, and Lucius clasped it. Civilis looked around the pool, but there was no one near, so he continued in a low voice.

"The raising of a cohort in Rome was engineered against local opposition. It took time to push the governor into acting. Centurion Crispus was chosen to lead the new cohort because of his 'old school' skills. Why did this happen? Because for a while now – over the last two years – we have picked up small pieces of intelligence that would indicate trouble may be building. Frustratingly it has never been more than tittle-tattle, and we could not see beyond the scant information."

Sweat was pouring off both men. Civilis paused as a slave approached and offered the men goblets of cool grape juice, which they gladly accepted. Then, as the slave receded, Civilis continued.

"I only heard about your meeting with the centuriate after the fact; they tell me old Secundus gave you a rough ride! I wish I had been there. However, it reinforced my belief that we have a problem. Your mission was not the greatest success, but it added evidence to the case. Rufus is reticent, but he is busy enjoying the good life, and I am told, some of the good wives of Caesarea."

Not *Governor* Rufus, thought Lucius. "Matters could involve more than Judean unrest. Our Frumentarii, or should I say *my* Frumentarii, have obtained another piece of information. Are you familiar with the Imperator's balsam estate at En Geddi?"

Lucius realised that the conversation was becoming serious at the mention of the Empire's dreaded secret service.

"I have heard of balsam but estates at En Geddi? No, I haven't."

"The oasis of Ein Gedi on the Dead Sea is one of the very few places that they can successfully grow balsam trees. They turn the sap from the tree into oil with exquisite perfume; the process is a secret. In fact, the town is now a major production centre. You will know that the oil demands an exorbitant price. After the Great Revolt, when Titus destroyed Jerusalem, the Imperator claimed the balsam groves of En Gedi and declared it a royal estate. The annual revenues went straight into the Imperator's coffers."

"A considerable sum?" Lucius asked.

"Believe it," Civilis replied. "However, what my Frumentarii have uncovered is a scam, creaming off a percentage of the oil and selling it privately. Just how much? I do not know at this juncture. But one of those involved admitted, under interrogation, that some of the revenue from the illicit sales goes to Tineius Rufus, Governor of Judaea."

Lucius was shocked.

"The governor? Surely not. He has an impeccable background."

"Lucius, I would not dream of saying what I have said unless I am certain of my facts."

"Surely then, if you produce this informer, the truth will come out?"

"It is not as simple as that, Lucius; the governor would just deny all knowledge, and we know whose word would be accepted, do we not? There is another complication; the man is dead!"

"That was not a good move, surely?" Lucius asked.

"It was not us, Lucius. Four days after they questioned the man, they found him with a slit throat in his cell. We thought we had been discreet but not discrete enough, or else he talked. But what is done is done. There is more. From what the Frumentarii have uncovered, there is an amount of 'turning a blind eye'; certain people are being paid off."

"Your Frumentarii have been busy." Said a grim Lucius.

"They are a team brought in at my request and with the full approval of the Imperator."

"Hadrianus himself?"

"I did not come to Judaea by chance, Lucius."

"But Gaius, why are you telling me this?"

"For the IV Cohort, we – and *we* shall remain nameless for now - handpicked every centurion that was sent back to Rome, especially Crispus. Crispus did not ask for you because of your service record. Instead, he was 'advised' you might be a good man to have as his Optio; 'advised' by me. Knowing your Equestrian status and background, you were watched as you trained and worked through your first commissions. Crispus was chosen for his reputation, and he needed an Optio we could trust – that person turned out to be you." Civilis continued, "Your conversation with Faustinus in Caesarea; was it his idea you visit your father?"

"It was."

"He was following my instructions. Reliable soldier, the Praefectus." Civilis looked about him, but their end of the bath was empty; there was no one within earshot. "Hadrianus' wish is to settle the *Pax Romanus* upon the empire. He wants all its varied tribes and clans to see that all can prosper under Rome's banner. It is why he is travelling the empire, seeing that the proper administration and people are in place. The Imperator has no desire to be a great soldier; he wants peace and prosperity.

After he visited the province two years back, it left him with a distinct feeling that all was not right but little hard evidence. Some years ago, you will know of the Jewish revolts in Alexandria; they taught us that these people fight like devils, so we have always been sensitive about Judaea. The governor was assuring us all was well, as were senior officers, but our independent intelligence was contradicting those assurances."

"I mentioned earlier about my doubts about the resilience of the Fretensis. Except for the centurions, the new cohort comprises soldiers with little if any connection to the province. But, as you well know, Crispus has moulded them into a fine fighting unit. There have been men we so wanted to include in the cohort that we have issued them with Roman citizenship."

"I heard," Lucius said, "and thought it was strange."

"It was not a normal procedure; It has been a long time since we raised military units in Italy, and it had well-placed individuals creating Hell. But, if my concerns are accurate, we have an Augean Stable to clean out here in Judaea. You do not yet understand just how important the IV Cohort may be in the coming days."

"Gaius," said Lucius, "I appreciate all you have told me, but why?"

"That is simple, Lucius. I want you as an informal contact." Seeing the expression on Lucius' face, Civilis added, "Don't worry, Crispus and I have talked this through. I have other tasks for Crispus."

"Informal contact?" queried Lucius.

"I want you to be on the lookout for suspicious activity; anything from soldiers spending money freely to relevant gossip or behaviour which is out of the ordinary."

"A spy?"

"Not a spy," said Civilis, "more an intelligence gatherer. I'm not expecting you to dress like a Judean and crawl around the desert. You've done your fair share of that recently. It's a role that involves keeping your eyes open and listening. We'll probably meet but not on any formal basis as I want this to be discreet." There was a pause. "Can you do this for me, Lucius?"

Lucius did not see that there was an option.

"Yes, of course, Gaius."

"Gratitude, Lucius. Don't forget, in this, you are serving the Imperator. Now, I think I'll turn into a lobster if I sit here much longer. Shall we try the *Frigidarium*?" Both men rose from the caldarium bath and moved to another large, highly decorated room housing the cold pool. The shock to the system prevented casual conversation. The two men were quickly out of the pool, dried by attendants and dressed. As they walked from the bath house into the sunlight, Civilis leaned towards Lucius.

"I intend to send out cavalry patrols across the area; I will find those damned tax farmers and the auxiliaries if it's the last thing I do. I'll also check out your forge too. We'll shake the tree and see what falls to the ground. I'll brief my officers to look out for anybody with the top of a finger missing – some interrogation might be in order.

When I've set matters running, you and I are heading for Caesarea as the Fourth is landing in a matter of days. I want them down here in Judaea quickly. Now, I have business, Lucius, but I'll be in touch. And, thank you. I was sure I was right about you."

At which point, Gaius Civilis strode off towards the Principia.

Capitulum X - Assassination

31 Martius. Year 16 of Imperator Hadrian

Lucius was crossing the parade area within the Aelia camp, heading back to his quarters, when a voice called out.
"Optio Petronius, sir!"
Lucius stopped, turned, and spotted the diminutive figure of Marcus Apollinaris approaching, followed by Sextus Postumus. The two came to attention in front of him.
"Stand at ease, soldiers," said Lucius, "What's the rush?"
Apollinaris and Postumus exchanged glances.
"We was having an hour of relaxation, so we visited the Actium Taberna for a drink. So we walks in, and guess who we sees sitting there as cool as Claudius?"
"Best you tell me, Apollinaris."
"You're right, sir. That Judaean we bumped into on the way into Beit Horon. You remember – the goat farmer, the one with the big scar on his face." Apollinaris spoke with a sneer of contempt. "He was on 'is own, so we gets our drinks and joins him. Dressed as soldiers, he didn't recognise us, so we gets chatting with him. Our friend is on his way to meet his cousin in En Geddi; they occasionally do business."
"Did you get his name?" Lucius asked.
"Yes, sir. Zacharya ben Hassan. I believed him to be genuine, but who knows?" Lucius nodded. "Anyways, we was just getting into detail when these six auxiliaries turns up and greet him like an old friend. They invite him to join them, and off he goes. When leaving, he stared me in the face and said he was sure we had met before. Then he was gone."
"If I may add, sir?" said Postumus. "We had little choice other than let him go with 'is auxiliary mates if you get my meaning, sir. It was no off-chance meeting; it was more of an extraction by the auxiliaries. Furthermore, ben Hassan's little finger on his left hand had its top missing, confirming just who it was."
Lucius considered what he had heard.

"Men, this may be a tall order. Can you quietly, and I mean quietly, try to get information on this ben Hassan. Such as, has he been here before? How often? Also, what cohort were the auxiliaries from – even better – some names? But do not push it; I don't want anyone thinking there is an investigation. If you find anything, let me know."

"Yes, sir," Apollinaris responded. "Leave it to us, sir."

"Keep an eye on Apollinaris' enthusiasm," Lucius said to Postumus. "Low profile. And, well done the both of you. I can confirm that we shall head back to Caesarea soon, so be ready to travel."

"It'll be nice to be back in the *Minerva*, sir," said Apollinaris.

"It will. Now, carry on both of you. Oh, and will you tell Optio Fimbria that I shall be at the *Neptune* this evening. Let me know if he can't manage it."

The two soldiers turned and walked away whilst Lucius continued to his quarters. Lucius returned feeling a lot cleaner and refreshed from his time in the baths though his mind was racing from the recent conversation with Gaius. Once inside, he opened his wooden chest and took out a roll of parchment. An ink bottle and pen followed, and he drafted a brief note for the Tribune. Lucius sealed it and found an idle legionary who he despatched to the Tribune's office with the message. He had not expected to have news so quickly.

The next port of call would be the *Neptune*. It was early for dinner, but he had promised to drop in on Miriam and check on her situation. He may not be indebted to her, but he felt responsible for the girl. Lucius shed his formal uniform and dressed in a tunic and cloak but, just in case, he still wore a dagger.

He strolled to the taberna, going through Gaius' information in his head. Add to that Apollinaris' and Postumus' recent contribution; he had a lot to absorb. As he saw it, there were four main elements. The Judaeans were plotting a rebellion, the governor possibly robbing the Imperator, and elements of an auxiliary, even a *Fretensis,* involvement. He could not believe his uncle could be tangled up in it all. But, when he boiled it down, the real problem seemed to be that there was such an absence of evidence to show, only well-placed suspicion. He was just wondering whether to talk to his uncle when he found himself outside the Neptune. It was early evening, and the establishment appeared not to be busy.

Lucius left the fading sunlight and ducked through the doorway in the taberna. His eyes adjusted and he quickly spotted Agenor, the landlord who welcomed him back. The man poured Lucius a wine, and they sat together for a few minutes as Agenor told Lucius that Miriam and his daughter Anaitis were getting along "like sisters". He was impressed with Miriam's removing a splinter deep in his foot "almost painlessly". The girl had been helping around the establishment, and Agenor said he would like a few more guests like her. Lucius laughed.

"You may not be so happy when she presents you with the medical bill!" At that point, the two ladies in question appeared and spotted the two men talking. As they approached, Agenor nodded at Anaitis, and father and daughter moved off towards the bar and began to organise and tidy. Lucius signalled Miriam to sit.

"Agenor tells me you are settling in?" The girl paused as she processed the Greek.

"I like Agenor, Anaitis," she said, "Good people. I like help." Her Greek was slow but understandable.

"That's good," Lucius said. "I also hear you have been doing healing work."

"Yes," Miriam smiled, a smile that charmed Lucius, "I see Agenor walk – er – not walk well. I ask him, he tells me of his foot. It is nothing. He had what I needed to mend foot."

"Well, he seems happy," Lucius said. They discussed the arrangements, and Miriam thought her room to be just what she wanted. She planned to buy some new clothes tomorrow and insisted that Lucius would be repaid. Lucius assured her the money was a "gift from Rome"; he had said the words before realising it might not have been the smartest thing to say to a Judaean, but she smiled and thanked him. He changed tack.

Lucius told her he would be returning to Caesarea to join his cohort, and he expected to be back in the future but was unsure when. She proposed that she remain at the Neptune for a while. There followed a three-way conversation between the two of them and Agenor. The outcome was that Lucius had paid for Miriam to be at the Neptune for ten days, after which Agenor would employ her in the inn. Then, she could move in with Anaitis when the time came. The girl's future seemed secure in the short term, and Lucius promised to visit when he returned to Aelia. She responded with a smile.

Agenor went back to the bar and briefed Anaitas, who smiled in their direction. Miriam reached across the table and took Lucius' hands.

"Lucius, how I thank you? I nearly dead, but I live." Lucius stared into her dark eyes, thinking that Caesarea right now, a little distance, may be the best option.

"Miriam, not all Roman soldiers are callous," seeing her expression change to one of puzzlement, "callous – err - hard-hearted, none-caring." She smiled and nodded – that smile again. "I did what I considered right, and don't forget Mordecai and my legionaries. They all helped you."

"And I thank when I see them, but you here, now." Lucius felt a little awkward but put the feeling down to her poor capability in Greek. He was wondering about the direction of the conversation when a voice behind him shouted,

"Petronius, where's my drink?" Lucius turned, and there stood Optio Porcius Fimbria in civilian garb.

"Porcius, welcome," said Lucius. Porcius' eyebrows raised, staring at Miriam. Lucius smiled.

"It is a long story. Meanwhile, Optio Porcius Fimbria, meet Miriam," he said formally, "Miriam meet Optio Porcius Fimbria." Porcius bowed his head.

"My pleasure entirely."

Miriam stood up,

"I help Anaitis. Thank you, Optio," and headed towards the bar where Agenor was working, and his daughter was filling beakers of wine.

"Goodness Lucius," said Porcius, "I don't have that effect on women usually!"

"Maybe if I share events of the last few days with you, Porcius, you may understand. But first, we need wine."

"A defined set of priorities. Crispus would be proud of you!" Porcius responded as he waved to Agenor.

Lucius spent the next half hour retelling his trek across Judaea with Mordecai, stopping the story at his arrival back at the fort. The dealings with Tribune Civilis would remain a secret. Porcius sat back in his chair and shook his head.

"I have to say, Lucius, truly the gods are playing with you, my friend. You arrive in the province, and in no time, you find yourself up to your neck in it!" Lucius wanted to say *you don't know the half of it* but restrained himself. "And what about the girl? Will you get her back to Caesarea?"

"I have promised her. I think we shall be -" They were interrupted by a desperate cry of "FRETENSIS!" coming from the street. Both men knew just what that meant; a fellow soldier was in severe trouble. The two officers looked at each other and leapt to their feet. They drew looks from the Taberna's customers as they bolted through the door. They spotted two men running down an alleyway to the left as they looked up and down the street. It was getting dark, though occasional flickering wall sconces gave a little light. All Lucius said was, "Let's go," and the two optios took off in pursuit of the men.

Speeding along the alleyway, they could see a commotion ahead. The closer they came, it was clear a fight was ending, with several individuals fleeing up the alley. One of those running left his departure a little late, and a grounded combatant sat up and swung his sword as best as he could from his awkward position. The blade struck the fleeing man on the calf muscle of the left leg. The man spun around and fell to the ground, after which one of the two men preceding Lucius and Porcius jumped on his chest, sword raised.

Lucius shouted, "Take him alive!" and the sword-bearer paused. By now, the two optios were upon the group and skidded to a halt. Lucius took in the scene; the light was feeble, but apart from the man who tried to flee, Lucius could see the remaining men were all soldiers. Two of them were the victims of the initial attack; one leaning panting against the wall and the other who had downed the fleeing attacker, lying on the ground bleeding. Whilst one of their would-be rescuers sat upon the wounded attacker, the other man turned towards the two new arrivals. Before he could speak, Porcius spoke up.

"I am Optio Fimbria, 1st Century, III cohort."

"Legionary Albus, sir," the soldier responded, "We heard the cry and got here just in time. Six of 'em bastards there were, fortunately, only armed with knives. Stuck one of the cunni, sir, but he made off with the others as you approached sir. Didn't stick 'im hard enough!"

Lucius was taking in the scene. The wounded soldier was still grounded and holding his side. The other was resting against the wall, leaning forward with his hands on his knees, hanging his head. He was a well-built specimen.

"Jupiter's mentula!" Lucius exclaimed, "Sextus Postumus. I did not recognise you in this damned light." The soldier looked up,

"Optio Petronius. You must have heard the ruckus then, sir?"

"The 'Fretensis' call, you mean, yes I did and… oh my god!" he looked at the fallen man, "That's Apollinaris." He knelt beside the stricken soldier. The victim looked up at him,

"Bit of a scratch, sir." He moved and winced, "Be good as ever soon."

"We'll see to that, Marcus." Lucius turned to legionary Albus. "Are you injured, Albus?"

"No, sir. I was charmed tonight."

"Right, get back to the fort and alert the Officer of the Watch and then get a medicus down here quickly." As he spoke, another thought hit him, "As you pass the Neptune, stick your head in the door and ask for a lady called Miriam to attend. Tell her it's severe cuts. Now go, fast as you can." Lucius said to Marcus, "We will get you sorted, Marcus, just hold on."

The injured Marcus smiled inwardly. The Optio had never addressed him by his first name before.

"What do I do with this cunni, Optio?" asked the soldier who was holding his sword to the fallen attacker's throat.

"Get him up, shall we?" suggested Porcius. "He might need some support. That cut is deep."

"Can we get a bandage of some kind on his leg," Lucius added. "I don't want him bleeding out on us. He has some questions to answer." In no time, the soldier had pulled the cloth from the man's head and torn it in strips, which he bound tightly around the damaged leg. It worked in assuaging the bleeding.

"On yer feet, cunni," the soldier said as he pulled the man up roughly, causing the prisoner to emit a groan. "Shut your face, or I'll shut it for you!"

Lucius approached Sextus.

"What happened here, Postumus?"

"We went for a wander around the vicus, sir. You know, seeing what we could see, given our earlier conversation. We were heading back to the fort chatting, when out of that side alley over there," he said, pointing to the particularly dark passageway, "came the sound of a screech and a black cat shot across our path and down the street. At the same time, I heard a voice cuss in what sounded like Aramaic. Both me and Marcus was instantly on alert, drawing our gladii when out they came. They carried daggers – the cat did for their plan, sir, even so, it was six against two. I gave the call you responded to, and the two lads came running. One of the cunni got Marcus before they decided that four gladii against six daggers was too much. Albus stuck one – it surprised me he got away because it was a good strike. Marcus clipped this bastard," he nodded towards the assassin who was standing with hands tied behind his back, "as he attempted to run. At that point, you and Optio Fimbria arrived, and you know the rest."

People appeared from the direction of the Taberna, some carrying torches; the lighting situation improved.

"Postumus, your arm!" Sextus' left arm already carried one bandage from a wound inflicted during the ambush. Now there was blood pouring from yet another injury.

"Worse than it looks, sir. Not deep, I'll get it covered."

"Optio Petronius." It was a woman's voice. Lucius turned and was face-to-face with Miriam. She was carrying a water bucket and a bag. She looked past him to Marcus lying on the street, and Lucius saw her expression change as she realised who the injured man was.

"Yes, it's Marcus. Can you help Miriam? I have called for the Medicus."

She turned to the onlookers who had gathered.

"Bring light." She instructed and knelt beside Marcus. The torchbearers met her wish. "Sextus, remove belt and sword." Postumus did so, and with little hesitation and to the concern of Marcus, she took out a short-bladed knife. Before anyone could react, she took Marcus' tunic and ripped the tunic open to the neckline.

"Priapus' cock!" said Marcus. His loincloth maintained his dignity. Just above the cloth was a gash across his stomach, weeping blood. Miriam's bag contained linens, courtesy of the Neptune Taberna, and the wound was washed, and a large pad placed upon it; she instructed Marcus to press it tightly in place. In the light, Lucius could see Marcus was looking pallid.

"Will need..." She made a sewing action with her hand. "Stay down," she commanded Marcus.

The sound of marching feet reached Lucius, the Officer of the Watch and his crew. Porcius left the group and made off to meet the new arrivals. He was back with Centurion Secundus, eight soldiers, a medicus and one of his orderlies carrying a stretcher.

"Optio Petronius, in the thick of it again, are we?" Lucius would not rise to his bait.

"I missed the action here, Centurion, but my men were attacked." He related Sextus' details to the officer. Meanwhile, the Medicus attended Marcus and instructed his men to get the injured man on the stretcher.

"So, where's this Judaean cunni we captured?" demanded Secundus.

Sextus' would-be rescuer stood at the rear of the gathering guarding the prisoner whilst Miriam was bandaging the captive's wound. Secundus pushed through and took one look at the proceedings.

"Get that bloody woman away from him!" Miriam stood up and turned around to face him. Knowing Secundus' reputation, Lucius knew this would not go well, so he stepped forward. "Get her away!" Secundus repeated.

"Sir!" said Fimbria. "This girl -er- woman has just helped dress Legionary Apollinaris' wound. I then asked her to attend the prisoner, sir. My motive is to keep him alive and in good condition for interrogation, sir." Marcus, lying on the stretcher, propped himself up on one arm as if on cue.

"Optio's right, sir. I am feeling better 'cos of what that lady did for me."

Secundus shook his head and, much to everyone's surprise, smiled.

"All right, all right. Medicus, take care of this man and get him to the infirmary." He turned to Miriam. "You, woman, will finish bandaging his leg and then kindly return from where you came. Optios, accompany the soldier with the prisoner. I will see you back at the fort." So Secundus, the watch, the medics, and Marcus set off for the fort. The audience of the curious drifted away.

"Miriam," said Lucius, "Thank you. Don't mind Secundus. He knows you were helping." Miriam pulled the bandage around the prisoner's thigh and knotted it off.

"I no mind Optio, Marcus is friend," she said with a smile, lit by the soft light of the torches. Lucius experienced a feeling he should not be feeling for a Judaean woman. They looked at each other in silence.

"Right then, let's be off, shall we?" said Fimbria. Lucius felt he owed Fimbria for his interjection.

"Thanks, Porcius. Secundus and I are not best friends."

"He's my centurion, Lucius. He is all bluster really and not such a difficult person as he can seem, though I know he can be heavy work at times."

At that, the small group headed for the fort, the soldiers taking much of the hobbling prisoner's weight. Miriam left them as they passed the Taberna, but not before seeing to Sextus' arm wound.

Lucius, Porcius, and Sextus had visited Marcus lodging in the infirmary within an hour. According to the medicus, Marcus was lucky. His wound appeared severe, but it was not so, in so much as the assassin's blade had sliced the flesh and only nicked the mass of stomach muscle. Nevertheless, they had stitched the wound, and the prognosis was a few days of discomfort. They would release him from the infirmary later the next day if all were well.

The three soldiers then reported to Centurion Secundus to complete any reports that may be required. They were also interested in the prisoner's interrogation. They found Secundus in the Watch Office seated behind his desk.

"Welcome, my friends, busy night, eh? Please sit." The offer was to the Optios. Sextus remained by the door at attention. "Relax, legionary; we are not on parade." Secundus leant forward on his desk, grasped his hands together and stared straight at Lucius. "No one fucking attacks legionaries under my watch. Who are these cunni, Optio? What in Hades' name is going on?"

"Sir, I have to tell you I have no idea," Lucius said, "but it was not robbery. These men meant to kill."

"Under the nose of a Roman fucking fort!" Secundus' face was reddening, "Under my fucking nose!" He was like a volcano, pressure building and about to blow. Porcius attempted to release some pressure.

"Has the prisoner said anything, sir?"

"No, and I have sent for two men who are persuasive in getting the reluctant to talk, and he will talk, I assure you." Secundus sat back in his chair, the volcano settling a little. "Two murders in one night would have been bloody embarrassing for me; I run a tight ship." Porcius frowned.

"Two murders, centurion?"

"Well, if they had killed our friend here and his mate," nodding towards Sextus, who was standing by the door, "it may have been three murders." The Optios both looked confused.

"*Three* murders, centurion?" Porcius pressed on.

"A Judaean, only about a quarter of a mile down the road to Bethany. He was found in a ditch with his throat slit. A cavalry patrol spotted him."

"At least not one of ours."

"True Optio, very true, and something we can handle. A little different from attacking Roman citizens in the streets." The volcano's output reduced to a mere wisp of smoke.

"Do we know anything about him? A local man?" Porcius asked.

"We are checking. By morning we shall have what we are looking for. Easy to identify, though, a red, jagged scar down one side of his face." Lucius sat bolt upright.

"Dark, heavy beard, about my height, muscular with the top of his little finger missing?" he asked. For what seemed an eternity, Secundus just stared at Lucius.

"So Optio, am I right? You are familiar with this man?"

"You are aware, sir, that I had been scouting for the governor?"

"Searching for your rebellion, eh?"

"I believe we met this man, or one very like him." He turned to Sextus. "What would you say, Postumus?"

"He fits the description, Centurion, and he was up to no good. He claimed to be a bloody goat herder – what a joke. The finger cut is a brigand's mark."

"Thank you for your contribution, legionary Postumus." Sextus, please don't mention the meeting in the Taberna, Lucius thought to himself, please don't. "So, you think this man was no friend of Rome then?"

"We proceeded upon that basis, Centurion."

"And you never saw him again?"

"No, but we saw others like him with the cut finger." It horrified Lucius that he had lied to his senior officer. He knew Sextus knew it too, and if he kept his silence, they were creating a conspiracy. They were in dangerous territory.

"Well, he won't be troubling anyone again, that's for sure. Interesting though; what is he doing here?" Secundus thought for a second. "Perhaps I should send a patrol up to Beit Horon and see what we can uncover." Secundus looked pleased with himself. "And I understand you are off to meet your friends from Italia arriving at Caesarea soon, so I better not keep you, had I?"

Lucius received the signal loud and clear, stood up, saluted, and left the office with Sextus in tow. Neither man spoke until they were outside where darkness had fallen. Then, when Sextus tried to engage Lucius in conversation, Lucius suggested they go back to his quarters before saying any more.

Lucius closed the door and signalled for Sextus to sit on his only chair whilst he sat on the end of his cot.

"Sir, I have to ask you a question," said Sextus. "You have my respect, sir, but I am a Roman soldier of several years standing, and there are things you do and things you don't do. You – no, we – just did something you don't do, lie to an officer. I am sure you have very good reasons, sir, but you have involved me, and I need to know what I have let myself in for." At that, the big man just sat and stared at his officer.

Lucius was fighting for a suitable response. Sextus was right; he had involved him, yet so much of what he knew was sworn to secrecy. However, Sextus deserved an explanation.

"I apologise, Sextus," he started. "Things are happening here in Judaea, and I have given my word I will not devolve those matters. I have involved you, and I wish I had not. My holding information back from Centurion Secundus was no reflection upon him. In many respects, it might be safer for you if you were unaware of my justification for doing so."

"I see." Lucius watched Sextus as he processed what he had been told. "So, we've a dodgy Judaean walking off arm-in-arm with brothers from the auxiliary. As soon as I heard of the man's death, I questioned that. If what I'm thinking now is even half true, this isn't a good situation."

"Indeed, we suspect murky business."

"You worried, sir?"

"The situation isn't good, so of course I am worried."

"Not talking about the situation, sir, I am talking about you." Lucius realised Sextus was about to surface a concern. "Someone tries to take Marcus and me out after taking out our Judaean friend. It seems that all of us that were on the road to Beit Horon are targets, and that would include you, sir."

"Could it be connected to your chat with our friend in the Taberna?" Lucius asked. Sextus nodded his head slowly.

"Could be. But we need to be careful. Perhaps the interrogation will shine a light on the situation. *Cac*! I'd forgotten. Marcus had found out that those boys who walked off with our now dead friend were likely part of a supply train up from En Geddi. I damn near forgot."

"Now, that is interesting. That would fit well with...." There was a sharp rap on the door. Lucius rose and opened the door to find an orderly standing in the hallway. He held out a parchment.

"For you, sir, from the desk of Tribune Civilis." He handed over the paper and marched away. Closing the door, Lucius sat down and read the document. Sextus waited.

"It would seem Postumus, that I'm required to return to Caesarea, and quickly at that. The Fourth is only a few days away. Crispus landed at Antioch three days ago and is marching them the three hundred miles. Does he ever let up?"

"Knock the lads into shape, sir."

"When was the last time you did a march of that distance, Postumus?"

"Quite some time, sir. We get the occasional march up and down to Caesarea, but it is not onerous. These days it is all about garrison duties and occasional patrols. I often wonder what it must be like to be part of a legion drawn up for battle. Dreams of my youth, Optio!"

"Something I too have never witnessed," said Lucius, adding, "though, against a small rebellion in Dacia, we formed up a vexillation of four cohorts. I learnt then that you will prevail if you stick to your training. Crispus says it often, and he's right. It was scary, but you stuck with your brothers and worked together; our casualties were few. The Dacians were wiped out. They fought hard, though; it was no rout."

"Fighting for their homes and families, sir?"

"Yes, Postumus, they were." Lucius paused for a few seconds. "Once we had dealt with the men, it was the turn of the families and the village. Not much left afterwards, but a few women and children were potential slaves. They must understand the price of taking on Rome."

"Woe to the vanquished, eh sir?"

"It's how it always was and always will be, my friend."

There came a sudden rap on the door, and it burst open. Tribune Gaius Civilis entered, and Sextus leapt to his feet, saluting. Lucius stood up more with a little more grace.

"Tribune, sir?" Lucius queried.

"I need to speak with you," said Civilis as he cast a glance at Sextus, who turned to Lucius, made his excuses, and disappeared through the doorway. Civilis closed the door behind him and sat. "Lucius, you recall the missing tax farmers. Well, the governor sent two centuries to determine what had happened to them and their auxiliary escort. What's left of those centuries have returned – about fifteen men, some of whom are in a bad way. It was an ambush about two miles from Bet Alin."

Lucius' jaw dropped in utter surprise at such a possibility.

"One hundred and sixty regulars?"

"Correct Lucius, the III Cohort. As you can imagine, Secundus is breathing fire, and I suspect the Governor will let him take the rest of the Third, supported by cavalry to wreak havoc and mayhem."

"Forgive me, Gaius, but what do we know about the enemy – their size, their make up?"

Civilis smiled ruefully.

"I wish the governor thought like that. He insists we are facing a bunch of irregular rebels. I am not sure and recommended a reconnaissance, but he and Secundus are Hades bent on revenge. They are both embarrassed, Lucius, not a good frame of mind for making reasoned decisions." Civilis sighed, "However, it may all be a useful diversion."

Lucius realised they were now getting to the real cause for this nocturnal visit.

"Lucius, you are one of the few that knows of my mission. You also know that Secundus has locked away the would-be-assassin you captured earlier. In a short time, the interrogators will get to work on him, and I suspect he will 'die' before he talks. I do not want that to happen. Instead, I want my Frumentarrii to interrogate him. I must have the truth from this man. That means I need to remove him from his current location to one I chose for my men to get to work. For that, I need your help and that of your legionary. I can contribute my two Frumentarii, but I daren't involve anyone else."

Lucius tried to take this in, and his head filled with questions.

"Are you saying Secundus would have the Judaean killed, Gaius?"

"Not all Lucius, but there are those who may not want him talking."

"So why don't you attend his interrogation with your Frumentarii?" Lucius asked. Civilis stared at Lucius and sighed. "I am sorry, Gaius; I've had a bastard of a day!"

"All right, let me explain. I do not want others to share in what the man divulges. It could be crucial and relevant to what is going on here. That is why I am sure they will not let him live."

Lucius considered this, and the mist clouding his thinking dissolved.

"I understand. You are my Legionary Tribune, Gaius. Tell me what you would like me to do."

"I've thought it through, and this might work. So, get your legionary and meet me outside the Principia at the watch change, in full kit – don't bother with shields - then we'll...."

The watch bell rang as the officer and his accompanying legionary crossed the small parade ground heading towards the Principia. As they approached the building, they witnessed the sentinels being replaced, as one Century took over duty from another. As the two men closed upon the entrance, Tribune Gaius Civilis strode out from the porticoed doorway, followed by two dark figures wearing cloaks and hoods. Civilis spotted the approaching Optio and waved.

"Perfect timing, Optio Petronius." He pointed to the two hooded individuals that stood behind him. "This is Septimus Lucanus," he said, pointing to the taller and slender of the two men. "And this is his colleague, Spurious Sextilius. They are the Frumentarii I mentioned." As he introduced them, both men nodded, and though the light was poor, Lucius was sure that Lucanus smiled as he was introduced. Sextilius, he was sure, did not. "Follow me. Optio, I would speak with you."

They strode off towards one of the towers positioned at each corner of the fort.

"I intend to remove the prisoner from Secundus' men before the interrogators arrive. I have arranged a location to take him so Lucanus and Sextilius can do what they do well. We shall be at the cell in a few seconds, so follow my lead. Brief your man, I do not want trouble, and I am optimistic there will be none."

Lucius fell a few paces back and briefed Sextus on the plan; what little of it he comprehended. A minute later, they entered the tower's base, descended a staircase, and came to a landing off which there were two doorways. The two legionaries positioned on either side of one of these doorways snapped to attention at the sight of the Legionary Tribune. Civilis stopped in front of the guarded door.

"Legionaries, I have come to remove the prisoner for interrogation. Please open the door." The two soldiers looked at each other before one turned to the Tribune.

"Sir, our orders are to ensure the prisoner remains here until the interrogators arrive, which I am told should be very soon." Civilis smiled.

"Your orders came from Centurion Secundus, no doubt?"

"Sir, they did."

"I am the Tribunus Militum Laticlavius, as you well know. I am taking full responsibility for this prisoner. I have here a document," he said, reaching under his cloak and producing a small leather parchment tube, "which will absolve both yourself and Centurion Secundus of all responsibility for the prisoner. You are dismissed, and I would like the key."

Two legionaries would not argue with the second in command of their legion, so taking the tube, they handed over the key, offered a salute and disappeared up the stairs.

"Secundus will be busy organising his column for tomorrow's foray to Bet Alin, but we had better move quickly." He turned to the two Frumentarii. "Lucanus, get the man and let's get out of here."

Lucanus took the keys, and he and his partner entered the room.

"That went as I had hoped, Optio," Civilis said, "without the application of muscle."

The prisoner was dragged out of the room; his injured leg was not functioning well, but Lucius guessed he could hobble. With Civilis leading the way, the party reversed course into the open air. They all followed Civilis to an adjacent tower, one used for long term storage. They travelled up the stairs to the second floor, where there was a small room into which they placed the prisoner. The room was prepared for what was to come. In one corner sat a chair with attached leather straps. On a side table lay an opened leather roll containing an assortment of unpleasant looking instruments, some of which could have served the Medicus well. The Frumentarii pushed the prisoner into the chair.

"Legionary," said Civilis, "would you stand guard on the door. No one is allowed to enter, by my orders." Sextus left the room, closing the door behind him. Lucanus pulled up a second chair to face the prisoner.

"Spurius," he said, "Would you pour our friend here a goblet of wine." Lucius, who was taken aback at the approach, looked at Civilis, staring at the prisoner. Sextilius did as requested and passed the goblet to Lucanus. In this light, Lucius could see that Sextilius was swarthy, bearded, and burly, a fact emphasised as he removed his cloak and hung it up on a random nail. By contrast, Lucanus was clean-shaven, well-manicured, and a real contrast to Sextilius. Lucanus handed the goblet to the prisoner.

"I suspect those rough legionaries did not look after you well," Lucanus said. "There is no need for unpleasantness. I am sorry we had to rush you on that leg; still, the weight's off it now." He paused as the prisoner hesitated with the goblet. "Oh, for Hades' sake!"

Lucanus took the goblet back and took a swig of the wine.

"Did I ask you to pour the best wine, Sextilius?" said Lucanus staring at the goblet, "This is good. It's certainly not poison." So saying, he handed the goblet back to the prisoner who cautiously sipped from it.

Lucanus assumed a relaxed posture in his chair.

"Let me tell you about this situation you find yourself in, Jew." It was said, with no malice. "My job is to obtain information, and let me assure you that between us, my friend Spurius and I never fail, the outcome is not in question. However, you have options." The prisoner perked up, listening intently. "You can answer our questions satisfactorily, and then we will have you off to the harbour and on a ship to Alexandria in no time. Once there, you can disappear, and no one will find you. The other option is to resist, in which case I shall call upon Spurius to employ his great skill at extracting information; this option is not so pleasant for you, of course."

To everyone's surprise, the prisoner barked back at Lucanus, "Skill? He is little more than a thug!" Lucanus did not flinch.

"In one sense, you are right, but Spurius' skill is not simply inflicting pain, oh no. His real skill is in keeping you alive while he inflicts pain. He can keep it going for days until he gets what he is after."

"I will not betray my brothers."

"Oh, but you will, you will; they all do, so why not cut the pain element out and just tell us what you know. More wine?"

Civilis spoke up,

"Lucanus, can we speak outside – Optio, with me." The trio gathered on the landing after closing the door. Sextus stood by the door, acting the disinterested guard. "We do not have days, Lucanus. I need this information before I am asked why I've removed the prisoner from Secundus' custody!"

"This I understand, Tribune. It is all about breaking their will. You see, some resist a little at first so that when they give us what we want, they can face their conscience by believing they tried to hold out. I suspect that Lucanus will crack him quickly; he is the best. Others? Well, they…"

"Let's get on with it." Snapped Civilis. The three returned to the room. Civilis approached the prisoner, who was now strapped to the chair by Sextilius in their absence. "I am sure you know who I am. If you've given me the information I want in the next hour, I give you my word you will gain passage to Alexandria. I will be back." With a wave of his hand to Lucius, he exited through the door. As they left, they heard Lucanus saying, "strip him." Lucius cringed. They were in the Tribune's quarters within a few minutes, having left Sextus on guard duty.

The two men sat around an ornate table positioned on a marble floor. A marble bust of Caesar was placed in a corner, mounted on a floor-standing pedestal. Silk drapes adorned the walls, framing the elegant window that looked out into the camp. It was all far removed from where the prisoner was suffering unknown degradations. The memory of the recent conversation with his two legionaries sprung to mind.

"Gaius, in all the activity this evening, I forgot to mention that my two men have reason to believe the auxiliaries that whisked away the dead Judaean bandit belonged to a detachment up from En Geddi." The Tribune nodded.

"All this is beginning to put colour onto what was an outline drawing. I do not want to extrapolate too much, but let's suppose the auxiliaries spotted their Judaean friend talking to two legionaries out of uniform. They may have assumed an act of betrayal. So, they took him off and...." He ran his finger across his throat. "Next, we have a squad of assassins after your boys and, from what I hear, if it weren't for a lucky black cat, they too would be...." He ran his finger across his throat again. Lucius frowned.

"But that would need cooperation between the six auxiliaries and the Judaean bandits?"

"Yes, Lucius, it would." Civilis stood up, picked up a pitcher, and poured the two men goblets of water. It was a break to think. When he sat again, he said, "It is En Geddi - Lucanus, and I am sure that the Imperator's oil is being skimmed off and sold. We have six auxiliaries linked to En Geddi killing a suspected Judaean bandit. We could be close to finding out more, but you know what worries me? It is not knowing the payoff for the bandits in all this."

"Get rich quick?" suggested Lucius.

"No one has identified any extravagant behaviour taking place. Of course, you know balsam fetches a king's ransom, and such behaviour could have been expected, but...."

"So, if they are selling the balsam, what are they doing with the money they are earning?" mused Lucius.

For an hour, the two men explored ideas about the situation but went around in circles. Finally, just before midnight, there was a knock on the door. Lucanus walked into the room.

"I can report Tribune," he said. Civilis nodded. "He held out then suddenly seemed to cave in. Tough one, though. His name is Chanock Marshak. He is not one of the ringleaders, but he wanted to go along with the little jaunt to bolster his reputation. I suspect that is why he was a little slow in making his escape."

"What did you get?" asked a frustrated Civilis.

"Right, sir. There's several of them involved at En Geddi. They skim off a small percentage of the balsam and send it in the regular provisions convoy to Aelia. Several legionaries are bribed not to find it at inspection points, but given auxiliaries move it, it is often waved through. As the wagons get close to the camp, they offload their cargo in a small village about two miles down the En Geddi road. Given the nature of 'the sale', the price will give the purchaser a big profit when sold onwards. From there, it's shipped secretly to Galilee, then Syria, and to Mesopotamia for sale. He claims there is knowledge of it on the Roman side but has no information about who's involved. Of course, he may be telling the truth. Spurius can be very persuasive."

"My men could identify the auxiliaries they met Gaius," suggested Lucius, "or we could arrange to ambush the next convoy."

The Tribune said nothing; he sat staring out of the window.

"Lucanus," said Lucius, "did you get any names?"

"Not for the major players, but he gave us two names from the assassins group, though I suspect they are long gone. But, unfortunately, he did not know which village they came from as they were assembled at short notice for the job."

"No!" Civilis said, turning back to the group. "When I was a boy, and in trouble, I used to admit to smaller misdemeanours and give my parents the satisfaction of punishing me. However, I hid my involvement in a bigger misdemeanour in doing so. So, he is hiding something, Lucanus, this stuff is good – and he knows it – but I suspect he may be sacrificing it to hide something else."

"Any thoughts, Tribune, before restarting with him?" Lucanus asked.

"By the Gods, I do. "Civilis responded. "I want all he knows about Simeon bar Koseba. In addition, I want all he knows about weapons manufacture and what happens to the Judaean manufactured weapons we reject. Finally, I want to know what happened to the Governor's informers. Oh, and just how high has the rot reached on our side. Get to it, Lucanus."

"Immediately Tribune," and Lucanus was gone. Lucius drank his beaker of water in one swig.

"Gaius," he said, "Should suspicions be confirmed as fact, what in Hades' name happens then?"

"Let's cross that bridge when we reach it, Lucius. Until then, it is up to Lucanus and his associate to do their work."

I don't know why, thought Lucius, but all this is not as random as it may appear.

Civilis seemed relaxed; the two men sat and talked for another hour. Much of the conversation covered life experiences, particularly stories of their youths. While Lucius' had a comfortable childhood and adolescence, he understood that Civilis' younger life was much more privileged though he talked in generalities with few specifics. Lucius raised the issue of the half-truth told to Centurion Secundus, and the Tribune assured him it would not be a problem. It was odd, thought Lucius, to have this casual conversation while the Judaean was suffering extreme torture so close by. Finally, there came a knock on the door, and Lucanus returned.

"Well?" said Civilis.

"He's dead, sir,"

"Damn it, Lucanus. I thought Sextilius was a master at this. So, what the fuck happened?"

Lucanus stood his ground.

"He is the best, sir. However, it takes time to wring them dry if we're to do the job well and extract everything from a prisoner. You needed the information quickly, and his heart gave out. Fortunately, we gathered information that will be of interest to you."

"Thanks be to Jupiter. So, what did you get, man?"

"Let's start with Koseba. He is the leader of these bandits – though you may want to refer to them as rebels – he detests everything Roman and wants to restore the Jewish Kingdom of Israel, so we are led to believe. The Judaeans greatly respect him. Koseba has been preparing for years, and the money from balsam oil sales was funding the purchase of weapons. They were selling the balsam as far afield as Mesopotamia and Parthia. The weapons rejected by the army are being made good and fed into rebel arsenals; we did not find out where they store the arms, but I would say there are several arsenals across Judaea. Incidentally, our man denied his people had anything to do with the death of Zacharya ben Hassan. They knew of him but were not aware of why ben Hassan died."

"And the informers?" asked Civilis.

"They were under Koseba's control. They fed the Governor just what Koseba wanted him to have. Then, once they had served their purpose, Koseba had them killed. The impression that the prisoner gave is that Koseba is ruthless."

"He must be because the information they fed to the Governor led to the death of several Judaeans over the last couple of years; his very own people!"

Lucanus nodded in agreement and looked as though he had more to say but was not keen – or sure – of how to tell it.

"Well?" demanded Civilis.

"Just before he died, Spurius extracted some additional information, sir."

"And?"

"How do I put this? He implicated the Governor and several officers in the En Geddi balsam fraud, and I am not talking about only auxiliaries – Roman officers are involved. Spurius extracted a few names before our man died, sir."

"Jupiter Maximus! So, it is as bad as I dreaded. But can the man be trusted? The risk with torture is that the victim will often tell you what they believe you'd like to hear. Just to make it stop." The legate paused to think. "Or possibly to sew disinformation and chaos amongst our ranks."

"There is that possibility, Tribune," said Lucanus. "There is one more thing, though." The two officers waited for the disclosure as Lucanus paused for a moment. "Well, sir, just before he died, he laughed. Bloody laughed! Coughed the stuff up he did, sir."

"Get on with it, man," Civilis snarled at the Frumentarii.

"He laughed and said, "Your too damn late, Roman… far too late." Then he spewed blood and died, sir."

"Yet another curse from a dying Judaean!" said Lucius.

Civilis leant forward and put his head in his hands for a second before looking up.

"You realise Lucius; this is one monstrous pile of *cac*!" He turned to Lucanus, "I'll join you, Septimus. Please send the legionary back to join the Optio."

"You will take this information to the governor, Gaius?" Lucius asked.

"I shall, and I pray this time he will grasp what is going on. Do I tell him that in one respect, he's funded the rebels by selling them Balsam? No. This stays between us, Lucius; do I make myself clear?"

"You have no worries on that score, Gaius; you have my oath if you recall?"

"Apologies, Lucius, I meant no disrespect."

"None was taken, Gaius. I'm not sure I would like to be where you are right now, my friend."

"Let's not talk about me. You need to get back to Caesarea and the IV Cohort. How are you in the saddle Lucius?" Lucius laughed.

"I'll manage not to fall off!"

"Good. By tomorrow morning, you will receive two documents from me. One will be for Praefectus Faustinas, instructing him to bring Caesarea to full combat preparedness. The other is for Centurion Crispus. Someone will deliver them to your accommodation. You and your legionary – Postumus? – will ride back to Caesarea with the First *Ala* at break of day."

"That would be with Decurion Manlius?"

"Indeed, Lucius. As I recall, he escorted your convoy to Aelia after your ambush. They are due back to Caesarea, so they will act as an escort for you. But, as of now, we act as if we have a revolt on our hands. Worsened by the fact that we have fuck all knowledge about what we are up against, damn it!"

There came a knock at the door, and Sextus strode in, coming to attention.

"I trust that wasn't too unpleasant, soldier?" Civilis asked.

"He had attempted to kill me, sir. The cunni got just what he deserved, sir,"

"I would have wished for more time with him, but we have confirmed some of our suspicions," Civilis said. "Right, you men both need sleep. The Optio will brief you, soldier, but you are back off to Caesarea at first light. I trust the next time we meet that we may be in better control of the situation."

Lucius and Sextus were pacing across a dark parade area heading to the barrack building within seconds. Lucius briefed Sextus as they proceeded.

"Postumus, I would like you to know that the Tribune knows everything – even that which we managed to avoid sharing with Centurion Secundus." Sextus chewed the information over for a few seconds.

"Thank you, sir. I feel much better knowing that."

"If there are questions, then you were working under the orders of the Tribune; that will indemnify you – me too, as it happens."

The two men proceeded and were in quarters, sound asleep within minutes.

Interludum IV

A Street in Capua

It could have been a street in any sizeable Roman town. It was broad, paved and lined with many shops selling everything from fine silver to kitchen implements. Some traders stood outside their emporiums, trying hard to persuade passers-by of the value that lay within. Others were closing their establishments as the first signs of the evening began to encroach upon Capua; the shadows lengthening, the temperature gradually falling and the prospective customers thinning out. Shutters were being closed.

Positioned between a shop selling fine cloths and a purveyor of jewellery and trinkets lay the 'Vine' tavern. It was more an open-fronted eating house with a lean-to front. The back was dark but cool, whilst the front was open, well-lit and gave a full view of the street. The vines growing up the side and front gave it a rustic appearance. On a table close to the street, two men sat with plates of lamb, cheese, bread and olives whilst sharing a pitcher of wine. To all appearances, two traders having some refreshment after a hard day's work; until one looked closer.

The two men wore caligulae, the regular soldiers' boots and beside each man, laid across the table, were two gnarled wooden sticks. These were vitis, three-foot lengths of vine carried by centurions of the Roman Army; traders these men were not. They were deep in conversation. Drawing closer, one would catch parts of their discussion; training schedules, equipment shortages, route marches and more of the language of military officers.

At a table next to the two officers sat a solitary figure also eating a meal. Dressed in relatively fine cloth, this individual was a civilian. As he ate, he appeared engrossed in the passing population, but he was listening in on the conversation between the two adjacent soldiers. He was dark-haired and dark-skinned. Some would say an Egyptian if asked to guess, and they would be right. Since the ignominious end of Mark Anthony, Egypt had been part of the Roman Empire, and Egyptians were not a strange sight in Roman towns and cities.

Before standing, the dark man finished his food, downed the last of his drink and pushed his plate away from him. He turned towards the two soldiers seated near him. The movement caught the eye of one of the centurions, a powerfully built man with sandy coloured greying hair. His skin was weather-beaten after many years of army service, though the eyes focused on the standing dark man were anything but weather-beaten. His hand moved to the pommel of the gladius at his side. The dark man often had that effect on people.

In three paces, the dark man stood before the two soldiers, both of whom had stopped eating and were staring at the interlope. Both men had determined that the dark man was unarmed in no time.

"My apologies, good sirs, for intruding upon your meal." The sandy-haired soldier nodded acceptance. "A little earlier, I could not help overhearing you mention a name. It was Petronius. May I ask if that would be Lucius Decimus Petronius?"

"And what business would it be of yours, stranger?" responded sandy hair.

"I knew him two years back. I trained him in swordcraft and combat skills."

"Well now, maybe you did, or maybe you didn't, but our conversation is army business." The soldier looked over to the dark man's table, "If you've finished your food, I suggest you move on about your business."

The dark man seemed about to speak but then to have second thoughts. He turned and walked out past his table and out onto the street. It was then that the soldier jumped up and called out,

"Atelius!"

In an instant the dark man turned and faced the caller.

"You know my name?"

"Come back here. Take a seat. I'll even persuade Quintus here that we share our pitcher with you." Puzzled, Atelius joined the two soldiers, sitting as instructed. The soldier called for an extra beaker. Atelius asked again,

"*You know my name?*"

"*I do. I needed to check if it was you. I'm Aurelius Crispus, Senior Centurion to the IV Cohort of Legio X Fretensis. This,*" he said, pointing to his colleague, "*is Quintus Facilis, who commands the 2ndCentury.*"

"*Clearly, you know who I am, but you still have to answer my earlier question, Centurion.*"

"*Lucius Decimus Petronius is my century's Optio - second in command of the century. He was hand-picked by me a while back, and I know him well. He has told me of you.*"

Atelius smiled,

"*Is he well? An Optio? An officer?*"

"*He is well as far as I know. He's in Judaea preparing for our arrival there. I'll pass your compliments on to him should you wish?*" Atelius did not respond but stared at Crispus. "*What is it?*" the soldier asked.

"*I'd like to go with you, centurion.*"

"*I can't stop you buying a fare on a boat, I suppose!*" laughed Crispus.

"*No, no,*" Atelius said, "*I want to join the army!*"

Quintus spluttered in his beaker, and Crispus' jaw dropped, which he recovered when Atelius' expression showed that he was serious.

"*Atelius, this is not like joining the local wrestling team. Why on earth do you want to join the legions at your age? You must be over thirty-*"

"*Thirty-two.*"

"*Yes, well, a point made.*"

Atelius took a deep breath, followed by a long sigh.

"*Sirs, you know me. I was a gladiator for eight years and rose to the top when I received the Rubus, and they made me a free man and citizen of Rome.*" Quintus spoke up,

"*' Saw you fight, mate. Must have been about six years ago in Rome. Yeah, you were good!*"

"*Thank you.*" Atelius continued. "*I am relatively rich and own property. So a successful gladiator can make good money.*"

"*And get the girls!*" added Quintus.

"Do you know, I woke up this morning after a wild night with a girl beside me. I never knew the cunni's name. If I drink, I might sleep. I have no real friends to talk of." Atelius stared down at the table, his face looking drawn. "I spent eight years fighting for my life. Gladiators do not have long-time friends; instead, we have a brotherhood. Outside the arena, we watched out for each other. Even though we understood that we might have to kill one another one day, it was nothing personal. It is what we did. I enjoyed those moments in the arena; I felt alive. I was king. You will think me mad, but I miss it. This life I lead now is killing me."

"The Roman Army isn't the arena, Atelius," Crispus said. "There is no king there; in fact, quite the opposite."

"I realise that, but my life is fighting, and in the army, there is brotherhood. So I can do what I am good at doing, using arms."

"You'd be working with young men, Atelius, fit young men, many over ten years younger than you. Could you handle that?"

"I train gladiators for a living. Anything they do, I can do, and better."

Quintus spoke up,

"Atelius, we shall be headed to Judaea in a short time. Unfortunately, the training period might exclude you from coming with us – it's not something you can do in a few days!"

"That's correct, but...." Crispus scratched the back of his head. Anyone who knew him said that this was his 'thinking' signal. "I had that idiot break his leg last week. If he ever gets right, it won't be for months, so at least I have a tent space to fill-"

"But Marcus, the process takes days just to get him into the army, let alone the training period."

"You're right, Quintus, but there are two factors that might enable the situation. First, the army has given me a lot of leeway in assembling the cohort. I will have to explain to the governor, but I'd rather apologise than seek permission given the timing." He turned to the Egyptian, "Second, Lucius has often spoken of you, which is more than I can say of his father!"

"He always wanted to be a soldier, that lad," said Atelius. "His father was wrong to have resisted it. Now he has lost a son, though he rapidly gained another!" Crispus scratched the back of his head again,

"Tomorrow morning, you'll report to the Campus Martius and ask for Centurion Pancus. You'll not see Centurion Facilis or me" nodding towards Quintus, "as you must do this yourself. I shall tell Pancus to put you through Hades and back."

"If you can do that, mate, you will be bloody Hercules!" laughed Quintus.

"Get through Pancus first," Crispus continued, "if you do, we'll meet the following morning to start inducting you into the cohort. Understand this Atelius, you'll be only a common tiro, and you must work your arse off to catch up on the training. It's up to you – there'll be no favours."

Atelius finished his wine and slowly placed the mug onto the table.

"I shall look forward to meeting you again, centurion, the day after tomorrow."

Capitulum XI - Training Camp

1 Aprilis. Year 16 of Imperator Hadrian

Sextus was at Lucius' door just after sunrise. Lucius was groggy, having had but a few hours' sleep, but he was ready to go. Close behind Postumus came two legionaries who collected Lucius's two chests.

"So, Postumus," said Lucius, "how are you on a horse?"

"I may not be leading the charge, sir, but I can handle myself."

"In that case, let's head to the North Gate where the cavalry should muster for the trip to Caesarea." The two men left the room and headed out across the small parade ground. The day was new enough to feel still fresh, which brought Lucius to life and cleared any grogginess the lack of sleep had caused.

"By the way, sir," Sextus said, "I still have this." He pointed to the bag that hung on his shoulder. Lucius laughed as he recognised Marcus' dispatch bag.

"In the name of the God's – I don't think we've even opened it Postumus!"

"Marcus would be upset if we'd left it behind, sir. He feels responsible for it. I dropped in on him to explain. He will follow on as soon as he can."

"That's good," Lucius replied, "I feel bad about leaving him, but orders are orders."

As they approached the gate, it was clear the cavalry was getting ready to ride out. Lucius spotted the crest of the commander, recognising the officer immediately.

"Decurion Manlius," he said. He held out his arm. "Caius, good to ride with you again."

"Optio Petronius," Manlius replied, "It seems your coming to Aelia did not augur well."

"The reason I came down to Aelia, Caius, was to see my uncle. Instead, I've travelled halfway around Judaea, and now I'm heading back to Caesarea without one of my men."

"I heard about the attack. I understand your man will recover?"

"He will, but he is in no condition to ride." As he spoke, Lucius saw his uncle approaching, accompanied by Civilis. The Decurion made excuses about checking that his men were ready to move and departed. Tribune Civilis approached Lucius.

"Ready to leave, Optio?"

"Indeed, sir, I was just discussing the ride with Decurion Manlius."

"Well, the centurion here just wanted to wish us a good trip." Julius Petronius stepped forward and held out an arm that Lucius clasped.

"Salve Optio, I'd hoped we could talk more. But I suspect you'll be happy to be out of this place," his uncle said.

"The visit was not what I was expecting," Lucius responded. "I'll be back, so we must pick up where we left off upon my return. The bonus will be that I should be with Centurion Crispus, so you'll have a lot of catching up to do."

"We will. And when you see him, tell him it's his turn to pay for the wine. Before he left for Italia, he fair cleared the Taberna and left me footing the bill, including the bill from the Taberna owner's daughter – or was it her mother?" He laughed at his humour. "I must be off, Lucius, may the gods be with you, and if not, keep your gladius close. Salute Civilis." He turned and made his way back towards the principia. Lucius turned to Civilis.

"I am sorry, sir, but did you say, 'us' a second ago; you are returning to Caesarea?" Civilis glanced at Sextus, and Lucius noticed the gesture.

"Sextus, can you get our horses ready; I'll be along shortly." The big legionary moved off towards the horse lines. When he was out of earshot, Civilis spoke in a lowered tone.

"Lucius, the governor has ordered me back to Caesarea to lead reinforcements back down here. I stress it was an order made against my protest, but he was adamant."

"So, what does this mean?"

"I do not have enough yet to act, but I can assure you the matter moves forward. It is likely that when we return, I will be in a better position to move. There is every possibility that the IV Cohort will be one of the units coming back with me, so you should be meeting your uncle again soon."

"Perhaps my next visit might be a little less eventful?"

"That maybe. I've ordered a cavalry patrol to seek out your weapons forge; they will leave a little after us. Also, I've asked your uncle for a daily report, so we should hear what they find. The Messenger Service is fast in these parts."

Looking towards the horse lines, Lucius spotted the Decurion waving in his direction.

"The Decurion is signalling us." The two men strode across to join the Decurion.

"We are ready, sir. Legionary Postumus has your horse Optio, and *Diomedes* is ready for you Tribune." As he spoke, a cavalryman walked a large grey stallion towards them.

"The best horse I've ever owned," Civilis said. Lucius turned to the Decurion,

"So, Caius, when can we expect to be in Caesarea?"

"I would say tomorrow evening, but some of my lads say they know a shortcut that could knock three hours of the journey. Tribune, you said you wanted to move swiftly?"

"I did, so let's get moving, shall we?"

Within a few minutes, the column was mounted. Lucius was at its head along with Civilis and Decurion Manlius. Sextus rode behind them, followed by the thirty riders of the cavalry *ala*. Each rider was helmeted and carried a spear and an embossed round shield, decorated with the boar of the Tenth Fretensis. They looked business-like, and Lucius felt good to be back with a body of soldiers – even if they were cavalry and not his beloved legionaries.

As they left the ruins of old Jerusalem behind them and headed towards the hills of Judaea, the Decurion ordered two pairs of scouts to ride parallel to the column, at each side some distance out. Given some of the recent events, he did not want to take any unnecessary risks. As they proceeded the day warmed up, and when the sun was at its zenith, the Decurion pulled the column up beside a large olive grove and suggested a short respite from the saddle. In no time, men were sitting in the shade of the olive trees whilst others tended to the horses.

"Sir, the shortcut I mentioned is about a mile along this road," said the decurion, "It's only a trackway and it will be hot and dry, but it should save us quite some time, and it means we can spend the night in Antipatris. Are you happy to take it?"

"I don't see why not," Civilis responded.

Thirty minutes later, the column was on the move, and as the Decurion had predicted, the turn off soon appeared. They headed up a valley trail, rising higher as they went. Good time was made with the hours passing quickly. Lucius could eavesdrop on conversations across a wide range of soldierly topics from the cavalrymen behind, including exploits amongst the whores and the copious amounts of drink consumed in tabernas. He and Civilis were debating the oratory of Cicero when a scout came riding furiously towards them, pulling up alongside the Decurion, who brought the column to a halt.

"In Hades' name Avitus, what's the rush?" Manlius asked.

"There is something you ought to see, sir," Avitus gasped, "over the ridge. Bloody hundreds of 'em, sir."

The Decurion glanced at Civilis before turning back to Avitus.

"Soldier, you will make a formal report. Now!"

"Sorry, sir." He swallowed and began. "On the other side of the ridge, we spotted a large - very large – camp, sir. At a guess, we estimate several hundred soldiers, sir."

"Hundreds?" a visibly shocked Decurion checked, "You said *hundreds* of soldiers?"

"Yes, sir. Mostly foot soldiers, but there may be as many as a hundred cavalry."

The Decurion was about to respond when Civilis raised his hand.

"Soldier. Are you sure? You tell us that across that ridge is a military camp containing hundreds of soldiers. I ask you again, are you sure?"

"May Charon take me if I am wrong, Tribune, sir."

"Then I think you'd better show us this camp. Decurion Manlius and Optio Petronius, you can accompany cavalryman Avitus and me. Let's go."

The small party broke away from the column and rode up the sloping valley side. As they approached the ridge at the top of the slope, Avitus' comrade walked down to meet them, saluting the tribune as he came to a stop.

"Respect, sir. With your approval, sir, I suggest we proceed on foot as this number of horses will raise a dust cloud which may be seen. Can I also suggest removing helmets; your crests may be spotted. No sign of patrols, but we can't be sure."

"Good advice Balbus," said the Decurion. After dismounting, the officers removed their helmets and hung them from their saddle pommels.

"So Balbus, what're your thoughts about this camp?" asked Civilis.

"Well, sir, best you look for yourself. It gave me a scare." Balbus said as he dismounted. "Thankfully, there's cover on the ridge, and we can overlook the camp from there safely."

The small party trudged up the dusty slope towards the ridgeline. The five soldiers dropped onto their stomachs for the last few feet, using the low-lying scrub as cover. None of them was prepared for what they viewed in the valley.

In front of them stretched hundreds of crude tents and accompanying fires – including several poorly erected shacks – but the sheer number of warriors shook them the most, many practising drills, others hand-to-hand combat, whilst others were gathered around instructors. They could make out horse lines at the far side of the valley, with cavalry drilling in line and column, a much less disciplined affair than Roman sessions, but this was undoubtedly an army in training.

"Cac," Civilis muttered, "this is more serious than I thought."

Balbus nodded toward a remote corner of the camp,

"Can you see that, sir? Past the tents at the foot of the valley side?" Civilis and the others squinted as they sought out what Balbus indicated.

"I'm seeing ballistas, aren't I?" Civilis asked. The ballista was a wooden device that could fire stones or bolts at an advancing enemy, a practical artillery piece. "Jupiter, these people are getting ready for some serious action."

"There could be nearly a thousand soldiers out there," Lucius said. "Their equipment looks haphazard and -." Then, two men suddenly appeared, their approach having been hidden by some larger bushes on the opposite slope to the right of where the five Romans lay. Armed with spears and small oval shields, they were roughly fifty feet away and heading towards the ridge where the Romans lay prone.

"Back!" hissed Civilis, and they all slid away down the slope. The Decurion spoke up.

"I suggest the officers return to the turmae. Balbus and Avitus to me."

Lucius and Civilis turned and retreated down the slope, but only for thirty paces before throwing themselves behind a low bush, enough to hide them from anyone on the ridgeline. When they looked back up the valley side, they saw the Decurion ambling up to the ridgeline. Hiding a few feet either side of him were Balbus and Avitus, crouched as low as possible behind what little greenery they could find.

Lucius watched in amazement at the decurion's behaviour on the skyline. Once there, he shouted in surprise, turned, and ran. In no time, two Judaean fighters appeared over the ridge pursuing the soldier, one drawing back his spear to launch it at the decurion's back. At this point, several things happened quickly. First, the fighters spotted the Turmae waiting in the valley below, distracting them for a second. Then, as they hesitated, Balbus and Avitus appeared from either side, their long falcata cavalry swords in hand. The fighters were disadvantaged as the two cavalrymen were too close for spears to be effective. At the same time, the Decurion turned to face the two Judaeans.

The right hand of the two men turned and swung his shield in front of him to block Avitus. Dropping his spear, he reached for his sword. Unfortunately, he was a fraction too late; just before the shield could protect him, Avitus' long sword thrust into his side. Avitus barged the man's shield as the injured man faltered, knocking him flat on his back. The nimble Roman finished his work with another rapid thrust.

Balbus was coming at his man from the soldier's shield side. The Judaean turned to face Balbus, keeping his shield to his front whilst swinging his spear in a vicious arc towards Balbus' head. Fortunately, the Roman was inside the spear's radius, but he still took a severe blow on the side of his helmet, which caused him to falter for a moment. The Judaean pulled back his spear and readied a thrust; it was halted only by the Decurion's falcata cutting deep into his neck. Balbus' antagonist fell, dying to the ground.

"Cunni!" spat Balbus at the dying man, rubbing the side of his head. "How'd we miss these two?"

The Decurion cleaned his blade on the fallen Jew's body, returning it to its scabbard.

"Job done," he said as he pushed the sword home. "They got lucky, Balbus – to a point. First, roll the bodies behind some scrub, so they are not obvious to anyone looking over the ridge, then re-join us in the valley."

The cavalry commander descended to where Lucius and Civilis were now on their feet. The three officers returned swiftly to their mounts and re-joined the Turmae standing by on the road.

"Good work Manlius," Civilis said, "That was quick thinking."

"It may've been, sir, but it shouldn't have been necessary."

"True, but you made good the error."

When they joined the waiting troopers, the Tribune said,

"Manlius, call for your two best riders to return to Aelia. Give them details of what we have seen and tell them to report to Centurion Petronius to brief the governor. They should take separate routes. You know the drill."

"Immediately, Tribune." The Decurion walked off towards the middle of the patrol, signalling two men. Civilis turned to Lucius,

"Optio, I can tell you your suspicions have been validated. We face a potentially serious revolt, and we'll need to hurry, or this could quickly get out of hand. Frankly, we have damned little intelligence upon which to make any sort of plan." The two men mounted their horses. "Let's get back to Caesarea. I'll pull together the units we have there and be braced to act. But, unfortunately, I suspect your IV Cohort lads will be busy earlier than they thought!"

"Crispus will rejoice in it, sir," Lucius replied. The men talked a little more before the Decurion returned.

"Caesarea, Manlius, with all the speed we can muster," called Civilis as he kicked his horse forward.

As the column moved onwards, Sextus drew up alongside Lucius.

"Some fun and games up there, sir?"

"There's numerous armed rebels over that ridge, Sextus. Several hundred in number. Whatever it is, it has begun."

"Best we get back to soldiering then, sir," Sextus replied. "All this creeping about ain't my style if you know what I mean. Also, my nose is twitching something awful."

The rest of the journey back to Caesarea was uneventful. It felt to Lucius that as they moved through Samaria, ever closer to Caesarea, the friendlier the reception they received from the villages on the way. It was midday as they rode into the camp at Caesarea; the Decurion was correct; the shortcut had saved hours, even allowing for the distraction on the way.

Lucius had presumed there would be time for refreshment once they arrived, but it was not to be. So instead, he accompanied the cavalry to the Principia.

"Come with me, Optio. Decurion Manlius, stable your horse and rest the men," Civilis ordered.

Halfway through the journey, Lucius' backside had reminded him it was some time since he had done any distance in the saddle. He slid down from the saddle, grateful to be on his feet again. It was necessary to jog to catch up with Civilis, who was already disappearing into the interior of the building. They strode down the long marble corridor to the Tribune's office, where a clerk sat in the corner sorting despatches.

"Legionary. After the next watch change, I want you to have the Praefectus and all senior centurions in the meeting hall. You can include all junior tribunes in camp too. I don't care who is doing what; they will be here. I also want you to gather whatever decent maps we have of Provincea Judaea." He paused for a second, "I nearly forgot, will you ask Decurion Manlius to attend. Understand?"

The legionary who had leapt up in surprise at his senior officer storming into the room promptly snapped to attention.

"Sir! All senior centurions and tribunes plus Decurion Manlius, here, after watch change, with maps, sir!"

"Good. See it, soldier." With that, the legionary was gone.

Civilis had briefed Lucius as to his plans as they rode. He was confident that this was no local insurgency but a full-blooded revolt; consequently, the Legion must assume a full war footing. His concern was that the legion had approached matters in a piecemeal fashion; cohorts here, centuries there, resulting in them being knocked about.

He sat in his chair behind his desk and rested on his elbows.

"This is a mess, Lucius, and we need to get back control. This rebellion is centred in Judaea. I want to get the cohorts here in Caesarea, all bar one, back to Aelia. That will get us up to full strength in Judaea. Crispus and the IV cohort should be here any time; I'll hold them, along with a remaining cohort as a reserve. I'd better alert the Sixth Legion in Galilee if they need to be ready to move. If we can crush this quickly, all the better, but I shall need to inform Rome of what is happening. We need to get the governor back here too; it is risky having him based in Aelia – I should be there."

It amused Lucius that here he was, a mere Optio, sharing war strategy with a senior tribune. However, he was unsure what was expected of him and decided he was no more than a sounding board.

"I am sure once you get the centurions together, you'll be able to construct a plan, Gaius."

"I'm sure we will, Lucius, but it will be based upon weak intelligence. There is so much we don't know, a fact that could have major consequences upon our actions."

Civilis stood, turning to stare through the window with a view across the camp. Lucius could not imagine all the issues that must be racing through the Tribune's mind. Instead, he had a glimpse of the loneliness of command, and he realised how much he missed his role in the cohort where life was more straightforward. There was one matter nagging at him, however.

"Gaius, may I ask a question?"

Civilis turned to look at his companion,

"Ask away."

"The Governor and the information you uncovered...." Lucius stalled, realising he was treading on dangerous ground.

"It involved you, Lucius; it's fair enough to inquire," Civilis paused for a few seconds. "In one respect, the less you know, the better, but I've asked for advice from others far from this place. So, can we leave it there? I trust your man Postumus can be discreet?"

"He is solid, Gaius."

"Good. Now, we have a little time before the watch changes. Get cleaned up and get some food. Then, be back in the hall for the arranged time." At which point, the two men parted, and Lucius walked to the Minerva. His arrival caught the landlord, Sistus, by surprise, and Lucius had to stall any detailed conversation until later in the day. While washing in his room, Sistus arrived with bread, soup, olives, and some wine, all of which Lucius hurriedly consumed before heading back out and returning to the principia.

As he approached the building, he headed straight to the hall, where Caius Manlius joined him.

"Council of War, Optio?"

"I suspect it will be Caius, but as fine as a horse maybe, this time I will be marching. My arse will be mighty relieved!"

Manlius laughed,

"You did alright for a stubble hopper, my friend!"

They turned into the meeting hall. It was not a large room, but five rows of benches were squeezed in. A raised dais accommodating two empty chairs was positioned at the end where the two men entered. On the wall behind the chairs was a mural of a red boar, the legion's emblem. Already the senior centurions of the three cohorts present at Caesarea sat talking together on the second row of benches. They looked old and grizzled compared to the young tribunes that sat in front. These were young men undergoing the military aspect of the *cursus honorum*. Most came from Patrician families or the rich *Novo Homos*, the 'new men'.

Lucius felt discomfort in his stomach as he recalled the last meeting with senior legionary officers. Still, this was the Tribune's meeting, so he shouldn't be the focus, though he wondered why he was required to be here. As he chewed over the situation, Civilis walked in, followed by a clerk with a large, rolled map attached to hooks on the back wall, all but obscuring the legion's red bull. All the officers present stood up upon Civilis' entry. The clerk stood back and viewed the map, nodded to himself, and left the room. Lucius stood by a bench behind the others and watched as Civilis lowered himself onto the curule chair positioned in the centre of the dais.

"Please sit," said Civilis with a wave of his arm. "First, my thanks for attending this meeting at what I appreciate was rather short notice." There were mumbles around the room, after which the Tribune continued. "You may have heard rumours about trouble down in Judaea. Well, I am here to convert those rumours into fact. Frankly, brother officers, we have a huge pile of *crepitus* on our hands. We have lost men, and I suspect we will lose more before getting this sorted. If I sound pessimistic, it is because I am." The audience looked to each other and back to the Tribune.

"So, the goat fuckers are looking for a fight, sir?" The speaker was Flavius Gallianus, the senior centurion of the V Cohort. An experienced veteran of twenty-nine, he was accustomed to trouble, but he detected something more serious judging by the concern visible on the Tribune's face.

"Yes, Centurion Gallianus, I believe so." Civilis thought for a moment. "I have asked Optio Petronius to attend us here. I suspect he was the first officer of the Fretensis that detected anything untoward. Upon raising his suspicions, he received somewhat of a rebuke. As it happens, I have confirmed what he suspected, but extremely late in the day. Nevertheless, I think it might be useful for us to listen to the story he has to tell. That done, we need to make plans. Optio Petronius, would you join me?"

Lucius rose to his feet and strode to the front. He approached the Tribune, snapped off a salute and turned and faced the audience.

"Relax, Optio. I suggest you start at the beginning, but maybe we can omit some minutiae."

Lucius recognised the warning about omitting any references to the governor's possible involvement. Well, he thought, here I go yet again! He took a deep breath.

"Sirs, I am Optio Lucius Decimus Petronius, IV Cohort, 1st Century. My role in being here was to help prepare the imminent arrival of the cohort into Caesarea...."

Twenty minutes later, Lucius ended.

"... we arrived back this morning. Sirs, you now know as much as me. From what I have seen, I can support the Tribune's description of where we are; in a huge pile of *crepitus*!" He turned to the Tribune, who pointed to the chair beside him.

"Better stay up here, Optio. I want the officers to have every chance to question both of us on what we know. The more information they have, the better we can plan a response." Lucius sat and there followed a myriad of questions, noticeably Lucius thought, from the centurions, except for a young junior tribune, Aemilius Iuncus, who asked some testing questions. It was an hour before they finally devised a plan. Civilis sent for refreshments.

After all the talk, the plan was surprisingly straightforward. As soon as the IV Cohort arrived at Caesarea under Crispus, centurions Quintilianus, Gallianus and Vincinius would march their cohorts south to Aelia. Quintilianus' IX and Vincinius' X cohort would remain in Aelia as reinforcements, whilst Gallianus' V cohort would escort the governor back to Caesarea. Manlius' cavalry turmae would accompany the downward journey and then return with the governor in a protection and scouting role.

Once at Aelia, the IX and X cohorts would function as a defence force for Aelia; they were not to move out into the province. Vinicius scoffed at the idea that the rebels would attack Aelia, but the Tribune insisted. If anything happened to the

Imperator's newest colony, one named after him, there would be Hades to pay.

The Tribune announced that he would lead the three cohorts back to Aelia; Lucius assumed that the governor must have rethought his decision to have the Tribune in Caesarea. After the announcement, the Tribune closed the meeting, and the group dispersed.

"Would you remain a moment, Petronius," the Tribune requested. He waited until the hall was clear before continuing. "Lucius, I want you to keep Postumus close. He will expect to return to the fifth, but I would be happier if he is with you."

"You believe he might talk about what happened?" Lucius queried, "I've assured you he is solid, Caius."

"You may well be right but find him some task or other. I don't want him going to Aelia right now."

"I'd miss him dogging my heels; I'm sure I can dream up something for him." At which point the two men parted.

It was getting late in the day, so Lucius decided to return to the Minerva and have some of Octavia Trianus' good cooking and her husband's excellent wine. So, he left the Principia but had only gone a short distance when a voice called out his name. Stood close by was Junior Tribune Iuncus. Lucius threw saluted, coming to attention.

"Relax, Lucius, please." Using his first name took Lucius by surprise. "Your report was good. Detailed and to the point."

"Thank you, sir."

"For Jupiter's sake Lucius, call me Aemilius – we are in private." This puzzled Lucius. Had he missed something? Tribune Iuncus – or Aemilius as he would prefer, laughed. "If you could see your face, Lucius!"

"I am sorry, sir – err - Aemilius, but I do not understand."

"Well, old Marcellus would have been impressed with the report." Lucius shook his head as he recalled his boyhood tutor. The old man was Greek, and Lucius attended a small class of five boys for over three years. Then the fog lifted.

"By Hades, Aemilius! How long has it been? I didn't recognise you." Arms were proffered and grasped, and Aemilius threw an arm around Lucius' shoulder.

"It's been too damn long, my old classmate, too damn long."
Lucius stood back and took in his friend from years ago,

"You've grown!" They both laughed. Aemilius was the opposite of the dark, strongly built, bearded Optio. Tall, lithe, and sandy-haired, sporting a classic roman nose and sharp blue eyes, he looked the part of a patrician. However, when he laughed, he was the young boy Lucius remembered.

"We have catching up to do. What are your immediate plans? Food?"

"Pretty much. I am lodged in the Minerva." Lucius replied.

"Right, why don't we get out of this kit so we can be Roman to Roman. What do you reckon?" Aemilius, still the enthusiast that Lucius remembered him to be.

"If you are happy with basic but good home cooking, I suggest we eat at the Minerva. Then, I'll head back there. Get sorted and wait for you. A plan?"

Aemilius nodded,

"A plan," followed by, "It will be good for us to talk. See you then." Upon which Aemilius turned and made off towards the officer's quarters.

Capitulum XII - Tales from Home

2 Aprilis. Year 16 of Imperator Hadrian.

No sooner had Lucius entered the Minerva than Sistus insisted he was seated and told him of the rumours of trouble down in Judaea. Wine appeared, a welcome home from an old veteran, so Lucius gave him a watered-down version of events in Judaea, downplaying the seriousness of the matter. He escaped to his room. He had just changed when there came a knock on the door. Opening it, Sextus Postumus was stood in the doorway.

"Excuse me, sir," he said, "I was wondering about Marcus, sir?"

"Apologies, Sextus, I haven't seen you since we returned. However, the Tribune has issued an order for Marcus' return to Caesarea as soon as he's fit to travel."

"It's just, sir, that I hear the Fifth is going down to Aelia the day after tomorrow. We're just waiting for the Italian lot – sorry sir - the Fourth to arrive. So, given you won't be needing me, sir, I thought I could re-join the lads in the 1st Century."

"By *Dis*, Sextus, the news carries fast in this place!"

"Just the gossip, sir."

Lucius was caught in a spot, recalling the Tribune's words.

"Sextus, I may have a role for you in the next few days. The Fifth will return quickly, so can I suggest you re-joining then?"

Lucius thought he detected a flicker of disappointment pass across the soldier's face, but he perked up.

"As you wish, sir."

As he turned to walk away, Lucius called him.

"Sextus." The soldier turned, "Thank you, and believe me, I mean it."

"Thank you, sir. Good night." With that, he left. Lucius felt terrible about what he had just done. He trusted Postumus, but orders are orders, and he had little choice. He was unsure what he would do with Sextus over the next few days, but he needed to get creative quickly.

Lucius returned to the bar where Sistus had set him a table a short while later. Sistus' wife, Octavia, rushed over and welcomed him back. Thankfully, she did not want to explore the military situation in Judaea. They were discussing the menu when Aemilius Iuncus walked into the Taberna. Shorn of his Tribune's paraphernalia, Lucius could see more of his friend from years ago. Seeing Lucius, he joined him and Octavia. He was a charmer as he told her the word was, she was a goddess of cooking, and he'd come to worship in her temple. Lucius was surprised that one from the patrician class could be completely at ease with this ex-soldier's wife.

Food was ordered a few minutes later, and a pitcher of wine was placed on the table.

"Well, who'd have thought we would bump into each other in Caesarea?" Lucius said.

"It's a small world, the Roman Empire!"

"So it is. You know, Aemilius, I hadn't thought about old Marcellus for some years until you mentioned his name; how he used to whine on about Virgil. *Fortune shines upon him who dares!*"

"If I cannot move Heaven, I will raise Hell," countered Aemilius.

"The thing is, Aemilius, we still remember it!"

"We do. Do you remember how the old man ragged you relentlessly about your namesake, the poet Petronius and the *Satyricon?*"

"Don't remind me. At least we are not about to join the *Banquet of Trimalchio*. I don't think we would stoop to such a level of vulgarity. On second thoughts...." The two men laughed. "I suspect Octavia would throw us out for all your charm."

"Tell me," said Aemilius, "how are you finding the army? It's been a while, hasn't it? I see your equestrian background has achieved officer rank for you."

"It's treating me well, old friend. I've had much to learn very quickly. I believe I have been fortunate to end up serving with Aurelius Crispus – he's an 'old-school' soldier and has taught me much. And you?"

"My family has plans for me. My father is a senator, as you well know. So here I am doing a period in the army to move me along the *cursus honorum*. I have been out here for about nine months, mostly at Aelia. I am a bureaucrat handling army organisation. Sometimes I envy you legionaries, believe it or not."

"Yes, well, it was my father's plans that brought me to where I am too!"

"I know," Aemilius said. Lucius looked at him inquisitively. "Lucius, I know the story. Your father is a rich and influential man and mixes at high levels. I am very aware he was not happy with you going to the legions – not happy at all. I also know the consequence."

"He has disowned me and adopted a son to be what I would not."

"Yes." Lucius became absorbed in his thoughts, and Aemilius watched him for a few seconds.

"Lucius, your father adopted Antonius Aminus, your other uncle's son. The older Aminus had died, so it was an opportunity from the gods for your father. He was the right age too."

"Aemilius, you are exceptionally well informed, my old friend," Lucius said. "How is it so?"

Aemilius took a large, deliberate swig of wine from his goblet, returning the vessel purposefully onto the table.

"Lucius, I carry news. Antonius Aminus will marry my sister, Atia, in two months."

Lucius' mind raced upon hearing what Aemilius had said, quickly concluding that he did not care. He had chosen his life in the legions, and that was that. But then, he glanced at Aemilius, who was looking not a little nervous.

"Your sister is what?" Lucius demanded, his face a mask of shock. "What did you say?" Aemilius recoiled.

"Lucius – my sister – she is marrying-" Lucius burst out laughing.

"I am joking, my friend. I couldn't resist it." He adopted a more serious demeanour. "I'm sure my father sees a dynastic marriage that'll raise his family status. I say *his*, not my family, as I'm married to the legions. My uncle, Julius of the Sixth and Aurelius Crispus of the Fourth, are my family. You see, you may return to Rome in two years. Me? I've a term to serve. So, let's forget my father, your sister, and Antonius. We two are here in Caesarea and, courtesy of Octavia, about to have a fine meal."

An expression of relief spread across Aemilius' face.

"Thank the gods, Lucius. I'd expected you to be upset."

Octavia arrived with the meal; two large plates of freshly cooked pork. The two men discussed their shared past and their lives since they had both parted. Both men being unmarried, the subject turned to the fairer sex. As Aemilius talked eloquently about girls in Rome he had known, images of Miriam bat Yaholem interrupted Lucius' train of thought. He realised he hadn't thought about her since leaving Aelia, but now she came forcefully into his consciousness. He was concerned she was now in a region that was becoming dangerous. However, she was in Aelia, so he decided not to be overly concerned.

The conversation moved on to matters political back in Rome and talk of the Imperator's travels; it was only recently that the Imperator Hadrianus himself was in Caesarea, part of a tour that seemed to go well. It was then that Aemilius asked,

"What do you think of Tineus Rufus?"

Alarm bells rang in Lucius' mind. Be careful.

"Well, as you know, I have only met him twice; both cases were formal meetings. He seemed to be on top of matters." Lucius laughed, "I can't say I thank him for sending me off into the wilds of Judaea, though!"

Aemilius joined in the humour,

"Well, you survived – what's the problem?"

"Why do you ask?"

"I'd have thought you may have embarrassed him. If you'd not rattled cages, he, the governor, may have been none the wiser until Judaea blew up in his face. Some are asking how we did not spot this coming?"

This was not a conversation an Optio wanted to have with a Tribune – even if he was a Junior Tribune.

"I'm the new arrival Aemilius, and my feet have hardly touched the ground since I arrived, so I am unable to say why we didn't have better warning. All I did was to tell it as I saw it."

"Better late than never. Civilis seems to warm to you."

"Thrown together by fate. Now we are back here in Caesarea, I suspect I will go back to being a simple soldier and him to be the legion's senior tribune."

"He's only been with the legion a matter of months. He seems to know his business, but…."

"But?" Lucius asked.

"I mentioned him in a letter to my father. When he replied, he could find out little about him, so I tried to bring it up in conversation, but he was evasive."

"Perhaps he's just a personal man; not everyone shares their life story with everyone they meet."

Lucius was beginning to feel a level of discomfort with the conversation when Aemilius suddenly changed direction.

"Lucius, you may be right. So, tell me more about your trip into Judaea as a trader…." Aemilius received a detailed account of Lucius's experience with his small team, by which time the pork was consumed, and the two men had moved on to dates and fruit. Aemilius declared that he needed an early night.

"Thanks for the meal, Lucius. After all these years, it is great to find an old friend in the legion. I shall let my father know we've met again, and I am so pleased you are relaxed about my sister's forthcoming nuptials." He prepared to leave, throwing his cloak over his shoulders.

"Great dinner and thank you again." At which he left the Taberna.

Lucius sat thinking over all that his old friend had said to him. Then, as he was about to return to his room, Sistus joined him.

"Good to have you back, sir. I hope you enjoyed your meal."

"It was excellent, Sistus. Please tell Octavia it was one of her best."

"I will, I will, sir. Was that Tribune Iuncus you dined with?"

"Correct, Sistus, it was."

"By Jove, I'll have the governor in next!" Lucius smiled, but then Sistus' face turned to a more serious countenance. "As I said earlier, I hear stories from down the road, sir. Stories of legionaries getting themselves killed, sir. In numbers too. Now, we can't be having that, can we?"

"There's a problem, Sistus, I can't deny it, but plans are afoot to sort it."

"I hope so, sir." Sistus looked uncomfortable, shifting in his chair. Lucius sensed he wanted to say something.

"What is it, Sistus?"

"You see, sir, we have this Jewish woman, getting on a bit like, come in to help with cleaning and the like. She is always mumbling about 'bloody Romans this' and 'bloody Romans that.' She's harmless, sir. Well, she told Octavia that her son had run off to join a fella by the name of Koseba who was raising an army to fight the 'bloody romans'!"

"I may've seen that army," Lucius said. "Must've been a thousand strong, I reckon, well equipped too."

Sistus raised his eyebrows and shared a knowing smile.

"She was talking many thousands!"

"*Cac*! I hope not!" Lucius responded. "Anyway, we are sending reinforcements down to Aelia to deal with them, whatever size their army may be."

"That's the other thing, sir; she says they have spies everywhere, so they will know just what 'the bloody Romans' are about to do."

"Damn it, Sistus, this was a good evening until you sat down."

"I thought you ought to know, sir. This *cac* will get worse before it gets better, sir."

"You're right. We may need to speak to your cleaner friend. I wonder if there's anything else she could tell us?" Lucius stood up, "Sistus, thanks. I've had enough to think about for one night. Busy day tomorrow, so right now, I am off to bed."

Capitulum XIII - The Fourth arrives

5 Aprilis. Year 16 of the Imperator Hadrianus.

Three days later, as he was finishing his evening meal, a legionary approached Lucius.

"Optio Petronius?" Lucius nodded. "The Praefectus wishes to inform you that news has arrived saying the IV Cohort will arrive around the middle of the day tomorrow. Do you have a reply for the Praefectus, sir?"

"I do, soldier. Please inform the Praefectus that I'll join him after the morning parade if he finds that convenient." Then, the legionary was gone with a salute and a 'Yours to command sir'.

"That'll be good news then, sir," said Sistus, who was hovering close by. "Your old mates are arriving."

"And a touch of normality at last."

As Lucius spoke, a further legionary entered. This one was casually dressed and headed for Lucius in some haste. It was Sextus Postumus.

"Sir, have you heard the Fourth...." Lucius raised his hand to interrupt an enthusiastic Sextus.

"For once legionary Postumus, the army was faster than the legionary rumour mill. Yes, I have heard the news." He stood. "But right now, I'm off to my cot."

Sextus spoke up.

"Given tomorrow's events, I'd better get your kit sharpened up, sir."

Lucius replied, "If I know Aurelius Crispus, there'll be a whole cohort getting its kit sharpened up tonight, ready for a grand entrance tomorrow. So at last, we can all get back to some regular soldiering, eh, Sextus?"

"That's as may be, sir," the dour soldier replied, "but my nose is twitching again."

218

Over the previous three days, Lucius had visited his contacts in Caesarea. He and the prefect spent additional time organising the facilities for the IV Cohort. Lucius enjoyed the normality that came with military business. However, he was also preparing for his removal into regular barracks.

Lucius expected to miss Marcus, but Sextus proved adept at getting things done. Sextus was much cheered by a note from the patient in Aelia, who was recovering well and hoping to be back to the V Cohort soon. Lucius had smiled when he heard the news, quipping that the way things appeared, the Fifth may be in Aelia before Marcus got back to Caesarea.

The V, IX and X Cohorts drilled furiously and held combat training. However, there were continuing reports of trouble in Judaea. To everyone's shock, the rebels were hammering the Fretensis, and a sense of foreboding lay across Caesarea. As a result, soldiers began to adopt a more serious tone, with talk of marching south to 'bang some Jewish heads together'.

Although rumours abounded, no one understood how the Jewish forces achieved such success; yet successful they were. Finally, however, Lucius thought *this is no longer my problem; I'll be back as an Optio of the IV Cohort.*

About the middle of the following day, Lucius was outside the walls of Caesarea, standing alongside several senior officers on the edge of the drill field. Beside the officers, a small podium was erected for the Tribune Civilis to address the IV Cohort upon its arrival. Lucius was grateful for Sextus' handiwork with his equipment, utilising the 'magic' cleaning fluid they had acquired in the vicus at Aelia. His Lorica positively gleamed in the brilliant sunlight, and he felt comfortably on a par with the senior officers. Behind the officers drawn out in several lines were two centuries of the V Cohort, acting as a ceremonial guard for the unfolding event.

What had initially appeared as a cloud of dust away to the north slowly transformed into an approaching body of soldiers moving south along the coast road towards the city. Caius Faustinas, the Camp Prefect, leant towards Lucius; smiling.

"Back to work very soon, I think, Optio."

"I shall not be sorry, sir," Lucius replied.

After a time, the soldiers marched onto the drill field, heading to the left of the officer group. The Legate ascended the few steps and stood on the podium, looking quite the part in his finest armour. The feathers on his helmet rippled gently in the slight breeze. At the head of the approaching column, four files wide, Lucius could make out his friend and mentor Aurelius Crispus, the senior centurion of the IV Cohort. His height placed him a head higher than many of his men; he was not one to be missed.

As the lead century drew close, the 2ndCentury pulled out from behind it and adopted a parallel path to its left. The 3rdCentury quickly did likewise to the second, a manoeuvre copied by the remaining three centuries. By the time they came to a standstill, drawn up in front of the Legate, all cohorts were aligned side-by-side. In front of each century stood the century's centurion and its *signifier*, who carried the unit's small identification flag on a pole, accompanied by the century's *tesserarius*, the administrative officer responsible for organising the watches and such military tasks as necessary. Each century's optio was found at the rear of the body. For a few seconds, there was absolute silence as the cohort stood in readiness.

Senior Centurion Crispus stepped forward and marched to Civilis, the Tribunus Laticlavius, waiting on his podium. Saluting very smartly, he said,

"IV Cohort, missing one officer, is yours to command, sir."

The tribune cast a glance at Lucius before announcing,

"I believe we should make the cohort entire, Centurion."

Without moving his head, Crispus glanced at Lucius. His voice boomed.

"Legionary Semellus. Step forward." The command's volume caused some in the officer group to visibly wince; Lucius could not suppress a smile, which the centurion did not miss. A soldier was visible from behind the 1st Century as he made his way to the front. As he passed the front of his unit and turned in the direction of the grouping at the centre, it became apparent that he carried a six-foot pole, topped with a small silver orb.

As the soldier approached, Lucius stepped forward to face him. Legionary Semellus came to a smart stop in front of his

Optio and held out the *hasti*, the Optio's badge of rank, for him to take. Lucius took the pole, and Semellus turned about and returned smartly to his file.

"Optio, take up your position," snapped Crispus, and turning to Legate added, "Establishment now complete, sir!"

Lucius shouldered his *hastile* and rejoined his century. As he marched to his position at the rear of the century, he received nods and smiles from his comrades. When he finally took up his place, a soldier in the rear rank was heard to whisper,

"Good holiday, sir?"

"If you need to break the silence, Legionary Domitius, I can arrange a few days of latrine duties!" responded Lucius. The only reaction was sniggering amongst the rear ranks.

"Men of the IV Cohort, I gladly welcome you into the body of the Tenth Legion. Expectations of you are high, for your creation was on the wish of Imperator Hadrianus. You will soon have every opportunity to prove yourself; your brothers based in Aelia Capitolina face a rebellion by Jewish insurgents that we will ruthlessly extinguish. You have good officers and have trained hard, and I know you will not let your brothers down." He paused, then punched his fist on his breastplate and then rose it to the sky, crying, "Hail Caesar!" To a man, the cohort mimicked his action, as did the watching officers, and a second 'Hail Caesar' thundered across the Campus Martius and over the walls of Caesarea.

Three hours later, having implemented the accommodation plans organised with Prefect Faustinas, Lucius sat with Crispus in the centurion's office. Crispus was nearing forty years old but looked not a day past thirty. His blue eyes and sandy hair added to his youthful appearance, albeit greying slightly. Add his height and physical build to this, and he made an impressive soldier. He was also very fair, a strict disciplinarian, and his soldiers loved him for it. He asked nothing of his men that he would not do himself, which was quite understandable given his role model was the divine Julius Caesar. He always carried a copy of Caesar's *De Bello Gallica* in his baggage.

Lucius had just completed a detailed recounting of his time in *Provincia Judaea*.

"This is a sorry state," Crispus said with a sigh. "It should never've come about. The tribune's suspicions have become fact, I fear. The Governor's been most unwise."

"I'm sure the Legate will brief you tomorrow," said Lucius, "but the IX, X and V cohorts are heading to Aelia very shortly. The fifth will collect the Governor and return him to Caesarea."

"If I am not wrong, that'll leave just the IV at Caesarea?" Crispus checked. Lucius nodded. "And what of Legio Sixth Ferrata up in Tel Shalem. What are they up to?"

"I understand they're on full alert," Lucius answered. "They haven't committed troops. After all, their patch is Galilee which is still quiet."

Crispus had many questions, not all of which Lucius could answer. They were deep in discussion about the Jewish rebels when Claudius Paullus, the 1st Century's *tesserarius,* joined them. He reported that the centuries were installed in barracks, and the baggage distributed as they spoke. Crispus invited him to sit and join him and Lucius. Lucius always thought Claudius looked like he should be running a taberna somewhere. He was short, slightly rotund and red-faced, not quite the image of the fearless Roman soldier. However, he could march as well as any of them and had a fine organisational mind, capable of many things at once! Crispus would not be without him.

"Good to have you back, Lucius," he said. "Crispus and I have got a surprise for you."

Lucius had a puzzled look.

"A surprise?"

"Well, you decide." Claudius rose and opened the door to the office. He called out.

"Legionary. Attend the centurion!"

A tall, dark soldier clad in a tunic, weapons, and helmet marched in and stood to attention. Lucius stared at the man – familiar, but then not – and then he sat bolt upright.

"By the Gods! Atelius! What in Jupiter's name are you doing.... a legionary?" He jumped up and offered his arm to the dark man, who took it, smiled and said,

"You see, Lucius – err – sir, I was not happy in Capua." In a short time, he had retold his tale, ending, "I feel I've been reborn."

"We've a first-class legionary here," butted in Claudius, "Only needs to be shown something once, and he's got it, eh, Atelius?"

"It's the standard of trainers we have here in the legion," quipped Atelius.

"Excuse me," Lucius said, "when it comes to training in combat, there's few to match this man." He nodded in Atelius' direction.

"As I well know," added Crispus, "and like a few others of our legionaries have found out during training!"

Lucius was still standing. He asked,

"You are the 1st Century?" asked Lucius.

"I am, sir. Centurion Crispus arranged it."

"Well, this is something I never expected. I thought the temple of Venus would fall before we met again, Atelius. I hope we can get back into regular sword practice again – indeed, I insist!"

The tall, dark legionary smiled, nodding his head,

"That is something I would look forward to, sir."

Crispus arose, followed closely by Claudius.

"We have business, Claudius. I suspect our Optio and the Legionary have some catching up to do, so let's get going." The two men left the office.

For the next hour, the two old friends shared their lives since they last parted, and the barrier between officer and legionary fell quickly away. Atelius' story, following his decision to join the legion, was one of hard work and sheer determination. It was the tale of a man adrift, with no goal and a great sense of loss before that decision. Lucius told of his initial time in the legions and how he was hand-picked by Crispus, not just for the IV Cohort, but for his century. However, he deliberately omitted some of the more recent details from his account.

Later that night, reflecting upon the day, Lucius detected what he thought may be the hand of fate. Joining his unit again, he had reconnected to his recent past. Now a further past thread, Atelius, had been woven into the tapestry. He had an uneasy feeling that matters were coming together, presaging who knows what.

Capitulum XIV – The end of a century

The end of a century

Legionary Felix Antonius gradually came to, regaining his senses. The first sensation was one of confusion; the last thing he remembered was marching along with his comrades, but now he was face down on a hard, dusty surface. No sooner had this sense flooded his brain, his body, particularly his left-hand side, howled out in pain. His eyes opened wide, and he looked into a dark, shadowy void. Antonius' befuddlement grew, and he groaned with the pain.

His mind took in what his eyes were relaying to it. A Legionary shield lay across him, though some light shone through a split in the middle of the shield. He gingerly moved his shield arm, which caused him to grimace with pain, but thankfully not the stabbing, piercing pain of a broken limb. Antonius deduced that his arm, though damaged, was functional. Gritting his teeth, he pulled the limb clear of the arm brace on the back of the shield. Split, the wooden device slipped off his body, both parts in a different direction.

Antonius viewed his local surroundings; only a few feet from where he lay sat a vast boulder. As he turned his head, he realised even his neck ached. He could see other boulders strewn on the crude roadway he and his comrades had been marching. Then it hit him that strewn amongst the boulders were the bodies of Roman soldiers. As he turned to look behind him, close by lay a Legionary, and it took him a moment to discern that the soldier's helmet was out of shape. He then understood the unlucky soldier's fate. Antonius cursed his century's bad luck to be marching along the roadway at the time of such a rockfall.

Antonius moved his legs, and though the pain may have been extreme, he had no broken bones. He deduced that a moving boulder must have struck him, but his shield saved him, explaining why the left-hand side of his body was so painful. He gradually rolled onto his backside and sat upright. His body complained, but the process worked. Now sitting upright, Antonius had a better view and could take in more of his surroundings. His head began to clear, and the observation capacity increased caused him to gasp. Rockfalls do not fire arrows! Arrows protruded from the bodies of the fallen soldiers. Antonius was witness to the aftermath of a planned ambush that destroyed his century. He began to realise that he was very fortunate to be alive, having been overlooked by the century's attackers.

Antonius' instinctive reaction, understanding the reality, was to reach for his gladius, and much to his relief, it was still in its scabbard. His pilum was nowhere to be seen. It seemed to Antonius that the best strategy would be to get clear of the area as soon as possible. It would involve getting onto his feet, which he knew would be painful – as might walking be – but he must stand. He took a deep breath, gritted his teeth and was shortly on his feet. As he arose, he pushed the remains of the shield to one side, making a scraping sound as it did so.

From behind Antonius came a not dissimilar scraping noise. Antonius swung round to face the sound, gladius in hand with all sense of pain forgotten. A few feet away ran a rainwater gully, dry and dusty. A large boulder sat bridging the ditch, and from underneath it, a dusty legionary began to extract himself. Antonius recognised the soldier.

"Octavius! In Hades' name, what the fuck happened?" Antonius was euphoric, knowing he was not alone.

"Jewish Cunni is what happened, brother. We was marching along when these bastards come rolling down the hillside at us," nodding towards the boulders, "We wasn't stopping them things with a shield; the column got badly knocked about. Then, still staggering from them rocks, they showered us with slingshot and arrows. The next thing we knows, hundreds of the bastards came down the hillside." Legionary Octavius Latius looked around at the scene of carnage. Latius continued. "I were plain lucky. I falls backwards into the ditch in the chaos with the bloody rock on top of me! Ditch saved me tho'. The cunni was careless and missed me under the rock. From what I could reckon, they appeared to be keen to collect weapons, an action that means we are still here, brother."

"So, what now then?" Antonius asked. 'What now' became a search for any other surviving legionaries. A quest that sadly bore no fruit. Falling rocks, slingshots and arrows had dealt death, with more slain by the sword and spear. It had not all been one-sided; the two soldiers found several blood trails leading back up the hillside; the Jews extracted their dead and wounded. However, the sad fact was that Antonius and Latius were the only survivors of a century of almost eighty soldiers.

There were some positives from the dreadful task. The two soldiers came across skins of water and bags of bread, cheese and some meats. The water was most welcome, but appetite, they had none. However, they realised they would need food on the march back to their base. Antonius hoped that getting his body in regular motion would help ease some of the pain he was experiencing. He also understood it was crucial they left the area as soon as possible; pain or no pain.

"I can promise you one thing, Octavius," he said, "if we get back alive, I'll most certainly sacrifice a beast to Mithras – maybe two of the fuckers!"

"That'll be a good day for Mithras, brother, because I'll be with you – but two? Don't want to be too generous!"

Capitulum XV – Death in the vicus

4 Aprilis. Year 16 of the Imperator Hadrianus

Marcus Apollinaris wandered past Aelia's drill field, enjoying the warmth of the sun on his back. The area was full of drilling soldiers, encouraged by loud centurions bellowing orders and waving their vine sticks. The past few days had seen Marcus confined to the small infirmary that served Aelia's sick and injured, so he found the fresh air and sunlight reviving. However, he was limited to light duties as his stomach, though healing well, needed some respite from heavy use. Physically, Marcus felt pleased to be up and about. Mentally, though, it was somewhat different.

Marcus was a worried man. His physical recovery was not the only reason to be released from the infirmary; the infirmary was overflowing with wounded and dying soldiers. Marcus believed himself to be part of the finest fighting organisation the world had seen, yet the wounded kept arriving. Those he spoke to talked of ambushes, skirmishes, and night attacks where the roman soldier was coming off worst. These, thought Marcus, were the survivors – many never made it back to their bases. Moreover, these events seemed to be happening across the region surrounding Aelia Capitolina. Marcus was beginning to believe that the army was being beaten, a thought that would be hitherto unthinkable.

Marcus decided that his best course of action was to return to his unit at Caesarea as quickly as possible. It seemed the road north was still functioning, and his orders stated as soon as he was fit to travel, he should report back. Well, he considered himself capable of travel. It was thinking of Caesarea that brought Miriam into his mind. During his time in the infirmary, he wondered how the Jewish Christian girl was faring. It took only seconds before he decided he would visit the taberna where she was staying; perhaps she would like to head north with him to her relative in Caesarea.

He visited his quarters for a change of tunic. Off duty or not, given his recent experiences, he kept his gladius with him. As he passed through the North Gate heading towards the vicus, he noticed a gate guard with his arm wrapped in a bandage.

"Been in the wars, brother?" Marcus asked the bored-looking soldier.

"Two days ago, coming in from Bet Shehan with provisions. Forty of the pricks hit us. We drove 'em off, but they're fucking lunatics!" he gestured to his arm, "Got this from a spear. Luckily, not too bad; it didn't get me off duty."

"Me, I've just spent days in the infirmary. They had a go in the vicus for Jupiter's sake."

"That was you, was it? We heard about it. Bastards. Something is not good here, brother."

"You may be right. I am off for a drink. Take care, brother."

So, Marcus was not alone in his concern. He walked the short distance along the road to reach the vicus. It was its usual self, a hubbub of activity with folk coming and going, many of them like Marcus, off-duty soldiers. But, as was ever the case, it was the smells that Marcus related with the vicus. The aroma of different foods, of leather, forge fires and the fuller's barrels, to name but a few of the many odours assailing him. Before he knew it, he was outside the Neptune. He pulled his tunic straight and adjusted his sword belt before entering the relative darkness of the taberna. His sight slowly adjusted.

"'ello darlin'," a voice addressed him from one corner of the bar. Marcus turned,

"Well, well, a sight for sore eyes! How are you, girl?"

"I'm alright, lovey, but how is our hero?" Anaitis asked. Marcus gave her a quick rundown of his time in the infirmary. "Well, that's fine, but what happened to the little bugger that did it to you? So we never heard no more?"

"I expect he got what was coming to 'im." He ran his forefinger across his throat. "I thought I'd drop in on Miriam."

"She'll be holding court outside." She nodded towards the rear exit from the inn that led into a large enclosed courtyard, popular with most drinkers. "You may 'ave to join the queue, though." Intrigued, Marcus went through the door into the bright sunshine. He was taken aback at the sight that befell his eyes.

Miriam bat Yahalom was seated at a broad table, her baskets holding herbs before her. A mortise and pestle sat on the table, as did several roles of cloth and a large bowl of water. At the side of the table, three bandaged soldiers stood waiting for her attention. A fourth soldier stood with one foot on the bench beside Miriam as she dressed a slight wound on his thigh. Marcus stood, fascinated; she seemed so confident in what she was doing, and the soldiers seemed to hold her in some awe.

She had not noticed Marcus as he moved into the corner of the yard, shadowed by the spreading arms of a cedar tree. Deftly, she dressed the soldier's thigh wound, the arms of the second and third soldier and a cut across the side of the fourth soldier's neck. Each soldier leaving the courtyard was effusive with their thanks, tossing small coins into a bowl. When they left, Miriam reorganised her table and sat back, taking a drink of water from a goblet. It was then she spotted the fifth soldier standing alone in the shade.

"Come legionary, how do I help, please?" Compared to when they first met, her Greek was improving. He stepped forward. A huge smile spread across Miriam's face.

"Marcus! You are well, yes?" Dark locks fell out of the sides of the headscarf she wore. With her dark eyes and full lips, Marcus had entirely forgotten how attractive she was.

"Yes – yes, I'm much better, lady. Light duties only for a while, but it's good to be out of the infirmary. How're you faring?" A female voice answered the question from behind.

"She helped a legionary whose wound was going rotten – an overnight cure it was, an' she has not been idle since!" Anaitis joined the couple in the yard. "She won't take no money and the tips they leaves, she spends on bandages and powders. Told 'er, she's bonkers!"

Miriam laughed,

"I do as Yeshua wish, Anaitis, you know." Then, her face grew serious, "Tell me, Marcus, your injury good, yes?"

"I've been better, lady, but it could have been so much worse."

Anaitis returned to the taberna, closing the door behind her so the two friends could have some privacy to catch up. Marcus' tale was dull, having been trapped in the infirmary for days, but Miriam's was very different.

One evening, a soldier arrived with his tent mates to drink at the tavern. It was not a joyous occasion; one soldier suffered a severely infected arm. The soldier did not look well; he and his tent-mates had come to drink his arm farewell. The medicus had declared it must come off before it gets any worse. They informed Anaitis of the event, who mentioned it to Miriam. Miriam persuaded the poorly soldier to let her apply a poultice. He had nothing to lose. Miriam had soothed the angry arm by the following day, and the soldier received a stay of execution. He would return for a new poultice each day. His career was saved, the 'healer woman' legend was born. Anaitis screwed up her nose.

"Some revolting concoction of herbs and fungus," she said, "yet it saved his arm. Would you believe it, Marcus?" The soldier nodded. "Now soldiers come every day. Still, they buy a beer or a wine, so Agenor is pleased!"

Marcus smiled inwardly; a soldier would much rather have a good-looking young lady wrap bandages around his thigh than some battle-scarred medicus at the fort. But it couldn't be denied, she had applied a cure that probably saved one of his brother's life. Since the outbreak of regular violence, business was brisk. An hour must have passed when Miriam suggested they go for a walk. There was a while left of good light, and she needed to refresh her stock of herbs. She knew just the place amongst the ruins beyond the vicus. As they left the Taberna, Miriam told Anaitis what they were about.

"Nice to meet again, Marcus," she said with a smile. By then, they were out on the street, carrying her large baskets to bring the crop home. Several hundred paces away from the vicus were the ruins of what had been a sumptuous residence that must have boasted a large walled garden. All that remained of the residence were blocks of stone and rubble. Much of what was the garden lay covered in strewn rocks. However, hardy herbs had taken hold over the years – initially planted in an orderly manner by a careful gardener – and now they grew wild and free across the area.

The soldier and the healer began to harvest the herbs. The healer was clearly in charge, directing the soldier what to gather and what not to gather, for some of these herbs could be damaging. After some time, the light began to weaken, and they both stopped collecting, baskets overflowing. Miriam removed a small skin from one of her baskets and offered Marcus a drink.

"You know," he said, "I reckon when I leave the legions, I will take up farming – that was very satisfying."

"Farming more than cutting, Marcus," Miriam responded. "You bend much. How is wound?"

"Aches a bit, but no more'n that."

"We go back taberna, I look at for you."

"There's no need, lady, really there isn't. But, talking of going back…," he looked around him, "the light is fading fast. Manoeuvring among these rocks is tricky in the daytime, let alone dusk. So we should get going."

"We shall -," A commotion in the distance interrupted the conversation; it was coming from the direction of the vicus. Miriam looked at Marcus,

"Marcus. What sound is that?" The volume of the commotion began to rise.

"You tell me, lady - but I don't likes it!" The noise became louder, pierced by screams and shouts, the source of which now appeared to emanate from the edge of the vicus closest to them. Marcus' instinct cut in.

"Get down," he barked at Miriam as he pushed her to the ground. He fell to the ground with her, and they crawled behind two large blocks of stone. "Stay still and remain quiet." He came to his knees and pushed himself up to see over the top of the large block. Flowing around the side of the vicus opposite him was a large body of armed men. He had seen their ilk before when they ambushed the waggons heading for Aelia Capitolina. He dropped back to the ground.

"An attack. Jewish rebels," Marcus hissed. "We must stay hidden, lady." Miriam nodded; there was fear in her eyes. The cacophony of noise from the vicus continued. Marcus knew only too well what was happening, though he wondered where the legionaries were. He looked at Miriam shaking beside him. "It'll be over soon, lady. Believe me." And so, they waited.

They never saw the two rebels almost upon them until it was too late. They were big men, but the fading light hid their details. Marcus could see they were armed with swords and shields. His brain started to process the situation and consider an escape route. Miriam stared, petrified, then she began to whisper a prayer. Marcus had made the mistake of placing his gladius in a basket as it kept getting in his way,

collecting herbs. His mind frantically thought out a plan; we will look like civilians in this light with no visible sword.

"Well, well, well. What've we got here?" sneered the man nearest to Marcus.

"For the god's sake, get down," Marcus replied, "The Romans are coming." He pointed in the direction opposite to the vicus. The two soldiers instinctively dropped to one knee and looked in the opposite direction to the two would-be fugitives. Then, unseen in the dusk, Marcus slipped his hand into the herb basket and withdrew his gladius from its scabbard.

"I don't see any accursed Romans. What are you..." Marcus leapt at the man. As he plunged the sword into the rebel's gut, he experienced excruciating pain in his abdomen. The fallen rebel's colleague, briefly taken aback, recovered swiftly. Marcus faced him, his midriff screaming in protest.

"You Roman cunt!" shouted the remaining rebel and approached Marcus. He was a big man, and Marcus presumed a strong one too; Marcus' defence would be paltry against such a physique given his state. The rebel continued, "Gutting you'll be a pleasure, short-arse, an extreme pleasure." He moved towards Marcus, who retreated but came up hard against the blocks he and Miriam had been sheltering behind.

"I'm sorry, lady, this didn't work out," Marcus muttered into the now falling darkness where the girl lay. His stomach was throbbing, and it hurt to lift his sword into a defensive stance.

The rebel raised his sword for the killing blow. To one side of the rebel's head, a silhouette of an arm appeared, the fist gripping a rounded object. The arm whipped across, and Marcus heard the *thump* as the 'object' hit the head. The rebel did not fall to Marcus' amazement but stood frozen on the spot. Marcus gritted his teeth, screamed, and thrust his gladius into the chest of the warrior. The man sagged down onto his knees, and Marcus pushed him backwards, pulling his sword free.

The body fell at Miriam's feet. She stood rooted to the spot, shaking uncontrollably, staring at the dead rebel. Marcus stared at her for a few seconds – she'd saved his life; there was no doubt about that. Then the noise from the vicus intruded, and he remembered just how precarious their situation was. At the same time, his old wound was vigorously complaining. He wiped his sword on the dead man's tunic and returned it to its scabbard before putting a hand on each of Miriam's shoulders.

"Lady, you saved both our lives. If it were not for you, that would be us bleeding out on the ground. I could not have done it on my own."

Miriam's teeth chattered as she shook; she looked to the fallen Jews and spoke in a whisper.

"You…shall…not…kill."

Marcus held her in a firm grip.

"Look at me, lady, look at my eyes," he said, giving her a mild shake. "You didn't kill anyone. That was me done it, but what we done was save life. Two live, one dies. It could've been two die and one lives. We had no choice. Alright?" Miriam started to take deep breaths, and the shaking receded. "That's better. Now, we have to get out of here, and quick about it too!"

Just as he spoke, a horn sounded in the distance. Then, three blasts resonated across the area: an unambiguous, intentional signal.

"A cornicen! About bloody time, the lads are coming!" No sooner had Marcus stopped speaking than a second horn, this time a much higher pitched sound, transmitted its signal. Marcus went to peer over the blocks they had sheltered behind. Two sights struck him. The first was burning buildings; the vicus was on fire. The second were the dark, fleeting shapes swiftly pulling back from the vicus and retreating into the distance. "They're bloody legging it! They're pulling back!"

When Marcus turned back to Miriam, she held the two baskets of herbs that had survived the whole ordeal. Her countenance had changed.

"Marcus, I needed. Peoples hurt. We must go."

"Hades' fire, Lady, you're a strange one. Let's head back, but it won't be pretty, let me warn you."

The failing light, assisted by the rough ground covered in blocks from the old Jerusalem, slowed their progress. As they closed upon the vicus, the flames from the several burning buildings lit their way. As they joined the roadway that led into the settlement, Marcus could hear the shouted commands from the arriving Roman legionaries. However, the burning buildings were only a portent of what was to come. When they turned onto the main thoroughfare of the place, the road was littered with dark mounds that Marcus knew to be bodies. Milling around the bodies were freshly arrived legionaries; others had gone in pursuit of the fleeing Judaean rebels. Yet others were scrambling to find water to extinguish the flames.

As they moved onto the street and toward the Neptune, a voice called out from behind them.

"Stand where you are. Do not move!" It was a voice you did not argue with. "What's your business?"

Marcus turned to face a sergeant and three legionaries, all looking like they meant business. A grin spread across Marcus' face.

"I guess better late than never, Tesserarius Tetricus?" he said. The officer stared at Marcus, who identified himself, "Legionary Apollinaris, V Cohort. The ambush south of Gophna?"

"Well, well, Apollinaris. You seem fond of a scrap then?" he nodded towards Miriam, "and who is your lady friend then?" The word 'lady' was laden with sarcasm and suggestion. Before Marcus could reply, one of Tetricus' legionaries spoke up,

"I knows 'er sarge. She's that healer woman the lads were talking about."

"She has family at the Neptune," said Marcus. "It is just down the road."

"I know it," Tetricus replied. "Come on; it might be easier if we took you. It may not be a pleasant visit, even if it has missed being torched."

The small group made their way along the road, stepping around bodies and avoiding marching groups of soldiers. Though not all buildings were on fire, the smoke and heat became all-pervasive as they walked. By the time they reached the Neptune, eyes were watering, and their throats were dry. The discomfort was forgotten at the joy of seeing the building intact. Tetricus had orders to carry out, and Marcus and Miriam found themselves alone at the entrance to the taberna.

"Let me go in first," Marcus suggested, drawing his gladius. The rebels were long gone, but he was not taking any risks. He entered the building. One small oil lamp burned, casting a dull yellow glow across the main drinking area. There were bodies; Marcus counted five. Beside the lamp was a taper, and Marcus spent a minute lighting other lights that sat on small shelves about the room.

Three dead lay on the floor and two across a table, all attended by the dark shadows of spilt blood. Marcus detected a sixth body lying on the staircase that led upstairs to sleeping quarters. It was one of Anaitis' girls. Sprawled headfirst on her back, exposed to the waist and with her throat cut. Her blood ran down the steps and pooled on the floor. A noise caught Marcus' attention; he turned to see Miriam staring at the slaughter in the entrance. Then a loud moan broke the silence. Marcus rushed to the side of the bar where the landlord of the taberna lay hidden by an overturned table.

He lay on his back, his clothing appearing a shiny black in the yellow light of the oil lamps. Ignoring his complaining stomach, Marcus knelt beside him. His eyes were open. He attempted to speak, but what sound he made was unintelligible. Then, turning to Miriam, Marcus called her to him. She gasped as she recognised the victim, quickly understanding they could not save his life. She knelt beside him, her clothing became stained with blood, and she held his hand.

"Dear God", she spoke in Aramaic, "he was not one of us, but he was a good man who wished no ill of anyone. So I beg you, in Yeshua's name, to look kindly upon his spirit and close your arms around him." Tears ran down her cheeks. Marcus' Aramaic was enough for him to understand.

"I'm sure he will hear you," he said, seeking to comfort her. Miriam nodded then spoke straight to the dying man.

"Agenor, where is Anaitis? Where is she? She's not here."

Agenor' eyes flickered, and with a free hand, he moved a finger to make a weak pointing gesture. Miriam and Marcus looked to where he was pointing. It was the room's bar area, just a few feet away. Marcus looked back to Miriam, but she shrugged, so Marcus stood up and went to the bar. There was no sign of a body. He was about to turn back when he spotted a large cupboard at the end of the bar that ran under the counter. Several plates and bowls lay scattered on the floor, some broken, along with various utensils and flasks. Marcus walked to the bar's end and swept the debris away with his foot. Then, he reached down and opened the cupboard door.

She was a young woman, sitting with her knees pulled up to her chest and hands covering her ears, only just fitting into the confined space. She emitted a piercing scream. He had found Anaitis. Marcus and Miriam had the petrified girl out of the cupboard and sitting on a bench within a moment. She was too terrified to notice Agenor's body on the floor. Miriam had her arms around her and was trying desperately to soothe her. Anaitis rocked back and forth, staring at the floor and began to sob; deep sobs racked her body. Marcus caught Miriam's eye; she responded by nodding him away. He understood that a Roman legionary did not have the aptitude to calm distressed females.

Marcus checked out the rest of the taberna. There being no other bodies, he presumed the other occupants must have fled at the time of the attack. As he came back down the stairs, sidestepping the body of the young girl, the door to the taberna opened. Tetricus stood in the doorway, assessing the scene. He spotted the two women, and with a level of sensitivity that surprised Marcus, he spoke in a soft voice.

"Teams are collecting the dead, and I have two lads outside ready to clear this out," he nodded to the bodies. "They'll be cremated or buried in the morning."

Marcus pointed towards Agenor's body.

"That one is one of ours, tesserarius, an ex-marine."

"Right, I'll see that the lads know. We are separating our people from the others. Ours will get full military rights." He paused and looked across at the two women. "I'll give you a few minutes. Best you get them away before we come in and start hauling the corpses out, don't you think?"

Marcus agreed, and after Tetricus stepped out, he approached the women, suggesting to Miriam that she get Anaitis upstairs and to bed. When he had been lighting the lamps, he had spotted a large pot over the dying fire. He suggested bringing Anaitis a bowl of broth, still warm, to help her sleep. It was something his mother used to do for him when he was young and upset – it usually worked. After Marcus had prudently moved the corpse on the stairs within a few moments, Miriam helped the distraught girl towards her bedroom. Marcus filled a bowl with broth and ascended the stairs when Tetricus returned, accompanied by two civilians carrying a long wooden board between them. He motioned Marcus to proceed as the men approached the first body for removal; this was their job, not his.

A few minutes later, he returned downstairs to see the two men removing the last body: Agenor.

"I'll see he gets a proper funeral," said Tetricus. "This whole situation is going tits up. Why didn't we see this coming?" Marcus shrugged in response.

"My officer saw it was coming, Tess', but no one listened. Time and again, he said something's wrong – even the centurions refused to hear."

"They'll bloody listen now – we've lost so many men and now this. It's death by a thousand cuts. If we're to protect what's left of this place," Tetricus looked around over his shoulders, "as well as Aelia, we'll be thinly spread."

"Can't call in men from the outposts? There are auxiliaries too, surely?"

"Well now, officially, I'm not told much, but I've heard they're all knocked about. We haven't had a messenger from En Geddi for two days. I tell you, Apollinaris, this is a screw up of Jovian fucking magnitude!"

"There's little you or I can do to affect it, Tess', except clean up the mess." Marcus changed tack, "I'd like to remain here tonight, Tesserarius. I'm on light duties as it is, so I'll check in tomorrow morning."

"Don't see an issue with that soldier. I'll let the watch know I've granted permission. There'll be patrols here from now on, so you won't be alone. Any hint of trouble, get out. Sleep well."

Tetricus' news was disturbing to Marcus. It appeared the Roman authority in Judaea was collapsing. He found it hard to believe the bandits were bettering Roman arms. Nevertheless, it passed through his mind that the best plan was to get back to Caesarea in short order. While he contemplated possible means of doing so, Miriam returned from settling Anaitis for a night's sleep. She was dreading what nightmares the girl would have.

Quickly she settled beside Marcus and placed two beakers of wine on the table.

"We work hard for this," she said. Marcus smiled; her Greek was getting better but not all the way there yet. "And when drink, we have broth."

Marcus lifted his beaker to drink,

"Here's to a few days of calm, Lady." Miriam lifted her beaker and paused,

"Marcus, I thank you for my life. Soldier have killed me if you did not him kill."

Marcus sampled his wine and placed the beaker down.

"Miriam, if you had not stunned him like you did, he would have killed me first and then you. So, you have saved *my* life." He laughed, "Let us be grateful that we are both alive!"

"Yeshua not want me dead; he guide your hand."

"Then let me drink to Yeshua's health," Marcus replied before downing his wine in one gulp.

Capitulum XVI – Panic in Aelia

5 Aprilis. Year 16 of the Imperator Hadrianus

The sun shone as Marcus walked from the vicus towards the camp's main gate. On a piece of ground behind the vicus, smoke arose from the funeral pyres of the slain Romans from the previous attack. In addition, 'civilian' burials and cremations were taking place.

Before leaving the Neptune, Miriam had dressed Marcus' wound. Fortunately, his injury appeared to be recovering well, for all the pain he felt when he fought the rebel. He had been given firm instructions to take good care of himself. As he was leaving, Anaitis appeared. She was drawn and her spirit low but was trying hard to achieve a sense of normality.

It occurred to Marcus that this was the first time he had been this close to the impact of war upon civilians. Whilst the attack on the vicus was little more than a large raid, it was a life-changing experience for many survivors.

Approaching the gate, he witnessed a high level of comings and goings; along with the usual traders and off-duty military, he noted many better-dressed people passing through. The closer he came; he could hear the rumbling of a multitude inside. Arriving at the gate, he strolled up to one of the sentries.

"What's going on, brother?"

"Panic, brother, they've all gone crazy! It seems the citizens are terrified that Aelia will be next on the rebel's list."

"We'll never get 'em all inside the fort!" exclaimed Marcus.

"Not my problem, brother," shrugged the sentry, "I leave that sort of *cac* to the tribune."

Marcus entered the fort. There were hundreds of people milling around. Military officers were mingling with them, trying to apply reason and logic, but the sense of panic was palpable. It was a situation that appeared to be spiralling out of control.

He pushed past clusters of concerned, frightened residents, heading towards the Watch Office to check back into the fort. The Watch Officer informed him that he had a few minutes to don his uniform and report to the Camp Prefect's office. In his case, it appeared that 'light duty' means desk work involved in the mass of administration that goes with running a Roman Fort. Marcus shrugged, thinking that it beat the drill field hands down.

Cassius Cornelius was a wealthy man, an owner of a villa on the Capitoline Hill in Rome. A few months back, he left Rome to visit many of his business ventures across the Empire. An Equestrian of the highest order, he has more than a passing acquaintance with the Imperator and a good relationship with at least half of the Senate. His wish to curry favour with Hadrianus brought him to Aelia Capitolina, assisted by his factor, to set up a trading venture in the nascent colony. Cassius knew of Hadrianus' enthusiasm for the colony to grow into a city. If Cassius invested in that objective, it would pay healthy dividends.

This morning he had been rudely awakened by a visit from several more worthy – or perhaps wealthier – residents of the colony. Judaean rebels had attacked the vicus, burning down important buildings and slaughtering the "collaborators". Cassius invited them to join him for breakfast; they wished to see the governor, who fortunately was in the camp, and demand protection. Were they not Roman citizens? Was it not their due? Citizens, they may be, thought Cassius, but some of his breakfast guests were Jewish and knew only too well what their fate would be if they fell into the rebel's hands. Against his better judgement, Cassius volunteered to go directly to the governor's office and ask for an audience. Having seen his guests out of the door, he interrogated his servants. To his dismay, it seemed the nervous guests were accurate in their account of the previous night. An inkling of concern crept into Cassius' mind.

Later that same morning, Cassius Cornelius entered the governor's office in the principia. Tineus Rufus, the governor, was at his desk when a clerk announced the arrival of the equestrian from Rome. Rufus stood.

"Cassius. It has been too long. When did you arrive?" Rufus took in his old acquaintance. Tall, slim with the look of an aristocrat; The classic Roman nose, the salt and pepper hair and the countenance. It could be mistaken for arrogance, but Cassius was socially skilled. Today he was playing the wealthy equestrian.

"Three days ago. I didn't bother you as you have your hands full," Cassius replied. Rufus pointed to a chair, and the two men sat facing each other across the governor's large desk. The conversation began with a catch up on the situation in Rome, mutual acquaintances, and the discussion rambled for a few minutes. Rufus then moved back to the matters in hand.

"All excellent, Cassius, but I feel this is more than a social call."

A servant placed glasses of honied water in front of the two men. Cassius lifted his glass, sipped the contents, and returned it to the table with deliberation before recounting the early morning visitation from the 'worthies' of Aelia Capitolina.

"In many respects, Tineus, they are no different from me. We are investing in this place as the Imperator would wish, and they, like me, are concerned."

He did not tell the governor that he met with a centurion who happened to be the brother of one of Cassius' main business partners back in Rome on his way to the camp. The picture that he had painted was worrying, to say the least. To Cassius, who had served in the legions as a legate years ago, the situation was precarious.

"We are getting on top of it, Cassius. Yes, we were caught unprepared, but we'll soon have a grip on matters."

"Tineus. Last night the rebels came damned close to destroying the vicus. I am told they destroyed anything of military utility. So, you can understand the worry that the people of the colony feel?"

"Of course, of course, I do," Rufus replied, "and we shall reassure them."

"Aelia needs a permanent guard unit, Tineus. The citizens believe they will be the next target of the rebels. Are you able to spare some cohorts? The people need to see action; they're in a state of near panic."

"I'll see who can be spared. It may not be several cohorts. We're having a tough time with these Jews."

"Can't you pull reinforcements down from Galilee? The Sixth Legion is but a few days away."

Rufus shook his head.

"How can I, when I am not sure if trouble may break out in the North?"

There came a knock on the door, and a clerk stepped in.

"The Primus Pilus to see you, sir." He said.

"Damn!" Rufus sighed, "I'd forgotten we were to meet this morning," he said to Cassius. Then, turning back to the clerk, he asked him to show the soldier in. The Primus marched in and stood to attention.

"Please sit down, Quintus. Now, have you met Cassius Cornelius? An old acquaintance and an Equestrian from Rome. Cassius, this is Quintus Vorenus, Primus Pilum of the Tenth."

"My pleasure, sir." Vorenus smiled as he said, "I'll bet you wish you were back in Rome!"

Cassius laughed.

"It's good to meet our senior centurion. I trust we'll be safe in your hands?"

"Quintus, can you give Cassius your view?" asked Rufus. The centurion gave the governor a raised eyebrow. "You may be frank, Quintus."

"Right, sir. It's a fuck-up, sir. We'd have reports of trouble, and we'd send a century or two out to sort it like we always have. We get to the source of trouble, expecting the usual handful of bandits, only to find bloody hundreds of them. Other times, we get there, and they're gone. Then, on the return journey, they ambush us. We've lost a lot of men that way, sir." He paused, nodding his head as if to confirm his last statement. "Well, we got wise and moved in bigger units. They hit us from the hillsides with slings and arrows, then pull back and disappear. Other times, after pelting us, they attack in the hundreds before pulling back and disappearing again. It's hard to give chase up those hillsides in our kit!"

"Sounds familiar, centurion," responded Cassius, "Similar tactics to those used by Fabius Maximus; he drove Hannibal mad with his hit-and-run approach. It can wear the opponent ragged. Enough of tactics, though. What do you think their strategy is?"

"You won't like it, sir." Quintus paused, took a deep breath and sighed. "I'm certain we're in trouble, sir, big trouble. I've never seen this before. It's been planned, and it's been coordinated. They have the weapons. They've trained well. We ain't up against simple mountain bandits. Don't ask how they did it, but we missed this coming. We're facing a serious revolt."

There was silence in the room. Cassius spoke first.

"I wondered, centurion. Attacking a vicus outside a Roman fortress is utter folly or the mark of a very confident commander. Do we know who is behind this, Tinius?"

"Assuredly? No. But there's a bandit leader we'd like to know more of; one Simeon ben Koseba. His name has cropped up in several interrogations, but we know little about him, except that some of his men call him 'the Big One'."

"It would be good to know more about the man and quite what he wants from all of this. I am assuming you are making Rome aware of what is happening?" Cassius stood, "Centurion, Tinius: You are due to have a meeting, so I'll get out of your way." Cassius turned explicitly to the governor. "So, I tell the citizens of Aelia that they will get legionaries to protect the town?"

The centurion also turned to the governor with a quizzical look on his face.

"Can we manage that?" Rufus asked him.

"It's possible, but it will impact on our capability to mount as many external patrols – it could limit our intelligence of what the rebels are up to out there."

"Can I remind you that Aelia Capitolina is one of the Imperator's favoured projects," Cassius interjected.

Rufus conceded.

"Do the best you can, Quintus."

Resigned to doing a lot with an ever-dwindling resource, the centurion nodded. He had a horrible feeling about this.

Thankfully the following week was quiet. Marcus spent his time as a clerk with his wound recovering well. He spent most evenings at the 'Neptune', where Miriam had restarted her medical practice. With Miriam being busy, Marcus spent some time with Anaitis. They talked, and as they did, the withdrawn, shocked girl began to come out of the mental shell she used as a retreat. She told him how Agenor shielded her as the rebels invaded the inn, giving her a few seconds to hide, fearing discovery and unpleasant death, but it never came. Staff and customers begged for mercy, screaming as they died. The greatest horror was listening as her good friend was being raped. Anaitis thought the girl had broken free, for she heard footsteps on the stairs, but a scream and then silence followed them. She knew yet another friend was dead. Between sentences, tears rolled down her cheeks. Marcus did his best to encourage her to look forward, to rejoice that she still lived and was safe. This was new territory for the soldier.

The panic in Aelia calmed down, and life seemed to return to normal superficially. True to his word, the Primus allocated a cohort to Aelia's protection. People felt assured to see shields and spears patrolling the perimeter. However, it was not business as usual because much of the produce that came into the town no longer did so. The Judaean countryside seemed to have closed. The rumour mill said that the size of the rebel army was such that it was consuming all the local produce. Even so, people relaxed. They may face rebels, but the Roman Army protects them!

Calm appeared across the region of Judaea. Primus Pilus Vorenus welcomed this; it gave him time to reorganise his sadly depleted forces. However, along with several of his centurions, he was nervous. What exactly was going on out in the hills of Judaea? Why this cessation of activity? The last messenger from Caesarea gave word that two, possibly three, cohorts would march south. In addition, the new IV Cohort – the Roman cohort – had arrived. Vorenus felt his resources were being severely stretched, guarding the fort, and patrolling and garrisoning Aelia. He would welcome some reinforcements.

During the week, Cassius Cornelius wrote a letter. It went to Rome, and the content spoke frankly about the situation in Aelia and Aelia. Cassius had spent time as an officer in the legions fighting in the Empire's heart as a younger man. He knew of Hadrian's concern about the Tenth Legion. Whilst they trained regularly, their genuine real combat experience was minimal. This fact may not be a big problem when policing a province and chasing bandits, but this situation was different; they were facing what seemed a determined enemy in large numbers. Cassius also tried to make arrangements to return to Damascus – or Rome – and became anxious when warned by the military that travels in the countryside was considered unsafe. "Are we under siege?" he demanded. The reply; "Your words, not mine, sir."

Cassius sat in the atrium of his rented villa in Aelia with his factor from Damascus.

"Well, Atticus, seven days and no reports of attacks or fighting of any kind. Maybe they have thought better of taking on the might of Rome?"

The Greek smiled. He was middle-aged with the look of a favourite grandfather—a deception he used with devastating effect in his business deals.

"I pray to the gods you're right, my friend. Who can tell what is in the minds of these crazy people? They seem to love arguing and fighting! Let's just hope all remains still for a few days longer."

Atticus' wish - and prayers - were to be denied.

Marcus Apollinaris was sleeping soundly on a bed in the 'Neptune'. He had a day off before returning to full military duty, and he was going to enjoy his day, starting with a late rising. His plans fell apart as soon as Anaitis burst into his room. She shook him awake. Marcus realised she was trembling and very frightened. To his surprise, she threw herself on him and hugged him close.

"It's beginning again, Marcus; it's coming back!" She started to sob. Marcus held her for a few seconds before gently pushing her back so he could look into her face.

"What's beginning, Anaitis? What's 'appened?"

Between sobs, she related what she had picked up on the street. A raid on Aelia – dozens slaughtered - families massacred – Jews expelled – no help from the army. Marcus moved her to one side and swung out of bed, not the least embarrassed being dressed only in loincloth and bandage.

"What you've heard is likely exaggerated, Anaitis, but let's find out what's 'appened, shall we?" he said, reaching for his tunic. As he put it on, Miriam appeared at the door. She took in the scene.

"Anaitis, it be fine. They will no more come – they done their worst." Turning to Marcus, by now donning his heavy studded military sandals, she said, "Not good for Aelia, Marcus. Many dead. Many Jews. Why not the soldiers to stop them?"

"Damned if I know, lady," he replied, "but I'd better be getting back to the fort. Take care of Anaitis. She's had enough of these doings!"

Anaitis stood facing Miriam.

"I'll be alright – really, I will. I'm sorry." She turned to Marcus. "Please, be careful, Marcus."

"Look *meum mel*. I'm a bloody soldier; 'careful' does not come into it!" Then he smiled, "I'll be back. Count on it." At which point he disappeared through the doorway.

Not much after, Legionary Apollinaris reported to the main office. Until returning to Caesarea, he was to be attached to the VI Cohort under Centurion Petronius. Jupiter, he thought, from one Petronius to another! The clerks could not understand why he burst out laughing. He quickly moved to his accommodation in the barracks and attired himself in full legionary uniform, collecting his shield and pilum before locating the VI Cohort. He found the cohort forming up on the drill field. One look at the men mustered there told him they were short-handed. He reported to the centurion. Julius Petronius looked Marcus up and down.

"Well, Apollinaris, you don't put the fear of Jove in me, but the beggars can't be choosers, eh? Still, if you are one of Gallianus' Fifth, you can't be too bad. You'll be in my century, fall in."

Marcus saluted and turned to take his place with the men of the 1st Century.

"Apollinaris, stand where you are!"

Marcus froze.

"I knew your short arse was familiar, soldier. You came down here with Optio Petronius of the Fourth, did you not?"

"Yes, sir!"

"Got ambushed?"

"Yes, sir!"

"In that case, you may be of some use after all. Get fell in – quickly!"

After some thought, Marcus decided that he had just received a compliment. And so began Marcus' time with the VI Cohort.

Cassius was dining with the Imperator, discussing the state of the roads across the Empire. Hadrianus was talking about building new and better roads when there came a terrifying scream from the kitchen area of the palace. The second scream awoke Cassius, taking him from the Imperator's palace back to his rented villa in Aelia Capitolina. In a second, he knew something was wrong. He swung his legs out of bed and shouted for his servant, who stumbled into his sleeping chamber a few seconds later. Cassius despatched the man to determine the cause of the commotion. Meanwhile, Cassius dressed, taking care to strap on his belt and gladius. His manservant rushed into the room as he finished dressing, severely agitated.

"Domine, it is terrible. They are dead!"

"In Jupiter's name, who is dead?"

"Your neighbours Domine. In the villa, all dead."

At this point, Atticus appeared in the doorway, fully dressed.

"Cassius, what is going on?"

"I suggest we find out, my friend."

The two friends left the villa. At the next villa along, a throng of people was gathering to their right. The two approached a mixture of sobbing women and concerned men, all frightened. One of the crowd spotted the two figures coming. Seeing them as men of substance, he called the people to part and allowed the pair access to the building.

As they passed through the doorway, they entered the vestibulum where two servants stood, clearly agitated.

"Domine, Domine, you must come with us," the elder of the two spoke, "the master is dead - they are all dead!"

"Show me," demanded Cassius. The two servants led Cassius and Atticus through a beautifully laid out atrium decorated with paintings. Nothing seemed more normal. They passed out of the building into a small peristylium, a small colonnaded garden; three bedrooms lay side-by-side along one wall. The servants went to the first room, pausing at the open door.

"We do not wish to enter Domine," said one, standing to one side. Cassius strode past the men and into the bedroom. He soon came to a stop, shocked at what he saw. He heard Atticus take a sharp intake of breath as he saw what lay before them. They were both overwhelmed by the tangy odour of blood.

A young couple lay in the bed – each could have been sleeping – except for the gaping smile of a slit throat. The surrounding bedclothes darkened with blood; splatter ran down the walls that Cassius could not miss. His attention was instantly drawn to a word scrawled on the wall beside the bed – painted in blood, big and bold; 'COLLABORATORS'.

"In my time as a legate in the Thirteenth, and I've seen blood and gore, yet this still shocks me, Atticus. Here lie two young people, butchered in their beds."

"Did you notice the *menorah* in the vestibule Cassius?" Atticus asked. "This is a Jewish family," Cassius remembered a fleeting glimpse of the seven-branched candlestick. "When I rented our villa, they told me this family were spice merchants."

"This is assassination Atticus, simple assassination. I'll warrant you nothing will have been taken. This is the work of the rebels. What's more, they got clean away with this in Aelia!" Anger crept into his voice. "Where was the damned army?"

A cough interrupted the conversation; a servant stood in the doorway to the bedroom.

"Excuse me, Domine, this way, please." He pointed towards the adjacent bedroom.

"Don't tell me there is more!" said Atticus. They left the corpses behind and followed the servant to the next door; he hesitated before entering. Cassius had no such hesitancy and entered this smaller bedroom. As he took in the sight, too late, he closed his eyes. A young dark-haired girl, she could have been only seven years old, lay upon the bed. The stroke that slit her throat must have been so violent that her head was nearly severed. She lay in a sea of blood. Cassius pivoted away and opened his eyes to see that Atticus remained outside the door.

"I'd stay where you are, my old friend. You don't want to see what lies inside. She was only a-"

"Domine, there is more," interrupted the servant. Irrationally, Cassius nearly cursed the man before noticing the tears streaming down his cheeks.

"Show me," he said, "Atticus, stay here." And so, he entered the third bedroom where a young boy lay dead upon his bed. Like the girl - presumably his sister - his throat slashed, though more cleanly than his sibling's. Then, again, the tangy, metallic, pervasive smell of blood; even worse, flies had settled on the wound and the bloody bedclothes. Cassius left the room and breathed in deep lungfuls of fresh air.

"By the gods, Atticus, this is a bad business. It's a young boy in there – six or so years old. Died the same way as his sister and parents." An officer and two legionaries appeared in the peristyle. The Optio realised he was facing two men of substance, particularly the taller one equipped with a military gladius.

"Optio Porcius Fimbra sir, III Cohort. You would be?"

"Cassius Cornelius, Optio. I am an Equestrian and here on business from Rome." He paused before throwing in, "and ex-Tribune to the Thirteenth Legion." He nodded towards Atticus, "This is my factor, Atticus Diomedes."

"I understand, sir, that this villa was attacked in the night?"

"You're bloody well right it was attacked!" The anger returned. "Centurion Vorenus assured me he'd protect the colony. So, what happened to the army last night? Knocking back amphorae of the best Falernian?"

"I am sorry, sir. The colony's still under construction. You'll know that walls have yet to be built. We can detect an attack such as that which attacked the vicus, but small groups of two or three men...." He paused for a second. "There are not enough of us to prevent that."

As Cassius listened, he shook his head.

"Apologies, optio, arrangements for guarding the colony are not your responsibility." He pointed to the bedrooms. "We have the parents in one room and a child each in the other two. Throats well and truly cut. The parent's room has the word 'collaborator' painted in blood on the walls. A terrible business."

"Sir," Said Fimbria, "this scene is repeated across the colony; twelve households that I know of, just like what you've described. Mayhem is breaking out."

"Jupiter, this is so bad!" Atticus exclaimed. Cassius laughed wryly,

"Bad? This is catastrophic." To the optio, he said, "I take it the victims were all Jewish; no Greeks, Romans, Syrians…?" Fimbria nodded. "That means the rebels had specific targets, and someone must've led them in, or at least identified the targets."

"You may be correct, sir. I have passed villas where the surviving Jewish families are already throwing the servants out – they've arrived at a similar conclusion to you, sir."

"This is looking very bleak, Optio."

"Excuse me, sir, but you mentioned you were a Tribune in the Thirteenth?"

"I was, Optio."

"Then, can I ask, as a military man, your view of the current situation?"

Cassius paused for a few seconds before responding.

"I don't believe you would want to, or should, hear my answer to that question."

"Right, sir. I'll round up the servants; see if there's any missing."

Capitulum XVII - Unrest in Galilee

7 Aprilis. Year 16 of Imperator Hadrian.

Lucius had enjoyed his first full day with his century. They had spent several hours on the drill field performing battle drills before applying the learning in mock combat with other centuries. The 'Italian Cohort' members were full of enthusiasm and looked forward to facing the rebel Judaeans. The bruises and cuts that some legionaries bore spoke volumes for their eagerness to fight. Lucius thought such enthusiasm might be driven by a desire to show the older hands that the "new boys" were up to the task at hand.

As the soldiers were leaving the field, Centurion Aurelius Crispus approached Lucius and suggested dinner together. They still had to catch up on all that had happened since Lucius' departure from Italia. So, Lucius suggested they leave the fort and dine at the Minerva.

Two hours later, both men sat at a table in the taberna. They looked forward to a satisfying meal and an uninterrupted discussion on military matters. But unfortunately, the plan quickly threatened by Sistus Trianus' effusing over Lucius' return. Once Sistus had left them, Lucius offered Crispus an account of his adventures in Judaea.

It was two goblets of wine and one meal later before Lucius finished his account. Apart from a few questions to clarify what he was hearing, Crispus sat and listened to what his optio had to say. When Lucius finished, the centurion pushed his chair back a little from the table and relaxed.

"I had an hour with the Tribune this morning," he said. "I'd agree the situation is not good. We seem to have been caught napping. How the Judaean Jews got away with all of this is beyond me. All I can say is that they planned carefully, with a lot of forethought. And they've been planning for quite some time, too."

"The realisation that this was more than just banditry came too late," Lucius said. "We repeatedly sent out centuries that the rebels overwhelmed. Unfortunately, we were slow to learn the lesson, and it has had a high price in men."

"Well, we can't undo what we've done," the centurion said. "However, I'm sure we've adopted the learning has and now things in Judaea will get done differently, if for no other reason than the fact that Julius Petronius and six cohorts are in Aelia. He'll have'em knocked into shape and will teach the rebels it's unwise to mess with the Fretensis!"

Lucius laughed at the mention of his uncle.

"I wouldn't want to be the rebel who gets too close to Centurion Petronius!"

Crispus smiled before a serious countenance crossed his face.

"I understand from the Tribune has involved you in his, shall we say, investigations?"

Lucius looked around the Taberna to ensure they would not be overheard. He had omitted from his earlier account the incidents where he had worked for the Tribune. He was more than a little embarrassed that he had done so, withholding such information from his commander and mentor. Crispus could see the difficulty his optio was experiencing.

"The Tribune will have demanded complete discretion from you. However, he has briefed me. If certain well-placed individuals had been skimming off the Imperator's balsam, then we have an unpleasant situation. If the balsam was being sold to Judaeans who were using it to buy weapons, we have a situation which is orders of magnitude greater." The centurion pulled his chair back to the table and lent forward in a conspiratorial posture. "The rebellion is making matters harder for us, but the Tribune's determined to dig to the bottom of this cesspit! Between you and me, be ready to march south at short notice."

"To what aim?" Lucius asked.

"I'm sure the Tribune will make that clear when the time comes. However, he wants to use the fourth for whatever he has in mind." The centurion looked at Lucius, and the Optio was sure he was weighing up his following words. After a few seconds and then a much lower voice, Crispus went on, "Are you familiar with Civilis' background?"

Lucius shrugged.

"He seems to be working his way up the *cursus honorum*, a *Quaestor* at an early age, so I suspect he will go far."

The centurion gave a knowing smile.

"Oh yes, be assured he will go far." He paused, as if still weighing up his words. "Part of the picture he has painted is very true. However, and this must be between you and me, the part he does not make public is that he appears to be very well connected, and I mean outside of the army."

Lucius considered Crispus' words.

"You'll be telling me next he is the Imperator's bastard younger brother!"

Crispus smiled.

"I'd rule nothing out." Crispus laughed. "If it helps, I trust him. I am telling you this, Lucius, because you need to understand what you are becoming involved in. He has not been specific with me, but I sense that this business goes beyond mere army corruption in Judaea."

"But why us?" asked Lucius.

"The creation of the Fourth in Italia wasn't part of his plan, but it became an opportunity that Civilis grasped. In his position, he was unsure which officers were trustworthy. Then along comes a new cohort raised in Italia, its legionaries untainted. Civilis approached me in Italia not long after we'd begun raising the cohort. He considered me trustworthy." He laughed. "We then spent some time surreptitiously vetting the officers we brought with us. You may recall that three of them were "called back" to the province. It's not that we found anything concerning them; it's just that some of their connections made us feel uncomfortable."

"So, Aurelius, you've known about this situation for quite some time?"

"Correct." The centurion nodded. "Civilis identified you early on as someone he might bring closer in when the time came. I don't know what he led you to believe, but he was only too aware of your background. As I said earlier, I'm convinced this is much bigger than just a corruption issue. There is something else too." Lucius' eyebrows raised. "There is a worry that several legions have become soft, simply policing provinces, seeing little action and frankly, getting lazy. I suspect there is an element of that here in Judaea. The lads have complained that I've been overzealous in training, too many route marches. Well, I've trained them as they used to be trained – hard. The legate is expecting a lot from the Fourth I suspect."

"Well, no doubt when he wants us to know more, he'll tell us," Lucius responded. "Perhaps he needs the fourth cohort to -" The return of Sistus to their table interrupted the conversation. Sistus homed in on the empty plates and associated breadcrumbs.

"I see you enjoyed your stew, Sirs." Sistus gathered up the plates and brushed down the table and made to leave before hesitating. "Optio Petronius, you recall I mentioned the old lady that comes into the Taberna and does occasional cleaning?"

"I do, Sistus," Lucius said, "in fact, wasn't she the one that had a rather suspect son?"

"Well, that's it, Sir," Sistus came back. "It's her birthday tomorrow, and she let slip to my missus this morning that he'll drop by her place tomorrow evening. It is meant to be a secret visit, but the old girl's mind gets addled – she had her children late in life you see. She thinks telling you something in a whisper will keep it a secret!"

The centurion looked puzzled.

"Aurelius, I am sorry. Let me explain," said Lucius. He outlined the earlier conversation that had taken place between him and Sistus.

"So, let me understand this," said Crispus, "Sistus Trianus, you're saying that one of the rebels is going to visit his mother close by tomorrow night. Is that right?"

Sistus nodded, confirming the centurion's summary.

"Sistus, you had better sit down," Crispus commanded, "we need to have a chat."

By the time the two officers had left the Taberna, they extracted from Sistus and his wife Octavia the background to the cleaning lady and where she lived. Although it was vague, they also had a general description of her son; fortunately for the Romans, the old lady, Aliza, had talked about him to Octavia.

As Lucius and Crispus returned to the barracks, they hatched a plan to apprehend the rebel. Their return route swung them past the home of Sistus' occasional employee. It surprised Lucius as the area she lived in comprised villas and three-storey buildings, not the typical artisan's accommodation in which he expected her to live. Instead, she had the ground floor of one of the larger units, built to quality beyond the standards used in the multi-storey residences in Rome's subura. Lucius made a note to ask Sistus about the background of this lady. By the time the two soldiers had returned, their plan for the next day was complete.

The following day was typical in the life of a garrison soldier. First, Lucius arose and attended a parade of the Fourth Cohort where daily orders were issued, after which he mustered with his century and the day's various tasks discussed and duties allocated. The latter part of the morning he spent on the drill field. Then, in the afternoon, he addressed some of the administrative responsibilities that fall to a century's Optio. Only part of Lucius' mind was focused on his duties; the more significant part was thinking hard about what would happen later that day.

Crispus sought out Lucius that afternoon, and the two men ran through and finalised their plan. As the sun became lower in the sky and evening began to draw in, Crispus and Lucius met with six legionaries. To the uninformed observer, the legionaries could well pass as labourers; all wore cloaks over their clothing, and some with hoods pulled up over their heads. Any casual observer would not detect swords and daggers worn around the labourer's waists. One soldier was carrying cloaks for the officers to wear.

The party of would-be workers passed through the Gate where Lucius and Crispus deposited their helmets, something no hood would conceal. The plan was simple. The disguised legionaries would loiter near the building along the rebel's route. Crispus briefed them that the target was tall and would stand out. The minute he approached the old ladies' door, they would close in and seize him.

They were near the point where the group would split up, with Lucius and Crispus leading, when the centurion suddenly held up his hand, bringing them to a standstill.

"Look ahead," the centurion whispered. "See what I see?"

Lucius stared forward and saw the focus of Crispus' attention. An old lady walking their way accompanied by a tall young man.

"Castor and Pollux!" Lucius exclaimed, "It's them."

Crispus looked over his shoulder.

"Take your lead from me, boys. Do not uncover but be ready."

The party remained standing as the two approaching figures drew closer. The old lady, aware of them, continued her progress. Crispus started to walk towards her, and when only a short distance separated them, the woman and her companion came to a stop. Lucius was expecting tension within the couple and was surprised there was none. The old woman's younger companion showed no sign of fight or flight. Using Greek, Crispus spoke first and in a remarkably gentle tone for a Roman soldier.

"Tell me, mother," he said, "would you be Aliza?" The woman did not reply immediately. Instead, she looked at Crispus, gave Lucius a visual inspection, and then looked between them at the men behind. Finally, she spoke.

"I'm on my way to see you."

Lucius turned to look at Crispus, who was still facing her, his eyebrows raised in puzzlement.

"Coming to see me?" Crispus asked. Lucius studied the woman. Her hair was grey, and she was of short stature. He thought that her lack of height was natural, not brought on by her age; she appeared to be in good physical condition. The light was fading but sufficient to give a hint that this lady may have once been a fine woman.

"You are Roman, are you not?" she asked abruptly. Crispus attempted to feign indignation, spreading his arms and shrugging his shoulders. His acting failed. "I've been around Romans long enough to tell you that a mere cloak is no disguise. Given that stance and you are doing the talking, I'll assume you are in command." Crispus smiled and slowly nodded his head.

"Mother, you see me for what I am, and I can't deny it. Centurion Aurelius Crispus. So, if you are coming to find me, you've been successful; tell me your business."

"That's not something I want to discuss in the street. My home is two minutes away, and you and him," she nodded towards Lucius, "are welcome to join Jacob," she placed an arm on the young man's shoulder, "and me in a bowl of soup and some bread."

Crispus hesitated.

"Pah! Forget the soup and bread if you wish, but I'm not discussing matters standing in the street." She turned to Jacob, "You have nothing at all to fear about Jacob. You may be interested to hear what he has to say."

As she spoke, Lucius watched Jacob and noticed that he would look anywhere rather than catch someone's eye. Naturally, this made Lucius uncomfortable with the man.

"Right, mother," said Crispus, "We shall all return with you, but my men will stay outside."

And so it was that five minutes later, the two officers were seated at a table opposite Aliza and Jacob. When Sistus described Aliza's son, the two men assumed a tall stature would mean a muscular, stocky build. The reality was different. Jacob was quite the opposite, tall but of a slight physique. His hair was dark and his beard full; even his eyes seemed dark, though Lucius had yet to make eye contact with him.

"Well then, mother, you'd better tell us what this is all about." Said Crispus.

"Jacob's a good boy, though he's not the shiniest shekel in the purse. He's told me things that I believe you should know. But first, I've something I need to say." She had set beakers of water on the table, picking one up, she sipped from it. "I have no love of Rome. What I am doing this evening is for the sake of my beloved Galilee. I'm old enough to have seen what taking up a sword against Rome means; blood and butchery for those who take on the conquerors. We've learned to accommodate Rome in this part of Israel, for scripture tells us that Rome will pass, and the Messiah will come in time. We must be patient." She took another sip from a beaker before turning to Jacob. "Jacob, I want you to tell these men what you have been doing over the last several months."

Still staring at the table, Jacob spoke in a monotone voice. "I was working at the bakery about a year when they told me that Judaea was going to throw out the Romans very soon. I've always wanted to be a soldier, and it would be great to give the conquerors a kicking." Lucius and Crispus exchanged looks. "So, I filled my backpack with clothes and some money I'd saved and went south, didn't I? Well, after abouts a week, I find the camp, didn't I? I cried 'cause they didn't want me as a soldier, no, they puts me in the bakery to work. Well, I thought, at least I am part of the army, didn't I?"

"So, to all intents and purposes, you were a baker?" Crispus asked.

"At the start," Jacob responded, "but they asked me to help store and prepare weapons, so I said yes, didn't I? I had a great skill in sharpening blades, didn't I? 'Sharp as a razor,' they used to say. I did a real good job, and they liked me. So, I worked really hard with the weapons, didn't I?"

"Perhaps we could find you a job here in Caesarea," joked Crispus. He wanted the boy relaxed and off guard.

"I'd like that," the boy responded. "So, I explained to them that my father was dead for a long time and my mother brought me up, didn't I? I told them it was mother's birthday soon and I would like to see her, didn't I? They said I could have a few days, so home I came, didn't I?"

"Was your mother pleased to see you, Jacob?" Lucius asked softly.

"She was angry 'cause I just ran off, didn't I? She said I shouldn't go back. It would all end in tears, and we'd all suffer. I told her that much of Galilee was ready to rise against the conquerors, didn't I?"

"And what did mother say, Jacob?" said Crispus, looking at Aliza as he spoke.

"She said I was stupid and should never have got involved. She said there would be blood and death, and it must be stopped. The rebellion would not be good. She said we have to warn the authorities." He stopped. He finished as he began, staring at the table. Lucius had not seen a single eye movement during his words.

Crispus stared at the boy for a few seconds and then turned to Aliza.

"So, mother, you'd confirm that what Jacob told us is very much the story he gave you?"

"Yes, it is, and it's why I was coming to see someone at the camp."

"And you Jacob, you are sure that rebels in Judaea told you that Galilee was close to rising in revolt?"

"It is as I told you." The boy replied, never lifting his eyes from the tabletop. Crispus rose out of his seat and strode to the door, opening it and calling to his men, who were quickly in the room. Crispus addressed them.

"Soldiers escort this man back to the camp. He is to be handed over to the officer of the watch and held until I return."

Agitated, Aliza jumped up out of her chair.

"You can't take him. He has told you all he knows. What more is there? It is not even as though he was a soldier – he's just a lad, a simple lad who doesn't know what he's doing half the time!"

"Mother, we need to understand what Jacob did, saw and heard when he was in Judaea." He was speaking calmly. "It's not my intention to harm Jacob. I think he's a simple lad, deluded, but simple. So far, he seems to have been honest with us, and once we have interrogated him, I would argue for his release."

"How can I trust the word of a Roman?" She stood with her hands on her hips and chin pushed forward; Lucius thought she looked fierce. He braced for flying fists. Crispus was unruffled,

"I'll tell you what, you may come to the camp each morning for the duration that we hold Jacob and satisfy yourself that we're not harming him. I hope to resolve the matter quickly."

The hands slid from the hips, and her chin pulled in – she appeared to deflate as she turned to Jacob.

"Jacob, I want you to go with the centurion and answer questions he may ask you. Be a good boy, don't trouble the centurion, and you will be home in no time."

Jacob looked forlorn, almost childlike, and nodded his head twice without muttering a word or looking up at anyone.

"Thank you, mother," said Crispus. "Do not lose sight of why you brought Jacob to us. You may not believe it, but even we Romans would rather avoid blood and slaughter."

Two minutes later, Aliza was sitting at the table, wondering if she had done the right thing. Those Judaeans were very persuasive.

The sun had long set; Aurelius Crispus and Lucius sat on either side of a table in the room off a long corridor in the principia. Meanwhile, Jacob was in a secure room on the same passage. There was no escape through the locked door. Centurion Crispus had placed a burly legionary on guard in the corridor.

"Well then, Lucius, what's your take on young Jacob?" Asked Crispus of Lucius. The Optio thought back upon what had happened in the room along the corridor over the last two hours.

"Do you know," he began, "when I was a boy, I used to play 'Hannibal' with my mates. We'd split the group in two; one side was Roman, and the other was Carthaginian. Next time we met, we'd change roles, ensuring that everyone would have a turn on the winning side. Young Jacob is a simple lad, and all he is doing is playing a grown-up version of Hannibal. To him, it's just a game, and I suspect it will remain so until he sees the shedding of blood."

"I think we are on the same tablet," said the centurion. "What about the information he has given us?"

"There's truly little detail from him, but that is not surprising given his state of mind. We know he found his way to a rebel camp and joined them. I imagine they saw him for what he was and put him on safe, simple duties. Whilst he could not give us firm numbers, he was clear there were "hundreds and hundreds" of them. It is a sizable camp, and I'm wondering if it's the one we stumbled across on the way back to Caesarea."

"In which case," said the centurion, "all we have is a confirmation of what you saw earlier. So, it may not be a second camp."

"Yes, you're right about that. Confirmation of a second camp would have been useful intelligence indeed." Lucius responded. "However, what has he told us about how well equipped they are? He has mentioned many of the weapons are identical to ours, and we know how they came about getting them. He has confirmed that they have basic siege weapons, such as crude onagers and some catapult-based devices."

"Now then," said the centurion, "what would a bunch of glorified bandits want with such weapons? They must have some target in mind."

"And we need to understand what that target is, yet Jacob claims not to know. Although, to be fair, I could understand the rebels not mentioning it; in fact, it's likely a guarded secret."

"That may be so," said the centurion, "the question is, is he holding back on us? Should we let our professional interrogators loose on him?"

Lucius felt some discomfort when he thought of interrogators working on Jacob. He knew they would beat the boy until they got an answer to their questions. It was often a successful approach, but sometimes the victim would give any answer to stop the pain, which resulted in a lot of wasted effort before the realisation dawned that the information was meaningless. Also, he had a slight sense of responsibility for Jacob. It was because his mother was an employee, if not a friend, of Sistus back at the taberna. Crispus could see the hesitancy in Lucius' face. Lucius spoke,

"I think the boy is genuine, Aurelius."

"Lucius, we're officers in the Roman army; 'think' is not good enough, we must be sure or at least as sure as we can. But, for the moment, I'll reserve judgement regarding the interrogators."

Lucius felt embarrassed.

"You are right, Aurelius," he admitted. "Apologies, we must be sure."

"So, what else did we get?" Asked the centurion.

"A lot of information about himself and his trip up and down to the camp. We have some names; he recognised 'Ben Koseba' but denied seeing him. Likewise, the name 'Akiba' got mentioned, but as with 'Koseba', he never saw the Rabbi. The most important piece of information we gleaned was the talk in the camp of the next "rising" in the province, in the Galilee region."

"I'd agree with your assessment, Lucius." Said the centurion. "The boy mentioned it was common talk around the camp. Had he only a single source for the rising Galilee, I may be more suspicious." The Optio nodded his head in agreement with the statement. "I'm persuaded that this lad is a simpleton, and what he tells us is genuine." The centurion continued, "We must inform the Sixth *Ferrata* in Tel Shalem as soon as possible. However, I shall run the situation by the legate for his approval first."

"It's a pity that we've so little to go on," Lucius said.

"Indeed," agreed the centurion, "but what the Sixth *can* do is smother Galilee in patrols. They have the good fortune of being forewarned by what is happening, something we lacked in Judea, until you belatedly raised the alarm, that is. In addition, the people of Galilee are better disposed to Rome than those of Judea, so raising a rebellion will be a much more arduous task for its instigators."

The centurion stood up, ready to leave.

"Lucius, I suggest you get something to eat, then get some sleep. I'm off to brief the legate. I'll take his advice on what we do with the lad next door." Saying such, Aurelius Crispus was away.

Capitulum XVIII - Vengeance

13 Aprilis. 16th Year of the Imperator Hadrianus

Legionary Marcus Apollinaris arose from his cot. His thoughts went to the events of the previous hectic day; servants thrown onto the streets, panicked residents of Aelia trying to storm the gates of the camp demanding protection and some even loading carts and heading out of the colony. The army veterans living in the colony were much more stoic about the situation. Within hours, these men formed an Aelia Militia, ready to take up arms once more to defend their new homes. By evening, matters had calmed, but the tension across the new colony was palpable.

Along with his other seven new tent mates, currently living in a wooden barracks, Marcus washed in cold water, dressed, and headed with his mates to the refectory. The routine was standard for any legionary based on a fixed camp. After eating, they would don the full military attire of the mail Hamata, Gladius, pilum, and the iconic large Roman shield, the scutum. They would then muster for a full parade. This day was no different.

Equipped with all the paraphernalia of the legionary, Marcus and his comrades made their way towards the drill field. Approaching the point of the parade, many more soldiers joined them. There was not much of the usual banter; instead, the conversations focused on the previous day's happenings. As they cleared the last buildings and moved onto the edge of the field, they heard a voice say,

"Blood of Zeus, what's the tribune doing here?" followed by,

"Not just the tribune, brother. The bleeding prefect is with him!"

Standing beside a small podium, stood tribune Civilis accompanied by Caius Faustinas, the camp prefect, and several military tribunes. Marcus wondered if, following the previous day's events, they would announce the evacuation of Aelia. He thought better than to share his thoughts. Marcus and his group joined the rest of his century, and in quick time the cohort formed up in ranks and files, flanked on either side by other cohorts from the garrison at Aelia Camp.

A command went out for the cohorts to "be ready, and the legionaries stood silent, awaiting further orders. Ascending the five steps of the podium, the tribune walked to the middle of the platform, where he stood looking out across the mustered cohorts; the impact of the recent fighting with the Jewish rebels was clear to see. None of the cohorts were near full strength. The question was, could they fight back and regain control?

"Soldiers," he began, "I would be dishonest to both you and my Imperator if I did not say the rebels have caught us off guard. We have many injured brothers in the camp, and sadly, some brothers have not returned and will not be doing so." His voice was soft and measured. "A few days ago, the rebels attacked the vicus and murdered many of the Artisans and residents that you've befriended over the last several years. So many of the dead had served this legion, lending us their skills and knowledge.

"The night before last, the same rebels came by stealth into Aelia, where they butchered whole families as they slept in their beds; yes, fathers, mothers and even the infants died." The legate paused, sweeping his eyes across the gathered multitude. When he began again, his voice was more demanding and louder. "Brothers, the time has come – perhaps belatedly – to show these rebels who it is they are fighting. The time has come for us to avenge the dead of the vicus and those families slaughtered in Aelia. I intend we teach our enemy a lesson he'll not forget in a hurry." The gathered legionaries cheered and stamped the butts of their pilums on the ground. The legate let the soldiers vent their emotions before raising a hand to request silence.

"Soldiers, I have briefed your centurions regarding the forthcoming operations. The cohorts will now fall out of parade and re-muster to take instruction from their officers." Gaius Civilis, the Tribune Laticlavius of the 10th Legion, stood down from the podium.

A short while later, the Sixth Cohort stood formed up in front of its senior centurion, Julius Petronius. He ordered his soldiers to stand at ease and outlined the previous night's plan.

"Right lads, the Legate said it was time to teach these Judean *cunni* a lesson, and I intend that this cohort ensures they learn the lesson well." Legionary helmets nodded in agreement, accompanied by low murmurings of support for the coming project. "We have allocated each cohort a particular rebel target. Two hours' march from here is the village of Tel-Salem, lying in the Judean foothills. We know the village is associated with banditry, and it is likely that it is providing men for, and supporting, the revolt. Our mission is straightforward; we will devastate the village and all those in it; no one will survive. We shall secure any cattle or livestock and returned return them to the camp. After this raid, Tel-Salem will cease to exist."

The Senior Centurion let this information sink in before continuing.

"When we are close to the village, I will share the tactical plan with each century's centurion. They shall march from this point in one hour."

They put the hour to effective use as soldiers supplied themselves with water and filled their snap sacks with basic sustenance for the day's work. Weapons were sharpened and equipment checked.

One hour later, just as the day was getting hot, six cohorts marched out of the camp, each heading for a different destination. For Marcus, it was along the dusty road that would deposit his century close to the village of Tel-Salem. Marcus joined in the banter between soldiers common with marching men; he thought how good it was to be back to regular soldiering. Sometime later, the cohort came to a halt; it was time to brief for the attack on the village.

"Damn it all," Marcus said to his comrades, "I was enjoying the walk!"

One of the cavalry scouts screening the cohort came trotting down the road and drew up alongside Centurion Petronius as the cohort came to a stand.

"The way ahead is clear, sir," said the rider. "The village is quiet. I'm sure they don't have the slightest idea we are approaching."

The centurion acknowledged the report, and the rider rode back the way he had come. Petronius called his junior centurions to him and shared the plan of attack. Briefed, they returned to their centuries to prepare them for action. Marcus' commander, senior centurion Petronius, called his Optio, Signifier along with his standard, and tesserarii together to run through the plan.

The first three centuries would surround the village, their role being containment; nothing was to pass them, nothing was to escape. The remaining three centuries would then attack the village, moving straight along the road. When the cohort had full possession of the village, which Marcus took to mean that all the residents were dead, the containment centuries would move in and salvage whatever grain or livestock was available. The next task was to burn or otherwise destroy all the buildings in the village. Before reforming the cohort, Centurion Petronius spoke to his century.

"Soldiers, this'll be a bloody business. This action will be no regular fight. I ask that you think of this task as a justified execution. The odds are stacked immeasurably against the murderer when the executioner's sword swings for his neck; so, it is here. Do not forget the people of the Vicus. Do not forget those innocent families in Aelia butchered sleeping in their beds. What we do today is righteous vengeance on behalf of those who cannot be here. Your optio will take command of the century as I shall lead the main attack."

The cohort continued onwards along the road that approached the village. A little distance away from the village, the containing centuries left the path and entered the scrub and bushes that clung to existence on the stony hillside. As the rest of the cohort stood waiting to give them time to take up position, the three centuries formed the cordon around the village.

Marcus found himself positioned in an area heavy with dense thickets. His nearest comrades were thirty feet away from either side of him; they took a sentinel stance looking towards the settlement. It comprised buildings, square and box-shaped, so typical of Judaea. Marcus noticed that the back walls that faced the Roman cordon had very few windows, allowing soldiers to take position unseen. It was a sizable settlement, and no one in the cohort could be sure what resistance level they would meet. If the three centuries involved in the direct attack encountered a setback, whistles would blow, ordering that the legionaries of the cordon to reform back on the road, ready to support their comrades.

Though it must have been only a few minutes, to Marcus, it felt like an eternity before he heard the tramping of soldier's boots on the distant road, a sign that the attack had begun. A matter of seconds later came the sound of screaming accompanied by a cacophony of crashing and banging; doors were being broken down. It frustrated Marcus not to see what was happening; he half hoped someone would attempt an escape so that he could get involved.

He listened to the sounds coming from the village; it was the screams of women and children he could hear—no male voices. There was no sound of combat, indicating the settlement had no protection. Instead, what he was hearing was butchery, pure and simple.

In front of him, a thicket rustled. Startled, Marcus took a pace backwards and drew his gladius from its scabbard. As he did so, a young woman, crouching low, appeared before him. Though Marcus was taken aback - and his face showed it - *her* countenance reflected the absolute terror of a hapless victim, expecting a painful death. Marcus did not enjoy the thought of killing a defenceless woman, but as a Roman soldier, he had his orders. His gladius arm swung back, low, ready to come forward in the stabbing thrust for which the weapon bore a notorious reputation. In enacting the movement, he looked into her eyes, causing his arm to freeze. Just for a second, he found himself back in the Neptune, looking into the terrified face of Anaitis.

It was a physical shock for Marcus, and he knew he could not kill this woman. He looked to his left where his fellow legionary, back turned, was pissing into a bush. To his right, his comrade was fixated on something in the distant village. The woman remained frozen in fear, staring up at Marcus. He lowered his sword and flicked his head sideways, a signal for her to pass. There was no look of gratitude on her face as she darted past, still in a crouch, a frightened fugitive from the killing ground in the village.

Marcus replaced his sword in its scabbard. He fell back into a sentinel position, wondering if he had imagined the incident. Hell continued to reign in the village; the screaming seemed relentless. Marcus attempted to rationalise his recent behaviour. A survivor or two to tell the tale would add to the message's strength, enabling a loud signal for the Judaean rebels. No harm done then, yet whilst he was a craftsman at bending the rules, it was the first time he had disobeyed a direct order. Still, what's done is done and will have negligible impact on the day's business.

The noise in the distance did not diminish, yet it was becoming mere background music to Marcus, so when a piercing scream split the air, he jumped. The sound had come from behind, and he spun around - several feet away, a cavalry scout sat on his horse, his spear point embedded in something that lay in the bushes at his mount's feet. While unable to discern the spear's target, in his heart, he knew exactly what it was.

"You fucking infantry need to stay awake, don't you?" The cavalryman sneered as he tugged his spear out of its recent kill. "This Jewish bitch crept right past you, under your bloody noses!"

The legionaries on either side of Marcus had turned at the sound of the scream.

"Well, we thought we ought to give you something to do," said the legionary on Marcus' right. "I think even the cavalry could kill an unarmed woman."

The cavalryman just laughed at them.

"The first rule of combat," he taunted them, "is that you have to be awake!"

His heels kicked the rib cage of his horse, and he was gone.

"Damn cavalry," one of Marcus' comrades cursed, "she may not have even come from the village. She could've been out and about collecting berries or herbs, you name it, brother."

"I suspect not," Marcus responded, "but it's possible. Anyway, these donkey lovers aren't the smartest at the best of times!"

Laughing, the soldiers took up their allocated positions yet again.

"This will be over soon," one soldier said, "there can't be many left to -"

A roar from the village interrupted the man, followed by the clash of metal on metal.

"Fuck me!" The soldier continued, "that sounds like a scrap; the *cunni* are attacking the lads."

No sooner were the words spoken than the sounds of whistles rang out above the noise. With no command, Marcus and his fellow legionaries turned to the left and jogged back the way they had come. It took two or three minutes before the men arrived back at the road and formed up into centuries. Senior centurion Petronius was back at the head of the column accompanied by the two centurions in command of the second and third centuries, along with their Optios. In seconds, the group split up, and the officers returned to their centuries. Petronius spoke to his century.

"Right, lads, this won't be complicated. We will move along the road and take on the first sizable rebel group we see. The other centuries will seek their own targets." As he spoke, he tightened his helmet with its distinguished red cresta running side to side, in combat it was the instant indication of his status and location. Centurions lead from the front and Petronius wanted his men to know his position – he could not afford to lose his helmet!

Marcus watched as his centurion turned to face front, issued a command to move, and in an instant, the century was on its way to action. Marcus held his shield close to his left and his spear to his right as they marched. The centurion marched them at double pace, and they soon passed between the outer buildings of the settlement. Bodies lay in doorways, in gardens, and at the side of the road; what Marcus saw confirmed the screaming had been women, children, and the old. Ahead of him were the sounds of desperate combat; swords and spears colliding with shields and armour, men screaming and cursing as they fought. The cries of the dying.

The centre of the village comprised a small open square built around a large, tall tree. To the side of the tree, there stood a covered well. Tired from fighting half a century of legionaries, a large band of rebels reformed its ranks on one side of the square. The legionaries also backed off to reform their ranks and deal with their injuries. The situation had become a stand-off between the two forces. It was shocking to see several legionaries face down on the ground. They would not be arising again.

The rebels chanted and jeered at them as the 1stCentury marched into the square. Petronius wasted no time; he turned the century from a column into two lines behind the bloodied legionaries facing the rebels. Now closer, Marcus could observe that the rebels had also taken a beating. Their shouting and jeering were an attempt to maintain morale in the face of an additional threat.

The large cedar tree and the well stood between the legionaries facing the rebels and the 1st Century. Marcus could see that these objects would hinder any spears unleashed on the enemy. They would need to get closer, but there was no room behind the legionaries to the front. They were backed up to the tree and the well, blocking the First's line of fire. The jeering from the rebels increased in volume. Marcus wondered if they were about to charge the tired legionaries that stood before them.

Petronius shouted at the centurion commanding the legionaries to his front. Petronius turned to the 1st Century and ordered them to open their ranks, to leave a three-foot space between each soldier. The soldiers of the First completed the manoeuvre. Still facing the enemy, the other century retired backwards. Flowing around the tree and the well, they slipped through the spaces between the 1st Century's soldiers. The instant the soldiers cleared the lines of the First, Petronius ordered his men to close their ranks again. The manoeuvre left the First facing the rebels, preparing to charge them. Now in the front line, Marcus stood peering over the top of his shield. Nervously, he looked across at the screaming horde, whose single goal was to kill him and his fellow legionaries. Furthermore, the Romans were not facing the bandits of old but well-equipped soldiers who were bloodied but determined.

Petronius gave the order to march; within seconds, the First stood upon the ground that the earlier Roman unit had occupied. They came to a stop when the centurion gave the order 'ready pila'. Marcus and the entire front line took one pace forward and lifted javelins to the shoulder, bracing for the throw. Marcus chose a target amongst the agitated rebels, who were continuing to shout insults. Finally, the command came to 'loose pila', and with all his strength, Marcus hurled his javelin at his target.

The Roman javelin, or *pilum*, was a purposely designed throwing weapon. The top third of its length was iron, topped by a penetrating spearhead. This iron section fitted to a wooden shaft, held in place by a pin. If the weapon missed its target, the pressure of impact on the ground would cause the pin to snap, disabling the weapon, rendering it useless to the enemy. If it hit its target, it did its work. Should it lodge in an enemy's shield, any attempt at banging it on the ground to dislodge the weapon would cause the steel shaft to bend. Thus, the shield becomes useless, burdened by the bent javelin.

The rebels facing Marcus' century raised their shields. The rebel shield, round and smaller than the Roman shield, offers less protection. Marcus tracked his weapon as it bounced off his target's shield, flew over a shoulder, and penetrated the chest of a soldier behind him. Not all spears found their mark, but enough did. Cries and loud groans came from the rebel group, followed by a roar as they charged at the Romans.

Having thrown the javelin, Marcus' right hand sought his gladius. By the time the rebel charge began, he stood shield to shield with his fellow soldiers. There was just enough room for a gladius blade between each shield, presenting the advancing rebels with a prickly shield wall. The rebels crossed the separating space in less time than it took to take a breath but allowing the Romans to brace for the impact.

Marcus took the onslaught on his shield and was face-to-face with a wide-eyed Jewish soldier hacking Marcus' shield to clear the way for a blow on the head. The man was screaming in a language Marcus did not recognise, spewing spittle! The Roman kept his shield up and his head down; he and his century had long trained for this. Along the line, rebel bodies pressed and hacked at the Roman wall until Petronius gave three short blasts on his whistle and every legionary in the front rank responded by pulling the shield's left side inwards a little way. This action exposed the right side of their attacker. Doing likewise, Marcus thrust his gladius through the gap into the side of the rebel, attacking his comrade on his right.

Marcus withdrew his gladius, as did all the legionaries, reforming the wall. On the other side of the shield barrier, injured and dying Jews slid to the floor. Marcus noticed his frantic adversary had disappeared, replaced by a spear-wielding warrior. He thrust his spear at Marcus' head, causing him to duck down behind his shield. Then, using his shield, Marcus heaved forward with as much energy as he could muster. At the centre of the Roman *scutum* was a large bronze boss, which could serve as an effective weapon if pushed with force, knocking an antagonist off his feet.

As Marcus' bronze shield boss smacked into his opponent's shield, the man fell back. His antagonist unbalanced, the Roman stepped forward, bracing for a deadly thrust with his gladius. A horn blared from behind his attackers, and instantly the rebels drew back and, in a choreographed move, turned and fled the village square. They retreated between the houses that lined their side of the square. It was no fighting retreat; it was flight. Marcus was cheated of his kill.

Behind the shield wall, Marcus and the legionaries were enraged by the manoeuvre's speed and suddenness. Their swords had tasted blood, and the appetite was growing.

"Let's get the bastards, lads, kill every one of the *cunni*!"

As one, the soldiers surged after the rebels, determined to finish what they started. They had held the rebels, killed a sizeable number of them, and now felt victory within their grasp. No different to his legionary brothers, Marcus was up for the kill. As they funnelled into an alleyway between two houses, Marcus spotted the transverse plume of centurion Petronius' helmet leading the way. The century compressed, barrelling down the alleyway, belatedly spotted roof tiles raining down upon them. Two soldiers fell to the ground to the front, causing chaos as those following along the confined pathway tried hard to avoid stumbling over the bodies.

Centurion Petronius slid to a stop on the gravelled surface. Then, turning back to his men, he shouted, "Testudo!"

In seconds, legionary shields provided a roof and protective walls for the unit, significantly reducing the impact of the falling tiles.

"Four men at the rear, into that house!" roared the centurion, "Century, follow me." Four legionaries at the rear of the column, accompanied by their optio, began kicking down the door of the identified building. Now clear of the bodies, the rest of the century moved on at a jog.

In a matter of moments, the legionaries burst clear of the houses and into the surrounding bushes and scrub wood. The ground fell away for several hundred paces before rising into the hills. The only movement was that of six distant rebels running towards the hills. The centurion and his men ground to a halt. *Where were the rest of the rebels?*

"Perhaps they're escaping on their 'ands and knees, behind the bleedin' bushes!" said the century's joker.

"Hades, where the fuck 'ave they went?" A legionary asked. Centurion Petronius scanned the countryside before him, disappointed that the rebels seemed to have disappeared. Still conscious of the mission objectives, he turned to speak to his men,

"Soldiers," he began, "we're here to destroy this village, and that's what we'll do now. Apollinaris!"

Marcus, who was only standing a short distance from the centurion, jumped at the sound of his name.

"Yes, sir."

"Take two men with you. You should find our wagons have entered the village by now. There are several bags of prepared torches on them. Get two bags each and meet us back in the square, and we can set to razing this place to the ground. Is that clear?"

Marcus confirmed his order. Tapping two of his comrades on the shoulder, he 'suggested' they accompany him to find the wagons. The trio pushed their way through the century and back along the alleyway. They had gone a short distance when they came upon the optio and the four legionaries detailed to clear the house of its tile throwers. The job was done. Passing the building, they saw the bodies of two Jewish boys lying in the alleyway, both broken in their fall from the roof.

Reaching the square, they passed a gaggle of soldiers caring for their brothers felled by the roof tiles. One victim was dead. A second looked due to cross the river Styx anytime, and a third moaned loudly, showing that Chiron was cheated this day. As

Marcus observed the victims, what little pity he may have had for the two boys disappeared.

Arriving at the far side of the square, the cohort's carts rolled to a standstill. Marcus and his comrades approached them and were soon in possession of two sacks of torches. They re-joined the First as it formed up on the far side of the square. Centurions from the cohort's centuries, all defined by their transverse, red-crested plumes on their helmets, were approaching Centurion Petronius. It was clear to Marcus that Petronius wished to confer with his century leaders, and as the thought ran through his head, Petronius looked across, raising his hand, palm outwards. Marcus' small band picked up the message and came to a standstill, dropping the torch bags at their feet.

Petronius gathered his centurions around him and the cavalry decurion joined them. Marcus was close enough to eavesdrop on the conversation.

"So, Octavius," said Petronius, looking the decurion straight in the face, "were your men asleep? How in Hades' name did these *mentulae* surprise us as they did? You must have seen them approaching?"

"Believe me, Centurion," replied a puzzled decurion, "I stationed my lads as agreed. We didn't see anyone approach." He threw both hands into the air. "Trust me; they must've been here all along, hiding in the buildings."

"Then what you are telling me is that this was a carefully prepared trap?"

The decurion pondered the question for a second or two.

"If it was a trap, centurion, then the bait came at a terrible price for them. I would find it hard to believe that even fanatical Jews would sacrifice their families to kill Roman soldiers."

"A fair point," said Petronius. "Any of you others have any thoughts?"

"It may be, just maybe, that we were unlucky with our timing."

The speaker was Aurelius Bilbus, a centurion of the 3rd Century, an ageing but competent soldier who came to the centuriate late in his career. He had Petronius' complete confidence. "If Octavius is correct, it must mean that for some unknown reason, the rebels were within buildings on the edge of the village. Maybe they were briefing for a raid - given they gathered - at the same time as we launched our attack."

"Well, now is not the time for an inquisition," said Petronius. "We need to get this mess sorted out and get back to Aelia before dusk. So, here's the plan. The 2nd Century scours the village. Take possession of any Roman weapons in the hands of the rebels. Render useless all remaining weapons. Stack them in a single house. Burn it to the ground along with all the others. The 3rd Century rounds up livestock and grain and assembles near the wagons. Given the lack of foodstuffs entering Aelia, they will rejoice when this lot arrives. Slaughter injured livestock and throw some down the well. 4th Century count Jewish casualties, execute the wounded. I do not wish any Jewish corpses moved. Leave them where they fell as a clear message to their kind. Then collect our dead and injured. The 1st Century is to torch the village once the previous actions are complete. I would like them done with speed so we can get out of this godforsaken place. All other centuries form upon the road. My thanks to you, centurions – to your work!"

The centurions departed to join their centuries and carry out the indicated actions.

A short while later, the village was ablaze. The fires roared, and every so often, a tongue of flame leapt to the sky as a roof imploded. A plume of dark smoke signalled the village's demise to the surrounding countryside. Buildings falling into alleyways and across the narrow roadways covered many corpses. The intense heat consumed others.

Formed up on the road with wagons to the rear, the cohort was ready to move off. One wagon carried injured legionaries. The other wagons transported the booty taken after the action: chickens and goats. A motley drove of cattle and sheep under the care of a few legionaries followed the wagons. Then, fanning out on either side of the road to ensure there would be no more nasty surprises on the return journey to Aelia, were the rest of the cavalry. Finally, on command from Centurion Petronius, the whole body moved off.

With his mates of the 1st Century, Marcus marched at the front of the column. Petronius had his men marching at alert, carrying their shields and spears ready for action, making the march more demanding. However, the soldiers soon fell into their stride, and as the crackling, smoking village fell away into the distance, they relaxed. Marcus was uncomfortable with what they had done.

"You know, lads," he said to the soldiers on either side of him, "I'm uncertain just how effective all that was."

"What do you mean, brother?" Asked one of his comrades.

"Well, we was told that what we just did was to discourage the *cunni* from hurting us in the future."

"Yeah, I suspect they'll think twice before trying that again!"

"I'm not so sure," Marcus said, "if I was a rebel with a family, I'd fight all right, but ensure I gets back to my wife and kids. Now, if the Romans had slaughtered the wife and kids, I wouldn't give a fuck; all I'd want to do is kill Romans, lots of 'em!"

The soldier on the other side of Marcus nodded his head.

"Fair point, mate, but if we've made the Cunni hate us more. They'll die harder."

"Well, one thing's for sure, lads, it's not for us to question our betters. Only time will tell."

Capitulum XIX - The storm breaks

13 Aprilis. The 16th year of the Imperator Hadrianus

The return journey was easier work than the outward journey, for much of it was coming down out of the Judean hills and comprised a long downward march. As the heat of the day faded, the soldiers of the first cohort were looking forward to unburdening their bulky lorica segmentata and tucking into an evening meal. The general atmosphere among the cohort was improving. Joking and banter amongst the men increased as they marched.

Not far outside of Aelia, they approached a convergence between their road and one coming in from the East. As they approached the junction, they spotted two riders in the distance, heading towards the cohort. As they came closer, it was apparent that the riders were military, but strangely, they were carrying neither shields nor lances. Two of the cohort's screening cavalry broke off to intercept the two equestrians. The cohort kept up its pace as the two dishevelled troopers and escort caught up with the cohort on the junction.

The rider's condition made it apparent to the foot soldiers that something was wrong. As the horses came to a stop in front of him, Centurion Petronius brought the cohort to a standstill. Marcus studied the riders and their beasts; a sorry pair, lacking shields and spears, and only one wearing a helmet. They looked as though they had been riding a long time over a long distance; even the horses appeared dusty, let alone the riders. Positioned at the head of the cohort, Marcus could overhear the conversation between Petronius and the lead rider. There was an initial exchange of names and ranks before the rider said,

"We are two of a small group of survivors from En Geddi. The town is now in rebel hands."

"Jupiter!" said Petronius. "What the fuck happened?"

"Can my brother and I have some water? We ran out earlier today. We're parched. Then I'll give you the story."

Petronius called for water for the riders. Two legionaries offered water bottles, the contents of which the riders gulped down. Then finally, the spokesperson, who was simply the most experienced soldier out of the two, told of the events at En Geddi.

"As you know, the *Cohors I Milaria Thracum* garrison En Geddi with close to three hundred men. Centurion Magonius Valens is our commander. It has been noticeably quiet of late, not a lot happening. Then, around sunrise four days ago, all Hades broke loose. They hit us with a full-scale military assault. Hard to say how many, but some say over two thousand!" The auxiliary looked amongst his audience to respond to the number of rebels. He got one. "A small group of us got isolated and pulled back to the stables. We lost a few doing so. We mounted up and charged through the rebels. Six lads went down." Again, he paused for effect. "One thing, though, has stuck in my mind over the last four days; it was their war-cry."

"Which was?" Petronius asked.

"Jerusalem," the soldier replied.

"Fuck me," one of Marcus's comrades said, "the bastards are heading our way, brothers!" The soldier had verbalised what the whole cohort was thinking. Men were weighing up the fighting strength of the Tenth Fretensis against the estimated numbers of rebels. Even allowing for some centuries still stationed on garrison duties, the number of soldiers in the Aelia should cope with the rebels.

"We'll treat this lot of cunni as we treated their mates," a voice exclaimed.

"Silence!" Petronius bellowed. He held his gnarled vine stick, the familiar badge of rank of the Centurion, high in the air. "The next man to so much as a whisper will get this across his back." The cohort fell quiet. Petronius turned to the cavalry commander.

"So then, what happened to the rest of your men?"

"They are about four miles back, taking shelter. Frankly, some are at the end of their tether. We have skirmished twice, resulting in some injuries. Tullius and I rode ahead to find help.

If you could spare a cart and a few soldiers, sir, I'll bring them in."

Centurion Petronius stared at the ground, stroking his chin, saying as he did so,

"There may be more of the sneaky bastards out there, soldier." His head rose to reveal a determined look on his face. "No, we shall do this properly. Here's the plan...."

With a small cavalry escort, the carts and livestock moved off toward Aelia. The cohort, accompanied by one cart, prepared to move along the road the auxiliaries had approached from. The Thracians remounted, ready to lead the way. Petronius had put the unit on alert, and each legionary was prepared should they be attacked.

Orders rang out, and the cohort trudged along behind the Thracian on horseback, a more sober unit than the one that had come to a standstill a few minutes earlier. Marcus' mind raced, turning over what he had just overheard. For all the bravura of his mates, it occurred to him they might not be dealing with rebels any longer. Instead, they were facing an army. He consoled himself that a Jewish army would be no match for the drills and training of a Roman legion.

They passed two small, empty villages as they moved eastwards, though Marcus thought he saw the odd face at a window but couldn't be sure. Finally, they approached a valley with sides covered in large scrub bushes after an hour. The Thracian rider brought his horse to a stop. He made a loud, distinctive whistle, and from behind a distant bush, a man stood. The Thracian waved to him. The man waved back and said something into the bushes at his rear. Instantly, men appeared.

Some men were in fair shape, while others were in poor condition and needed assistance to descend. The Medicus jumped down from his waggon, took up his bag and ascended the slope to help the exhausted auxiliaries from En Geddi. Centurion Petronius turned to his column,

"1stCentury, two tent parties, fallout," he said. "Give these lads a hand." Marcus and his immediate comrades laid down their spears and shields and moved to assist the exhausted auxiliaries. One soldier, who was poorly, was being laid on the ground at the foot of the slope by two of his fellow auxiliaries. Identifying him as the worst affected of the group, the Medicus attended the soldier. He ordered the injured soldier's two mates to get water from the waggon, and he began treating the injured man.

Marcus approached as the Medicus was cutting the soldier's tunic to access a wound in the man's side. He looked up at Marcus.

"Get me a bucket of water as fast as you can."

Marcus did not have to be asked a second time and soon returned with a canvas bucket slopping with water. As the Medicus washed the wound, the soldier mumbled deliriously. Marcus squatted down by his head and put a hand on his shoulder.

"You'll be alright, mate," he said, "you're in good hands now, and you won't have to walk. We've a nice comfy waggon to take you back to camp."

The soldier continued his mumbling and Marcus lent forwards to hear.

"So hot....I remember well....my father told me....the balsam....after all we gave....look what the cunni have done....no more bloody drill...."

Marcus squatted upright again. Had he heard correctly? However, he was sure his hearing was fine. He caught the Medicus' eye, gave him a querying look, glanced at the wound, then back to the Medicus. The man shook his head; this one was unlikely to make it. Leaving the Medicus with his bucket, Marcus stood up and went to the wagon where the auxiliaries were quenching their thirst and devouring bread. He approached one and, pointed to the soldier being tended by the Medicus, asked,

"What's your mate's name?"

"Mynos Kipula. Unlucky fucker. The last skirmish, late yesterday, after we'd driven off the attackers, an injured cunni we thought dead, stuck Mynos' side with a spear." He sighed. "We did our best, but I fear the spear was tipped with poison."

"It is," Marcus said. "I suspect he will be with the Chiron by nightfall."

Before Marcus could ask further questions, Centurion Petronius ordered the two tent parties to return to the column. Along with several exhausted comrades, they loaded auxiliary Kipula onto the cart. Within a matter of minutes, the column was backtracking at a good pace, intent on reaching Aelia Capitolina by nightfall.

"People, people, let's not get ahead of ourselves," said a frustrated Tineus Rufus. The meeting as it was heading off in a direction he had never intended. When the news of the fall of En Geddi reached Aelia, Rufus had believed it a good idea to assemble the town's leaders and the Roman command to discuss the situation.

Governor Rufus had summoned Quinctilius Varus, governor of the colony of Aelia, to the principia. Varus had served as a centurion in the Fretensis before retiring and settling in the new town. Varus had brought along his deputy. Lucius Fabius. Rufus had felt it was politic to invite Cassius Cornelius, a wealthy Equestrian from Rome, and an old friend of the Imperator. In addition, Quintus Vorenus, the Primus Pilus of the Fretensis, was present. Finally, sitting alongside Rufus were two of the legion's military tribunes. Rufus continued.

"We cannot even consider conceding ground to these rebels. Fortune was on their side when they surprised and overwhelmed the *Miliaria Thracum* at En Geddi. Here at Aelia, we are ready and prepared, and what is more, we are Legion regulars – not auxiliaries. Just because they used the word 'Jerusalem' as a battle cry does not mean they are about to overwhelm us. Far from it!"

Quinctilius Varus pursed his lips; he did not share the Governor's confidence. A heavily built man, the bulk of his body being pure muscle, many of the old soldiers in the colony looked up to him. When he spoke, people listened.

"Governor, you are right," he said, whilst his body language spoke differently. "A legion protects Aelia. However, after the fighting and skirmishing of the last few weeks, it's a depleted legion. The fort is defensible, but may I remind you, the colony itself has no protecting walls. Should the rebels come, defending Aelia would be a messy business."

Rufus let out a noisy sigh and slammed the palms of both hands down onto the table.

"Is there anyone of you that believes these rebels would attempt to attack Aelia?" He demanded. There was a silence as Rufus' audience stared meaningfully at the table. Then, after a few seconds, a voice spoke.

"May I say a few words, governor?" It was Cassius Cornelius who had broken the silence. Rufus nodded. "In the brief time I've been in the colony, I've met and talked to a good number of the Jewish business community living amongst our ex-soldiers and Roman merchants. So, I am naturally curious and have tried to understand what is happening in Judaea."

"I would welcome your observations, Cassius," Rufus responded. "Anything that will help us eliminate this problem needs saying at this table."

Quintus Vorenus inwardly smiled; Cassius's relationship with Hadrianus caused Rufus to be so diplomatic.

"Thank you, Governor," said Cassius, "Here is what I have learnt. For many centuries, Israel, which the Romans call Provincia Judaea, has been their home. Throughout Israel, their religion has been paramount.; in fact, they refer to themselves as 'God's chosen people.' Israel was a nation governed by its priests, and the heart of the priesthood was the city of Jerusalem. Israel became a client of Rome's, and the relationship functioned well until the great revolt in the time of Nero. We know that that revolt ended when Titus took and destroyed Jerusalem, the heart of the revolt." Cassius paused and looked around the group. Heads were nodding, and there seemed to be no disagreement with what he had said. He continued. "Since that time, the Jews have yearned to take back Jerusalem and to rebuild their grand temple to their God. The relationship until the Great Revolt was a partnership. Now it is subservient, ruled by their conquerors – interestingly, that is the term often used by the Jews to describe Romans. Is this just an interesting history lesson? No, it is not!" The heads stop nodding. Many of those present stared at Cassius.

Quintus Vorenus raised his eyebrows – 'here it comes,' he thought to himself.

"Governor, Tribunes, this is no political revolt against Roman authority. The joy of such revolts is they can be suppressed - politics, as we know, is a constantly moving feast. No force like theirs, driven by political belief, would be crazy enough to attack Aelia and its fort. Here though, we face a fundamental, deep-seated religious belief century old. We are facing a force that believes fervently that its God is on its side. With him, they will overcome whatever Rome should throw at them. Yes, governor, I strongly suspect these rebels will come to take back their city and rebuild their temple."

Instantly, the tension in the room was palpable. An equestrian merchant from Rome had contradicted the province's governor, the Tenth Legion's commander. Quinctilius Varus sat up in his chair.

"Well," he said, "I spent my military career in the province, and Cassius Cornelius' description of these Jews would fit with my experience. Their lives are governed by their god and the teachings of their prophets. Some of it is downright strange, but me, I was raised in Egypt." He shrugged his shoulders.

Rufus was staring at the marble surface of his desk, his face giving no trace of the emotions that seethed within. There was a realisation slowly dawning, and for him, it was potentially a nightmare. The horror was that Aelia might not be defendable against the oncoming Jewish horde. He turned to the most experienced military man in the room, his trusted First Spear, the legions primus pilus, Quintus Vorenus.

"Primus, how do you see this situation?

Vorenus did not rush to answer and sat for several seconds looking beyond the Governor, out through the window behind him. Then, realising that every head in the room was looking at him, Vorenus spoke.

"Sir, we're in no easy position," he began. "The fighting has knocked the lads about in the last few weeks. Yes, the recent retaliatory raids have boosted morale, but the number of fighting men is lower than I would like. We could do with the cohorts currently in Caesarea." He paused as he marshalled his thoughts, realising that what he was about to say could significantly impact everyone in the room. "The question is, if attacked, could we successfully defend both Aelia and the fort? Governor Varus is correct that the colony has no walls and will be difficult to defend against a determined attack by overwhelming numbers. Especially if we have to defend the fort simultaneously."

"Let me understand this, Vorenus," said Rufus slowly and deliberately, "in an attack, you do not think the fort and the colony are both defensible. Am I right?"

Vorenus had a long, distinguished career behind him and had been in sticky situations before. But it had been a long time since he had felt this nervous.

"That reflects my opinion, sir."

"Thank you, Centurion," Rufus said officiously. "Let us suppose the Primus is correct. What are the options open to us?"

It was Lucius Fabius, Varus's deputy, who spoke up.

"It would appear everything hinges upon *if* the rebels will attack us… and when?" He had everyone's attention. Fabius was a successful merchant and one of the first to open a business in the new colony. He was young to be deputy governor of a colony, but he had a sharp mind and good administrative skills. "First, we must address the 'if', and I suspect that the 'when' will sort itself out. Second, we need a plan. If they come to attack, it would seem we must evacuate Aelia."

There were audible gasps throughout the room. Rufus' nightmare loomed large; evacuate Aelia. Aelia, a colony founded by and named after Imperator Hadrianus. The absolute ignominy of it! It could well be career-defining. If it came out that he may have had a role to play in causing this crisis, may the gods help him. This was never meant to happen. One of the two Tribunes, Gaius Sallus, interrupted his thoughts.

"I may have an idea regarding the 'if' Governor."

"Go on, go on," Rufus snapped. The Tribune was typical of many of his rank. They sent a young man to the legions for a year as part of his training. He would then move on to bigger and better things. Usually, such individuals formed a staff for the legion's commander. While well-educated and often bright, they were not always the most effective military operatives. This one proved the exception.

"Well, sir, we know the rebels are coming from the east. Therefore, we should establish a scout base half a day's ride from here, where we will forward patrol to detect any advance by the rebels. The scouts will report back four times a day, so if even surprised and captured, the lack of a report would alert us."

"A good proposal, sir," said Vorenus. "The Legate sent word of a large rebel camp to the north, so perhaps we could do the same in that direction."

The Tribune looked pleased that the legion's primus pilus had supported his proposal. Rufus, however, was uncomfortable.

"And if the word comes, you suggest that the population of Aelia, along with the legion, walk away? We do not fight?"

Cassius responded.

"Governor, you may recall the great revolt in Britannia. It was during Imperator Claudius' reign."

"History was never my strong point - but do continue."

"Thank you. In Britannia, a warrior queen called Boudicca revolted against Rome. Her first move was to sack the new Roman colony at Camulodunum. The military general at the time, was an officer called Paulus. They pressed him to attack Boudicca, but he realised that throwing soldiers piecemeal against the British horde would fail. So, Paulus held back, allowing Queen Boudicca to sack the Roman port of Londinium and the settlement of Verulamium until he was ready to pick the time and place to destroy the British. Though vastly outnumbered, the legion destroyed the British horde. If at any point Boudicca destroyed Paulus' legion, the whole province would have arisen and thrown Rome out of Britannia." Cassius paused as the story sunk in with his audience. "Governor, if your legion attempts to defend the colony and is beaten in doing so, I beg you to think through the consequences. The Jews will have retaken their holy city and defeated a Roman legion; Rome is no longer invincible. The entire area, Judaea, Syria and even Aegyptus, could revolt against Rome."

Rufus knew he was in a difficult position, and whatever decision he came to, his career was in the balance. Yet, no one in the room spoke as the pressure piled up on the governor.

"Vorenus, I suggest we take the Tribune's suggestion," said Rufus, "and place a scout base to monitor any attempt by the Jews from En Geddi to move on us. Also, your suggestion regarding a similar base to the north has value. Do it. There will be no attempt to desert this colony until we have a confirmation from the Primus Pilus that we have a genuine problem." He paused. "Are we agreed?"

Heads nodded. Quinctilius Varus, the colony's governor, spoke up.

"If I may, Governor?" Rufus waved his hand. "I'd like to alert the population so they can be ready for an orderly evacuation. I fear if we do nothing until the rebels are approaching, the result could be chaos."

"That may make sense," said Primus Vorenus. "Getting everyone out will be a major challenge. We assume that we're in enemy territory until we get thirty miles north of here. Additionally, we're led to believe a force north of here may need to be dealt with. This may get very messy."

"So, the citizens should prepare to move at short notice?" said Rufus. "Can you be sure that alone will not cause panic?"

"Let me coordinate with the Colony Council, governor," said Varus. "I'm sure we can manage this. At least doing it this way, we've the luxury of time. Leave it, and it will be chaos."

The meeting continued whilst they agreed on minor details before Rufus' visitors filed out of the room. Last to leave, Quintus Vorenus paused in the doorway and turned.

"Governor, can I have a moment with you – in private?"

"Of course, Quintus. Please sit." The Primus Pilus sat facing the governor.

"Sir, you're the governor of Provincia Judaea besides being the commander of the Tenth Legion – the entire Tenth Legion." He paused as his words sank in. "The situation is worsening. We've a major revolt on our hands that could become a war. As this legion's primus, it's my humble view that you need to be back in Caesarea. It's much too risky for you to remain bottled up here in Aelia."

"So, you want me out of here, Primus?"

"Immediately, sir. You'll be able to take complete control from Caesarea and defeat these *cunni*!"

"By the gods, Quintus," exclaimed Rufus. "Do I sense you believe you may be unable to get out of this place?"

"I wouldn't go so far, sir, but we don't want you in the middle of it all. We need to get you out. Perhaps we can get Tribune Laticlavius Civilis back down to take over?"

"We could, we could," Rufus responded as he thought through the Primus' proposal. He weighed up what he saw as reputational damage against his survival. "I'd get ready in two days -."

"Excuse me, sir. Now. I fear the window of opportunity may close fast."

"What!"

"I've a small group of cavalry turmae standing by. Moving fast, you'll be well clear in a short time."

For once, Tineus Rufus was left speechless, though strangely relieved. Whilst a defeat in Aelia would be disastrous, it would cover all the tracks of some shady dealings.

As the sun was dropping from the sky, Marcus Apollinaris stepped into the Minerva taberna. After the day's exertions, his century had been dismissed and given the night off. He wanted to get away for a few hours, so he washed, donned a clean tunic, left his new mates, and headed for the Minerva. Unfortunately, the Taberna had yet to re-open for business; it may be some time before Anaitis felt up to re-opening the business and employing staff. Marcus grimaced as he wondered if time was on Aelia Capitolina's side?

"Marcus!" a voice exclaimed, "You're back safe. I prayed to Diana for you." Anaitis rushed up to him and embraced him, squeezing him hard.

"Only the good die young," Marcus joked. Anaitis released him and stood back.

"You must be hungry. Let me get you some food. I still have some amphora of wine, too." She moved off towards the kitchen, and Marcus followed her. She busied herself preparing a meal for the soldier as Marcus leaned against the door frame.

"How is Miriam?" he asked.

"Oh, you won't have heard," she replied, "The medicus is so short-staffed, they've asked if she'd help in the infirmary, just changing bandages and applying poultices and the like. Many of the lads treated here at the Neptune spoke up for her. They came for her this morning."

"Funny old thing, eh? Jewish girl helping Roman soldiers injured by 'er own kind! A lone woman in that situation – it's unheard of. The medics must be desperate."

"No, Marcus, you're wrong," Anaitis said forcefully. "She's a *Talmidei*. I'm told that the rebels are murdering them if they refuse to fight for them."

"You're right, and we saved 'er from that during our jaunt with the Optio."

"What's more, she can well care for those injured lads. So many of them trust her now."

Anaitis put down the knife she used to prepare the meal and walked over to the door, facing Marcus. Her countenance changed.

"Marcus, is it true?"

"Is what true?"

"That a rebel army is coming?" Her lower lip was trembling. "They will attack Aelia… kill us all…" She threw herself at Marcus and sobbed into his shoulder. "I can't face it again, Marcus. I'd rather kill myself. I've lost Agenor - I don't want to lose you."

Marcos closed his arms around her. There were no helpful facts to share with her, but he thought to reassure her. He pushed her back so he could look into her face.

"Anaitis, this is Hadrianus' colony, protected by the *Fretensis*. We're prepared for them. Hey, we trounced them today, didn't we? They will not get near you." It was then that the last words she spoke became clear. "And I am not going anywhere."

She clung to him yet again, kissed him on the neck and then on the lips; it was no simple kiss between friends and Marcus felt his body responding. For a while, body pressed hard against body, and tongue explored tongue. Marcus felt desire surging through him as he squeezed Anaitis closer. His hands slid down to her buttocks. She mimicked him, pulling them both crotch to crotch, an act that betrayed his state of arousal.

There came the sound of footsteps, followed by the creaking of an opening door. Instantly alerted to someone entering the taberna, the two would-be lovers froze and then leapt apart.

"I'll finish your lunch, Marcus," Anaitis said as she turned back to the table where the components of his meal sat, ready to come together on a plate. "See who it is."

Marcus straightened his tunic, left the doorway, and walked into the primary room of the taberna. Miriam closed the front door behind her and turned into the room as he did so. A look of surprise crossed her face, followed by an enormous smile.

"Marcus, I am happy see you. You returned."

"I told you I would. Me? I'm difficult to kill." He felt his body returning to normal as the sexual tension abated. He wondered if Miriam could see his discomfort. "I 'eard you've been recruited?"

"A *capsarius*, yes. Bandages, poultices; simple things. Many men poorly. I like help them. Some are boys." She paused, "But you. You went to fight. How was it?"

Marcus could hear her Greek was developing, especially when not so long ago, she spoke only Aramaic. Before she could answer, Anaitis appeared with a plate of meats and bread accompanied by a welcome beaker of wine. Marcus waited to respond until she placed the meal on the table and sat opposite him. Miriam joined them.

"Let me tell you...." Marcus recounted the events of the day. The woman grimaced at some detail and other times showed concern. A tear ran down Miriam's cheeks as he related the death of the young fugitive. She found the whole episode gruelling. Miriam did not miss that Anaitis leaned ever closer to Marcus across the table as the story was related. Finally, his account was over. All he omitted were the words of the dying auxiliary soldier; they were for certain ears only.

"I hear at infirmary rebels may come to here," Miriam said, wiping her eyes, "Important people at a meeting this evening."

"Marcus says the legion will stop them," interjected Anaitis. Miriam noticed her friend's facial expression – it appeared Marcus was becoming her hero.

"Marcus, will Lucius return with more soldiers?" Miriam asked. It was apparent that working in the infirmary would expose her to a more realistic view of the situation. Damaged, the mighty Tenth Legion was not the fighting machine it was.

"They don't let lads like me in on those decisions, Miriam. I 'eard about a meeting too, so a plan'll be formed, you can be sure."

"I am little afraid, Marcus." Said Miriam.

"No need," Anaitis interjected. "Marcus says the legion will protect us!"

"I am sure they will," Miriam said, placing her hand over Anaitis'. Marcus recognised the expression of concern on Miriam's face, a concern he also shared. "I am sure they will."

They talked for some time, a meandering conversation, but kept coming back to the current situation. Several times, Anaitis declared her faith in the legion to protect them. Though Miriam concurred, Marcus was sure she was feigning simply to calm her friend. Eventually, Marcus told them he had to return to the barracks. As he prepared to leave, Miriam gave him a brief hug, saying, "Thank you for being our friend." The hug surprised Marcus, given the conservative nature of Jewish women, but it was only the hug, a 'big sister' hug. Anaitis, in total contrast, hugged him tight and close. Marcus prayed she would not kiss him in front of Miriam, and the gods answered his request. He left.

As he walked back through the dark streets of the vicus, Marcus' mind was in turmoil. If Miriam had not arrived when he did, he would have had Anaitis on the table. From what he had seen many times, he knew she had a desirable body, and it would have been a fuck he would have enjoyed. Even as he walked along, he felt the first stages of arousal. However, the other half of his mind, his conscience, responded differently. Does she really want me, a mere legionary and not exactly the finest physical specimen? (Sextus Postumus jumped into his mind) Perhaps she would give herself to any man who could rescue her from this frightening situation. Am I nothing more than a branch thrown for the drowning swimmer to clutch? He shrugged and said to no one in particular,

"If I get a shag from it, so what?" Two passers-by gave him an odd look before carrying on their way.

Marcus did not return to his barracks but sought the centurion's mess. He entered the fort, and even without beacons burning on every corner, he knew exactly where to go. They designed every Roman fort across the empire the same way; know one, know all. In front of the doors into the mess were two soldiers in full military apparel bearing javelins and stood behind their shields. Marcus approached one sentry.

"Marcus Apollinaris, Fifth Cohort, to see Centurion Petronius. Ninth Cohort."

The sentry looked Marcus up and down before telling him to wait. The man turned, placed his shield against the wall, and disappeared inside the building. Again, Marcus waited as the other sentry eyed him up and down.

"Must be urgent this time of night," said the sentry. "Centurion is probably just getting settled in."

"I don't think he'll mind," Marcus replied, "and I'd rather be falling into my pit. I was on one of today's operations and I'm knackered!"

"Heard we whacked it to the *cunni*!"

"We did, but there weren't many of 'em, brother. Women and kids, but few men."

The sentry laughed.

"Do unto them what they do unto us, 'eh?"

"Fair enough," Marcus replied, "but then we found them En Geddi survivors."

"Fucking auxiliaries, some job of defence they put up!"

"They were outnumb -."

"Legionary Apollinaris, what on earth do you want at this hour?" Centurion Julius Petronius walked through the doorway, followed by the first sentry.

"Sir, I would like a word," he said. He looked about him at the sentries, "in private, please, sir."

"Come." The centurion moved towards a dark corner where they would not be overheard. Marcus followed. "Well, Apollinaris, what is it you have that is important enough to drag me away from my wine and brothers?"

"Maybe nothing, sir, but I thought you should be told like. It's about them auxiliaries we came across earlier today…" and Marcus related the tale of the dying auxiliary, Mynos Kipula. "…and I realise it ain't much, sir,"

"You've done the right thing, legionary. But don't forget, these conspirators tried to kill you; anything you come across is worth reporting back. So, there was just one mention of balsam: 'The balsam…. after all we gave…. look what the *cunni* have done….'?"

"Yes, sir."

"And this Mynos Kipula is dead?" the centurion asked warily.

"Yes… well, actually, lasts I sees of him, we were all sure he was a goner – poisoned spear tip, sir."

"So, he *might* have survived?"

"I 'spose so, sir. Possibly."

"Right." The centurion spoke the word with a sense of finality. "Get some sleep. And gratitude for coming to me. Good night legionary." With that, Centurion Petronius strode back to the mess block and disappeared through the doorway. A yawning Marcus headed back to his bed.

It was a new day, and the sun had just reached the forum in Aelia Capitolina. It was built in brilliant white marble, befitting its status as the centre of a colony named after the Imperator. Multiple shops selling all kinds of wares, foods and spices ran around its edges. As the colony grew, the forum became a busy hub. Today it heaved with concerned citizens, answering the call for an urgent assembly. Standing on a rostrum at one end of the place, a man stood in a brilliant white toga. The crowd listened to the colony's governor, Quinctilius Varus, outline the colony's current situation. The more he spoke, the greater the concern of the crowd.

For many, their worst fears were taking on form. They had invested heavily in creating this new colony, and now Varus was telling them to prepare for an evacuation, which came as a shock. The invincible Roman army protected them – this kind of thing did not happen to Rome's citizens. Many passed through the stage of shock and shouted questions at the governor. How had this happened? Surely Caesarea would send help? Who is responsible for this coming about?

The colony's councillors were at the foot of the rostrum, looking uncomfortable. The adjacent crowd shouted questions towards them. Some threw more than questions; fruit, bread or whatever they had to hand. At that point, legionaries filed into the square and took station. The governor had prepared well. The crowd, not used to this situation, fell silent.

"Citizens," cried Varus, "preparations for evacuation are a cautionary move. I hope we shall remain – indeed, that is the plan. However, should the worst happen, we must be ready. We are Roman citizens. Let us not descend into some Dacian rabble."

The crowd grumbled, but no projectiles took to the air.

"I need you to be ready to move at short notice. First, prepare bags and valuables – then carry on as normal. In the next few days, if we must leave, I shall post guidelines in the forum to tell you how much you can take and where people will assemble. Then, in a week, I hope to be telling you to unpack. But I promise you, should we have to leave, we shall soon return."

"What about my stock?" a lone voice cried.

"And mine!" another tradesman called out. Comments and jeers accompanied the questions. Varus did his best.

"My friends, our goal is to preserve life. Unfortunately, we cannot save businesses and livelihoods. However, I stress, we may not have to implement an evacuation; it is a fall-back plan."

The crowd rumbled again.

"Where's *the* governor? Why is he not talking to us?"

Varus baulked at answering, his discomfort visible.

"Well," the voice called again, "Is it a secret?" Again, the crowd rumbled. Varus could evade answering no longer.

"He is returning to Caesarea to take control of the province and organise a response to the situation."

"Oh yeah? When is he 'returning'?" the heckler cried, supported by the crowd.

"He left last night," Varus said. The uproar ensued. The crowd pushed the councillors at the foot of the rostrum back, some toppling over as the crowd surged. Varus held his position on the rostrum as a file of legionaries pushed forward to protect him and his councillors. If it could be thrown, it was. Cries of "We've been deserted" and "We're abandoned" filled the air. At one point, an entire basket of fruit sailed through the air, just missing the governor and crashing into some legionaries positioned behind him. The situation had turned nasty.

A whistle sounded above the noise. It gave four long blasts. A regular drumming noise began by the end of the fourth blast; *thump – thump – thump*. The crowd paused and looked around for the source of the noise and its meaning. They quickly found the source. Now surrounding the forum, legionaries had drawn their swords, beating them on their shields. The crowd stilled. This was not a Roman mob; they were hard-working citizens who had lost control. They quickly perceived the message being sent by the soldiers – silence fell across the forum.

Holding his ground on the rostrum, Varus raised his arms in the air. The drumming stopped.

"My friends, we are all in this together. One thing is for sure, unless we stay together, we will not come out of this as we would like. Believe me, these soldiers," he said, pointing out the troops positioned on the perimeter of the forum, "wish to be getting to grips with our enemies, not our people. If we get behind them, we may not have to evacuate Aelia. If we must leave, it is they who will protect us. There is no option. Working together is the only way forward." Varus pushed his luck. "Is there anyone who will not fall in and work together to get us prepared for whatever may come?"

Varus was unsure if the silence was a complete agreement or fear of the shiny gladii presented by the legionaries.

"I suggest we return to our business or homes. I will post notifications in the forum each day. Please read them and follow the advice and instructions given."

Sullen but accepting, the crowd moved away. The whistle sounded again, giving two short blasts. Swords crashed back into their scabbards, the sound reverberating around the square. Varus stepped down from the rostrum, joining Lucius Fabius, his deputy.

"Lucius, I want a meeting of councillors in one hour. Kindly ask the Primus Pilus and the tribunes to attend. Oh, and we might as well have Cassius Cornelius in on this too – he is a friend of Hadrianus and might be a useful ally."

"I can arrange that Quinctilius."

"If we need to evacuate, we will do this properly. However, I fear we may be reliant upon the legion to keep order. Those last few minutes were an uncomfortable experience."

"They were frightened, Quinctilius. Frightened people behave irrationally."

"That, my friend, is just what worries me."

Capitulum XX – A time to leave

16 Aprilis. Year 16 of the Imperator Hadrianus

'It is time for a fight!' This was the message received by Legio X Fretensis during the morning legionary parade. There was no mistaking it, thought Marcus as he stood in ranks with the legionaries of his adopted cohort. Senior centurions (but no sign of the Primus) and a handful of tribunes were briefing the soldiers on the situation. The rebels had taken En Geddi. Scouting parties were out to act as an early warning of any rebel advance. Then came the thunderbolt — the governor had departed the night before, returning to Caesarea. That's it, thought Marcus. There's a storm coming, and it will rain *cac* all over us. When the parade broke up, the men of the legion mustered in their cohorts to receive more detailed orders from their centurions.

It was as expected: check all equipment, swords, javelins, armour, footwear. The list went on. The Keeper of the Weapons would be a busy man this day. There would be some rebalancing of centuries, evening out the numbers between them. A myriad of minor details, all indicators that the legion was moving to a war footing followed this. The days of policing rebels were over. Marcus awaited the order to dismiss as the parade ended when a young tribune joined senior centurion Petronius.

"Men, you know what you have to do, so let's get it done." Petronius bellowed. "Legionary Apollinaris, report to me once we fall out. The cohort will dismiss." Centurions repeated the order to their centuries, and the soldiers moved off to attend to their duties. Marcus remained in place while the soldiers departed, then marched across to where his senior centurion and the tribune stood, smartly presenting himself. Much to his surprise, the Primus Pilus joined them.

"Rest at ease, Apollinaris," said Quintus Vorenus, the Primus. He turned to the tribune who stood beside him. "This is Tribune Gaius Sallus. We'd like to talk to you. Centurion Petronius, feel free to return to your cohort. Come, let us walk." Julius Petronius left the group, and the trio of tribune, centurion and legionary walked across a near-empty drill field. "What I say is confidential, Apollinaris. If a word leaks out, I shall flog every piece of flesh from your back, after which I shall rip off your head and shit down your throat. Do I make myself clear?"

"Very clear. Sir!"

"Good, that is understood. How is your injury?"

"Given the *cunni* tried to remove my arse through my stomach, it's doing well, sir. It reminds me it's there sometimes."

"Good, I need you to be fit," said the Primus. "I have a job for you, assisting Tribune Sallus."

Here we go again, thought Marcus, weighing up Sallus. He was young, most likely from a senatorial family, here for a year before going back to join the political circus in Rome. He probably hates soldiering, thought Marcus.

"Given your cohort is in Caesarea," said Vorenus, "you could say you are a bit of a spare *mentula* here in Aelia. In your favour, Centurion Petronius' nephew spoke highly of you in your role, supporting him. I want you to do the same for the Tribune here." He said, nodding towards the young officer. He ploughed on. "We understand the rebel army may head this way. If it is, we plan to evacuate Aelia." Marcus stopped in his tracks; the other two had moved a pace forward before they stopped and turned.

"Apologies, sir. *Evacuate* Aelia?"

"Correct. I hate this as much as the next soldier." The distaste was clear in the Primus' face. "Look, we're outnumbered, but worse, Aelia has no walls we can defend. The governor's concern is the civilian population. If the Jews get into the town, it'll be carnage. We're not beaten. We're making a tactical withdrawal. Then we come back and fuck the *cunni* once and for all. Let me continue."

"Apologies, sir."

"When – if – we evacuate, the legion will function as protection for what'll be a substantial refugee column. There are many ex-soldiers in the colony. They've already formed an ad hoc militia, and they're already coming forward to volunteer for the legion. So, we should have extra swords to protect the withdrawal, covering for lost men. That'll be straightforward to plan, but we need an urban cohort in Aelia in this situation. This unit can administer and control the civilian element, put together a waggon train and keep it moving once we go. This could be a tough operation all-around, legionary. However, the last thing we need is a horde of panicking civilians. Understand?"

"Yes, sir."

"Good. We're picking some of the ex-legionary volunteers to formalise the existing ad hoc militia. They'll police the civilian element of the evacuation. They'll work under Tribune Sallus here, and I want you to act as his aide, as you did for Optio Petronius, with the rank of Watch Officer. You'll work alongside an ex-centurion who'll take practical command of the new militia.

Do not get above your station Apollinaris. You will deal with the colony's populace, organising, and keeping order, so you'll need a rank. It will give you authority and enable you to enforce the decisions that you need to make. The Watch Officer rank is one that Tribune Sallus and I have created for this situation. The minute we reach Caesarea, you will return to your cohort and take up the duties of a legionary."

It stunned Marcus. Arriving at the drill field, he expected another day of drills, make and mends, and all the usual activities in the day of a life of a Roman Legionary. But now, his world just turned upside down. Watch officer, but not a denarius extra pay, bloody typical of the Roman army!

"Right, legionary, I'll leave you with Tribune Sallus. He is now your officer. I remind you; we have not announced this plan yet. The people have been told that we only are *considering* the possibility of an evacuation. Should we have to leave, we will then announce the reorganisation of the Militia. Over to you, Tribune. I need to be off to meet with the colony's governor."

"Very good centurion." Vorenus turned and smartly strode off. Gaius Sallus looked the part. A polished helmet with a flowing white plume. His cuirass was of white pressed linen, and his boots were of red leather. Beside him, Marcus felt plain, but at least his segmentata was highly polished. "Let's talk as we walk, legionary." Marcus wondered what his fellow legionaries would think if they should see him hob-knobbing with a military tribune.

"Right then, Apollinaris. This is all not what it may seem. Fact: we do not know just how many ex-soldiers will volunteer. Fact: when they do, the ones we get will be those unfit for legionary duty – cast-offs and misfits. Our principal role will be to organise the assembly of an evacuation column and then to ensure it keeps moving in good order. Our centurion is Julius Gracchus; he left the Tenth eight years ago."

The two men talked for some time, circumnavigating the drill field twice, and Sallus shared his thoughts. They talked through how the militia would operate and how they might manage moving two thousand civilians from Aelia up to Caesarea, given many would make the journey on foot. He was hopeful the militia might be close to numbering one hundred. Sallus had concerns about the fitness of the cohort for making the journey – its members would have been out of the legion for some time, enjoying a softer living. They had already failed legion selection. After a little longer, the two agreed to meet later that day, along with ex-centurion Julius Gracchus.

Over the next two days, the volunteers came forward. The legion picked the fittest of the men, who were sent for retraining; it would be busy on the drill field. Those rejected by the legion were passed across to Centurion Gracchus. Gracchus may have been out of the legion for many years, but he was still lean, tall and had a mean look that belied his good nature. He must have been a tough centurion in his prime, Marcus thought. He knew the centurion would require junior officers to build his watches, while Marcus' role was more administrative. In this early stage, he was to capture the general details of the volunteers and any specific information Gracchus required from them.

What these men had lost in fitness, they made up for in enthusiasm. It was said that the most miserable soldier was the retired soldier. Well, the volunteers were bubbling with enthusiasm for their new role. True, they had not made it to the legion, but they would be back in arms. At the end of the two days, they had eighty-six ex-legionaries eager to go. They would muster on the drill field and be formally inducted into the militia the following day. Sallus and the centurion would then take them through the plans for the coming days.

The militia mustered on the drill field by mid-morning the following day.

Marcus strode onto the drill field where Gracchus stood before the century of volunteer rejects. His heart dropped. Accustomed to viewing fit, battle-ready Roman soldiers on parade, what he gazed upon was anything but. They had no uniforms and wore a myriad of styles of clothing. Most looked like they were in their forties, some a little older. Many had 'run to seed', but not all. Some were tall, others shorter. Some were greyer than others, some shaven, others bearded. It was a motley crew. However, their bearing stood out; their erect stance showed they had served, arms by their sides, eyes straight ahead. These men had been soldiers; they could become so again.

Marcus joined Gracchus.

"Ready when you are, centurion," he said. Gracchus nodded and took a deep breath.

"Right, you lot. It looks like it must have been back in Vespasian's time since last you stood on a drill field. I suspect some of you even stormed Jerusalem with Titus!"

A ripple of laughter ran through the motley crew.

"Fuck me! If I am going to tell a joke, I'll fucking let you know. Understood?" Absolute silence greeted him. "Right then. The legion needed topping up with veterans 'cos we are in a bit of a crisis, and you were good enough to volunteer. Fed up with the wife, are we? A warrior's life looked attractive. Well, guess what, you lot turned out to be the veterans the legion didn't want – the rejects. And do you know what the legion did? The bastards gave you to me!"

Inwardly, Marcus smiled. His earlier assessment of Gracchus' nature as a centurion was to the mark. The man continued.

"Yes, I got given the *cac*! Now, some of those bastards think I'm no different from you, so I intend to change their minds.

Also, I don't enjoy commanding *cac*, so you lot will change their opinion. Am I right?" Much to Marcus' surprise, the response was robust to a man.

"Yes, centurion!"

Gracchus softened.

"Good lads." He hardened again. "In two or three days, it's likely we must abandon Aelia. Leave your families to sort themselves out as you'll be busy – very busy. If you're told to do something, do it – the faster, the better. Shortly you'll get a detailed briefing but let me introduce our Watch Officer." Gracchus turned to Marcus, "Captain Marcus Apollinaris."

Marcus stood forward, not sure what to say. He was conscious some of these men had put in more service than he. If all else fails, he thought, bull it out.

"Welcome to the militia, brothers. I knows the legion thinks we're *cac*, and the way to change that is for us to do the job. You lads 'ave a wealth of experience, let's use it. Centurion Gracchus'll be your line commander. My role is as the Tribune's administrator," – he would not call himself a clerk – "and ensure that you and the column gets what it needs like. I've screwed the legion for swords, javelins, and helmets for you. You'll get 'em later."

Marcus took a step back, handing the century over to Gracchus.

"Right, you lot," he called. "Let's see how much you've forgotten!" Within seconds, the militia century was marching about the drill field. Marcus looked on. They surprised him. After several minutes of watching the old soldiers work up a sweat, Tribune Sallus appeared beside him.

"A fine body of men, 'eh Apollinaris. Well, what do you think?"

"Actually, sir, I think they may be fine for the job." He laughed, "They ain't crack legionaries, but for herding civilians… maybe."

"I hope so," the tribune responded. "I suspect by the end of this accursed business they will have been sorely tested, and we'll know if they *were* ready for it."

Not long after, Marcus and a small team was scouring Aelia, finding and documenting wagons for the evacuation. They commandeered waggons 'for military use', which caused some aggravation. Wagon owners wanted to keep their wagons for their escape and were reluctant to release control over their vehicles. It was a slow start, but gradually collected more and more waggons, and they moved off to the assembly point. At that point, Marcus handed the role over to a newly appointed militia tesserarius and set off on yet another task. They would need to commandeer provisions and arrange a stock of fresh bread to be produced just before departure from the colony. Fortunately, he was accompanied by a local militiaman who knew the businesses, enabling them to target the more significant suppliers. Again, more arguments, the main one being who would pay. Marcus promised they would issue them a note authorising payment later – if they survived to collect, thought Marcus.

He felt guilt, but he almost wished the evacuation would happen, so he could see all their work produce practical benefits. Meanwhile, militia recruit's families were told their men had volunteered to join a legionary militia. They were sworn to secrecy about their actual intent. It was a secret that lasted all of one hour. In no time, the rumour mill was working flat out. At the end of the first day, Marcus was exhausted in his new role.

People became used to seeing Marcus scurrying around the town, posting the information the governor had promised. Being Captain of the Militia was an active role, and Marcus only got back to the Neptune taberna once. It was evening, and he dropped by to check on Miriam and Anaitis. Miriam was absent, working in the infirmary, but Anaitis was there. She was not alone. An old friend of Agenor was visiting, concerned how Anaitis was faring since the old sailor's death. He was a good man, and together, the three of them ate and drank. The chief topic of conversation was the forecasted approach of the rebel army.

Marcus noticed that Anaitis had applied cosmetics, and he could not help but notice how attractive she was. The thin cotton chiton she wore aided and abetted the attraction, tied closely at the waist. It was indeed not working attire. Several times she glanced at Marcus, her eyes transmitting inviting messages. The news that Marcus was now the watch captain brought more wine onto the table. A wrong move, thought Marcus, as Amyntas' old friend liked his wine and stayed to drink more. If the old man was to go.... Marcus felt his body responding to his thoughts.

The door to the taberna sprang open, and a middle-aged man, equipped with a helmet and sword but not much else in terms of military attire, burst in.

"Captain Apollinaris, sir." Marcus still had not become used to being addressed as 'sir'. Still, he was an officer, a militia officer maybe, but an officer to a new cadre of soldiers.

"What is it?" *Cac!* He thought, she gets away again.

"I'm told you must report to the principia. Tribune Sallus sent me, sir."

"What goin' on then, soldier?"

"No idea, sir, but there's a lot of running about, sir. Please, sir, they said it was urgent like!"

Marcus rose from his seat and slung his cloak around him. As he tied his helmet strap under his chin, he turned to his host and her guest.

"Apologies and gratitude for the wine and food. It was cracking." He was about to turn away when Anaitis launched herself from her seat, crossed to Marcus and hugged him tightly, then looked him in the eye.

"They're coming, aren't they? The devils are returning?" She buried her dead in his shoulder, every curve and projection of her body pressing against him. Marcus wanted her, but knowing he had to leave, he reluctantly untangled himself from her.

"If there's any danger, I'll be looking out for you, Anaitis. Believe me. Though I hate to, I have my duties, and I must leave."

Marcus nodded to the older guest, who smiled back.

"Gods be with you, brother," the older man said. "I'll keep a close eye on her. You just do what you need to do."

Marcus turned and headed out of the door, followed by the messenger.

"Lovely lass, if I may so, sir."

His instinctive reaction surprised Marcus: he was about to tell the man to mind his own business. He got a grip and said,

"Yes, she is." His conscience pricked; was that jealousy?

Marcus picked up on the sound of activity across the camp, building a sense of foreboding. Approaching the principia, it was clear there was heavy traffic through the front entrance. Entering the building, he spotted Gaius Sallus waiting in the main corridor, deep in conversation with Centurion Gracchus. The tribune spotted Marcus approaching.

"Apollinaris, good, you've made it. There's a meeting about to start, and we need to be in it. Scouts rode in not so long ago; the rebels are moving in this direction." Marcus looked from Sallus to Gracchus.

"How long do we 'ave?"

"We'll find out, brother, but rumour says three days," Gracchus said. "My view, we need to be out of here in two."

"I suggest we go in," said Sallus.

The assembled officers listened to the confirmation of their suspicions; the enemy *was* approaching. Gracchus had not lost his soldier's intuition or his ability to detect rumours – the tribune presenting the situation confirmed the rebels could be outside Aelia in three days. If the populace and legion were to make their escape, they needed to get away in two. The meeting ran on for an hour, and when it was over, Sallus and his two officers retired to a small office where they would be undisturbed. The three sat at a small table.

"In two days," said Sallus, "we shall leave Aelia. I cannot believe it, but it is a fact." The tribune looked at his two lieutenants, who hung on his words. "I will not beat about the bush, men. This may be a defeat for the Roman army, but it is not a rout. We are pulling out of Aelia under our terms, and we shall be back." Marcus thought he saw a tear run down the young man's cheek. His whole body seemed to sag. "In military terms, our group is at the bottom of the heap; a century of past-it soldiers acting as a would-be militia." He paused for a few seconds, his face hardening, and his hand slapped the table. The previous demeanour evaporated as he sat bolt upright. "Well, let me tell you both. We have a responsibility to the citizens of this colony, and it is one we will not shirk! I am damned if we lose one person on this retreat through our omissions. I will expect every, yes, every man to perform his duty as well as any regular soldier."

Silence filled the room, and Marcus watched a teardrop run down the tribune's cheek and fall onto his cuirass. Gracchus broke the silence,

"Your centurion and watch captain are yours to command, sir. We'll make it happen."

Marcus, not one for grand speeches, said,

"We can do this, sir."

Another period of silence passed, after which the tribune composed himself.

"Right," he said, "to action then. We've planned it, so let's do it."

A few minutes later, the three soldiers left the principia. Militia teams were to patrol the town, announcing that the evacuation was imminent, telling people they could only take what they could carry. Wagons would be available for their baggage. Marcus' primary role was to organise the assembly of wagons, so he took six men and set off across the colony. He estimated he had the use of just over one hundred civilian wagons and carts, big and small and of many types: eighty wagons for food and baggage, the rest to carry the infirm and fatigued. The food wagons would need to be sent to the stores to load, so they planned with Gracchus to alert those people for a visit from the militia soon. It will be a busy two days.

One piece of the tribune's advice lingered in Marcus' head; whatever situation, never forget that the common good of the colony and its citizens comes first. Marcus discovered what the tribune meant in the two days following the Principia meeting.

Marcus was a soldier who believed the Roman army could best any enemy; he was supremely confident in risky situations. However, civilians think differently. He had never seen the panic he was now seeing in Aelia. As a result, he and his men needed to become harder and more ruthless than he had ever imagined. The one resource the militia didn't have was time; it was simply not possible to spend hours persuading the owners of wagons to hand over their vehicles, taking them to the assembly point. The militia soldiers quickly developed a patter explaining why the wagons were crucial to the citizens' survival. If that failed to reach the citizen's sense of common good, they resorted to a more forceful approach. Some citizens behaved irrationally, ignoring all instructions. At one extreme, they attempted to bring far more possessions than they could carry – "We need our wagon". Some arrived at the assembly points with barrows of possessions. At the other extreme, those who had offered wagons for the evacuation changed their minds. Marcus instilled in his men the tribune's ethos. All this resulted in resorting to physical force, which was unpleasant for his soldiers, especially having been these people's neighbours a few days ago.

The matter came to a head on the second day – the planned last day – when a miller would not allow the militia to remove his wagon and his store of grain and flour for the journey. A row ensued with the miller and his two sons that spilt out onto the street, where the three men faced off four militiamen. No one can recall the sequence of events, but an altercation quickly developed. The watchers, at first quiet, became extremely aggressive, and they threw small missiles at the militia. The militiamen withdrew. It was not long before they returned, led by the tribune, accompanied by Gracchus and Marcus, along with twenty well-armed militiamen.

In no time, the bodies of the Miller and a dead son still lay in the street. In front of such a display of force, the crowd fell silent. The silence hung for a few seconds before Tribune Sallus stepped forward to the bodies. Marcus placed his hand on the pommel of his sword, ready to act. The tribune spread his arms.

"Citizens of Aelia, listen to me. I am Tribune Gaius Sallus of the Tenth Legion." He scanned the crowd to ensure he had their attention. He had. "I am charged to see that you are all taken from this colony to safety." He ignored several expressions of disbelief from the crowd. "I am a Roman soldier, and I shall carry out my duty, a duty to *all* the citizens in this colony, including you." The tone of voice changed, as did the body language. "Therefore, I will not, I repeat, not let any single person place the safety of the many at risk." Sallus looked down at the two bodies. "I regret, no less than any of you, what lies at my feet. It is a tragedy of substantial proportions but understand this; the evacuation is for *all* of you, and it will take you to safety. You have two options; follow the procedures or face the consequences." The audience was still as it took in the Tribune's words. The officer let them dwell on the subject for a few moments before continuing. "Citizens, the militia and the army are here to protect you, but *we* cannot do this alone. We need your help to make this evacuation happen. Together, we can get you to safety. There is only one other alternative; the enemy is approaching, and the gods help us if they find us still here!"

The assembled citizens remained silent for a few seconds more before a voice called out.

"We're with you, Tribune." Another, "We'll help you!" Yet another, "Mars be with the Legion!" The tension evaporated. Sallus saluted the crowd,

"Citizens," he cried, "Let us go forward together!" He turned and re-joined his troops. "Soldiers, collect the flour and grain." It surprised Marcus to see citizens rushing to help load the wagon. A small group removed the bodies from the street. As four men removed the Miller, each holding a limb, Marcus couldn't help but overhear a whispered comment.

"This bloke was a bastard. He was always overcharging for his bread. He had it coming to him, anyway." The comment drew supportive mumbles of affirmation.

The officers and militiamen called to the event made their way back to the assembly area north of the colony. Marcus' opinion of his commanding officer went up by a leap – young as he might be, he could handle himself in a tight corner.

"Our Tribune is quite the orator," remarked Gracchus.

"He's a good'un," said Marcus, "that was nasty. Could've gone either way."

"Indeed, it could," Gracchus agreed. "It was our militia that worried me. But don't forget a few days ago, they were citizens. They may have had friends in that crowd. If it got rough, what would they have done?"

"That includes you, brother?" Marcus asked. Before giving Gracchus a chance to answer, he added, "Let's pray to Mithras that we'll never 'ave to find out. We'd better see 'ow things are going at the wagons."

In due course, they arrived in the assembly area to find the attitude of the citizens had changed. A holiday atmosphere seemed to prevail. To Marcus, they were behaving as if going on an adventure rather than fleeing for their lives. Families followed the instructions to bring their belongings for loading before returning home for a last night's sleep in their homes, ready for an early departure the next day. They filled the lines of wagons with their baggage whilst other waggons took on board assorted supplies: food, flour, skins of water and a few amphorae of wine.

They had set guidelines detailing what weight and volume each citizen could bring with them. Many arrived, accompanied by their slaves, overloaded with baggage. They struggled to push their way between the wagon lines, loaded everything from bulging bags to possessions in blankets. There was constant bickering as militiamen explained to the more overloaded that some of their loads would have to remain. Families wishing to share a vehicle with friends or neighbours caused additional strain on the organisation. The situation was further complicated by many families insisting on leaving a slave overnight to guard their possessions. To compound the struggle, others pushed in the opposite direction against the flow of laden citizens, heading home for what would be the last time.

For Tribune Sallus and his team, there had been little time for the thorough organisation of the evacuation they would have wished. They attempted crude social structuring. The head of the column would see the propertied citizens. Artisans and general tradespeople would take the middle, with general workers sent to the rear. Then there was a matter of slaves, who would be a drain on resources but there was a worry that some might attempt to join the rebels if left behind. It was decided slaves would accompany the column, staying close to their masters, but would always remain on foot.

"This is a bleedin' ant's nest - ain't nothing but organised chaos!" Marcus exclaimed to Gracchus as the two stood watching the proceedings.

"Two fucking days, brother. I think we done good, but two days to organise something like this, well, it's not going to be great – is it?"

"Yeah, well, it's still a solution. It ain't perfect, but what's the option?" Gracchus did not respond, and both men continued to gaze on the 'organised' chaos before them. "Right then, are you happy we'll 'ave enough provisions by this evening?"

"I believe so, we've…"

Both men returned their focus to the job at hand.

Even though some citizens initially treated them as a joke, the militia had risen to their new task. In no time, the legion issued equipment to them. The watch appointed a Keeper of the Weapons, who worked miracles in acquiring much of anything needed. Now wearing mail coats, *lorica hamata*, they looked more like soldiers. To enable easier identification, they initially had been issued with bright yellow armbands. Once properly equipped, Marcus questioned the use of armbands any longer. They were now identifiable as more than just citizens with swords, but the men had grown to be proud of their armbands, so they retained them. Marcus felt a particular pride when the men presented him with a bright yellow sash to wear around his waist.

That evening, Sallus suggested to Marcus that he get a good night's rest as it would be an early start in the morning. Having checked that Gracchus did not need him, Marcus headed straight to the Neptune and Anaitis. He found her talking with a group of women. Their conversation focussed upon the coming evacuation. As Marcus walked in, the woman turned to him.

"It's the militia!" said one.

"Here's trouble!" said another.

"No, not at all – he's a friend," Anaitis interjected, "the one that found me after…" She had no comfortable description of her traumatic experience.

"So," said the first woman, speaking directly to Marcus, "we're off to the wagons at sunrise?"

"We are," said Marcus. "Take my advice and get there early. Take your ticket to the wagon assembly area – the militiamen will show you which is your wagon. You should get to ride sometimes, walk at others. But, if I was you, I would go to bed because tomorrow'll be a long, hard day."

The meeting wound up, and the women left. Once the door was closed, Anaitis stood up and approached Marcus.

"I thought you'd be too busy to see me," she said.

"I promised I'd take care of you," said Marcus. He omitted to add that the Tribune had ordered him to rest. "Where's Miriam?"

"She's at the infirmary preparing the wounded for movement. She's hardly ever here since they asked for her help, coming in late and leaving early in the morning. Miriam is anxious about some soldiers that are being evacuated on wagons."

"It'd be much worse if we left 'em behind, Anaitis."

The girl put her arms around Marcus.

"Is this just a quick visit or…" She leant back and untied his helmet strap, lifting the helmet off his head and placing it on a table beside them. Marcus did not resist.

"I have a few minutes, no great rush," Marcus replied. He felt the tension flow through his body as she pushed against him.

"Then let's make the best of the time we have," Anaitis replied and kissed him hard on the lips before her tongue probed his. "Upstairs," she murmured. Almost mesmerised, Marcus followed her dutifully to the stairs. Climbing the staircase, she pulled a ribbon, and her chiton fell onto the stairs behind her. Marcus looked upwards – Great Jupiter, he thought, I am about to shag Venus.

An hour later, walking through the vicus towards the fort gates, a puzzled Marcus was mulling over what had just taken place. It was unlike anything he had experienced before, incredible, but…. He had never experienced a woman as skilful in bed as Anaitis. The sex was unbelievably good, but…. In between bouts of furious lovemaking, she told him, panting, how she loved him, but….

He orgasmed quickly, but she kept working on him, bringing him back to form within a few minutes. It was no time until he spasmed again, moaning in sheer pleasure and falling back on the bed, a spent man. Had she even noticed, he wondered, because she continued her arousal techniques until he gave his all a third time? He felt like she was somewhere else, and he was being used. Finally, he was all done and had to calm her down; her body drenched in sweat – they both were – he held her firm on the bed whilst the panting slowed, and she relaxed.

"Anaitis, I don't have the word -."

"I love you, Marcus," she clutched him close, "Please don't leave me. I can't face --"

"Sssh," Marcus soothed, "I have to return to the militia, but I'll take care of you, my honey. When you come to the wagons tomorrow, ask any of the militia - they wear a yellow armband - to find me. All right?" The girl nodded, her head resting on his shoulder. "Thank you for a night I won't ever forget. Now, I have to go." He took her head in his hands and kissed her before slipping from the bed and dressing. She watched him in silence. He kissed her again before letting himself out of the taberna.

Now, back in the street, Marcus was trying to understand what had just happened. The frightened, timid girl he knew became someone else in bed. He had followed her upstairs thinking she was Venus, but had he made love with the shade of Cleopatra? It was as though she was possessed. He loved it, but it was a little scary. Was this an entanglement that he wanted? He decided to wait and see how it developed, but he had other more threatening matters to deal with in the short term, and a good kip would help with the coming challenge.

Before the sun's first light, Marcus was up, dressed, armed and ready for the day. All he could think of was Anaitis and the previous night's torrid encounter as he prepared for duty. Setting out for the assembly area, he disciplined himself and focussed on the task at hand. He knew Gracchus had patrols in the colony whose roles were to ensure the town was cleared of civilians, driving the tardier towards the assembly point north of the camp.

The militia was divided into small teams. Each team was allocated to care for several wagons. They would 'manage' the townsfolk attached to those wagons, ensuring who would walk and who would ride at any given time. Other militiamen would move along the column, used as and when needed. Thankfully the legion would be guarding and protecting the column.

By the time Marcus reached the assembly point, Sallus and Gracchus were ready and waiting. Gracchus assured the other two men that all would go to plan. But then, the sound of marching feet and the unique call of the cornicens interrupted their conversation. Marcus turned to see a sight that never failed to send a shiver up his spine, a legion on the march.

Led by the Primus Pilus, tribunes, and the legionary eagle, row after row of soldiers clad in steel Segmentata marched past. The iron fist of Rome. The complete body came to a stand alongside the column.

Marcus turned to his two companions,

"What the fuck are we doin' retreating?"

"It's galling; that's what it is." Said Gracchus.

"I share your feelings, men," Sallus responded. "Don't forget that the Jews will not fight us on an open field. They will avoid it at all costs. They outnumber us and will use that advantage should we try to defend the colony. So we have to save the citizens." They watched as the ranks of legionaries passed. "After that, we shall trash the rebel bastards!"

"I pray to the gods I will be there," said Gracchus.

"I trust we shall all be there, centurion," Sallus said. "Apollinaris, it will be a while before we move off. Can you keep an administrative eye on things? Any problems, let me know." Then, turning to Gracchus, "Centurion, your men are all engaged as discussed. Any issues make Apollinaris aware, and he can brief me. I wouldn't expect any help from the legion; we are at the bottom of the pecking order. Ah, here comes Varus."

Soon to be ex-governor of an ex-colony, the colony's governor was striding purposefully towards the trio.

"I'll be off then, sir," said Marcus. "See how it's all working out."

"I'll accompany you," volunteered Gracchus.

"Might be best," said Sallus. "Gracchus, can you get someone to locate my horse?"

"Indeed, sir."

The two men headed into the massed ranks of wagons and the sea of civilians milling about. Two red-faced, puffing militiamen walked past, saluting as they went.

"Gods bless them," said Gracchus, "They may be keen, but I am not sure how they'll last the march!"

"Julius," Marcus said, using his forename to stress the importance of the question to follow. "What's your take on this evacuation? Do you think it'll work?"

"Marcus, I've been long out of the legions, all of ten years. However, I have to say I never recall a stunt like this being pulled. If the bastards leave us alone, we could make it intact. If they don't, only the gods can predict, but I suspect Charon and his ferry will be busy."

"We've planned everything except what to do if attacked."

"That's for the legion to handle, Marcus. Our job will be to keep the civilians protected as best we can." He shrugged, "You know, get them under cover from slingers and archers – under the wagons – whatever. Of course, it depends on what the ground is like when they hit us – if they hit us."

"It might be useful to make that clear to the men, Julius. I suspect they'd want to get one-on-one with the rebels!"

"Just before we move off, I'll call a briefing."

A member of the militia marched up and saluted badly. Marcus thought Gracchus would dress him down, but the man was sincere, just ten years out of practice.

"Captain Apollinaris, sir. There's a lovely piece asking for you. Reckons you would know who she was. She's by my wagon, sir?"

Marcus eyed the man up. A little bulky now, but he had the thick neck from wearing a steel helmet for sixteen years and the legs of a man who had marched across the empire. He was pushing forty years, he thought.

"Thank you, soldier…?"

"Miniscius sir, Antonius Miniscius."

"Good work, Miniscius." He turned to Gracchus, "Centurion if you don't mind?"

"Crack on, Marcus. Does she have a sister?"

Marcus laughed.

"Be careful what you wish for, centurion."

"Well, until then, I have an appointment with a horse!" said Gracchus with a loud guffaw.

Two minutes later, Marcus and Miniscius swung around the rear of a wagon crudely adorned with the number twenty-three to find Anaitis pacing the ground. She saw Marcus approach and rushed towards him. Marcus flashed her a cautionary look.

"Anaitis, it's good to see you." Thankfully, she received the message and did not wrap him in a hug. She stood close by. Marcus turned to Miniscius,

"Gratitude, Miniscius. Stay local if you can." Then, the militiaman moved off about his duties. "Anaitis, are you okay?"

"I am. Miriam had to go with the legion, so I'm alone."

"It will be difficult for a few days, but we'll soon be away to Caesarea."

As he spoke, she moved closer and surreptitiously took his hand.

"Marcus, I am frightened," she said. He squeezed her hand.

"My honey, beyond the wagons, a Roman legion is forming up. So, You-err-we will be well protected. We'll have cohorts to the front and rear of the train, as well as on either side. We got cavalry out scouting, so we gets the earliest warning of trouble. You really are well protected, my honey."

All these facts seemed to calm Anaitis, assuring her she safe. However, the grip on Marcus' hand did not loosen. Out of the corner of his eye, Marcus spotted Miniscius.

"Miniscius," he called, "I need a word, brother."

The old soldier re-joined the couple at the side of the wagon.

"Anaitis," began Marcus, "This is Antonius Miniscius, who was an experienced legionary until his retirement. Antonius is takin' care of your wagon, and I'll ask him to make sure 'e keeps you safe." He turned to Miniscius, "Antonius, this here is Anaitis, a *particularly* good friend. Makes sure she don't come to no 'arm during the journey?"

"It'll be my pleasure, Captain Apollinaris," said the old soldier, "she'll be in safe hands." He beamed as he appraised the young woman who stood before him.

"So, there you goes, Anaitis," said Marcus, "you have me, Miniscius, the militia as well as a bleedin' Roman legion protecting you. Ain't nothing going to hurt you girl!"

She appeared to relax a little. Marcus was relieved as he was still worried she might throw her arms around him in a declaration of affection, embarrassing him in front of the soldiery. He was about to suggest she should climb into the wagon and relax when he noticed Miniscius was staring at something over Marcus' shoulder. Marcus turned to see what was holding his attention. Distant but fast approaching was Centurion Gracchus accompanied by an Optio. Much to Marcus' relief, Miniscius had the foresight to gently take Anaitis' arm and guide her towards the wagon's rear, leaving Marcus alone.

"Apollinaris," Gracchus said as he fast approached, "this is Optio Gratix. He organises the evacuation of the wounded. He'd like a word."

"Legionary – I am sorry – Captain Apollinaris," he began. He flushed. Another young one thought Marcus, but he's no Petronius. "We have decided that we should have just a single combined military and civilian column, so the plan is to merge the medical wagons with the civilian wagons. If attacked, it will make defence much easier. We are talking about fifteen medical wagons in total."

"I takes it these are full-size military wagons, big uns?" Asked Marcus.

"Yes, they are mostly drawn by oxen."

"Fifteen?" Marcus queried with an element of surprise.

"That is correct, Captain. Ten wagons carry injured men, and five will be almost empty."

"Five'll be empty?" Marcus again queried.

"Yet again, you are correct, Captain," the Optio answered, "the empty five wagons are for the wounded or injured incurred during the journey. Gods forbid we should have to defend this column against rebel action, but we must be ready. We are dealing with civilians here. No doubt a number will fall off wagons – or even under the bloody things!"

"Right then," said Marcus, "so how're we going to make this work then?"

Ten minutes later, they had constructed a simple plan. They would line the civilian wagons up in eight long columns. The medical wagons would form a further line in the middle of the eight refugee columns upon arrival. It would be a tight squeeze, but it meant that once the column left Aelia behind, they would position the medical wagons in the centre. Satisfied with the plan, the optio returned from where he came.

Civilians arrived in droves, reminding Marcus of lost sheep. Centurion Gracchus stood with his hands on his hips, observing the developing chaos around him. Shouting out their wagon numbers, militia soldiers stood on their wagon's driving seats, trying to act as beacons for their passengers. Marcus noted that the cheery atmosphere he had seen the previous day had evaporated. The civilians moved silently amongst the wagons seeking their allocated vehicle. Many looked stressed, and several women were crying. The reality of the situation sank in as they said goodbye to their homes, unsure if they would ever return. Marcus had seen nothing like this before.

The centurion and the watch captain took in what they saw before them. In their minds, each tried hard to accommodate what they were seeing—each was handling their own emotions.

"By Jupiter," Gracchus declared, "I just pray that this will work."

"It should, Julius," Marcus said. "Over the last couple of days, the boys have issued each civilian with a ticket – it shows the wagon they'll report to. We worked out the number of tickets for each wagon just right. Next, we'll check each wagon to ensure no buggers moved about. Don't forget, the fit 'uns bloody well walk! I'm sure we can do this, brother."

"You and Sallus seem to have the organisation sorted," said Gracchus, "I was thinking more about moving this lot…" he held his arms towards the oncoming civilians, "to Caesarea in one piece."

"Brother, we was told to sort out the wagons and provisions. We done that. The problem of getting this crowd to Caesarea is the legion's," responded Marcus, "what we does, is looks after the civilians."

"Fuck me," said Gracchus, "only a few days ago, I was a retired centurion, and the only worry I had was the quality of my olive harvest!"

Sometime later, the medical wagons arrived. As Marcus had expected, it was a tight squeeze positioning the column of fifteen wagons into the centre of the lines of refugee wagons. Marcus learnt that if the horns of oxen can fit into a space, then the wagon it is pulling can also fit. He stored the fact away in the back of his brain, hoping one day it may be useful knowledge.

Anaitis spotted Miriam, joining her immediately alongside a medical wagon. Marcus was relieved. He believed they would keep him busy in the coming days, and Miriam would be good company for the girl. Yet, he questioned why such thoughts made him feel guilty?

Much to his surprise, Gracchus arrived on horseback. A spare horse accompanied him. It was two seconds before the realisation dawned on Marcus. The look on his face broadcast his emotions.

"You can ride, can't you?" asked Gracchus. Marcus could ride, though it had been some years since he had been on the back of a horse.

"Err... yes, of course," he blustered, "it's just that... well, it's been a while."

"For Hades' sake, man, this column will be at least two miles long," said Gracchus, "If you think I'm running up and down it at my age, you've got another thing coming!"

"Bleedin' Minerva," said Marcus, "I'spose I'll 'ave to give it a go then."

Conscious of his rank of Watch Officer and that several of the populous of Aelia Capitolina were now watching him, Marcus whispered a quiet prayer to the gods and approached the spare horse. He knew, once mounted, that the saddle would hold him firm between its four raised corners. It was the journey between ground and saddle that made him nervous. Gripping one of the four saddle corners, he jumped and pulled himself up. Much to his relief, whilst messy, the upward journey was successful, and he found himself in the saddle atop the horse. The latter had not moved during the operation and stood placidly awaiting a command. It felt strange to have his legs dangling free and his feet not placed firmly on the ground as an infantryman.

"Well now, that was impressive!" said Gracchus. He pointed towards Marcus' horse. "They'd said she'd not be leading any cavalry charges, but she'd be up for trotting – maybe that's for the best, 'eh?

"Maybe." Marcus found his confidence and realised why cavalrymen were so arrogant. They spent much of their time looking down on the infantry!

"Right! Let's trot," said Gracchus. He turned his horse's head, kicked its flanks with his heels, and rode out of the column.

"Oh well, here goes," Marcus spoke under his breath. A turn of the head, a kick of the heels, and his horse obeyed. In his mind, the horse was already named 'Trotter'.

A little later, both men sat mounted by the roadway the immense column would take to leave Aelia Capitolina. On foot, several militia soldiers stood by, ready to tick off the wagons as they passed and to deal with any issues that might arise. The leaving process was due to begin when Tribune Sallus joined them.

"We can do no more," he said, "but I will admit that I thought we had bitten off more than we could chew. My gratitude to you all." He aimed his words not just at Marcus and Gracchus, but at the small cluster of militiamen who stood around.

"Yours to command, sir," said Gracchus and the entire group saluted the Tribune.

Capitulum XXI - The column

19 Aprilis. Year 16 of the Imperator Hadrianus.

Engrossed in his thoughts, Lucius stared out of the window across the camp. It was amazing how he had slipped back into his rank's routine and enjoying his role. The morning legionary parade, the cohort parade, the training, the marching and all that went with his position. Friendships put on hold when he went ahead to Judaea, renewed. Lucius was back to doing just what he trained for.

News from Judea filtering through to Caesarea was sporadic. The colony was living on borrowed time; indeed, the cohort would be going south to assist, something that filled the new soldiers of the Fourth with apprehension. The cohort had yet to prove itself in action. Crispus had trained them hard – more than necessary - determined they would be ready when the time came to fight. While in Italy, one day in Capua, Lucius became concerned about the level of violence during training. Several legionaries hobbled off the training ground. Carried off sitting on his shield, one commented to Crispus, whose response was terse.

"After this, a battle will be easy."

Fortunately, Crispus had the leadership skill to make his cohort proud of their bruises. To Lucius' surprise, the soldiers apologised to Crispus, staggering off the training ground. The centurion gave them a soft whack with his vine stick and encouraged them to 'work harder on it'. Lucius knew Crispus to be one of a kind; a man soldiers wanted to follow. Many junior centurions tried hard to emulate him but never quite achieved it.

A figure, whose red helmet cresta ran crossways, intruded into his view of the camp. Lucius snapped out of his reverie as Crispus powered towards the building entrance. Lucius turned from the window and moved to open the door. As soon as he had reached the door, Crispus swept in, strode to the window, and turned to face Lucius, removing his helmet as he did so.

"Optio Petronius, avoid staring out of the window early in the day. You'll have nothing to do later!" he said as a smile broke out over his face. Lucius laughed, but the smile faded. "Developments Lucius. I'd welcome your thoughts."

"Of course, Aurelius," Lucius replied, using the informality they adopted when alone together. "Go ahead."

"Well, our would-be Jewish rebel and his mother have disappeared. Vanished."

"Eliza and Jacob?"

"The very ones, optio, the very ones. I requested a patrol drop in to see how they were faring."

"Have they been abducted?" asked Lucius.

"If they have, their captors were kind to them." Crispus replied, "They seem to have taken plenty with them and left the place tidy."

"Threatened, then. Perhaps they were threatened and fled."

"I've thought of that. It's an option." Lucius felt there was more to come, but an option was rapidly developing in Lucius's mind, so he shared it.

"There may be another answer, Aurelius…" he paused.

"Go on," instructed Crispus.

"We've been had." Crispus smiled,

"I've trained you well, Lucius. It had crossed my mind."

"What've we heard from Galilee?"

"All reports say there is no change to the usual. A few *Romani ite donum* slogans daubed on walls, but little more."

The two men stood silently for a few seconds, contemplating the ramifications of their thoughts.

"So, we've held Legio VI back from reinforcing Judea to prevent a non-existent revolt in the north — in Galilee?"

"I fear it may be so," said Crispus, "relieving the pressure on the rebels in Judea. But it's worse, Lucius, much worse. Sit down." The two men sat on either side of the office table, Crispus placing his helmet on one side. "We've received word the rebels have seized En Geddi. They've overwhelmed the *Thracum*, a handful of survivors getting through to Aelia."

"Hades, that is shocking. The *Thracum*? Pushed out? As auxiliaries go, they're a tough bunch. By Jewish fighters?"

"Come on, Lucius, what you saw on your journey back here would show that these are not 'Jewish fighters'. We're up against an army." Said Crispus, stressing the 'army'. "However, it gets even worse. Apparently, the battle cry of the Jews is 'Jerusalem'. The *Thracum* survivors are saying Aelia is their next target."

Lucius made a mental leap.

"So, we're off to Aelia, Aurelius."

Crispus laughed.

"Don't be too enthusiastic, Lucius. Not yet, we've no orders, but the governor will have a plan for us. Until then, we wait."

"Fair enough, but the messenger service between here and Aelia has become sporadic. Suppose we don't hear?"

"The boys of the messenger service are bloody tenacious. If anyone can get through, they'll do it. If we get no word from Aelia, the tribune will have to decide on a course of action."

"So, the cohort has to carry on waiting until we get word from the governor, who's down in Aelia."

"That's about it, brother," Crispus said.

"Well, whilst we wait, I've an issue I need to discuss with you," said Lucius. "It's about the situation with Legionary Postumus. I understand the tribune's concern, but I can't leave him kicking his heels for very much longer."

"Funny that," said Crispus. "The other day, his centurion was asking after him - I suspect Legionary Postumus has had a word with him. I think it's time we returned him."

"We've talked, and he's prepared to swear an oath on Mithras he'd repeat nothing of his work with the tribune. I trust Postumus. I'd have him in my century any day."

"Leave it with me," said Crispus. "I'll talk with the tribune. With what is coming, I'm sure they'll need him back in his century."

"Gratitude, Aurelius. So, now we wait. And I guess we get a little more training in!"

The two officers could not have known that the wait would be much shorter than either of them expected. A few minutes after the conversation, the guards on the main gate into Caesarea spotted a cavalry unit fast approaching. As they came closer, it became clear the unit had been riding hard, evidenced by the glowing sheen of sweat on the horses, marred in places by patches of dry dust clinging to the flanks of the beasts. Whilst the sentries identified the unit as Roman, it was not clear until the horses were upon them that, in the centre of the troop, rode the governor of *Provincea Judaea*. The new arrivals broke protocol, failing to stop, galloping into the town towards the camp. The sentries smartly saluted before being engulfed in dust and the stench of horse sweat.

It had taken the governor's troop the best part of four days to reach Aelia. The principal routes held by rebels forced the troop to follow mountain tracks and other byways. However, they had the foresight to attach several experienced scouts to the troop; without them, they may be still in the saddle or, even worse, dead.

That afternoon, Tineus Rufus had briefed Civilis, his second in command, the junior tribunes and senior centurions about the situation in Aelia Capitolina. All realised that a problem had developed into a crisis by the meeting's end. The concern was the plan to evacuate Aelia should the rebels move upon the colony; not in living memory could any of the officers recall such a venture. The senior centurions, Crispus included, champed at the bit to move their units south to defend the colony. As part of the case, Crispus shared his belief that they had been subject to a misinformation strategy to hold back troops in the province's north. Rufus did not take this well until Crispus pointed out that, as a result, the north was likely to be safe for the time being. As an outcome, they put all units on notice to be ready to march the following morning.

When Crispus returned to the Fourth, he immediately briefed his centurions and optios. Shortly afterwards, the IV Cohort formed upon the drill field. Crispus informed them they would soon see action and were instructed to prepare and then reassemble in full marching order at the next morning parade.

The legionaries would carry all they needed on their backs. Lucius's options were more comfortable; what he required and was not wearing would go to the cart designated for officer's equipment and other items the cohort would need. Lucius packed a small knapsack of essentials. Upon returning to the drill field, he found Crispus deep in conversation with the tribune, Gaius Civilis. The tribune spotted Lucius approaching.

"Optio Petronius... Lucius," he said as he held out his arm. Lucius clasped it. "I need to get down to Aelia Capitolina and, literally, in double time. I was exploring the options with Aurelius here."

"The Tribune has every faith in the Primus," said Crispus, "but he's less confident with the junior tribunes. As second in command of the legion, he believes he needs to be with the evacuation when it happens. There is too much at stake not to be. Fuck knows how Rome will react to all this!"

Out of nowhere, Miriam bat Yaholem entered Lucius' mind. He felt sure she would be in the column. The greatest optimist would not deny that a refugee column was no safe place to be if attacked.

"Lucius?" Crispus interrupted his thoughts.

"Apologies, Aurelius," said Lucius. "Yes, I understand. Surely, it's too dangerous for a cavalry unit travelling alone, no matter how fast it travelled?"

"Precisely, Lucius," said Crispus. "The governor's experience in returning confirms that. The tribune and I were considering other options."

"It's not my intention to travel with a cavalry unit," the tribune said. "I shall march with infantry and cavalry scouts." The tribune paused, and Lucius could see he was weighing his words. "It is not a straightforward decision to make," he continued. "The cohorts are ready to move south to Aelia. They comprise experienced soldiers, and now we have the IV cohort available too. My concern is that none of the cohorts have seen major action for years; the *Tenth Fretensis'* combat experience has mainly been policing actions. Another quandary is the IV cohort." Saying so, he turned to Crispus. The centurion picked up where the Tribune stopped.

"It's like this, Lucius," Crispus said. "Going against us is that, apart from our officers, our lads haven't seen action. But, on the positive side, the Fourth has done little else than train hard for battle. Me? I believe the cohort's motivated and ready to fight."

Thoughts of Miriam bat Yaholem were still drifting around Lucius' mind, and the urgency to protect the refugee column grew. Added to this, he agreed with Crispus. It must be the Fourth that escorts the tribune south.

"I agree with Senior Centurion Crispus," he responded formally, "though I'd say the cohort's motivated and *wants* to fight."

"Lucius is correct, sir, they *want* to fight," said Crispus added, "and sir, these lads are young and fit, and I've had them marching their arses off. They can move and move real quick!"

The tribune nodded, his focus on the ground. Both centurion and the optio realised he had to make a tough decision – one upon which his career could depend. The two men remained silent, leaving the man with his struggle. Finally, after what seemed an age, he looked up from the ground. He stared each of his companions in the eye.

"May the gods be with me. We shall leave only a small auxiliary force here at Caesarea. I will speak with the other senior centurions; they will move south to support the evacuation. Meanwhile, the IV Cohort will go with me, moving ahead at a forced march to reach the colony quickly. I hope to Jupiter we can get there before the evacuation begins. So, we will see just how well your lads march, Aurelius Crispus."

The centurion tried but failed to suppress a smile.

"The IV Cohort won't let you down, sir," he said. "They will be formed up here on the drill field and ready to move within the hour."

"I will join you then. I am trusting Mithras will be with us in what we do."

Seconds later, the three men moved swiftly to ensure that the other Caesarea cohorts would be ready to take the road south the next day.

The orders meant the unit was on a war footing from the minute the Fourth left Caesarea. Shields would remain in their leather covers until they entered Judaea itself, where they would be naked and ready for action. They would wear no cloaks today; uncovered, the column would appear as a metal snake, the sun reflecting off the armour. Each legionary carried not just a shield, but also two javelins. Lucius thought in the event of a surprise attack, they would be ready. He scanned the mass of gleaming helmets from his station at the rear of his century.

Lucius sensed a nervousness in his stomach. The IV Cohort had been in training for so long that he would often dream of training drills. Usually, the training was tough, as were many of the route marches that Crispus utilised to bring the men to peak fitness. But no matter how you looked at it, training was training. Now the training has ceased. The second they passed through the main gates of Caesarea, the world would be quite a different place. When these soldiers now faced an opponent, that opponent aimed to kill them.

"Well, optio," said a soldier in the rank in front of Lucius, "we're the boys who will save Aelia!"

"You'd do well to look to the front and listen for your orders," Lucius responded. "This'll not be a jaunt in the countryside, so pay attention and remember your training."

My gods, thought Lucius, I sound like Crispus!

The thought had just passed through Lucius' mind when the tribune joined the cohort, mounted upon Diomedes, his striking white stallion. He brought the horse to a halt in front of the cohort alongside centurion Aurelius Crispus.

"Legionaries of the Fourth. We are about to march south as the vanguard of a relief force for Aelia Capitolina. I am of no doubt you will have picked up on the circulating rumours about a sizable rebel force, described by some as an army, approaching the colony. You may have also heard talk of evacuating the colony. Shocking as it may seem, it is an actual possibility. Therefore, it has become crucial that the element of the *Fretensis* here in Caesarea move south with some urgency to support the cohorts in Aelia. Centurion Crispus tells me you have trained hard, and today we shall test that training's efficacy, for the urgency demands we move at a forced march pace. If you find the going tough, just remember the many citizens of Aelia who will pray to the gods for your arrival." He sat very straight in his saddle, drew his sword and punched it into the air above him, shouting, "*Fretensis!*"

As one voice, the cohort replied,

"Fretensis, Fretensis, Fretensis!"

The sound of the cornicen filled the air, followed by Crispus' voice bellowing a command. Within the second, four hundred and eighty legionaries of the Fourth Cohort marched from the drill field and moved towards the distant main gates of Caesarea. Lucius slipped into his marching pace, following the cohort's regular tramp – tramp – tramp. Once clear of Caesarea, he knew the pace of the tramping would increase.

An hour later, the banter that takes place between marching legionaries had died away. The joking and laughing, replaced by grim determination. He knew legionaries had the capability of closing their minds to complaining muscles and sore feet, instead grimly focusing on the pace, the tramp after tramp after tramp, as the cohort continued south. It amused Lucius to think that never had the citizens of Aelia been the focus of so much determined legionary thought!

They planned to spend the first night camped outside the town of Antipatris. It would be usual for the legionaries to carry everything they needed during the march. However, this march was different, and speed was of the essence, with the soldiers of the Fourth being unburdened of cloaks, tents, food, and other paraphernalia. It was all being carried in mule carts at the rear of the cohort, ensuring a few more miles of coverage during the day.

The cohort approached the town of Antipatris as the sun was lowering in the sky and fast approaching the horizon. Lucius' thought went to his last visit to the township as part of the supply column commanded by tesserarius Tetricus. Antipatris was in Samaria, a region of the province which had shown no recent disturbance; in fact, the Samaritans always held an element of antagonism for Judaeans, one deep-rooted in their history. Given this, and that the cavalry scouts accompanying the cohort had ranged miles ahead to find nothing concerning, they felt safe in spending the dark hours here. The following mule carts arrived carrying tents and provisions. They swiftly erected a tented encampment outside of the town - there would be no visits to tabernae tonight!

Whilst Senior Centurion Crispus walked the camp talking to his fellow centurions, Lucius stayed with the 1st Century, mingling with his legionaries as they fed. Whilst he heard a continuous flow of complaints about uncomfortable footwear, poor-fitting armour, and a myriad of other complaints, the overall morale of the soldiers was high. Lucius felt everyone was aware this was their first proper mission, and they would not let the Legion down. Lucius watched a group of soldiers eat their rations and noticed that Felix Calvus, the century's *Signifier*, the standard-bearer, had joined him. A second later, Claudius Paulus, the *Tesserarius,* joined the pair.

"Lucius," said Felix, "you got a second?"

Lucius read the question to imply that the officers would like to talk out of earshot of the eating legionaries. So the trio moved away a distance. Lucius knew these men well. They were some of the first recruits to the new IV Cohort and became the officer cadre of the senior centurion's 1st Century. When the Fourth arrived in Caesarea, apart from Centurion Crispus, these were the two people Lucius sought and with whom he shared wine.

"Claudius and I were just talking about the situation in Aelia," said Felix, "and we know the lads have taken a bit of a beating down there, so we can understand the need for evacuation. But it is fucking galling running from a bunch of Jewish rebels."

"If it's any help," said Lucius, "what we are facing is much more than a 'bunch'. They're well organised, trained, and motivated to fight. So whatever happens, brothers, don't underestimate these people."

"In that case, it's even more worrying," said Claudius.

"What do you mean?" Lucius asked.

"There's a lot of citizens to evacuate," explained Claudius. "However you look at it, they will make slow progress. What's saying the rebels won't overhaul them as they progress?"

"First," responded Lucius, "we don't know for sure that an evacuation will happen. If we, the Seventh and the Eighth, can get there in time, it may be we can hold Aelia."

"Pray to the gods you are right," said Claudius. "Should they leave the colony before we arrive, this could all get very messy."

"Possibly," said Lucius, "but right now, I need some sleep. Tomorrow will be another testing day, so, brothers, I will see you in the morning."

At the first light of dawn, the cohort awoke, fed, stowed their tents on the mule carts and left the town of Antipatris behind them. In no time at all, legionaries' thinking moved to focus on the pace of the forced march. The route planned was the quickest approach to Aelia; the cohort would march southeast to Arimathea and then follow the road to Gophna.

Lucius felt strange to be following the same route he had taken a few short weeks ago. His initial journey had a simple aim; to spend a few days visiting his uncle in Aelia. He smiled as he considered how naïve he had been. He could never have imagined what was to develop in such a scant time since the attack on the supply column. What he then thought of as simple banditry turned out to be a jigsaw piece of a significant rebellion against Roman authority.

Once the cohort left Antipatris, it moved into Judaean territory. The soldiers had been marching with leather shield covers in place up to this point. Today, they removed them, placing them in the mule carts that followed the cohort, lightening the legionaries' load. In addition, the cavalry scouts doubled their activity compared to the previous day. Everyone behaved as though they were entering enemy territory rather than the south of a Roman province.

Taking brief breaks through the morning, the Fourth marched straight through Arimathea. They allowed a more extended break for lunch on the far side of the town. The afternoon saw them approaching the town of Gophna. Lucius was convinced that it was here that the rebels planned the attack on the supply column. He felt very much in unfriendly countryside. He recalled the phrase that legionary Sextus Postumus would often use; his nose was twitching!

They set up a camp outside of Gophna. Tomorrow would see the Fourth entering Aelia.

"This reminds me of a beehive," said Marcus to Centurion Gracchus. The two men sat on their horses on the edge of the assembly area north of Aelia. Drawn up in front of them were four long lines of waggons of all different shapes and sizes. Much shorter than the others, in the centre stood a fifth line: the infirmary waggons. To the waggons' right, the best part of the remaining fit soldiers of the Fretensis stood, ready and waiting to march. A thronging mass of people filled the space between the waggons. By this point, the swirling movement within the masses had slowed as people found and attached themselves to their allocated waggon.

And what a mass of people it was. Marcus thought it strange to see such a mix. The wealthy classes were used to living within their white-marbled Villas, mixing amongst themselves. The Artisans and traders would live in their plastered premises, and they too would remain within their domains. Now it was as though all the people of Aelia Capitolina had been thrown into a colossal amphora, shaken up and poured out. Though planned for, there had been little time to arrange waggons by social strata in the rush to organise; everyone was jumbled up.

Earlier, centurion Gracchus had dismissed his men following the last meeting before the huge column set off. He acknowledged they worked in uncharted waters; they had never attempted an evacuation the likes of this in living memory. He stressed their focus must be the welfare of the citizens. It would be important that everyone occasionally rested, taking a ride on their waggon. No matter what social status, the fit and healthy should shoulder their share of the walking. Food and water distribution were yet another responsibility, the militia ensuring that all were favoured equally. Should the column come under attack, their role was a shepherding one, leaving the primary defence of the column to the legionaries. "We shall only fight if it gets down to the Triarii." Gracchus had said, referring to the last line of older, experienced soldiers in the Army of the Roman Republic. Should the Triarii be engaged, the business is desperate. Now the men of the militia had dispersed.

"Beehive? Well, brother, let us hope we don't get stung!" Gracchus responded. Marcus laughed, saying,

"Well, Julius, from where I'm sitting, that would make Tribune Sallus the Queen Bee!"

"Would it indeed?" Said a voice from behind Marcus, who did not need to look to know the voice owner. Marcus turned his horse about to face the Tribune.

"Apologies, sir," said a red-faced captain of the watch, "I was jesting."

The discomfort in Marcus' face was apparent.

"I should have you flogged for insubordination," Sallus said, grim-faced.

Marcus wriggled in his saddle, and the visage of discomfort grew even more extreme.

"I... I... What I mean...."

The Tribune's face broke into a smile.

"Let that be a lesson to you, Apollinaris, to be a little more careful with what you say and when you say it," Sallus said, "however, I think a little light humour might be a positive thing." Then, he turned to Gracchus. "We shall move off in a few minutes. Is everything prepared?"

"With respect, sir, who in Hades could honestly answer that question? We've done all as discussed, but is it enough? Only Jupiter knows, sir, and he ain't telling!"

Smiling, the Tribune nodded his head.

"I understand your feelings, Centurion. Perhaps we should ask Jupiter to keep an eye on matters as we progress. The occasional useful tip from the gods might prove immensely helpful in this venture."

The three men sat in silence for a brief time, each dwelling upon what was to come in the ensuing days. Finally, the current reality intruded when a rider approached. He saluted the Tribune and informed the group of the departure from Aelia. Message delivered, the rider promptly rode away.

"With your permission, Tribune, I'm off to do a last check on the lads," said Gracchus, as he turned his horse and rode back amongst the lines of waggons and carts.

"Apollinaris, I need you at my side for a while," said Sallus, "I'm afraid I intend to use you as a messenger. I suspect there will be coordination issues that will need sorting, especially on the first day. Gracchus and his men can keep the column functioning."

"You mean, just like a staff officer?" Marcus responded. The Tribune Sallus laughed.

"Apollinaris, if you want to see yourself as a staff officer, please go ahead," he said, "but at the end of this, I suspect you may have much more respect for the position!"

"Always been the top of me list, sir - staff officers, always -".

The sound of a cornicen filled the air, and the commotion and noise from the assembly of waggons fell silent. The instrument's command did not need explaining; the thousands present, soldier and civilian, knew what it signalled. For the first time in history, a significant colony was being abandoned in the face of an enemy. However, the abandonment was no guarantee of safety. While the civilian refugees prayed they would live to see Caesarea, the soldiers filled their minds with thoughts of the bloody retribution they would exact when the time came to return.

Hundreds of tramping feet could be heard from beyond the column, accompanied by the rattle of the soldier's metal lorica segmentata. Sallus turned to Marcus.

"The column will not move until the two lead cohorts are ahead. Thus, we shall have a cohort flanking on either side of the column and the remaining two cohorts following in the rear."

The first cohort cleared the column and marched up the evacuation road as he spoke. Roman legionaries marching, not towards but away from the enemy, caused Marcus discomfort. In his mind, he reiterated the logic of the venture, but it refused to sit easily with him. As the II Cohort overhauled the static column, Marcus experienced a yearning to be in their midst. It is what he knew and what he did – soldiering.

The Tribune earnestly watched the II Cohort move smoothly onto the road when he turned again to Marcus.

"Apollinaris, will you get over to the lead waggon and tell them to get moving? They are to keep as close a distance as possible behind the II Cohort. The cohort commanders have orders not to pull away from the column."

Marcus snapped off a salute with a sense of involvement in something unique and of enormous importance.

"Yours to be commanded, sir."

What a strange sight. Waggons and carts of different shapes and sizes, snaking back a long way down the road. In front of, beside and behind, a mass of people of all ages and genders walked with the waggons. Julius Gracchus had seen similar sights during his service in Dacia, but never the size of that before him. He had never expected to see such a retreat involving Roman citizens. He watched the column, occasionally spotting a bright yellow armband of a militia soldier. As he had expected from the start of this venture, he did not have enough men to manage what he saw before him now. It would get tougher before they reached their goal. But the citizens appeared resigned to their lot as they plodded alongside the disparate range of vehicles.

The column moved at a walking pace, determined by the speed of the slowest waggons; the infirmary waggons drawn by large oxen. Fortunately, driving along a paved Roman road made for good going. Gracchus knew that as they progressed, people would tire, but he had explicit orders. The column must maintain speed. He worried there would be a shortage of resting spaces on waggons. But for now, three hours after leaving Aelia, he was relaxed with the situation.

The plan was to head West, towards the town of Lod, via Emmaus, where they would meet the main Roman road that runs up northwards from Gaza to Caesarea, following the coast.

The first night on the road saw the militia run ragged in the attempt to see everyone fed. Fortunately, nobody went hungry. Once the refugees had eaten and turned to sleep, the officers and several militiamen held a late-night meeting.

"Good job, they're all bloody knackered, or we could have had a riot in our hands!" exclaimed one militiaman.

"The easy bit is behind us, men," said Tribune Sallus. "Our job is to hold this column together. So, who has any ideas about food distribution? Unfortunately, we cannot go through this again tomorrow."

Thirty minutes later, the men made their way towards their waggons, a decision made. Between them, Marcus and Centurion Gracchus would group waggons into six and appoint three passengers to coordinate food supply for their group. Marcus summed up,

"It won't be perfect, but this is a crisis, ain't it, an' bugger all's perfect in a crisis."

As soon as the sun rose into the sky, the militiamen were banging on the sides of waggons, announcing that the column would move off shortly. It was wishful thinking! The refugees took an age to be ready to move. This did not surprise Marcus; he recognised the first morning on the road would be difficult, and matters would move faster once the refugees had established their routines. Meanwhile, the Legion formed up around the column, champing at the bit for quite some time before it was ready to move.

Thanks to the Roman road, the column achieved excellent progress. There was little resistance to the many wheels rolling across its surface. As the column moved through the hills of Judaea, the road climbed, exerting the beasts harnessed to waggons.

Marcus spent much of the morning riding the length of the column and organising food distribution groups. Every hour, the column would stop for ten minutes to rest the passengers and animals alike. Ablution habits between the social strata in the column made Marcus smile. The Artisans and small traders would walk some feet away from the column to do what was needed. The property-owning class provided Marcus' amusement; they would seek a remote, discreet bush; sometimes queueing up for the privacy offered. Meanwhile, they would be under time pressure – nobody wanted the indignity of running to catch up with their waggon!

Not long after midday, as Marcus was returning to the head of the column, the leading two cohorts came to a stand and, likewise, the column itself. Marcus joined Tribune Sallus and Gracchus.

"What's going on?" he asked.

"I suspect we shall know soon enough," answered Sallus. As soon as he had uttered the words, a cavalryman appeared from behind the cohorts and galloped towards them. He brought his horse to a stop and saluted Sallus simultaneously.

"Compliments of the Primus, sir," he said, "Could you please attend the head of the column."

Sallus turned to his two officers.

"You two had better come with me," he said, "it might save me having to repeat myself later on."

The Tribune and his officers, accompanied by the cavalryman, rode past the cohorts to the head of the column. There they found the two centurions, two tribunes and a small cluster of cavalry scouts, all dismounted. The team from the column came to a stop, dismounted.

"Welcome, tribune," said Quintus Vorenus, the Primus Pilus, the Legion's most senior centurion. "The Scouts bring us details of a potential problem." He turned to greet the tribune's companions as he spoke the words. He stopped with a look of surprise on his face. "May the gods preserve us! Legionary Apollinaris, my favourite bad denarius, you seem to turn up at the strangest of times."

It was said with a smile, for which Marcus was grateful.

"Apollinaris is acting as my aide," Sallus said. "He has been very useful to me."

In contrast, the Primus turned to Gracchus.

"Julius Gracchus by Jove, it's good to see you again."

"You too, Quintus. So, what's the problem?"

Vorenus turned to one of the cavalry scouts.

"Tell them just what you have told me."

"Right, chief," the scout said, pausing a second to marshal his thoughts. "We was pushing ahead up the road and about to rest the mounts when Cato 'ere," he nodded to one of his comrades standing on the outside of the group, "spotted movement further up the valley. So we dismounted, secured the horses, and got as close as we dared. The long and short of it is the *cunni* are laying an ambush, sir..."

"An ambush?" queried tribune Sallus, "but we have the protection of a legion, for Jupiter's sake!"

Vorenus looked to the Scout.

"Give them the details." He instructed.

"A *big* ambush, Tribune. As you'd expect, the rebels are well concealed, but it's a large force. I reckon well over a thousand men - possibly more! As we watched, they began placing themselves along the sides of the valley. An ambush that size, sir, it 'as to be us they're after."

"Forgive me, soldier, but are you sure about the numbers waiting for us?" asked Sallus.

"Me and the lads, Tribune, we are good at what we does." He skilfully put the Tribune in his place.

"I've no reason to doubt the scout's report. Been working with them for some time. They've never let me down." said Vorenus, "So given the facts presented to us, what do we do?" There was no immediate response from the surrounding men, so he continued, "One option is to send the legion forward and fight it out. The enemy will be well concealed and slippery to fight – they are light in arms and are nimble. Added to this, they may well outnumber us. In addition, it would leave the waggons unprotected," his eyes met Marcus' eyes. "… apart from the militia – but eighty against hundreds?" Again, he paused, but drew no response from the group. "Brothers, we need a second option."

There was a shuffling of feet as the group members attempted to look like they were thinking the problem through. Nothing was said for several seconds before the lead Scout spoke up.

"With your permission, chief," he said deferentially to Vorenus, "there may just be another option, but it is not an easy one."

Every head turned to face the Scout, who showed signs of discomfort at being so exposed. Finally, Vorenus nodded and waved his right arm through the air, a clear signal for the Scout to proceed.

"Well, chief," he began, "a few minutes' ride up the road, there's a junction with a smaller road, which leads off northwards, to our right. Branches of the road feed off to several villages. However, it re-joins this route about twelve or thirteen miles further north, just south of Lod. It's a typical Judaean road; it's hard but not paved, and it has the width to handle the waggons."

"The Gods may smile upon us after all," said one tribune. Heads turned towards Vorenus, absorbing and thinking through what he had just been told.

"Right then, what you're saying is if we take this route, we will bypass the rebel ambush and come back onto his road a good number of miles to the north of where we are, just short of Lod?" asked Gracchus.

"That's correct, chief," responded the Scout, "but there's a problem. At the point where the rebel bastards planned to ambush us, there's a track, also running northeast, which joins up with the road what I've just mentioned."

"Again, let me understand this," Vorenus said. "You're implying the rebels could use this track to cut across country and attack us on this new, second route?"

"They could, chief," the scout replied, "but they'd be moving on a narrow track while crossing the hills that separate the two roads. If they try it, it ain't gonna be quick."

"And where this track joins our alternative route, what is the ground like?" Asked Vorenus.

The scout was developing some confidence in the situation.

"I knows this area pretty well. As it happens, we've used it for training in the past, and I've ridden this track a few months back, so I knows they'd struggle with such a large body of men. Where it meets the road, what we are talking about isn't complicated, chief," He paused for a second to construct his answer to Vorenus' question, "the track comes down from the hills in a narrow defile. A short distance before it meets the road, the sides of the defile fall away to a slope that runs down to the road."

"It sounds like we could get past the track before the rebels could cross the hills," Sallus said. Vorenus was about to answer when the newly confident scout replied.

"The junction's about 10 miles up the road, sir. It's about a similar distance for'em taking the track. We wouldn't maintain the column speed once we got onto the track. But, depending on how quick the bastards detect our diversion, there's a chance they'd get there quicker."

"Damn it!" said Sallus.

"Well then," interjected Marcus, "we're just gonna have to go faster. Can't see any other options."

"What would the Roman army do without your penetrating military insights, Apollinaris?" said Vorenus. "However, in this case, I believe you are correct."

"Thank you, Primus."

"Don't push it, Apollinaris," Vorenus said, "but you have a point. We *shall* take the secondary route. Aginthus' III Cohort and Petronius' VI Cohort, currently at the column's rear, will forced march to where the track meets the road, ensuring they get to the junction first. Coming down from the mountain, the rebels cannot deploy fully, drawn-out along the defile, and their frontage will be narrow where the track hits the road. The job of the two cohorts will be to plug the exit of the track as it comes down from the hills." Vorenus looked around him at the assembled group; there were no questions. "If we're lucky, maybe we will pass this junction by the time the rebels arrive – *if* they arrive. If we're unlucky, the Third and the Sixth will hold them at bay while we pass." Then, turning to the Scout, he said, "You had better pray to the gods that your description of that junction is accurate, brother."

Vorenus had no sooner finished speaking when Centurion Octavius Secundus arrived accompanied by two other centurions, all from the rear cohorts. Vorenus said he would brief the newly arrived officers and suggested that Tribune Sallus and his two militia officers returned to the column and made ready to move. Time was now of the essence.

The militia trio debated what to tell the passengers as they rode back. The militiamen would require briefing too. What concerned Sallus was the possibility of panic amongst the waggons. Leaving a well-constructed, paved road to travel on a bare hard earth equivalent would be noticed by the refugees. The conclusion was that people would have to be told, but the changing course would be positioned as a cautionary measure, already in the plan.

"Thank you, Miriam," Anaitis said to her friend, "I'm grateful to be doing something whilst we travel."

"It is good to have you looking after the injured," Miriam replied, "it means medics can give their time to the soldier's wounds."

The two women had spent some of the previous evening together, and the result of their conversation was Anaitis joining the medical section on the infirmary waggons. Anaitis was no medic, but she could move amongst the patients with water and juices and support the team. However, Anaitis was finding it difficult sitting in a waggon with little to do; her mind would not let go of the possibility that they would be attacked by Jewish rebels. During the previous evening's conversation, Miriam sensed the anxiety in Anaitis; she was more stressed than many of the passengers. Miriam decided Anaitis needed to be busy. The following day, she spoke to the medical officer, who was sympathetic to Miriam's suggestion that Anaitis join the section as a helper. That Anaitis was familiar to many soldiers, who often visited Aelia's Vicus, helped influence him.

None of the medical section was sure why the column had stopped, but they used the opportunity to move between the waggons, attending to their patients. The wounded had become used to the novelty of having a female medical assistant; they also learned that daring to step outside of the medical relationship earned a quick slap down. Nevertheless, Anaitis was welcome and put a smile on the soldier's faces. They remembered her from the Neptune Inn, a favourite legionary drinking hole.

At the waggon's front, Miriam was changing the dressing of a young legionary with a cut to his thigh. Meanwhile, at the rear, Anaitis was helping a soldier sip from a beaker of water; he was so ill that she held his head in a position to take down the drink. Miriam had earlier warned Anaitis that this patient would not see the sun set. The patient on the cot next to Anaitis' soldier had a leg injury, but one that was clearly on the mend. He was a seasoned legionary who considered his wound would be yet another badge of honour for service to Rome.

"You're the lass from the Neptune," he said to Anaitis, "Me and my tent mates used to drink there and do a bit of gambling."

"I am," said Anaitis, remaining focused on the dying legionary, nodding her head.

"Yeah, I never forget a face," the soldier continued, "and it wasn't just the drinking and gambling. I hope you brought your two mates with you. They were right juicy, those two. I always fancied the one with the little tits – she always got me off in no time!"

Anaitis froze, and then after lying the dying soldier's head gently onto the pillow, she stood. She glared at the guffawing soldier.

"Bastard!" she spat, "bastard!"

The smile disappeared from the soldier's face, and his jaw dropped.

"I… I was only…." He stammered.

"They are both dead – butchered!" Anaitis turned away and fled the vehicle, dashing off before stopping amongst the scrub and bushes lining the roadsides. Miriam had heard the expletives. She tied off the bandage on her patient's leg and went to the waggon's rear.

"What happens?" she asked the soldier who was the target of Anaitis' venom.

"I only asked about her two mates from the Neptune," he said, "I didn't know they was dead. I didn't mean to upset her."

Miriam left the waggon and went to join Anaitis, who stood back to the column, sobbing, tears flowing down her cheeks.

"They're dead, Miriam, my friends – they're both dead. He didn't give a *cac*!" Miriam put an arm around the distressed woman.

"Yes, Anaitis, they are dead. It is hard," said Miriam, as she remembered her murdered aunt, uncle and cousin. She was close to tears herself but suppressed her emotions. "No matter how you try with it, the… what is the word… sorrow, has to come out." Anaitis attempted to gather herself, wiping the tears from her cheeks.

"I'm sorry, Miriam," she said, "it was what he said. It all suddenly rushed up inside of me."

"I know, I know," said Miriam, "I think of family. It is like that too." The two women made their way back towards the infirmary waggon. "Anaitis, soldier mean no harm. Days ago, your friends would laugh at words, very funny – and take his money. Soldier did not know they dead."

"I can see that," Anaitis said, "I'll try to ensure it doesn't happen again. I wish I was as stoic as you, Miriam. I'd forgotten that it was not so long ago that you lost your family."

"Yeshua's teachings tell me that my family are with the Lord and when he call me, I will see them."

"I wish I had your belief," Anaitis said.

"Lucius saved me, or I be with them now."

Anaitis noted how she mentioned Lucius' name with some reverence, something she had witnessed before.

"Miriam, would I be right in saying a certain Roman officer has captured a piece of your heart?"

"Me?" said Miriam, "a Jewish healer who follows Yeshua. A Roman officer? Anaitis, your head is poorly!"

"Miriam, in this *cac* world, I could believe anything right now."

An overweight militia man appeared from behind the infirmary waggon and approached the women.

"Miniscius, what are you doing here?" asked Anaitis.

"One of my passengers has gone off to join a cousin in another waggon. So, we have a space now on our waggon."

It took Anaitis a moment to understand the implications of what Meniscus had said. She turned to Miriam,

"Miriam, last night you said your waggon was a long walk from the infirmary waggons." She nodded towards Meniscus, "Our waggon is just two up, very close. So what Meniscus is saying is that we have a place for you. I would love to have your company."

"That very good," said Miriam, "I thank you, Miniscius."

"No need," Miniscius responded, "if it makes Anaitis happy, then I'm happy. After all, Captain Apollinaris instructed me to take very special care of Anaitis here. However, we are about to move off, so I suggest you return to the waggons right away."

Anaitis was now all about efficiency,

"Come, Miriam. We must get back. There is work to be done." She set off at a pace to return to the infirmary waggon. Miriam followed.

"Anaitis, 'very special care'? Who talks of hearts?" she asked.

Ignoring the question, Anaitis returned to her station on the infirmary waggon. She went to a bucket at the waggon's rear, which contained fresh lemons. Taking one, she sliced the lemon and squeezed the juice into a beaker, added water and walked to the front of the waggon. The soldier with the wounded leg was watching. She silently offered him the drink. He took it from her.

"I didn't know about your friends," he said, "I was genuinely fond of Lydia."

"I know," said Anaitis, "Enjoy the drink. But, unlike drinks at the Neptune, this one's free." Saying so, she returned to her duties.

Marcus was standing in front of the lead waggon whilst he rested Trotter. Whilst doing so, he watched as the III and VI cohorts marched past at speed. They turned from the well-paved Roman road onto the hard earth Judaean road that led upwards between two ridges of hills.

"Gods be with you, lads." He muttered to no one in particular. The whole procession moved forward once the second advance cohort pulled away from the column's static lead cohorts. Marcus stood his ground as the waggons and hundreds of pedestrians passed him. The mass of people seemed to hold up well. Several pedestrians were now walking with one hand gripping the side of a waggon, being pulled along. So far, there had been no drama, but the alternative route would be much more challenging going underfoot, and matters might worsen.

As the civilian waggons rolled past, the militiaman responsible for their cart gave Marcus the agreed 'thumbs down' signal to show all was well. Then, after a few minutes, the infirmary waggons approached. Marcus remounted and, as he did so, spotted Anaitis' fair hair. At the same time, she noticed him and gave him a wave. Then, turning, she spoke to somebody hidden behind the high sideboards of the waggon; Miriam appeared and waved.

"Does all go well?" called Anaitis.

"All good so far," replied Marcus, "we're movin' onto the back route. It'll be safer, but it'll get a little rougher for the waggons, so bed your patients down well. We'll be okay. I must go forward. Good luck."

Saying so, he kicked Trotter in the flanks and rode towards the front of the column. He reflected on his recent words and prayed that his confidence would be rewarded. But unfortunately, his conscience told him otherwise.

"Jupiter," he said to no one, "I'll be developing Sextus' damned nose if this goes on!"

Marcus' concerns grew when the lead waggons rolled onto the alternative route. Hard road it may be, but it had never been used to carrying the number of waggons that made up this column. He knew the going would become difficult for the vehicles in the rear half of the column. They would struggle along a track broken up by the leading waggons. In addition, life would be hard for those on foot walking alongside the waggons. One factor was apparent, the column's rate of progress would be much slower. Speed would be a significant issue, giving the rebel band more time to clear the hills and prepare a new ambush. He envisaged that the III and VI Cohorts were in for some hot work.

They had been moving along the road for an hour when the first problem arose. A large cart snapped an axle. Part of Tribune Sallus' planning had foreseen such an event. The militiamen on the waggons local to the damaged vehicle, accompanied by civilians, removed people and possessions from the cart and pulled it off the road. The cart's occupants were re-homed before the column moved on. Marcus arrived at the scene halfway through the process. Watching the militiamen working so effectively to remove the hold-up filled him with satisfaction. He felt paternal regarding the militia and was proud his band of "rejects" were working so well.

When the men had cleared the road, Marcus joined them.

"Better get upfront and tell them to get moving again," said one, wiping his hands in his tunic.

"Well done, lads," said Marcus, "you done that well."

"You know what they say," said the hand-wiper, "you might take a legionary from the army, but you can't take the army from the legionary."

Marcus laughed

"Too bloody true that," he said as he turned Trotter to face the head of the column and rode off.

The IV Cohort's overnight stop outside of Gophna was uneventful. As the first rays of dawn lit up the countryside, mule carts were loaded, breakfast eaten, and the Fourth set out for Aelia. It was a rigorous marching pace, but legionary morale was high. Today they would march to the relief of a colony founded by the Imperator. Little did they know their expectations were to be far from reality.

Lucius could see over the helmets and forest of javelin points well enough to observe the tribune and his junior tribunes leading the cohort from his position at the rear of the leading 1st Century. As a centurion, Aurelius Crispus had every right to be mounted. He marched. Crispus was not a man who would ask his soldiers to do one thing while he did another. With full military paraphernalia, the mounted officers looked a fine sight as they led over four hundred legionaries, all with polished armour and helmets – Crispus saw to that! As he marched along, Lucius was dreaming of the past glories of the Roman army, only snapping out of his reverie when he saw the tribune's arm raised into the air, signalling a halt. The cornicen rang out, relaying the command to the files of legionaries. Lucius could see a rider had joined the mounted party at the head of the cohort to the front.

Lucius moved from his central position at the rear and stood at the formation's right flank, enabling Crispus to signal Lucius' should he require him. After some conversation at the head of the cohort, Aurelius Crispus did just that. The call went out for the cohort's centurions and optios to assemble.

"A very interesting development," said Tribune Civilis, sitting upon his mount looking down at the gathered officers. "It would appear that a short distance ahead of us, our enemy is preparing an ambush."

"Then we should persuade them otherwise," said one centurion.

"From what the Scout has said, I do not think we are the intended subject of the ambush," said Civilis. Then, turning to the scout, he continued, "perhaps you would brief the officers on what you have seen." He dismounted; the tribunes and the Scout followed suit as he spoke.

"There's four of us scouting ahead. The road in front follows the valley, taking a right turn then running straight for half a mile, before swinging round to the left." He ensured everyone had taken in the information he had just shared before continuing. "As usual, we keep off the road but sweep both sides of it. I was on the right flank." He turned and pointed to the ridge on their right, where the road turned right and disappeared behind it. "I rode to the top of the ridge, which gave me a full view of the straight stretch before it turns left behind a second ridge. I saw, on either side of that straight run, a very large body of soldiers, deliberately preparing an ambush."

"How many?" Asked Crispus.

"Exactly? Difficult to say," the Scout responded. "There is heavy shrubbery lower down on the valley sides. There are many already in position and well concealed. If you want my gut feel, I will say there are well over two thousand men, maybe more, around that corner. There was a steady flow of men arriving from over the ridge on the opposite side to me. Cavalry was going back and forth from the direction of Aelia."

"Thank you," Civilis said to the Scout. Then, turning back to officers, he said, "So men, what are they up to?"

"Well, we can rule out banditry," Crispus said, "they're preparing for something much more serious. But, as we've spotted no enemy scouts, it would make me think our scouts are correct in their deductions. We aren't their target."

"If you are right, Aurelius," responded the tribune, "it is possible they are unaware of our existence."

"My thoughts, exactly – we'll have the element of surprise if it comes to a fight."

Whilst Lucius listened to the conversation, his mind dwelt on the purpose of the ambush. Almost as though the tribune had connected to Lucius' flow of thought, he asked,

"If the Jews are not planning to ambush *us*, what then is their target?"

As the tribune finished his question, a thought struck Lucius.

"Hades and damnation!" He declared. All heads turned in his direction.

"Optio Petronius, is there something you would like to share with us?" asked Crispus. Lucius knew he had the focus of the entire group.

"Apologies, sir," he said to the tribune and turning back to the group, he continued, "A large ambush requires a large target. We're marching along the principal route from Aelia to Caesarea. Consider what large target would move up that road?" He scanned the group, waiting for an answer. None came. "Before we left Caesarea, I heard talk of abandoning the colony – an evacuation – to save the citizens. Unfortunately, we know the messenger service is hardly functioning, so we're getting little information from Aelia. Well, the thought occurred to me we might be unaware an evacuation had begun. So, a large refugee column, along with what remains of the *Fretensis,* is moving northwards, into a trap."

"If you are correct, Optio Petronius, then Hades and damnation it is." Then, said the tribune, "Your thoughts, men?"

The size of the ambush was a concern, and though discussion flowed for a few minutes, it found no other purpose for the enemy action other than to destroy a large target coming from Aelia. That enemy soldiers were emplaced would show that they planned for the trap to be sprung this day. Crispus felt it was time to move the discussion onwards.

"Well, whatever the target is, we have to make sure our enemy has a terrible day. There is no point in us charging up the road behind a wall of shields – I suspect we shall be overwhelmed. So, brothers, we need a plan."

A flurry of conversation ensued as they considered several approaches. They all involved surprise, the chief advantage the Fourth had over their enemy. A centurion pointed out that the

Fourth would not be alone; there would be little doubt whatever may come up the road would have an escort. Whilst acknowledging the fact, another officer pointed out communication with the escorting soldiers would not be possible. Lucius, noticing that Crispus said little but knew he was following the conversation. His helmet removed, scratching his head, the centurion weighed up what he heard. Finally, after a while, he spoke.

"There's been some good thinking, brothers," he said, "I've listened, and I have a plan. There are a lot of these bastards around the corner; we *must* beat them. Remember, they are not Roman soldiers. They are insurgents. I've always believed that a few professional soldiers with high morale can defeat a much larger disheartened enemy. That, my good friends, is what we shall do – with some help from the rest of the *Fretensis*."

The tribune and his junior tribunes had deliberately stood apart from the officer group. These centurions, all experienced professional soldiers, excelled in a situation such as this. Hearing Crispus' last spoken words, they moved closer. The centurion continued.

"Each century will form up two tent units wide, which will give us five rows per century. We are going up that hill," he nodded towards the ridge the scout had mentioned. "We shall stand just below the ridgeline, formed in line. I accept we shall be broad, with little depth. I plan to let the *cunni* spring the trap – whatever the target – and get them engaged in combat. The Fourth will move over the ridge and down the hill, making as much noise as possible. I want our officers," he said as he glanced at the tribune and his tribunes, "spread across the rear of the cohort. Let them think we're more than a single cohort. I want the bastards below, engaged with the escort troops, to realise we've trapped them, with legionaries before and behind. I intend to create panic. Panic is infectious, and all we'll need is for a few of the bastards to run; the rest will follow. I remind you we are not facing seasoned professional soldiers."

Crispus' reputation was such that only the briefest conversation ensued before the officers returned to their centuries and adopted the new formation. Within a short time, the Fourth was ready and waiting. Lucius noticed a change in the men of his century. The low-level murmuring, so often present among soldiers waiting for further instruction, was absent. Lucius understood. For the first time, these men formed up to go into action. They did not know how they would be by the end of the day.

Crispus sensed the same. He walked along the shortened column of soldiers, talking as he went.

"Brothers, there's every chance that shortly we'll engage the enemy. Further down the valley, they have set a large ambush," he said, avoiding mentioning the size of the Jewish force, "We intend to move up the ridge to our right so that when they spring the trap, we'll descend the hill and assault their rear. This'll be your first action, and the unknown always holds fears. You were trained by the best," he paused as a snigger ran through the cohort. "Remember your training and listen for your orders. Do that, and this day holds no fear for you. And remember, 'your sword will save your life!'" Strangled laughs ran through the cohort as Crispus quoted his well-worn adage. No one said anything, but the vast majority prayed he was right.

Crispus returned to the head of the column and joined the cornicen who stood ready and waiting, expecting the next command to be sounded via his huge circular trumpet.

"Well, Arrius Phillipus," said Crispus, "the time comes for us to advance upon the enemy. Sound the -" A rider was approaching the column, galloping along the paved road. Crispus recognised the man as another of the cavalry scouts. The tribune rode forward a few paces to meet him, and Crispus stepped out to be with his commanding officer. At one point, Crispus feared the cavalry scout would collide with the small command group, but at the last moment, he pulled up, snapping off a salute as he did so.

"Tribune Civilis, sir, the rebels are moving!"

"They have seen us?" Asked the tribune.

"No, sir. As we watched, two riders came at speed from the direction of Aelia. They talked with what appeared to be a small group of officers – we was at some distance, sir – and the next thing, orders was being given to form upon the road. Now, sir, just where they placed the ambush, a small track runs northeast, up over the hills. Before they was even fully formed up, their column head turned off the road and took the track. They were still moving out when I left."

"Cac!" spat Crispus.

"Thank you, scout," said the tribune, "you are right to report this quickly."

"Indeed," said Crispus, "tell me about this 'track' they've taken."

"Well, chief," the Scout responded, "that's just what it is – a track. Mainly used by shepherds for moving goats and sheep. It runs for several miles, as I recall, finally meeting a road on the other side of the hills."

Crispus removed his helmet and scratched his head.

"What in Hades name are they up to?"

"They must have received word that the subject of their ambush would not be arriving." Said the tribune. "Perhaps they are simply going back to where they came from."

The tribune's answer did little to satisfy Crispus' concerns. Instead, he continued to scratch his head.

"This road on the other side of the valley; how well do you know it?" he enquired of the scout.

"We – the Legion, that is – has used it, chief. A centurion will often turn off the Roman road coming south from Caesarea and use the alternative. It's heavier going, but if the lads have grown soft in Caesarea, it helps toughen'em up a bit."

Crispus nodded his head,

"Yes, I believe I've been down that road. It was quite some time ago." Then, he turned to the tribune, "Sir, I think I know what may be going on."

"I'm glad someone does," the tribune responded, "Let's hear it, Aurelius."

"They intended to ambush a large target. Let's suppose Optio Petronius was correct in believing the target was an escaping column from Aelia. If I am not wrong, the road on the other side of the hills that our Scout refers to breaks off from this road about nine or ten miles south of here. After passing several small villages, it re-joins a similar distance north of us. We passed the northern end as we came south, unaware of any significance." He looked at the Scout.

"That's about it, centurion."

"Now, this track the rebels have taken intersects that road," Crispus continued, "and I am wondering if they are moving to reposition their ambush. Maybe scouts from the Aelia column detected the trap in time to turn off the Roman road and take this Judaean road by way of diversion. The Jewish bastards have realised this and are moving over the hills to catch them as they take the diversion."

"Aelia column?" the Scout asked in amazement. Crispus briefed him.

"Fuck me! This is bad, fucking terrible," came the response.

"It is, but it's not over yet." Crispus turned to the tribune, "Sir, with your permission, I'd like to pursue the rebels. The fundamental plan does not change. If they find and attack the column, we'll hit them in the rear as planned."

"I do not see that we have many options, Aurelius," replied the tribune, "our duty must be to the citizens of Aelia." He turned to the Scout. "I need one of your men to intercept the cohorts following us. It would be ideal that they turn onto the road we suspect the column has taken and march to meet them. However, they must not head to Aelia. Do it now and do it quickly."

It took a few minutes for the Fourth to reform into regular marching order. Crispus no longer planned a forced march; the last thing he needed was for the cohort to bump into the rebels' rear; remaining undetected by the Jewish force was a crucial part of Crispus' plan.

The cohort moved forward into the bend that lay ahead, expecting a straightforward march, before turning off up the hillside track. However, the scouts brought the cohort to a stand again. The path was narrow, restricting access, and hundreds of Jewish rebels were milling about, waiting to move onto the track and follow their comrades. Had the Roman force marched around the bend, they would have been visible to the waiting rebels, and all Hell would have broken loose. As it was, it was going to be a lengthy wait for the way to clear. Crispus used the time well, ordering the legionaries to don their helmet covers and cloaks, minimising the risk of sunlight reflections alerting the enemy of their presence.

As the cohort neared the track they would follow, it became clear to Crispus he would have to adjust the column, currently spaced at the standard six legionaries wide. To the benefit of the cohort the large Jewish force preceding them had flattened the ground on either side of the path, crushing small scrubs and kicking loose stones to one side. As it would be safer, Crispus marched the cohort in two files width, keeping them on the track; he could not afford to have too many sprained ankles or damaged feet in this situation. Being a smaller force, the Romans were onto the path with only a slight delay, forming a column of over 400 men. The Scouts ranged ahead, ensuring the distance between the cohort and the preceding Jews. The last thing he wanted was for an observant rebel rear-guard to spot the following body of men. Should the cohort be detected, it would be a complete disaster.

As the day ground on, both forces climbed higher into the hills. For the cohort, their enemy determined any rests; if the Jews stopped, so did the Romans, keeping their distance, just out of sight. So Crispus ordered the cohort's carts to follow on at their own speed, which meant they were falling behind the nimbler legionaries. The consequence was as the centurion was acutely aware, that each soldier was carrying only a little sustenance – they had expected to eat in Aelia that night. Having to fight on an empty stomach is not reassuring.

As the Fourth approached the ridge marking the summit of the range of hills they had been sending, the Scouts informed Crispus that the enemy had ended their march for the day and was bivouacking where they stood. Fortunately, the ridge separated the two forces, so the tribune permitted a camp – or rather, imitating their enemy, bivouac. There could be no fires, for it would be too much risk even with the separating ridge between the two forces. Legionaries sharing whatever food remained and wrapped in their cloaks settled down for the night. Fortunately, the air was cool as opposed to cold. Crispus posted a watch. The Scouts camped on the back slope of the ridge, checking for any rebel movement. There was none. All was quiet.

The morning brought a bonus; the night had been clear with a bright moon, and the team Crispus had left with the carts, kept moving in the dark. They, too, were aware that the Fourth would have little food and that they had supplies, albeit limited, on the carts. They arrived in the middle of the night, and they issued food in the morning. As the sun rose on a new day, Crispus' legionaries were up and ready in quick time; there was nothing to pack or stow away, no tents to dismantle. As they passed a limited breakfast to each soldier, there were smiles on faces. One cheery soldier joked.

"If you can't catch a rabbit, a mouse tastes grand!" It was a sentiment shared by many. But, like the previous day, they wasted the efficient preparation. A scout informed the officers that a delay was likely.

"The vanguard's moving, sir," he said to the Tribune, "but I suspect it'll be a wait before those at the rear move on. From up the ridge, they look like a monstrous viper sliding down the hillside."

"I pray that by the day's end, we may cut off the snake's head," responded the tribune.

"Now, that'd be something to look forward to," responded Crispus, "in the meantime, sir, while we wait, I'll check on the men." The tribune indicated his approval, and Crispus walked back down the track, chatting with his soldiers as he did so. Banter it may be, but the centurion was gauging the morale amongst his un-blooded legionaries. He felt the men were coming to terms with imminent action; the jokes and the usual whines and moans were reappearing, but overall, they were quieter than usual. That was to be expected. Given the situation, it satisfied Crispus that all was well. But he knew the coming day would test his confidence.

Capitulum XXII – The junction

24 Aprilis. Year 16 of the Imperator Hadrianus.

Never had Marcus Apollinaris so appreciated the skill of the army's road builders. They made it possible to move legions, siege trains, and baggage swiftly across the empire. Sadly, the 'road' the column moved along – or more realistically, struggled along – was not constructed by *any* engineers, let alone Roman engineers. It was being churned up by the wheels of the many carts and waggons. Within the first few hours, four waggons had been abandoned; they had developed wheel and axle problems. Losing the waggons meant more people were on foot, and their baggage was distributed across the remaining waggons. Marcus looked to the sky and thanked the gods it was an expanse of blue; should rain arrive, the broken-up road would turn into a quagmire.

Given the issues around the travelling surface, the column covered only a few miles before dusk approached, and progress ceased for the day. The evening gave the militia time to reallocate passengers from abandoned waggons to other waggons. It was clear that if the attrition rate continued most citizens would be on foot within a few days.

The reduced legionary escort posted centuries along the length of the column. Those not on sentry duty, grouped into small bands, camped from the column's front to its rear. Should an attack occur, it meant a body of legionaries would respond wherever the enemy struck.

Marcus rode the length of the column accompanied by centurion Gracchus. People lit small fires once food distribution was done and gathered around for nourishment.

"They're bloody shagged, Marcus," said Gracchus. "They're not used to this. After all, you could walk across the expanse of Aelia in no time at all. Even that would've been a trek for many of this lot!"

"You're right, Julius. The enthusiasm when we first set out has gone. Look at them now, and this is only day two," said Marcus. "This will become gruelling. Some of our lads will find it hard too – don't forget, we got the legion's rejects."

"Same thoughts, brother, and I've been using what I've got between the ears," Gracchus said, touching his helmet. "If we sent word ahead to Caesarea, I wonder if it would be possible to arrange a support column to head south and meet us in Samaria once we get clear of Judaea?"

"Jupiter! Carry on like that, and Tribune Civilis will see you as a threat," joked Marcus. "But, yes, good thinking, brother. Talk to our tribune — see what he thinks."

"I'll do that." The centurion responded.

Aginthus' III Cohort and Petronius' VI Cohort moved forward up the road at a forced march. Claudius Aginthus, the senior officer of the two centurions, took his orders seriously to reach the junction of the road and hillside track seriously. It may be dusk, but he will keep moving.

"I know there's a risk to marching in the dark," he said to Optio Porcius Fimbria, who had joined him at the head of the cohort, "but we have to be sure we get to the junction before the enemy. We've a full moon, and the sky is clear - the risk is worth taking."

"Is Centurion Petronius with you on this?" asked Fimbria.

"He is. I do not intend to march through the night simply to get some distance under our belts before we rest. I'll send some scouts forward whilst we still have some light left."

"It'll be good to see our objective," said Fimbria.

"You are right, Porcius, and one of my reasons to reach the junction soon as we can is to gain some breathing space to consider positioning the cohorts."

Aginthus' risk paid off; the Third and the Sixth travelled several miles in the dark before establishing an overnight camp; the moon was high in the sky by that time. With his task in mind, Aginthus had the cohorts formed and moved shortly after daybreak. They hurried onwards, and it was not long before a scout reported they were approaching the junction, their objective. The forced march had worked; the junction was clear of enemy forces. The two centurions rested their men just short of the junction upon arrival. Aginthus and Petronius went forward accompanied by scouts to inspect the ground in front of them.

Standing on the road, they looked up the track from which the rebels would have to disgorge. Higher up, their pathway ran through a steep-sided valley, but as it approached the road, the valley sides fell away, and the track ran down a steady open slope to the road.

"We need to be on the slope, Julius," Aginthus said to his colleague, "the more we keep'em compressed in that valley, the better."

"You're right, brother; they'd have a slight downhill advantage but limiting their frontage would cancel the benefit. What would you estimate their frontage would be if we met them at the top of the slope?"

"I'd say eight to ten men wide," Aginthus replied. "they're not heavy infantry, so let's go for ten."

"Right then; upfront, we have three holding lines, each of twelve legionaries - effectively a wall of shields." Petronius continued, "The remaining legionaries will form up to their rear in lines of the same number. We rotate lines in turns, releasing javelins and retiring to the rear. If our enemy's concentrated within the valley, it'll be like pig-sticking – if I was them, all I would want to do is back off." Aginthus laughed.

"Good plan, Julius, and we'd still have the II Cohort standing by. However, I've a niggle that once the goat-shaggers realise we block their exit, they will scale the valley side, swing around, and attempt to attack us on one or both flanks."

"Given that," said Petronius, "then it might be expedient to split II Cohort in two, so it can serve as a flank guard. They could also rotate with the blocking cohort if the going gets hard."

"Well, it sounds like a simple plan, the type that tends not to fail!" Aginthus gave a grim laugh, "It is about time that Fortuna smiled upon us. I mean, the odds are that we must be due a success against these bastards."

"Cheer up, brother. You never know, our assumption may be wrong – perhaps our goat shagging friends have all gone home."

"After the marching we have done in the last day or so, I'd be bloody disappointed if the bastards don't turn up. I feel I need to beat the Hades out of someone, and I'd much rather it was one of them!"

"Time will tell," said Petronius, "but meanwhile, let's get the lads in a position where they can rest but move to fighting stations as soon as the Scouts spot the Jews approaching. The only question is, which cohort carries out what role?"

Aginthus reached to the ground, picked up a stone, and stood with his hands behind his back. He then stretched his arms forward with his fists clenched.

"That's simple," he said, "which hand? Left, or right?"

Lucius Petronius was at the head of the IV Cohort. Centurion Crispus had gone back among his legionaries' elongated column, ensuring all was well and consulting with his centurions. In Crispus' absence, Lucius was accompanied by the century's tesserarius. Just behind the two, marched the signifier and the century's cornicen, all leading the century of over 80 men, a scene repeated five times along the column.

"Is there a plan in Crispus' mind?" Tesserarius Claudius Paulus, asked of Lucius.

"Until we see what is facing us, I suspect that'll be difficult. Crispus has likely worked out several scenarios, but he's yet to share them with me."

"It'll be messy if we're forced to fight along this track. There's damn little room for manoeuvre."

"That's true, Claudius," responded Lucius, "but it'll be worse for them. The surprise should be with us. Add to that the fact we'll hit them in the rear – where they'll position their second-rate men – we'll have the advantage."

"As long as the bastards don't spot us."

"I guess Crispus'll do as he planned yesterday – wait for them to be engaged before we hit them. One reason the scouts are way out front is to avoid our forces colliding and giving the game away."

"Well, Aurelius Crispus knows what he's doing, so I'm sure the Fourth will do well."

"You've yet to see a major action, have you, Claudius?" Lucius asked.

"A scrap or two, Lucius, but nothing like this."

"Well, as the man says, it's a case of listening out for orders, obey them as trained, and you will find it's soon all over – even if it's been a slog," Lucius said, "What new soldiers fear most, the killing, is just a blur; the training sees to that. After the action, the feelings hit you – hard – but that is normal. Then, the next time out, it's easier and gets so each time you're engaged."

"Well, I keep praying to Mithras that I carry out my duty well," said Paulus.

"I think even the hardest veterans do the same, Claudius, and you can count me in too!"

Lucius had just finished speaking when a cavalry scout arrived at the head of the column.

"Where is centurion Crispus?" He asked Lucius.

"He's back down the column checking on the centuries. You'll find him easily enough but take care the path is narrow – it'll be a tight squeeze. What's up?"

"The bastards are up to something!" At which point he dug his heels into his mount's side and moved off down the column. Lucius could imagine the expletives which would greet him as he pushed past the marching men. Claudius Paulus, the tesserarius, turned to Lucius.

"*Cac*! I wonder what they're up to?"

"Well, Claudius, in my experience, your enemies are always up to something," Lucius replied with a laugh, reassuring his nervous tesserarius. "If it's something important Crispus will inform us."

Experience told him that a scout arriving at speed is a signal that action is close when at this proximity to the enemy. He wondered how the century would react to the scout's arrival. He was sure the tension would rise amongst the men following him.

It was not long before the scout passed the century in the opposite direction, heading back down the meandering track from where he came. Then, just a few seconds later, a breathless Crispus returned to the head of the column. He fell into step alongside Lucius and the tesserarius.

"Developments, men," he said, "the scouts have spotted small groups of rebels clambering up the valley sides – left and right. This bloody valley has so many twists and turns; their view of what's going on isn't good. However, the lad that just came in reckons that these groups number around fifty men each. What pisses me off is that we've no way of knowing just how many groups have left the rebel column."

"Did he say how far we are from the junction?" asked Lucius.

"Reckons we are about 3 miles off," Crispus responded, "which would make the head of their column about a mile from the junction, would be my estimate. What's your thinking?"

"Their principal force delivers the punch. The lads rush to face it, and they get hit on the flanks, left and right."

"My concern too, Lucius. However, I'm still convinced that if we can smash the main force, their ambush will fail."

"In principle, I would agree, sir," Lucius replied and paused before going further.

"Spit it out, lad."

"Well, for them, what is failure… or success, for that matter? What is their aim?"

"Go on," Crispus said.

"We are agreed that the odds are high that their target is a column coming from Aelia. The column will comprise many civilians, with the best part of a Roman legion protecting it. Yes, the rebels may've knocked the *Fretensis* about a bit, but the legion can still put up stiff resistance. The Jewish force is sizable, but is it big enough to overwhelm our lads and destroy the column?"

"If they were legionaries, certainly," answered Crispus, "a rebel militia… I'm not so sure. Maybe – maybe not. However, our objective *is* clear; we hit the main body in the rear and kill as many of the bastards as we can. I want to panic them, Lucius. If we can do that, I'm sure they will break."

"I've no doubt we'll strike them hard. My concern is the men they are sending out of the valley," Lucius replied. "You see, I am not so sure they expect to destroy the column, just wreak havoc upon it. What eventually arrives at Caesarea is a shamble of the dead, along with wounded and exhausted survivors. It means the rebels will've taken our primary base in Judaea, followed by the arrival in Caesarea of fleeing refugees. What signal would it send across the region? You, of all people, understand the importance of morale, Julius."

"Jupiter, Optio Petronius!" Crispus looked agog at Lucius, "what the fuck difference does all that make to our position right now? Our job is to kill the bastards in front of us — simple."

"It is sir. It's those men they're sending out either side of the valley that worry me. If I'm right about the objective, I believe they'll be sending out archers and slingers. Their one goal will be to create carnage within the column."

Crispus did not respond. He went to scratch his head, only to find he was wearing his helmet.

"Dammit!" He thought a while longer. "You could be right, Lucius. Those men *are* being placed on the hilltops for a reason. And yes, they *are* in an ideal place for distance weapons. The *Fretensis* will have little that could retaliate. So, my smart-arsed optio, I am in no doubt you wish to make a proposal?"

It had been a busy day so far. The long column, preceded by two cohorts of legionaries, continued its slow progress, continuing to churn up the road as it went along. The rough conditions caused other waggons to fail, throwing more people onto their feet. It was becoming more challenging for those walking. The waggons were now becoming permanent homes for the women and children whilst the men proceeded on foot. Morale was sliding, and most citizens had one desire; to get clear of Judaea and reach the relative safety of Samaria.

The column's watch officer, its centurion and its commanding tribune, rode at the head of the large train, reviewing the day's actions. Knowing this to be the day when the column would pass the potential ambush point, they had arranged that the militia instruct their passengers what cover to take in the event of an attack. The choices are limited; should all movement stop, hide in or under a wagon.

"The trouble is, sir," said Marcus Apollinaris, "you sees 'em coming at you with a spear, but you don't sees the bloody slingshot. That is where they *will* get hurt."

"Marcus is right, sir," agreed Julius Gracchus, "and if possible, the legion wants the column to keep moving, so there ain't much sense in trying to hide under a moving wagon. But we cannot fit everybody aboard waggons. So, if they attack us, the column will come to a stand – it has to."

The tribune absorbed what the two men had said for a few seconds. Then, finally, he recognised the reality that lay in their statements.

"I suspect you are right, Gracchus. If they ambush us, it would be a case of handling things as they come. The risk of panic worries me, and that's why I wanted everyone to have instructions on how to react should they attack us. It's a comfort, even if it is a false one!"

The militiamen had briefed the column passengers earlier that day, focussing on safety if attacked. The column leaders doubted the efficacy of the advice, but the passengers needed guidance for it to appear that matters were under control. Nevertheless, all three men voiced their concerns, driven by an internal belief that an attack would rapidly lead to chaos amongst the waggons.

"Problem's made worse by the fact we've lost nine more waggons this morning," Marcus said, "so we have more people on foot and less shelter." In response, Gracchus gave a grim laugh.

"I'm praying to Mithras that the *cunni* take a wrong turn in the hills!"

"True, we are basing everything upon the belief that the rebels were coming this way," Tribune Sallus said. "For all we know, they may have turned off the track for another destination."

"Wrong turn – right turn," interjected Gracchus, "as long as they turn, I shall be a happy centurion!"

They rode in silence for a while, becoming mesmerised by the gleaming helmets of the I and II Cohorts to their front, rocking side to side as they marched before them. Then, finally, it was Gracchus who snapped them out of their trance.

"It looks like a Scout reporting to the First," he said. Marcus and the Tribune squinted their eyes as they looked to the front, dazzled by the sunlight shining off the marching helmets.

"You could be right," responded the tribune. "We're due some good news!" Then, after remaining with the officers of the preceding legion for a brief time, the scout joined the officers at the head of the column. He saluted the tribune.

"The III and VI Cohorts have arrived at their destination and are in position. There is no sign of the enemy. The primus, Centurion Vorenus, intends to maintain the current pace, which means we should reach the junction in about two hours."

"Thank you," responded Tribune Sallus. "Please pass my compliments to the primus as you return."

The Scouts saluted again, turned his horse, and rode back past the marching legionaries.

"Well, brother Gracchus, we'll soon see if Mithras hears you," quipped Marcus. The tribune was deep in thought. He surfaced a few seconds later.

"Gracchus, I want you to get down the column and ensure the waggons are as close together as possible. I want the column to be as short as possible."

"Very good, sir," Gracchus replied as he turned his horse's head. The tribune had not finished.

"There is something I need to be very clear on," he said. "Should they attack us, and things go badly, I shall order the column to move at full speed to get clear. Those are our orders if you recall." He turned to Gracchus. "I am counting on our escort holding the attackers off for such a time as we are away. I appreciate it will make it exceedingly difficult for those on foot and exhaust the animals. However, it *will* be the lesser of two evils. Our goal is to protect the citizens but accept we may lose a sizeable number if it comes to a fight. Go to it now, Gracchus."

The centurion galloped off.

"Let's hope Mithras *is* with us, sir," Marcus said.

"Let us hope so, Apollinaris," replied the tribune, "if they attack us, we shall need all the support we can get."

Slowly, the column followed the lead cohorts around a sweeping left bend. Tribune Civilis and Marcus caught sight of Roman soldiers in the distance. It was a clear sign they were approaching the junction. They had no sooner spotted the activity ahead when Centurion Gracchus arrived from his ride along the length of the column.

"The waggons are closing up, sir," he said, "and given the junction will be on our left, I have advised everyone on foot to walk on the right-hand side of their waggons."

"Well done, Centurion," the tribune responded. "There is little else we can do."

"Our escort has moved to the wagon's left, so anyone coming out of the hills will have to get through them first," Gracchus added.

As the ambush point neared, the officers fell silent. Butterflies seem to flutter around in Marcus' stomach, even though things seemed calm at the junction. As the column closed on the intersection, he could see the hillside track falling out of its valley onto a widening plain before joining the road. Where the track exited the valley, a cohort stood in a lengthy column, the front lines plugging the exit. On either side of the column stood two blocks of legionaries, ready to support.

"I wouldn't want to 'ave to work my way through that lot," Marcus said to no one in particular. Gracchus laughed; the tribune did not respond. Sticking to plan, the column's lead cohorts, remaining on station, were now marching past the junction.

"By my estimates," the tribune said, "it would take the best part an hour or more to get the column past this point, and that is an optimistic expectation. Until then, it is at risk. So, I suggest we remain at the junction to see the last waggons past."

It amused the tribune and gave him a little relief to see that his two officers placed a hand on the pommel of their swords without being aware of their actions.

Not so far away, back along the track, the Fourth drew closer to the rear of the rebel force. Centurion Crispus, moving forward with a scout, had removed his helmet to avoid advertising his presence to the enemy. From their vantage point, the two men could only see the rear of their antagonists waiting on the road.

"They've shed many men into the hills, chief," said the scout. "They are equipped lightly and climb well."

"Bugger it!" Crispus replied. "We will have to keep our eyes on our flanks as we move forward. I'm counting on the fact they're not expecting us."

"They've done nothing to show they've seen us," the scout said. The two men turned to return to the cohort when the sound of distant shouting reached them.

"Well, brother, we shall soon find out if they are expecting us or not." Crispus donned his helmet and jogged back to his waiting men, tying his helmet strap as he went. In Crispus' absence from the century, the Optio moved to the front to take temporary command. Crispus arrived back to find Lucius, Tesserarius Paulus and Signifier Calvus waiting for him, all three looking very expectant.

"Did you hear the noise from down the road?" asked Crispus as he approached the three officers - they had. "Right then, we're going in. It will be tight, but I want a wedge on me, six files wide. Tell'em to watch their bloody footing. I don't want anyone falling – not packed as tight as they'll be. It'd be chaos!" He paused for a second or two and rubbed the side of his helmet, causing Lucius to smile. "It'll be straightforward, as we get them in sight, we'll go from march to jog – it's crucial we stay tight – and we'll drive hard into their rear. Before we hit, I want the loudest roar we can manage and, once amongst them, as much noise as possible. I aim to terrify the cunni! Mithras be with us." The officers fell back into position.

Crispus turned to Lucius, "Get the other centurions here – and the cornicen--I'll need to brief them."

Lucius jogged off to the rear.

Marcus, Tribune Sallus and Centurion Claudius Aginthus stood on the exact spot where the track joined the road. The men of Aginthus' III Cohort stood on either side of the VI Cohort, blocking the point where the path would enter the short plain that lay before the road. Thus, the track was well and truly blocked. Marcus contributed little to the conversation, aware that Aginthus was a full-blooded centurion as opposed to Gracchus, whose 'centurion' status was vastly different.

So, as the tribune and the centurion discussed the situation, Marcus watched the column trudge past. It looked a pitiful sight, the people appeared ragged, if not a little dirty, after several nights on the road. Occasionally a wagon would pass, and children's heads would appear above the sideboards. Even for them, the initial sense of adventure had waned. The stance of many showed that severe fatigue was setting in. But Marcus would not let this affect his morale. Two facts kept him buoyant: the tribune had sent to Caesarea for a relief column to head south, and Marcus knew that once they re-joined the northbound Roman road, they would soon be in Samaria, and the threat of attack would recede.

As he watched, the medical waggons rolled past. Marcus was conscious of searching for Anaitis amongst the passengers, but the waggons had high sideboards, which restricted his view. He wanted to assure her all was going well. He spotted Meniscus, who waved in recognition, and Marcus replied, returning the acknowledgement.

"Well, Apollinaris," Tribune Sallus said, turning away from the centurion, "with half the column passed, perhaps we should return to the head." Marcus turned to the legionary, who stood a little distance away holding the reins of their mounts and signalled to him to approach. Trotter neighed and made her way towards Marcus. The legionary tugged on her rein to pull her back, then collapsed to the floor.

"What the fuck?" said Marcus. As he spoke, a minor explosion of dust and stone erupted at his feet, followed by a further eruption a few feet away. "Slingshot!" Centurion Aginthus swung around, looking for his century's trumpeter.

"Trumpeter," he bellowed, "We're under attack!" The target of his communication placed the brass instrument to his lips and began his call. One made redundant by a mighty shout from the track. Hundreds of Jewish rebels charged the narrow Roman blocking line. Centurion Aginthus left the small group at the run to join his cohort. Marcus watched in fascination as the two forces met. The Roman line shivered but held, and he could see the first of the deadly Roman javelins fly over the heads of the blocking legionaries to land amongst the attackers. The noise from the fight surprised Marcus; he had long forgotten the sounds of an actual battle. Men roared, men screamed – often as they died – and metal clanged upon metal, metal thumped into wood in an explosion of sound. Marcus thanked Mithras for the foresight of sending the III and VI cohorts forward. If the screaming horde advancing down the track had got amongst the waggons, it would have been a disaster.

"Apollinaris! The waggons – they're under attack." The tribune ran to his horse. Marcus turned to see chaos descending over the waggons. The evacuees were on the right side of the column that shielded them from the slingshot's source, but not all. These latter people indicated trouble. Several fell to the ground, while others clutched the parts of their bodies impacted by the slingshot, screaming as they did so. Marcus looked upwards to the ridge that ran alongside the road to find it lined with rebel slingers. Some were confident enough to creep down the hillside to get a better shot.

Marcus leapt onto Trotter and rode to the nearest militiaman.

"We're goin' to increase speed. We must get this lot," his arm swept across the vista in front of him, "moving and get to Hades away from here. Pass the word down the line – I'm headed up to the front." With that, he dug his heels into Trotter's flanks. He had considered moving along the sheltered side of the column, but what he saw gave serious concern. So many passengers fled from the waggons onto the opposite slope away from the hill where the missiles originated. It would be a slow passage for anyone horseback manoeuvring around them. So Marcus took the risk and rode along the exposed side of the column.

Trotter was falling into a steady gallop when another horseman drew up alongside Marcus.

"Tribune's upfront," Gracchus shouted. "We need to get these people away from here."

"Fair point, brother," said Marcus, "but it'll be like herding sheep while the fucking wolves are dining on them! Some buggers are even running off."

"Their choice – their choice," was the only response from Gracchus.

Suddenly, he remembered it had been years since he had galloped a horse, and he remembered it differed from trotting up and down the length of a column. It was very much to his relief that he was still in the saddle as they joined the tribune near the head of the column. Tribune Sallus, accompanied by two militiamen, had moved down along the column, demanding the waggons moved to full speed. The principal rebel attack was against the centre of the column, and it took an effort to persuade the wagon drivers of the urgency of maximum speed. They had to overcome their tendency to preserve the strength of their animals.

"I'll get 'em shifted," declared Marcus. He kicked Trotter and rode back along the column, making his wishes quite clear to anyone within earshot. "There are people fucking dying back there!" Marcus bellowed, walking his horse down the column, "the sooner you get your arses moving, the more people we'll save – including you!"

Much to the officer's relief, as the whips cracked over the backs of beasts, the waggons picked up speed. Finally, Gracchus and the Tribune caught up with Marcus, who was about to repeat his diatribe for waggons further down the line.

"As orders go, quite unconventional Apollinaris," said Tribune Sallus, "but given the situation, most effective. I'll take over here. I want you and Gracchus to round up the idiots who fled the waggons and get them back into place. Keep them all on the safe side and as close as possible to the waggons. Go to it."

As the two men were about to ride off, he added, "Some of those unconventional commands might serve well, Apollinaris."

The two officers saluted and then paused for a second as they saw the two lead cohorts flowing around the column, as they reversed direction and marched back to the sound of battle. Every so often, a century would fall out and create a protective screen between the hills and the column.

As he rode, Marcus kept gesturing to the front of the column, shouting, "Move, move, faster, move!" His life experience of civilians in situations like this told him they would act in two ways. The first was to run screaming, as many had already done so, away from the violent threat. The second was to be petrified, mesmerised by fear, and to do nothing. In Marcus' mind, the simplest solution was to issue orders. These offered hope and achieved obedience. Even faced with wolves, he thought, we can still round up the sheep.

The next few minutes were hectic as the two riders, and several militiamen, tried to persuade, cajole, and force the frightened people to return to their waggons. Many women with their children, were cowering behind bushes and scrub, desperately trying to shield their offspring.

As Marcus rode among refugees begging them to return, he passed a young mother and her small child sheltering in a shallow rainwater gully. He approached them, and the mother looked up. Marcus was hit with a flashback. It took him back to the village, being attacked by his cohort. The face had appeared from behind a bush, the young woman in fear of her life. For her, discovery by a Roman soldier meant death. It was the eyes, the sheer desperation in her big black eyes, the knowledge that the end was coming, her time was over. Marcus took pity and let her pass; she would not die that day. But, alas, soon after, she lay slaughtered. Marcus was again staring into her eyes.

"Lady, you can't stay here. You're not safe. Get back to the waggons." He pleaded. The woman shook her head, the look in her eyes unchanged, petrified. "If you stay here, you will die. At the waggons, you will find friends, and we have more soldiers arriving to protect you. Think of your child. It has every right to live."

As Marcus looked into the woman's face, He knew his responsibility was to all, but he would not leave this one to her fate. There was a slight change in her face, and the muscle tautness brought on by fear eased.

"Please," begged Marcus, "we don't have time." The woman's gaze moved to a child and then back to Marcus, and he knew she was relenting. "Come on, quickly," he said, "I'll take you both, but it must be now." She stood holding a child's hand, and Marcus could see it was a boy. "Pass him up to me." She obeyed and lifted the boy into Marcus' arms. "Right lad, we'll play at being soldiers." The boy looked at his mother, who managed a smile, and Marcus felt the boy relax; fear had fled, and games had begun. "We are off to save the column," Marcus said cheerfully to the boy. He turned to the mother. "Hold on to my saddle," and they moved off towards the column.

It was no time before Marcus handed over the mother and child to a small group of concerned women huddled up to the side of a wagon, safe from any incoming missiles. He continued with his mission. Glancing up to the ridge, the number of rebels was growing. Looking between the waggons, Marcus glimpsed the protective screen of legionaries that now lay between the rebel force and the column. He felt a little easier. The waggons moved as quickly as they could go. Frightened waggoners continued to lash their animals, hoping they may go faster. The clearest indicator of speed was the pace of the people on foot. Many refugees were struggling with the pace. Marcus wondered how long they could keep it up.

He turned his horse towards the head of the column to see two riders approaching him. Marcus came to a stand, and the two men pulled up beside him.

"The Third and Sixth would appear to be holding them at the junction," said Tribune Sallus, "and the attack on the column is slingshot. If we can get the waggons out of range, we may well get through this reasonably intact."

"Let us hope so, sir," Gracchus responded. "We've rounded up most of the 'runners', but not everyone – they'll just have to take their chances."

"Right then, as long as we keep the walkers this side of the waggons and keep 'em moving, it won't be long before we're in the clear?"

"If the gods are with us, I believe so," said the tribune.

"There'll be more casualties before we get passed," Gracchus said, "and we've taken a good number so far, so it'll be crucial to keep up speed. With your permission, tribune, I'll check on my men and the waggons." The tribune nodded, and Gracchus rode away.

"I'd love to get at the bastards, sir," Marcus said.

"I share that feeling, Apollinaris, but our job is keeping the column moving and rescuing as many citizens as we can. After that, we must leave the rebels to the legion."

The waggons progressed along the road, protected by a screen of legionaries standing behind their shields on the column's left. At the junction, the Roman 'plug' was holding, the fighting furious, but the plan was working.

They may have hoped the gods were with them — but they were wrong.

Optio Lucius Petronius waited at the trackside and watched as his century led the Fourth into its first battle. Crispus had moved the cohort to a position where the enemy was just visible, a few hundred feet to the front. The leading ranks formed a wedge with Crispus at its point. An order rang out, and the whole cohort jogged forward. Lucius had faced this tactic in training; the metallic rattle of the lorica segmentata in time with the heavy tramping of the legionary's boots and a wall of shields approaching at speed. When Lucius last experienced an infantry wedge, it was in training. He thought it must be terrifying to be facing the sharp end for real.

Crispus was right; the enemy had placed the weaker men to their rear. These rebels relaxed as the length of their stretched-out force convinced them it would be over by the time they reached the junction. Two soldiers, slouching on their spears at the back of the column, turned to check out the growing noise behind them. Their jaws dropped, and they turned again, screaming at their colleagues. When the rebels understood the threat and attempted a defensive formation, the Roman ploughshare drove into the column's rear. Bodies flew left and right as the wedge struggled to maintain the formation as they passed across fallen bodies—the ranks following dealt with any Jews still showing signs of life. Lucius thought the tactic would lose momentum, but it worked as planned.

Lucius turned to the thirty legionaries that Crispus had allowed him to co-opt. He and these men had another mission. They were going to climb the hillside to understand better what the rebels were doing.

"Soldiers, stack your shields to the side. They'll only hinder us." Lucius was aware of the strange looks he received and the reluctance of his men as they took turns to ground their shields. One of those soldiers was a dark-skinned legionary, showing little reticence and smiling as he lay down his shield. Lucius was thankful that Atelius was amongst the group.

"Men," said Lucius, raising his voice above the sound of the tramping feet and rattling armour, "we know the enemy has been getting soldiers away up these valley sides. They're lightly equipped and nimble. We don't know what they're up to, and we're going to find out. You could call this a scouting mission in force – it's not an attack. So, what I intend…."

A minute later, the small force was climbing up the hillside. It was manageable but steep enough that several legionaries wished to dispense with their armour. They understood why they had abandoned their shields. As they approached the top of the hillside, Lucius brought the party to a stop. He moved ahead alone to see what lay ahead on the ridge that overlooked the road. The pause gave the sweating legionaries brief respite to recover from the climb.

Lucius removed his helmet before raising his head as he approached the top. A short way to his right, standing along on what he presumed must be the ridgeline, were many slingers busy about their business. Beyond them, in the farther distance, was a large body of men armed with spears and shields – infantry! It all confirmed that the report of men moving into the hills was correct. They must have left the enemy column earlier when it was easier to ascend to the ridge. Lucius recognised they were facing a capable enemy. Given how the disruption of rebels' earlier plans, they had recovered effectively from the setback. As he observed, yet more rebel soldiers appeared from the valley, having climbed its sides.

Lucius slid a short distance back down the slope to where his men had waited. He shared with them a verbal picture of what he had seen.

"... the nearest credible threat to us is the infantry. So, I intend to move along the valley top and prevent the rebels from escaping up the valley side, leaving the Fourth and the units at the other end to squeeze and destroy the bastards. So, let's be about it."

Before they moved off, Lucius sent a soldier back down to the track. He recommended Crispus put another force up onto the other side of the valley, blocking any retreat in that direction. Lucius' group clambered up the short distance before standing on the ridge. He ordered a two-file formation, and the column moved along the ridge, in parallel with the unseen track below. They had only gone a short distance when several heads appeared above the ridgeline, enemy soldiers about to exit the valley.

"*Fretensis!*" cried, and the Romans surged forward. The rebels tried to clear the valley side and gain a footing on level ground – three of them made it. They did not stand a chance, one dying before he even drew his sword. Enthusiastic legionaries jumped onto the slope, landing on top of surprised rebels. Within a matter of seconds, a dozen bloody bodies lay on the ground or down the incline. It was a successful action, but several legionaries whose enthusiasm got the better of them found themselves many feet down the slope. Seeing another rebel group on their way up the hillside motivated the legionaries to return to the main body hurriedly. They appraised Lucius of the situation and he did not hesitate.

"Men, collect the bodies and then roll them down the valley side onto the next group," he ordered. "let's see how that affects their enthusiasm for a fight." They consigned the bodies down the valley side. Two corpses went a short distance and stopped, but the remaining gathered momentum and rolled towards the upcoming enemy. There were shouts from below, showing a state of confusion amongst the climbers.

"They don't like it, sir – that's for sure!" commented an Aramaic speaking legionary. The shouting continued for several seconds before a more dominant voice seemed to gain control. Lucius looked expectantly at the legionary. "They never saw us, sir. They're confused, but the big voice is ordering them on."

"Right, I want two ranks, ten paces back from the slope," Lucius ordered. "We'll hit them just as they find their feet. Do it, now." They quickly achieved the formation. Seconds later, they heard the scraping of sandals clawing for grip on loose rock accompanied by the chinking of metal. Each legionary braced to fight—then all went quiet. Down on the slope, caution was being applied. Lucius had kept himself and his men well back from the head of the incline, keen not to give the enemy any sign of what was waiting. Given his lack of information about what awaited him on the crest of the slope, the enemy commander adopted an appropriate cautious tactic.

Six well-spread groupings of three men came into the Roman's view, clearing the slope at speed. There was confusion in the Roman ranks for a few seconds as they now had enemies to the left, right, and front. The Jewish leader had been cunning. Then the groups rapidly became three groups of six men – left, centre and right – and screamed they charged the block of legionaries. "What I wouldn't give for some shields," thought Lucius. He was about to shout the order to stand fast when Atelius broke ranks. Then, from the front rank's middle, he hurled himself at the central band of rebels, his sword in his right hand and his pugio dagger in his left.

Lucius yelled, "Charge," hoping to the gods that his men would have enough sense to group effectively to counter the enemy assault. The forces clashed, and a general melee broke out. On the right of his force, Lucius joined those legionaries defending that wing. The usual intuitive fighting focus overtook Lucius. The struggle moved back and forth for a brief time, and then it was over. The rebels were all down – most dead – but three legionaries also lay on the ground. A silence fell over the scene, the only sound being that of panting legionaries and the occasional moan of an injured combatant. Reality slowly returned Lucius. A voice spoke up.

"Well, fuck me, brother, when you said you was a gladiator once, you was not fucking joking, was you?" The silence was broken, and Lucius could noticed the men in the centre staring at Atelius.

"Jupiter Optimus, did you see that?" said another. Atelius stood a little apart, sword in hand and dagger in the other, his armour splattered with blood.

"Brothers, where I came from, I couldn't count on a shield for protection," he held up his two weapons, "these were my defence – maybe a spear."

"And glad you one of us, brother!" a voice said.

"Optio done alright," another voice said.

Lucius studied his small band of warriors. A number were buoyant, the vocal ones, while others were withdrawn, and several were on their knees beside their fallen comrades. He knew it would be dangerous to allow them to loiter, dwelling on their feelings generated by their first genuine combat.

"I want the rebel bodies down the slope, joining those we sent earlier," he said to them, "let's get to it – straight away. Now!" The soldiers' trained instinct to obey had them moving the slain rebels, dragging the corpses to edge, and rolling them off. As they were doing so, Lucius looked across toward the slingers and, beyond them, the infantry.

The infantry's attention was drawn to the road in front of them, which the Romans from their position could not see. A few slingers called their mates and pointed at the Roman group on the ridge. Lucius felt they were debating whether to change from their current targets to his small group.

"Job done, sir," said a voice behind him. Lucius was about to turn and reorganise his men when half a dozen slingers formed a short line facing the Romans. They were a distance off but well within the range of the deadly missiles. The slings rotated above the slinger's heads. He, too, wished they carried their shields.

375

"Slingshot! Everyone – now – down the slope, beneath the ridge. Move. Move. Move!" he shouted. Taking a second to react, the group followed in the dead Jews' path before falling prone. One soldier screamed before reaching safety, pitching forward over the ridge, and rolling downwards. Two of his comrades grasped him and prevented him from sliding amongst the corpses that littered the hillside. The slinger's victim quickly recovered and crawled upwards.

"He got whacked on his leg by a rebound," a voice said, "the shots fell just short. He's a lucky bastard!"

Lucius realised that his expedition was ending; he could not ask his men, shield less, to move across open ground against slingers. It would be suicide. The curve of the hillside meant he could not see the track where his comrades were trying to crush the Judaean force. As he looked, he detected no further attempts to escape the valley. Finally, crawling to the top of the slope, he took in the view. While a tiny number of slingers were still looking in their direction, the rest had returned to firing missiles onto the road.

"Soldiers, we've achieved our goal of stopping the rebels escaping; we can achieve little more. So, we'll give the slingers a short while to settle back into their work. After that, we go back up the slope and return to the point we ascended and re-join the Fourth. When we get back up on the level, move quickly."

"Sir, what about Octavius and the others?"

Lucius understood the concern for the three fallen soldiers.

"When this day is won, we'll recover them, and they'll receive funerals befitting their bravery," he replied, "Right now, the focus must be upon the living."

The group returned to the ridgeline, jogging towards the point of descent. Lucius paused, scanning the scene to his front, and was about to join his retreating band when what he saw caused him to freeze.

While not able to see the ambush site in the valley below him, he had a clear view across the valley to the opposite side. A swarm of locusts caught his eye, flowing over the ridge and descending into the valley. The realisation soon dawned; these were not locusts; it was a trap, and it was being sprung.

Capitulum XXIII - Decapitation

24 Aprilis. Year 16 of the Imperator Hadrianus.

"These Jews are fucking fanatical," said centurion Claudius Aginthus, commander of the III Cohort, to his colleague Julius Petronius, the commander of the Sixth. "The bastards are throwing themselves at us." The two centurions stood a small distance from the Third, still blocking the hillside track. The Sixth was straddling the blocking cohort to prevent any flank attack.

"Fucking fanatical they may be," responded Petronius, "but they die like any other man, and your lads can see it happens."

"We shall," agreed Aginthus, "but we're taking losses. For every one of ours, we've got to take several of theirs. Narrowing the front and pouring pila into their compressed column worked well, but we're now out of pila." His fellow centurion listened, nodding his head as he studied the proceedings at the blocking point. The Jews may die like any other man, but their zeal for killing Romans astounded him.

As he watched, two rebels attempted to jump over the first rank of Romans. They must have been helped to propel themselves to such a height. The tactic was simple: disrupting the Roman line could enable the enemy to penetrate it. Aginthus had seen such tactics before, referring to it as the 'human ballista'. The two rebels landing upon a rank of legionaries caused it to buckle. There was a frantic scurry before they hacked the two to death and the rank reformed. The enemy doubled its efforts to attack the Roman front, but seeing the tactic fail, they dropped back into a defensive position. Dozens of bodies hindered combat. The Jews may die like ordinary men, Petronius thought, but they don't run like them; something had to be done.

Petronius' nodding ceased; the decision was made.

"It's time to rotate the cohorts," he declared, "pull out all but your front six ranks. Then we'll form up your rear, so we'll take over your position as you retire. It makes sense; we have pila so we can hurt the bastards." Pretorius slapped Aginthus on the back. "Come on, Claudius, let's get it done. We'll break'em."

The rotation of cohorts went smoothly – as to be expected from well-trained soldiers who were familiar with the manoeuvre. Neither centurion could know that the Jewish bravery was driven by the fact there was nowhere for them to retreat. The cohorts blocked their exit, which had never featured in their plans. Attempts to escape up the steep valley slopes ceased once they saw the Jewish bodies littering the hillsides. Lucius' work had been effective, as had a similar party operating on the other side of the track. However, neither officer knew that a Roman blocking action at the rear of the Jewish formation was penning them in. The fighters may be fanatical, but they were also becoming desperate.

As Petronius had predicted, storms of VI Cohort javelins fell upon the Jews, exacting a terrible price. Bodies prevented either side from coming into physical contact; footings amongst the slain were hazardous.

The III Cohort, having exchanged positions with the Sixth and now acting as a flank guard, enjoyed the much-needed break. Reviewing the situation stood Centurion Aginthus and his optio, Porcius Fimbria.

"Our losses so far have been light, Claudius," said Fimbria above the noise, "but those bastards are taking a Hades of a hammering. Why don't they pull back?"

"Well, what they lack in military skill," replied Aginthus, "they make up for with fanaticism!" He nodded towards the front line, "These people hate us with a vengeance. Their religion says they are the chosen — the rest of us are worthless. There is only one solution for their sort. Destroy them all."

"That may be," Fimbria said, "but at this rate, we'll still be at it at tomorrow's sunrise!"

Aginthus gave a grim laugh.

"We do what needs to be done and – what's going on?"

Out of the corner of his eye, the centurion had spotted movement. The centuries holding the defensive line between the hillside and the column were now flooding past the waggons to reach the column's right flank, which faced the opposite eastern hillside. Fimbria followed Petronius' gaze.

"They're moving position – good gods! The hills Claudius – what the fuck is that?"

Aginthus knew only too well what "that" was.

"Cac! This is about to get interesting." He looked towards his cohort, "Optio Fimbria, rest time is over. Form up the Third. We're switching flanks. Oh, and you'd better let Petronius know he's on his own."

Marcus Apollinaris rode along the 'safe' side' of the column. Lying on the floor of their vehicles, refugees maximised the protection of the wooden sideboards. Leather waggon coverings also offered a degree of safety, not always the case with other lighter materials. The pedestrians, walking closely in the shadow of the waggons, had learnt to shelter under the waggons where ever possible. Life was relatively safe for the legionaries, knelt upon one knee behind their shields. A hit from a slingshot on the helmet may debilitate at this range, but the helmets offered only small targets.

The initial panic amongst the passengers and walkers had subsided. The expression on their faces was now one of grim determination. Between them, he and Gracchus had ridden the length of the column, encouraging people to come from under the waggons and keep moving along. They told them it was only a matter of time before they cleared the area and left the ambush behind. Marcus felt some sense of satisfaction; the enemy was using slingshot from a distance, and he was hoping that attack would comprise little else. The two cohorts at the hillside bottled up the real threat. Maybe, just maybe, they would get away with this.

"Jogging along nicely, sir," a voice called out. Marcus turned his head to see Miniscius, marching beside his waggon, amidst a group of pedestrians.

"Any casualties?" Marcus asked.

"One nasty, some bruises," the militiaman replied, "the nasty'll be okay. The shot bounced under the waggon and hit his ankle. The leg isn't broken, but he'll hobble for a day or two."

"If we can keep moving, we have a good chance of getting clear," said Marcus.

"The Third and Sixth are doing a grand job, sir," Miniscius said, "The young lady is fine, sir. She's just behind in the second medical waggon. They're a bit safer than these." He nodded towards the vehicle beside him. Marcus had been so engrossed in his thoughts, unaware, he had just ridden past the medical section. The waggon he was alongside had a small group of weary and frightened civilians walking alongside it. He attempted to motivate them.

"I know it's tough, but keep going, everyone. If we maintain speed, we'll soon be away from here." The response he received from a well-educated voice took Marcus by surprise.

"I do so hope that to be the case, Captain, because frankly, the sooner we get the fuck out of this place, the happier I shall be." Strange, he thought, the posh ones should be all up front! Still, under these circumstances....

"You are not alone in that, my friend," Marcus responded as he turned his horse to return the way he had come. Seconds later, he dismounted, tethered Trotter, and nimbly climbed into the second medical waggon. The waggon's high sideboards and leather covering shielded its patients from the slingshot. Anaitis sat at the front of the vehicle, looking back upon six infirm soldiers. Marcus could not suppress a smile; a mother hen and her chicks, he thought.

"Marcus – thank the gods – you are well," the young woman said, rising to her feet. Anaitis would have appeared inebriated to a casual eye as she navigated between the poorly soldiers sitting along the rocking waggon. Marcus' helmet, lorica hamata and yellow sash did not encourage a hug, much to Marcus' relief. Instead, standing in front of him, she placed her hands upon his shoulders and looked him up and down. "You're not injured?"

Marcus responded with a humourless laugh,

"It'll take more 'an a few bastard bits of lead and stone to 'urt me!" Seeing her face bore a concerned countenance, he broke into a smile, "I'm fine, *meum mel*, seriously, I'm fine. How're you coping here?" As she spoke, she straightened the sash he wore around the waist.

"We are managing, it gets – "

"The lass does great," said a voice from the front corner of the waggon, "don't she, lads?" A series of approving grunts answered the question. Anaitis smiled.

"That's Cassius," she quipped, "We fell out at first, but he does what he's told now!" Then, as his eyes adjusted better to the dim light of the leather-clad waggon, Marcus spotted a body swaddled in cloth and bound by string. Anaitis saw his gaze. "That's Arius. He went to meet the ferryman some time ago." Marcus looked at the men.

"We'll get you out of this, brothers, if it's the last fucking thing we do!" He turned to Anaitis, "I have to go." He surprised himself by leaning forward and kissing her on the cheek. Before he knew it, he was astride Trotter, riding past the grim-faced citizens, towards the head of the column. He had not gone far before the great snake of waggons ground to a halt. Marcus kicked his heels into Trotter's flanks, his anxiety level rising. In a matter of seconds, he could see the source of the problem. A large ox-drawn waggon pulled out of the column along the rough ground that ran beside the road.

The cause of the waggon's diversion was the vehicle preceding it in the line; it had lost a front wheel and now sat at a precarious angle in the middle of the road. Its human cargo climbed down onto the road, sheltering, clustered against the side that gave them protection from the projectiles falling out of the sky. Marcus could see the next waggon in line turning off the road to follow its predecessor, bypassing the breakdown in front of him.

These vehicles at the front of the procession enjoyed a suitable track surface. Further down the line, the pressure of scores of wheels caused the compressed earth road surface to break up. It made the going more difficult. Difficult or not, the verges of the track were far more dangerous; comprising small rocks and occasional gullies, they could be a treacherous trap for any waggon.

"Hold yer ground," Marcus shouted at the driver, about to move his waggon onto the verge, "You must stay in line – the verge is too risky."

He had just finished speaking when the waggon moving along the verge gave a loud crack and lurched to one side. Its front wheel shattered by a rock embedded in the sand at the track's side. The passengers, comprising women and children, began screaming and leaping down from the broken vehicle. Marcus rode over to them.

"Get back inside," he yelled. "I'll get help. DO NOT leave the waggon!" Ahead he could see the vehicles at the column's front were still moving, their drivers believing that movement equated to safety. However, as the small convoy moved away, two riders rode furiously towards broken vehicles: centurion Gracchus and tribune Sallus. They pulled up alongside Marcus. The following dust cloud enveloped them as Gracchus carried out an immediate assessment.

"The one in the rough," he said, nodding towards the waggon sitting broken on the verge, "can go to Hades. This one…" He nodded at the vehicle squatting in the middle of the road, "we get sorted. So, let's get that wheel fitted back." A small band of militia men joined them, two of whom were already rolling the wheel back towards the waggon. Marcus felt a sense of pride that these men, the legion's rejects, were one step ahead of their centurion. "Good lads," the centurion encouraged, "get that bugger back on and get moving again."

Some male civilians who had been accompanying the waggon joined the remaining militiamen and some from the following vehicle. Ignoring the occasional slingshot, they all gripped the chassis of the waggon and lifted it. When presenting the wheel to the axle, it was quickly apparent that the axle had suffered minor damage on impact with the track.

"*Dis's Balls!* It's goin' to need a bit o'work," said a militiaman. "It shouldn't take too long. Let's get this bastard propped up – and be quick about it!"

"Do your best, men. We need to get moving as soon as possible." Sallus said to the assembled company.

As he finished speaking, a civilian screamed and fell to the ground clutching his shoulder – a piece of slingshot had found its mark.

"Oh cac!" Gracchus shouted.

"I suspect he will survive," said Sallus.

"Not referring to him, sir," Gracchus replied, "Look." He pointed to the eastern ridge that lay beyond. It was not high and fell towards the road on a long gentle slope. Thousands of Jewish rebels were descending the hill and approaching the road.

The column's course followed the valley bottom. To the column's left, the western valley side was composed of a short, steep slope covered by a blanket of scrawny grass and a liberal covering of low, windblown bushes and scrub. The decline eased as the hillside approached the road, turning into a gentle slope before reaching the road. The track taken by the Jewish ambush force cut down through this side of the valley to connect with the road.

To the east, similar grass and bushes covered the column's righthand side. However, it was different as it descended more gradually to the road, making it a greater distance from its easterly ridge to the bottom of the valley. The nature of the left side would mean that any force descending would come down at speed in some disorder, whereas on the right, the gentler slope would permit a more ordered approach. This concerned the members of the *Fretensis* and the observing militia. The vast rebel force flowing over the East ridge came to a stop about a quarter of a mile from the column.

The column's sudden halt, compressing the space between waggons, complicated matters. Initially the threat had come from the western, left slope of the valley. Roman legionaries frantically squeezed between waggons to form a defence line against the enemy now coming from the right, eastern side. Frightened civilians further compounded matters. In attempting to move from the 'safe' easterly side of the column, they impeded soldiers going the other way.

"Well, this is a fucking *cac* storm if I ever saw one!" said a legionary, struggling as he pushed his way between the rear of a waggon and the head of an ox. The beast was unconcerned and relishing resting from his labours. The legionary barged into two people fleeing in the opposite direction knocking them to the ground. "Stupid cunts, can't you see we are trying to save you!" he screamed at the prone civilians.

"Shut the fuck up and get moving," a centurion shouted, looking in frustration at the melee behind the legionary. He broke free and joined his comrades on the right flank, forming into line. Claudius Aginthus, commander of the III Cohort, watched as his defence line grew. His men appeared from between waggons on either side of him for some distance, frantically looking for their signifiers to locate their century. The remaining IX Cohort centuries, protecting this so-called 'safe' side, were thinly spread. In either direction, as far as Aginthus could see, legionaries flowed through the waggon train to face the mass that had descended the right-hand slope. He knew the outcome would all depend upon timing.

Fighting to suppress the signs of fear growing in his gut, Optio Porcius Fimbria, second-in-command of the Third's 1st Century, stared to the front. A mere quarter of a mile away, an enemy force took formation, yet only half his century had fallen into line. Fortunately, his signifier was one of the first to pass through the column and take a position, enabling the century's men to rally to the standard. The first century's centurion doubled up as the III Cohort's commanding centurion. A busy man indeed. That left Fimbria in control of the century, his first taste of command in action. He must be seen to be in control. He focussed upon the mass to his front.

"Move! Move! Move!" he shouted towards legionaries appearing from the other side of the waggons. "The century will form four lines." The century's tesserarius pushed recent arrivals into line, and an organised block of soldiers came together. In a brief time, the tesserarius reported to Fimbria.

"Century formed up, sir, down ten men, wounded or dead," he spoke loudly and formally before adopting a more conversational tone, "By Hades, I wish we had our pila to face this lot." He gestured towards the rebel force. "First contact will be on the shields."

"You're right, and the line is much thinner than I would have wished. I realise we have the First and Second upfront and the Tenth and the Eighth to the column's rear, but there's a lot of the bastards facing us in the middle!" he said, "All the cohorts are down in numbers. The last few weeks have exacted a price. Whatever happens, we cannot allow them to get through to the waggons. It would've been helpful if they'd kept moving."

"Why'd they stop?"

"The gods only know that—must've been a breakdown," said Fimbria. "Still not moving, they can provide shelter for civilians on foot."

"A small mercy from the gods," quipped the tesserarius, "and I'm praying for another."

"And what would that be?" asked Fimbria.

"Simple. That Petronius and the Sixth can keep the rebel cunni trapped in that fucking valley."

"I think that's something that deserves both our prayers, brother."

Drawn up in four lines, the men of the 1st Century waited. To their right, the other centuries had formed up; the cohort now stood ready. Legionaries braced, left foot forward and right foot back, and the shields to the fore. Their deadly gladius swords held parallel to the ground, prepared to stab swiftly forward. The signifier carrying the century's identifying number on a tall pole stood in the slight space between centuries. Behind each century stood the Optio, ensuring formation was maintained, ready to take control should his commander fall. Finally, the centurion and the tesserarius stood waiting to lead their men in action to the century's front.

As Fimbria looked down at the line, he wondered if all the men shared his nervousness. Tradition said that Roman training, discipline, and battlefield structure would enable a body of legionaries to withstand ten times their number. His gaze turned to the enormous rebel force before them, and he sincerely hoped tradition would prove accurate. The enemy had formed up similarly to the Legion, large blocks of well-armed men led by officers to the front. To the rear, Fimbria could make out several small units of cavalry. To no one in particular, Fimbria said,

"They told us these bastards were nothing more than bandits—I think someone made a mistake."

"And a fucking big mistake at that!" responded the tesserarius. No sooner had the man stopped speaking, there came a roar from the enemy. The entire line began moving forward. Fimbria turned to his men.

"Century," he shouted, "close up and brace!" All along the front rank, shield met shield, presenting a red wall that not even a fly could penetrate. In the second and third rows, the men pulling their shields to their left braced the legionary to their front with the right shoulders. It would be crucial that the front rank did not buckle when the enemy smashed into it. Fimbria and his tesserarius took station in the centre of the second rank.

As the enemy closed upon the Roman lines, Fimbria quickly analysed the century's antagonists. They may have resembled a regular army from a distance, but as they closed, the picture changed. Most men wore helmets in the enemy's front ranks, carrying shields and spears. Further back, the uniformity fell away; some carried swords, others spears and many more wore the traditional sura headgear rather than helmets. This should have helped bolster Fimbria, but the sheer numbers now charging towards him eroded his confidence.

The enemy came on at a steady pace until, sixty feet away, they broke into a mass charge, howling as they came. Fimbria watched until the gap closed to a few feet before shouting,

"Brace! Brace! Brace!" As he shouted, the Roman lines tensed, and no sooner had the air left his lungs, there came an almighty crash of wood on wood, coming together at speed. Fimbria felt himself being pushed back a small distance as his frontline buckled. Every legionary had been in this very situation, many times, on the training grounds. They knew how to absorb the impact, bending like a branch in the wind, only to spring back into place. If they could stabilise the front rank's wall of shields, then the gladius could begin its deadly work. Grunts, groans and bellows of encouragement filled the air, and the line straightened.

Banking on the application of sheer mass and numbers, the Jews pressed up hard against the Roman shields. Well, thought Fimbria, they had made the classic mistake in attacking a wall of shields. The darting gladii would demand a price for such a move. The legionaries in the front rank presented a well-defended target to the enemy, crouching behind their shields and protected by their helmets. Desperate to break through the wall facing them, the Spearman, holding their weapons above their heads, stabbed down into the second rank of legionaries.

Fimbria stood behind his front rank, ducking spear points, attempting to monitor the century's situation. Mere feet to his front, wide-eyed, screaming, spitting attackers hammered the Roman shields, filled with a burning desire to kill - and yet, he felt strangely calm. His nervousness was all but gone. Then, two airborne bodies were falling towards him in the blink of an eye. One fell upon the legionary to Fimbria's right, and the other crashed into Fimbria's chest. As Fimbria was thrown to the ground, he heard a deafening roar from the attackers.

The body lay on top of Fimbria, and he felt it frantically struggling to arise, only for it to fall back where it lay, unmoving. Then, as a soldier dragged the body clear, he regained his senses and struggled to his feet.

"You injured, sir?" A voice asked.

"I'm fine, I just –" The optio was suddenly and violently knocked backwards by the retreating legionaries to his front. Their attempt to absorb the charge from the revitalised rebels had failed. He was back on dirt, trodden on, before being reburied under two fallen legionaries. Fimbria found himself unable to move, trapped not just by the weight of the bodies, but hampered by the two large shields that lay over them. Confined as he was, his helmet prevented any attempt to turn his head. His line of vision was fixed at ground level. The footwear passing him changed from the heavy Roman military sandals to a different design completely. With horror, he realised he was now in enemy territory.

The sound of the fighting continued, confirming his men were putting up stiff resistance to the onslaught. Finally, he realised he had little choice other than to play dead, which was not difficult given the blood from the fallen legionaries lying across him, seeping into his clothing and staining his armour. The bodies would occasionally twitch when a combatant stood on them, and a growing pressure convinced him the heap of bodies was increasing.

He wondered how his century was coping without him, but he was sure his tesserarius would do a competent job in his stead. The fight was not how he had expected to experience his first battle. All thoughts of glorious charges and turning the enemy to flight had gone. All he wanted to do was escape the dead weight that held him tight to the ground.

The voices he could hear screaming, shouting and sometimes howling were foreign. Whilst not understanding a word, the tone told him the enemy was not getting all their way. The sound of sword and spear crashing with wood showed his men were still close. They had not been forced back. It was still a contested fight. He pinned his hopes of survival on that fact and offered a heartfelt prayer to Mithras.

The inside of a leather-covered infirmary waggon was a discrete, claustrophobic environment. Sitting on a stool at the front of the waggon, Anaitis watched over five badly wounded legionaries. Her only view of the world was through the open rear of the waggon. When soldiers came into view, streaming right to left, away from the enemy, she became concerned. What was happening? Moving to the end of the waggon and peering out, she clarified the situation. They were moving *towards* the enemy.

"Oh, great Arduinna, help and preserve us," she said, reverting to her mother's Gallic traditions as she retreated into the depth of the vehicle.

"What's going on, lass?" said Cassius, her old antagonist.

"Rebels, hundreds and hundreds of them coming from the other hills." As she spoke, she trembled; arms and legs shook, "and they're coming for us."

"Don't worry about them bastards," Cassius said reassuringly. "The lads'll sort 'em, just you see."

Anaitis sat stiffly, limbs trembling, staring fixedly through the back of the waggon. She felt helpless, with no option other than to await the Jewish army. She was barely aware of the rustling noise to her left before Cassius spoke again.

"Here, lass, take this." She remained rigid. "Come on, take the bloody thing." His voice became sterner. The girl turned her head and stared at the wounded soldier, offering her his sword. He was insistent she took the weapon. "Keep it with you, lass. If there's any bother, keep it behind your back. When you get close, scream like fuck and stick the bastard in the gut."

Slowly, a trembling arm rose, and her hand closed upon the grip of the sword. Surprised at how light it was, she laid it across her lap and her gaze returned to the rear. In no time, the sounds of battle filled the air. Inside the hot, stifling atmosphere of the infirmary waggon, there were few clues which side prevailed. Legionaries passed by as they moved towards the action, but as the fighting continued, Anaitis did not move. As the noise of combat grew and the action moved closer, the fixed stare did not change. Instead, the knuckles of her right hand turned white as she held the gladius in a vice-like grip. And suddenly, her greatest fear became a reality.

A bearded rebel soldier, his head clad in the traditional cloth sudra, appeared at the vehicle's rear. Agitated and panting, he attempted to see into the relative darkness of the waggon. As he discerned the contents, he grinned. Anaitis' heartbeat doubled, and for a second, she closed her eyes, praying she had seen nothing more than a fear-induced apparition. When she opened them, he was mounting the rear steps.

The warrior paused and took in his surroundings, the grim smile fixed on his face. He balanced his sword in his hand and selected his defenceless target. As she watched, a wave of anger rose within Anaitis, and she jumped up from her stool. It distracted the man from his task, and he turned to face her. She had forgotten to conceal the gladius. The Jewish warrior shook his head in wonder, smiling as he did so.

"So, the little pussy wants to fight the Wolf?"

He spoke in Aramaic, so Anaitis understood the threat. Terrified she may be, but the anger—rapidly becoming rage — subjugated the terror. Still smiling, he raised his sword and closed upon the rigid girl, standing trembling and fixed to the spot; so close she smelt his breath. The fighter knew that none of the prone soldiers could assist her. Cassius' words echoed in her head—scream like fuck and stick the bastard – but her arm could not move. Wishing not to see what was coming, she closed her eyes.

"Well, let's see what Roman whore blood looks -" It wasn't a scream but more than a cry that caused Anaitis to open her eyes. The warrior was on his hands and knees in front of her. On her left, a legionary was clutching his stomach and moaning; she realised he had kicked the feet from under the rebel. It had hurt, the scream evidence of such, and it had done the soldier's wound no good. An incandescent rage punched Anaitis into action. Not an efficient sword stroke by any definition. It swept from above the girl's head to hit the fallen warrior at the base of his neck. A howl of rage accompanied the stroke.

The blow was weak, and whilst penetrating through clothing and cutting skin, it did not disable, but it had the strength to knock Anaitis' antagonist flat to the floor. Desperate to see where the threat came from, he rolled onto his back, his sword rising to defend himself from the demented fury that stood above him. Too late. His last vision in this world was of a wild-eyed, red-haired woman plunging a sword, now held point down in both hands, into him. The end of the blade penetrated deep into the rebel's neck. Anaitis dropped onto her knees, straddling the fallen soldier. The jugular artery severed, blood spurted upwards, drenching her face, shoulders and chest.

"You fucking bastard!" she screamed as the sword rose to fall upon his neck a second time.

"You murdering son of a whore!" The blade fell again. Pushing themselves up on their elbows, some of the waggon's residents watched, fixated.

"You butchering cunt!" The blade fell again. More expletives, more blood and more strokes from the gladius followed. Then she stopped. The waggon floor ran with blood, and several of the prone soldiers, half-sitting, became sprayed with the red fluid.

For a few seconds, the girl remained kneeling across the corpse of the dead soldier as if in quiet contemplation. Then slowly, she rose, never taking her eye off the body at her feet, the head lying detached. Once fully upright, she took three deep breaths, bent forward and reached towards the dead man's head. She gripped the sura that enveloped it with her left hand and then stood again.

"Steady lass, steady," said Cassius gently. The other soldiers stared, fixated, except for the leg-kicker clutching his stomach and moaning in pain. Anaitis gave no sign she had registered Cassius' words. Carrying the head in one hand and grasping the gladius in her other, she walked to the rear of the waggon and stepped down to the ground. Turning to her left, she faced the mayhem of the fighting taking place a few feet ahead of her. She moved towards the noise. The Roman defenders had their backs to her. As she approached them, she became visible to the Jewish attackers.

In this small pocket of the battle, things quickly changed. As they saw the vision in front of them, the Jewish fighters became so distracted that they became defensive. The apparition was out of place on a battlefield, a woman liberally doused in blood. It matted her hair. White eyes stared out from the blood splashed face, her clothing scarlet and in places turning black. In one hand, a bloody gladius, and in the other a human head - clearly recognisable as a Jewish head. The defending Romans sensed the change in the attackers, to the point a legionary dared to snap a glance in the direction of the enemy's gaze.

"What the...? Fuck me!" His comrades could not resist a look, and the fighting came to a stop; the soldiers amazed. The bloody Anaitis walked to the Roman line. An expectancy hung in the air. Later, one legionary told his mates he thought a thunderbolt would crash into the ground. Standing amongst the legionaries, the bloody apparition swung the sura-clad head forwards and backwards, the arc increasing with each swing. Though the soldiers on both sides knew what was about to happen, nobody moved. The small pocket of fighting had become like a marble frieze. The sound of battle around them added to the surreal situation.

The woman swung the head forward in a great arc and released it. It took to the air on an upward trajectory before falling, hitting the ground and rolling amongst the attacker's feet. All the Jews stared aghast, fixated at the head lying at their feet.

"*That* is for Lydia! *That* is for Cynthia!" she shouted at them, "and *that* is for Agenor!" The arm holding the gladius rose slowly until the sword pointed directly at the Jewish attackers. "Kill the bastards," she screamed at the legionaries, "Kill every fucking last one of them!"

A legionary instantly took the initiative, leaping into the space between him and his antagonist, thrusting his gladius into the man's stomach. In the blink of an eye, the gods of war were on heat again. She reached the rear of the waggon and slowly fell to her knees. Where she remained still, in acceptance of whatever would follow.

"Give me six of your shields!" Watch Officer Marcus Apollinaris shouted to a tesserarius from the IX Cohort that was protecting the column's flank. "I need cover to fix this waggon and get'em movin' again."

As he spoke, there was a minor explosion on the ground just to his right, as a piece of slingshot hit the dirt, causing a puff of dust to rise. The slingers on the hill had eased off somewhat; presumably, Marcus thought, because they were running out of shot. Having seen one of the leading waggons come to a halt and tilt to one side, they directed their fury towards the group, attempting to repair the vehicle. The legionaries with their shields would form a protective screen. Seeing the enemy was still up on the hillside, the tesserarius sent six men across to the waggon. Close to its side, they created a hide that was three shields wide and two shields high.

"Right, you lot. Two of you grab the wheel. The rest of you lift the bastard waggon!" Marcus was shouting to the gaggle of civilians cowering around the waggon. They now realised they had the enemy on both sides. Five women with two children crouched, sobbing, sheltering from the slingshots. The men stood around hopelessly, and Marcus' words stung them into action. Fortunately, the problem was a broken retaining pin on the axle, which had allowed the wheel to become detached, neither the axle nor the wheel being damaged. As Marcus spoke, the waggoner came rushing from the front of the waggon, brandishing a spare retaining pin.

"This'll fix it, chief," he said as he approached the repair party, who were preparing to lift the rear of the waggon. He fell to the ground, stone dead. Accompanying his death was a cacophony of rattling slingshots impacting the shields screening the frantic citizens. An adolescent boy, seemingly oblivious to the surrounding dangers, dashed over to the fallen waggoner. Retrieving the axle pin, he dashed back to Marcus, proudly presenting him with the crucial device.

"Get behind the shields and bloody stay there!" Marcus said gruffly and then relented, "bloody fit job, lad." He turned to the group. "Right, let's get this waggon lifted, and you two be ready with the wheel."

Half a dozen pairs of hands grabbed the side of the waggon, not without some groaning. They lifted it so the axle was clear of the ground and quickly married up the wheel, which was slid into position. Then, dropping the pin into place, the waggon was ready. Marcus looked at the fallen waggoner.

"Cac!" He said to no one before turning to the group sheltering under the shields. "Can any of you lot drive a waggon?"

A young man, some might still consider a boy, hesitantly raised his hand.

"I can... I mean, I have...."

The child who had recovered the axle pin stared up at the boy with a puzzled expression. Marcus realised they were brothers. "*I have.* A couple of years ago on uncle's farm," he said to the boy, then turning to Marcus, "Really, I can do it."

Marcus wondered where the boys' parents were, for no voice raised resistance to the offer. Unfortunately, there were no other volunteers.

"Right lad, off you go. But be careful. We need to move at speed but not at the bloody gallop." He slapped the newly promoted waggoner on the back. "You'll be just fine." As he spoke, the women and children climbed back into the waggon, a voice saying,

"You're staying with us, young man, and not joining your brother upfront!"

Marcus untied and mounted Trotter. He told the shielding legionaries to report back to their tesserarius. Riding up to the front of the waggon, he approached the newly appointed waggoner, now clutching a set of reins in one hand and wielding a long whip in the other,

"Get moving," he called, "and don't stop 'til you are well clear of this bloody place!" The young waggon driver took a deep breath, swung and cracked his whip. The ox stepped forward, the waggon wheels creaked, and the whole assembly was underway again. "Well done, just keep movin'" Marcus turned Trotter and rode back down the line of the waggons telling all who could hear that they would shortly recommence the journey out of Judaea.

Marcus felt elated to have the column underway. But as he rode, the feeling abated, and reality took over. To his left, lines of Roman legionaries held off a rebel attack coming from the eastern slope. On the western slope, to his right, slingers hurled their shots at the column, though the rate of fire had lessened. As he proceeded along the length of the column, Marcus noted that the fighting became fiercer.

The people of Aelia, trapped in and beneath the waggons, looked terrified. Marcus dreaded what might happen should the rebels break through the lines of legionaries. However, upon being told that the waggons were recommencing their journey, the look of relief was palpable. Then came the realisation that it might be a few minutes before their waggon was underway, and the fear returned. Meanwhile, the gap between the defending legionaries and the waggons was gradually shortening.

Two riders were approaching at speed. As they closed, he recognised Tribune Sallus and Julius Gracchus. The two men pulled up alongside Marcus.

"It is touch and go in the centre," said Sallus, "that is where they mean to break through, I'm sure of it."

"It's bloody close to our infirmary waggons," Gracchus added. "If the line breaks, they'll be on the edge of the breakthrough."

"Fuck!" said Marcus, feeling as though a thunderbolt had hit him. Anaitis and Miriam were in waggons that rebels could overwhelm.

"I'm sorry, Apollinaris," the Tribune said. "Gracchus mentioned your–err—situation."

Marcus struggled to suppress his emotions.

"Gratitude, sir. The good news is the waggons upfront are moving again. If the Legion can hold these bastards off long enough, we may still escape."

"Indeed, we may," responded Sallus. "Look, centurion Gracchus and his men are doing a fine job—as, may I say, are you—but I believe the infirmary waggons need special attention. Can you get down there and make sure everything is in order."

Never had Marcus experienced the sensation of wanting to kiss a Tribune, a feeling he fortunately ignored!

"I'm on my way, sir," he replied. As he kicked his heels into Trotter's flanks, Gracchus called after him,

"Fortuna be with you, brother."

Marcus was aware that Gracchus knew he would need every bit of good fortune the goddess could give him.

"Are those waggons moving yet?" asked Centurion Julius Petronius as he arrived at the rear of his VI Cohort, which was blocking the exit from the hillside track. Bodies were scattered along the frontage between the opposing forces to the extent fighting was becoming impractical. It was turning into a stand-off. Petronius was focussed on his objective; prevent the Jews from disgorging out of the narrow valley until the column was clear. When he left his narrow front line, Roman and Jew, a few feet apart, stood glaring at each other, separated by a carpet of corpses and groaning, mutilated bodies.

"Fixed to the spot, sir, not moved in a while," a tesserarius replied, "and there's a sizable enemy force on the other side of the waggons."

Petronius detected a hint of concern in the soldier's comment.

"The Third has gone to help deal with them. It's what we do with these bastards," Petronius said, pointing towards the Jewish force facing his cohort, "It's a slaughterhouse out there. It'll be difficult to do any more than hold them in place for now."

"At this rate, sir, we'll be bloody building a camp here tonight!" the tesserarius joked, "and if we—Hades, what's going on?"

A roar smothered the rattle and crashing of distant battle. The column separated the two men and the battling soldiers, but the roar was clearly audible. Other soldiers sought its source, but the waggons obscured their vision. As the roar died away, the familiar sound of battle turned frenetic. The centurion shared his tesserarius' earlier concern.

"That sounds as though your 'large enemy force' is attempting to break our lines," he said with a coolness that belied his inner tension. "I think I'll watch developments for a while."

For a short while, little seemed to change as the sounds of frantic combat continued unabated. Centurion Petronius later described what happened next as 'a wave crashing between rocks. Dozens of Jewish fighters poured between the waggons and formed into separate groups facing the rear of the VI Cohort. They were a short distance away, and Petronius instinctively knew their plan. Within seconds, the dozens became hundreds.

"Fuck! They've broken through! Tesserarius, get the cornicen and the signifier up here — now!"

The junior centurion commanding the century at the rear of the cohort shouted an order to take his century from a line into ranks. It would not be enough to combat what was coming, but it was a practical first step. His men pulled out of the blocking group and lined up to face the newly arrived Judaean force. The centurion joined Petronius, whose mind was racing.

"Stuck between two groups of the bastards, sir. Formation?" asked the centurion.

"Not too many options, as I see it. The century directly engaged with the *cunni* on the track will maintain its position. They ought to hold them until we sort this *cac*. Meanwhile, the remaining centuries six deep, with ends of the line meeting the valley sides, will stop the bastards outflanking us. This won't be pretty; we'll get the centuries to form either side of your lads." His face turned into a grimace. "I feel the hunter is becoming the prey."

"This is the Roman army, sir, *cac* happens," he spat at the ground, "we'll manage."

"Well spoken, brother," said Petronius, "These bastards will find out that the cornered boar can prove to be an extremely dangerous beast," he said, referring to the legion's symbol.

The tesserarius returned with the cornicen and signifier, all red-faced and breathing hard, much aware of the urgency. Quickly, the signifier had planted his standard in front of the century, already drawn up to face their antagonists. The cornicen sounded, repeating its call several times. The many, many hours spent on the training grounds proved their worth. To the untrained eye, the legionaries frantically moving into position from column to line may have had some resemblance to chaos. The lie to that resemblance lay in the fact that within a brief space of time, the cohort stood facing the enemy, a block nearly fifty men wide and six men deep, each century's centurion at the front. A single century to the rear continued to block the Jewish force on the track.

"Hold 'em on the shields!" Petronius shouted to all who could hear, "Let 'em tire and then kill 'em all!" The centurion hoped the matter-of-fact delivery of his words would help boost morale. However, he was not blind to the fact that the enemy severely outnumbered them. As the cohort formed its line, more and more rebel forces negotiated their way through the column of waggons to join their comrades facing Petronius' VI Cohort.

No sooner had Petronius finished speaking than the enemy charged, hurling themselves onto the cohort's shields. The Jewish charge caused the line to buckle with its significant advantage in numbers. But a frantic effort by the legionaries ensured it was held. Petronius threw himself into the front line to give his men some encouragement, a common practice that resulted in a high turnover of these officers in times of war.

Petronius was shaken by what he saw, though none of his men would ever have guessed. It appeared there must be thousands of rebels attacking the column and taking on the *Fretensis*. Where have they come from? How on earth had they built up the capability to field so many men? When did they train? Finally, how in Jupiter's name did this happen right under our bloody noses? Julius Petronius was skilled in combat and the product of many years of training. Yet, right now, he was professional, but also angry. He repeatedly punched his shield forward, the large brass boss on its front cracking ribs on impact. His gladius was thrusting to his front like the darting tongue of an adder, burying itself in his antagonists.

It came at a cost. In the frantic frenzy at the Roman front line, Petronius had not noticed that his right arm was bleeding. He could not help but felt the blow to the side of his helmet, where the cheekpiece probably saved his life. Pain in his left shoulder told him that all was not well in that part of the fighting machine either. Many of the men that stood on either side of him experienced similar, but, like Petronius, the desire to slay their opponents was paramount. In situations such as this, the brain ignores the body's signals regarding its condition. Instead, it was fixated on whichever enemy stood to the fore.

Three regular thumps on the back brought him back into the rational world.

"Sir! Sir! To the right. To the right!" his tesserarius, Vibidius Nasca, was screaming to be heard over the din of battle.

"Pulling back, I'm pulling back!" Petronius shouted at the legionaries to his right and left. As he stepped backwards, the two soldiers swiftly moved to protect the gap on either side of him. The two soldiers recovered their positions as a second ranker took Petronius' former position in no time. Pressure off, he looked across to where Nasca was excitedly pointing. The cohort's right wing was breaking up.

"They're throwing all their recent arrivals onto our right," Nasca shouted. "The line's giving way!"

When the enemy broke through the line of waggons, it left Petronius with minimal choice of strategy. He had hoped that wedging his cohort between the two valley sides would give them the best chance to hold the attackers. Unfortunately, badly outnumbered, his right wing was collapsing, and he knew the strategy had failed. Every second now counted; he was in a race against time before the superior enemy numbers rolled up his outflanked line.

"Nasca, come with me. Be quick about it!" He pushed through the ranks of legionaries to the rear where his cohort's standard and the cornicen stood. "Form a defence square," he shouted at the cornicen, "Sound the command. Now!" He turned back to Nasca. "Get over to the lads holding the track. They need to get back here before the *cunni* shaft'em up the arse!"

Petronius knew that more enemies would pour onto the battlefield once the track was unblocked. With the situation being what it is, he had no choice – it was a matter of the cohort's survival. Again, the training paid off and quickly the VI Cohort formed the square. As the rear ranks manoeuvred into the square, the front ranks paid an exorbitant price in holding off the enemy. The centuries on the right wing had taken a mauling. The legionaries who formed the square now numbered only three-quarters of the original line. Petronius knew the situation had moved from bad to bloody desperate.

The cohort stood in a square, with standards in the centre, where Petronius positioned himself. Around him stood a denuded century, kept as a reserve to plug holes in the defence. The battle had paused. The Jewish forces were surrounding the Romans but keeping their distance. Petronius and Nasca stood helplessly watching as hundreds of Jewish soldiers poured down from the track, reinforcing their comrades surrounding the square. Petronius felt the need to offer some encouragement when he recalled his earlier comment to Nasca.

"Men," he shouted at the top of his voice, "You are Roman soldiers! You will teach these bastards that a wounded boar is a dangerous fucker! They're going to see that the price for killing this boar is much too high – they'd be better hunting rabbits!"

Laughter rang through the cohort.

"They're all right, sir," said Nasca. "We can still kick the *cac* out of the fuckers!"

A voice from one side of the square suddenly shouted,

"Rabbits!" His adjacent comrades took up the cry, and in no time, the whole cohort chanted, "Rabbits, rabbits, rabbits!" By the third 'rabbit,' gladii crashed upon shields in time with the new battle cry.

"By Mithras," Petronius said to Nasca, "I believe we may yet kick some *cac*. Let's hope it's enough."

No sooner had the words left Petronius' mouth than the opposing Jews let out a deafening roar and assaulted all sides of the cohort's defensive square. Petronius stood in the middle of the formation, closely watching the fighting. The cohort had practised this defensive manoeuvre many times previously, defending against fellow Romans. However, no amount of practice prepared Petronius for the sensation of being trapped. First, they must defeat their antagonists; otherwise, every legionary in the cohort would be in Hades by sunset.

The legionaries of the Sixth gave a good showing, but the enemy's numerical advantage was telling. Every time they slew an enemy, another took his place. Yet they could ill afford the casualties they were taking. Petronius was yet to commit his reserve, though he knew that time was close. Finally, he came to terms with the fact that the cohort would not long survive the onslaught.

The Jews fought with an intensity that few legionaries had experienced. It appeared their lives were unimportant, with many throwing themselves into attacks on the Roman lines that were nothing short of suicidal. Occasionally, they would account for a Roman death. The Jews could replace their fallen, and the Romans could not. The Jewish tactics followed no military manual. They screamed, they shouted. They hurled themselves at their opponents. Some even threw themselves to the ground and lashed out with their swords at legionaries' ankles, attempting to cripple them.

As Petronius watched, he knew that defeat was only a matter of time for all the training and the morale.

Though they were not to know it, the Fourth had reached a similar position to their comrades blocking the Jewish force attempting to leave the defile. Both parties stood apart, their combat zone covered in the dead and dying, their ability to fight severely restricted. The day was warm, and though the fighting took place in the shade of the steep-sided valley, the legionaries stood panting and sweating, grateful for the break in the action. As they looked across the bodies strewn across the trackway, they observed their opponents were in a similar condition.

"This is an impasse," said Marcus Crispus to the tribune, "we could be at this for days, Lucius. It's like digging a mine – we just keep hammering away."

"They must be blocked at the other end of the defile," said Tribune Civilis, "which means they're trapped. Do you think surrender is a possibility?"

"Not with these bastards! I suspect it will be a long, hard, bloody slog."

Lucius Petronius stood with his centurion and the tribune looking towards the enemy. He took in Crispus' comments.

"Well, if we keep a steady rotation of centuries-" Lucius stopped mid-sentence, "Jupiter, there's movement!"

There was movement. It was slow at first, but it gradually increased as the Jewish column in front of them, save for a small rear-guard, moved away down the track.

"Right, we had better make ready to follow. Whatever blocked the *cunni* from exiting the valley is blocking no more," said Crispus.

"I'm not sure if that's a good or a bad sign," Lucius said.

"Well, if legionaries were blocking them, they are no longer doing so. A bad sign."

"Fourth to the rescue, then?" Lucius quipped.

"Get me the Scouts," commanded Crispus. "I need to know what the fuck is going on down there."

The IV Cohort was formed up in a column in a short time. The cohort's waggons had caught up with them some time previously, and they loaded the gravely wounded; the walking wounded were also left in the care of the medics. The enemy rear-guard had backed off and disappeared down into the valley. Crispus briefed the Scouts to follow the Jewish force and report back immediately once they understood the situation at the bottom of the valley. He would feel happier once he knew what he faced. So, the Scouts moved off ahead to trail the Jews, whilst Crispus took the cohort along the path they had taken.

The track went through slow twists and turns, making a distant view impossible, but as they marched, sounds of battle, at first a distant rumble, grew clearer. Then, it became apparent to all who heard it that the cohort was moving towards the first major action of its brief existence. Time passed until one of the Scouts returned at a gallop, jumped off his horse and reported to Crispus and the tribune.

"A large Jewish force is attacking the waggon train. There would seem to be a major fight taking place. Just where the track breaks out to meet the road, there's a cohort surrounded," the scout paused for breath; he had ridden back at speed, "from where we were, we couldn't pick up a lot of detail, but I'd say it's not good."

"How far?" asked Crispus.

"Not a mile. After about three-quarters of a mile, you'll get a view of what you're up against."

"We have to get down there. And quickly," said the tribune, "that's the *Fretensis* getting knocked about."

"Right then," Crispus had made his mind up, "let's get moving; we'll plan as we go!"

The column moved off, instructed to lengthen their stride as they did so. Time was now of the essence. Crispus had the 1st Century at the head of the column, and Lucius marched in the optio's position at the rear. It did not miss him that, like the previous day, the reality of imminent action suppressed the usual banter within the men. But, unlike before, they could hear battle and knew they were about to be hurled headlong into it. They had trained and trained again, but if you got it wrong today, it would not be a centurion's vine stick that hit you; it would be a weapon embedding itself in your body. Every man pondered his response to facing death or injury.

"Cheer up, lads," Lucius called out to the rear ranks, "we've practised for this since Italia. Just remember your drills. Remember your training – Oh, and for Mithras' sake, listen for commands. It'll be noisy where we're going."

"How many are there?" A voice asked. The question touched upon memories from Lucius' boyhood.

"Let me ask you a question. Has anyone here *not* heard of the Spartans?" There was a general mumble confirming knowledge of Sparta and its soldiers. "It was said of the Spartans that they never ask, 'how many?', but simply ask 'where are they?' Those lads, they were true warriors. Well, we are Roman soldiers, much superior to Greeks. So, whatever we face down there, we aren't worried. We just get the job done."

There came a buzz of approval. But within a distance of a few paces, all fell silent again.

As she climbed back into the waggon, Anaitis grasped the feet of the corpse that lay there and unceremoniously pulled it out of the vehicle, bouncing it down the steps, and dragged it to one side. Anaitis then returned to her stool at the front of the infirmary waggon. As she passed its occupants, she drew comments from the soldiers.

"You gave it to him, good and proper!" "You'd make a legionary, girl." "He deserved what he got—he'd of killed us all." "Remind me never to upset you!". They were in awe of this young woman who could hack the head off an enemy. If not a little frightened of her.

Lowering herself onto her seat, she reached out for the adjacent bucket of water. Taking a rag and soaking it, she slowly wiped the blood from her cheeks. Cassius, the soldier she once considered an antagonist, watched as the sensation of the cold liquid drained the anger from her.

"You all right, lass?" he asked tentatively. She stopped what she was doing and turned to look at him. He tried not to react to seeing hair clotted with drying blood, the front of her clothing likewise. Yet out from this apparition, there now stared a white face. The contrast was startling. She let the cloth fall back into the bucket and held out her hands, rotating them as she inspected them.

"It seemed like a nightmare," she said, speaking in a monotone, "but it wasn't, was it?"

"You know, it must've been bleedin' terrifying," Cassius responded, "but you did what had to be done otherwise we'd all've copped for it." A smile crossed his face. "Now, you done it with a little more gusto than I would've, but you got the job done."

"I was angry, Cassius. I still am," the woman said, staring at the bloodied floor, "the bastards that killed my friends, they will not kill me – or us. Yes, it was terrifying. I went for the fucker. I wanted to kill him – to cause him pain, to feel what my friends must've felt."

"You did that all right!" said one patient.

Outside, the din of battle went unabated, and the lines ebbed and flowed. Yet the legionaries were holding back the waves of Jewish rebels. Anaitis continued to wash her face as though everything was normal. Then she snapped out of it when a soldier moaned in pain. It was the legionary who had kicked away the feet of Anaitis' victim. She left her seat and went to him, dropping onto one knee. His blanket was darkly stained. She gently pulled it back and revealed the price of bringing the rebel to his knees. The soldier's stomach wound bled profusely, a grimace of pain on his face, soaked in sweat. All this was beyond her. She was no medic. She turned to Cassius, who was the most conscious and alert of the passengers.

"I must get help for him. It's the best I can do."

Cassius, whose leg injury allowed him to adopt a sitting position, remained still for a second, listening.

"It sounds like we are a little distance from the fighting, but I suspect it's scrappy so keep your eyes open and take care. Take the gladius."

Anaitis stared at the weapon which lay on the floor at her feet.

"No, I don't want to touch one of those ever again." She made her way to the rear of the waggon and stepped out into the brilliant sunshine. The body lay where she had left it, looking especially gruesome without its head. A short distance away, Roman and Jew were fighting one another with relentless fury. Not far off lay a soldier with a yellow armband. She knew immediately who the body belonged to; Miniscius. For a second, the horror surged within her. She fought it, taking deep breaths one after another, forcing herself to get a grip. Finally, the panic receded, and she focussed upon her task. Anaitis knew that she would find the waggon where the medics were based a few waggons back along the column. Her surroundings frightened her, but a sense of normality returned now that she had a meaningful goal, and she set off. She passed two waggons that contained sick and injured men.

Then, ahead, was a unit of legionaries drawn up facing the direction of the enemy. Approaching, she realised they were protection for what had become a busy medical post. Wounded soldiers were being carried in for treatment, and as she got closer, she beheld dozens of men laid out on the 'safe side' of the waggons. The medics moved between their patients, tending their wounds, but they were under pressure coping with the number of injured. As she approached, she attracted some rather strange looks. She realised how she must look to them. They were familiar with blood. It was their business, but a woman on a battlefield?

She passed a stretcher, and as she did so, the man upon it clutched his stomach and let out a scream. Anaitis jumped, startled by the suddenness of it. She felt an urge to help the wounded legionary – to do something, at least. An adjacent orderly, seeing her surprise and confusion, grimly laughed.

"Don't worry about him, girl," he said. "It's the quiet ones you need to worry about. If he can scream like that, there's life in 'im yet."

Anaitis moved on, spotting a medic to who the orderlies deferred; he appeared calm and in control amidst all the hectic activity. She had found someone with authority. He also looked vaguely familiar. She hurried across to him, attracting the now expected look of surprise on his face.

"My, my. I'd say you've been in the wars, young woman."

"Please, sir. I need your help." She pointed with her arm, "Three waggons down, there's a young legionary. He's bleeding badly, and he's very poorly. Can you help him?"

"*You* have a poorly legionary?" The medical officer spread his arms and rotated his torso. "Look around you, young lady. *You* have a poorly legionary? Believe me, *I* have some too!"

Anaitis realised that her mission was failing. Frustration built up inside her.

"But he helped save our lives!" The pitch of her voice rose. "He kicked our attacker, and it opened his wound. Please, you *have* to do something!"

"Now, you look here, young woman, I have a duty to -"

"Anaitis!" Both the medical officer and Anaitis turned towards the voice.

"Miriam," said Anaitis, instantly recognising her friend, who had just risen from attending a patient. She had bloodied cloths in both hands and the general air of dishevelment about her of someone very overworked.

"You know this woman?" asked the officer.

"She good friend," Miriam replied, "she helping care for injured. Since two days ago."

"By Jupiter, covered in all that *cac*, I didn't recognise her!"

"Miriam, please help," Anaitis begged. "He saved us, and he's going to die."

Miriam looked at the officer, a silent request for permission. The officer nodded his head and then called to one of his men.

"Fundanius, I want you to go with Miriam and–err – her friend. One of our patients has taken a turn for the worse. Take a stretcher with you; I'm sure the three of you can get him back here. Now go - and be quick about it."

"Thank you, sir. Thank you," said Anaitis, an enormous sense of relief flowing through her. Anaitis led Miriam and the orderly back to her waggon. As they went, she kept a nervous eye on the fighting not far to her right; the line was holding, but the general din of battle, the screaming and shouting, frightened her to the core. The little group passed two vehicles and approached Anaitis' waggon. Just before she turned towards the waggon's rear, she registered a rider approaching, but in the heat of battle, she thought nothing of it.

As he rode Trotter back along the column, Marcus Apollinaris was confident he would reach Anaitis' waggon before it moved forward once again. Marcus was relieved to see the column moving again. Hope rose that if the Legion could hold back the Jews for a while longer, the great train of waggons might get clear of the ambush. He spotted his objective, and reining Trotter to stand, hitched her to the vehicle. He walked swiftly to the rear, only to bump into the small stretcher party.

It both surprised and confused him. A medical orderly stood opening a stretcher, assisted by a woman liberally stained with blood. She talked avidly to the orderly as he, listening, focused on the task at hand. A second female was ascending the few steps that led into the waggon. To make matters more surreal, a headless corpse lay to the left of the stretcher party. The bloodied woman sensed his presence, for she turned and looked straight at Marcus.

"Marcus!" she cried and moved towards him.

"Good gods – Anaitis! What the fuck?" No sooner had he spoken the words than she was hugging him. Then, gently pushing her to arm's length, he asked, "Anaitis, what on earth happened?"

"He came to kill us.... Cassius gave me his gladius.... I killed him, Marcus. I killed him dead. The boy helped me.... He kicked his feet away.... he's bleeding... we have to save him. Meniscius, he is.... dead." She took deep breaths between the terse statements, and her chest heaved; she broke into deep sobs. Marcus drew her to him. Perhaps not behaviour becoming an officer in the midst of battle, but it was only human.

"Sorry, brother," the orderly interrupted the caring cameo, "but I have a casualty that needs moving to the Medicus." The second woman, now standing on the waggon's rear, turned.

"Miriam!" said Marcus, startled at seeing her. Miriam carried a wooden box. The telltale pieces of white linen poking out from under the lid left Marcus in no doubt that it contained bandages and medical accoutrements.

"Marcus, it is good you here. I will tell all, poorly soldier needs help, very now." Amidst it all, Marcus creased a smile at her improving but broken Greek. For a second time, Anaitis went to arm's length, as he spoke softly.

"*Meum Mel,* stay right here. I'm going to help the orderly," Holding her head between his hands, he added, "I will be back shortly." Marcus moved away and mounted the waggon. Miriam knelt beside the prone, bloody body of the intended patient. He was lying at the back of the waggon, which would make extraction all the easier. The orderly joined her and laid a stretcher at the feet of the infirm men. Space was tight, and he gently pulled Miriam away from the soldier and took her place.

"He ain't made a sound for a while, brother," Cassius volunteered. "Ain't good - seen it before."

The medic felt for a pulse in the soldier's neck and lent close over him, listening for any breathing sounds, but he found neither pulse nor breath. Marcus and Miriam watched on expectantly. Finally, the medic looked over his shoulder and shook his head.

"He'll be negotiating the ferry fare with Charon," he said, rising from his crouch. "Help me get him on the stretcher. Then we'll lay him down outside."

Marcus and the medic manoeuvred the body onto the stretcher and out of the waggon. Marcus nodded towards the headless corpse.

"We'll put him around the side; nowhere near that bastard!" Then, the body lowered, the orderly recovered his stretcher.

"I've got to get back. Gratitude for your help, brother." At that, he was gone. Marcus and Miriam joined Anaitis, who had watched the proceedings with tears running down her cheeks, the deep, racking sobs falling away.

"He saved us. Had he not brought the rebel down, we'd all be dead," she sobbed, deep, wracking sobs.

"Yes, he very brave," Miriam responded gently, "and he want you be brave, Anaitis."

"Miriam is right, Anaitis," Marcus added, "the soldiers in the waggon need your help. Come on, let's get you back inside." Anaitis resisted.

"Marcus, Miniscius - he is dead." She pointed to the corpse in the near distance. "He is dead," she repeated. Marcus struggled to remain calm.

"Anaitis, he died a soldier doing his duty. He would be proud of that. A soldier to the end."

Saying this, Marcus helped Anaitis back into the waggon. It was only then that he noticed the great bloodstains that ran across the waggon floor. Even the soldier's blankets carried heavy stains.

"Fuck me, brothers," said Marcus. "Have we been sacrificing a bull in here?"

"No bull, brother, just a Jewish bastard. Young lass did for 'im. Took 'is head." Cassius rarely chose his words carefully. Marcus turned to Anaitis – this was a day of surprises. Now he better understood her bloody clothes. In his mind's eye, he was having trouble picturing this slight girl removing the head of the Jewish soldier. Anaitis stared at him, expressionless. Marcus took in the surroundings. In the corner, Cassius, leg heavily bandaged, sat propped up. Two other men had pushed themselves into semi-sitting positions whilst another lay flat on his back, but conscious. The fifth man lay quietly, eyes closed and oblivious to the world.

"She done all right—we owe her," said one recliner. Marcus manoeuvred Anaitis back to the stool. He squatted in front of her. He spoke softly.

"We should move shortly, and then hopefully this'll be over, I'll be back. That's a promise," caressing her cheek, he continued. "Once we get away from here, it'll be right." Then, standing, he turned to the prone soldiers.

"Men, the waggons upfront are moving again, so I expect you'll be on your way soon," he said, addressing soldiers. "The lads are holding the ambushers off; it should give the column a chance."

As he spoke, Miriam was adjusting a man's blanket. She jumped up and turned to Marcus.

"We cannot move. Many injured men at the Medicus' waggons – too many for waggons."

"Oh *cac*!" exclaimed Marcus. His responsibilities returned and swamped him. "Miriam, take me to the Medicus. We must get these waggons moving."

Miriam nodded and moved to leave the waggon, with Marcus following her. Suddenly, he pulled up, staring down at the unconscious soldier. A nagging, uneasy sense of recognition came over him. He knew he should rush to the medic, but there was something important he was missing. He turned back to the vehicle's passengers.

"Brothers, who is this man?"

"Not one of us, brother," came a reply. "The orderlies said he's an auxiliary."

The recognition hit Marcus like a punch.

"His name's Mynos Kipula. He's an auxiliary that escaped En Geddi. I thought he'd died from poisoning." Marcus, aware he could wait no longer, leapt out of the back of the waggon. Then, grabbing Trotter's reins, he followed Miriam to find the Medical Officer.

Marcus understood the problem as soon as he arrived at the medicus' waggon. What was once a medical centre was now a bloody military aid post in the middle of battle. Hitching Trotter, Marcus crossed over to the Medical Officer, who was ending a hurried conversation with two very bloody orderlies. Marcus introduced himself.

"Yes, I know who you are. What do you want?"

"Sir, in front of us, the column's movin' again, which means the infirmary waggons I've just left will be on their way," Marcus looked around him. "Can't see this lot going anywhere. The trouble is, sir, all this is blocking the waggons behind."

"Well then, that's not too big a blockage then, is it?"

The comment puzzled Marcus,

"There's nearly half the column behind us!"

"Technically, you are quite correct, Watch Officer," the Medicus responded. "However, you seem to be unaware that ten waggons back from where we stand, the enemy has recently broken through the column. They are engaged with the III and VI cohorts blocking the enemy's approach from the hills."

"Cac! Then they're cut off – nearly half the bloody column is cut off!"

"Let us just say that their fate lies very much with the X and V Cohorts bringing up the rear." The Medicus surveyed his surroundings. "Now, I am sorry, but I have men very much in need of my services." The man moved off to join one of his orderlies who was struggling to calm a recent arrival. Just before he engaged with the orderly's patient, he turned back to Marcus and called, "when you get moving, do not take any of *my* waggons. We're going to need them."

Miriam had been standing back but now joined Marcus, who was still recovering from the shock of the medicus' news.

"Well, he's a cool one. 'Their fate lies in the hands of the X and V Cohorts...', I mean…" he mimicked the officer.

"Marcus, look what I see," Miriam said, pointing to the chaos that was the aid post. "I am glad he that way."

"You're right, lass," Marcus replied, getting a grip of himself, "his lads looked after me when the bastards had a go." He paused as he struggled internally with what he had heard, "But there's 'alf the column back there, bleedin' stuck on this bloody road!"

"The soldiers will help."

"I pray to Mithras they do," said Marcus, "but you've got to get back to Anaitis. Take 'er back to 'er own waggon and get the Hades out of here. Better be quick about it, lass, or they'll be gone without you."

"No, Marcus. This place is mine. The soldiers need my help. I cannot leave."

It took Marcus aback.

"Miriam, listen," he commanded, pausing for a second, "what you hears is battle, and there ain't no promise we'll win it. You could die here!"

"I listen, Marcus. Now, you see," she swung to face the centre of the aid post with her arms open wide, "the hurt soldiers cannot leave. I cannot leave." She turned back to him. "You go. Take Anaitis and waggons and go. Please. We meet after."

She was right, and Marcus accepted her logic. He decided to re-join Gracchus and the tribune to ensure that all the waggons positioned ahead of the aid post would drive clear of the ambush. Marcus stepped up to Miriam and put his arms around her.

"The gods be with you, Miriam."

She returned his wishes with a smile.

"Yeshua guides me," she replied softly.

Marcus mounted Trotter. Before he rode away, he looked around. To one side of the column, legionaries fought with the rebels. Ahead, he could see that the column, protected by more of his comrades, was underway. Behind him, the waggons stood static, and a little further down, the enemy had penetrated the line of vehicles. Beyond that point, he did not know what was happening to the rest of the waggons. At his feet was the aid-post, filling with injured and dying soldiers. Within it was a woman he considered a friend, and the enemy could capture her. Given she was one of their own, he knew there would be no mercy shown. He cursed.

He went directly to find Anaitis. Pulling Trotter up at the rear of the waggon she currently occupied. He did not dismount. Speaking from his horse, he begged her to return to her waggon, explaining that, "for the time being," the infirmary waggons would not be moving. She must take herself to safety. She assured him that is what she would do.

Wishing her well and a promise he would return, he turned Trotter towards the head of the column, kicked her flanks, and the elderly mare showed she still had a turn of speed in her.

The downhill track took a final sweeping right turn, which enabled Marcus Crispus to have the first view of the battlefield ahead, albeit a narrow one. It told him what he needed to know; there was a cohort in dire straits, needing help if it was to survive. He brought the Fourth to a halt and called for his centurion's and optios. Once they had arrived, he briefed them.

"This'll be straightforward," he began, "We move at double pace. With me, the 1stCentury will exit the track and form into line. Following centuries will form on my left and right, bringing the cohort into a wide line. The line will likely move forward before our wings are complete, so the last centuries onto the field must march quickly. I regret the haste, but our friends are in trouble. Clear?" Heads nodded. Compared to the cohort's drill capabilities, this was basic manoeuvring but done at speed. Crispus continued. "The minute we step off in line, let's get gladii banging on shields — I want to scare these fuckers. They're surrounding a *Fretensis* cohort, so we'll surround *them* and kill the bastards. Any questions?" Several of the large crestas sitting across the officer's helmets shook, indicating there were to be no queries. "Let's get this done. Go," Crispus finished, waving his officers back to their stations.

Lucius walked swiftly back to his position at the rear of his century. He may be facing the most significant military action of his career, but something else occupied his mind. As Crispus talked, a fellow officer whispered to him that word was the cohort they strove to help was the Sixth - his uncle's unit. This fight had suddenly become personal to Lucius. As the briefing continued, he attempted to view the fighting, but distance meant he failed to identify his relative's helmet cresta. For Lucius, speed was now of the essence.

Allowing a brief time for the centurions to return to their units, Crispus ordered to march at a double pace. Yet again, Lucius observed the self-imposed silence of his century. Every man focused on the oncoming fight. As the cohort descended the track, the advantage of height was lost, so Lucius' view of the battlefield became limited. His uncle was his lifelong hero, a man who had influenced many of his major life decisions. Lucius' determination to fight only grew.

The lead century, Crispus at its head, approached the point where the track left the small valley. As a new cohort, the legionaries of the Fourth had never seen battle. Here, they had their first taste. The fight here made their action back up the valley a mere skirmish. Where the track met the plain, it was covered in corpses. In places, the cohort had difficulty stepping across the dead. Many of the slaughtered wore the accoutrements of Roman soldiers, unsettling the passing legionaries. Lucius visually searched the bodies in fear he may see his uncle amongst them. Fortunately, no fallen Roman wore the great transverse cresta that marks out a centurion of the Roman army.

The cohort left the carnage in the valley behind them, marching onto the plain where the fighting took more lives. Crispus took his century from file into line and then stood. The centuries following took positions on both his flanks. Lucius, moving to the middle of his century's revised formation, looked between the helmets of the three ranks to his front, and the fighting was plain to see. The Sixth would appear to have no intention of going down without a fight; the rattle, groaning and howling of battle evidenced their intent.

As promised, Crispus did not wait long before giving the order for the cohort to advance in line towards the Jewish fighters surrounding the Sixth. As they moved, the enemy spotted them. More and more of the trapped cohort's assailants turned towards the advancing Romans. Those who spotted the approaching Fourth screamed to their comrades, still intent on destroying the surrounded VI Cohort. Their faces turned from a look of surprise to one of fear as they understood the situation. The width of the approaching cohort meant it would envelop them. When that happened, there would be no escape for the rebels.

"Beat your shields!" yelled Crispus, positioned in the front line at the very heart of his cohort. This fight would be their baptism, and he would be with them throughout. The 1st Century took up the rhythm instantly, and within seconds the entire line throbbed with the rhythm. The bravest of the Jews quickly turned, disengaged from their current fight, and formed a line facing the oncoming Romans. Others of weaker hearts slid around the encircled VI Cohort, moving away from their oncoming nemesis, planning to flee back the way they had come, towards the waggons.

From his position in the rear, Lucius detected the hesitancy of their enemies. An adherent to the 'Crispus' doctrines of war, he recognised a weakness instantly. They were no longer sure of themselves, which would lose them the fight. Taking a deep breath, he yelled, "Fretensis, Fretensis, Fretensis," the name being called to the timing of the gladius' beat on his shield. By the sixth iteration of the word, it became a full-blooded cohort chant. Lucius did not stop chanting. Instead, he yelled even louder, his heartbeat rising. He clenched his gladius, his knuckles white. For the Fourth, the killing was about to begin. Yet a detached, rational corner of his mind prayed that the cohort would come through this with honour. Everything he had done, everything he had experienced, had been leading to this moment.

Centurion Julius Petronius stood in the centre of his beleaguered VI Cohort, carrying out a mental computation. They fought like lions, but the legionaries' attrition rate told him the fight would not last much longer. With his reserve century committed, there were no tactics left to play. The enemy may have succeeded, but Petronius had the satisfaction of knowing his boars exacted a high price. Focussing on a weak point in his defensive wall and how best to shore it up, he was distracted by his name being shouted. Petronius turned, half expecting to find his line collapsing. Instead, he saw excited legionaries pointing towards the track they had been blockading earlier.

"Reinforcements, sir," one legionary yelled above the noise of the fight. The centurion moved to see what it was his men were pointing out. Sweat may be trickling into his eyes, but his vision was still functioning, and he looked at a Roman cohort pouring down from the hillside. A flood of relief surged through Petronius. The drowning man had a lifeline. But he must hold out a little longer. One of his optios appeared at his side, looking somewhat worse for wear.

"Who are they?"

"Damned if I know, Flavius," Petronius declared, "the thing is, they're here. Let's make sure all the lads know it – if we can hold on a short while longer, we may shag these bastards yet. Come on."

The two men separated and, shouting over the din of combat, encouraged the remaining legionaries with the news. But unfortunately, little more could be done as the defence line shrank inwards. It was time for every sword to demand its price from the enemy.

Petronius threw himself into the line that faced the direction of the approaching cohort. He had watched soldier ants devour a large black dung beetle as a boy. It amazed him how the semi-armoured beetle, for all its twisting and turning, disappeared under the ever-growing multitude of ants. As he faced the screaming, howling mob of hate in front of him, he knew how the dung beetle felt. Pieces from the rim of his shield spun through the air as weapons crashed against it. One second, he faced a sword, next a spear, and he even spotted vicious-looking agricultural tools in action.

As a soldier beside him fell screaming to the ground, Petronius wondered if they could hold until the relief arrived. It was said that desperate times demand desperate measures. Petronius had a desperate idea. He crossed to the cohort standard-bearer, who stood in the middle of the defensive ring.

"Rufus, when I shout, I want you to waive that standard in the new arrival's direction," he shouted to him, "whatever happens, just keep waving it in their direction. Have you got that?" The signifier nodded his head and stood ready to obey instructions. Petronius moved back towards his defence wall. The approaching cohort was forming into line whilst on the move to his joy. Its commander appreciated that time was not on the side of the Sixth. Petronius moved to implement his idea.

"Legionaries now hear this," he bellowed. "I want you all to cheer as loud as you can. Then, to those facing our approaching brothers, point towards them and cheer if you're able. Now, do it, lads!" Optio Flavius Maximus took up the exhortation.

"Come on, you grunts," he shouted. "The old man may have lost his mind, but what have we got to lose?"

Those whom the gods would destroy, they first make mad. Any impartial observer of the Sixth would believe the gods had marked this cohort for destruction. The unit, surrounded and outnumbered, fighting with a sense of desperation, broke out into cheers. Anyone observing would think they rejoiced in death.

The impact on the attacking forces was immediate; the intensity of the fighting slackened. Their antagonists were confused. Cheering aside, soldiers not that instant in combat pointed at the advancing cohort. The signifier, holding the prize the Jews would love to take, waved the standard. Several of the attackers glanced over their shoulders in the direction indicated. They could not miss a Roman cohort advancing in line even with the restricted vision. As they looked, the sound of rhythmic drumming flowed over them.

Initially, the tone of the Roman cheering sounded forced, but it turned genuine. A voice shouted out.

"Brothers, it's time we killed these fucking rabbits!" Drawing on every ounce of energy in their tired bodies, the legionaries fought with new vigour. A chant began, and it grew in volume.

"Rabbits! Rabbits! Rabbits!"

Petronius joined his signifier in the centre. He continued to wave his cohort standard and spread around the defensive circle. The other standard-bearers followed suit. He thought he detected a slight hesitancy in the Jewish resolve as he watched.

"Aemilaneus Rufus," addressing the signifier personally, "I believe the Sixth might just survive this scrap. Our little ruse may yet pay off."

"Mithras willing, sir." Just before the oncoming cohort launched itself at the surrounding Jews, the signifier read its standard through the myriads of helmets and airborne dust. "Great gods, sir! It's the Fourth. It's that old sod Crispus and your nephew!"

It frustrated Lucius that Optios were stationed at the rear of a century, whilst the action took place at the front. This was a long-standing practice, for if the centurion fell, the optio would take command of the unit. A benefit of his position was a clear overview of the fighting. He watched the First shudder to a halt from the rear as it crashed into the rebels. The banging of Gladii on shields ceased, as did the chanting, quickly replaced by the sounds of hand-to-hand combat. Even though Lucius had several ranks of legionaries to his front, he could see the large horsehair cresta, the *crista*, positioned ear to ear on his centurion's helmet. Julius Crispus served as both a marker and a leader for his men. His would be big boots to step into.

The 1st Century had come to a halt, and spellbound Lucius watched the outer centuries turn inwards, their aim to entrap the enemy. How ironic, Lucius thought, for that is very much what the enemy would have done earlier in surrounding the 6th Century. But unfortunately, the Jews were not blind to what was happening. Large numbers pulled back out of the trap, heading back towards the static waggons. It would only be a matter of seconds before soldiers of the Fourth could clasp arms with those of the Sixth.

"Jupiter's name!" cried a soldier close to Lucius. "What are those silly buggers shouting?"

"Sounds like fucking 'rabbits' to me, brother," came the response.

"The poor sods've lost it," came another.

"Na, brother. Old Petronius loves to be prepared; they're arranging their dinner!"

The soldiers returned to the business at hand. The collapse came when those Jews who could escape the fight did so in a desperate rush. In an instant, Lucius' century surged forward, and the two centuries' soldiers intermingled. Shouts of joy filled the air as the exhausted survivors of the Sixth savoured the fact that they would live to see the sunset. Some soldiers briefly embraced before returning to business. The trumpeter of the Fourth sounded a general advance. Lucius knew that this was going to be a chase.

"IV Cohort, advance at will and finish the bastards!" Crispus bellowed, "Get on with it." But, as groups of centuries stormed forward, the discipline and precision of the initial advance disappeared. Crispus passing close to where a tired centurion Petronius stood with his survivors raised a gladius in recognition. Then, following the fast-moving hounds of the 1st Century, Lucius passed his uncle engaged with his survivors. He could hear his uncle's familiar voice ringing out.

"VI Cohort, are we going to let the children of the Fourth do our work for us?" There came a brief pause before, "I'm damned if we are. Let's get to it, lads." The pack of hounds grew larger.

It was quickly apparent to the Jews, desperate to escape and gain the safety of the hillside that a barrier lay in their way. On their advance, it had taken several minutes for their hundreds of soldiers to negotiate a passing through the static train of waggons. Their current problem was straightforward. Frantic fighters, having little time to escape in the other direction, threw themselves under the vehicles and scrambled out the other side. The flow was too slow. The sheltering refugees they slaughtered on the way through lay strewn beside and under waggons. Moreover, bodies impeding their passage hindered the Jews' escape. It held hundreds of fighters up, unable to get clear.

With no time to organise a defensive line, the Jews faced several hundred armoured, vengeful Roman legionaries. Some Jews escaped, slipping away along the sides of the column in both directions. The Roman defensive screen on this side of the column had done little apart from shelter from incoming slingshot, the intensity of which had long since fallen away. These Romans would relish the opportunity to mop up the Jews that chose such an escape route.

Lucius found himself in a massive melee with all sense of order in his century gone. It was one-sided. Lucius had not been present for the attack on the *vicus,* nor did he witness the butchery in Aelia. He had only recently seen the condition of the column and glimpsed the civilian bodies strewn around. What drove his anger was the surety of what the Jews *intended* for the column, and Miriam, too; she must be somewhere in the column. The image of the young healer powered his gladius into another victim as the red mist descended.

The bloodbath continued until, as though driven by a single mind, the Jews threw their weapons down, placed their hands in the air, and fell to their knees. It was a surrender. It was over. Lucius paused for breath when a spear, thrown aside by a terrified, surrendering fighter, arcing towards the ground, tore a gash in his upper left arm. He did not see it coming, nor could he identify the owner of the discarded spear.

He felt as if someone had thrown a bucket of cold water over him. The tension and single-minded focus on killing disappeared, replaced by a heightened awareness of his physical condition. His arm was pouring blood, and it was complaining furiously about being ripped open.

"Hold your gladii!" Crispus commanded, concerned that his men were now hacking down kneeling Jews. Good slave bounty was being wasted in the heat of the moment. The soldiers obeyed, the haze of battle evaporated, and some sense of normality returned to them.

"Fuck me, chief," a voice beside Lucius said, "the bastards 'ave landed one on you. You'd best give me your shield." He turned to those that could hear, "'ere lads, the optio has copped for one."

Within minutes, Lucius' arm was bound in cloth. It was not precisely what a medicus would have approved of, the fabric having seen much service in a legionary's knapsack. Finally, however, the flow of blood from the wound was stemmed.

While receiving 'medical' attention, his legionaries secured the many Jewish prisoners. Lucius then sought his commanding officer and spotted the broad horsehair cresta not far away. Crispus was engaged with soldiers securing a Jewish fighter. He spotted Lucius approaching.

"Optio Petronius. Injured?"

"It was a spear, thrown down at the surrender. All the way—" he nodded in the hillside's direction, "-from there to here without a scratch. And then some idiot dumps a spear! The lads believe I'll survive!"

"Well then, that's splendid news." Crispus turned to the prisoner. "So, look what we have here. Not your common soldier, I think."

Lucius studied the prisoner. He wore a fine muscled cuirass. Medium height, long dark hair, neat beard and physically in good shape -- except for some facial abrasions and a bloody left leg. Lucius thought it a pity that the blood was ruining a fine pair of soft leather boots.

"I would say, sir," Lucius responded, keeping the conversation formal, "that we've an officer on our hands." The prisoner had adopted a fixed stare, gazing at the horizon, showing no recognition of their words. The two officers conversed in Latin. Lucius believed the prisoner's conversations would be in Greek or Aramaic.

"Your assessment would be correct, optio. This feller might give us some useful understanding of what the Hades is going on in Judaea."

The snort of a horse caused both to turn in its direction, to see the Tribune Civilis dismounting. He joined them.

"For their first major action, your men performed well, Crispus," he said. "However, it is not over yet. Get your cohort through the waggons and let's drive these impertinent rebels back into the hills. Those that got away that is." He looked the prisoner up and down. "And what do we have here? He would appear to be a man of substance."

"He is," responded Crispus, "and we intend to pull his knowledge of this rebellion out of his head. Quicker the better, sir."

"Nasty leg wound. Don't let the bugger bleed to death on you, centurion." The tribune turned and remounted his horse. "Now, let's get your men formed up on the far side of these waggons. See to it." With those parting words, he left them. Crispus turned to the two soldiers securing the captive.

"I don't think he will bleed his life away," he said to them, "but, when this all dies down, get him to the Medicus and have him patched up. Then bring him back to me. Right, Optio, let's go join the lads on the other side."

Seconds later, the cohort's orders were being relayed by the cornicen. It was not long before the entire cohort, less a small prisoner guard, formed up on the far side of the column. The VI Cohort returned to where it made its stand against the Jews. A high number of injured legionaries would need help—several who would not be seeing the sunset that day.

Since leaving the junction, the head of the column had made good speed, driven on by the desire of the waggon masters to reach safety. Unfortunately, however, three men were riding ahead of a much-foreshortened train of waggons.

"We are pulling away, Marcus," Gracchus said, "and there appears to be no attempt by the rebels to come after us."

"Then we may yet salvage something from this mess," Tribune Sallus responded. "I pray the Legion can protect what we left behind. I cannot believe how many men the Jews have mustered."

"Fair point, sir, but I reckons it's worse'n just that." Marcus Apollinaris chipped in. "They won't 'ave gave up on Aelia to attack us. There'll be another force doing for the colony. The bastards 'ave a lot of fucking swords!"

"I fear you may be correct, Apollinaris." The tribune gave a deep sigh. "I suspect once we get to Caesarea, there are going to be questions to answer. How could we have been so blind that we never saw this coming?"

"I'm sure you're correct, sir," Gracchus said. "Right now, Apollinaris and I have several waggons to look after. So, with your permission, we'll ride back and check that everything is in order."

"Of course," agreed the tribune, "Do a waggon count whilst you're at it. Have a care for those on foot; we're doing quite a pace, and I don't want to exhaust them. The enemy has done enough damage already."

Marcus and Gracchus turned their horses and rode back down the column. Marcus had an ulterior motive for the small mission; checking on Anaitis' welfare. As they rode, Gracchus peeled off to speak to some of his militiamen. Marcus continued to the end of the train, seeking Anaitis' waggon. Looking back along the road, he observed the column was now clear of the ambush, much to his relief. Finally, he found the vehicle he sought and peered into its dark interior. Several faces returned his stare: women, children, and an elderly man. But no Anaitis.

"Where's Anaitis, the lass helping the medicus?" he asked. One of several men, following the waggon on foot, responded.

"She went off this morning—not been back. Haven't seen her since, friend."

Marcus' heart plunged into his stomach. If she wasn't here, it meant she was with Miriam and the medicus. In the centre of the ambush. He looked back down the road, and in the distance, he could catch glimpses of the ongoing fight. Rising smoke showed waggons were burning. He fought back an impulse to gallop

Trotter back to the junction. He was still staring, his mind in turmoil, when Gracchus arrived alongside him. Gracchus knew whose vehicle this was. Even with cheek plates obscuring much of Marcus' face, he surmised all was not well with his comrade.

"She's not there, brother?" he said. "Must have remained with the medicus."

"Never came back to her waggon, brother."

"She'll be safe. After all, the best part of the Legion is protecting her," encouraged Gracchus.

"I'm sure you're right, brother," a despondent Marcus replied. "I *pray* you are right."

"Right then, we've got thirty-four waggons, and my lads tell me that those on foot will run if it guarantees safety from the murdering rebels!" Gracchus dropped back into centurion mode, "So we need to get back to the head of the column and report to the tribune. Let's get going." It had the desired effect on Marcus.

"That's good, brother. Perhaps if we get more distance under our belt, we can give them all a break." Tribune Sallus was where they had left him, two horses' length ahead of the first waggon, pulled by an ox with the most expansive horns Marcus had ever seen. For a big heavy beast, it was struggling with the pace, which reinforced Marcus' view that it was not just the citizens that would relish a rest.

The road now ran through a wide valley lined with low hills, running straight ahead, allowing excellent visibility. When the two riders located the tribune, they found him gazing intently ahead. Without looking at them, he asked,

"Do you see what I'm seeing?"

The two officers peered towards the horizon. Whilst Gracchus' eyesight was not what it used to be, Marcus always claimed to have the eyes of a hawk. True or not, he detected movement in the far distance.

"There *is* something, sir." As he spoke, there were flickers of sunlight reflecting from the subject of their gaze. They all witnessed it, even Gracchus. "Reflections, sir, off armour— them's bloody soldiers heading our way!" Cac thought Marcus. We may have escaped the Fox only to run into the wolves. This is not their day!

"Is the rear clear of the rebels?" the tribune asked.

"It is, sir," Gracchus responded.

"We are halting," said the tribune, pulling his horse up and raising an arm into the air to signal to the lead waggon it was to stand. "I'm not fond of rushing into the unknown."

Marcus understood the hidden command.

"Well, we don't have no scouts, so I'll volunteer." He did not wait for a reply but kicked Trotter and rode forward. The approaching body of men was more than a mile away, but Marcus did not take his eyes off them. As the gap between the rider and the oncoming force reduced, it was clear this was no skirmish party but a large body of men. A sense of foreboding overtook him. As the distance between him and the on comers foreshortened, he brought Trotter to a sudden halt. He slapped the horse on the side of the neck and laughed.

"Fuck me, Trotter! We're saved! It's the Roman army, late as usual, but the buggers are here!" Marcus turned in his saddle and waved towards the head of the column, indicating that Gracchus and the tribune should join him. The three were face-to-face with Centurion Antonius of the VII cohort in no time. Antonius had brought his cohort to stand bringing the VIII cohort to a halt at their rear.

"Salve, Antonius," Sallus greeted the commander of the Seventh, "I would waste little time, centurion. The remains of our column, along with the Fretensis, are under attack from a large Jewish force." Then, he turned and pointed back to the column, "we have got these free of the ambush, but a good half remain trapped."

"Salve, Tribune. That explains the smoke we could see. I will leave you a century, though I suspect you are safe here. We have seen nothing on the way." He spent a few seconds assessing the tribune's companions. "Sir, if one of your men could brief centurion Decimus behind me, I would be moving and at a fast pace."

"Leave that to me," Sallus responded. "You get moving straight away. Just follow the smoke. You will see it all soon enough." Then, turning to Gracchus, he said, "Julius, please move down to the eighth and brief centurion Decimus as to the situation."

Gracchus put his heels into the horse's flank and sped off past the VII Cohort, already moving off in the junction's direction. Marcus and tribune Sallus watch the cohort pass. The Eighth followed in their rear, led by centurion Decimus, escorted by Gracchus. Decimus was getting his briefing on the move. Gracchus peeled off and joined his companions as the cohort passed the two observers. They continued watching until the cohort was away down the road.

"Perhaps the gods are smiling on us after all," said Marcus. "The lads will be kicking some arse in no time!"

They headed back to the stationary column and, approaching the waggons, they saw that many of the refugees had abandoned their vehicles. Several sat on the ground, escaping the claustrophobic atmosphere within, relishing the fresh air. They sat in the shade of their vehicles, a gesture of relief now the enemy had gone. As the two cohorts passed, everyone was back on their feet and loudly applauding. If Decimus was correct, they were indeed safe, Marcus thought, so let them relax.

"Gracchus, I want you to make a rough assessment of how many refugees we have lost," said the tribune. "I'm sure your militia will assist." Then, the officer turned to Marcus, "Apollinaris, I want you to assess our provisions. – these people are going to need food. Oh, and check the water situation whilst you're at it."

Gracchus rode off, and as Marcus turned away from the tribune to face the column, it occurred to him that counting would be a quicker task than it would have been first thing this morning.

For Porcius Fimbria, the day's events had not covered him in glory. Knocked to the ground early in the attack, his soldiers rescued him when the enemy receded. On his antagonist's next push, he went down again. He remained for some time trapped under dead bodies and fallen shields, a fact that saved his life. Then yet again, a pushing back of the rebels permitted a rescue.

He fought on furiously, wishing to recover his soldier's dignity. Unfortunately, it was not to happen.

The substantial Jewish surge towards the waggons and beyond, had cut Fimbria's III Cohort in two. The Jew's objective was to liberate their comrades held on the hillside track. For Fimbria's contingent of the Third, the fighting line became very ragged and broke up into several resistance pockets based around individual centuries. Fimbria re-joined his century to continue the fight, none the worse for his time lying in the dust.

Both sides were tiring. The Jewish fanaticism was still there, but its edge had dulled. The legionaries were fighting by the military manual, their aggression also lacking bite. It occurred to Fimbria that the end of the fight had to be approaching. The gladius would not determine the outcome, only the sheer will of the individual soldier to carry on. The thought had barely passed through Fimbria's mind when a soldier cried out.

"What the fuck?" he yelled, looking towards the breach. Fimbria sheltered behind a shield and looked in the direction the soldier indicated. a few Jewish fighters scrambled out from underneath the adjacent waggons and fled back up the hillside. Fimbria barged his Jewish opponent with his shield, snatching a longer glance. There were now dozens appearing from beyond the waggons and making for the protection of the hills.

"They're coming back through the waggons! The bastards are running!" a voice cried. And they were. As a lessening number of swords and spears crashed into Roman shields, the din of battle appeared to fall away. It's happening, thought Fimbria. The infection began at the vehicles but rapidly spread down the Jewish line. They were tired, and the sight of comrades fleeing collapsed their morale.

"Come on, brothers," called invigorated legionary, "let's finish the *cunni*!"

His comrades roared in response, and leaping over the dead and wounded, they took off in pursuit of the fleeing Jews. They quickly dispatched he walking wounded, the low-hanging fruit. They soon discovered the fitter of their prey was both fast and agile. The ever-increasing uphill slope became their advantage as the armoured legionaries tired. Realising most rebels would escape, their officers brought their men to a stand.

Fimbria's frustration improved when he returned with his century. All along the Roman defence line lay hundreds of corpses. It had not been a one-sided fight, for he spied many legionaries amongst the dead, though those Romans had exacted a terrible price on the Jewish attackers. In no military order, Fimbria's men returned to the lines as individuals. The day was at its hottest. They had not drunk for over an hour and under the armour and heavy padding, it drenched in sweat. They may be tired, but they elation set in. They had fought. And they had won.

As the group approached what had been the defence line, strewn with corpses, Centurion Aginthus approached Fimbria.

"How are you, Porcius?" The officer inquired.

"Apart from spending part of the fight on my back, I'm fine," Fimbria responded, "but we drove the bastards off." Fimbria expected a supportive response. Thew centurion's response took him aback.

"They punched a hole through our defence line—through *my* cohort. If you look down the column, you will see smoke from burning waggons. In this section of the line, they came damn close to overwhelming us several times. We held them, but at what cost, I wonder? I suspect we shall find the other units suffered as badly, possibly worse, as we have. The final ignominy is that so many of the bastards escaped. This was not a victory for the *Fretensis*. We merely survived the day."

As he spoke, two cohorts approached, appearing from the head of the column, leaving a cloud of dust in their wake. Each unit marched in perfect formation. Row after row of damage-free shields positively glowed in the sunlight. The javelins moved before them like a small forest, and the hundreds of polished helmets emitted a constant flicker of sunlight. Aginthus and Fimbria stood motionless, watching the procession pass. The centurions at the head of each cohort saluted Aginthus as they passed.

"It's the Seventh and Eighth," observed Fimbria.

"Antonius and Decimus," responded Aginthus.

"I seem to recall a time when the Fifth looked as they do," Fimbria observed, "Such is war."

"Such is war, indeed. But it was never Rome's intention to construct her legions for the parade ground. We were ever intended for battle. A damaged shield is a mark of honour." Aginthus sighed, "Oh well if nothing else, the Legion is now complete."

"If the seventh and eighth had arrived earlier," said Fimbria, "it may have been a different story."

"Let me tell you, Fimbria, I have served with Gaius Antonius and Achilius Decimus for years. Their late arrival will not have been for want of trying," said a protective Aginthus.

"I did not intend to infer anything otherwise, sir."

"That's good then," the centurion replied. "I suggest we see if we can sort out this fuck up and get these damned waggons moving again."

Capitulum XXIV - Aftermath

24 Aprilis. Year 16 of the Imperator Hadrianus.

Leaning on his shield, Lucius Petronius let it take his weight as he watched the VII and VIII Cohorts march into view. With the enemy fleeing to the hills and two fresh cohorts arriving, he knew the fight was over. Now would come the reckoning, tallying the dead and injured, both military and civilian. Lucius did not expect it to be a pleasant experience. As he rested, Aurelius Crispus joined him.

"You should get that arm looked at, Lucius," he said. "The infirmary waggons are just a little way up the column. We can handle matters here." The centurion called to a passing legionary. "Soldier, take the Optio's shield and keep it secure until he returns. You are?"

"Legionary Adventus, sir. 2nd Century."

"Best you get you gone, Lucius," Crispus instructed Lucius. "Seek out Adventus when you return."

Lucius knew a subtly masked order when he heard one. Aurelius' suggestion made sense; as battle tension leached from his body, he noticed a throbbing ache in his left arm when he attempted to move it. Lucius had no wish to leave his century, which had just completed its first action, but his arm was telling him otherwise. He gave his shield to the soldier and made his way towards the infirmary waggons. Groups of legionaries hindered his progress. As he passed by, he overheard snippets of conversation, recounting stories of bravery, analysis of the new enemy, and debating how the battle had proceeded. It was the natural wind down from an orgy of violence. The centurions would understand, and it would be a little time before the men returned to ranks.

Smoke was still rising from the burning vehicles at the column's rear. Lucius walked past the waggons where the rebels had breached. So many civilians lay amongst the Jewish fatalities, mingled with the slain legionaries from Aginthus' III cohort. He knew only too well that there would be similar scenes along the column. The legionaries' next duty would not win them glory; their tasks would be onerous.

The aid post was a nightmare. Lucius had never seen its like before. Injured soldiers lay all around the waggons, many moaning in pain, whilst others lay ominously silent. Amongst the casualties, accoutrements of war lay scattered, removed by the medical orderlies to enable rushed, early treatment, more focused on saving a life than aiding recovery. On the perimeter of the aid post, queues of soldiers were waiting patiently to have their injuries attended to. These were the lucky ones who would boast of their wounds by nightfall. Then, set over to one side, was a row of men laid on the ground. They made little noise. Lucius knew these to be the soldiers who would not survive. The focus of the medics was on those they could save.

Lucius smiled as he thought of himself discussing his 'battle honour' with his comrades, injured by an abandoned spear! What he was seeing was predictable. The consequence of a major fight but one omitted from the accounts of victories told to the Roman people. What Lucius was not prepared for the number of civilians.

Apart from the lack of uniform, they were little different from the legionaries. Many lay upon the ground, and even more stood in queues, though the civilians formed separate lines. Seeing injured women and wailing children in this place shocked Lucius. The enemy respected neither gender nor age. There were even civilian doctors working with the Medical Optio's team. Yet more casualties from across the column arrived. Struggling to comprehend, Lucius remained fixed on the spot. Then, whilst taking in the scene from Hades before him, he sensed someone beside him. Turning, he came face-to-face with a centurion, one with the look of many years of service.

"Salve, optio, this is your first time?" the officer asked in a gruff voice. Lucius was becoming used to old hands assessing his age -or lack of it- and assuming a lack of experience. He was aware that his age did not always sit well with his rank.

"No, but the last time was in Dacia, sir," he responded. Finally, his conscience got the better of him, "but this is the largest action I have seen."

"Sad that your first big one should be such a fuck up," he said, "if it hadn't of been for the new cohort, the so-called Italians, arriving when they did, it might not've been such a happy ending." A small crease of a smile appeared on Lucius' face. The centurion spotted it. "Well, well, well. By Jupiter's balls, you're from the fourth?"

"1st Century," was all Lucius said.

"So, new cohort, new optio, then." Patting Lucius' back softly with his uninjured hand, the other being a bloody mess, "From what I hear, it was well done, optio."

"We were lucky that we had the advantage of surprise, sir."

"Well, you know what they say, optio. Victory is half strategy, half luck. Today, we were in luck," he studied Lucius' arm, "and what's more, you've got yourself a battle honour."

Lucius pressed the bandage over his wound; it was hurting like Hades. The two men stood for a short while, taking in the scene in front of them.

"This is the element of war no one talks about, optio. The glory of victory, eh?"

Lucius emitted a grim laugh.

"I understood our drills were meant to be the battles. This today should've been a drill!" He looked around him, "It's the women and children—the non-combatants—that's strange to see."

"I grant you that; it's a strange sight for a medical post. But I can tell you this, from twenty years serving the legions, that civilians have always been the victims of war—Harden your heart, lad. What you see here are *our* people. I can assure you before this is over, we will slaughter *theirs*." His tone changed to one more serious. "Policing a province is one thing. Fighting a war to keep it is something quite different." Lucius let the words sink in and was about to reply when an orderly holding a steaming bowl of water approached.

"Officers, two waggons down, that way," he said hurriedly, showing the way with a nod of his head before continuing his way.

"That sounded like an order to me," the centurion joked. "Better follow me, optio, before we end up in the *cac*!" He followed the orderly's instruction, Lucius likewise.

The officer's aid post was immediately identifiable by the sea of helmet crestas. The area was calmer than the main aid post and with far fewer casualties. Officers stretched out on the ground, surrounded by attentive medics, but the vast majority stood patiently in queues. Lucius and his newfound friend joined the end of a line.

"What happened to your hand, sir?" Lucius asked. It would be likely some time before the orderlies would treat him, and he thought the conversation might make the time pass faster. The centurion lifted his hand and turned it at the wrist. Its colour was dark, and where large bloodstains had left the flesh visible, it was swollen. The officer did not move his fingers.

"Simple really," he began, "I'd just stuck one of the bastards. My gladius was still in his guts when, what I can only describe as a hammer on a pole, swung down and hit the back of my hand. It hurt like Hades, and I was fucked!" Then, looking down at his sword sitting its scabbard, he added, "It was one of my lads that recovered my weapon. I should add, he did so *after* sorting the bastard that did this." He nodded at the damaged limb. Lucius studied the proffered hand more closely.

"I don't see any bones," he said reassuringly. "It's badly swollen, and the skin's been split. You will not be swinging a vine stick for a while, but hopefully, it'll mend."

"Bleedin' better had," his friend replied, "it's taken me fifteen years to make centurion, and I ain't giving up yet!" After a momentary pause, he rested his hand on his chest and asked,

"So, what happened to you?"

Lucius gave his fellow officer a brief account of the surrender of the Jewish fighters that resulted in him gaining what was technically a non-combat wound. He was then subject to a series of questions about the IV Cohort and its involvement in the day's actions. Lucius lost track of time, but the conversation ended when an orderly joined them in due course.

"Who's first?" he asked.

"I think age and seniority have it," joked Lucius. The centurion smiled and held out his left, undamaged arm to Lucius. Lucius went to raise his left arm, only for a stabbing sense of pain to overwhelm the limb. It made him wince and sufficed to persuade him moving the arm was not a great idea. The two men looked at each other and burst out laughing.

"Good talking to you, optio…?"

"Petronius, sir. Lucius Decimus Petronius."

"Celer. Plotus Celer. III Cohort. 2nd Century." As the centurion identified his unit, Lucius' eyes widened. "Yes, the Third. Your uncle's cohort. Your lads saved our skins today. Like I said earlier, it was well done. Good to have met you, Petronius."

"I wish you had told me earlier, sir. But, before you go, a question: what in Jupiter's name was all that about rabbits?"

The medical orderly was looking a little impatient with the two men. He was in a hurry, but you don't rush a centurion. The centurion laughed at him.

"I have to go, Petronius. I'll leave you guessing on that one. Vale, brother." Accompanied by the orderly, the officer disappeared around the side of the waggon.

No sooner had he gone than another orderly approached Lucius and took him from the queue. Shortly, he sat on the stool, his upper arm relieved of its bandages. They both studied his wound. The medic had carefully washed the exposed flesh, and the result was not a pretty sight.

"You're lucky," said the cheerful sounding orderly, "it's more of a gash than a cut."

"My gratitude, orderly, I'd no idea I had such an abundance of luck."

"Apologies, sir. What I meant was the wound isn't deep, nor the muscle severely damaged." He rose to his feet, looking down upon his patient. "It will need honey and binding—it's too ragged to stitch—and we will need to change the bandage daily for a while, but you'll mend, optio."

By the time Lucius left the medic, his left upper arm treated, bandaged and resting in a simple cotton sling, the sun was moving behind the hills that enclose the valley. His limb ached and was very stiff, but the orderly's prognosis had dispelled any fears of permanent damage. He felt a sense of elation; the day was ending; both his cohort and his century had performed well in their first action. His only niggling concern was to learn of the casualties they had taken. He was keen to re-join his men, who would be celebrating. They had become soldiers.

As he retraced his steps, passing the main aid post, the failing light now being assisted by burning torches, he saw the medics were still hard at work. As he stood watching, it surprised him to see that the injured were still being brought in. The flickering torchlight compounded his earlier impression that he was viewing Hades. To be fair, he thought, order *was* taking the place of chaos. He had seen enough, turned and promptly strode on— to come to a sudden halt as he collided with a passer-by in the half-light. He quickly stood back.

"Apologies, I should have—Miriam!" Mirroring Lucius, the woman stepped back a pace, regaining her composure. She peered at the tall, young officer in front of her; he removed his helmet.

"Lucius? It is you?"

"It is, but…" he looked at the surrounding scene, "what in Jupiter's name are you doing in this place?"

"I helping wounded people." He recalled she was a healer, and he saw a tenuous connection. Finally, she registered his bandage. "Lucius, they hurt you."

"A damned fool dropped a spear on me," he told her, "but the orderly says it'll heal."

"That is good–,"

"But you, I'm glad to see you're safe. With all that was going on, I should find you here, in a legionary medical post!"

"In Jerusa — Aelia, I helping sick and wounded Roman soldiers. When leave Aelia, I stay with them." As she spoke, she repeatedly looked over her shoulder as if expecting a summons at any moment. She carried a small wooden box that contained folded strips of cloth, like the one wrapped around his arm.

Lucius realised she would be exceedingly busy if she were part of the medical optio's team. He, too, wanted to get back to his century but found himself reluctant to leave.

"Miriam, it's so good to see you." His words earned him a broad smile, "and I realise you must get back to the injured. If I come back later to this waggon, can we catch up on what's been happening?" It took her a moment to translate his words before replying,

"Lucius, I like that… very much. Please forgive, I go." She reached for Lucius and lightly squeezed his healthy arm before turning and returning towards the flickering lights of Hades. Although for a few moments, there was no pain from Lucius' wound, he had never felt so good—even if he was reluctant to admit it, he was experiencing the emotions of a schoolboy who just had his first kiss.

"Optio, pull yourself together," he said to no one in particular. Then, donning his helmet, he set out to find his century.

Meanwhile, Miriam returned to the aid post, where she put the box of folded linen alongside similar containers, all empty, in the facility's centre. She suppressed her concern that she had removed the last such box from the supply waggon; they would address the consequences when the problem arose. There were just too many other pressing issues here and now. A medical orderly approached her and asked her to assist a legionary standing silently at the head of a waiting line of wounded. She crossed to where the soldier stood.

"I wash, and we bandage wound. Yes?" He was young and in mild shock and simply gave her a nod. He needed stitching, but there was a queue for that pleasure, so Miriam decided she would wash his injury, lightly cover it and send him to wait in line for the medicus. She did as she had done many times that day, and he was quickly off to join the others. No sooner had he gone when someone called her name. She turned to see the medical optio beckoning her. He stood with two serious-looking, battle-weary legionaries who held a captive between them, roped around the neck and hands.

The man carried signs of violence; his face bruised, bleeding from several places, but his principal wound was a deep, bloody cut to his thigh. Miriam saw the soldiers were physically holding him upright. His clothing showed that this Jew was not an ordinary soldier. Though his weapons had gone, the finely embroidered tunic broadcast quality. What armour he may have worn was long gone. She thought it sad that his fine boots should be caked in his blood. Built like an athlete, heavily tanned with long inky hair and a neat beard, this was an officer.

"The centurion wants this one kept alive, Miriam," the medical optio said. "Can you clean him up and get that leg dealt with? We may have to waste a stitch on him." Miriam searched for a stool, located one and placed it before the two legionaries and their prisoner.

"Please. He sit, and I help him," Miriam said. Satisfied with what he saw, the optio grunted and walked off to his next emergency. His captors pushed the Jewish officer onto the seat. He grimaced as he attempted to sit without bending his damaged limb. Miriam got a bowl of clean water and a linen cloth. She knelt in front of the prisoner, soaking the fabric as she did so. His wound had gathered dirt, and she moved to wash it. As the wet linen touched the ruptured flesh, she looked up to see if it caused him pain. As she did so, he spat in her face.

"Traitorous whore!" he said in Aramaic, Miriam's native tongue. She froze as one of his captors kneed him in the back, nearly knocking him off the stool.

"Bleedin' do that again, Jew, and I'll fucking kill you personally—do you understand?" The soldier sounded like he meant it, but the captive failed to respond. He grimaced in pain when the soldier's knee pushed him forward onto his damaged leg. Miriam maintained control. Wiping the saliva from her face, she rinsed the cloth and returned to the wound. As she did so, he spoke again.

"You are one of us, bitch. How can you help these dogs?" he continued to speak in Aramaic, quietly, conversationally, not wanting another punch in the back. "You are a Jew. Have you no shame?"

Miriam paused what she was doing.

"I would help any injured soldier. Do I not help you, my friend?"

"Do not dare to call me 'friend'. I fight to recover Israel for the Lord God—and you? You give succour to our vile oppressors, those who would enslave us," as he spoke, he sneered, "and at night, I expect you open your legs and offer them your cunt. Roman slut!" His words shocked her. She focused hard on cleaning the wound again, giving her time to consider a response to the diatribe. She could feel her heart pounding, and her shock turned to anger. Finally, she ceased attending to his injury and sat back on her ankles.

"You *'fight* to recover Israel for the Lord' by killing Romans?" she asked.

"Are you also blind, woman? Of course, we do."

"You claim to be a Jew?"

"Have you lost your mind?"

"Then you'll be familiar with the tablets Moses brought down from the mountain?"

"You are a mad bitch!"

"His first commandment was, *thou shall not kill*. Yet you claim you are recovering Israel for the Lord God, but breaking his most important command to do it?"

"You impertinent bitch!" The volume had risen somewhat, and a guard yanked on the rope tied around his neck.

"Shut it, Jew! One more word, and I'll smack you where it hurts!"

Miriam turned her face from the prisoner and cleaned his injury in silence. When she tried to dab the moistened cloth on the abrasions on his cheeks, he pulled his head away, having none of it. She flung the fabric back into the bowl and stood.

"I am finished. The wound needs the needle," she told the soldiers. The two men dragged the captive to his feet, and she stood face-to-face with him.

"I am a follower of Yeshua. You? You kill Romans, but also my people. Why?" she demanded, then answered her question. "Simply because we obey the command of Moses—*thou shalt not kill*." She glared at the prisoner before turning to his escort and slipped back into Greek, "Take him medicus, will not be gentle like my cloth!" Her gaze returned to the prisoner, moving back into Aramaic. "With much use today, I fear needle be very blunt." She turned her back on him as the two soldiers dragged the hobbling man away.

Once they were gone, the horrors of the day and her recent interaction overwhelmed her. Collapsing onto the recently vacated stool, she put her head in her hands. Many of her people had died that day. She wept – copiously.

"We should get back down there," said Centurion Gracchus. He was with Tribune Sallus and Marcus Apollinaris on their horses, looking back down the road that the foreshortened column had just passed before coming to a halt. Just over a mile away, beyond several twists and turns in the road, they could see smoke lazily drifting into the air.

"It would seem the rebels have left us. It appears the hillsides are clear," Sallus observed, looking to both hillsides. "The ninth stayed alongside as we broke free, so, fortunately, we have our screening troops with us. I'm sure they can keep this part of the column safe along with what militia we have. First, I need to understand what has happened to those who remained at the ambush." The Tribune paused for thought. "Gracchus, I want you to remain here and work with the ninth to make sure this element of the convoy will be safe overnight. Apollinaris and I shall ride back to determine what is happening at the rear."

After further conversation with the IX Cohort commander, the tribune and his watch captain rode towards the column section that had failed to disentangle from the ambush.

The scene was different from the one they had fled. The rebels who had hurled themselves against the waggons had gone. Instead, relieved civilians were mixing with Roman soldiers, many of the latter hauling corpses away onto the hillside. The riders passed several rows of fallen legionaries, respectfully laid side-by-side.

"Not much wood for funeral pyres, sir," Apollinaris said to his tribune.

"You are correct, Apollinaris," the Tribune said, "the scrub around here would not cook a rabbit."

"We'll be taking the lads back then, sir?"

"That is a decision for the Tribune Civilis. If we have enough water, it may be what we do." Sallus was referring to the practice of wrapping bodies in woollen cloth and keeping them cool by regularly soaking in water. "And there he is." Sallus pointed towards a cluster of conversing soldiers, two of whom were mounted. Apollinaris recognised the tribune's helmet cresta and alongside him another easily recognisable helmet decoration, that of the Primus Pilus, centurion Quintus Vorenus. The men approached the group.

"Ave, Gaius," Tribune Civilis greeted Tribune Sallus, "is the head of the column safe?"

Sallus gave the tribune a concise report; the passengers were as well as expected.

"Thank Jupiter for that," Civilis responded. "We have several better citizens in those waggons. Had they been badly mauled, there would have been Hades to pay back in Caesarea!"

"Then we should be grateful for small mercies," quipped Sallus. "With your permission, Captain Apollinaris and I wish to assess the rest of the column and --."

"Well, well, well." All eyes turned towards the Primus, Centurion Vorenus. "Apollinaris, you keep turning up and this time wearing a sash! Did I hear you referred to as 'captain'?"

Some years ago, as a much younger legionary, Marcus had was caught 'liberating' a skin of wine from the officer's stores. It had been Quintus Vorenus, then a senior centurion, who had dealt with the offence. Ever since that day, whenever their paths crossed, Marcus met with deprecating banter from Vorenus. By now, it was a behavioural quirk of the centurion's, and they both realised it was harmless. Nevertheless, Sallus' reaction surprised Marcus.

"With all due respect, centurion Vorenus, Captain Apollinaris has been most diligent in his duties and has served me well in difficult circumstances." His tone said he would brook no argument.

For a second, the Primus was speechless. Marcus suppressed a smile. Effectively, the Primus ran the legion. The tribunes were young men sent to experience the army and serve as staff officers before they moved on to complete their political careers.

However, these men were often from the ruling classes of Rome. It was time for the Primus to apply some of the tact and guile that helped him achieve and hold his position.

"Apologies, sir," he began, "legionary – er – Captain Apollinaris and I have a long history. I know him to be a first-rate legionary, requiring, shall we say, a little guidance now and again."

Marcus saw an opportunity to place some credits into his relationship with the Primus. So he turned to the Tribune.

"If I may, sir. It is said that insulting your friends in such a way shows how deep the friendship is."

"Our *militia* captain has a fine way with words, sir," Primus commented. Sallus was keen to move forward.

"So, Primus, how is it at the end of the column; I see smoke?"

"It was tough down there, sir. The lads put up a stiff defence, but the fight still ended up amongst the waggons. We lost citizens, but many fled up the hillside. Fortunately for us, the predominant enemy force on those slopes was further up the road, in the middle of the column, so once clear of the vehicles, they were relatively safe – but not before the rebel *cunni* had fired half a dozen waggons. If the rebels had not retreated when they had, it might've been a quite different outcome." The Primus paused; when he continued, it was in a more sober tone. "I'm afraid you've lost several militia, sir. I counted several yellow sashes amongst the dead."

Marcus immediately racked his brain, trying to remember which of the men Gracchus had posted to the rear of the train of waggons.

"And the rest of the column, Primus, did the rebels make contact?"

"Fortunately, apart from the road junction itself, we held them off. You see…"

Marcus was still searching memories of faces in his mind when he noticed the Tribune Civilis had manoeuvred his horse alongside Trotter. As the Tribune discussed the waggon situation with the Primus, the Tribune turned to Marcus.

"Well, Apollinaris. You seem to have recovered from your wound?"

"It behaves itself, sir, but likes to remind it's there now and again." Marcus lowered his voice, "Sir, do you knows about the auxiliaries that escaped En Gedi?"

"It was mentioned in one the last dispatches out of Aelia Capitolina. A mere handful of men, I understand."

"More'n that, sir. It's that business about the balsam. One survivor…" and Marcus gave an account of the finding of the En Gedi survivors. He paused at the point when the survivors and the fourth set off to return to Aelia.

"Dammit," Civilis spat, "we are always so close but so bloody far from the facts!"

"Well, sir," said Marcus, "we may be closer than you think."

"Say more."

"Our friend, Mynos Kipula ain't dead, sir. I reported it to centurion Petronius but given the fight and all, he won't of seen you yet."

"Jupiter Almighty man, do you know the whereabouts of this Kipula?"

"I do, sir," replied Marcus, "He's as sick as a pregnant whore in one of the infirmary waggons. At least, he was when I last sees him."

The tribune sat silent upon his horse absorbing and thinking through what he had heard. Then, suddenly, he was all action.

"Tribune Sallus, I need Apollinaris for a while. Apologies." Sallus turned from the Primus and looked questioningly at Marcus. Marcus raised his eyebrows and shrugged. "I'll get another of the tribunes to accompany you on your inspection." Civilis then turned to the Primus, "Quintus, four of your best men - quickly." The Primus turned his horse and trotted over to a unit of soldiers engaged in sorting the dead, Jews from legionaries, and engaged with them to obtain the necessary men.

Within minutes, Marcus and the tribune were making their way towards the infirmary waggon trailed by a squad consisting of a tesserarius and three legionaries.

"I want to seal the waggon off. This man Kipula has information that I want. I suspect he is alive only because some were sure he was about to die. That must not happen," said the tribune, "Who else is in that waggon?"

"There was six of the lads," Marcus answered, "but one of 'em laid down his shield. So there's Kipula, who's out of it and four of 'em who'll live. Oh, and a woman, sir."

The expression on the Civilis's face was both one of puzzlement and surprise.

"A woman? In the infirmary waggon?" he asked, "by the gods, I'm aware we try to take good care of our injured, but I think I draw the line at supplying women!"

Marcus laughed out loud.

"Apologies, sir," said Marcus, "she's not a medic like, but she's lookin' after the lads. You know - water, food and checking their bandages—that sort of thing."

"Is she Jewish?" the tribune asked. Marcus, developing a comfort conversing with the legion's commanding officer, responded quickly.

"No, sir. She's 'alf Gallic and 'alf Egyptian. From the vicus at Aelia." Marcus realised he had shown more than just a passing connection with the woman in the waggon as he said the words.

"Tell me, Apollinaris, do you have this level of familiarity with everyone you meet?"

"No, sir. But this lass, Anaitis, ran the Neptune taberna in the vicus. So we all knows 'er well."

A short distance from their destination, Marcus and the Tribune Civilis dismounted. So close to the legionary aid post, many soldiers in the area observed the small party arriving. With his fine sculpted armour, sweeping helmet cresta, grieves and finely filigreed gladius, the Tribune Laticlavius of the Tenth Fretensis was hard to miss. Soldiers were already discussing why the commander should have arrived in their midst. Those closer to the small group came to attention and saluted the commander. The tribune dismissed them with a wave of his arm, saying,

"Be about your business, men. You can ignore me." They quickly arrived at their destination. Turning to the accompanying tesserarius and his men, he briefed them on his requirement. Giving no intricate detail, he clarified that no one apart from legionary medics was to enter the waggon. As dusk fell, he ordered Marcus to provide a brazier to keep the vehicle's rear well lit. "So, Apollinaris, let's have a look at our man. Soldiers, take up your positions."

Marcus moved quickly to the rear, wishing to enter before the Civilis and to signal Anaitis he was strictly on business. He was sure once she caught sight of the tribune, she would understand the situation. Unfortunately, as the light was fading outside, visibility inside the covered vehicle was not good, but enough for Marcus to see that Anaitis was not present.

Cassius was sitting in his corner where he had been for the last several days. He looked to see who was entering his temporary home, grateful for a variance in a monotonous routine. He smiled as he recognised Marcus from his previous visit, but his face straightened upon seeing the tribune. Cassius punched off a salute, or the best he could manage, sat on his backside with his leg in a bandage. Three other men came out of their slumber and groggily recognised that a senior officer was in the presence. One prone figure did not move – Mynos Kipula.

"Legionaries, please relax. This is not an official visit," said the tribune. Marcus pointed to the one soldier that remained still.

"That's Kipula," Marcus said.

The commander turned to Cassius, who appeared to be the most alert of the vehicle's residents.

"Has this man said anything during the journey?"

"E's started moanin' and mumblin', sir. Not as though we can understand a word," Cassius responded to his superior officer.

"Well, legionary...." Civilis paused.

"Finatus, sir, Cassius Finatus. 2nd Century, III Cohort."

"Well, legionary Finatus, should our friend talk, you will make the sentinel outside aware of the fact; he will know what to do." The tribune made to leave, but changing his mind, turned back to legionary Finatus. "How good is your memory, Finatus?"

"Good enough to admire your new gladius, sir." A look of surprise crossed the tribune's face. "A while back, when you first arrived, you inspected the Third. Of course, you wasn't carrying that gladius then."

"You've convinced me, Finatus," the tribune responded, "so anything our friend here might say, I want you to remember – accurately."

The legionary attempted another sitting salute.

"Yours to command, sir."

As the legionary commander and the watch captain left the waggon, Anaitis appeared, struggling with two buckets of water. Seeing the two men, she stopped and gently lowered them to the ground. Her face reflected the confusion in her mind. On the one hand, she wanted to throw her arms around Marcus, yet on the other, she was aware she was in the presence of a senior Roman officer. It was the Tribune Civilis that broke her paralysis.

"You must be the lady from the taberna?" He looked Anaitis up and down. She was cleaner than she was when Marcus left her, but her clothes remained bloodstained. She had tied her hair upon her head, but the bloody matting was still visible. "It looks to me as though you have been very thorough in your job."

"Gratitude, sir," was all Anaitis could say. Marcus covered her confusion.

"At one point, the fighting was hard in this area. The lady here," Marcus nodded in Anaitis' direction, "was kept very busy, like."

"I'm sure the legionaries appreciate your service. A rare woman would put herself in harm's way to care for our legionaries. My gratitude to you." The tribune turned to a sentinel. "This lady has a free pass to the waggon, but no one, regardless of rank, may enter except the medicus." Then, turning to Marcus, "We have business to be about."

Marcus managed a discrete smile in Anaitis' direction as he left.

The two soldiers arrived at the regimental aid post in no time at all. The sun was setting behind the western hills, and the area was lit by burning torches mounted on poles. Visibility was good enough for those present to recognise the legionary commander in their midst. Once again, Tribune Civilis gave the order to be at ease. He signalled an orderly who promptly approached. He requested and received the location of the medical optio.

The tribune made clear to the optio that he had a particular patient who should be afforded all possible care; he was not to die. He did not explain further and received a confirmation that they would comply with the request with. Shortly after, Marcus left to acquire a brazier for Kipula's waggon and arrange a guard schedule that would remain in place until the column arrived at Caesarea.

Lucius Petronius returned to his unit. The carts following the Fourth had arrived, and his comrades offered basic sustenance. A level of exhilaration remained amongst the soldiers. They had been blooded, no longer recruits. They were now soldiers. Added to their elevation to the ranks of the soldiery, they were also heroes, having saved the Sixth from destruction. Lucius sought his commander, whom he found engaged with two of the cohort's centurions. Crispus paused the conversation as he saw his junior officer approach. Arm in a sling, Lucius saluted with his good limb.

"Optio Petronius reporting back for duty, sir."

"A little worse for wear, eh, Optio," quipped his commander.

"Nothing too serious, sir," Lucius responded. "The men seem in good spirits."

"And so they should be," said Centurion Quintus Facilis of the 2nd Century, "A few hours ago, they'd no idea how they'd each perform. Now they know. They've passed the test."

"True words, old friend. But tomorrow morning, they'll wake up," added Centurion Petronius. "That's when they'll realise several brothers are no longer with them. That's when they'll learn that victory always demands a price."

"But today, Fortuna was with them, so let 'em celebrate; they earned it," said Facilis, "and what's more, I'm celebrating too. All those hours of bloody training paid off!" The third centurion chipped in.

"Fuck rejoicing - let's eat. We will be busy tomorrow getting this shambles -" he pointed over his shoulder with his thumb in the column's direction, "- back towards Caesarea. I suspect we'll be too damn busy to worry about victory's high price."

Lucius joined the men of his century and entered the banter as they ate their meagre rations. He was the butt of several 'one-armed man' jokes, but he enjoyed the relaxed company after what had been a tense day for all of them. He felt guilty because he knew he was only going through the motions before leaving to meet Miriam. Fortuna smiled upon him. The day's emotions demanded a price, and soon, several legionaries bedded down for the night. It was not long before Lucius apologised to the handful of diehards still recounting the events of the day and slipped away.

By now, the sun had departed the sky, which was ruled by a bright moon. Even on the darkest night, Lucius would have located the infirmary waggons by their glowing braziers. Arriving at the aid post, he waited on the edge of the flickering amber light cast by the burning wood. Removing his helmet, he slowly paced along the periphery of the amber glow. Surprise took him when Miriam suddenly appeared at his side. She did not come as expected from the aid post, but her waggon further up the column.

"Lucius, you have come."

"I said I would. Let's walk." They moved away from the glow of the aid post, and their eyes quickly adjusted to the moonlight. Two large boulders sat side-by-side a little distance away. "We seem to have found some seats."

"Are we safe?" Miriam asked.

"I don't think our friends will be back tonight," Lucius replied as the couple chose their seats. They sat facing each other, knee to knee. "So tell me, Miriam, just how have you ended up working for the medical optio?"

Time passed as Miriam recounted her experiences since Lucius had left to return to Caesarea. He let her talk, asking only the occasional question for clarification. The matter-of-fact delivery of her story took aback Lucius. Whatever dropped in her lap, she just got on with it. Mixing with the Roman army had enhanced her Greek. Lucius related the experiences that brought him to this place. By the time his story closed, the moon had risen higher in the sky.

"... and so, here we are together, in the Judaean hills, sitting on rocks in the middle of the night." Lucius ended.

"My aunt, be not happy! She want my cousin with me," Miriam said. Under the moonlight, the world was grey, but it did not prevent Lucius from seeing the smile on her face.

"It would be no different in Rome," he said, "and we'd meet because our parents wanted it to be so." As the words left his mouth, he remembered Miriam's parents were long dead. "Apologies, Miriam. I forgot about — "

"It was a long time. Do not worry. Lucius, you have family?"

She listened, not interrupting, as he related the family history that resulted in him joining the legions.

"So, Lucius," she said, "we are both without family."

Since she had appeared, Lucius experienced a growing sense of nervousness in his gut but knew its origin. He knew what he wanted to say but found it more difficult to cope with this situation than facing the enemy. It was like entering an icy river; he could struggle into the water a little at a time, suffering the cold, or he could jump. Lucius jumped.

"Then we could start a family," He proposed. Lucius spoke the words before he realised his choice was not quite what he intended! "I mean... what I wanted to say was...."

The girl leant forward.

"Lucius, I do not understand. Start family?"

Lucius realised he had jumped only to find himself back on the riverbank. He could walk away or attempt another jump. He tried again.

"Miriam, at times when I least expect it, you keep coming into my mind. I–I–," he stammered, "I have strong feelings for you." Well, that's done it, he thought. But unfortunately, the nerves did not recede. Instead, the sensation grew worse as he waited for the response. Lucius suspected she was checking her translation to ensure she had understood his meaning. Then, gently, she placed a hand upon his knee.

"Lucius, I am a Jew from hills of Judaea," she said softly, "a follower of Yeshua, yes, but still Jew. You are Roman. You have your gods. You are Roman officer. Between me and you is wide river."

"Miriam, I am Lucius Decimus Petronius, a man," his voice betrayed a sense of frustration, "you are Miriam bet Yaholem, a woman."

"I know this, Lucius. You are good man. You saved me from rebels. You pay taberna for me. In your Latin, 'gratitude'."

"That was nothing," Lucius responded. "I did what I wanted to do." A silence fell across the pair, and it was a little time before Lucius spoke. "Miriam, let's forget the world and who we are for a moment. If it were just you and me, could there be a tomorrow for us?"

"A tomorrow?" she asked. Lucius saw he was stretching her understanding of Greek.

"A future for us, together?"

Miriam listened, translated, and then placed her hands on his arms and looked straight into his eyes.

"There is no need to ask question. You have been in my mind."

"Miriam, then I am sure," Lucius said. "You have become precious to me. The rest we'll just have to work out."

She leant forward, holding him by the shoulders. His brain dismissed the scream of pain from his arm.

"I would like, Lucius."

Interludum V

Koseba and the rabbi

Surrounded by his officers, Simeon ben Koseba stood in the centre of the forum in Aelia Capitolina, the very heart of Hadrian's colony. It was now in the hands of Jewish rebels. The forum, its new marble, brilliant in the midday sunshine, sat uncommonly quiet with its shops closed, with many ransacked. All around lay the detritus of a hurried departure. The emptiness of the place diminished the size of the small band of soldiers. Ben Koseba, the 'Big One', looked around him and raised his arms to the azure sky.

"This day, we claim Jerusalem for the Lord God of Israel!" Those surrounding him shouted their approval. They were elated, whilst at the same time incredulous. They, simple foot fighters from the hills of Judaea, had swept the mighty Roman army from this place. The hand of God must have touched them. Ben Koseba spread his arms wide and slowly turned on the spot.

"He hath swallowed down riches, and he shall vomit them up again: God shall cast them out of his belly."

"The Lord of hosts is with us. The God of Jacob is our refuge!" came a response. Sounds of agreement passed through the group.

"Harken," ben Koseba commanded, "collect your companies and scour this place for anything that may be of use to our forces. No man is to take any item for themselves, for such behaviour is a pollution. We shall gather them later to sell and fund our army, after which we will raze this Sodom to the ground, and Jerusalem will arise." Again, a ripple of approval ran through the assembled fighters. "Company commanders, return to your men and carry out the order."

Most of the accompanying soldiers left the forum. Ben Koseba was alone with his closest lieutenants. The day was growing hot, and under the shade of a portico, ben Koseba espied a table with benches. It was not long before they were sitting, enjoying the cooler air.

"For years you've planned for this, Simeon," said Yohanan, "and it has proven all the naysayers wrong. The oppressors didn't raise a sword against us. The hand of God was in this."

"My brothers," began ben Koseba, "I must confess that I did not expect this. I realised it would be hard for them to defend this place—it has no walls—and yet I failed to consider that they would abandon it. The world must hear of this. Those reluctant to join us will see that our victory here is the will of God."

"Then let's trust in God that the fighters we sent to reinforce our companies attacking the refugee column will be as successful," a voice replied.

"It was the lack of defence in this place," ben Koseba refused to speak the Roman name for the settlement, "that allowed us to send reinforcements to our brothers. God's hand is in all of this," he continued, "but do not expect them to destroy the retreating column. It's protected by a legion—a damaged one—but a capable force. The orders are simple; ensure that the evacuation is not a success. Hurt them badly. We will have the element of surprise, but once they recover and organise, we shall pull back and escape."

"Simeon, you don't believe we can defeat legions?" one of his officers asked.

"Yehudah, have I taught you nothing?" ben Koseba's tone stiffened, "I have spent years preparing. Yet, I did not expect Jerusalem to fall so easily into our hands for all my planning. That enabled me to send many more men to attack the retreating Roman column, something unplanned. The day we destroy a legion will be a day that is meticulously prepared. Never, ever underestimate the Roman army. They have not conquered so much of the world by incompetence. Throwing great numbers of soldiers at them will not guarantee a victory." His tone softened again. "Yehudah, be patient, my brother. Look around you. Jerusalem is ours, and soon Judaea will be. Israel, too, will be reborn and restored to God. Yes, Rome will respond, but with careful preparation, we can make the price in blood unacceptable to them."

The small group of officers seated at the table were ben Koseba's inner sanctum. They prepared with him for the holy war upon the Romans. But, unfortunately, one soldier was missing, Amos, absent leading the troop reinforcements sent to attack the Roman refugee column.

"Will we move north? Perhaps harass Caesarea?" asked the ever-enthusiastic Yehuda. "Will Galilee rise for the cause?"

"Be assured that the bloody Samaritans will do fuck all!" said a voice at the end of the table. Samaria sat between Judaea and Galilee and was no friend of the former. Koseba raised two hands in front of him. Then, when all fell silent, he spoke again.

"A spider does not rush back and forth, chasing flies. Instead, he patiently builds his web and waits until the fly comes to him. The fly may be bigger than the spider, even so, it is trapped and devoured." Koseba studied the faces of his lieutenants; what he saw assured him they understood the analogy. "My brothers, I have learned much about the Romans. Long before they stamped their boot on Israel, there was a time when they fought a great Carthaginian general named Hannibal Barca. He crushed Rome's army, and Hannibal's forces ranged across Italy. Did the Romans surrender? No, they did not. Fabius Maximus, an ageing senator, took their limited forces and adopted a hit-and-run strategy. Hannibal did not know which way to turn, lashing out in all directions. Meanwhile, Rome's boys grew of age, and it rebuilt its army."

"The Romans destroyed Hannibal?"

"They failed," Koseba replied, "but they fought on and eventually, an exhausted Hannibal went home." Then, yet again, Koseba paused and stared into the faces of his men. Had they received the message? "My brothers, the fight will be long and bloody, but I intend to send the Romans home. We shall prevail."

"Simeon, what of this place?" An officer asked.

"We will raise a body of men from the hills to come and take this abomination down, block by block, stone by stone, in the same way, the oppressors reduced Jerusalem to rubble. Then, my brothers, we shall begin building a new Jerusalem and a new temple." Sounds of approval ran through the small group.

"Meanwhile, we move to the next stage. Every camp throughout Judaea must now be ready to fight."

Over the preceding years, ben Koseba had been preparing the hundreds of villages across Judaea. Every village had become an arms depot. Since his earliest planning, Koseba had always referred to the villages as 'camps', seeing them purely as military assets. This network of settlements, divided into military regions, would be ben Koseba's spider's web. Knowing the call would come to revolt, their menfolk had trained in using the stored weapons. He would trap the Romans in his web, enabling his field armies to destroy them.

"Regional commanders, your chief role now is to make sure your people are ready for the fight to come. The whole of Judaea must stand shoulder to shoulder against the Roman. There can be no neutrality in this fight. If you are not with us, you are against us. We must eradicate anything that stands against us." Koseba looked around the table into the eyes of his men. His icy stare reinforced the message. "Until now, we have had the element of surprise, but from today, the Romans are alerted. The sheer determination of our people will decide the outcome of what we have begun today; grasping their freedom."

Out of the corner of his eye, he spotted a small group heading towards them. It comprised four people: one leading, riding a donkey, and three on foot. Koseba swung around for a better view, and his officers mimicked him. Their leader knew only too well who was approaching. Finally, a short distance from the officers' table, the arrivals came to a standstill, and the rider dismounted. He took three paces forward, clear of his companions, stood and spread his arms wide, looking up into the sky.

"Praise be to him that loves Israel," the man said loudly, "for he has shown his people his great mercy and returned Jerusalem to them."

Koseba rose from his bench, his officers likewise. The general opened his arms and addressed the new arrival.

"Rabbi Akiva, I am honoured to welcome one of our greatest sages to the city of Jerusalem, a city that lies in the hands of its people — your disciples too, are most welcome." He looked upon the Rabbi, a man he considered an enigma. He was aged, but still dressed well in a fine, full-length tunic of mixed colours. A prayer shawl lay across the shoulders, each corner carrying a coloured tassel. Yet it seemed to Koseba that whatever the rabbi wore never seemed to sit well upon him. Perhaps it was because Rabbi Akiva was not a typical Rabbi.

Akiva ben Jusef's family were agricultural workers. Akiva had seen many years of manual labour before entering the Beit Midrash, the Centre for Jewish learning, in Jamnia, which had become the centre for Judaism after the fall of Jerusalem. Akiva looked as though he had spent years working in the fields. He was not the product of the system that trains its rabbis from a young age. His skin had never lost its leathery appearance, and they sometimes described his hands as shovels. His greying beard was long and often thoroughly dishevelled. As he walked, he rocked slightly from side to side because of his bowed legs.

Akiva was forty years of age before entering the Beit Midrash and put his labouring life behind him. The latter fact drew Koseba to Rabbi Akiva, a man who understood the people. The other attraction was that, like all 'converts', Rabbi Akiva was a zealous follower of his religion. For all his differences, over the last 20 years, the Rabbi's reputation had grown, and he was now considered one of the great sages of Judaism.

"General Koseba," the Rabbi said, "as a younger man studying under the great Rabbi Yohanan, I would often dream of standing in front of a new temple in Jerusalem. Returned to its people, its priests offered sacrifice to the Almighty One. His hand has been upon this place, and it has partially fulfilled my dream. All praise be to Him."

"Indeed, Rabbi," Koseba responded, "the hand of the Lord - and the sword arms of my army." If Koseba saw the slight frown that ran across Rabbi Akiva's face, he ignored it. "Come, Rabbi, join us at the table. These are my senior officers who all had a hand – along with the Lord God's – in bringing us back to Jerusalem."

The three disciples accompanying Rabbi Akiva glanced at each other, hearing what they perceived as a disrespectful reply from the general. It was now Akiva's term not to react.

"It would honour me to join you, General Koseba."

Full introductions made, the next hour saw the conversation touch upon the plans for the city and the liberation of Judaea in the future. Akiva was resolute that the Roman colony of Aelia Capitolina should suffer the same fate as Jerusalem at the end of the Great Revolt; levelled to the ground. The colony was "unclean" and an "abomination unto God". He was as adamant that a new temple should arise upon the site destroyed by Titus after the Great Revolt.

While many of the rabbis in Jamnia were nervous of Simeon ben Koseba, his planning and preparation impressed Akiva. After the terrible destruction of the Great Revolt and the strictures placed upon the Jewish people, there was a natural fear of upsetting the developing relationship with the Roman administration. Koseba recognised the weaknesses of earlier Jewish revolts; the internecine religious bickering, the constant struggling for military leadership and the complete lack of planning. His officers often heard Koseba referring to previous struggles. "They knew what they didn't want, and they fought against it. Sadly, what each party wanted was quite different!"

The Rabbi Akiva was zealous. His focus was upon establishing a nation governed by the laws of Moses. It was not about relationship building with the Romans. In Simeon ben Koseba, he saw a man who could move his focus forward.

"Your planning has been meticulous, General," the aged sage said. "There seems to be little you have not considered. God is guiding your hand."

"Rabbi," the general responded. "Grand plans are usually worthless, but I believe planning is crucial. The Romans have the might on the battlefield, but we have the strategy, and we shall defeat them."

"I often a pray that it is so," the rabbi responded, "but I recall a sage once saying that whilst it is right to prepare for the lion, sometimes it is the mouse that brings you down!" Koseba said nothing for a moment and then chuckled. "General, what amuses you so?" Akiva asked.

Koseba knew that all eyes around the table were now focussed upon him.

"I had a little brother. Some of the family named him Gakhbar, *the mouse - he was always darting here and there* - I had not thought about him for years."

"Had?" the rabbi asked.

"He became sick in mind, and my father sent him to a relative in Alexandria. I have not seen or heard from him since that day."

For the soldiers around the table, this was a revelation. The general never talked about his past life or family matters; it was like a window opening slightly and letting in some light for the observers.

"I know of your sister, general, but I never knew you had a brother. I am sorry you have lost him, but the Lord works in strange ways."

"Well, rabbi, I suspect he is one mouse I do not have to plan for."

Capitulum XXV – Return to Caesarea

25 Aprilis. Year 16 of the Imperator Hadrianus.

Fortunately for the IV Cohort, their carts, complete with tents, had arrived the evening of the battle. Rising with the sun, the legionaries, still buoyed by their victory, were in good spirits. For them, it was another day in their careers as Roman legionaries. For Lucius Petronius, he sensed he was moving into a new career phase. Having lost his mother early in his life, emotional investments with women were unknown to him. For much of the time, his relationship with his father had been good, if not rather formal. Lucius always saw himself as self-contained, but he edged the container open last night. He experienced the urge to tell everybody about the woman he had bared his heart to, but that could not happen. So, for now, their feelings must remain between the two of them—a secret.

Tribune Civilis called a meeting of the centuriate. It was practice in the *Fretensis* that senior centurions were accompanied by their optios. It meant that should anything befall a cohort's commander, the optio could step into the centurion's role. Lucius had not long risen before Centurion Crispus joined him and the two men set off to the meeting point.

The Primus had chosen a position away from the column, on a plateau a short way up the valley's eastern side. It gave the officers some privacy and would be cool in the ridge's shadow from which the Jewish force had attacked the column. Lucius and Crispus quickly located the meeting, its position indicated by the number of broad crestas. They joined the group, which formed a semicircle around the Primus. The tribune stood alongside the legion's senior centurion, watching his commanders. Being amongst the last to arrive, the luxury of a rock seat was not available to the officers of the Fourth; they would stand. Every senior centurion was present, though Lucius observed several bandages and dressings amongst them. The optios were in a similar condition, and Lucius felt he was in like company; several arms were in slings.

"Brothers, yesterday was a fuckup," began the Primus, "we escaped by the skin of our teeth. Had the attackers overwhelmed the Sixth, the enemy would've rolled over us. That it did not happen is purely down to the timely arrival of the Fourth. In my view, Centurion Crispus deserves a *Corona Obsidialis*." Some heads turned towards Crispus, while others nodded sagely. They awarded a Corona Obsidialis to an officer who raises a siege, something many felt they had recently experienced. The centurion continued, "However, history will record that the Fretensis drove the enemy off, but let's be in no doubt how close it was. The evidence of that is in the injury reports. We've paid a high price for the safety of the column." He allowed a few moments of silence whilst each officer contemplated the losses amongst his men. Lucius was grateful that the Fourth had lost only four soldiers. The Fourth's fight was not the gruelling struggle faced by most of the legion; the two late-arriving cohorts excepted. Primus Vorenus nodded towards the tribune. "We've decided to transport our dead to Caesarea. Last night a relief column of twenty waggons arrived and is currently up the road, working its way around the waggons that escaped the ambush. Several of those waggons will take our fallen back to the colony. Scouts have ridden ahead to prepare them for the waggon's return. Our brothers will have fitting funerals."

Civilis stepped forward.

"Soldiers, it is imperative we move the column as swiftly as possible. The route we are on re-joins the Roman road a few miles to the north, and we will then be clear of Judaea. Once we are moving on a paved carriageway, we should be up to Caesarea in no time. That, men, is our aim. Even if your centuries must carry children on their shoulders, then so be it; whatever it takes." He ran his gaze across the assembled company, the pause giving seriousness to what he had said. "The Primus will share our plan with you."

Sometime later, the officers left the meeting and returned to their cohorts to explain the plan to their subordinates.

"Well, young Petronius, did you get the message?" Crispus asked Lucius as they walked back. After a second's consideration, Lucius responded.

"We head to Caesarea with all speed, come what may."

"In terms of process, you're correct," Crispus responded, "but the underlying message was that we get out of here damn quickly because if the Jews come back in the numbers we faced yesterday, we 're fucked!"

"Do you think they will?"

"If you asked me that a week ago, I would've said that I don't think they will." Crispus stopped, and he looked back towards the ridge the enemy force had swarmed across the previous day. He was bare headed, carrying his helmet, allowing a hand to scratch his head. "But you're asking me today, not a week ago, so I'd have to say I don't know. And that, Lucius, that makes me very twitchy."

Once the centurions had returned to their cohorts, Roman efficiency kicked in. They loaded the newly arrived waggons with their cargoes of dead and injured, leaving some vehicles to carry tired citizens, still traumatised from the previous day's events. With the militia working frantically, the waggons at the junction were ready by the middle of the day. They would soon connect with those that had escaped the attack, waiting a mile ahead. They positioned the cohorts throughout the column, ready to offer protection in case of further attack.

Crispus had formed up the Fourth alongside the column, ready to step into position between the waggons when they moved off. The century's officers stood to the front, passing the time of day, waiting for the orders that would begin the journey. Aurelius Crispus interrupted the conversation.

"Well, what do we have here then?" he said. His fellow officers turned their heads in the direction Crispus was looking. They saw the bulky figure of centurion Octavius Secundus of the II Cohort walking towards them. The idle chatter stopped as the officer approached. He halted a few feet short of the group.

"Optio Petronius, a moment of your time," he said

Crispus muttered under his breath.

"You never know with Secundus if it's an order or a request!"

"Of course, sir," Lucius replied and joined the centurion. Secundus suggested they walk. They moved directly away from the column. Until well clear, the officer said nothing, and Lucius' puzzlement grew. They stopped after a short distance, and Secundus turned to face Lucius.

"The Fourth did well yesterday; in fact, for a new cohort, you did bloody well."

"Thank you, sir," Lucius replied, confused why they had to leave the column for such a conversation.

"The Primus' comments regarding the *Obsidialis* were well spoken." The man paused, and Lucius could detect a sense of discomfort in his face. Then, after a few seconds, he continued. "Some time ago, you told a meeting of the centuriate in Aelia of your suspicions about Jewish intentions. I harshly belittled your view in front of my comrades."

"Sir, I can understand my views may've been outlandish and-"

"My opinion may have been valid in the circumstances, but Optio, my behaviour was not. I think myself to be an honourable man. I wish to apologise, and I also wish to Mars that we'd listened to you." The centurion held out his hand.

"There is no need, sir, to-"

"There very much is, Optio," Secundus said, pushing his arm further forward. Lucius grasped the offered forearm. "Thank you, Optio Petronius."

"Sir, if it's any comfort, I suspect my report was too late to change anything."

Lucius knew that a group of 1st Century officers watched them not so far away. The senior officer scratched his head. Secundus and Lucius walked back to the group. In response to Crispus' expression of puzzlement, Secundus explained.

"Optio Petronius and I were just catching up." Upon which he turned on his heel and walked away. Lucius filled them in as to the conversation.

"Well now, that's a bloody rare happening, Lucius," said Crispus with a laugh. "Consider yourself honoured!"

The sun had just passed its zenith when the main body of the column moved forward. It was a slow start, as it had to pause occasionally to allow cohorts to take up their positions. Not long after, the column connected with the element that had escaped the ambush. Once again, the great snake of waggons made its way along the twisting and turning road until it re-joined the Roman road towards Lod. It found itself parked outside of the town at the day's end. The tribune decreed that whilst the legion would remain with the column, the refugee colonists from Aelia Capitolina were free to visit the town. The column was clear of the Judaean hills, and it was time to give the travellers a break.

That evening, myths were born as shops sold out of goods and taverns ran dry. Throughout the night, well-fed citizens returned to their waggons, loaded with an array of provisions. Some were even better dressed than when they set out. Many struggled to find their way back to their waggon, their brains befuddled by some of Lod's finest wine. Nevertheless, they celebrated their survival and regained a sense of normality, forgetting for the time being the uncertainty around what the future held. The traders in Lod would not forget the night the column passed through. Meanwhile, the legionaries watched the goings-on with envy, but they knew they would eat good food and sleep on a soft cot in a stone barracks soon. Their time would come.

At daybreak, the column reassembled, ready to move on. The soldiers showed little sympathy for the aching heads that so many citizens experienced. This day was to be a long one. The column would travel to the port of Joppa and from there take the main Roman road up the coast to Caesarea.

Marcus Apollinaris rode Trotter down the length of the column, pleased with himself. Since leaving the junction, matters had gone well. He had encountered a few slight problems, but nothing that could not be dealt with. He had even managed time with Anaitis the previous night, which involved a stroll into the surrounding countryside that had become greener and far lusher away from the mountains. Inevitably, they lay together under the light of the moon. Afterwards, he dwelled on how lucky he was with the developing relationship. Again, Anaitis had taken complete control, and by the time she collapsed beside him, they were sweating profusely and found themselves completely drained. Yet, as lucky as he felt, there remained a niggling doubt that something was not right. But he pushed the niggle towards a dark recess in his mind. Rising, he threw an arm around Anaitis, and they strolled back to the camp. He was one lucky man.

Lucius Petronius joined centurion Aurelius Crispus at the head of the Fourth. Two men had spent much of the previous night talking through the Tenth Fretensis' situation. Crispus was sure the legion would soon reorganise and march south to recover Judaea and Aelia Capitolina. Lucius thought matters would not resolve that quickly. Conscious of the enormous numbers of fighters the Judaeans could put out into the field, he felt the Fretensis, badly depleted, did not have enough men to take on those forces. They needed to recruit more legionaries, and their training would take time. However, there was common ground between the two men. They both wondered if the Sixth Legion, the *Ferrata,* based at Tel Shalem in Galilee, would join the campaign. Crispus was worried that they may see the *Ferrata* clearing up the *Fretensis'* mess, a sentiment Lucius shared. However, once the command to march was sounded, the matter slipped out of Lucius' mind as he fell back to take up station at the rear of his century.

Five long days later, Marcus Apollinaris experienced another of those moments when the organisation and method of the Roman army made him feel immensely proud. As he waited on Trotter, he looked around him at what had been the long column of waggons that had arrived at Caesarea several hours earlier. They currently drew the vehicles up into relatively short lines. Marcus was not sure how many, but he watched a legionary close by who was busy at the head of one line. Having hammered a wooden post into the ground, he hung from it a board emblazoned with the number twenty-seven. Beyond him, more lines remained numberless. Horses, mules, and oxen were being led away for watering, feeding, and rest.

Before the vast waggon park stood many tents, shelter for those who did not have room in a waggon. Traders had set up stalls in a hurriedly created market. Alongside stood waggons loaded with amphorae of water. Meanwhile, the refugees from Aelia Capitolina waited patiently at their waggons until formally given their freedom to move about. Most of them would not stay long at Caesarea. Some would head for Damascus, while others continued north to Antioch. With their families and several of the more successful business class and the colony's council members would get accommodated in Caesarea.

Marcus's current task was to implement a census of all surviving refugees and identify the waggons to which each was attached. The team of militiamen moved amongst the waggons, collecting names, releasing the travellers with each waggon once the information was secured. Marcus believed the danger had receded for these people, and some normality would slowly return. It all seemed to be going to plan, not only for the living, but also for the dead. He knew that in the field outside of the town, edging onto the coast, Roman efficiency had constructed several funeral pyres for the fallen legionaries. They were large pyres, each large enough to carry the bodies of four soldiers. Marcus would like to have been able to pay his respects, for he knew some had fallen in his cohort. Before he became too maudlin, horses pulled up alongside him. Julius Gracchus and Tribune Sallus joined him, recently having left a meeting with Caius Faustinus, the Camp Prefect, discussing handling the many refugees.

"More work for us, Marcus," Gracchus said. "When we've completed the census, we are to draw up lists of no more than 500 names. The lists will grant groups of refugees access into Caesarea at a specific time. It appears the 'old man'," referring to Faustinus, "doesn't want to swamp the place!"

"You would be best to create the lists by vehicle numbers," Sallus suggested. "It would make communicating the information much easier."

"The lads'll be a while yet, sir," Marcus responded. "They're collecting names by waggon. But, once done, we'll be able to draw up the groups quickly."

"That is good," Sallus said. "They are keeping everyone in the waggon park tonight, so the first groups go into the town early tomorrow. I want a rota drawn up and circulated by sunset."

"Yours to be commanded, sir," chipped off Marcus' tongue, "I'll be off to check on the lad's progress then." He kicked Trotter's flanks, nudged his neck, and rode forward. As he moved off, he whispered to no one in particular, "From militia captain to bleedin' clerk, don't you just love the army?"

Marcus had a vested interest in riding back into the waggon park. He recently heard of the plans to house many refugees in Damascus and Antioch. The last place he wanted Anaitis was anywhere other than Caesarea, which meant he would have to ensure that she was not on the refugee list, getting to the militiaman in her waggon file - before he got to Anaitis.

Lucius Petronius sat on his cot, glad to be back in the legionary barracks, reviewing his recent return to Caesarea. On the day of arrival, they had positioned the IV Cohort at the rear of the legion. It had bemused the soldiers, for marching in such a position is a dusty place to be and, on a dry summer's day, an unpleasant experience. Consequently, the most junior cohort traditionally occupied the position. It appeared the Fourth had gone from yesterday's heroes to today's greenhorns.

As the column entered the approaches to Caesarea, the escorting cohort broke away and headed for the town's main gates. As they approached the entrance, the cohorts marching ahead of the Fourth stood to alternating sides of the roadway. Each column then turned inwards, facing each other. Finally, Aurelius Crispus marched the Fourth towards the gates, entering the human channel of cohorts. The legion broke into cheers as the Fourth marched through, beating their swords on their shields. If a cohort could not qualify for a *Corona Obsidialis*, they were certainly going to receive the thanks of the legion.

Marching in his position at the rear of the cohort, Lucius had never felt so proud. Such applause and recognition from fellow legionaries was one of the greatest plaudits for a soldier. Looking forward, Marcus could see heads turning left and right, revealing beaming smiles. Like the men of the Fourth, he too was emotional, and the dust of a Roman road was a small price to pay for the pride they were feeling. The deliberate consequence of the legion's manoeuvre meant that the Fourth, first through the gates, accompanied by the tribune and the legion's Primus Pilus, led the legion through Caesarea. The legionary standards marched with them. Lucius knew he might be experiencing a once-in-a-lifetime event.

Later, sitting on his cot, those emotions still physically lingered. An additional bonus to the day came from the tribune's announcement that the Fourth would have the next four days free of all duties. Other matters had also gone Lucius' way. When the legion broke away from the column on the approach to Caesarea, the waggons carrying the fallen moved off to where the funeral pyres awaited to consume their subjects. In addition, the medical vehicles departed and followed the *Fretensis* into Caesarea. It was a relief to Lucius; he had heard the rumours that they would send the refugees onwards to Damascus and Antioch. With the medics in Caesarea, he knew Miriam would be in the town caring for her patients.

There were a few hours of light left, and Lucius wished to locate Miriam. It would be important that she find her uncle, as she would need accommodation. He rose from his cot, stripped off his military garb, and donned a plain civilian tunic and cloak.

Not much later, Lucius and Miriam left the hospital behind them, heading towards Caesarea's large forum.

"Your arm – it is good?" she asked. Lucius confirmed it was comfortable. She looked about her.

"Lucius, this place. It is so big. The buildings… I have never seen before. Is Rome like this?" Lucious laughed,

"Rome? Rome is many, many times bigger than this Miriam. With thousands upon thousands of people living there. Caesarea is just a colony."

"It scares me," she responded.

"So, tell me, do you have any idea where your uncle lives?"

"I have been lucky," Miriam replied. "I helping soldier who thought he know uncle."

Lucius laughed.

"So, you just bumped into a soldier who just knew your uncle!"

"No, Lucius, not that," Miriam retorted. "Soldier ask me why I come Caesarea. I tell him my uncle Jacob is carpenter, he very tall man and always has hair tied at back. People remember him and Rebecca, his wife. She is Carpenter. Soldier drinks at taberna near uncle's workshop."

"That's a lucky break if the legionary is correct. So then, which direction do we go in?"

"It is big, wide road from forum. A short walk soldier's taberna is right side, uncle's workshop left."

"Well, that's not far, so we should be there fairly quickly. When did you last visit your uncle?"

"Four years ago, he and Rebecca visit uncle and aunt at farm. Was quick visit."

"Just passing by?" asked Lucius.

"It is difficult." Miriam paused, and Lucius sensed she was struggling for the words. He wished he spoke Aramaic and made a mental note that it might be helpful, given he was serving in Provincia Judaea. "My aunt and uncle follow Yeshua–like me. Uncle Jacob and Aunt Rebecca, they do not."

"So, they are conventional Jews, then?"

"No, they are…." But, again, she struggled, "nothing."

"Nothing?" asked a slightly incredulous Lucius. Miriam nodded. "No Jewish god, no Roman gods; no other gods?" The young woman nodded; she seemed too embarrassed to say as much. "How interesting. I'm not sure I've met anyone who has no gods."

Miriam found her voice again.

"Lucius, Uncle Jacob, good man. Is different."

"Well, my honey, I look forward to meeting him."

The street they moved along ran into the forum, and on the other side, Lucius spotted a road such as the soldier had described, being wider than the other exits. As the sun dropped in the sky, traders were still busy at their work with customers aplenty. Lucius and Miriam passed through them purposefully, getting past the hustle and bustle as quickly as possible. Lucius would have loved to have taken Miriam's hand, but he worried about the unwanted attention it might attract. He wore a plain civilian tunic, but all and sundry could see he was a Roman. The quality of his clothes spoke volumes. Whatever Miriam's religious convictions, in the eyes of the populace, she was a young Jewish woman. The two of them, Roman and Jew, in public and unaccompanied, raised the odd eyebrow in the crowd. Taking her hand would be a step too far, and they both recognise this, always keeping a space between them.

The soldier had accurately described the road; it was wide and very straight. Within a few seconds, Lucius spotted the taberna in the distance. Pointing out the destination to Miriam, it occurred to him they had not discussed how they would approach the carpenter and his wife. Would they offer Miriam accommodation? In Lucius' view, it was a big ask. He raised it with Miriam.

"I am family," she replied. That was it—no further comment. Lucius realised that he had much to learn about Jewish traditions. He imagined the bartering that would occur if this situation arose in Rome.

They approached the carpenter's workshop from the far side of the road and stood outside the taberna taking in the business. Running across the front of the building was a large lean-to that turned and ran down one side. Fronting the lean-to, there ran a waist-high wooden wall. It was well constructed, equipped with pull-up shutters for when not in use. Inside, a man crouched over a workbench with a chisel, concentrating on gently tapping a mallet onto the chisel's wooden head. Miriam dabbed Lucius on the arm.

"That is Jacob. Come," she said as she stepped out to cross the road in the workshop's direction. Lucius followed in her wake. When she stopped, she stood at the entrance. Lucius halted a respectable distance behind. "Jacob bat Yaholem?" she asked. The carpenter ceased his tapping but remained leaning over his workbench.

"And who would want to know?" The voice had a distinctive, deep resonance. Lucius was silently grateful the man had responded in Greek and not Aramaic. Miriam paused two seconds before answering.

"Your niece. Miriam bat Yaholem." For a second, the man did not move; then, he stood up slowly and turned in the voice's direction. Yes, thought Lucius, he is tall. The carpenter looked Miriam up and down before a smile spread across his face.

"Miriam, by all that is good, you have grown up." He placed his mallet and chisel on the bench and walked across to the entrance, hugging his niece. Then, turning towards the interior of the workshop and the door that led into the building proper, he called out, "Rebecca, come here. I have a surprise for you." Then, turning back to Miriam, he said, "She will be so happy to see you."

Glancing over Miriam's shoulder, the carpenter spotted Lucius as he stood watching the proceedings. The man visibly stiffened.

"Are you going to introduce me to your friend?" He moved slightly away from Miriam as he spoke, and Lucius interpreted it as positioning to shake hands. It gave Lucius his first full view of the carpenter. Tall and powerfully built, he had a full Jewish beard, with his hair pulled back into a horse's tail. The hair that had once been jet black betrayed his age, speckled with grey. A large brown leather carpenter's apron protected his tunic. Lucius was about to proffer his hand when Rebecca disrupted the scenario.

"Heavens above! Miriam, it is you! You have become a woman!" The small group of three promptly turned as Rebecca rushed across the workshop to throw her arms around her niece. If the carpenter were a memorable character, Rebecca would also be one not to forget. The first surprise was that she dressed almost identically to her husband with woollen leggings to maintain some female decorum. Like her husband's, her hair was drawn back and was speckled with grey. What struck Lucius immediately was not the commonality with her spouse, but her one differentiator. She was also ageing, but he thought she must have been beautiful when younger. Even with age, the high cheekbones, the full lips, and the large dark eyes would turn any man's head. It all seems so incongruous in the attire of a carpenter. She hugged her niece and then stood back to take her in. "What a wonderful surprise, Miriam; it is so nice to see you." Then, just as her husband did a few seconds earlier, she spotted Lucius. "Oh, you have company?"

"Yes, she does," a husband responded, "and I've a suspicion it is Roman company."

"Uncle Jacob -."

"Miriam, I think we can drop the uncle and aunt now that you have grown," the carpenter said gently.

"Jacob, Rebecca, I have much to tell. First, you are right that my.... friend -" she flicked her wrist to indicate to Lucius that he should join the small group, "- is Roman. He is optio IV Cohort. He is Lucius Decimus Petronius. He saved my life."

"Miriam, what on earth happened?" Carpenter's wife asked. Before Miriam could reply, the carpenter's deep voice cut into the conversation.

"If you saved my niece's life, the family's indebted to you. The least we can do is offer you refreshment. So, let's go inside and hear what Miriam has to tell." He held out a hand to Lucius and Lucius shook it, though he felt the invitation was recognition of debt rather than an act of friendship.

As they moved through the workshop, they passed all the paraphernalia one would expect to find in the carpenter's workshop: workbenches, treadle, lathes, chisels and mallets and a fair amount of half-finished furniture and cabinets. However, what caught Lucius' eye lay in one corner of the workshop, where a magnificently carved bull sat close to completion. The bull sat collapsed on the ground as the figure of a man plunged a knife into its neck. The carved creature's size was that of a dog, but the detail stunned Lucius; he expected the frozen cameo to move at any minute.

"That is magnificent," said Lucius, gesturing towards the carving. "Mithras?" he asked, surprised to find the effigy of a Roman military god in a Jewish workshop.

"I do the routine stuff," the carpenter said. "The bull is Rebecca's work; Mithras slaying the bull. The piece is for the new Temple of Mithras. She's been working on it for weeks."

They entered the principal room of the building, and three of them sat around a simple wooden table whilst the carpenter's wife produced bread and olives, complete with a large jug of fruit juice. The table surprised Lucius. It was of a worn condition and design found in many simple homes in Caesarea. Noticing Lucius looking at the table, the carpenter said,

"You were expecting something of better quality and construction, my new Roman friend?" he said, "I'm afraid that I'm too busy applying my skill to customer's requests to spend time on my tables." He laughed. "Rebecca's sister is a highly skilled seamstress, yet she dresses like a washerwoman!"

Lucius smiled and recognised the truth in the carpenter's words.

"I understand, my friend, but a soldier is quite different. In his case, he *is* the product. If he is of poor quality, he dies."

"I can see that," the carpenter replied. "I think I will just stay with my carpentry."

Rebecca joined the trio at the table, handed them beakers and wooden platters, and invited them to eat. She sat beside her husband.

"Miriam, it is so good to see you again," the carpenter said. "You said you have so much to tell. My ears await your words."

Miriam returned the olive she was about to pop into her mouth to the plate, pausing for a second to gather her thoughts.

"I will tell you news in Greek," she said. "Lucius will understand. He is not long our country." She flashed Lucius a smile. "Jacob, I am hurt to tell your brother Ephraim, my uncle, is dead."

Rebecca took a sharp intake of breath. The carpenter also returned his food to his plate. He reached across the table and took Miriam's hand.

"Miriam, when you arrived, accompanied by a Roman and didn't mention my brother, I knew your visit was not simply social." Rebecca placed an arm over her husband's shoulder. The carpenter continued, "Before this year is out, I believe thousands will be dead, but my brother is my brother. I would like to understand what happened before I grieve for him." Miriam took a breath and was about to speak when he added, "and what happened to you, my girl?"

Miriam turned to Lucius.

"It will be easy for me if I speak Aramaic." Lucius nodded in response.

"I understand."

It took Miriam quite some time to tell a story that began with her leaving her life as a Judaean country girl working on a smallholding in the hills and ending with her many miles away as part of a medical team in the Roman army. Carpenter and his wife remained silent throughout. Occasionally, a name would arise that Lucius recognised. Understanding nothing else of what she said, Lucius focused on the small group's facial expressions and how they changed in unison as the subject of the conversation altered. He combined the names with facial expressions, which gave him some idea of Miriam's story. Finally, she came to an end, followed by a few moments of silence, broken by the carpenter. He turned to Lucius and spoke in Greek again.

"It seems that I've a debt to the Roman army for the life of my niece." The bullish, vocal presence that Lucius had first experienced was now much softer. Perhaps, he thought, it sounded tired. "Invariably, whenever we met, Ephraim and I used to argue over religion – I've little time for it—and he thought Rebecca should spend more time in the kitchen. We saw little each other, but we both felt the bond of brotherhood. Ishmail, our son, used to look forward to Ephraim's and Natanya's visits. It will disappoint him to hear the news. Now, Ishmail and Miriam are all that's left of the family."

Rebecca reached across and took his hands.

"Jacob, Ishmail is safe, and Miriam has walked through the valley and is with us safe and sound." She squeezes hands.

"Perhaps we should be thankful that the news was not worse. We've been granted a small mercy." The carpenter slowly nodded his head. Lucius felt as though he was an intruder on a very private occasion. He pushed back his chair and stood.

"Excuse me. I'll get some fresh air and leave you alone for a while."

Suddenly, the voice was back.

"Nonsense, sit down, my Roman friend – perhaps I may call you Lucius – and eat. It is what it is, and I know I shall often recall my time with Ephraim, but life continues. Rebecca is right." He turned to Miriam. "You cannot have anywhere to live. Rebecca and I would welcome you here. Since Ishmail left us, we have just been rattling around on our own." Miriam glanced at Lucius, then turned to her uncle, who had not missed the glance. He smiled. "Perhaps I should've added that Lucius would be a welcome visitor."

"Jacob, Rebecca, that good of you both. It make me happy to be in your home." She followed with a minute of Aramaic, but it was apparent that the decision overjoyed all parties. The carpenter then turned to Lucius.

"It is decided, then. Let us set aside these juices," he said, pushing his beaker to one side. He left the table, disappeared into an adjoining room, and returned with a pitcher of wine. "Perhaps a small celebration is called for; my niece is safely home in Caesarea." As the carpenter sat down, his wife went to fetch new beakers.

"Jacob, you have a son?" Asked Lucius.

"Ishmail, yes I do." He turned to Miriam. "How many years has it been since you last saw Ishmail, Miriam?"

"Five years? He was older than a child but still a boy." Miriam responded. "Where is he today?"

"It will surprise you," the carpenter answered. "Caesarea is by the sea, and Ishmail always had a fascination with boats. An old friend of mine has a fishing boat and is a partner in a trading galley. He said Ishmail was a natural sailor, so he taught him everything he knew: navigation, ropes, sails, tides – you know – all that watery stuff." He emitted a deep, resonant laugh. It was not so funny, but the others joined in the humour. "He sailed for my friend for, it must be, two years. Then he shocked us all – he joined the Roman Navy." The carpenter, noticing Lucius' eyebrows raise, laughed again. "Don't worry, Lucius, he's not an oarsman. He works on the deck. Also, he must be good at it because he's now in charge of men."

Lucius's thoughts returned to his sea voyage from Italy to Caesarea on the galley, commanded by Trierarchus Amyntas. For all he knew, Ishmail may have been a crew member.

"So, he's seen a lot of the Empire, then?" he asked.

"He seems to remain local. Egypt, Cyprus – that kind of area," the carpenter replied.

"Will he be home soon?" Miriam queried.

"You'd better ask his captain that question," came the answer. Then the carpenter deliberately turned to Lucius. "My fellow countrymen butchered my brother and his wife, not Romans or their auxiliaries, but fellow countrymen. My niece, nearly murdered twice. They drive the Roman army out of Judaea. What is going on, my Roman friend? I hear there is even crazy talk in Galilee!"

"In truth, Jacob, we grew complacent. A clever, devious man named Simeon ben Koseba patiently and carefully planned a major revolt against Roman authority. When he was ready, in his own time, he trounced us completely."

"What'll happen?"

"Let me just say," Lucius responded, "I'm thankful to the gods that Miriam is safe here in Caesarea, for I fear Rome will unleash all hell upon Judaea."

Lucius Petronius walked along the Cardo Maximus the next day, which ran southward through Caesarea. Following the road, he passed through the wall built by King Herod centuries earlier, leaving the colony. He dressed as a citizen, clad in a tunic and light cloak with a hood resting on his shoulders, which conveniently hid his left arm, sat in its sling. Only his heavy caligulae on his feet betrayed his military origins.

Not far beyond the old Herodian gate, several tombs lined the road. It was a Roman tradition that burial always takes place outside the city boundaries. To find cemeteries dressing the approaches to towns was not uncommon. Lucius' destination was a large tomb adorned with a fine equestrian carving on its side. He estimated the work to be half life-sized, yet it would not be missed by a passer-by, the intent of the tomb's occupant, as it was Lucius'. It was here that he had arranged to meet Miriam. The road ran through some light woods past the graves from where pathways meandered down towards the coast. While exploring these tracks, Lucius intended to get to know Miriam better and share his past with her.

The cemetery approached, and he spotted Miriam studying the carving on the side of a large tomb. Pedestrians and carts plied the busy roadway, and Lucius was nearly at her shoulder before she turned towards him.

"Lucius!" She looked him up and down. "You come."

She was in a full length light blue tunic. In addition, she wore a head shawl that fell across her shoulders and lay wrapped around her neck, concealing much of her hair.

"And you look lovely!" She stepped forward and kissed him on the cheek.

"It is good to see you. Your arm – is better?"

"Becoming so; sore but improving. The medic says three days before I can get rid of the sling, so roll on tomorrow. Let's walk." They set off down the road, Lucius keeping an eye out for one of the sea-bound tracks. Very conscious of the woman walking beside him, he maintained a polite distance.

"You know Miriam, this is strange. In Rome, things are so different. My father would've identified a family like ours who'd have a daughter of marriageable age. They'd agree to the relationship, arrange a dowry, and they would organise a marriage. I'd have little to do with it - and no choice." A few seconds passed before Miriam responded. She needed to translate and comprehend.

"Dowry, Lucius. What is dowry?" she asked.

"The girl brings money to the marriage. It's an old tradition."

"Ah, *Nedunyah*," she said, "we have like that too. In Judaea, it is father who tells his daughter."

"It is strange to wander so publicly with a woman," Lucius said. A frown came over Miriam's face. "Is there something wrong?" he asked. She stopped walking and turned to face him.

"Lucius, are we right?"

"Right?"

"I am Jewish girl from farm in Judaea," she shrugged and held her arms out, "only now I learn Greek. And you," she stood back looking him up and down, "You from great city Rome. You Roman officer. My people and your people fight."

Lucius understood her feelings. The two came from different worlds and social positions, but inside him lived a rebel. He had walked away from the city of Rome and his father, intent to do what he believed. He looked at the woman before him and trusted his intuition in this matter.

"Miriam, the other night, I said we'd find a way through. I promise you, we'll do so," he said, "Let's keep walking. There is much to talk about."

Just down the road, they turned up onto a track that led in the direction of the coast. Over the next two hours, they talked. Lucius gave her his life story; it was a slow process as the world of Rome was an alien concept to the girl from the Judaean hills. Her story was simple, as she had told Mordechai when they found her at the farmhouse. When Lucius considered the circumstances of their first meeting, he was amazed to think she was now an accepted, albeit temporarily, part of the Medical Optio's team in a Roman legion.

They were heading back through the woods towards the road when Lucius stopped. They faced each other.

"Miriam, I don't want us meeting in the shadows forever. He drew her to him and kissed her. For a second, she tensed before relaxing in his arms. Finally, he released her, and she took a step backwards, her shawl fallen from her long black hair, and smiled at him.

"Roman officer always find way!" she said and laughed. She hugged him, and then they both continued towards the major road. Just as they approached the broad, paved carriageway, Miriam stopped.

"Lucius, I must—er…" she pointed to the greenery that grew between the tall tree trunks. A second passed before Lucius understood.

"I'll wait for you at the road," he said, pointing towards the junction that lay a short distance ahead. As Miriam disappeared amongst the greenery, Lucius ambled towards the carriageway, chuckling to himself. A fine bay horse was cantering his way at the intersection, the rider exuding confidence of one accustomed to moving on horseback. Lucius stood back to allow the rider to pass.

"Great Jupiter," he declared, "Mordechai!"

The horseman pulled in the reins, and the beast slowed from a canter to a stand. The rider looked down at the nondescript man who had addressed him, his expression passing through puzzlement to surprise.

"Lucius Petronius, what on earth--." At that moment, Miriam reappeared and realised who the young woman was. "Miriam!" His mind worked quickly. A Roman officer in civilian garb is coming out of the woods with a young Jewish woman. A smile quickly spread across Mordechai's face. "My friends, I will not speak of this to anyone." He effortlessly slid from his saddle to the ground. He approached Lucius and held out his hand.

"Salve, Mordechai, believe me, this isn't what it looks like!" Lucius said, grasping the other man's wrist. "It's good to see you, my friend. What brings you to Caesarea?"

Mordechai noticed the arm in a sling, partly hidden by Lucius' cloak.

"Your arm?"

"I was in a small scrap, but it is mending."

Mordechai turned to Miriam.

"You are keeping well?" He didn't wait for an answer and responded instead to Lucius' question. He nodded to the track the other two had recently traversed. "Let's get off the road. You never know who might pass." He set off down the pathway, walking his horse, Lucius and Miriam following on behind. Mordechai spotted a clearing in the woods and moved off the track. The area, cleared by woodcutters, had several tree trunks lying around, probably for later collection. They made suitable temporary seating in the short term, and once Mordechai had tied his horse's reins to a branch, the trio sat.

"So, Mordechai, just why have you returned?" Lucius asked. Mordechai, staring at the leaves at his feet, looked up directly at Miriam. Lucius read his mind. "My friend, Miriam would not repeat what she hears here. I assure you." Mordechai smiled.

"To be truthful, Lucius, it is nothing the world will not know about shortly."

"Go on."

"Abandoning Aelia Capitolina has had consequences," he began. "It is now in the hands of Shimeon ben Koseba. He –."

"We had little option," Lucius interrupted, "the colony has no walls, and they heavily outnumbered the legion. Had we stayed, it may have been a glorious last stand but a defeat nonetheless."

"But for the first time in hundreds of years, the Jewish people have sole possession of the spiritual home of Judaism. Lucius, are you familiar with Rabbi Akiva?"

"It's a name I've heard in passing. Isn't he involved with the rebels?"

"He is wise sage," answered Miriam, who was striving to keep up with the Greek conversation, "they say, a wise man."

"Miriam is right," Mordechai confirmed. "He is a great sage who has many thousands of followers. He has declared Shimeon Ben Koseba to be 'Bar Kokhba', which means 'son of the star'. The prophesied King Messiah, who would come and prepare the way for the coming of the one true Messiah. The one who would restore to Israel the kingdom of heaven and the rule of the Lord."

"There shall step forth a star out of Jacob," quoted Miriam in Aramaic. Mordechai raised his eyebrows.

"You have learned your scriptures, Miriam."

"The Book of Numbers. It tell of the Messiah." She replied.

"This is all very interesting," said a mildly irritated Lucius, "but what does it mean?"

"One of our greatest sages declares one of our greatest warriors, who has just liberated Jerusalem, is the prophesied King Messiah, said Mordechai, "and it means that the whole of

Judaism will rise to support him. Moreover, many will return to Judaea to fight by his side. In short, this revolt has turned into a holy war."

"This Akiva, the great sage," said Lucius, "are all the other rabbis behind him?" Mordechai laughed.

"I think I mentioned to you once before, Lucius, we Jews are never happy unless we are arguing amongst ourselves," Mordechai replied. "Rabbi Yohanan ben Torta heard Akiva's declaration. He laughed at him and said that the grass would grow through Akiva's cheeks before the Messiah came to Israel!"

"So, it's not a foregone conclusion that this will become a holy war?"

"Lucius, the minute Rabbi Akiva made his declaration, his followers fled the *Mishnah*, the religious school, to spread the word that the Messiah was coming. So, no matter what Rabbi Yohanan may believe, it is already too late."

"So what brings you hotfoot to Caesarea?" Lucius asked.

"I carry a message for the governor from the rabbis in Jamnia." Mordechai paused. Lucius knew that in sharing the content of the message, he was moving close to breaking a confidence. "Naturally, I was not a party to the writing of the letter."

"If you were to guess the content," said Lucius, "what do you think it would be?"

Mordechai hesitated. Miriam stared at him, focusing hard on keeping up with the Greek to Aramaic translation going on in her head. Mordechai was biting his lip as he struggled with his conscience. Finally, he spoke.

"Shimeon bar Kokhba has lit a fire that burns throughout Judaea. The many in the Mishnah in Jamnia wish to disassociate themselves from the revolt. No matter how successful bar Kokhba has been, they fear he will bring down terrible destruction upon Israel." After a very brief pause, he smiled. "Of course, I'm only guessing."

"Mordechai, forgive me, but I have a question." Lucius looked earnestly at Mordechai. "You are a Jew. Do you believe this man to be the Messiah?"

In response, Mordechai laughed.

"Fear not, my friend, I am not about to slaughter you on the spot!" Quickly he became serious again, "In Scripture, there is a range of criteria to determine the Messiah's coming; one of which is the return of the ten tribes of Israel to our land before a Messiah can appear." He looked about him and continued, "I am not sure I can see the return of one tribe, let alone ten. Does that answer your question, Lucius?"

"Apologies, Mordechai. I mean no offence."

"None taken, my good friend. Though I suspect that Miriam and I could debate Messiah's for the rest of the day!"

"God sent Yeshua," Miriam said. Lucius's mind was racing, and he had no wish to delve into a theological debate on Jewish belief. He also wanted Gaius Civilis, the tribune, to be the first to receive the information that Mordechai carried with him. Civilis could then approach the governor with a prepared plan.

"Mordechai, I would like to arrange an initial meeting with the legion's second in command. He could then accompany you to meet the governor."

Even before he responded, Mordechai's expression signalled he was not comfortable with Lucius' suggestion.

"My friend, I'm acting as an ambassador for the Mishnah at Jamnia. So they instructed me to address the governor only."

"I understand," Lucius said, "May I have your permission to take this news to the tribune Civilis– no one else?"

For a few seconds, Mordechai's face betrayed a puzzlement.

"Lucius, is there something happening here?" he queried.

Lucius could not mention the ongoing investigations that may implicate the governor.

"Not at all," he responded. "The governor is shaken up by what's occurred, and he has his hands full with the refugees from Aelia Capitolina. Consequently, the tribune, in his role of Tribune Laticlavius, has taken responsibility for directly organising the military response to the revolt."

"So, why don't I ask for a meeting with both the governor and the tribune?" Mordechai suggested, "Two rabbits with one slingshot!" A clever build on his proposal, thought Lucius.

Lucius turned to Miriam, unsure how much of the conversation she had understood.

"Miriam, I'm sorry, but we must return quickly." The girl nodded her head. Then, turning to his Jewish friend, he continued, "I'll escort you, Mordechai. It'll make matters easier for you. I'll pass by the barracks and get myself rid of this civilian garb on the way."

As they headed back past the cemetery towards the gates of Caesarea, Lucius had a distinct feeling that the intended few days of rest were about to be cut short.

Lucius Petronius, accompanied by Mordechai ben Zakkai, strode into the Praetorium. The clerk, who had heard the approaching sound of iron-studded military sandals on the marble corridor, sat back in his chair and assumed an air of self-importance.

"Yes?" It was all the man said as he gave them a nonchalant glance. Lucius resisted the urge to punch his lights out: instead, he announced who he and his guest were, and they were here for a meeting with both the governor and the tribune. The clerk pointed to a marble bench and suggested they sit until the governor "was ready."

It had been a hectic few hours since Lucius had met Mordechai on the edge of the woods outside Caesarea. The two had seen Miriam back to her uncles' carpenter shop before going back to the barracks, where Lucius clad himself in his best parade dress. Messengers sped to the tribune and the governor's office, stating the importance of the intelligence that Mordechai was carrying from the *Mishnah* in Jamnia. Not waiting for a reply, two men then set off for the Praetorium, chancing that the messages would have the desired effect. They both understood there might be some delay involved. Their understanding turned out to be accurate.

"Mordechai, you said that the news you carry will soon be common knowledge," said Lucius. "So what is the purpose of your coming here?" Then, after a brief pause, he smirked and added, "I know you are not privy to the contents of the letter."

"I cannot betray the confidence, my friend, but the letter's content will be revealed soon." As he spoke, Mordechai was staring at the floor between his feet. He remained in that position for a few moments longer, then sat upright. "I can tell you this. The sages are uncomfortable with what has transpired. I suspect they want to make that position clear to the governor. But please, Lucius, I really cannot say more."

Lucius took in the Jew's words, nodding as he absorbed them.

"So, you're saying we are not facing the solid wall of revolt in Judaea? Not everyone is keen that the country should take up arms against Rome. Am I right?"

"The letter, my friend, wait for the letter."

"Apologies, Mordechai, I didn't mean to--"

"Optio Petronius, salve!" Tribune Laticlavius Gaius Civilis marched into the room. The two men, involved in their conversation, had missed the approaching footsteps. Lucius immediately stood and saluted the legion's commander. Civilis turned to Lucius, "How's the arm? Getting better, I trust. And who do we have here?"

"Sir, this is Mordechai ben Zakkai. He carries a letter for the governor from the sages at Jamnia."

"A letter for the governor? I am sure it'll interest him, but what is my role in this meeting?"

"Apologies, sir," Lucius responded, "I have not seen the letter. However, I believe it may contain important military intelligence."

Lucius was conscious of the clerk listening to the conversation. Lucius stared directly into the tribune's eyes and flicked eyeballs in the clerk's direction. Thankfully, the tribune understood.

"Well then, we shall have to get this letter read, shall we not?" Civilis turned to the clerk. "Make the governor aware I am here." The clerk slowly pushed his chair back and ambled towards the large doors that led to the governor's office. "And get a move on!" snapped Civilis. He turned to Mordechai. "You must be the ben Zakkai that has assisted the governor with intelligence before, if I recall correctly. If I'm not wrong, you accompanied Petronius here on his clandestine mission before all Hades broke loose in Judaea."

Mordechai had risen at the entrance of the tribune. He was standing tall and straight, adopting the persona of an emissary from Jamnia. He made a slow bow from the hips.

"It is an honour to meet you, Tribune Civilis. May I also say that I'm grateful for your attendance at such brief notice. Given the circumstances we are in, I imagine you are a busy man."

"You are perceptive, ben Zakkai, and also a master of understatement."

The clerk appeared in the doorway, and all heads turned in his direction.

"The Governor requests you join him, sirs." Lucius smiled to himself at the change in the clerk's attitude - it doesn't do to upset a legionary tribune. Lucius and Mordecai stood aside to let the Tribune lead the way, and the three men passed through the doors into the governor's office.

The office differed from Aelia's, where Lucius had last met the governor. That room had been a practical workspace compared to this. They designed this office for one purpose; to reflect power and authority. The floor was highly polished marble, as was the top of the enormous table positioned in front of the rear wall. Two ornate floor standing sconces, unlit, stood in the corners next to the desk. Black wooden cabinets lined one wall, their facias expertly carved with military imagery. For Lucius, the workmanship brought Rebecca's carving skills to mind. In another corner, sat upon a mottled marble column, was a large painted bust of Imperator Hadrian. Tineus Rufus, the governor, stood with his back to the trio who had just entered his office, staring out of the window, enjoying the cooling breeze that passed through.

"Welcome," said the governor. He remained looking through the window. "This must be the first peaceful moment I've had in quite some time. I fear your presence means my peace is shattered." He swung round to face the newcomers. "Find yourselves a stool and let us sit." Saying so, he walked back to his desk and sat. "Gaius, sit yourself here," he motioned to the side of his desk, "You two here," positioning Lucius and Mordechai to the front. They had established the pecking order. "It is a pleasure to meet you again, Optio Petronius. It seems long ago you warned me we might have trouble amongst the brigands. I hope to the gods you are not back to bring me more doom-laden prophecies!" He chuckled at his humour. *Cac,* thought Lucius, that's just what I am about to do. The governor continued.

"Ben Zakkai, I was wondering if I would ever see you again. Under the circumstances, you are a brave man to show your face here in Caesarea." He wafted a hand in Lucius' direction. "I hear the optio believes you carry important information for me. From none other than the rabbis at Jamnia, I understand." So, thought Lucius, the governor's clerk had large ears!

Mordechai reached into a shoulder bag and pulled out a sealed scroll.

"Domine, the rabbis at Jamnia entrusted me with this letter me. I was to deliver it to none other but yourself. In doing so, I discharge my duty. It would honour me to carry any reply to the sages, should you so wish?" As he spoke, he laid the scroll upon the desk in front of the governor.

Rufus took up the scroll and examined it. He gave the tribune a quizzical look.

"Gaius?"

"Sir, this is as much news to me as it is to you," Civilis responded. Rufus opened a small drawer and withdrew a pristine pugio.

"Right, let us read what the rabbis have to say, shall we?" He used the knife to cut the sealed ribbons that held the scroll. Rufus then used both hands to hold the scroll flat on the table. He read the contents of the letter. Lucius noticed the air of confidence around Rufus change as he proceeded through the text. By the time he had finished, his face bore a look of concern. Using one hand, he passed the letter across to Gaius Civilis. The tribune read the contents and returned the letter to the governor, whose tenor changed again.

"You had better explain what the fuck is going on, ben Zakkai. One of your precious rabbis – or sages, as you prefer to call them," he sneered, "has declared holy war on the Roman

Empire. Yet, the rest of his chums write to me, saying it was not their fault. He had broken from the consensus. Just who in Hades does this Rabbi Akiva think he is?" Mordechai was subject to a withering stare. The Jew shuffled in his chair, pulled himself together, and replied.

"Dominus, in my reply, let me answer your last question first," he began, "Rabbi Akiva ben Joseph is one of our most respected sages, yet he is an enigma. He was over forty years old and the son of a farmer before he became drawn to the Torah. He does not have the background of a typical Rabbi. We have a saying; there are none more righteous than the converted. I can say this of Rabbi Akiva. He would wish for nothing more than the coming of the Messiah and the re-establishment of the kingdom of Israel."

"Somewhat more than a wish, ben Zakkai," the tribune said, "our intelligence tells us that this man has been actively working with the rebels over some time."

"As I said, Domine, Akiva is an enigma," Mordechai responded, "but he has a huge following, not just across Judaea, but across the entire land of Israel. The Rabbi visited Jerus – Aelia – after the withdrawal. He returned to Jamnia, and in a consequent meeting of the rabbinate, he declared Shimeon ben Koseba to be 'Son of the Star'." The two senior officers both adopted puzzled expressions. "In our scriptures, there is a prophecy, Dominus, which refers to the King Messiah as 'bar Kokhba', which translates to 'Sun of the Star'. Some rabbis argued with him; they must satisfy other conditions before they can recognise a Messiah, but it was too late, the word was out."

The governor had reverted to his withering stare.

"Ben Zakkai, look me in the eye and answer this question. Do you believe this ben Koseba is, in fact, the son of the star, Bar Kokhba?"

"I know he is not," Mordechai stated. The speed and content of Mordechai's statement surprised Lucius. Believing something and knowing something are different. He wondered if the two senior officers had picked up on it. They had.

"You *know* he is not?" the governor asked. Lucius thought he detected a fluster in Mordechai before he responded.

"Er - as I have said, Dominus, there are several other conditions, all currently unmet, for a Messiah to appear."

"Please go on, ben Zakkai," the governor requested, "Do enlighten us."

"There are several criteria, some greater than others," Mordechai said, "but there is one major factor that must happen before the King Messiah can arrive to prepare the way for the saviour Messiah." He paused, expecting an interrogation around the subject of messiahs, but none came. "The ten tribes of Israel, currently scattered across the world, must come together as one, truly as God's people. It is written and has not yet come about. Therefore, bar Kokhba cannot be the King Messiah."

Lucius was listening intently. When Mordechai stopped speaking, he responded.

"If that is so, how is it – "He stopped. Turning to the governor, he said, "Apologies, Dominus, it was not my intention – "

"No, no, carry on, optio Petronius; it was my question too."

"Given the criteria," Lucius said, "then why are the people of Judaea rising behind a false messiah?"

Mordechai sighed, slowly shaking his head as he did so.

"Dominus, Rabbi Akiva ben Joseph is one of our greatest and oldest sages. As I have said, he has a huge following across the people of Israel and especially in Judaea. If one such as Rabbi Akiva believes ben Koseba is the Messiah, then they will blindly follow. I hope, Dominus, that you will have noted that the *Midrash* in Jamnia has not declared Koseba to be a Messiah. They know only too well the doom he will bring down upon Israel."

The governor and the tribune exchange a glance. It was the tribune who responded.

"The impression I have from reading the letter your rabbis have written, is that they recognise we will retaliate, and it will not be good for Judaea. But they are saying they are not behind this bar Kok - Ben Koseba, so would we leave them alone in any ensuing conflict; in effect, keep clear of Jamnia. Am I right?"

Mordechai stared at the marble tabletop as he considered the question. Then, after a few seconds, he lifted his head to face the governor directly and responded.

"Dominus, not all the rabbis wished for what has come about. Some have tried to talk sense to many who would lift the sword against Rome, but the belief in Akiva ben Joseph is strong. It has been like tossing a burning torch into a dry bush; the fire has almost been instant and is running out of control." The Jew paused before continuing, "Dominus, this is a terrible, terrible moment for Israel."

There was complete silence in the room for a moment, and no one moved. It is clear to Lucius that the governor would have to decide. A scraping sound split the silence as Tineus Rufus pushed back his chair, stood, and returned to his window. He took in the view as his mind worked. Finally, he turned back to the trio sitting at the table.

"Ben Zakkai, I found your rabbis to be affable people when Imperator Hadrian visited Judaea. They were respectful to the Imperator and gave no hint of disaffection to him." His tone was soft and amiable. "I believe what you tell me to be accurate and that the rabbis would rather have no part in what is taking place in Judaea. I would go so far as to say I have an element of pity for the situation." He walked back to his chair and sat. When he spoke again, he adopted the voice of a Roman governor and the controller of two Roman legions. "However, I am placed here by Rome to ensure peace and prosperity in the province, that is something from which benefits both the people and Rome. But, if the province takes a path of revolt, peace and prosperity will be secondary to the rule of the sword. Rome will simply not tolerate rebellion and will do everything in its power to crush those that would rebel against its authority. I have little option in the matter. It is what Rome and the Imperator would expect of me."

Mordechai sat rigid in his chair, speechless. He tried to find words to respond to the governor when Rufus continued.

"However, I would not wish to make those who would hold little truck with rebellion suffer unnecessarily. But I need to be sure that those people are truly against what is happening. Therefore, I have a simple proposition for the rabbis in Jamnia. Should they hand over Rabbi Akiva ben Joseph to Roman authority and declare this not a holy war, I will ensure that the

Roman sword does not enter Jamnia. Over the years of politics, I have learned that it is deeds, not words, which make the man. Let your rabbis persuade me by their deeds, and it will truly convince me of their neutrality."

Lucius sensed Mordechai stiffening in his chair.

"All I ask is you take my reply to Jamnia," the governor continued, "the responsibility for the decision is not yours."

Mordechai stood, his chair hard scraping the marble floor. The Jew bowed formally to the governor.

"Dominus, I thank you for your consideration and it would be an honour to carry your reply, however sad it makes me, back to Jamnia. With your permission, I will return immediately."

"Of course, I'm grateful." The governor turned to Lucius. "Optio Petronius will escort you out of Caesarea."

Lucius stood, and he and Mordechai headed to the door. The governor interrupted them.

"Ben Zakkai, please understand I bear no personal ill will to the rabbis. You are most welcome to remain in Caesarea if you return with their decision. For now, goodbye."

The last words the two men heard as they left the room came from the Tribune Civilis.

"Rome will have to be informed, sir. I can…"

Capitulum XXVI – Herbs and lust

25 Aprilis. Year 16 of the Imperator Hadrianus.

Lucius and Mordechai stopped for refreshment on their return to the gate at a street taberna. It was a stunted conversation, Mordechai's mind elsewhere. At the gate, Mordechai mounted and bade his friend farewell. Then he headed southwards down the road, taking him back to Jamnia. Lucius watched him depart with a sense of foreboding. Would he ever see his friend again?

As he returned to his quarters, a legionary accosted Lucius, requesting that he report immediately to the tribune's office. So, two hours after leaving the tribune, Lucius was to re-join him.

Whilst the tribune's office may not be as grand as the governor's, it was still fine accommodation. It was very comfortable with its marble floor, rosewood desk, and a view across Caesarea. The clerk, who admitted Lucius, left the room, leaving Lucius to stand at attention in front of the tribune's desk. The door closed.

"Take a chair, Lucius," Civilis said. "Sit easy." Lucius understood that this was to be an informal meeting. As he sat, the door opened, and the clerk entered carrying a tray, upon which sat a jug of wine and two finely coloured wine glasses. Civilis spotted Lucius' eyebrows raised at the sight of the glassware. "You know, Lucius, we are both equestrians, so we don't have to act like uncouth soldiers all the time."

The clerk filled the glasses and left.

"So," Civilis went on, "how is our friend ben Zakkai?" he said, pushing a glass towards Lucius. Before answering, Lucius took a sip. The wine was full flavoured.

"Not watered, Gaius?" Lucius asked. "I trust this isn't to loosen my tongue!"

"I'd hope I would not have to stoop so low."

"Maybe not, Gaius, but after a few of these, I would probably tell you anything."

"It is I who am going to do the telling. But before I do, let's return to Ben Zakkai. How was he?"

"He said little about the matter we discussed between us. I would say he was melancholic."

Taking a large sip of wine, Civilis then slowly returned the glass to the table, marshalling his thoughts.

"A few days ago, I enjoyed an excellent dinner with a Jewish merchant and his son, both Galileans. They have supplied the army at Caesarea for many years with horses, tack, saddles, cavalry shields, and other wares. The father is well affected to Rome. He is retiring soon; His son will take over the business. It would be fair to say that the Prefect and the decurions well respect them.

As you would expect, the conversation focused on the tumult in Judaea. However, they were both clear they did not expect Samaria and Galilee to follow suit. They explained why, and I would like to share what they told me. You know of the last great revolt put down by Vespasian and Titus, which saw the destruction of the temple in Jerusalem?"

"Yes, I have a copy of *De Bella Judaea* in my baggage," Lucius replied. "I thought it might be useful in understanding the country."

"Good. Until that time, the Jews had centred their religion upon the temple. Their religious beliefs based on codes– scriptures he called them – were written centuries ago and impacted their daily lives. Yet, they claim the scriptures came directly from their *one god*." He took another large sip of wine. "Even with the gods, the Jews have to be different!" He placed the glass back on the rosewood desktop. "Did you know, as Titus broke through the walls of Jerusalem, the Jews were fighting between themselves over who controlled their great Temple? It made our job of destroying the place easier. Now, we come to the interesting part."

"In the last days of the siege, the Jews used a coffin to smuggle one of their sages out of Jerusalem—at least Cleopatra chose a carpet. A little more dignified I'd say. But, then again, I suppose the sage had no intention of seducing Vespasian!" he chuckled at his humour. "It seemed he wanted was a meeting with the General. The sage was trying to negotiate a settlement to stop the fighting. The general would not play the game and ordered the sage confined. Before being removed, the Jew told Vespasian that he would be a great leader of Rome soon. The general sent him off with a flea in his ear. The story goes that during the night, a dispatch rider rode into the general's camp with news that Imperator Nero was dead and the army in the East had declared Vespasian as Imperator. Vespasian was so impressed with the sage's prophecy that he called the Jew back to his tent and said he would reward him by granting him one wish. The sage requested that he and his fellow sages–or Rabbis– be permitted to form a religious centre in Jamnia after Jerusalem should fall. Vespasian granted the wish."

"I recall the tale. It's in *The Jewish War,* Josephus mentions it," Lucius responded. "But you're not telling me this for entertainment, are you, Gaius?"

"It is merely a preamble to my key point," Civilis said. "With most of the priests, zealots, and other religious leaders dead, it meant that the Rabbis could take control of the Jewish religion. This is where it gets interesting, Lucius." Civilis took a sip of his wine. "Yes, this is indeed a pleasant wine." Returning the glass to the table, he continued. "Until that point, their law was written and god-given. For centuries, in any debate about law or morality, the priests fell back upon the scriptures. According to our merchant, now, things are quite different sixty years later. Over that time, the Rabbis began interpreting the scriptures and producing many new laws. My merchant said that they control all aspects of people's daily lives. Early on, any rabbis who argued against the changes faced ex-communication or execution. It seems the Jamnia rabbis took few prisoners."

"So, you say that the Rabbis have control of Judaea?" Lucius asked.

"Precisely. So, who has been driving this change - a man considered one of their greatest sages?"

A smile crossed Lucius' face.

"Rabbi Akiva ben Joseph." He said solemnly.

"Exactly. But let us go further. This rebellion has been in the planning for quite some time; it is not spontaneous. Are we expected to believe that this has taken place in the face of *disapproving* Rabbis at Jamnia? The Rabbis, with their stranglehold on life in Judaea, let this happen against their will?"

Civilis picked up his glass of wine and poured what remained down his throat, returning the glass to the table.

"Will you refill that for me, Lucius - the sheer audacity of the Jews makes me angry. *We really did not want this war. Please do not attack Jamnia.*" He mimicked. "Do they think we are that stupid?"

"But Gaius, Mordechai mentioned the criteria for a Messiah to arise," Lucius countered, "For example, the tribes of Israel must come together as one." He refilled their glasses.

"You are correct, Lucius. But, as my merchant friend pointed out, those criteria were part of the old written law. The Rabbi's addition of so much more new law of their interpretation to the written scriptures has resulted in Judaeans accepting the rabbi's word as the word of their God. Therefore, if Rabbi Akiva ben Joseph says it is so, then to a Judaean, *it is so.*"

Lucius absorbed the tribune's words; but he needed to clarify his understanding.

"Gaius, the governor must surely know what you've just shared with me."

"Yes, Lucius. He does."

"Then the meeting we had with ben Zakkai was a sham. Why?"

Civilis sipped his wine before replying.

"It involves several factors, Lucius. First, please understand we cannot treat with these people. This uprising must be crushed and crushed brutally. Since the great rebellion that Titus put down, we have experienced repeated revolts from the Jews across the Empire. We have yet to hear formally from Rome, but when the orders arrive, I suspect no mercy for the Judaeans."

"I fully understand Gaius, but why the game with ben Zakkai?"

"That was the governor's idea," Civilis said, "ben Zakkai has been useful to him in the past. He sensed that the man was uncommitted to the revolt, adamant that this Bar Kokhba character is not a messiah. So the governor gave him a reason to return to Caesarea in the belief that he would stay here. You heard the offer."

"I did, and I hoped that Mordechai - ben Zakkai - may have given me some hint of his intentions as he left Caesarea. But, sadly, he didn't."

"The governor believes he will return," Civilis said. "ben Zakkai is well-informed on the goings-on at Jamnia. I suspect he knows more about Bar Kokhba than he has let on."

"Does the governor think he'll make a Josephus out of him?" Lucius asked, referring to the Jewish officer from the earlier great revolt, who, when captured, changed sides and joined the Romans.

"That I don't know, Lucius. What I know is that he sent ben Zakkai off with an offer that the rabbis have to refuse."

"So, we wait?"

"We do, Lucius, we do," said Civilis, "but we have a major task in front of us." He pointed to a table in the corner of his office, "I have the Fretensis' establishment returns sitting on that table. With dead and wounded, we're only six out of every ten men fighting fit. The word has gone out for recruits, but the situation isn't good. The Fourth is the only unit that is up to strength. So far, I've resisted pressure to allocate centuries from the Fourth to other cohorts." He took a large drink of wine. "On an entirely different matter, do you recall legionary Marcus Apollinaris?"

The question called Lucius off guard.

"I do. Quite a character. He was with me in Judaea before all hell broke loose. He often marched close to the edge, don't tell me he's overstepped the mark somewhere."

The tribune laughed,

"Quite the contrary, Lucius. I've been requested a promotion to tesserarius by a tribune who's worked with him in the evacuation. Apollinaris was an 'officer' of the militia we formed as a train guard. It seems he's been invaluable. The militia is retained to settle several refugee groups into Caesarea and then act as an urban cohort. That'll relieve our hard-pressed regulars of unnecessary duties. The militia centurion concerned is a competent ex-legionary centurion, who would like Apollinaris to serve as his tesserarius."

"Even if I wished to, it would not be my place to argue with a Tribune," Lucius responded. "Apollinaris is a good soldier, if somewhat unconventional."

"That may be, but he's served us well in a matter with which we're both acquainted. Apollinaris came across a legionary in a group fleeing from En Geddi, who was injured by a poisoned tipped spear. He was very poorly and rambling. Apollinaris may've only been on the periphery of the matter in question, but he was smart enough to pick up on the man's ramblings. He had them reported back to me. I ordered the best care for the wounded legionary. The medical optio gave him over to the Healer Woman—you may have heard of her – and he has recovered. He is being interrogated."

Lucius's body muscles tensed when Civilis mentioned 'the Healer Woman'. He had no idea Miriam was building a reputation such that the soldiery had given her a name. The tribune noticed him tense in his chair but put it down to his interest in the subject.

"Tribune Sallus did a fine job with the refugees. If he wants Apollinaris attached to his militia as a tesserarius, I'll not stand in his way. But it doesn't end there. What I'm about to tell you is subject to our agreement on secrecy; you will recall?"

"I do, Gaius. I assure you of my promised discretion," Lucius said.

"Good. The legionary that Apollinaris discovered has talked, and I believe what he's told us. You remember the matter of the balsam being sold to the Jews?"

"I do. The story was that the governor was buying off the bandits."

"Your recollections are accurate, Lucius. That is what our wounded legionary confirmed. Auxiliary Centurion Valens recruited six legionaries, working at night, to cut out a supply of balsam and load it on the cart driven by Jews. The legionaries were all sworn to secrecy, receiving a small bonus. Our poor fellow thought he was on official business."

"Did Centurion Valens survive the attack?"

The tribune sat back in his chair, picked up his glass and swallowed the contents, looking pleased with himself.

"That is the question, Lucius. I believe our legionary has given us the answer. It seems a sizable group of survivors from the attack came together in the hills beyond En Geddi. Some wanted to go to Aelia, whilst others felt that much too risky and proposed heading north towards the camp of *Legio VI. Ferrata*. They split up, with our legionary and some others heading to Aelia and Centurion Valens leading a group towards the *Ferrata*. We know what happened to our man's group. I've recently sent an enquiry to the tribune of the *Ferrata* to find out if the other group made it to the camp."

"And if he did?"

"I shall bring him back to Caesarea for interrogation. It must be discreet, certainly, until we know what was going on between the garrison and the Jews in the town."

"Well then, Gaius, we'll have to hope that our centurion reached the Sixth," said Lucius.

"Only time will tell," the Civilis responded. The tribune's tone noticeably picked up. "In the meantime, I should let you get back to your men. The fourth has excelled, and I've learned never to underestimate Aurelius Crispus. It may be some time before we have another crack at these accursed rebels, but it's important to make sure our cohorts are in a state of readiness." He reached across his desk and picked up the container of wine. "But, before you go, Lucius, I believe it right and fitting we finish the contents of this jug."

The next day Lucius re-joined his men, busily regaling him of stories of their three days leave in Caesarea, leaving him with the impression that the tabernae of Caesarea were now more profitable than ever and the whorehouses likewise. Then, with Centurion Crispus busy on legionary business, it fell to Lucius, 'the one-armed optio', to march the 1st Century onto the parade ground and put them through drills. In cases of hangovers and heavy heads, one hour on the drill field was a proven remedy.

As the sun climbed towards its highest point, Lucius gave the men a break of a couple of hours, a make and mends, gave them time to maintain their equipment and repair any damage that may have occurred over the previous days. Afterwards, he moved them back onto the drill field for personal combat training. They ended the day practising attack drills against the 2nd Century. After several practice sessions, the men were tiring. Lucius had pushed them hard. He knew of Crispus' concerns that sitting around in Caesarea could soften the cohort. Long route marches were on the agenda.

With drills finished, the century stood down. Lucius accepted an invitation from Claudius Paulus and Felix Calvus, the Tesserarius and signifier, to join them for an hour in the baths. Before bathing, slaves oiled the three officers, employing strigils to scrape the oil and parade dust off their bodies. The three then plunged into the hot caldarium, relaxing as they talked through the century's adventures in the recent past. Next, the tepidarium, the water cooler, closes the skin's pores. What followed, the frigidarium was a shock to the system. It was a cold-water bath and, after the preceding two baths, it took the breath away. There was no conversation here, but upon exiting the pool, Lucius felt invigorated. Next, Lucius' two comrades suggested a meal in Caesarea – Paulus knew a taberna where the girls were exceptionally accommodating. Lucius declined; he had other plans.

Lucius parted company with his companions, heading back to his quarters where he donned a fresh tunic and cloak, ones he thought would pass as a civilian. As he headed back out into Caesarea, dusk's last rays dropped behind the surrounding buildings. It was not long before Lucius found himself outside of Jacob's workshop. Hoping that Miriam would be home, he knocked on the workshop's door. Much to his surprise, it was she who opened it.

"Miriam!" he exclaimed. The girl looked perplexed.

"Yes, it is me." With her dark hair drawn tight behind her head, a stained apron protected her dress, speckled with tiny green flecks, and her fingers coloured a faint green, there was a distinct air of dishevelment about her. Then, holding her stained palms up in front of her, she added, "Look at me, I prepare herbs."

"Apologies. What I meant was – I was expecting Jacob to answer the door." She grasped his confusion.

"Jacob and Rebecca, they take work for the…" she paused, then found the word, "Mithraeum and tonight attend feast." Lucius glanced over to the space where the carving of the man grappling with the bull had sat. "Lucius, it very good to see you. Please, come inside."

Lucius stepped into the main house, closing the door behind him. Miriam hugged him when he turned back into the room, planted a kiss on his cheek, and then stood back.

"I missed you," she said. "Let me get drink. You like some food?"

"It's been a long day, Miriam; some food would be good."

She looked at his left arm, still in a sling.

"Your arm? It is well?"

"It's fine. I'll be rid of this damn thing in a couple more days," Lucius answered.

Rushing across to a table covered in fresh herbs, she quickly swept them into baskets which she stored away. Within minutes, apron gone and tidied up, Miriam joined Lucius at the table with food and wine. Lucius was relating the events between mouthfuls of chicken stew since he and Mordechai parted company with Miriam the previous day. Some detail he had to omit, but she understood what had happened. As his story ended, Lucius said,

"It is curious how religious beliefs can touch us all, beliefs that have taken Judaea to war."

The young woman spent a few seconds absorbing what Lucius had just said.

"If people believe, they struggle." She looked Lucius in the eye. "Your gods make Rome conquer us?"

"We have gods for many situations, Mars being the god of war, for example. But do the gods tell us to fight, to build an empire? I think not."

"But you have faith in many gods?" Miriam asked. Lucius did not reply immediately. Instead, with his head lowered, he stared at the table for several moments before raising it again.

"You know, when we win a great battle, we say the gods were with us. When we lost, they were not. That may be the case, but I ask myself, why do they let us lose? Why don't they warn us of defeat? Tell us not to fight? Have I ever seen a God?" He sighed, "I can only be truthful with you, Miriam. I often have my doubts. Crispus is right. If you're going to win battles, you train, train and train again. It's skilled soldiers and not gods who bring victory. Having said that, we are a superstitious lot." His tone picked up. "You trust your one God, Miriam?"

"I do, but sometimes hard. The world has much pain. I wonder how Yeshua's father allow suffering. I think he gives freedom, we make choice of pain."

"But, Miriam, you did not choose the death of your parents or that of your aunt and uncle. The horrible sights you saw fleeing Aelia Capitolina were not your choice," said Lucius.

"You are correct," she said as she refilled Lucius' beaker. "Yeshua said these things we must overcome."

"He is right in that," said Lucius. "We learn from our adversity."

Miriam looked puzzled.

"This… adver-sity?"

Her becoming so fluent in Greek, he had forgotten that she could only speak Aramaic not so long ago. He laughed.

"Apologies, Miriam. Adversity is something that is difficult."

She reached across the table and took hold of his free hand.

"I have a religious… adversity," she said in a severe tone. "I would like to talk with you."

Lucius laughed.

"Given what I have just told you, *meum mel*, I am hardly the one to advise you!"

A smile creased her face.

"It is simple adversity, Lucius." She hesitated as she collected her thoughts. "Yeshua was a Jew. Jews have strict rules. My aunt would teach me about men. When we go to village, she would make boys go away. My Uncle would find husband for me. Only then could I know men. It is Jewish law."

Lucius saw an inconsistency.

"I thought the Christians had renounced the Jews?"

The girl's reply held an element of fervour.

"They follow false disciple Paul, who say religion is for all. Yeshua told of one twist his words!"

"Right. But your relatives kept many of the Jewish customs. I understand."

Miriam squeezed his hand, keeping the pressure in place.

"Thank you, Lucius. That is my.... adversity." She gazed into his eyes. "You understand?"

Lucius was not confident he understood.

"So, Jewish custom is your adver – problem?"

"Yes!" she said, as though all was now clear. Lucius put his left hand on top of hers.

"I am sorry, Miriam, but I am not sure I understand. What part of the custom is the problem for you?"

"Lucius, Lucius, before I have not felt this." Again, she paused for words. The exchange became more complex for Lucius, as she battled with a language not her own. "I have seen pain. My aunt and uncle murdered. The vicus. Fleeing from Jerusalem and fighting. I help medicus with casualties. Young men, many die crying for mothers. Many people die – children too." Lucius could see her eyes glistening.

"But you got through it all, Miriam," he said.

"Yes, yes," a tear rolled down her cheek. "Now there is to be war – a terrible war. Many more will die. Jew, Roman, others– "

"But we will protect you in Caesarea."

"But you, Lucius. You are soldier. You will fight! I cannot lose you." The pitch of her voice rose. "I cannot!"

Lucius tried to reassure her.

"Miriam, I agree we had our arses kicked in Judaea, but we've got their measure now. Rome will sort this out; it'll not be mainly Roman legionaries dying. I promise you."

"Lucius, I do not wish to spend my life sad for lost love."

"You won't, Miriam, you really won't," Lucius said. But it puzzled him. "Miriam, how is this a *religious* problem for you?"

Letting go of Lucius' hand, sitting upright on her stool, she placed both hands on the table.

"Lucius, I go against what was taught. Against my religion. I want you. Is wanting love so bad?" Saying this, she rose, untied her hair, and let it tumble across her shoulders. Lucius remained on the stool, stunned, as he interpreted what Miriam had just told him. Rising from his seat, moving to face Miriam, resting a hand on each of her shoulders, he could sense her shivering, and it was not from the cold. He looked into her in the eye.

"Forgive me if I am a little taken aback, *meum mel*, but the only time women have made that proposition to me, there's been a price attached!"

"I promise, no price. Please love me, now!"

She clasped him. They kissed, and any control between them evaporated. He pushed Miriam back onto the table where she sat trembling, as she awkwardly loosened her robe. Lucius removed his tunic and what followed was outright abandonment. Miriam, lying back upon the table, shuddered as waves of unfamiliar sensations and emotions engulfed her. The negligible element of rationality that still occupied a corner of her mind was finding the experience strange, frightening, a little uncomfortable, but also pleasurable. Then, Lucius froze.

Lucius, panting, looked down at the naked girl lying prone on the table. He had never intended it to be like this. He felt ashamed of himself. I have crossed the Rubicon, he reflected. Our relationship has altered forever. What had taken place was altogether different from his previous sexual encounters. He had visualised something more romantic: a comfortable bed, perfumes and all the accoutrements of Venus. But what was taking place was a raw, primitive bonding, the girl lying naked before him, supine, glistening with sweat, akin to a sacrifice.

"Miriam, I'm sorry. I didn't mean it to be like this…. on a table…. forgive me, please. I don't know what possessed me to treat you like that. You're not a vicus whore."

He held his arms out towards her; she took them and drew herself to her feet, flinging her arms around Lucius' neck, holding on as her breathing normalised and heart rate settled down.

"My love, I do not understand – no person teaches me this," she said. "It scared me.... But I do not have the Greek to tell you my heart."

Lucius' hands passed down her back and grasped her cheeks, pulling her close.

"Miriam, *meum mel*, you deserve better than this."

Her response was all efficiency. Backing off, she picked up her crumpled clothing.

"Lucius, my love, bring clothes. Come with me."

Doing as directed, he gathered his clothing and followed a still naked Miriam into a modest chamber set just off the primary room. Lucius had no chance to take in the place, apart from a lit candle and a pitcher of water upon a table beside a draped window. Miriam sat on her bed and invited him to join her.

Lucius was cradling her head on his chest as her fingers wandered in small circles on his stomach a little while later. Why this woman, far removed from sort he had experienced in Rome? She was attractive, but that wasn't it. He felt so complete right then and there; it was a new experience. As they lay flesh against flesh, he was at one with her. He surrendered all rationality when her fingers were too much to bear.

Later, after several sessions of gentle lovemaking, Miriam again lay beside Lucius.

"Is this bad, Lucius? Am I any different from whore? I remember prisoner. He was angry with me. He said I open my legs for Romans."

"To begin with, I am just one Roman!" he quipped before taking a more sincere tone, "And this Roman is in love with you, Miriam. However, at some stage, we must consider the fut-" Miriam placed a palm across Lucius' mouth, warning they should be silent. They could hear Jacob and Rebecca arriving back from the feast as they listened. Fortunately, they presumed Miriam had retired to bed and would be asleep.

Having given the couple enough time to fall asleep, Miriam saw Lucius out of the house. It was a lingering farewell in the workshop, neither wanting to part. After holding each other for a while, he headed back to the barracks. One fact he was certain of with his seed laying in Miriam's body; she was no longer an innocent country girl from the hills of Judaea. She was now his woman. And he felt good.

For the IV Cohort, the next week was a blur of drilling and route marches. His arm functioning again, Lucius led many of these activities in the 1st Century because of Crispus' involvement in receiving and training recruits, putting his recent skills learnt in Capua to good use. Crispus had insisted they should work the men hard, wanting to avoid any chance of 'barracks belly' as he called it. If the senior command had a plan, it was known only to a few, so Crispus was determined his cohort would be ready for instant action. The drills were helpful for Lucius, as he became comfortable leading large bodies of men. He quickly realised he enjoyed the role. He rushed off two notes to Miriam but was too tired in the evenings for any form of socialisation.

On the third day of drills on the drill field whilst showing a legionary the best technique to parry a spear thrust and kill the spearman, Lucius spotted a solitary figure standing on the perimeter of the field. He returned the legionary's weapons, who, re-joined his regular drill partner. Lucius turned towards the lone figure and squinted. Mordechai!

"Carry on, soldiers. I shall return shortly," he called to his men. With that, he strode quickly towards his friend. As he approached, Mordechai smiled, but not the regular smile one might give to a friend; it was a smile of resignation. It said, good to see you in a bad situation.

"So, my friend, you've returned," said Lucius. "What news?"

"We may be friends, Lucius, but please do not patronise me,' Mordechai responded, "I believe you well knew what Jamnia's response would be."

"My friend, believe me, at the time the governor made his proposal, I thought it a tall order," Lucius explained. "Only after you had gone, did I realise it was an offer made to be refused. Apologies that it had to be you bearing the message."

"Accepted. Lucius, you are an optio, not a governor, tribune or general. You and I are just the foot soldiers in this great, bloody game. I hold you no grudges."

"But you've returned, my friend, even though the rabbis have rejected the governor's offer?"

"I have returned. But with a heavy soul and the conscience the weight of a stone." It surprised Lucius to see Mordechai's eyes well up with tears. "Lucius, can we walk?"

"We can." Lucius turned towards his century, working hard on their drills. He spotted his tesserarius gesticulating at a soldier who had dropped his javelin and called out to him.

"Tesserarius Paulus, take over the drill until I return!" The distant tesserarius turned towards his officer and saluted. Then he promptly returned to remonstrating with the errant legionary. "Come, Mordechai; I recall a bench that sits in the shade of a large tree, close to here."

The two men walked away from the drilling legionaries.

"Lucius, what I say is to a friend. God forbid, but I have few of those," Mordechai began. "I tried to explain to the Rabbis that no fight against Rome would end well. Ben Koseba may have had success, but it would not be long lasting. After all, in the Great Revolt, we destroyed the entire Twelfth Legion but still lost the war." For a few minutes, the conversation dwelt upon other failed Jewish rebellions and the outcome for the Jews. They soon approached the bench that Lucius and prefect Faustinas had shared just after Lucius' arrival in Caesarea – it seemed years ago. Fortunately, it was unoccupied, and the two men sat. Lucius removed his helmet. "This may sound like I've lost my mind, Lucius, but I hope that Rome acts and finishes this business as quickly as possible."

"By the gods, Mordechai. There would be many of your own who would have your head for such a thought!" Lucius said.

"They would. But I have good intentions behind what I have said. The least damage that ben Koseba can do before being beaten, the less terrible the Roman reaction will be. Of course, Judaea will suffer for what it has done, but punishment for a major misdemeanour is less than that for a capital crime."

Lucius considered his friend's last statement and could discern logic in his words.

"I think I understand," Lucius said. "You want to limit the penalties Rome may issue upon Judaea?"

"Yes, I do. A quick victory might make the Imperator Hadrianus more magnanimous."

"So, why are you back here? To advise the governor?"

"No, Lucius, there is little I can tell him about military strategy. However, I passed the rabbi's response on to him, and he has invited me to stay."

"Ah, so Josephus was to Vespasian what you are to Rufus, my friend."

Mordechai laughed,

"I'm no writer or historian, my Roman friend," he said before falling back to his previous demeanour. "My loyalty is to Israel. If ben Koseba successfully implements his plans, we'll face a bloody war indeed. He's no fool, as I suspect Rome is understanding. We have two choices – limited damage or a complete disaster. I want no responsibility for destroying my country." He paused momentarily, then spat out, "We must stop Koseba – or he'll destroy us all!"

Lucius let a minute pass for the vitriol to calm.

"I suspect that once we have the recruits, the Fretensis and the Ferrata will move south and sweep ben Koseba out from the hills, Mordechai. We know what we're up against." In his mind, it took Lucius back to when he was persuading Miriam she was safe; it was a strange feeling of repetition. "It'll be over soon enough."

"I'm sure you are right, my friend. Meanwhile, I'm not welcome in Jamnia. I wasn't sure I would get out of the place with my life. They told me I must be with the enemy if I was not with them. If it was not for their hubris of sending an insulting reply to the governor, I might well be dead. So, you'll understand why I prefer to stay here."

"So, you are persona non grata then? Exiled?" Lucius asked.

"Very much so, my friend, at least in Judaea," Mordechai said, "and it's difficult."

"Can I ask you something?" Lucius shared the story that the Civilis had told him at their last meeting, about how the Rabbis had effectively taken over Judaea with a regime of their own, sometimes even conflicting with age-old teachings. When he had finished, he queried Mordechai on the story's integrity.

"It's true that since the Great Revolt, things have transformed. They had to, given the disaster. It's true. The Rabbis have a powerful hold over Judaea – what they say is law."

"So that is why you knew the governor's request would never be accepted by them?"

"Exactly. Exile is the right way to describe how I feel right now. My only motivation is to stop ben Koseba and his accursed war!" Lucius thought Mordechai looked desolate. "There's something else I had for the governor. During the attack on the waggons fleeing Jerusalem – I am sorry, Lucius – Aelia, you seemed to have captured one of ben Koseba's key lieutenants. I don't think you were aware of that. It seems he's still a prisoner."

"That's useful intelligence, Mordechai. He'll know a lot, far more than an ordinary officer."

"Lucius, thank you for your time, my friend," Mordechai said. "I must be away and arrange the accommodation the governor has organised for me. But, surprisingly, at his expense!"

For the refugees from Aelia, many of whom had stayed in Caesarea, accommodation was in short supply. However, the tribune had found Mordechai a room at the Minerva tavern, where ex-legionary Sistus and his wife ran the establishment.

Lucius returned to the parade ground to find his century being marched back to barracks under the command of Tesserarius Paulus.

"They're knackered, sir," Paulus said. "I think they'd appreciate a day's stand-down."

"They've been hard at it, I know. I'll speak to Centurion Crispus when I see him."

With that, they entered the barracks.

Interludum VI

Herod's palace

"So, Yehudah, you've been with the Big One for some time then?" The young man asked, staring at his comrade's left hand, missing the top of the little finger. The other man laughed as he raised his hand in front of his face.

"Yeah, I was one of the last. You know, before the rabbis put a stop to the practice." He turned his hand, "I am proud of it, though; it beats any fancy uniform."

"It must have hurt, surely?"

"They gave us something to drink, which blurred my mind." His eyes fixed on the horizon over the shoulder of his inquisitive friend as he recalled the procedure. "It was quick. They ran a knife around the finger and pulled back the skin. Then, a neat chop with a sharp blade, and they pulled the skin back over the cut and tied it with twine. They pushed the finger into a bowl of brine – Moses, did that hurt – and they cut the excess skin away. Job done." The listener winced. "It's nought, all over with quickly." The story was told with bravado, but Yehudah did not share that he went through the experience with his eyes tight shut, jaw clenched, and breath held; he didn't want to spoil the story.

"Well, Yehudah, I'm with the rabbis on that one!"

It thrilled the young man to be asked to escort his area captain and one of his key lieutenants to the gathering called by their leader, Shimeon ben Koseba. The two men were lounging against a wall that surrounded the open square in the centre of Herodium. Many similar men were massed in the courtyard, companions and guards for those attending the meeting within Herod's old palace. Yehudah and his comrade Zachariah had ridden to this place from their hometown of Capharabis, accompanying their captain. Their horses awaited at the foot of the great mound that was Herodium. The overall commander of the Jewish forces, Shimeon ben Koseba, had assembled a meeting of his senior officers in the town. In the eyes of the Jewish soldiers, for they were bandits no longer, ben Koseba was a wonder. He had achieved what no Jewish leader in the past ever had; he had pushed the Romans out of Judaea. The revered Rabbi Akiva ben Joseph had declared that Koseba was Shimeon bar Kokhba, the foretold warrior Messiah. However, to the soldiers, he would always be the Big One.

"Maybe it wasn't so important," said Yehudah, "they meant the cut to be a test of bravery. Yet we Jews, with or without it, kicked the Romans arse!"

"And we ain't finished yet," added Zachariah with youthful enthusiasm. Yehudah's face took on a serious tone.

"We're not finished, my lad." The square they waited in stood in front of Herod's old palace, on the top of the great mound. Yehudah wistfully looked out across the rooftops below and across to the hills of Judaea. "These hills may be free of the Romans, but the bastards'll be back. The Big One will know this, and he'll have a plan. I fear your sword will taste much blood before we're finally and utterly free of Rome."

"When do you think they will come, Yehudah, before summer or will they wait until-"

The great wooden doors that served as the entrance to Herod's palace creaked open, and men flooded out of the building, moving with a sense of purpose.

"I suspect we'll know better when Eleazer joins us," Yehudah said as he scanned the stream of men leaving through the palace doors, "and here he comes."

Eleazer ben Menashe did not look like a fearsome warrior. He was young, his beard was thin, and he was of light build. His face still bore the flush of youth, but what struck most people upon meeting him was his piercing blue eyes, which were rarely seen in Judaea. They seemed to look right into your being, which made many people uncomfortable in his presence. He may be a captain of a region, but he dressed plainly in a tunic, the typical clavia of the region, which bore two broad vertical stripes front and rear. A woollen cloak covered the clavia hiding his baldric and sword. A bag was slung over his shoulder. As he approached his comrades, his face spread into a smile. If his eyes made people uncomfortable, his smile was such they would quickly warm to him.

Shimeon ben Koseba did not appoint Eliezer Ben Menashe for his skills as a warrior. Eliezer had two skills that impressed: superb organisation capability combined with natural leadership. When offered command of the Capharabis area, Eliezer turned to the older, more experienced fighters in the room. He explained he was no master of the sword. To his surprise, the men declared that there were plenty of those. They lacked what he could bring. Eliezer melded his men into an efficient fighting unit whilst earning a reputation for his military strategy. He ran the Romans ragged in his region and inflicted many casualties on Legio X Fretensis.

As he approached his waiting escort, he could not help but smile; they were such a contrast. Yehudah, a fighter of many years of experience and well respected by his comrades became Eliezer's chief lieutenant. He may have flecks of grey in his otherwise dark hair and the look of a rustic shepherd, but it belied a superb fighting ability. Additionally, the man had an extraordinary knowledge and understanding of the Judaean hills. He knew places where a general could hide an army. And then there was young Zachariah, inexperienced, rosy-cheeked but keen to earn Eliezer's approval. Eliezer saw a reflection of his youthful self in the lad, and he thought he had promise. If he could only overcome his lack of confidence.

"You've eaten?" asked Eliezer.

"Not long ago, chief," said Yehudah. "How'd it go in there?"

"We can talk as we go. Let's mount up, there is work to do, and we need to get back."

Descending the hill that Herodium sat upon took a few minutes and Eliezer remained silent. His two companions knew he would talk when he was ready. It was not until they mounted and on the open road, the commotion of the town behind them, that he spoke. Due to the heat, they were walking their horses, which made the conversation much easier.

"The Big One has plans that reflect his name—big ones!" His two companions moved their horses closer to Eliezer and waited for more from the leader. It was forthcoming. "He plans to begin the rebuilding of the Temple."

"All praise to the Lord of Hosts, but that'll be a lifetime's project," said Yehuda, "I'll be long gone before that is complete!"

"His thought is to build a small temple, so sacrifice and rituals can quickly begin again."

"That'll piss off Hadrian. He thought he'd shagged our plans for a temple!"

"Possibly. But that's not everything. The Big One intends to over-stamp Caesar's coins. So we shall very soon be using Jewish shekels, stamped in Jerusalem."

Yehudah slapped his thigh.

"I like this man. He always said he'd set up a free Jewish state, a land governed only by God's laws. And now, he's showing us he means it."

"There's more, Yehuda," Eliezer said, "He intends to retain the existing Roman districts, each having a parnas to act as mayors. Each district will give taxes, but there'll be no money going to Rome; it'll all be for the state of Judaea. There'll be strict observance of the Law – Hebrew law. He's banned Pagan practices, as well the heresy of Christianity, along with its followers."

Yehuda was about to respond when Zachariah cut into the conversation.

"The Big One has said those who don't fight with us must be against us. Those Christians have made their choice and must live by it. The Lord will not tolerate heresy!"

The other two riders exchanged glances; it was rare that Zachariah spoke out with such force.

"By Caesar's arse, when did the Christians piss you off, lad?" asked Yehuda.

The fire subsided in Zachariah, and it left him feeling not a little embarrassed.

"They didn't - haven't–what I mean, it is what the Big One has said, and he is right."

Eliezer laughed.

"He is? Well, I must let him know!" He saw that he was causing the young man even more discomfort. "I'm sorry, Zachariah. You are, of course, correct and right to say so. There won't be many followers of Yeshua left when this war is over." He let the words sink in and for Zachariah to recover his self-respect before he continued. "However, there's work for us. The Big One has decreed that we fortify every village and town and do it with haste. The Romans will return, and he intends to make life difficult for them. With the settlements fortified and our knowledge of the hills, they'll rue the day they tried to retake Judaea."

"Do we have any word when they'll return, Eliezer?" asked Zachariah.

"We don't," their leader said, "We suspect they'll want to lick their wounds and reinforce their cohorts before returning. However, the Sixth Legion in Galilee has yet to engage. So, my guess is they'll attack simultaneously from different directions. But let's not forget, they must come into the hills, and when they do, they'll be fighting on our ground - and we outnumber them too."

Capitulum XXVII – Seeking the rabbi

6 Maius. Year 16 of the Imperator Hadrianus.

Aurelius Crispus gave the century a day's break from drilling—but not regular duties; no, he was not that soft. Crispus sought Lucius, who was conferring with Claudius Paulus and Felix Calvus about the next morning's exercises at the end of that day. The little group was in the refectory, having just finished supper.

"Optio Petronius, we need to talk," Crispus called across the room.

"We can conclude this later," Lucius said to his fellow officers. He rose from the table and crossed to the doorway, where Crispus waited. Lucius was not sure quite what to expect. Had a 1st Century legionary stepped across the mark somewhere? "Yours to command," he said as he pulled up in front of Crispus.

"Come on, lad, let's find someplace that flapping lug 'oles can't hear us." He strode off towards the Praetorium and found an empty room after trying a few doors along the main corridor. "This'll do. Grab a stool." Lucius did as instructed. The two men removed their helmets, and the atmosphere became more informal. "Well, Lucius. It seems your chum Ben Zakkai has been quite useful to us already."

"He has?" Lucius asked, his interest piqued.

"Yes, he has. He tipped us off to a prisoner posing as a junior officer who, it turns out, is one of Ben Koseba's right-hand men. The interrogators promptly set to, and he's talking. Thank Zeus we took steps to ensure he lived."

"The man must have been cunning for us to miss his rank for so long?"

"He was, and for such a 'lowly officer', he had an arrogance to him that should have alerted us," Crispus said. "Still, to business. He let slip that our friend Rabbi Akiva likes to visit where he became inspired to join the religious ranks. Did you know he was not a young man when it happened? He had been a simple farmer until then. I digress. He goes off for two days for 'prayer and reflection'," Crispus sneered. "He always goes on the anniversary of the day he left his village. What's more, we have that date!" Lucius was wondering just where the conversation was leading when Crispus continued. "And Lucius, my boy, we are going to grab him!"

Lucius suppressed his reaction to the news.

"That's interesting, Aurelius, and how do we do that?" The response was not quite what Crispus had expected. Still, he ploughed on.

"He goes to the village. It's called Serifin, not too far from Lod. It's about seven miles or so from the coast."

"So, we're going to march through Judaea, seize him and bring him back to Caesarea?" There was a distinct tone of sarcasm in Lucius' voice.

Crispus laughed.

"If it were that simple, Lucius. No, we shall sail down the coast, go ashore, grab the bastard and sail him back to Caesarea."

"Aurelius, who exactly is *we*?"

"I've volunteered the IV Cohort for the job." The news stunned Lucius. Crispus continued, "It's only a possibility right now. We'll need to consider its feasibility. If we can get this bastard, Lucius, it'll change the face of this war." Lucius thought quickly. There might be some sense in the idea. He recalled Alexander the Great's maxim, "Kill the King". Akiva may not be the 'King', he believed Ben Koseba filled that role, but Akiva must be the Crown Prince. Capturing him would be a massive blow to the Jews. Sitting back in his chair, crossing his arms, he said,

"So, when do we plan?"

"Tomorrow morning in the Tribune's office. You, me, Paulus and Calvus for now, not forgetting Tribune Civilis. We'll involve the navy if we think it's a practical plan. Don't say a word to anyone; simply tell the others they will attend. We have to keep this scheme deep within the smoke."

Walking back to his quarters, Lucius admitted the prospect of another task in the field excited him. He had thought that the coming months might be a life of constant drilling and marching, but now he faced something much more meaningful and vital in the struggle to regain Judaea. He had to crush an urge to rush over to the carpenter's shop and share the news with Miriam. That could never happen.

The following day Lucius was joined by his tesserarius and signifier. As instructed, he made no mention of the meeting's purpose. At the Principia, Crispus greeted them, and they all proceeded to an appropriate office. Civilis was waiting for them, and they all took seats around a table after pleasantries. The tribune began the meeting.

"So, men, we have been presented with an opportunity. The question is the feasibility of it. Let me precisely describe what we have." Civilis then ran through the facts given to them by the prisoner. Lucius smiled as he saw the surprise on the faces of the two junior officers.

The meeting lasted over an hour. The outcome was a preliminary plan that would involve a bireme arriving at a disembarkation point near the settlement an hour before sunrise. Disembarking, legionaries would march through the growing daylight towards the village. Five tent units would be tasked with blocking the road from Jerusalem, and the remaining units would seek and arrest the Rabbi.

The navy would need to be approached to enable the century to start beach embarkation and disembarkation drills once a bireme for the raid had been selected. Initial exercises would be in the daytime, but later they would be at night. That was possibly the simple part, causing Crispus to raise valid questions.

"In the darkness, how do we spot the landing site? If we go ashore miles up the coast, we'll have a cock-up on our hands. Will we know for sure Akiva will be there? There is a war on, and he may vary his routine. Do we even have any idea of the layout of this village?"

Civilis nodded as Crispus spoke.

"Valid points, Aurelius, and damned important ones too. I doubt our prisoner has ever been to the place." For a few moments, there was silence as all parties considered Crispus' question. It was clear that the application of military force was straightforward; its precision counted. Then Lucius broke the silence.

"We need to inspect beforehand. Even better, to have a unit in the area to spy out the village, confirm Akiva's presence and to guide the boat in."

"Well," said Crispus, "it didn't take you long to get there!"

"You are correct, Lucius," Civilis added, "and as our experienced scout from a previous operation, could you do it?"

"Me?" Lucius asked in disbelief.

"Lucius, your work for the governor was exemplary," said Crispus, "and we need an officer's eye on this. An accurate understanding of the situation will be an essential component of the raid." There was a silence as Lucius considered Crispus' words. As a final push, Crispus added, "It's a village – not a bleedin' fortress. You'll have no trouble with it."

Judging he had limited options, Lucius agreed to the proposal.

"All right, I'll do it." Everyone smiled. "But I want the men from the governor's operation with me. Ben Zakkai is a jew and speaks Hebrew, Aramaic, Greek, and Latin. Postumus is Gallic and looks it. Apollinaris could be from anywhere on *Mare Nostrum*. Me? I could pass as Greek. Also, I want Atelius along as he is African."

"Ben Zakkai!" Crispus suddenly blurted out, "Fuck me, lad. He's one of them!"

"In Mars' name, Lucius," Civilis exclaimed, "Are you taking an army?" Crispus sat in his chair, his jaw slack.

"Ben Zakkai is one, and yet he isn't," Lucius replied. "He worked well with us before. Had they not allowed him to return from Jamnia, the Jews might have executed him. However, he understands Jews, which may be useful on the ground."

Civilis supported the concern about Mordecai ben Zakkai before moving on.

"So, Optio," he said, "Do you have as much as a hazy idea about how you intend to accomplish the task?"

"Yes, sir. Simply, we are off to join Bar Kokhba. Well, at least that'll be the cover story."

"Hades, you think quick, lad!" said Crispus.

"It just hit me," Lucius responded. "We'll hide in plain sight; we shall appear as their friends. It's what we did in the last operation, and mostly, it worked."

"Take whomever you need, Lucius," Civilis said, "and we must speak with the fish-heads about boats. We'd better get a move on. We have three weeks for this to come together."

Two days later, Lucius was sitting in an office, waiting for a knock on the door. It came, and in walked Marcus Apollinaris. The legionary had orders to attend without knowing who he was meeting or why. Seeing Lucius sitting at the table brought a look of astonishment.

"Hades' breath! Optio Petronius, sir." He came to attention.

"Relax, tesserarius."

"I wasn't expecting to see *you*, sir. What's happening?"

Lucius studied the soldier, now wearing the dress and trappings of a junior officer. But, beneath it, still recognisable, was the Marcus that he remembered. He was short, somewhat dishevelled, and looking mildly shady, along with his memorable Roman nose.

"Congratulations on your promotion, Marcus. You must have impressed someone!"

"Tribune Sallus, sir. Primus wasn't too happy about it."

"I can imagine!" Lucius retorted. "We need to talk. And by the way, you are an officer now, Marcus, and we are informal, so please, it's Lucius." Marcus seemed taken aback by the simple gesture.

"Thank you… Lucius. That means a lot."

"That's fine. What I am about to share with you is extremely secret. If you spill a word, you'll be a soldier again quicker than you can say 'flogging'. Understood?"

Marcus nodded in confirmation. Continuing, Lucius shared the intention to snatch Rabbi Akiva. There was no interruption.

"Have you talked to the others?" Marcus asked when Lucius fell silent.

"No, I'm briefing you first as a fellow officer. We'll both talk to Postumus and Atelius. Leave Mordecai to me. He might need some persuasion."

"Right you are... Lucius. When do you want to meet the lads, then?"

"I suspect soon. A clerk at the entrance is holding them there if I'm not mistaken. He awaits a signal from me to give them entry."

So it was that a few minutes later, Postumus and Atelius joined the two officers. Upon entering, they came to attention. The confusion on Sextus Postumus' face was unmistakable.

"Relax, men, and please sit down," Lucius instructed. Marcus spotted his old friend's puzzlement.

"Not my doing, brother," the new tesserarius replied, "I'll tell you about it after."

"Atelius, my apologies," Lucius said. "These two know each other well, and I have mentioned them to you in the past but let me introduce you." Lucius ran through a brief explanation of the relationship between them all. The dark African slowly nodded as Lucius talked. "When we finish here, I suspect they'll have some questions for you, Atelius. But I stress," he turned to Marcus and Sextus, "Atelius is here because he is the most skilled swordsman I have ever seen. I've learnt a lot from him in the past."

After a warning about secrecy, Lucius briefed them. It relieved him to see the enthusiasm they displayed once he had finished. The only query came from Sextus.

"Mordechai is a Jew, sir," he said. "Do you trust him with this?"

"I've yet to speak with him, Sextus, but I've reason to suspect he might want to help."

It had been an hour since the sun rose clear of the horizon. The men had breakfasted and waited to go ashore. There was little to do whilst the boat pushed forward, tacking against the prevailing wind until then. Lucius leaned back against the large bow timber of the vessel, looking astern along the deck. Atelius, Sextus and Marcus squatted together on the wooden boards, playing dice. Mordecai stood detached from the players, gazing towards the streak of land just visible on the horizon. The two weeks had passed quickly, and here they were, about to embark on another audacious foray into Judaea.

It had not been easy persuading Mordecai to take part in the seizing of Rabbi Akiva. Though he was fiercely against what Akiva was promoting, the prospect of securing Judaea's most famous sage made him hesitate. Then he began what almost seemed to be a confession.

As a juvenile, Mordecai became wild. He was so often in trouble that his parents sent him to an uncle in Alexandria. It was to no avail, as the young man promptly joined one of the many Jewish gangs to be found in that great metropolis.

"I became what, back in the days of the Great Revolt, many would know as a *Sicarii*. I learnt to handle myself in a fight and to become almost invisible when required. Walking through a crowd, I could assassinate a man and escape unseen. Yet, I was desperately unhappy and then two years on, I met a Rabbi called Tarfon. I felt an immediate connection to the man, and he to me. He recognised something in me I had not even seen myself. In a matter of months, he had helped me recognise that my raging inner anger would only get me killed. I determined I must leave the world of gang warfare, bribery and murder. Death was the only acceptable way out of the gangs, so they smuggled me onto a galley heading back to Judaea one night. I had some money, the clothes I was wearing and a letter of introduction to a Judaean Rabbi."

"The Rabbi was Eleazar of Modi'im, a well-respected Sage, known across the province. He realised shortly after meeting me I would never become a Torah student – I could have told him that. Notwithstanding, he thought me to be bright and intelligent. Realising I had to change my way of life, I became Eleazar's right-hand man, bearing messages, managing his schedules and serving as his security. I felt I had discovered a new father, my genuine father having died whilst I was in Alexandria."

Mordecai paused for a second. Lucius sensed that the real story was about to come.

"The Rabbi was a Haggadist, one who believes in the traditions of Judaism. The contemporary interpretations being imposed upon the 'old law' by the latest generations of rabbis did not rest well with him. Previously they had excommunicated sages for actively defying the reforms, so Eleazer kept his views himself, bar a select few. But of late, he has become more and more apprehensive about the path the Rabbis were walking. He recognised only too well how damaging a significant fallout with Rome could be to his beloved nation. The rabbi argued Jamnia should reach out to the governor – my last mission. He thought of the Judaea that *might* remain after another revolt against the Empire, expecting only defeat. Our religion would require re-establishing. By now, I shared the Rabbi's opinions on the futility of a further insurrection. I would do whatever it takes to finish the rebellion and do it cheerfully."

It occurred to Lucius that Mordecai had avoided questioning the cause for his "inner anger", but he did not consider it was the moment to push the man.

The mundane, shabby merchant craft that bore them south would shortly turn inland. It would then hug the coast in a northerly direction. It was a manoeuvre designed to convince anyone detecting the boat that it had come from the south, from the harbour at Gaza.

Lucius reflected on his small group. Three weeks back, he told the group to abstain from shaving and cutting their hair. He wished to appear as travellers from afar. They wore not a single item of Roman attire, even the weapons they carried. He was confident they could visually carry off the deception. No one could be certain what they would come up against ashore, so they would have to proceed with care, and looking the part they were portraying would be necessary.

Mordecai turned from looking out to sea and went to the bow to join Lucius. "The day is warming. We must head inland soon, my friend," he stated. "We need daylight time to locate the village."

"I am sure we will turn any minute," Lucius replied. "The triarchus knows this coast well."

No sooner had he spoken than a command rang out, and the vessel turned towards the shore. The crew scrambled to adjust the sails and the rigging.

"It seems the triarchus has large ears!" Mordecai said. The boat heeled, picking up momentum as the sailcloth became swollen with the breeze, when captain approached the two men at the bow.

"We'll be at the coast in a short while," he called to Lucius, "and we shall go north, putting you ashore before mid-day."

Lucius acknowledged with a wave.

"Marcus," he called, "Will you all come over here?" The three players picked up their dice and secured their stakes in their purses, joining Lucius and Mordecai in the boat's bow. "Right, a last-minute run-through of the plan – what there is of it!" The remark drew a chortle. "So, Marcus, perhaps you would care to take us through it."

"Right you are, Lucius," Marcus answered, stressing the name. "We're all on first-name terms, lads. No fucking 'Optio' or 'legionary' no more. We are civilians – rebels, in fact. I 'ave to say, you bleedin' look it to me!"

"The feeling's mutual," responded Sextus.

"If the triarchus lands us in the right place," Marcus continued, "it should be easy to get off this log and onto dry land. There's a beach that goes back a quarter of a mile, then a short belt of grassland, too sandy to farm, before we reaches the first fields. Luckily for us, a track runs parallel to the coast at that point, just as we reaches the fields. So we takes it, heads north and shortly after, turn east and it leads to Serifin. Simple, really!"

"A member of the II Cohort grew up in this locality, and he gave us the information. It's good," added Lucius.

"Right then, we follows the track, and it leads us to this Serifin place. At a steady pace, we should get there before sunset. We bowls in, bold as anything, 'cause we are there to help. Then, we gets talking to the locals and see if this Rabbi Akiva is in town. If he is, we 'leave' on our journey to join up with the rebels at Lod." Marcus paused for effect. "Of course, we don't go far.

Soon as it's dark, we double back to the beach, where just before daylight, the 1st Century arrives in their bireme, guided by the fires we will've lit. Simple lads, ain't it? After that, Centurion Crispus takes over, and we can relax."

"Serifin's a small village," Lucius said, "so it shouldn't be too hard to identify just where Akiva is residing. The main group cannot squander time searching for him."

"So, if all goes well – if – our swords should remain in their scabbards?" asked Sextus.

"That's the idea," Marcus retorted.

"A sword in a scabbard is a wasted resource," Atelius quipped. He grinned, his teeth gleaming white against his dark skin. "It is much more effective when it is in the body of your enemy. It was a Lannister that said that to me ages ago."

The group stared at him.

"Too much sea time, Lucius," suggested Marcus, "the sooner we get 'im ashore, the better."

Lucius was the first over the side of the boat, landing in knee-high water. The remaining four of the group followed him. Sextus turned back to the vessel and took hold of two large sacks containing wood shavings and kindling passed by a sailor. The contents would start the fire to guide the bireme with its cargo of Roman soldiers in the dark to its embarkation point; they were taking no chances. After a few well-wishes, two sailors using long boat hooks pushed the boat away from the shore whilst others raised the sails. Sextus sought and found a convenient hollow a little way in from the shoreline to hide his bag of fire making materials.

The five men had a look of travellers who had made their way from afar. The clothes were shabby. They carried snap sacks and water skins over the shoulder and footwear, which had seen many miles. No man wore the same sword, which added to the allusion of a ragged group from across the empire.

"We've got a walk before us, men," said Lucius, "I've allowed two hours to reach Serifin. So, let's get started. May the gods....." He caught Mordechai's eyes, "... or *his* God, be with us."

The travellers set forth across the sand and onto the rough grass. They came across the track, and Lucius attached a sizeable yellow cloth to an adjacent large thorn bush to mark the point. It would appear torn from a tunic by the thorns to the casual observer. Nevertheless, it would serve them to identify the landing point upon their return.

A little later, the track moved into a very different landscape. Unlike much of Judaea, the coastal plain was greener. They began to pass cultivated fields and orchards, cared for by farmers living in small hamlets. The group tensed each time they passed labourers working on their crops until Marcus gave several of them a wave. The workers returned the gesture.

"Come on, lads," he whispered to his comrades, "this lot are supposed to be our mates, so, better treat them as such." Enthusiastic as always, the next group of labourers received a "freedom for Judaea" greeting from Marcus.

"Better not forget whose side you're on, man," Atelius said.

"Don't worry, brother," Sextus responded, "Marcus is on the side that pays him!"

They followed a well-defined pathway created by many years of use, servicing fields and hamlets by this point. The first proper test came when a small number of men appeared, leading two laden donkeys. Lucius asked Mordecai to lead any conversation as they passed. When they met, the two groups stopped, and Mordecai led the exchange, leading in Greek. He explained how they had come ashore and were off to join the Judaean forces fighting the Romans. They had been told to head for Serifin and then onwards towards Lod. The labourers greeted them with enthusiasm pointing down the road and indicating that Serifin was a short walk away. They parted company. Once out of earshot, Lucius spoke up.

"That seemed to go well. I didn't detect any suspicion of us."

"These were simple labourers," Mordecai said, "It may not be quite as easy when we get to Serifin. I'd recommend we all visit our storylines, so they're fresh in our minds when we arrive at the village."

"A good suggestion, Mordecai," said Lucius, "if we're going to be there for a little while, we're bound to be asked more detailed questions; our stories must hold up."

They spotted the village of Serifin when it was a mile ahead of them. As they approached, Lucius reminded them that they had one objective: to identify if Rabbi Akiva ben Josef was present; it would also be helpful to know in which house he was staying. They had no plan so that improvisation would be the order of the day.

Serifin was a typical Judaean village. It consisted of small, square houses laid out on a rectangular plot. The places were often connected and shared a first-floor sun flat. Stone buildings used for artisan purposes were separated from the others. All walls on the outside of the village were windowless, and they had bricked any space between properties up. Serifin was defensible against raiders and bandits, apart from an arched entrance. Additional stone-built outbuildings were external to the village, all interspersed by olive and citrus trees. Lucius estimated the settlement would house one hundred or more people.

"Don't forget," said Lucius as they approached, "we are here to take simple refreshment, for which we will pay, before moving on to join the Judaean forces in Lod. We'll go straight in through the archway. Try to look weary and tired."

Moving on, they approached the arched entrance, the sounds of voices and children playing reached the group. Just as they were about to enter, a labourer walked under the arch and came to a sudden stop, surprised by the six strangers. Mordecai spoke up.

"Blessings upon you, my friend," he greeted the startled resident in Aramaic. "We are five tired and hungry travellers, on our way to Lod to join the forces repelling the Romans from Judaea. All we ask is some refreshment before we continue our journey." The fellow stared suspiciously at Mordecai, who added, "and of course, we shall pay for any refreshment."

"You had better follow me," the man said, turning and walking back through the arch. After a glance at Lucius, Mordecai followed, as did the others. Entering the village, the archway behind them, brought the sound of conversation to a stop as people gawked at the five strangers. "Call ben Israel!" the labourer shouted to a group of people gathered in one corner. Turning to the small band, he said, "Wait here." They came to a standstill. Then a few moments later, a figure appeared, and much to the group's dismay, two heavily armed soldiers accompanied him.

It was evident to Lucius that this was the village elder. He was of the indeterminate age when he could be fifty or sixty years old. His full beard was losing its battle to maintain its colour, but not yet grey. If his hair was the same, it was not apparent as he was wearing a brightly coloured headdress. Compared to the labourers they had seen, he dressed well. The trio approached until the soldiers stood, allowing the elder to come forward and speak.

"Shalom, strangers to Serifin. I am Daniel ben Israel. Blessings be upon you," he spoke in Greek, then, with ceremony out of the way, "and how may we help you? You appear to be well travelled." Mordecai responded, sharing the same information he gave the labourer at the arch. "Well then, the Lord would not smile on us should we turn down such a request, especially as you travel in his cause. I welcome you not just to the village of Serifin but to the liberated Judaea. Come, there is a table set up, and I shall ask women to arrange some refreshment in return for a few shekels."

Understanding Greek, the group smiled and indicated their thanks. They sat on long benches on either side of a wooden table in no time at all. The elder called some women who joined them and gave instructions to provide refreshments for the visitors. The two soldiers remained. Each stood at opposite ends of the table.

"So, you've come to fight with us, then?" The questioner had all the hallmarks of a veteran. He was muscular and carried a deep scar across his cheek, which gave him a menacing appearance. He wore a black leather cuirass, which gave the impression it had seen better days. Head swathed in cloth, he was equipped with a long sword, a sword belt across his chest, and was grasping a spear. His partner was little different, except he lacked the cuirass and wore a headdress of a contrasting colour.

"If you'll have us, friend." It was Atelius who spoke. "We heard that you boys are kicking Roman backsides, and we've…" he nodded towards his small group, "… all good reasons to rejoice in that and lend you our support. Have you been in the fight?"

The soldier turned to his mate, and they both laughed.

"Our swords have sent several Roman cockroaches to meet their *many* gods. They'll be disappointed to find there's only one!" His countenance turned severe. "But you are not of the faith?"

"I'm Jewish, my friend," Mordecai responded. "My companions have common cause with us, and their swords will stand with ours." The group nodded approval.

"Listen, friends," Lucius said, "the Romans have become complacent. They're more concerned with young boys and pretty statues. Judaea has caused a tidal wave. When others see that the Romans are gone from Judaea, they'll understand they are beatable. That is why we are here."

The second soldier joined the conversation.

"Well, friend, you're not alone. There are many coming to Judaea to fight with us. The Big One welcomes them all."

Women approached with bowls of fruit, meat and bread, and they carried water and juice. The 'travellers' began a welcome lunch.

"So, are you expecting the legions in Serifin?" Mordecai asked the soldiers.

"If they did, me an' Amos, here, would hold the dogs back!" The soldier laughed at his joke, and the group followed suit. "No, we are escorting the rabbis."

"Sorry, brother, you're what, exactly?" Mordecai probed.

"Well, Rabbi Akiva, blessings upon him, comes home to Serifin every year, they tell me. Given the situation, they sent us along to keep an eye out, if you know what I mean. In reality, we are running messages and the like."

"Moses!" exclaimed Mordecai, "The great Akiva is here?" Like a well-scripted play, the other 'travellers' shared puzzled expressions. "Forgive my friends; they'd not understand. They're gentiles, after all."

"I wouldn't expect any less from them," the soldier said with a look of disdain. "Yes, the sage is with us, along with others."

"He's a great man," Mordecai said, "and the spiritual leader of our nation." He was speaking for the benefit of the group as he maintained the charade.

"I think that's why there's more of 'em this year. Now the Big One has kicked the cockroaches out, the rabbis are discussing how we run the new state." said the soldier.

"The world is profoundly changing, my friend. The Lord is blessing us," Mordecai said. "Rabbis? How many has the great sage brought with him?"

"There's ten of them. They are in the two buildings at the end of the square."

"Ten rabbis, you say. We will soon have the whole Sanhedrin in the village!" Mordecai joked.

Meanwhile, Lucius' mind was processing what he had just heard. Should they revise their goal so they seize all ten rabbis? If not, how would they identify Rabbi Akiva in the darkness? Would Mordecai be able to pick out the Rabbi in poor light? All he could do was report back to Crispus when the century arrived; the decision would be his.

As the meal continued, they conversed with the soldiers. The village elder reappeared as they stacked the wooden bowls and downed the liquid refreshment.

"My friends, I have good news for you – particularly your feet. We have a waggon load of produce leaving for Lod. They have begun loading. At least two of you can ride, so if you take it in turns, it will be a much easier journey for you all."

Mordecai, leading the performance being laid on for the villagers, responded.

"Daniel, you and Serifin have the grateful thanks of five weary travellers. If I may show my gratitude…." He paused and, reaching into his purse, took out several shekels and placed them on the table. "Your offer of transport is most kind and gratefully received."

The elder tilted his head sideways and gave Mordecai a puzzled look.

"My friend, you look and dress like a bandit – a fighter, and yet your language does not fit your appearance."

Lucius tensed and prayed that no one noticed him do so. The two soldiers, still present, stared at Mordecai.

"Daniel, my friend. If only you knew the story, but it would take too long to tell, and it's not exciting." He laughed as he spoke the words, throwing his hands in the air. If there was any tension forming, it was dispelled.

"I confess, these are not the easiest of times, and the beast that is war does not care who it sucks into its deadly game. So walk with the Lord, my son," said Daniel.

"Blessings upon you, Daniel," Mordecai responded, "let us scruffy bandits get out from underfoot. Where may we find the waggon bound for Lod?"

"Through the arch, look to your left and you won't miss it. The driver and his mate are expecting you."

A few moments later, discussing their recent experience, the group stood a short distance from the loading waggon.

"Ten bleedin' rabbis!" Said Marcus, "in Zeus' name, ten of 'em."

Lucius turned to Mordecai. "If it came to it, Mordecai, would you be able to separate Rabbi Akiva from the others in poor light?"

"My friend, that would depend upon the situation. But would it not be better to seize all ten and remove them to Caesarea? Just think of the impact that would have."

"That's a decision for Crispus. We can discuss it later," Lucius responded. "The issue now is how we slip away and return to the beach."

"We go a mile up the road, hit 'em over the head, then head back, skirting Serifin as we go," said the ever-practical Sextus.

"It might work," said Atelius, "who'll expect us to be going back the way we came?"

"Well, it seems as good a plan as any," Lucius said, "we'd better introduce ourselves."

The group crossed to the waggon, where labourers filled it with great sacks of vegetables and crates of fruit bound for sale in Lod. A giant ox waited in its harness. Meanwhile, the waggon master stood beside his vehicle, watching the team of labourers. Lucius approached the man and introduced himself. The Master had was briefed and suggested that Lucius and his companions sit in an adjacent tree's shade until loading finished. As the vehicle was only half laden, Lucius suggested that it may be a while before they moved off.

As they sat under the tree enjoying the enforced idleness, the five men reviewed the course of action.

"You know," said Sextus, "if there's just two of them riding up front, we could slip away when the chance offers itself. With that amount of cargo, they ain't going to be able to keep an eye on us at the rear."

"That's a possibility," replied Lucius, "by the time they miss us, they could be miles along the road. I couldn't see them returning to raise any alarm."

They agreed that a furtive approach would be better than an assault on the waggon master and his mate. The conversation progressed, and they developed a plan to return to the coast. Once clear of the vehicle, they would split into two and make their way back to the beach; small groups, if seen, would not attract as much attention as a large group. Lucius was halfway through saying that he thought they had been lucky so far when Marcus sat bolt upright.

"Oh *cac*!" he exclaimed, "you just pushed the gods too far, Lucius." His comrades turned to see what had caught his eye to spy four cavalry troopers riding towards them. "They look like auxiliaries to me, but they can't be. Not here."

"They may not be," said Sextus, "but we know where they got their kit from, don't we?" The oncoming riders carried large oval shields, spears, and helmets, looking very much like Roman mounted auxiliaries.

"Just stick to our story, lads," said Lucius, "hopefully, they'll pass by into Serifin."

It was not to be. The cavalrymen approached the waggon master, exchanged a few words, and crossed to the group sitting in the tree's shade.

"The Waggoner tells me you're bound for Lod to join the Big One's army," said one of the riders. He would appear to be the commander of the small troop. Lucius stood, followed by the others.

"That we are," he replied, "and some of my comrades have travelled a distance to get here so Lod will be a welcome sight. We plan to hitch a ride on the waggon." The cavalryman nodded his head.

"So I'm told," he said, nodding towards the master, "and you'll be well-received in Lod. Also, you won't be alone. We've seen a steady trickle of foreign volunteers in the last few days. It would seem kicking Romans is appealing to people way beyond Judaea!"

"Well, there ain't been much of that going on, so it appeals to me," Marcus responded.

"That's good," said the cavalryman. "I have some documents for the rabbis." He slapped a saddlebag. "We'll drop these off, find a drink and join you. I'm in no rush to get back, so we are able to escort the waggon to Lod. I'll fill you in about what's been happening as we go."

Lucius felt his mouth turn dry. The plan seemed to go so well, and now it was all at risk. He realised that at some point, sooner rather than later, they would have to rid themselves of the cavalry troopers.

"There's no need for us to tie you down," Lucius said, "I am sure we'd be quite safe on the road to Lod."

"It's no problem, friend," replied the cavalryman, "It would be a bit of a break for me, to be frank."

Lucius could see the man was not to be deterred.

"Well, a briefing would be useful. We've little detail on events; it would be good to hear," Lucius said, "We'll be here when you're done." The cavalryman gave a brief acknowledgement before he and his comrades disappeared through the archway into Seraphin.

"Well, my friends, we seem to have a minor complication," commented Mordecai.

"Nothing a sharp blade cannot resolve," said Atelius, "We'll need an element of surprise. Ideally, we need them dismounted." There followed a few minutes of discussion about how to overpower the four cavalrymen. Sextus came up with the idea that the group adopted. At a point not too far from Serafin, Sextus would swing a punch at Atelius and the two would begin a fight. The others would try to pull the men apart, creating a commotion attracting the troopers. When close, Lucius would issue a command, turning on the soldiers. It was a rough plan having many variables, but they believed it could work.

"It *has* to work!" Lucius said.

In due course, as the labourers completed their task, the cavalrymen returned. Much to the group's surprise, one horseman galloped past the cart and disappeared up the road in Lod's direction.

"Urgent dispatch," said their commander, "he'll be alright on his own. There is little between here and Lod we need to be worried about." Lucius caught Sextus' eye; the look signalled one less to contend with. In no time at all, the loaded vehicle moved off. Lucius and Sextus sat with their legs dangling over the rear while their companions followed on foot. Two cavalry troopers rode their horses to the front. However, the commander joined the 'recruits.' He began to relate tales about the fight against Rome.

"The Lord must be with us, for we have driven the cursed legions from the land of Judaea." The Roman spies nodded and grunted their 'agreement' at the appropriate places. Then, after a while, the cavalryman announced he would re-join his comrades, riding off towards the waggon's front.

"Jupiter Optimus, he could talk my mother-in-law into the ground!" said Marcus.

"What?" exclaimed Postumus, "Mother-in-law? You were never married, brother!"

Marcus rolled his eyes.

"It's fortunate he didn't ask about our backgrounds. I am not sure how well the stories would hold up under a close interrogation," said Lucius. He changed tone. "I think it is time we acted. Sextus, Atelius, are you both ready?" Both the men confirmed. "Mordecai, Marcus, we shall initiate the attack as we will be on our feet. Take a rider each. Sextus and Atelius give up the sham when we move and get up as quickly as possible. We'll need your help."

They all checked their weapons. Then, having done so, they turned to Lucius, awaiting the command to begin the diversionary fight.

"I bruise easy, brother, so don't punch me too hard," said Marcus to Atelius, attempting to ease the tension.

"When you're ready," said Lucius.

"You African cunni!" shouted Marcus, turning and landing a punch on Atelius' solar plexus. The African recoiled, stood, and then flung himself at Marcus. Being a much larger man, he had Marcus on the ground and underneath him. As he swung punches at Marcus, the smaller man deflected the flying fists, pounding his knees into Atelius' body. Both men swore loudly. Lucius, Sextus and Mordecai waded into the fight to separate the two combatants while deliberately failing to succeed but making much noise in the process. Meanwhile, the commotion had resulted in the waggon coming to a standstill.

Their efforts were rewarded when the three cavalrymen came trotting down the side of the vehicle to investigate the tumult. The commander leaped from his horse. He rested his spear against the side of the waggon, leaving his shield strapped across his back.

"I thought you came to fight the Romans," he declared.

"They've been arguing on and off all day. Now, this!" said Lucius as he pulled on Atelius' neck. The officer pushed his way into the fray until he stood over the fighting men. Then, he went to draw his sword.

"Put an end to this," he shouted, "you're supposed to be soldiers."

"You're right, there," said Sextus, "that's just what we are." As he spoke the words, he withdrew his weapon from its scabbard, and before the trooper could react, he thrust it upwards into the man's stomach. His face screwed up in pain as he collapsed to his knees. Before he reached the ground, Lucius and Mordecai made their moves. First, the latter leaped at the closest rider, who was frozen in horror, driving a dagger into his groin and pulling him from his mount. Then, as Mordecai stabbed the rider, the horse turned sideways. Lucius, dashing past the animal to get to the other mounted soldier, ran into the horse's rear haunches, knocking him sideways, offering his target a reprieve.

Outnumbered, the remaining trooper gathered his wits about him, turned his horse and spurred it forwards. Lucius cursed as he realised he would not catch the horse and rider. Then, seeing the commander's spear resting against the side of the waggon, Lucius ran to it, and after bracing for a second, he hurled it after the fleeing rider. The weapon was a classic hand-to-hand fighting spear. Sadly, it was not a Roman pilum, the throwing javelin favoured by Roman legionaries.

It fell short of the rider and buried its head into the horse's left rump. The beast screamed and leapt into the air, but its passenger clung on, shouting and encouraging the horse forwards. Several strides later, the weapon fell to the ground. Lucius cursed but saw the disappearing horse develop an unmistakable limp, a small consolation.

"Well, at least you won't be going anywhere," he said to no one in particular. He turned to see his comrades standing over the bodies of the dead cavalrymen.

"I 'spose two out of three ain't too bad," quipped Marcus.

"I've injured the horse," said Lucius, "so unless he meets someone on the way, our friend won't be raising any alarms for a few hours or more. The sun will be setting by then, so if Fortuna is smiling on us, we may still be in the clear."

They were still looking at the bodies, backs to the waggon when Sextus turned.

"Now, lad, you really don't want to use that, do you?" the big legionary said. The others turned to see to what he was referring.

The waggon master's mate, a boy of about seventeen years, stood pointing a rusty spear at Sextus. Lucius saw the boy was sweating, and his breathing was rapid. He was of light build and was no soldier. His spear tip, amplifying the nervous shakes of his body, was wobbling back and forth. The two stood still, staring at each other. Lucius saw the young man's resolve fading. Even without his armour, Sextus would appear a formidable opponent. Then the spear was lowered. The confrontation was passing. Sextus relaxed and his weapon pointed downwards.

A loud cry shattered the scene as the waggon master appeared, wielding a sword, rushing towards the gathered group. Jumping back to avoid the man's blade as it arced towards him, Lucius tripped over one of the bodies. As he fell, he was aware of two things: Atelius leaping forward, lunging, blade first, for the waggon master. The second was a scream; it was the youth with the spear. Lucius scrambled to his feet, and the scene that met his eyes was shocking and unexpected.

At Atelius' feet lay the waggoner, not dead but pumping out blood at such a rate he would not survive, even if Atelius permitted it. The youth lay dead on his face in the dirt, with a deep cut to the neck, administered by Marcus. More shocking was to see Sextus on his knees, clutching a spear driven two hand's-widths into his stomach. Mordecai rushed to the fallen legionary, knelt, and supported him. Marcus held the spear, preventing it from tearing Sextus' wound as Lucius gently lowered him prone on the ground. The others joined them. The damage was mortal; it would only be a matter of time.

They gazed upon their fallen comrade, who was sweating profusely, his breathing laboured. Lucius took hold of his dagger and ripped open Sextus tunic, cutting around the impaled weapon. The wound was oozing blood.

"Pull it out," said the wounded soldier between gritted teeth. Marcus looked hesitant. "Pull it out, now!"

Lucius held Sextus down, and with a sudden tug, Marcus pulled the spear out, ripping further flesh as it did so. It may appear impossible to scream through a clenched jaw, but Sextus did. The force of Lucius' weight on this chest limited the writhing, but the wound gushed blood. Mordecai appeared by the body with a large cloth to compress the wound and staunch the flow. Sextus seemed to relax a little, though shock was setting in.

"My nose didn't twitch - I missed it," he said softly, "Well, this is it. But, please, brothers, you know what you have to do." His companions looked from one to the other as the awfulness of the request sank in. "Don't fuck about." Sextus' right arm lifted from the ground, and his hand reached for his friend, still holding the bloodied spear. "You would honour me, Marcus. Just do what needs to be done and let me escape from here. Fortuna be with you." Marcus looked around despairingly.

"*Irrumabo, Irrumabo.* This man is my friend. Why me?" he cried, holding his arms out to the sky.

"It is because you are his friend, Marcus," said Mordecai, "no one wants to die at the hands of a stranger." He placed his hands on Marcus' shoulders, "There is only one path for Sextus to walk now, and he would walk that path with a friend."

Lucius felt a debt to Sextus, but they had to get away; they could not hang around. The risk of being caught was so high.

"Mordecai, help me sit Sextus upright." Lucius's mind recalled the injured soldier at the attack on the Aelia-bound convoy; it was never easy to slay one's own, a mercy as it may be. In no time, they sat Sextus up, the legionary groaning as they did so. Lucius looked up to Marcus, who stood weapon in hand, dismayed to see tears falling down his cheeks. The soldier stood before Sextus. Lucius had loosened Sextus' tunic, exposing the left shoulder. Marcus lowered the sword until its point settled just behind Sextus' collar bone. Sextus glanced up, nodding his head.

"Farewell, brother. Go with the gods." Marcus thrust down hard on the weapon with a grunt, and the blade sank silently into Sextus' body. For a second, the wounded man stiffened, then he was dead, his body crumpling back into Mordecai's and Lucius' arms. Blood began to pour from Sextus' new wound as they lowered him tenderly to the ground. For a brief while, no one spoke.

"I suggest we gather all the bodies and lay them at the side of the road," said Lucius. He was sure he knew what the others were thinking. He was also feeling uncomfortable. "We shall have to leave Sextus. He was pragmatic. I am sorry, but he would understand."

They accomplished the task, and the group assembled at the back of the waggon.

"It's time we split up," said Lucius. "One pair can skirt the village to the north; another to the south." He glanced at the sun, which sat low in the sky. "Most of the labourers will be thinking about home, so be wary. There is not much sunlight left."

"Make sense to me," Marcus said, "why don't I team up with Mordecai and take the southern route; you and Atelius go north?"

"That's fine by me," responded Mordecai. As he spoke, he spotted the two riderless horses grazing at the side of the road. "I have an idea."

Mordecai and Marcus on horseback within a few minutes; shields across backs, helmets on heads and spears in hands.

"This is all right, this is," quipped Marcus, "just like being back on Trotter." He drew a few puzzled looks, but before he could explain, Mordecai spoke up.

"We'll take the road and ride straight past the village. Should we meet anyone, a friendly wave and we'll keep moving. We'll be back on the coast well before you, Lucius, if this works. Marcus and I'll prepare the fires." Apart from wishing their friends good luck, there was little more to say, and the two riders rode off toward Serifin.

"Right, Atelius," said Lucius, "we'd better get off this road." He was ready to move off when he moved to where the bodies lay. Dropping to one knee, he withdrew a coin from his pouch and opening Sextus' mouth, placed the coin on his tongue. Then, closing the dead soldier's jaw, Lucius stood. "Goodbye, my friend," and then with more enthusiasm, "Let's go."

A full moon ruled the sky. Whilst the landscape had lost its colour, visibility remained good. On their way back to the coast, the few people they saw received a friendly wave; there was no contention. Once Serifin passed, Lucius and Atelius relaxed. The coastline was not far, and moonlight enabled them to find the bush with the cloth marker, signalling their turn towards the beach.

Arriving at the point where they landed, they looked around, disturbed to find no trace of Mordecai or Marcus.

"They should be here, Atelius," said Lucius, "so, where are they?" Then, in the dark to their rear, a voice replied.

"Right behind you." Both Lucius and Atelius swung round, each reaching for his sword and then relaxed. "Sorry, sir," said Marcus, "but we ain't taking no risks. Just had to be sure. Good to see you made it."

"You, too. Any problems?" Lucius asked.

"As expected, a few people saw us, but they seemed to accept we was Jewish cavalry; so, no, it were uneventful. Mordecai, 'ere, passed a few greetings in the local lingo, to good effect. Finally, we secured the 'orses just down the beach." Marcus turned to Mordecai, inviting him to comment, but the Jew stood silent.

"Is all well?" Lucius asked Mordecai.

"Apologies, my friends. I have to remind myself that what I'm doing is to preserve Jewish lives. It's difficult, and I'm sure most will never forgive me." He hesitated for a second before proceeding, "However, I am committed."

"I know it must be tough," Lucius said, "but don't be despondent. Our efforts in the morning may make people stop and re-examine what they are doing. That alone would be a worthy outcome that you've been party to achieving, Mordecai."

"Let us hope so," the Jew responded.

Lucius suggested a watch-rota, permitting each group member to get a few hours of sleep. They were all to be woken when the first signs of dawn appeared. A short while later, with Atelius on the first watch, the others, rolled up in their cloaks on a blanket of sand, were sound asleep – experienced soldiers can take their sleep anywhere.

An alert senior centurion Aurelius Crispus stood on the landward side of the *Diana*, a Roman military bireme. The ship's triarchus stood beside him, staring at the dark smudge of coastline half a mile away. They both sought two burning fires positioned on the beach, the signal for their landing point. Down the ship's length, sleeping soldiers awoke from their slumbers as below them, rowers ensured the vessel remained still in the water.

Not keen on sailing in the darkness, the Roman Navy liked to beach its vessels at night. Besides, it gave their leaky boats a chance to drain. This voyage was different. They had left Caesarea several hours ago and overnight had moved under sail along the coast. The bright moon had helped. The objective involved landing as early in the day as possible. Crispus planned a rapid seizure of Serifin. The first light of dawn was arriving, and sunlight was not far away.

"Are we in the right place?" Crispus asked of the triarchus.

"My centurion friend, as you can pick a battle site, I can pick a landing place!" he replied. "And I have been sailing this coast for several years. When you step on the beach, you are the master. At sea, I am he."

Crispus knew a put-down when he heard one. He chuckled.

"I hate fucking boats!"

"Relax, centurion. I will get you to – there!" In the distance, a glow appeared, gradually glowing brighter. "We need the second one.... come on, come on." Then, a second glow blossomed in the dark further along the beach as if to order. "Good. Now we need our lantern." A sailor was waiting on the bow, standing with an oil lantern burning at his feet, ensuring invisibility outside the boat. "Raise the lantern, Axios," commanded the triarchus. The man did as instructed, swinging the device to and fro.

For a few seconds, nothing changed ashore, both fires blazing. Crispus held his breath; the two fires were not signal enough, the bireme remained static in the water. Then, one fire appeared to flicker and die. Crispus exhaled.

"That's it," he said, "head for the remaining fire." Then, turning inboard, he called out. "Tesserarius, get ready to disembark. The lads are waiting for us."

Mordecai awoke Lucius, shaking his shoulder.
"It is time, my friend. Marcus is lighting the first fire." Sleeping on sand did not make for the most comfortable bed. Lucius came to his feet, his muscles complaining at the sudden movement.

"Marcus? I thought he was on the third watch."

"Indeed, my friend. He's sad about Sextus, so he sat up with me and talked about his friend. The minute the first sign of dawn appeared, off he went to start the fires."

"Do you think he's alright?" Lucius asked.

"He is sad, my friend, but I suspect he will quickly be back to normal."

Lucius shrugged his shoulders several times and swung his arms to shake off the stiffness he felt. Looking around, he saw one fire blazing, and the second, further up the beach, was fast catching up. As he gazed seawards, the definition between sky and water became apparent. Dawn had arrived. Turning back to the beach, he could see both fires blazing, and he watched for a few moments, then turned seaward once again.

"Lucius, look!" Mordecai said, pointing towards the dark grey surface of the sea. Lucius followed his directions. He could spy a small amber light, rocking back and forth.

"That's the signal," Lucius said to Mordecai. He turned toward the blazing fires. "Marcus, extinguish one of the fires. They're out there."

A few moments later, having extinguished a fire, Marcus joined the others as they waited, peering out to sea. A few minutes passed before a shape appeared creeping towards the shore, its form becoming more precise as the sun rose behind them. The visage was accompanied by a regular splashing sound of oars beating the water. Then all fell silent as the vessel glided towards the beach, oars raised above the water. It altered course to approach at an oblique angle at the last moment. Grinding to a halt, the ship rested, bow forward, on sand that sat just beneath the surface of the waves.

The sound of splashing of Legionaries disrupted the calm. The leading soldier's silhouette was recognisable by the distinctive crest running across his helmet. Followed by a stream of legionaries, he approached the fire.

"Ave, Optio Petronius, it's good to see you," Crispus greeted Lucius. Then, losing no time, he was straight to business. "Well then, is our man where we expected him to be?"

"Ave, centurion. Yes, he is in the village, accompanied by several other rabbis."

"Good, so we haven't wasted our time," Crispus responded. He turned and issued a short set of orders ensuring the century formed a column, ready to march inland. "The sooner we get going, the better. You can give me a full briefing on the go, Optio."

"I'll do that," said Lucius, "and we have a useful resource; we have cavalry." He turned to Marcus. "You'd better get the horses and your kit. It'll be good to have a couple of scouts." Then, to Atelius, he said, "You ride, Atelius?" The dark African nodded. "Then will you go with Marcus?"

Marcus laughed.

"From legionary to tesserarius, to scout – in a matter of weeks!" With that, he and Atelius disappeared along the beach to collect the horses.

Turning to Mordecai, Lucius said, "It may be better you remain with us, Mordecai. You never know when your local knowledge may be useful."

On hearing the words, Crispus' face took on a sceptical look. Lucius spotted it.

"As you suggested, sir, I will fully brief you as we march," he said in the feigned formality.

"It would be nice to be informed!" Crispus responded. With more than a hint of sarcasm. He then looked around. "Where is Postumus?"

"I'm afraid he has made Charon's acquaintance," Lucius replied, referring to the Ferryman who rows the dead across the River Styx into the underworld.

Un breve interludio

Isaac considered himself lucky. At one point not so long ago, when the fighting broke out, having a wife, three young children and two old parents to support would have weighed upon him. Isaac worried he would have to become involved. However, when he explained his responsibilities and produced food crucial for the war effort, the new authorities permitted him to remain on his farm.

He rose early this morning, as he had an extensive field he wanted to plough before planting his crop. The sun had arisen, though it was still weak. While busy connecting his plough to his only ox, working out how much he could accomplish before taking a break for breakfast, two riders, evidently military, trotted past on the road that lay below his farm. True, it was not a familiar sight, but a lot was happening these days that was unfamiliar; he was not unduly concerned.

Isaac joined the ox to the plough and gave it a light tap across its haunches. Recognising the signal, it moved forward. Isaac followed, ensuring the blade of the plough dug into the soil. After a few paces, he pulled the oxen's reins, and the combination came to a stop. A sound had caught Isaac's attention: tramp,

tramp, tramp. The sound emanated from the road, and as he turned to see the source of the noise, a marching group of soldiers appeared from behind a row of olive trees. A large horsehair crest adorned the leading soldier's helmet, dispelling any doubt that the soldiers were Romans.

His initial response was to panic. But it occurred to him that a company of Roman soldiers would have little interest in a man ploughing his field. Wars may come, and wars may go, but people always need to eat. So, he shrugged, tapped the ox, and continued to plough his furrow.

As the sun climbed into the sky and warmed the day, the century made excellent progress. The settlement of Serifin was not far ahead. The centurion had tasked the two riders to apprehend anybody moving towards the village they suspected was trying to raise the alarm. Lucius was taken aback when Marcus received his orders.

"That would give me great pleasure indeed!" He turned his horse and rode off. Mordecai picked up on the comment.

"He needs to get Sextus' death out of his system, and I suspect I know how it's going to do it. There will be blood."

"If all goes to plan, Mordecai," said Lucius, "he may not get the opportunity today."

As they closed upon the village, it looked as though Lucius' forecast would come to fruition. Their approach seemed not to have raised any alarm. A few hundred paces from the village, Crispus gave the orders, and two tent-parties set off to surround the settlement. The remainder jogged at speed straight towards the gated archway that provided entry. Lucius and Mordecai remained outside the arch as the century poured through, only following as the last soldier entered.

Serifin looked just as it had the previous day, but Lucius felt quite different entering the place as a Roman. There was no worry of discovery today. The inhabitants would know who he was, but the power was with him this time.

Villagers stood frozen to the spot, mouths agape at the sight of sixty Roman legionaries occupying their square. Crispus brought his men into formation, and Lucius and Mordecai joined him. There was a clatter of hooves as Marcus and Atelius rode through the archway. For a few seconds, Crispus stood thinking, scratching his forehead, before issuing orders.

"You riders, take the road towards Lod; I want the earliest warning should we have visitors." Marcus and Mordecai acknowledged the order and trotted their horses back through the archway. "Tesserarius, take three tents and position yourself across the Lod road. Optio Petronius, ben Zakkai and I will see about the business here." The two horses were being followed out by twenty-four legionaries in no time at all. In the field, they would be the regular occupants of three eight-man leather tents and their tesserarius. Several of the 'frozen' villagers moved. "Stay where you are!" Crispus bellowed in Greek, hoping most would understand. "Tent leader Frontus, take your men, round this lot up and guard them until we are done."

Eight soldiers broke off from the rear of the formation and herded the villagers into a corner of the village square. They were not gentle, a tactic applied to crush any thoughts of resistance. It was effective; the male villagers were sullen, while the women turned to tears; those with children drew them close.

Crispus turned to Lucius and Mordecai.

"Right then, now to the purpose of our visit to this delightful village, take me to the Rabbi."

Lucius pointed to the houses at the bottom of the village square.

"They're in there," he said, pointing. Crispus turned back to his formation.

"First four tents, with me, signifier, keep the rest here. Now, let's go," Crispus called as he set off towards the buildings Lucius had identified. They had gone only several paces when Daniel ben Israel, the village elder, burst out of a side building accompanied by the two soldiers Lucius had met on his last visit. Others were standing in doorways, and some with more incredible bravado stepped out into the street. The two Jewish soldiers stopped dead in their tracks, faces agog when they saw what was to their front. The spears they were carrying must have turned red hot in their hands, given the speed they threw them to the ground. A good decision, thought Lucius.

"You! You are Roman. What do you think you are doing? We fed you and made you welcome," the apoplectic village elder shouted at Lucius, "this is a peaceful village. So why do you bring soldiers here?" He was making a beeline towards Lucius, who, in response, drew his sword.

"Stay where you are," Crispus ordered the man in a loud voice, "and everybody else gets back against the walls–clear the fucking square-I don't expect to see anybody near it. Do that, and no one gets hurt. Now move!" Hesitantly, the locals moved back against the village walls or to the front of the houses built into the stone defences.

The centurion had achieved what he wanted within a few moments, and he continued heading to the buildings where the rabbis were to be found. He did not pause when he came to his objective; going to the larger building, he gave the door a mighty kick, storming in. Lucius and Mordecai followed in his wake, as did half a dozen legionaries. Lucius noticed Mordecai had wrapped his head scarf around his head, bandit style, just leaving his eyes clear.

They came upon a group of four rabbis sitting around a table, eating breakfast. It was a frozen tableau, and for a few seconds, it remained so. Crispus turned to Mordecai.

"Well?"

Mordecai pointed to the Rabbi, facing the incomers seated with his back to the wall. The rabbi was old, grey-haired, and with a long beard of the same colour. Lucius thought he could be eighty years old. The other three Rabbi showed all the signs of nervous concern, yet the more senior man appeared calm. He broke the silence.

"Welcome to our humble breakfast, centurion." His voice had a mellow timbre; it was firm for a man of his age, showing little sign of frailty. "You would be most welcome to join us, but I'm sure you are here on business other than your stomach."

"You… You are Rabbi Akiva ben Joseph?" Crispus asked incredulously. It took Lucius aback, too; he had expected someone somewhat younger, more virile, and aggressive. Was this the man who had helped the bandit Shimeon ben Koseba set the hills of Judaea alight?

"I am he," Akiva said. The expected resistance was absent. Seeming almost embarrassed standing before this old man and his three frightened friends, Crispus ordered his party to put up their swords.

"So, where are the rest of you rabbi friends?" Crispus asked.

"Studying their Torah, centurion," replied the rabbi, "but that is something you would not understand."

"Well, never mind that. Rabbi Akiva, I must ask you to come with us," Crispus said, then recovering himself, added, "It is not an option; you are coming with us!" One of Akiva's colleagues stood up, causing the Roman party to reach for their swords. He appeared the youngest in the group, Lucius thought, of a similar age to himself.

"Where are you taking the Rabbi?" He demanded. "You cannot barge in here and insist upon apprehending Rabbi Akiva!"

Crispus gave a short laugh.

"Well, at least one of them has grown a set of balls!" He paused. "So, just who would you be?" The young rabbi pulled himself upright and stared straight at Crispus.

"I am Rabbi Joshua HaGarsi, a lifelong disciple of Rabbi Akiva." Lucius felt he knew what was coming as Crispus' face reddened.

"Right then, Rabbi HaGarsi." He paused for a deep breath. "I am centurion Aurelius Crispus. My authority goes all the way up to a man known as Caesar Traianus Hadrianus Augustus, better known to you as the Imperator of Rome." As he spoke, Crispus' voice raised in volume. "Now then, if Caesar Traianus Hadrianus Augustus requires me to apprehend one Rabbi Akiva ben Joseph, that is exactly what I will do. Anyone, anyone who stands in my way, will feel the edge of my gladius. Do-I-make-myself-clear-rabbi?"

The young rabbi appeared to wilt under Crispus' threats. Nevertheless, he stood his ground, looking Crispus eye-to-eye.

"You are abundantly clear, Centurion Crispus," the Rabbi responded, "and I take you at your word. However, I wish to make a request of you. Wherever you may take our great Sage, I would wish to accompany him."

"You wish us to take you into custody?" Crispus said.

Mordecai stepped forward.

"Centurion, with your permission, I would speak with the Rabbi?" Crispus nodded, his eyes fixed on Rabbi HaGarsi. Mordecai spoke with the Rabbi in Hebrew and the exchange between the two men lasted barely a minute. Conversation over, Mordecai turned to Crispus. "Centurion, Rabbi Akiva, as you can see, is quite some age and is frail. Rabbi HaGarsi cares for Akiva's well-being. Might I suggest you allow HaGarsi to accompany the Rabbi? I'm sure we wish to have Akiva arrive in Caesarea in the best condition."

Crispus studied the ancient rabbi.

"It's a fair point you make, and it would save one of my men looking after the old man," Crispus said.

"Thank you, centurion," Rabbi HaGarsi responded.

"It's no favour," said Crispus. "It benefits me." Turning to the soldiers in the room, "Take these two outside. It's time we left this place." He looked Akiva up and down, which resulted in concerns about the older man's health. He faced Lucius. "Optio Petronius, do make sure he doesn't die on the way; he's going to need to ride as we will not, in any sense, be strolling back to the ship."

In no time at all, the century formed up in the centre of the village. Agitated, the villagers that had remained in the square sensed the imminent departure of the Roman force would take their great sage with them. Crispus called Mordecai and Lucius to join him. He pointed out a donkey and cart that stood awaiting the return of its owner.

"There you go, Optio. They built it for the job of transporting aged rabbis! Lucius, I want you and ben Zakkai to guard Akiva until we get back to the ship. Stick him on the cart. You can get HaGarsi to lead the donkey; it'll keep them both out of mischief." He had no sooner stopped speaking, went to cavalryman trotted through the archway into the village. It was Marcus and Atelius.

"Just checking you were still here, sir," said Marcus as he dismounted. "We've been a mile or so up the road towards Lod; all appears quiet." Crispus nodded.

"You timed it well, Tesserarius, we're about to move out. But, as we head back, I'd like you to keep patrolling our rear, just in case."

Lucius signalled Rabbi HaGarsi for him and Akiva to join him by the donkey cart. They quickly ensconced Akiva in the cart, and HaGarsi took the donkey's reins. Crispus looked about him and saw the time had come to leave. He indicated to Lucius that they should proceed the century. The vehicle headed towards the archway to exit the village.

Ben Israel, the village elder, stepped forward from the group of now unguarded inhabitants.

"Where are you taking the sage?" He demanded. "This is nothing but kidnap. He is a man of God, and the Lord will punish you for this!" He was closing upon Crispus, who was still standing with Marcus as he spoke. Crispus advanced a pace, openhanded, to push the man away. As he did so, the senior of the two guards Lucius' small group had met the preceding day, rushed to ben Israel's defence. The guard did not see Marcus drawing his sword, his view blocked by the village elder. As the soldier reached the elder, Marcus came from behind Crispus and, with a sharp punch, embedded his sword in the guard's midriff. After a second, he pulled the blade upwards with a vicious stroke.

For a second, everyone froze, apart from the guard, who sank to his knees and fell face down onto the cobbled ground. In the shocked silence, Marcus' voice could be heard.

"That's for the Sextus, you bastard Jew!"

A wail arose from the corralled villagers, and some men moved forwards in Crispus' direction. He had formed the century into a column, ready to move through the archway. Crispus shouted.

"Face right. Defence position." The unit did as instructed, and the advancing villagers faced a wall of Shields and swords at the ready, standing still. "If any person moves one step closer, they will die, believe me." It took a few seconds for Crispus' words to sink in before the inhabitants stepped back.

A few minutes later, the column was clear of the village and making its way back towards the coast. Crispus, Lucius, along with his small group, walked several feet ahead of the rabbi's cart; the century at the rear.

"All in all, that went well," Crispus said. "I'm sorry you lost your man Postumus, Lucius."

"Apollinaris has exacted some revenge for losing his brother, sir," Atelius chipped in.

"That he did," Crispus responded, "but the focus now is on getting those two," he nodded towards the two rabbis following a few paces behind, "onto the ship and back to Caesarea. Should we have any surprises on the way to the coast, I want you three to concentrate on ensuring the rabbis reach the ship. Is that clear?"

Un breve interludio

Isaac had made good progress with his ploughing. There was a way to go, but he anticipated finishing the work by mid-afternoon. This would enable him to get back to the farmhouse and attend to many of the minor jobs his wife had set for him. Aware of the bag over his shoulder that contained his lunch, meagre though it was, he fought the temptation to bring his ox to a standstill, relax, and take an early meal. Nevertheless, he brought the beast to a halt to take a drink from his waterskin.

As he did so, his eye spotted a movement on the road that lay beyond the field. He recognised the soldiers he had seen earlier but now moving in the opposite direction. However, the donkey cart leading the column drew his attention. It had not been there when the legionaries had passed before. He could make out someone sat on the small waggon and a similarly dressed person leading the donkey. Two men, by their dress, not soldiers, led the procession accompanied by a soldier with a red crest bracing his helmet.

Well, thought Isaac, they have been to collect the passenger in the cart and are returning. He did not know who they were. Frankly, none of it is his business. He returned his water skin to his bag, whipped the ox across his haunches, and the plough moved forward. He had work to do. It was somebody else's war, not his.

Capitulum XXVIII - Parthians

1 Iunius. Year 16 of the Imperator Hadrianus.

The 1st Century made excellent progress, and the village of Serifin was soon far behind them. The banter within the column fell away as the unit trudged back towards the coast. Lucius was sufficiently relaxed that his thoughts went back to Caesarea and Miriam. It was a quandary as to the direction the relationship should run. He felt greatly for her, but he is a soldier in the Roman army, and she, for all the subtleties of her religious beliefs, is a Jewess. He faced a hurdle because he wanted to be with this woman. She would be no backstreet mistress. He had to find a way of –

Two horses thundered along the column, halting by Crispus and his companions. Crispus brought the century to a halt. Marcus slid down from his horse - competently for a foot soldier, thought Lucius, and approached Crispus.

"Dunno where they've come from, sir, but there's a bloody big force of Jews on our tail!"

"Apollinaris, you're a tesserarius, damn it. Be more specific, man," Crispus snarled.

"Apologies, sir. There's a unit of Jews, as much as two hundred strong, approaching from the rear; half a mile – and I estimate they are gaining on us, sir," snapped Marcus.

"In Hades' name, how did you miss them?"

"They didn't come down the Lod road, sir. Dunno how they did it, but somehow, they did."

Crispus turned to Lucius.

"If we double the pace, we may outmarch them. The problem is the bottleneck when we arrive at the ship. The Jews would hit us as we try to board - a total fuck up!" Having pushed his helmet back on his head, Crispus was scratching his brow. "As we get to the coast, the valley narrows considerably. The century will stand fast at that point. Lucius, you will continue with speed, get to the coast and embark the rabbis. Am I clear?"

"Absolutely, sir."

"Apollinaris, you and Atelius will accompany Optio Petronius back to the ship. There will be no role for cavalry in this action." Marcus nodded and slapped his fist across his chest in salute. "Good." Crispus turned to his men. "Century will march, double pace."

Lucius understood why Crispus had insisted on so many route marches during training. The century moved at double their previous pace. It was well within the century's capabilities; even the donkey seemed to relish the faster pace. Soon the track left the fields and orchards behind and ran through scrubland. A few minutes later, Crispus ordered the command to stand and rotate until the century stood facing the way they came. The ground to either side was rough, strewn with small boulders and bushes. It offered some, if not absolute, protection for his flanks. He called to Lucius to keep moving, and so the cart party with its accompanying cavalryman headed for the coast.

Lucius noticed that the rabbis had been silent since leaving Serifin. He was sure they must have overheard conversations about the pursuing force. Even now, as they rushed for the safety of the coast and the awaiting bireme, they maintained their silence. Lucius felt guilty at having abandoned - no – left his century under orders. He wanted to be with them, fighting the common enemy. But he understood that the overarching aim was Rabbi Akiva's apprehension, and if achieved, the century would have completed its task.

They reached the bush marked by yellow cloth a little later, turning towards the beach, where the bireme waited. Marcus and Atelius galloped ahead to alert the marines to waste no time before boarding the two rabbis. Lucius noticed they had lowered ladders from the deck into the sea, approaching the vessel, permitting easy access to the ship. But quick enough to evacuate the whole century?

"Right, lads, this wall of shields should stop the bastards getting through to the coast." Crispus paced along his men's line, who had formed a defensive stance that blocked the valley. "Brothers, there's a lot of 'em, but remember this; they're only a bunch of bandits, while you are Rome's finest. I've told you before, and I'll tell you again, don't forget your training, and we'll do all right. Right, shields front!"

Crispus studied his men. They had done well in the Junction fight, but he knew that they had been a relieving force, not shouldering a significant burden of the battle. Today would be the first time they had faced an enemy assault. They looked tense. Outnumbered at least by two to one, he prayed the earlier fight had embedded enough confidence to carry them through the forthcoming action. A thought came into his head.

"Remember the sixth?" he cried. "Remember the rabbits?" There came no response until a lone voice called, "Rabbits!" In no time at all, the century was chanting the name of the long-eared, furry beast. After a few seconds, the enemy appeared.

Crispus knew that the Jews avoided full-on confrontation with the Roman army. They faced well-trained Roman legionaries, and in a conventional action, the Romans will exact a hard price from them. However, the Jew's goal would be to save Rabbi Akiva from captivity in Roman hands, and Crispus banked they *would* try a head-on attack, relying on their greater numbers. Crispus relied on the discipline and training of his legionaries. Time would tell whose reliance was valid.

Seeing the Romans drawn up across the pathway, the Jewish force came to a standstill. They carried shields and tall spears and looked like they meant business. Crispus watched as their officers convened a conference before separating and returning to their units. The Jews had drawn up facing the Romans. As the valley sides reduced the line's width, the Jewish line, with its more significant numbers, came deeper than that of the Roman century. Nevertheless, the Jews continued to keep their distance until a rustle of movement in the front ranks saw slingers slipping through to the fore.

"Shields up!" cried Crispus, "Second row forward." The front rank presented a line of shields facing the enemy, while the second rank lent over and placed their shields on top of the front rank's wall of protection, almost doubling the height of Crispus' defensive wall. No sooner were the upper shields in place than they rattled with incoming missiles. And so, it begins – thought Crispus.

Lucius took the donkey cart to the water's edge. The *Diana's* few marines stationed on the beach acted as a guard. He would be hard-pressed to differentiate them from the standard Roman auxiliaries, thought Lucius. They looked like they could hold their ground in a fight.

They had moved at speed with the cart, and it was a breathless Lucius that related the events back along the road. The Marines perked up at the thought of action.

"Be prepared to head inland, men," Lucius said. "Our century's outnumbered and needs all the help it can get."

The marine officer stepped forward.

"We'll be ready in a short time. You can brief us as we go." Then, turning to his men, he said, "Make ready… and do it with haste!"

"First things first," said Lucius, "we must get Rabbi Akiva secure on board."

"We are ready for that," the marine officer confirmed.

Lucius turned to the young man who stood holding the donkey's rein, "Rabbi HaGarsi, Rabbi Akiva needs to board the ship, and quickly. Mordecai, can you make sure the Rabbis get aboard? I'm going to speak to the triarchus."

Mordecai stepped forward and, with Rabbi HaGarsi, helped the older rabbi off the cart. Akiva stood between them and looked up at the bow of the *Diana*.

"My last journey in such a boat was when the Lord, praise him, had me visit Rome. I was younger then. Will I go to Rome again?"

"Caesarea, Rabbi," said Mordecai, "not such a long journey."

Lucius climbed a ladder and boarded the bireme within seconds, seeking the triarchus, the ship's captain. The triarchus found Lucius, having come forward to see what the commotion was at the bow of the beached vessel. Lucius explained the situation, and the triarchus decided to order the sea anchor pulled in, dragging his ship into deeper water. He could not risk boarding by enemy forces. A cry came from the stern.

"Vessel approaching!" Lucius looked alarmed, but the triarchus smiled.

"One of ours, Optio," the captain said, "Spotted her a while ago. It seems she's nosy! Better see what she wants, hadn't we?" The two men walked along the ship's side until they reached the stern. In front of them, a Roman bireme approached, dropping sail and using the oars to bring the large vessel to a halt half a ship's length from the *Diana*. A voice sounded across the space between the two boats.

"Is all well? We didn't expect to see one of ours beached here."

"I am transporting a century of the Tenth Fretensis," the triarchus called back. "I await their return for disembarkation."

Lucius saw that the decks of the opposite ship carried soldiers, not just a complement of marines, but legionaries. Lucius cut in before the commander of the bireme could respond.

"I am Optio Lucius Decimus Petronius, 1st Century, the IV Cohort, of the *Fretensis*," he paused for breath, "From which unit are your legionaries?"

As if on cue, an officer appeared at the bow of the bireme. The helmet cresta identified a centurion.

"I am centurion Flavius Martinus, 1st Century, II Cohort of the twenty-second *Deiotariana*. We are a vexillation bound for Caesarea. You are not with your unit, Optio? Nor with your uniform, I see."

Lucius ignored the jest, his mind running, a plan forming.

"Centurion Martinus, my century is holding the road a short distance inland. They are facing a body of Jews twice the number. I respectfully ask for your support, sir."

"Well now, Optio," Martinus shouted over the water, "the *Deiotariana* are never ones to shy from a fight." The centurion turned and spoke to his triarchus, his words lost to Lucius. However, the conversation's contents became apparent when the oars of the bireme stroked the sea, and the ship headed towards the beach. Lucius addressed his own ship's captain.

"Can you beach us again, as I would like to avoid having to swim back to the shore?" The triarchus laughed, shaking his head.

"Bloody army, you can't make your mind up!"

Not long after, Lucius was on *terra firma*, accompanied by Atelius and Marcus, complete with their horses. As Roman legionaries poured ashore from the bireme *Minotaur*, Centurion Flavius Martinus strode across to join Lucius.

"Right, Optio, if things are as you describe, we need to get moving!" Martinus was tall and of slight build, not your typical centurion. He had the look of someone who lives on the nerves, his eyes darting about him. Whatever, thought Lucius, if he's a centurion, he knows his stuff.

"Can I make a suggestion, sir?" Lucius asked. The man nodded. "Perhaps you'd like to ride. It will have a much bigger impression on the enemy; they may think you are just the first of many." The Marcus Crispus' school of morale had found a foothold in Lucius.

"Good thinking, Optio," Martinus replied. "My Optio can ride the second horse. Twice the impact?"

And so, the relief force moved off the beach, led by two mounted officers and eighty men, all keen for a fight. Mordecai remained on board as Lucius, Marcus and Atelius marched behind the two officers. Lucius wished Marcus would stop whingeing about the centurion stealing "his bloody horse!"

Marcus Crispus stood in the front rank beside Claudius Paulus, his tesserarius, sheltering behind their large shields.

"This lot differs from the bastards we faced at the junction," Crispus shouted over the din of the paused battle, "much more disciplined and better trained."

The Jews had launched three assaults on the Roman line, attacking, fighting ferociously for a period before pulling back to their start positions, where they would remain for some time before beginning another assault. There was no rest for the Romans, for as soon as the Jews pulled back, the slingers pelted the legionaries with deadly lead slingshots. They were better equipped than the soldiers the cohort had fought on retreat from Aelia Capitolina. One-on-one, they were no match for a legionary, but they were still a challenge with their discipline and equipment. Crispus had not thought they would be so tenacious. He had lost no men from what he saw, but a number had fallen back wounded. In the ground between them and the Judaean fighters lay several enemy. Crispus was concerned that if an injured man could not fight, he did not differ much from a dead man in battle, and the Jews could afford to lose more than him. As if reading Crispus' mind, Paulus called back to his centurion.

"Do we retire in formation, sir?"

"It's a long way to the beach, Claudius," Crispus answered, "and the *cunni* want their Rabbi back, so I am sure they will keep pushing on. I'm thinking that we need to have a go at them; a defensive posture is certainly not putting them off." Paulus nodded. Keeping his shield facing the enemy, Crispus turned to the ranks behind, shouting, "Prepared to advance, boys. We are going to take the fight to them." He observed a shiver run through the ranks as the soldiers braced themselves to move onwards. "Forward march!"

In unison, the Roman line moved forward at a steady pace. The Jewish soldiers, relaxing behind their slingers, suddenly tensed, and their officers began issuing commands. Then, as they closed to within fifteen paces of the Jews, Crispus barked out an order.

"Charge!"

The legionaries let out a roar and sprinted to close with the enemy, shields raised and to the fore. But, as the Jewish frontline bunched together to brace for the attack, the slingers found they had no escape as a horde of snarling Romans reached them. Trapped, some began to scream; they knew what was coming. Lightly equipped, with no form of armour, most died crushed up against the shield of their spearmen while some were knocked to the ground by large Roman shields. Others died as a shield's edge smashed into their face, while passing legionaries in the following line skewered other prone soldiers with their swords.

The air rang with the sound of crashing shields, swords clashing on metal, the roar of the aggressors, and the screams of the wounded. Initially, the Jewish line fell back, but their sheer numbers helped steady them as they held their ground. Leading from the centre of the front, Crispus sensed the forward movement stopping; they had extracted a high price from the Jews, who were now fighting back. In his heart, he had hoped they would run, but his head was telling him differently. He screamed out an order for the century to retire, which resulted in legionaries falling into line, shoulder to shoulder and moving slowly back towards the start point. Fortunately, the bruised Judaeans chose not to follow but to take advantage of the respite and reform their ranks for the next assault.

"This is going to be a fucking war of attrition!" Crispus shouted as Claudius Paulus appeared at Crispus' shoulder.

"We have six dead, sir, and we have a number more casualties."

"Dammit!" Crispus scratched his forehead. "Claudius, get back there and tell the walking wounded to head to the coast. They'll do no good here." Paulus disappeared back through the ranks. No sooner had he gone than Felix Calvus, the century standard-bearer was beside Crispus.

"What's the plan, sir?" "

"As it ever was, Felix. We block this road until those bastards go back the way they came; it's as simple as that." Crispus scratched his forehead again. "I want you to make sure this standard gets planted in the centre of the road. Then, should it come to it, we shall rally around it." Crispus noted the expression of concern on Felix's face. "Don't look so worried, Felix. I do not intend that it should come to that. They will break, I promise you."

And so, the 1st Century of the IV Cohort returned to his defensive position, albeit not as confident as they were when they initially set up the line across the road.

"What in Hades name is this?" called out centurion Flavius Martinus as he gazed at the scene that greeted him as they passed over a slight rise. Several Roman soldiers were approaching, staggering along the road in a state of distress. Martinus kicked his horse forward, accompanied by his Optio, with Lucius and his comrades running behind. As they closed upon the bedraggled group, it was clear they had suffered injuries. Some could move under their efforts, but others had to be helped by their luckier comrades.

By the time Martinus had stopped his horse and alighted, Lucius, Atelius and Marcus reached the group.

"Gnaeus!" Atelius gasped, recognising one of the bloodied men. "What happened?" Gnaeus was one of those who could walk unaided but who held a limp, damaged, left arm in his right. The left side of his body was stained blood red, and he looked pale. Finally, however, he mustered enough strength to relate the events occurring further down the road behind him.

"Thank the gods," said Lucius, "for one second, I feared we'd lost the Century!"

"If we don't get moving, Optio, then it might be so," Martinus turned to the injured, "you men, keep moving down the road." He then faced the rear of his column, shouting, "Rear tent party, fallout and help these men back to the ship. They have done honourable work this day."

In the time it would take a man to breathe a breath, Martinus was back in the saddle. His century had been marching at double speed, but he upped the pace even further. Martinus' decisiveness impressed Lucius. The man had assessed the situation quickly in no time, and the century was moving again. Lucius and Atelius were certainly not going to complain; it was their century they were racing to save.

Marcus Crispus stood with his front line, facing his Judaean opponents, awaiting the next onslaught. They had just repulsed an attack that had cost the enemy several dead and injured. All well and good, he thought, but six of his century suffered injuries too. They were already heading coastwards. While he was grappling with his adversaries, he began to believe that these men may not be Judaeans. They were fighting with a discipline he had not experienced in local soldiers.

"We're down by roughly twenty men, sir," Felix Calvus said, "most wounded, but six dead!"

"Let's be positive, Felix," Crispus replied. "After five assaults, we nevertheless have sixty men. And look at what we've done to them. Twenty, thirty dead?"

"Yes, sir. But we'll reach zero before them!"

"Brace the line, Felix. I believe they are about to try again."

No sooner had Crispus spoken than the Jewish force moved forward. No rush to attack. They came on at a steady pace, spears to the fore, shouting and chanting in a language he did not recognise. The men of the century stood behind their shield, sword in hand, anticipating the next hectic round of combat. They had been blocking the trail for some time, facing constant attack, many tired and thirsty. The sun high in the sky made their task hot work. Crispus knew there was little he could do to ease their position. He counted on the force opposite losing heart; after all, the century had killed a large quantity of the spearmen. Taking a deep breath, he braced for the impact of the approaching force. The spearheads came to within arm's length of the Roman shields when a voice ordered a halt. There followed a cry from the rear of the century.

"Jupiter, *Optimus et Superbus,* they're bloody Romans!" Crispus snatched a backward glance and could not believe his eyes. A Roman column, led by mounted officers, approached at a pace, beating their blades upon their shields as they marched. His head swung back to his front to see the enemy retiring in good order, spears still held to the forwards. Crispus saw his moment, their morale collapsing.

"We've cracked them, boys. Let's finish this. *Fretensis* Advance!"

The remains of the 1st Century threw themselves at their retreating opponents with a roar. Shields hit and parted the wall of spear points. Many of the enemy threw down their spears and desperately drew their swords. Unfortunately, it was often too late, for a furious Roman hurled himself at them, showing how fine a weapon a shield in trained hands could be – no more so than when accompanied by a thrusting sword, the famed gladius. For an instant, the spearmen considered resistance, but they broke and routed as quickly. The soldiers of the First gave a half-hearted chase; the heat was draining and muscles tired. Nonetheless, Crispus estimated at least sixty spearmen lay dead by the time they were out of sight.

As his weary but happy soldiers trudged back to their standard, Crispus strode to the rear.

"To whom do I thank for this timely arrival?" he asked the mounted centurion. The officer dismounted and offered his arm to Crispus.

"I am centurion Flavius Martinus, the 1st Century, II Cohort, of the *Deiotariana*," he said smiling, "and I'm glad to have been of service, though you seemed to be doing a fine job by yourselves. You must be Aurelius Crispus?"

Lucius, Marcus, Atelius, and a gaggle of officers from both centuries joined the two men in no time. General introductions were made, and they familiarised themselves with the situation. They decided that the Fretensis soldiers would tend to their injuries and prepare to move back to the ships. The *Deiotariana* century would guard the road and deal with surviving rebel fighters. Crispus ordered Felix Calvus to organise helping the wounded and prepare to withdraw.

He and Lucius remained to discuss the situation with Martinus. The centurion explained how his century was on the way by sea to Caesarea. It was to bolster the Fretensis until it filled its establishment after the losses in Judaea. He was in mid-flow when a legionary approached the group.

"Excuse me, sirs," he called out and gained the group's attention. "Centurion Martinus, sir, I think you need to see something over here." He nodded his head to his rear. Martinus raised his eyebrows.

"What's so important, soldier?"

"These Jews... well sir, Jews they ain't; they're fucking Parthians!"

Martinus and Crispus exchanged surprised glances.

"That explains their fighting capabilities," muttered Crispus.

A few moments later, a Greek-speaking Parthian stood before the two centurions, held in the firm grip of two *Deiotariana* legionaries. The prisoner was bloody, having received a sword cut across one side of his ribcage. A blade's width to the left, and he would not have been talking at all. Instead, he stared at the ground, his attitude surly. It transpired that the Parthian force, which had faced Crispus' century, were all volunteers. Rome was a significant threat to Parthia, so these men were happy to help a country currently giving Rome a good kicking.

"So, my Parthian friend, just how do two hundred men of fighting age appear in Judaea equipped with standardised equipment?" asked Martinus.

"Yes, and fight like a well-trained force?" added Crispus.

"We are volunteers," the surly prisoner replied, "The Jews give us weapons."

"Lying *cunni*," Martinus spat. Behind the prisoner, a dozen wounded Parthians stood in a group, surrounded by soldiers of the *Deiotariana*. "You men, line those bastards up," Martinus ordered. He turned to the group around him. "We need to set an example here – and we shall do so."

Lucius wondered why only walking prisoners survived. Were there no leg wounds beyond the light cut and scratch? Then he realised that Martinus' men had already dealt with them.

A moment later, except for the Parthian standing with the officers, the prisoners were lined up, held by *Deiotarianan* legionaries. They stripped the captives to the waist. Lucius knew what was coming, and given the Parthian's faces, so did they. Nevertheless, they did not struggle or protest, a sign, thought Lucius, of their professionalism.

A file of legionaries marched out and stood facing the captives. Then the Parthian standing with the officers, spoke up.

"Domine, I beg you. Spare our lives." The surliness turned to pleading.

"You, I will spare," said Martinus, "for I have a job for you." He turned to the line of prisoners. "You men are Parthian. The Judaeans, I understand. They misguidedly believe they are fighting for their land when it is Rome's land, *Provincia Judaea*. They are wrong, but I understand." He stood while his words sunk in. "But you - you who masquerade as volunteers - are mercenaries, foreign troops fighting for the Judaean rebels. There can be only one penalty for such behaviour, no imprisonment, no slavery; only death." Then, again, he paused before using a parade ground voice, "Soldiers, draw swords."

The line of legionaries facing the captives drew their weapons, pointing them waist high at the prisoner opposite them. It impressed Lucius when not a single captive flinched.

"On my command," ordered Martinus, "Strike!"

Each legionary, thrust with extreme force, punched his sword into the stomach walls of the man facing him. The soldier paused a moment before wrenching the sword upwards towards the sternum. Lucius watched, fascinated and repulsed, as the soldiers stepped back three paces, likewise the soldiers holding the men captive. The stricken men fell to the ground, but not before some spilt their entrails onto the floor before them. One dying man attempted to raise himself on his forearms, then fell face down. His life force departed. Others twitched limbs, and then all was deathly still. The only movement from the corpses were the rivers of blood, turning the adjacent ground red in several directions.

Martinus, seemingly unaffected by what had just occurred, turned to the one surviving captive by his side.

"You will return whence you came and ensure any fellow Parthians and rebel comrades are aware of what will befall them should they raise a sword against Rome. Rome does not tolerate rebellion." He turned toward a group of his men who stood close by. "Find this man a water skin. I'd hate to think he dies of thirst before conveying my message - get him out of my sight. Oh, and by the way, cut off his sword thumb. I don't expect us to have to face him again, and you better get the medicus to see to his chest!"

They led away the unfortunate Parthian to be prepared for his journey back to Lod.

"Only way to deal with these bastards, Aurelius, wouldn't you say?" Martinus said with an enormous smile.

"You summed it up well, Flavius. Rome does not tolerate rebellion, and the whole of Judaea needs to understand that fact," replied Crispus. "What about you, Lucius, your thoughts?"

Lucius' mind raced. The two centurions were adopting the classic 'no tolerance' approach. However, he understood that

Imperator Hadrian wished to bind the Empire together. At all costs, he wanted peace to enable his subjects to prosper. Lucius considered the responsive 'punch-on-the-nose' was not always the most intelligent response, even if effective in the short term.

"Well, sir, if we appear to be ruthless, it may cause greater resistance in the enemy. More of our legionaries die. If we had spared the wounded, sent them back, there is a - "

"What the fuck are you saying, Optio?" Martinus burst out, "that we show the *cunni* mercy? Have you forgotten that they've just killed a good number of your men?" He turned towards Crispus, "What is Rome sending us, Aurelius? Bloody children in armour!" As he spoke, he became louder, moving close enough to Lucius that his breath wafted across Lucius' face. Lucius did not flinch. Crispus reached out and placed a hand on Martinus' shoulder.

"Flavius! The men will hear you. Be minded you are addressing a Roman officer." A red-faced Martinus stood, staring at Lucius before his posture appeared to sag. When he resumed, his voice calmed.

"Aurelius, if one of my Optios spoke like that, he'd be looking for a new cohort."

"Centurion Martinus," Crispus addressed his counterpart in an officious tone, "I *personally* requested Optio Petronius for my century. In Aelia, this 'youth' saw something we all missed, yet the 'experienced' centuriate rejected his observations. The following disastrous weeks proved him to be right. I believe I made a fine choice, and he has yet to let me down." He turned to Lucius. "Come, Optio, we've a century needing our attention." Turning away, he walked back towards the men of the First, busy organising the transport of the wounded.

"Thank you, Aurelius," Lucius said.

"Whether or not I agree with you, Lucius, he insulted my choice in you; ergo, he insulted me."

"It was so sudden and unexpected," Lucius replied, "and I believe he was wrong with the execution. He did not bother to consult you, Aurelius. It was our fight and our casualties. A matter such as the fate of the prisoners should've been yours.

Hades, we could've gained detailed intelligence from them. Suppose the Parthians had sent them, it would - "

"Lucius, Lucius," interrupted Crispus. "You must understand. I would've done as Flavius Martinus did." Then, noting the look of surprise on Lucius' face, he continued, "Your view may have merit, but it is not for us to decide alone. You are talking about adopting a strategy that the whole of the army in Judaea would need to adopt to have any effect. A gesture from us alone would have little impact. And what of the soldiers?"

"The soldiers?"

"Yes, the men who have seen their comrades killed by these people. It would not be good for morale to let prisoners walk away. And, finally, I think both Martinus and I would get our arses kicked by the Tribune, and his mates, if we had allowed them to walk." Lucius did not respond. "Lucius, you are young. You see things differently and have novel ideas. Your upbringing has differed from those of the centurions that populate this army. Your proposal may be of value, but new ideas need a careful introduction. Many people, as you well know, can be hostile to change and those that bring it."

Lucius sighed.

"I got that wrong, didn't I?" he said. "Only, it seemed a senseless waste of intelligence and an opportunity to influence our enemies."

"Well, you may've been wrong, but Flavius Martinus' actions were also out of order," said Crispus, "but let's put it behind us." He looked Lucius up and down. "Perhaps it was being told what to do by a scruffy civilian that upset the man!" Both men laughed.

As they approached where the legionaries were making ready to return to the ship, Felix Calvus joined them.

"Sir, the men wish to take the dead back with us for proper funeral rites at Caesarea," he said. "They're happy to carry them on their shields. There are eight of them, and we've twenty walking wounded, ranging from cuts to some quite nasty penetrations."

"The horses," said Lucius, "we could mount four of the injured."

"Aye, we could – as long as our friend Martinus hasn't become too attached to his beast!" quipped Crispus. Then, he adopted a more serious tone, "Detail off four men to a body. I want all the armour recovered and discharged pilum retrieved. Those bastards are not having any of our kit, that's for sure."

Later in the day, in the best order possible, the 1st Century approached the beached biremes. Behind them marched the soldiers of the twentieth Deiotariana. At the head of the First, soldiers carried the dead upon their large Roman shields, using their cloaks slung under the shields, front and back, to enable the carry. Upon arriving at the vessels, the sad procession drew up in a row. Then, on command, respectfully lowered the shields and their cargo to the ground.

The marine guard, understanding the situation, called to the sailors aboard the *Diana*, who sought ropes and tackle to enable hoisting the fallen aboard. Both centuries boarded the ships and made ready for departure, wishing to be away. The dead they laid out on the deck along one side of the *Diana*, and they guarded the two rabbis in the rear deck cabin. The remaining soldiers settled down for passage. Lucius and his 'rebels' sat upon the deck close to the bow of the *Diana*. There was not much conversation between them; each sat staring at the deck before them, replaying the last two days in their minds. Finally, it was Lucius who broke the silence.

"Look, men, I too am saddened at losing Sextus," he began. "We knew him well, and he was a fine soldier. Yes, I too wish we could have recovered his body, but it was not to be. But I am sure it would please him to know the mission had succeeded and that we all returned unharmed. He would not want us to be morbid."

"Lucius is right." Mordecai added in support, "Your roles, Sextus' too, in this operation were crucial to its success. And we completed the job allocated to us, so Sextus did not die in vain; he played an important part in achieving our objectives."

"Understood, sir," Marcus said, "but there's a tally to be settled."

As Marcus finished speaking, several sailors pushed past the small group and disappeared over the side. Some loud groans from the ship's stern followed as other seamen turned the capstan which hauled the anchor rope inwards. The anchor was firmly lodged astern of the vessel and did not budge, so the boat began to slide backwards. Assisted by the sailors on the beach and the rowers below decks, the bow was soon clear of the water's edge. It was not long before the dripping sailors returned inboard, and the bireme gently swung out to sea. Further commands saw the mainsail raised, which caught the steady breeze. As the bireme got underway, a shout carried across the water.

"Ahoy, biremes, all well?"

Lucius stood to see a small Liburnian, like the one he had sailed across *Mare Nostrum* to Caesarea, hove-to not far off. The triarchus and Crispus rushed to the ship's rail. The ship's captain cursed.

"It's busier than bloody Ostia harbour, for Hade's sake!" He leaned out over the ship's rail. "The *Diana*," he called back, "transporting a century of the Tenth *Fretensis* back to Caesarea, accompanied by a century of the Twenty-second legion *Dieotriania,* following."

"Just passing," came the response, "In these times, I didn't expect to see the likes of you on this coast. I'm carrying mails and cargo to Caesarea. Neptune be with you, brother." The triarchus of the mail boat turned back to his business.

"Ahoy," shouted Crispus. Then, realising the speedy Liburnian would be in Caesarea harbour much before the heavier biremes, he called out a request, "Can you take a message?"

The triarchus turned back towards the bigger craft.

"Of course. Give me your message," Crispus took a deep breath and proceeded.

"To the governor of Provincea Judaea. Centurion Crispus reports his mission a success, and we're returning immediately with the prize. We've twenty wounded and carry six dead."

The Liburnian's commander repeated the message, which Crispus confirmed was correct. The two men waved, and the lighter vessel, sails filled, moved off at speed.

"So," Lucius said to his small group, "now it's official. It wasn't easy, so well done, you played your parts well."

"We wouldn't have it any other way – nor would Sextus," said Marcus, "Don't know about you lot, but I need some grub." Then, rising to his feet, he added, "It's all this sea air, innit?" and sauntered off.

Lucius went towards the ship's rail to join Crispus. As he passed the injured men, he stopped for a few moments to talk with them. With the absence of abdominal wounds, he prayed they would all recover. At the worst, one or two might not be running for a while.

He found Crispus corralled with the century's remaining officers, Paulus and Calvus, who all welcomed Lucius.

"I was just saying that this was our real baptism of fire," Crispus said, "and given the bastards were Parthian spearmen, and they out-numbered us, I consider we performed well." He paused, rubbing his forehead; no one spoke, there was more to come, "but I was damn grateful for Martinus' intervention."

"Mars was with us this today," Claudius Paulus said solemnly. "We had his favour."

"Or maybe we should offer a sacrifice to Fortuna!" Felix Calvus added, "Whatever, we got the orders done."

"Perhaps we should sacrifice," Crispus agreed before continuing. "Wasn't it Scipio who said, 'the more I train my legions, the luckier we become'?"

They all laughed until Lucius spoke up.

"The mission has been a success, but will the strategy prove so?" His companions gave him puzzled glances. "What I mean is, we've apprehended the Rabbi – who must be all of eighty years old – but will we attain the objective of bringing the Judaeans to their senses and finishing this rebellion?"

Crispus stared at the deck, again kneading his forehead.

"Frankly, Lucius, who knows? But what I know is that the 1st Century did as ordered."

"Well, let's get the old man back to Caesarea alive," joked Felix. "He looks like he is halfway to Hades already!"

"Right, Calvus, I am making you answerable for ensuring we hand him over, still breathing!" Crispus retorted. He turned to

Lucius. "When we get to Caesarea, stay with the boat until we are all clear, then you and your lads can take a couple of days rest – you've earned it."

"Gratitude, Marcus. I'll notify the lads. It'll raise their spirits." Lucius turned to leave.

"Oh, Lucius," Crispus said, causing Lucius to pause. "Also, talk to Postumus' Optio to ensure they release the funeral funds. We need to get Postumus' pot back to his family given the circumstances. I didn't know him well, but I understand he was a first-class legionary."

"He was, sir. We spent quite some time together - often in danger - but I regret I knew little about him." Lucius experienced a sense of neglect and associated guilt. They had fought together, yet he knew so little of the man who had gone to the underworld. Finally, he turned and trudged to the ship's bow.

Capitulum XXIX - Caesarea again

2 Iunius. Year 16 of the Imperator Hadrianus.

No sooner had the ships docked than they took Rabbi Akiva ashore, handing him and Rabbi HaGarsi to a waiting centurion. Lucius and his companions watched his detachment march off the quay and towards the large archway that covered the entrance to the dockyards. Beyond the gates, they could hear the buzz of a small crowd; word had leaked about the *Diana*'s notable prisoner.

A waggon came alongside to collect the dead, and a team of medics boarded. In no time, the only people left on the Diana were its crew and Lucius' small company.

"From this point, we're off duty," Lucius said, "I think a little recuperation in a taberna might not go amiss." So they passed through the harbour gate, where the assembly had dispersed. With the operation behind them, it lightened the temperament. Even Marcus, upset about the loss of his friend, cheered, sharing a joke with his companions. But, before getting to the punchline, he interrupted the story.

"Venus' pussy, it's Anaitis!" Lucius followed Marcus' gaze to see two women, shawls over their heads, standing on the corner of a road junction, observing the comings and goings through the harbour gateway. In a moment, Lucius realised one of them was Miriam. The watchers recognised their men.

Anaitis threw her arms around Marcus and held him close. Miriam was more reserved, but it did not concern Lucius; her smile spoke volumes. Anaitis separated from Marcus.

"When you didn't come out, we feared you was lying in the cart," she said, "when the rumour spread, we come straight down, but you never marched out!"

"It's a long story," said Lucius, "but we're here. Anaitis, this is Atelius." He gestured towards the large African, "the man who taught me how to use a sword. And this," pointing to Mordechai, "is Mordechai ben Zakkai. We've worked a lot together and again over the last two days." The small group descended into a babble until Miriam posed a question.

"Lucius, where is Sextus?" All conversation came to an abrupt halt. Marcus confirmed her fears.

"We were with him, Miriam, at the end," Marcus said, "and placed the coin for *Charon* upon his tongue."

It seemed to take the women a while to absorb Marcus' words.

"He was a friend to you, Marcus. I will pray to Yeshua for him." She placed a hand on his shoulder and squeezed it.

"Don't you worry, Miriam, they've begun to pay the debt, and I *will* collect all of it," he snarled. On hearing his words, Miriam's face adopted a frown. She began,

"Marcus, you —"

"Make the *cunni* pay!" Anaitis spat. Miriam looked at her, shocked.

"Brother, it is war; it's not personal." Atelius' deep timbre gave his statement greater gravity. "Grieve, then let him go."

"It's easy for you to —,"

"My friends, it has been a trying few days. But, as I recall, we intend to find some wine and relax." Mordechai was back in the role of diplomat.

"Mordechai is correct," said Lucius. "I propose we visit Sistus in the *Minerva*. His food is excellent – as is his wine - which I'm sure he would make available to us!"

"That's easily done," Anaitis chipped in, "because that's where I work these days."

With the loss of Aelia Capitolina, Caesarea had become home to the whole legion. The colony was busy, with soldiers out of the town working on maintenance tasks and road repair. Sistus had needed an extra pair of hands in the taberna. It took only a morning for him to see that Anaitis was proficient in her work and every good landlord knows the value of a good-looking young woman. When Sistus discovered that Anaitis' good friend was close to a certain Optio Petronius, they easily persuaded him that Miriam's minor business venture would bring additional customers to the *Minerva*. After all, she was a success in Aelia Capitolina. And so, Miriam set up her healing service under a lean-to at the taberna's side.

Sistus welcomed the party with open arms; his wife Octavia prepared a "homecoming" meal for the men. Looking shabby, Lucius' party drew some odd looks from the soldiery using the taberna, who were wondering why these scruffy individuals should be carrying swords. Sistus assured them that these were men about the tribune's business, and they left the group in peace. The two women sat drinking honey water, and the men drank their wine uncut.

Mordechai made excuses and left the group; "he had to attend to business." As Lucius and Atelius made steady progress through the large jug of wine, Marcus drank as though he were in a hurry. Finally, Marcus picked up his beaker in mid-conversation and rose to his feet. He walked, unsteadily, to where a group of soldiers had gathered.

"Legionaries of the *Fretensis*," he said in a loud voice, raising his beaker of wine in front of him. "I ask you to raise your cups in memory of my good friend and fine soldier, Sextus Postumus." The gathered legionaries were taken aback for a second before raising their glasses. A voice asked,

"Sextus Postumus? Of the fifth?" In response, Marcus nodded his head. "Fuck me! He was in my tent party - a brother. Are you sure? Sextus, dead?"

"He is with his ancestors, brother," said Marcus, "but I can assure you, so are the bastards that did for him." Marcus raised his glass again. "To legionary Sextus Postumus."

This time drinking vessels rose to a chorus of the deceased's name. Marcus looked over his shoulder to see Lucius and Atelius both stood with beakers raised. He looked back at the soldiers.

"Brothers, on Jupiter, I make this oath that the bastards will pay many times over for his death." Marcus staggered back to his stool, collapsing onto it in an undignified fashion. Lucius decided it was time to leave. Anaitis declared she would take care of Marcus, and placing an arm around his shoulder, she stood him up and led him to the stairs at the back of the taberna.

With Anaitis and Marcus gone, Miriam sat sipping her honey water while Lucius and Atelius stared into their beakers. The trance broke when Atelius spoke.

"Sir, when I was a gladiator, I saw many fighters and different techniques —"

"Gladiator?" inquired Miriam.

"I would fight other men in an arena, a spectacle for the crowds," Atelius explained.

"They hurt men?"

"Yes, they hurt some," the African said, "and others perish." Miriam was taken aback.

"You kill?" She asked in a soft voice.

"I was a slave, lady, often tasked to kill, and if I did not, then I got killed. Simple."

"I am sorry, Atelius, I no mean to...." She bowed her head, staring hard at the table.

"No offence taken, lady. I had quite forgotten that you would not have seen *ludos* in Judaea." Atelius turned back to Lucius, "Sir, different fighters and techniques. One type of gladiator was the *Murmillo*. They gave him a gladius and shield, and he was heavily armoured; very well protected."

Lucius nodded his head, saying,

"Yes, I'm familiar with this type of gladiator."

"Often," Atelius continued, "they would pitch a *Murmillo* against a *Retiarius,* who wore a little light armour and was equipped with a Trident spear and a net."

"Keep clear of the net, then?" quipped Lucius.

"That was something the *Murmillo* focused upon," said Atelius. "So, you have a well-equipped *Murmillo* wielding a deadly Gladius and shield against a weakly defended *Retiarius* with the spear and the net." Lucius was now listening closely, wondering quite where the tale was going. Even Miriam was attentive a she struggled to translate Atelius' words. "However, the *Retiarius* had an extra weapon, his manoeuvrability. He would dodge and weave, intending to keep the *Murmillo* chasing him. He would stab at the *Murmillo* with the spear, constantly moving backwards or sideways. It was not long before the heat and the weight of his armour slowed the *Murmillo* down. The

Retiarius needed a tired, lumbering *Murmillo* before he could cast his net, knowing his adversary would be slow to evade. Once entangled in the net, the *Murmillo* was as good as dead."

Lucius' face took on a look of bewilderment.

"Well, Atelius, that was very interesting, but your point is…?"

The African emitted a deep, resonant laugh.

"Domine, sir, do you not see it?" he asked. "We are the *Murmillos*. With our steel helmets, our *lorica Segmentata* armour, our great shields, and our *Gladii* swords - we are the *Murmillo*!" He paused for a moment for his words to sink in, "like the *Retiarius*, the Judaeans are light of foot and will not fight until they have us where they want us; tired and upon their ground, the hillsides of Judaea."

"I think I see the point you are making, Atelius," replied Lucius, "and to some extent, our experience bears out what you say. But it will be different next time; I'm certain the Fretensis will not be alone when we go back prepared for the fight."

Looking at Atelius' face, it was evident he was sceptical, but he drew back from pushing his case harder with the Roman officer.

"You may be right, sir," he said with a certain reluctance, "it will be a different situation in the next campaign. Yes, matters *may* be different." To the surprise the other two, Lucius laughed, saying,

"By the gods, Atelius, don't tell me Sextus has bequeathed you his twitching nose!"

"He informed me of his nose, sir. Some of his tent mates used to call him Cassandra because of his prophecies of doom. Sextus would laugh and remind them Cassandra was never wrong!" He consumed the dregs of his beaker. "Thank you for the wine, sir. Best I be away now." Turning to Miriam, he said, "It was good to meet you, lady. Apologies for my gory story!"

After arranging for some weapons practise with Lucius the next day, Atelius left to return to his barracks.

Lucius and Miriam thanked Sistus for his hospitality before walking through the darkening streets towards Jacob's house she now called 'home'.

Lucius had a day before he would report for duty with his century, and he planned to enjoy the respite. So, dressed in a civilian tunic, he strolled through the military camp heading for the centre of Caesarea. He had a rough plan to drop by the *Minerva*. Perhaps the more compelling incentive was the expectation that Miriam might be there, working with her potions and herbs. After that, there was weapons practice with Atelius.

He passed the practice arena, where Centurion Drax was cajoling a large group of recruits. Recalling his last interaction with the large red-faced centurion, Lucius did nothing to attract his attention. Meanwhile, Drax's recruits sweated in the hot sun, brandishing wooden swords and wicker shields, both of which weighed far more than the genuine military issue. These lads would be well muscled when they joined their centuries. The weapons training would not carry on all day, but there would be little relief for the recruits, who would be off on a gruelling route march after weapons training.

Further on, he caught sight of two centuries practising battle drills, one attacking the other. There may be no deaths by the end of the day, but there will be bruising and cuts. The training was hard. Convalescing soldiers were being put through their paces in one corner of the parade ground. The legion made every effort to make the soldier's limbs effective again and return these men as capable legionaries.

Today, none of this was of concern to Lucius. He strolled past the principia, marvelling at its fine marble architecture and its –

"Optio Petronius, sir." The voice came from a legionary hurrying down the steps that led from the principia's entrance. Lucius turned towards the soldier.

"I thought I would just blend into the background wearing this garb," Lucius answered. "It would turn out not."

"Sir, the Tribune Laticlavius requests that you attend his person." The legionary said as he snapped off a precise salute.

"Well then, we'd better not have the tribune kept waiting," said Lucius, reflecting on how short his day of leisure had been.

A few moments later, the tribune's secretary gave Lucius access to the office. Gaius Civilis had his back to Lucius, gazing out of the window, watching the same drills Lucius had observed. A plumed helmet and white leather cuirass hung to his left on the armour stand; a wide desk covered in scrolls and several wax tablets was positioned to his right. The man spun around to face Lucius.

"Forgive me, Lucius. Aurelius had informed me he had stood you down, but seeing you passing by, the temptation was too great! Please, take a seat." As he spoke, he went to sit behind his desk, requesting his secretary bring water for the two men. "So, it went well, Lucius?"

"We did as requested, sir. We have apprehended Rabbi Akiva."

The tribune frowned.

"That's very factual, Lucius. I detect little enthusiasm for a job well executed." The tribune paused for a second. "I recognise you lost a good man; working in close-knit groups, you feel the loss all the more." Lucius was biting his lower lip, and Civilis sensed there was more. "Is there something else I need to know?"

Hesitant to respond, Lucius needed to get something off his chest.

"Sir, I understood we were to detain a leading member of the rebellion. A fire-breathing, religious extremist who was driving the rebels into battle. In taking him, we would undermine their war effort." Lucius fell silent.

"And?" The tribune asked.

"We returned with an eighty-year-old man on a donkey cart and a younger Rabbi, his assistant. In doing so, we lost a number of good men."

Civilis took a slow sip of water, returning his glass to the desk.

"So," he said, "you are questioning whether it was worth it. Am I correct?"

"It's a question that keeps running around in my head, sir."

The tribune sat straight-backed in his chair, placed both hands flat on a table in front of him and took a deep breath.

"Optio Petronius, you are a soldier in the pay of the Roman army. We give you orders, and you carry them out to the best of your ability – and I think you have plenty of that. It is not for you to question those orders. They gave you them and you implemented them well; the intentions and goals behind those orders are not your concern. Is that clear?"

Lucius felt like a chastened schoolboy, the discomfort growing by the second. He sat upright.

"Apologies, sir," he said, "I had no intention to question your judgement."

The tribune relaxed in his chair.

"You've had the official line, Lucius," he said. "Now, let's converse as Lucius and Gaius, man-to-man. On the one hand, I will confess Akiva is a minor disappointment. But there was more to this mission than apprehending a man. So let me ask you, Lucius, how do you believe the rebels will have taken it; our pushing into Judaea at our pleasure and stealing Akiva from right under their snouts?"

Lucius thought for a second before answering.

"Before we landed, they must've been pretty pleased with themselves. It's not everybody that pushes a Roman legion from their homeland. I hear what you're saying, Gaius. Also, we demolished a unit of Parthians, who, compared to the Judaeans, are elite troops. So, yes, I'd say we knocked their confidence somewhat."

"Now you are thinking!" the tribune declared, "but who else is affected by the enterprise?"

Lucius thought for a few moments.

"I'm not sure I'm following you, Gaius."

"Think about it, Lucius. Who has had their arses kicked recently? Who has lost good soldiers to death and injury? All inflicted by jumped-up bandits from the Judaean hills?"

"I think I can see where you're going, Gaius," Lucius said. "Our demotivation. The lads need some good news."

"Yes, we do need good news," said Civilis, "because I have a problem, and it's one I must resolve."

"Problem?"

"Yes, it is called desertion."

"*Cac*! Desertion? From the *Fretensis*? Surely not!"

"It is not in big numbers," the tribune said, "but it has been growing. We recruited many of our legionaries from the province. The lure of earning Roman citizenship is great, and to be fair, we have some excellent soldiers. But seeing the Roman army getting a hiding from Judaean rebels sends a dangerous message – "

"— that Rome can be beaten," Lucius interjected, "added to which they have a high priest telling them that a messiah figure leads the rebels. So, Rome is being defeated at the wish of the gods – or in their case, a God."

"Perhaps the Imperator was right to suggest we need more Italian blood!" said Civilis. "So, you are now the wiser as to why your mission had a higher goal than Rabbi Akiva per se." He paused, then his tone altered. "So, Optio Petronius, I think you can pat yourself on the back for your work in Judaea. You achieved a lot more than you thought."

"That makes me a happy soldier, Gaius," Lucius answered. "It means that Sextus Postumus died working to accomplish something beyond apprehending an ancient priest! It helps."

"I'm pleased to hear you say that, Lucius. But there is more I require to update you on."

The tribune took another sip of his water and sat back in his chair, suggesting to Lucius that the conversation was about to change direction; he was not wrong.

"On a brighter note," the tribune began, "our people in Damascus found the missing centurion from En Geddi. He arrived here under guard some days ago. It did not take our *inquisitories* long to make him talk. All I can tell you is that there is a clear link to a much larger plot."

"A much larger plot?" Lucius asked.

"Beyond the province, Lucius," Civilis replied, "but I am not at liberty to say more; you must understand."

"Rome?"

"Do not push me, Optio."

"Apologies, sir."

"No offence taken, Lucius," said Civilis, "but given your earlier involvement, I thought it fair to wrap the matter up with you."

Lucius thought the meeting was ending. He was wrong.

"There is one last item I need to share with you. Some time back, a woman in Caesarea had two sons. One son, the elder, was a bright lad and strong-minded. In complete contrast, the younger son, by a couple of years, was a dimwit, a simple lad with little intelligence and a slow thinker. The boys grew up together until the older son went south."

Lucius was wondering just where the story was going.

"Not long after, the younger boy who turned to labouring for a living fell off a cart. He landed awkwardly and broke his neck; he was stone dead. Meanwhile, in Judaea, the older boy falls into dangerous company. One day he returned to visit his ageing mother, at which point the Roman army drops on top of him." The Tribune paused. "Does any of this sound familiar?"

"I think it does, but it was the simple lad that went South?" said Lucius with a slight sense of foreboding.

"No, Lucius, the dimwit was dead. The older lad fooled us; after all, he had years to learn the role of being a fool. He pulled it off and escaped south with his mother."

"*Cac*, and we never saw it! How could we have been so stupid?" Lucius' mood changed to one of embarrassment. "Do we know anything about him?"

"Yes, our spy network may be damaged, but some of it still functions," Civilis replied. "He is Jacob ben Hamodai, and it seems his key role in life is to stir up a rebellion in Galilee."

"And we missed him!"

"*Cac* comes along every so often, and we seem to have had more than our fair share!" Civilis joked. "I suspect that ben Hamodai has a hard job in front of him. We are not in Judaea, Lucius. The Galileans have worked with Rome and done well from the relationship. I do not see them appreciating anyone rocking that boat. So, don't be too hard on yourself."

The officer pushed his chair back and stood. "Shortly there is a meeting with the senior centurions and the tribunes. We kept them in the dark about the Akiva business, and I think it is time we gave them an account of what happened. Why don't you come along?" Standing in front of the tribune, Lucius looked at his civilian garb.

"Sir. Like this?" he asked. Civilis ploughed on.

"In the name of *Dis*, you went through the entire operation dressed as a scruffy rebel! It'll bring a little authenticity to the tale." Lucius appreciated that he was facing a veiled order.

"As you wish, sir."

"Good man, Lucius, we had better be going."

"May I ask, sir," said Lucius, "who is giving them the account?"

The tribune smiled.

"Did I not mention it? You are. Now, let's be going."

Attached to the principia was a moderately sized assembly room. A stunned Lucius did not recall the walk from the tribune's office to the room. Entering through the large double doors, Lucius came face-to-face with the senior officers of the Tenth Legion. He followed Civilis to the raised dais positioned in front of the meeting in a daze. The officers, all of whom had stood upon the entry of the tribune, responded to a wave of the senior officer's arm, indicating they should sit. Lucius only half heard him introduce the meeting and set the scene for the content.

"Fellow officers, I thought it best that you should hear the details of the events from the officer who led the small party into Judaea, beginning the operation. Optio Petronius, the dais is yours." Civilis stood down. Lucius gave himself a thorough mental shakedown and mounted the podium.

Standing on the raised platform facing the audience, it took Lucius back to the day in Aelia when his uncle had asked him to share his concerns about the Jews with the centuriate. It had not been a comfortable exchange, and the emotions came flooding back. He looked across the audience. There he could see Aginthus of the Third and Gallianus of the Fifth. His uncle sat next to Aurelius Crispus, wearing a beaming smile. To further his discomfort, he spotted Senior Centurion Octavius Secundus, the man who had given him a very rough ride during the earlier meeting. Towards the rear sat Centurion Flavius Martinus of the Twentieth *Deiotariana*.

Lucius pulled himself together. He had some tutoring in rhetoric at school, so he was not afraid of public speaking, and he assured himself a straightforward account of the events would be no problem. He cleared his throat.

"Centurions of the Tenth, tribunes, I shall relate the events that began when Tribune Civilis gained information from a captured Judaean on the whereabouts of Rabbi Akiva Ben Joseph. We knew we had an opportunity that might not arise again. Therefore, we needed a plan..."

The audience absorbed the account, and unlike his previous experience with the centuriate, he was uninterrupted. By the time he reached the point relating to their departure from Serifin, this confidence had returned. Crispus continued to beam from the front row. His uncle was looking at him like a proud father! Confidence returned. He decided to turn the tables.

"You will understand, fellow officers, at this point, I left the century to return with Rabbi Akiva to the waiting ship. With the greatest respect, I would like to request centurion Crispus to recount his actions with the enemy force that attacked us. I suspect you would find that most interesting."

For a second, the smile evaporated from Crispus' face. Then he laughed, shaking his head, stood up and came to the dais. He picked up the story from where Lucius had left off, relating the fight with the Parthians that ended with the arrival of a century of legionaries from the Twenty-second *Deiotariana*. He acknowledged his debt to the *Deiotariana*. Lucius could not help noticing that when Crispus highlighted executing the captured Parthians, there was a murmur of general approval through the gathering.

Lucius stood to one side of Crispus, catching Martinus' eye. The man smiled and nodded, enjoying the confirmation of his actions. Crispus ended his relation at the point where the Roman forces sailed away from Judaea.

The tribune approached the dais. Crispus and Lucius made way for him, taking seats in the audience. Civilis stressed the impact of the venture on Jewish morale and the positive effect on legionaries in Caesarea. He was approaching the end of his talk when the doors to the assembly room burst open, and two legionaries entered, positioning themselves at either side of the doors.

"Make way for Tineius Rufus, governor of Provincea Judaea." Draped in an immaculate white toga, Rufus swept into the room. As one, the audience rose to their feet, standing to attention.

"Tribune Laticlavius Civilis, forgive me. I thought you had finished, but I interrupted you," the governor said in the tone that showed that showed a feigned forgiveness, and that Rufus was about to take over the meeting. Then, turning to a still rigid audience, he waved his hand through the air and said, "My friends, please sit as I would have some words with you."

As he spoke, two legionaries appeared carrying a white, polished, curule chair and placed it on the dais, the tribune stepping down to make way for them. Rufus stepped up to the podium and sat in the chair. The tribune stood to his right.

"Soldiers of Rome," the governor began, "we have been through an arduous and trying period. The uprising in Judaea caught us by surprise; we had some warning, but it was too late. Abandoning Aelia Capitolina was painful as well as hard to bear. For the *Fretensis* marching away from an enemy leaves a bitter taste in the mouth. We have licked our wounds for weeks and rebuilt our military establishment. What I can tell you is that we are near the time when we shall end this rebellion." As he spoke, the manner of his voice hardened. "The recent successful operation to capture the Jewish chief priest is the start of our retaliation. After that, there will be no more running from Judaean rebels."

A murmur of approval ran through the audience, and then someone clapped; it was infectious, and within seconds, the entire gathering was enthusiastically clapping. Lucius thought back to his recent meeting with the tribune; the audience's behaviour confirmed his words. These men needed some good news. Then the governor lifted his hands for silence.

"A campaign is in preparation, and at this stage, I can only share general details with you. When we move, the *Fretensis* will move south. You will not be alone as the Sixth *Ferrata* will be doing likewise, heading out from Galilee. That will be two full legions closing on the north of Judaea. Meanwhile, the Twenty-Second Deiotariana will land to the south and proceed northwards into Judaea from Egypt. We will squeeze the rebels like olives in the press, except of course it is not their oil we seek, but their blood."

The audience's response was yet more clapping. Even Lucius became swept up in the euphoria of the moment.

"There is one thing I wish to make quite clear. Rome does not tolerate rebellion. When you move, you shall be ruthless; any town or village that resists will burn to the ground. Those rebels who resist will die, and their wives and children taken and handed to the slave traders. I have assured Caesar that once this is over Judaea, will never again lift its hand against Rome."

The governor paused while the clapping subsided.

"This will not happen tomorrow; it'll be some time from now. But I wanted you to know that we are past the nadir. From here, matters shall go upwards. In this chamber, I see all our senior centurions. So go back to your cohorts, soldiers, drill your men and be ready when the hour comes; it is soon approaching. I will keep you no longer. You have work to do. Gods be with you."

The governor rose to his feet, and the audience stood. He turned to the tribune, and they began a conversation while the centurions and tribunes departed the room. Crispus and Lucius were about to leave as centurion Julius Petronius intercepted them.

"Well then," he began, grinning, "you two are quite the heroes!"

"For Dis' sake Julius, leave off," said Crispus, "it was just a job."

"Seriously though, well done. Lucius, you are making your mark. Carry on like this, and you will be a tribune in no — "

"Centurion Crispus," called the governor. The small group of three turned to face the voice, all standing to attention. "Relax, my friends." Then, turning to Lucius' commander, "Crispus, a job well done."

"Gratitude, sir," Crispus responded, "as I was saying to Centurion Petronius here, it was a job, sir. Someone had to do it, and it fell to my century."

"No matter, Crispus," Rufus replied. "It was well done. But, Optio Petronius, left your uniform in Judaea, did you?"

Lucius blushed and felt awkward.

"Sir, I was off duty and was called into this meeting at short notice. Apologies, sir."

"Never mind." The governor turned to Civilis, "I believe Faustinus is awaiting us, Gaius, we best be away." Saying this, he withdrew, followed by the tribune.

Interludum VII – "They will rejoice in Heaven."

Some weeks had passed since the Romans' audacious seizure of Rabbi Akiva in the village of Serifin. The man previously known as Shimeon ben Koseva, now revered as Bar Kokhba, had called his area commanders and army captains to a meeting at Herodium, south of Jerusalem in the Judaean hills.

The attendees gathered in the citadel's lower courtyard, taking shade under the few olive trees or sheltering in the great walls' shadows. Serifin aside, these men were bolder and more confident than they had been some months ago, encouraged, if not unbelieving, of their success in driving the Romans from Judaea. It was said that Bar Kokhba rarely slept, being so busy with state and the military affairs of Judaea. He had boundless energy, and some said he could be in two places at once. The rebellion was over to those assembled at Herodium; a new state now established, and it was necessary to protect it.

The heat was becoming unbearable when the great Round Tower doors were thrown open. The air inside was cooler, and the officers and administrators collapsed onto the rows of benches spread across the floor. They faced a raised vacant table and chairs. A hum of conversation filled the room when a small doorway that concealed a staircase opened, and Bar Kokhba, followed by his senior officers, entered the room. All talk ceased. The officers sat while Bar Kokhba remained standing, facing his audience.

"My brothers, friends, and comrades, shalom. I welcome you to this place." He stretched his arms wide and swung from left to right. "Who would have thought that Judaea would be free of Romans?" Smiling, he lowered his arms. "We have liberated part of Israel from the pagan hobnail boots of Rome. Blessed is the Lord God of Israel, who has given us this glorious victory." There was a nodding of heads and a murmur of approval throughout the audience. "Now, we must move to solidify our new state. Work has begun in replacing the Roman administration with a Jewish one. Guided by the Torah, daily life for our people continues, sending a powerful signal of stability and permanence. Even as I speak, Roman coins are being overstamped with symbols of the nation of Israel. In doing all of this, we shall please the Lord and keep his favour."

"Great Nasi, a question," came a voice from the audience. Israel had not seen the rank of Nasi since the destruction of Jerusalem by the Roman general Titus many years ago. However, the Nasi was a prince of Israel, and the rabbis had awarded the rank to Bar Kokhba. The 'Big One' indicated the questioner should continue. "The temple, will we rebuild the temple?" Bar Kokhba welcomed the inquiry, smiling.

"Israel cannot be without Jerusalem, and Jerusalem cannot be without its temple." A further murmur of approval went through the audience; many were still euphoric about the achievement of Bar Kokhba, the Nasi, or as his men referred to him, "the Big One." "However, let us not delude ourselves that Imperator Hadrian and his henchmen will sit back and accept this situation. As we speak here, I know that they are plotting vengeance upon us. We must prepare ourselves to receive them when they come." The expressions of joy and euphoria faded. It was not over; there would be more bloodshed. Bar Kokhba allowed some time for that fact to sink in.

"Now we've beaten them once, with the Lord's help, we'll beat them again!" said an enthusiastic voice, the speaker convincing themselves more than the audience.

"Yes, we can beat them again," said Bar Kokhba, "but let us be clear what we are up against." Then, he turned to the officers sitting at the table beside him, "I have asked Captain Yohanon to study our foes."

The tall, lightly built Yohanon took to his feet as Bar Kokhba sat. Then, clearing his throat, he began.

"Shalom brothers. As the Nasi has said, the Romans will be returning to our land." Tall and thin, his voice was of a higher pitch than Bar Kokhba, and his nose was such that his appearance earned him the nickname 'the Hawk.' However, Yohanon's great strength was his intellect, and he served Bar

Kokhba as both strategist and spymaster. "So, what is Imperator Hadrian going to throw against the Lord's host in Judaea?" The question was rhetorical. "Our spies tell us that the Tenth Legion in Caesarea is replacing its dead and is making ready. The Sixth Legion in Legio would also appear to be made ready, so two legions to our north will move to attack us."

The audience, sitting in rows of benches across the tower's base, was still. Yohanan knew what would be going through their minds. They had beaten one Roman legion by the element of surprise, and here he was telling them this time they would be facing two readied legions. He had more to say which would add to their discomfort.

"You are aware of what took place in the village of Serifin and the loss of Rabbi Akiva. The survivor from that fight mentioned a relieving force, carrying distinctive blue shields. I believe the Parthians fought a century from the Twenty-Second Legion based in Egypt. Therefore, I must conclude that we will face this legion, moving up from their base and attacking us in the south. I expect three legions supported by some auxiliary forces shall attack us simultaneously."

Yohanan stood, his gaze scanning the gathering. Their discomfort was quite clear; three legions formed a dangerous antagonist.

"Brother Yohanon, can you be sure of this?" a voice called out.

"It is what I would do," Yohanan said, "it is a simple plan – what the Romans are good at – designed to crush us between legions." The audience burst into a noisy commotion while the Hawk stood motionless for a few moments before raising his arms, calling for silence. The room fell quiet, and many faces looked towards the man with the outspread limbs, which lowered. "Brothers, the Roman plan has one great failing – hubris. They know their mighty, armoured masses will overwhelm us like the way a wave rushes across the beach. But, brothers, the Lord is with us, and we shall defeat them!"

"Brother Yohanon, I ask again, how you can be so sure?" No sooner had the question been asked than bar Kokhba rose to his feet. Yohanan, seeing this, sat.

"I remember," he began, "when I was proposing we drive the Tenth Legion out of Judaea, some of you asked me how I could be sure that we would achieve such an objective." He paused as his gaze swung across the audience. Nobody moved. "To those who were with me at that time, I said it was all about understanding our enemy, who was arrogant and complacent, to the point of laziness. We used our understanding to beat them, did we not?"

The murmur of agreement built into explicit consent. Then at the back of the room, a man arose. His hair was speckled grey, and his skin creased like an old leather bag. He was the oldest officer in the room.

"Nasi, we all respect your leadership in driving the Roman dogs out of our land," he said. The audience fell quiet to listen to the man. "Your plan used the Roman weaknesses, and with the Lord's blessing, our efforts were successful." The older man saw the nodding heads of support for his words. "But Nasi, three well-prepared Roman legions are a different challenge to the one we faced previously. Could it not be time for negotiation with the Romans?"

Those officers sat on the top table, either side of bar Kokhba, turned to look at their leader. Bar Kokhba did not take direct challenge well, and his senior officers braced themselves for a violent response. The Nasi tensed, ready to deliver a tirade towards the questioner. Then he relaxed.

"Brother Levi, my old friend. You were ever the cautious one."

"Perhaps, Shimeon, that is why I have lived to grow old bones!" The use of the Nasi's name raised eyebrows in the audience.

"Or perhaps it is because my approach has avoided major casualties," bar Kokhba answered. "Do you think I have not planned this next stage? I have not identified our enemy's weakness?" The leader's voice grew louder as he spoke. "I will tell you how we will defeat three Roman legions and keep our newly liberated state intact. We play to the hubris and arrogance, their belief that their armoured legions can overcome all before them, that they are the invincible Roman army." He stood, his eyes sweeping those before him, daring a challenge. None came. "Brothers, we shall not stand and face them in battle. Do they believe we are so stupid? But we shall fight them, in our time and on our terms. I plan to run them ragged across the hills of Judaea where their armoured might will be of little help to them." He turned to Yohanan. "Tell them, brother, share the plan."

He, who some called the Hawk, arose and confronted the audience, as an exasperated bar Kokhba took to his seat.

"Brothers, what I share with you is for your ears only. If there is greater detail to give, we will share it individually." Looking out at the expectant faces before him, Yohanan knew he had their close attention. "Our many villages and townships are all fortified, and we shall fiercely defend each one if attacked. The hiding places are prepared, holding stocks of food and weapons, and local forces will utilise them to strike at the Romans and then vanish. These are our hornet's nests, from where we shall sting and fly away. Each of these attacks will be of small impact but repeated a hundred times, will cause severe discomfort to the enemy. We want them nervous. They will not know from when or where the next attack will come. Therefore, with the Lord's help, they will be greatly demoralised."

Heads nodded, and Yohanan could see the audience was buying his message.

"As many of you know, we have established three field armies. Unlike our foes, we can travel through the mountains, the ground upon which Rome's lumbering, armoured legions will be greatly discomforted. Like our local forces, the strategy is to strike with surprise, strike hard and then withdraw, but with much greater force. We shall use all at our disposal to hit them, be it rock, slingshot, spears, swords, or fire. By the time the enemy recovers, we disappear into the hills. In effect, the Romans will be unable to bring their strength to bear. With the Lord's help, the blood of our enemies will stain the valleys of Judaea."

As he finished his words, Yohanan turned to bar Kokhba, who signalled his lieutenant should take a seat. The Nasi arose.

"Levi, my brother, we have known each other for many years," he said, "do you consider your 'old bones' would survive this last battle?"

"Shimeon, if it must be a battle for Judaea, you know full well I shall be there."

The Nasi smiled.

"They will rejoice in Heaven, Levi!" He remained silent for a moment before going on, his voice developing a hard edge. "I say to you now, to every man in this room, that if you hold any qualms about what we are about to do, then walk away. I will hold no animosity against you and thank you for your service. Only if my captains have conviction will we win this contest. The Lord's Host has no room for the hesitant and the uncertain." The audience sat still, ears straining for any sound of movement, but none came. Standing, Bar Kokhba played upon the moment, reinforcing the commitment from his officers. Then he went on. "Now, I want each of you to report your state of preparedness. Also, anything you consider may be a hindrance to your effectiveness." He lowered himself back in his chair, feeling that the last pieces were all settling into place. His forces would give the Romans an extremely bloody nose indeed.

Capitulum XXX – Postumus' sixth sense

1 Iulius. Year 16 of the Imperator Hadrianus.

Out of uniform, Lucius Petronius sat at a table outside the *Minerva* taberna, facing the street. He had spent the last several weeks drilling with the IV Cohort. A great disciple of training, Centurion Crispus had driven them hard. But, as this day had involved a long route march, Lucius felt he had earned the taberna's refreshments. The other attraction was the chance to talk to Miriam, the *Minerva* now being the base of her healing practice. The sun was lowering in the sky, but the heat of the day was present, and a moderate breeze served to make his pleasure in a beaker of Sistus' wine even greater.

Occasionally, Anaitis would emerge carrying food and drink to other customers who, like Lucius, were savouring the cooling breeze. At the side of the taberna Lucius' knew Miriam would be applying herbs and poultices to the cuts, bruises and septic fingers that kept her busy during the day. Lucius hoped that her flow of customers would dry up, and she would appear from around the corner.

He was not alone. Sitting opposite him was Marcus Apollinaris. The appeal of the opposite sex also drew the freshly appointed officer to the Minerva. Since Aelia Capitolina, they accepted that Anaitis had become Marcus' woman. Lucius was envious of the ease of their relationship. However, he recognised it was straightforward for Marcus, as Anaitis was a woman from the Empire with no local attachments. Moreover, they both came from comparable backgrounds. But for Lucius, Miriam was a Jewess with a family in Caesarea. What is more, his and her lived experiences could not have been further apart.

The two men discussed their military activities of recent days, only to discover that their activities were similar. The training routines were reaching a peak. After detailing the ups and downs of his last route march, Marcus' posture became conspiratorial.

"Don't say you heard this from me, Lucius," he said, "but a couple of the lads in the tent unit were doin' guard duty down the principia yesterday. They earwigged two tribunes on their way out. From what they're saying, it sounds like we are off down south in three days."

"They were certain about what they picked up?"

"They was dead sure," Marcus replied, "so I wants to spend some time with Anaitis 'fore we goes. Hopefully not the last time!"

"Bugger me!" Lucius exclaimed, "it would take Mars himself to finish you off." Marcus laughed. "So, how is Anaitis, our slayer of Jewish warriors?" The smile disappeared from Marcus' lips.

"I worries about 'er, Lucius. She often moans in her sleep, even awaking screaming. I suspect it is more than just me being there," he jested, "No, she told me that. There's more. Sometimes I think the Vulcaes themselves possess her; she's ready to blow at the slightest irritation. Sistus has mentioned to me that he's had to speak to 'er a couple of times after customers have upset 'er."

"Perhaps one of you should offer to *Bona Dea*," suggested Lucius, "it might help." The Tesserarius nodded. "Don't forget, Marcus, it's not every woman who gets shut in a cupboard, all around her being butchered. It's not every woman who goes through attacking, killing, and beheading an attacker. She needs time."

Lucius was about to say more when the subject of their conversation appeared from within the taberna. She no longer donned the apron she had been wearing when Lucius last saw her.

"Optio Petronius, nice to see you. Does Miriam know you're here?" she asked. Lucius explained he was sticking around for Miriam to close shop for the day while chewing the cud with Marcus to pass the time. "Well, I am sorry to break it up," she said, "but Marcus is taking me to purchase a new bracelet before the market shuts." She held out a hand for Marcus to hold.

"Apologies," the man said. "I made a promise. Dunno about Mars, but I think Anaitis will kill me if I break it." In a moment, the officer and his woman were stepping away from the taberna, leaving Lucius alone. As he sipped his wine, the III Cohort approached in battle order. The men's faces, damp with sweat, and covered in dust, revealed the unit was at the end of a route march. The amount of dust hinted of a gruelling route, as it was unlikely that a regular Roman road would throw up enough dust to darken the legionaries' faces.

Watching the men go by with their javelins and shields, clad in lorica segmentata and wearing polished helmets, Lucius wondered if the rebels had any notion what was about to hit them. He was proud to be one of these men, a highly trained, professional soldiers' brotherhood. To command men such as these was an honour. (How could Atelius' have concerns about the suitability of the troops?) The Third marched passed him by and out of sight. Lucius finished his drink and left the table, heading to where he expected to find Miriam.

Head bowed, she concentrated on clearing her modest table. She gathered her herbs and medications into a narrow wooden box. Cloth and wrappings she placed in a wicker basket. It intrigued Lucius how precisely she secured her things. He had commented upon this attribute before, the reply being, "a place for everything and everything in its place." As she eventually closed the container's lid, she glanced in Lucius' direction, her face lighting up.

"Lucius, you surprise me. You no say you are coming."

"A pleasant surprise, I hope."

"Yes, yes," she said, smiling as she took up her box and basket, "let us walk."

Lucius held up a palm.

"Miriam, can we sit for a while? I feel I need to talk."

She sensed a change of tone in his voice.

"Lucius, is all right?" As she spoke, she returned to the bench behind her table. Lucius sat across from her.

"Don't be distressed, Miriam," he answered, "but I've heard something today, and I need to discuss it with you." However, the expression on Miriam's face showed his attempt to minimise concerns had not worked.

"Lucius, what is it?" For a moment or two, Lucius seemed to collect his thoughts as Miriam looked on. Then, as he spoke, he reached out and took both her hands in his.

"Miriam, you know what I – the cohort – the Fretensis – have been training for over the last several weeks," he began, "well, I understand it is going to happen soon."

"The soldiers go to fight?" She asked.

"They will, and I need to talk to you about that," Miriam said nothing but looked into Lucius' face. "Miriam, the people of Judaea have risen in insurrection against Rome. But the Empire and the Roman army do not tolerate rebellion. So, the consequence for Judaea will be something that in Latin we call "*vastatio*", which means devastation." He squeezed her hands tightly. "My love, have you any notion what that means?"

Miriam remained expressionless, her brain processing the information in her newly adopted second language. Then she bowed her head and spoke quietly.

"Many people die."

"Yes, many people will die." Lucius continued, "The nature of this type of war is not like a battlefield where soldiers kill soldiers. Women and children will likely go down to the sword. Miriam, these are your people, and I am a Roman soldier. Do you understand my worry? I fear I may have put you – us - in an impossible position."

Again, Miriam remained impassive as she took in what Lucius told her. Finally, she nodded but did not speak, retaining her gaze on Lucius' face. He chose to give her some time, and she remained sitting holding his hand. He dreaded the silence was a bad omen but continued clutching her hands. Unbeknownst to him, she was struggling to put her thoughts into Greek.

"Lucius, I explain," she said, her face softening, "I am from Judaea. I am a Jew and follower of Yeshua. Jew's country is Israel: Judaea, Samaria, and Galilee. Do you see fight in Samaria or Galilee? No, fighting is in Judaea. Bar Kokhba not speak for Israel." She paused, and it seemed to Lucius almost as though she was gathering conviction. She then continued. "Bar Kokhba killed my uncle and aunt. You and others take care of me, or I would be dead, too. He killed many *Telmidei Yeshua*. For much time, Israel has suffered foreign kings and princes. We have tasted bitter price of rebellion many times. Bar Kokhba his people are fools. They bring the *vastatio* down upon them. I will weep for them and pray to the Lord." Again, she paused as she processed her thoughts. "Lucius, you have no fault in this. The soldier obeys." She removed her hands from under his and then reconnected, reversing the previous grip. "No worry for me. I do not like killing, but I understand."

Lucius' expression flipped between amazement and relief.

"Miriam, I am so glad," he said, "I did not expect you to see it that way."

"We go to Telmidei meetings. When over, the men talk much. On the way home, uncle would tell us about their talks. He say many times that rebels did not talk for all. He said *vastatio* would come. He was right."

"I was so worried you would think of me as the enemy," said Lucius

"Lucius, what is happening is very sad. Killing is not answer. You did not make this happen. My uncle say, play with scorpion – you get stung."

"Killing may not be the answer, Miriam, but when Rome stings, it kills. What is coming is going to be bloody, and many will die." Lucius' countenance changed. He smiled, "But we have a little time yet. Let me walk with you back to Jacob's."

"I would like," she said, "but Lucius, please, I beg, do not be hurt." Then, she squeezed his hands in hers, "I no want to lose anyone more." Saying thus, she stood. "Come, I prepare food for you," she volunteered.

"And I would like that."

Lucius intended to make the best of what little spare time he would have in the next few days. However, there was a dark, growing sense of foreboding in the back of his mind. It convinced him Postumus had bequeathed him his 'sixth sense'.

Epilogue

Ever since he was a small boy, the young man called 'Gakhbar' had a curious habit of 'appearing from nowhere'. He would never jump up and shout "boo!". Instead, he would just appear, leaving people to wonder how on earth he managed such an apparition. Unknowingly, he was developing a skill, the ability to appear alongside a person who had never seen him coming. It would serve him well later in life. Right now, his skill was boyish fun and gave him much enjoyment.

His schooling ended for the day, Gakhbar found he had an hour to kill before his mother would have dinner on the table. His classmates had all returned to their homes, and he was alone wandering through the small town where he lived. It had been several months since the harrowing event he had undergone at his uncle's home. After a couple of difficult weeks, he had started to move on with his life, but he had become withdrawn and had begun to develop a temper. However, the view was that he would get over it with time and his parents tended to give him the space he needed.

Whenever Gakhbar was not being kept busy, his mind would disengage and turn to his beloved cousin Maria. In Gakhbar's mind the girl, who was indeed pretty, had developed the status of a goddess, a divinity of perfect beauty. Placing her upon a pedestal, Gakhbar worshipped her. He was of an age where the hormones of adolescence were overwhelming his body. Often, lying awake at night, his hands would slip below the blankets that covered him, and he would worship at her altar. He was angry, at times raging, that they had taken her from him. Maria had become an obsession.

He strolled through the township's dusty street, passing people busy about their business before the day's end. Merchants headed home with their donkey's load lightened after a prosperous day at the market. Gakhbar's good friend, whose family were traders, would be assisting his parents packing up, and the boy planned to find him. It was then, a slight distance ahead, that he caught sight of his brother talking with a stranger.

He was seven years older than Gakhbar, who was never quite sure what his sibling did for a living. Gakhbar was told that he was trading, buying goods from the hill farmers and artisans, and selling them in the towns around Judaea. In truth, Gakhbar had seen him several times with another man moving products in a cart, so he accepted his brother's story. He was gone for periods at a time, and this was one of those times, or at least it was until Gakhbar spotted him sitting on a bench under a large spreading tree. There was a low wall against where they placed the bench, just beyond the tree base. Gakhbar's mind started processing a route that would get him close to his brother without being seen. It meant leaving the road, going to the rear of the houses to his right, and working his way behind the modest wall. He would have no problem jumping over it and appearing alongside his brother. The plan swung into action.

He was past the rear of the buildings in no time. Avoiding the odd sheep and goat, he reached the wall. He dropped to his hands and knees and manoeuvred himself towards the tree. As he neared, he could hear the two men talking, and it registered that the conversation, while not a whisper, was a quiet one. He was almost in position to rise and climb the wall when the discussion became clearer. It was his brother's voice that was the first he comprehended.

".... so, as you can see, we've completed several jobs for the Rabbi. We've the sanction of the Sanhedrin. The rabbis agree that the Telmidei Yeshua is heresy, and we should eradicate it. So, we're doing God's work. Now you're back, and you must join the team."

Gakhbar's ears pricked upon hearing the phrase "Telmidei Yeshua."

"We'll be the hammer of God, my friend," declared the man. "I heard you had a surprise at a job a few months back?"

"My good friend, you could call it such," his brother's voice said, "I found out just before we proceeded that my little brother would be at the house. That was not an issue, as I knew he would have to be home, so we sat it out. Then, as I foresaw, he left, and we began to execute the task."

"But he returned?"

"I found out later that he had neglected to hand over a letter from his mother, so, yes, he came back. We'd dealt with the two adult Talmidei scum, and one of the boys was sorting the girl when the son bolted. He'd got the rear door open when Joshua threw his knife and stuck him. He staggered out. I followed and came face-to-face with my little brother."

"Moses! What did you do?"

"I shrouded my face with my headdress, and I was wearing black - as we always do - so he didn't recognise me. In the gruffest voice I could muster, I ordered him to clear off, which he did."

"God was with you that day, my friend. It would have put us in an awkward position had the boy recognised you."

"It'd have been a disaster," his brother retorted.

Gakhbar remained behind the wall in a hands and knees position, frozen rigid. He thought his heart had stopped, and he could not breathe. He was struggling to comprehend what he had heard, praying to God that he had misheard it yet - knowing he hadn't - when the shock set in. His brother had killed his aunt and uncle, Ishmael too. Alone, that would have been a nightmare, but it was worse. He had a hand in the death of Maria. The conversation continued, but Gakhbar did not hear it. Gradually, he gained control of his breathing and, still on hands and knees, reversed back the way he had come. By the time he was standing again, he was trembling and wanting to vomit. In his head, he was back at the house where his friend Ismail lay collapsed, dying, and the only love of his life lay slain inside. Again, he fought back the urge to vomit but failed.

He wandered for hours, missing his tea and causing his parents some concern. It was a slow process, but he took back control of his body and mind. He began to think. He knew he could not talk to anyone about what he had heard - they would not believe him. Gakhbar must avenge Mariah, and emotional finger-pointing was not the approach. Instead, he must take his time, continue as usual and formulate a plan. By the time

Gakhbar returned home, full of apologies to his mother, he was sure of one thing. He no longer had an elder brother. In his mind, he was dead. If Gakhbar had his way, it would not be long before his sibling was destroyed, too.

Acknowledgements

It is a lonely task authoring a book, with hours spent in no one's company but your characters. So, when a real live person volunteers to help somehow, it is much appreciated. I would like to recognise those who had some input in one form or another.

Firstly, my neighbour and good friend Brian Ward. Brian read the novel, suggested some beneficial scene modifications, and noticed inconsistencies. It was very helpful.

My friend Paul Loxley started to review, but died before I completed the story. Paul, I would have rated your view on the novel most highly. Rest in peace, my friend.

I must not forget Lottie Aston, an MA with distinction in Creative Writing, who has answered innumerable questions and stayed sane at the same time; after all, it is what daughters are for!

Finally, my wife, Bernie. Holidays would see me squirrelled away writing whilst she was enjoying the sun with family and friends. At home, I would be lost to my office for hours on end. Thanks for your patience, and did I tell you there is another novel (at least) to come?

Guy Aston.
Danum.
March 2022

A short extract from 'CATACLYSM! The Bar Kokhba Revolt. Book Two.

Marcus Apollinaris and Anaitis sat in the taberna opposite the carpenter's shop. It was where Miriam lived with her cousin and his wife. Marcus was a soldier who had faced enemies in battle before. His next task seemed more challenging than wielding a sword in a battle. He had brought Anaitis along. She was Miriam's close friend, and this was not a job he wanted to conduct alone.

He had awoken that day in a good mood. The Urban Cohort was functioning well. There was nothing urgent to worry about, and he was seeing Anaitis this evening. After a cheery breakfast, he joined the duty watch to receive a report of the previous night's activities. He suspected there would be little to hear. As his decanus finished his brief report, Marcus spotted Centurion Aurelius Crispus walking in his direction.

"Tesserarius, I need a word!" Marcus sensed he was not a happy man. There was no hint of a smile as the centurion stood his ground. The decanus read the signs.

"I'd better be off then, sir." And he was gone. Crispus joined Marcus.

"This will not be good, Tesserarius. I have to tell you that Optio Petronius didn't return with the cohort." Marcus felt as though a thunderbolt had hit him. "We can only presume the worst."

"Lucius... dead?" stammered Marcus, "Surely not. Are you sure?" He knew the question was stupid. There would have been soldier counts and checks made. It was hard to accept such a monstrous truth. The centurion's countenance softened.

"I'm sorry, Marcus. I know you two had become friends." Then, after a pause, he said, "There's another aspect to this. His young lady has not been told, and I think it best it comes from someone she knows."

"Sweet Jupiter, you're right, chief- you don't mean me, surely?"

"You've known her as long as Lucius, and I've reason to believe they were... close?"

"They are–were- sir. I'll take Anaitis. She's a good friend and another woman. You know how it goes, chief."

"Yes, clever idea Marcus," said Crispus. "I could accompany you?"

"No need, sir. Best I does it with Anaitis."

And that is how Marcus and his lover came to be sharing a table in a taberna opposite Miriam bat Yahalom's home. He and Anaitis rallied their courage with wine, bracing themselves to tell his friend that the man she loved was dead. He had rehearsed the words in his head hundreds of times, but he could discover no painless way of breaking the news.

As he downed his second drink, he recognised it wasn't all about Miriam; Lucius was a brother. They had fought together and shared other hazards, too. He tried not to show it, but his loss greatly upset him. Recently, he had lost Sextus Postumus, another close brother, and losing Lucius so soon after was challenging. Anaitis, who herself had suffered dreadful trauma in Aelia Capitolina, sensed Marcus' internal grief. She pushed her beaker away and took his hand.

"Come on, my lovely, let's get this done. We'll be pissed as farts if we carry on like this!" The comment drew a smile from Marcus.

"You're right, my love. Let's do it. Gods give me strength."

Jacob, the carpenter, Miriam's uncle, opened the door. The man was a little surprised to find a Roman uniform at his door but relaxed when he saw Anaitis.

"Can I help you?" he asked.

"Is Miriam at home? We need to speak with her."

"Is someone sick?" Jacob asked. Clearly, Miriam's reputation as a healer was spreading.

"No, but it's important," said Marcus, thanking the gods the family spoke Greek. Jacob let them in. As they entered the workshop, a woman dressed in men's working clothing appeared from the house at its rear. Marcus couldn't fail to notice her good looks. Like her husband, she had pulled her hair back into a loose plait. Yet, her attire did not detract from the fact she was a very handsome woman.

"My wife, Rebecca," said Jacob. "She is a woodcarver. She recently supplied a carving of Mithras for the new temple. Me? I'm just a simple carpenter."

"Hello," Rebecca said, "and you are?"

"Tesserarius Marcus Apollinaris and this is Anaitis, my... my... friend."

"Goodness, you are Miriam's good friends." She turned her head and called out. "Miriam, someone to see you." Within seconds, Miriam entered the workshop.

"Marcus, Anaitis, it is good to see you. What brings you here?" Unfortunately, her beaming smile and welcome were not returned.

"We need to talk with you, Miriam," Marcus said. Rebecca's intuition noticed the atmosphere immediately.

"Why don't we go inside and sit down?"

"Yes," said Jacob, also beginning to sense all was not well, "That would be an excellent idea. I'll lead the way."

By the time they were sitting around a table, tension was evident in Miriam's expression. This was not to be a cordial visit. It was Marcus who led the conversation.

"Miriam, the Fourth returned to Caesarea yesterday. They were beaten up. The Fifth, who were with them, were all but wiped out." A moment or two passed for the words to sink in, preparing her for what was to follow. "Sadly, Lucius was not with them." So there, he'd said it. Jacob and Rebecca tensed, and the latter placed an arm around Miriam.

"Perhaps he separated and makes his own path home," the girl said in her newly learned Greek. It struck Marcus how her Greek had improved. "He will be here soon."

"A possibility?" asked Jacob. Marcus sighed; his ordeal was not yet over. A tear ran down his cheek, and his family knew what was to come. He was now fighting his own grief.

"They fought in a valley – another bloody valley! The rebels laid a trap, a huge rockfall. The Fifth were to the front and were smashed. The fourth was behind like and managed some shelter. The rebels ran straight through the Fifth and into the Fourth. The lads were still shaken but pulled off a fighting withdrawal. Apart from withdrawal, there was no other way out." As he spoke, more tears flowed down his cheek. Miriam stared into a space somewhere over Marcus' shoulder. "A legionary thinks he saw Lucius go down under the rebel attack."

Rebecca hugged Miriam. Anaitis reached across the table and squeezed Miriam's hands. There they sat for some time, a frozen tableau that only thawed when Miriam spoke.

"You tell me Lucius is dead?"

"Centurion Crispus wanted to tell you hisself," said Marcus. "He held Optio Petronius in 'igh regard." Marcus wiped his eyes. "He was a friend and a good officer."

Tears flowed down Miriam's face as her chest heaved. First, it started with sobs; then she started gasping for air. Rebecca called her name, but she did not react.

"She's over-breathing. She's going to faint," she said, "Jacob, get water – now!" The command was late delivered, and Miriam's head slumped, chin on chest. Anaitis jumped up and was beside the unconscious girl in an instant, gently raising her head. Jacob came back into the room with a jug of water. Rebecca took a corner of Miriam's shawl, soaking it in the pitcher before placing it on Miriam's face. Like a drowning person breaking the surface, she came to and gulped a breath. Rebecca hugged her close, then turned to her visitors. "Marcus, Anaitis, thank you for your sad duty, but we'll take care of her if you leave Miriam with us."

Minutes later, Marcus and Anaitis were back again, sitting in the taberna. Each staring into their large cups of wine.

"I'd rather face the bleedin' Parthian army than do that again," Marcus said.

"I wish I was with her, Marcus; she's my friend," said Anaitis, "but I understand – she's family after all. There's no way of doing what you did gently, my lovely, but you did it best as you could." She reached across and took his hand. "You'll stay with the Urban Cohort, won't you? I kept thinking of me sitting where Miriam was, people telling me you was dead."

Marcus uttered a cynical laugh.

"I don't think the Primus Pilus would 'ave me back in the Tenth. The only reason the old bastard gave my promotion the nod was to get rid of me. So no, I suspect I'll be an Urban Cohort man for some time yet."

"Let it be so. Miriam's loss has made me realise what you mean to me."

Printed in Great Britain
by Amazon